MASTER'S REACH

ALSO BY S.K. RANDOLPH

VARTERELS' UNIVERSE™

(as paperbacks)

Part I - UnFolding

1. DiMensioner's Revenge

5. ConDra's Fire

8. MasTer's Reach

10. Jaradee's Legacy

Agothany 1 (Companion Shorts 2, 3, 4, 6, 7, and 9)

Part II - CoaleScence

11. Incirrata Secret

13. Corps Stones

16. Mocendi's Gambit

19. Queen's Quest

Agothany 2 (Companion Shorts 12, 14, 15, 17, 18, and 20)

Part III - Quickening

(a work in process)

Told with words and art,

contained in novels and companion shorts,

available in print and eBooks.

MASTER'S REACH

ILLUSTRATED BY THE AUTHOR

VARTERELS' UNIVERSE™
BOOK EIGHT

S.K. RANDOLPH

Cover & Illustrations by
S.K. RANDOLPH

MasTer's Reach: Illustrated by the Author (VarTerels' Universe Book 8)

Previous published as The MasTer's Reach

Cover design and art copyright © 2015-2026 by S.K. Randolph
Edited by L.S. Lane
Illustrated by S.K. Randolph
Book design by T. Krantz

ISBNs
Paperback 978-1-962777-13-1
eBook 978-1-962777-31-5

Self Published by S.K. Randolph
CheeTrann Creations LLC
Suite 316-160
1410 Valley View Drive
Delta, CO 81416

Web Site: www.skrandolph.com
Substack: skrandolph.substack.com
Facebook: http://facebook.com/S.K.Randolph11

No generative Artificial Intelligence (AI) was used in the creation of this book - the words and images were created by the author, a certifiable human being. 😉

Revised 2026

VU-127-J VU08-MR 260704-1557 | 231129 PIbtA VUPt-1 .vellum

*To Linda Lane, my editor, mentor, and friend
whose critical eye and knowledge of writing
have brought me to today
and
whose ability to give feedback without raising my hackles
is worthy of a medal*

VarTerels' Universe ™
Science Fantasy

MASTER'S REACH

The Planet of DerTah
Desert of Sherah
LeCur
Toelchoc Mts.
Fera Finnero
Nesune R
The
Eissua
Strait
of
Treeds
Shu Chenaro
Trinuge
Marauder Passage
Sea of Fire
Echems
Strait
Von Baar Peninsula
Bockettle
Soprano
Narrows
Atkis
Aksala
Ocean of VerDeas

Ocean of VerDeas
N
W E
S
Geran Island
* TiCeed
Wont Harbor
Triple Moon Strait
So Geran Passage
ZaltRaca
Sea of Minusa
* Inev
of DoOlb
Katilan Bay
* Nigat
TheDa
tatt
ay of rinuge
Tumon Harbor
Cape of Trinuge
Sea of Trinuge

MASTER'S REACH

Prologue

The children of many strive for what's right.
They follow where led by their galaxy's plight.
The Unfolding defines the direction they'll go
To bring to fruition its ultimate goal.

Near The Outer Rim on the little-known planet of Persow, the VarTerel of the Inner Universe sat in his cabin, staring out the window deep in thought. Troubled visions had left his heart hammering. Wolloh, his favorite former apprentice, had fallen to the ground in an exhausted stupor. The five children foretold in the ancient prophecies, scrambled through the Tinga Forests on DerTah, pursued by a Mindeco from RewFaar. Icy fingers of foreboding thrust him back to full awareness. *The concluding cycle of The Unfolding has begun.*

Relevart frowned and ran a hand through his mane of white hair. Uneasiness nagged. A scan of the cabin's main room brought him to his feet. *My quiet time on Persow draws to a close.*

Shivering in the early morning chill, he hurried to his sleeping quarters, dressed for travel, and stuffed a few things in a pack. As he straightened, his image in the mirror held him quiet. An illusive thought emerged and faded.

What was that? His brow furrowed as he made his way to the larder. A distant echo teased his memory, and once again misted into nothing. Aware the thought would reemerge at the right time, he downed a quick breakfast and returned to the main room.

His VarTerel's staff flashed into being in his upraised hand. A whispered word sent a stack of books and a pile of hiking paraphernalia sailing to a far corner. In the wall revealed by their sudden flight, a well-hidden door slid open.

With a touch of wistfulness, he surveyed his comfortable home. *I will miss this cabin and the mountains and forests of Persow.* He pressed his lips together. *The time has come.* A succinct phrase preceded the tap of the rowan wood staff against the floor. All but the secret entrance disappeared in a blur of muted colors. He stepped through the open doorway. The soft sound of its closing click melted into the vastness stretching in all directions.

Relevart paused. A shake of his head dispersed the momentary sense of befuddlement that accompanied his entrance into Mittkeer—the place where All Time and No Time existed in the same instant—the place from which he traveled through time and dimension.

The sole object in the boundless expanse, a large quartz crystal christened Froetise, glinted atop a tourmaline pedestal a short distance from where he stood. Froetise connected him to crystals throughout the Inner Universe and allowed him to track the progress of The Unfolding.

Peering into its center, he watched a trail of phosphorescence follow a small, iridescent bird up from the crystal's depths; form a spiral of glowing, white light; and, at his command, flare and vanish. In the clear center, the image of Elcaro's Eye in Veersuni, the sanctuary in the Dojanack Caverns on Myrrh, came into focus. Bloodied water stained the fountain crimson and splashed over the alabaster rim. Five pools formed on the stone floor. On each reflective surface, a different scene took shape.

Huge ferns and gigantic moss-covered trees filled the first pool. Hidden in their midst, five young people watched two monstrous creatures battle. The leather-scaled wings of one whipped the foliage into a tempest. The single eye of the other flashed. A predatory roar reverberated through the forest. A challenging howl echoed after. The young people crouched lower, clinging to one another in terror.

In the second pool, screams of anguish vibrated the air as soldiers met hand to hand. Knives gleamed in the white-hot sun. Blood sizzled on the desert sands. Men on both sides lay unmoving. A DerTahan bearded buzzard wreathed in flames lifted into flight, sought its target, swooped, and rose again, a Human form dangling from taloned claws.

An elderly woman in the third pool walked from the Tropal Gateway into the sunflower field in Myrrh. She pushed amethyst-framed spectacles up on her nose and peered between tall, leaf-covered stalks. A RewFaaran camp occupied the garden where the Guardian of Myrrh's cottage should have been. Removing her spectacles, she dropped them into a pocket, straightened her be-flowered hat, and stepped into the open.

The fourth pool's surface trembled as raven's hoarse caw echoed through a prison cell. A man sitting in the shadows extended a hand and stroked its blood-covered feathers. Footsteps approaching in the stone passageway grew louder. The hand withdrew, and the man disappeared. Raven eyes peered through the pitch-black.

A woman in the fifth pool stared through salt-spray-covered windows at the frothing return of the tide. The roll and pitch of the sea mirrored her inner turmoil. Tears overflowed summer-green eyes and slid down pale cheeks. Her hands shook as she retied a blue scarf, the sole reminder of her life in Idronatti.

Elcaro's bowl came into focus at the crystal's center. A scene formed on its surface.

Flames blazing from a fiery pit sent shadows dancing over a charred land. Above it, the dark green feathers of an enormous bird of prey glistened in the diffused light. It circled and swooped to a landing on a stone balcony. A cloaked figure materialized. Scarred fingers plucked at a silver and moonstone locket on a long chain.

The scene faded. Reflective pools evaporated, creating a reddish mist that dissipated as water once more spilled from alabaster palms into Elcaro's bowl, the only sound in the Sanctuary of Veersuni.

Relevart's throat constricted. The urgency in each pooled-image left no doubt that his quiet interlude had ended. At his command, Froetise shrunk to a miniature of itself. He snapped it into place atop the staff. Rowan sprigs and leaves wove a cocoon around it. Holding the staff high, he focused on his destination.

And The Unfolding continued.

1
Myrrh

Chilling dampness cut SparrowLyn AsTar to the bone. Miniature fingers tugged her hair taut. Slimy tongues spilled rank, smelling spittle down her face. Fear more deadly than she had ever known made her knees go weak. A light flared. Tiny winged creatures scattered, their screams bouncing off stalagmites and stalactites. Strong hands caught her falling body, lifted her, held her next to the beat of a heart. Warm breath brushed her cheek, and then nothing.

S parrow flung herself from the bed, her gaze bouncing from rough stone walls to a small oil lamp to a heavy curtain. *Where am I?* She gulped a breath, sank onto the coverlet, and pulled it around her shaking body. *Meos, of course. I'm in my quarters in the DeoNytes' home in the Dojanack Caverns.*

She hugged her bent knees tight to her chest. *Will the memories of the Cavern of Vascorrie ever stop haunting me?*

Her gaze settled on the empty bed beside her. *I wish you were here, Allynae. DerTah is so far away. And the twins... How can you and our daughters be on another planet?*

Determined to shake off troubling thoughts, she tossed the coverlet aside and slid to the edge of the bed. Her feet came to rest on a hand-woven rug, her eyes on a small portrait she had painted of the twins. *So much has happened since you girls took Torgin Whalend to Myrrh for his Sun Cycle Celebration. Most important of all, your father found me and met you. I wish we'd had more time together as a family before The Unfolding snatched you away. Sometimes, I wonder if I'll ever see you again.*

Determination filled her as she picked up the portrait and planted a kiss on the identical faces. "I will see you again and soon!" Returning it to its place on the ledge above the bed, she smiled. *You look so much alike, but I know just how different you are.* Her brown eyes narrowed. *Right now, you don't look the least bit alike. I can't believe how much you resembled your father, Ariehn, when you shape shifted a boy. Ira Raast...a good name. Nobody will recognize you as twins, and you're safe. I'm grateful for that, but I miss you so much.*

Sparrow forced her gaze away from the portrait, straightened her bed, pulled on her clothes, and picked up a comb. Stroke by stroke, she untangled the silky length of her chestnut hair. She shivered. Snippets of her nightmare taunted her. The subterranean cavern on Thera...the primavers... the tarwish... Rubbing her hands up and down her arms, she scrubbed the goosebumps away.

Vascorrie. Just the word makes me want to crawl back into bed and pull the covers over my head. Merrilea and I almost died there. One Man found us and carried her from the cavern. Someone else carried me. Who? One Man wouldn't tell me.

She nibbled her bottom lip. *What if I...* A small smile curved the corners of her mouth. *I'll do it.*

With sudden possibilities flooding her artist's mind, she hurried along the passage to the studio Yookotay, the DeoNyte Redael, had arranged for her use. She had arrived in Myrrh knowing she was a talented artist; but after the events of the past few moon cycles, her completed works had surpassed her wildest dreams. Paints infused with a drop of Merrilea's Myrrhinian blood transformed her canvases from ordinary to prophetic. Not only that, but the images carried life. They melded in and out of one another, showing the changes wrought by The Unfolding.

Until a couple of turnings ago, she hadn't tried painting on demand. Then, Myrrh's Guardian asked her to discover where the twins and their friends were on DerTah. Sparrow hadn't thought she would succeed, but she had.

Today, I'm about to try it again. I have to know who saved me in Vascorrie, who carried me away from certain death.

S eyes Nomed stood in the middle of his small sleeping cave in Meos, the DeoNytes' home beneath the Dojanack Mountains. He and Myrrh's Guardian, Almiralyn, had spent the last two chron-circles in Veersuni with the all-knowing Elcaro's Eye. Every piece of information shared by the fountain had verified their fear that the battle on the planet of DerTah continued to rage.

The image of the High DiMensioner Wolloh Espyro crumpling at the center of the arena at Shu Chenaro shocked and dismayed him. *What left Wolloh so weak? Did his companions hold the shields in place?*

He paced the small cave. The fountain's surface then pictured Esán and his friends teleporting away from Nissasa Rattori's army, only to land in the most dangerous place on the planet of DerTah, the Tinga Forest.

A frown tugged his scarred cheek. *Brie and Esán are well-equipped to take care of most situations. Torgin and Ira will do what's needed, but Desirol Telisnoe, the youngest son of the Largeen Joram of RewFaar, is a wild card— unpredictable and undisciplined.*

The fountain's next image left terror clutching at his throat as Nissasa Rattori's pet Mindeco slipped through an opening sliced in the shield to pursue the young people.

Nomed continued to pace. Elcaro's final sharing pictured the Raven Karrew injured and imprisoned in an enchanted cage. Almiralyn's horrified gasps had turned to heartbroken sobs. Realizing she needed time alone, he had returned to Meos to report their findings to Yookotay.

He came to a standstill. *Time is racing. I can't waste any more of it. I must tell Almiralyn I'm leaving for DerTah.*

Without a backward glance, he exited his quarters and strode down the passageway. As he reached the Meosian central square, Zugo, the son of the DeoNyte ReDael, his white fur and light blue eyes contrasting dramatically with the black of his skin, fell in step beside him.

"Almiralyn sent me to find you. She's pretty upset."

Nomed paused and peered down at the startling face. "What did she ask you to tell me?"

"Please meet her at Sparrow's studio. I'll show you the way."

Nomed smiled his crooked smile. "I think I can find it. Thank you."

Zugo touched his arm. "I've never seen the Guardian cry. Do you know what's wrong?"

"I believe she would have told you if she wanted you to know."

The young DeoNyte frowned. "Guess you're right. I'll go tell Father where you are."

Nomed walked briskly down the tunnel. *I hate to leave, Mira, but too much is at stake.* Again, time snapped at his heels.

Sparrow put the finishing touches on the painting on her easel and stepped back. A man, tall and lean and well-muscled beneath his black uniform, angled slightly away from her. Blue-black hair cut in loose layers brushed his broad shoulders. Dark, almond-shaped eyes held a hint of laughter. Beneath his well-shaped nose, a generous mouth curved into a charming smile that deepened a dimple in his right cheek. Added to his physical attractiveness was an aura of intelligence and power that overflowed the boundaries of her canvas.

She tipped her head and tapped her lips with a paint-streaked finger. "Who on Myrrh are you, and did you carry me from that horrid cavern?"

"That's Corvus. He rescued you from Vascorrie. He's also been helping the children. You've captured him beautifully." The Guardian of Myrrh stood in the entryway. Tear-stained cheeks and red eyes caught Sparrow by surprise. She had never seen her anything but calm.

"Almiralyn, what's happened?"

The Guardian tossed her long, silver-blonde braid over her shoulder and studied the painting. Beautiful sapphire eyes absorbed every detail. Her hand reached toward the canvas, then lowered.

Keeping her gaze on the painting, she said, "I contacted the Galactic Guardians and asked to resign my position as the Guardian of Myrrh."

Sparrow's mouth fell open. She closed it and swallowed. "Tell me I didn't hear you correctly."

"I *must* go to DerTah. And I can't go as Myrrh's Guardian. If Nissasa caught me, I would be his bargaining chip. So I must resign. There is a catch, however."

"What's the catch?" Apprehension surged through her.

Almiralyn stood still. Her expression made Sparrow's pulse quicken. "The Guardians will not allow me to leave unless someone will assume my position here. They have given me permission to ask you to take my place, at least temporarily."

Sparrow's brain scrambled around itself. Several seconds passed before she could make sense of what she had heard. She smoothed her dark hair back from her face. "You want me to be the acting Guardian of Myrrh? That's crazy, Mira. I'm an artist, a mother, a—" She sank onto a bench and covered her face with her hands.

Almiralyn sat down next to her. "Please, Sparrow."

The pleading in her sister-by-Joining's eyes made Sparrow want to weep. "How can I do what you do? I'm not trained to make the decisions you make."

"You are as gifted as I am, Sparrow. Besides, Yookotay will advise you."

"Yookotay is the ReDael of the DeoNytes. He's spent his life in the Dojanack Caverns, not dealing with the politics of the Inner Universe."

"I'll transfer my powers and my knowledge to you. I can do that, and you'll have everything you need to protect Myrrh."

"If you transfer everything to me, where does that leave you?"

"I would be like you assumed you were prior to discovering you are half KcernFensian and half RewFaaran."

"Please tell me why you're willing to give up everything, perhaps even your life, to fly off to DerTah?"

A tear leaked from Almiralyn's eye and slid into the corner of her mouth. She caught it on the tip of her tongue and licked her lips. "Nissasa has Karrew. He's hurt—even worse than when Wodash wounded him in the Cavern of Tennisca. I can't leave him there to die, Sparrow. He is—" Her shoulders heaved as a sob choked her.

"I know you care about Karrew but he's just a..." The look on the Guardian's face and her own experience in Vascorrie stopped her. "Oh, Mira, he's more than a raven, and much more than your protector."

"Karrew is Corvus, Sparrow. He is the man in your painting; the man I love more than anyone in the Inner Universe. I *cannot* leave him in Nissasa's hands."

Sparrow stared at the painting. It blurred, and Allynae's features came into focus. *I'd do the same thing to save you, Alli.* She took Almiralyn's icy hand between hers. "I will act as the Guardian of Myrrh until you return. And I will do it without robbing you of the tools you need to save Corvus. I have one request."

"Anything, Sparrow."

"Once he is safe, please find Allynae and the twins and bring them home to me."

"I'll do everything I can to restore your family to you." She began to cry.

Sparrow sat quietly. When Almiralyn's tears ceased to flow, she put an arm around her shoulders.

Almiralyn wiped her eyes on her sleeve and produced a watery smile. "I have one more thing to share before we inform the Guardians of your willingness to serve."

Sparrow searched her face. "And that is?"

"A special person is coming to help you."

"Who?"

"Do you remember Henrietta?"

Sparrow's heart steadied. Her resolve strengthened. "Of course. She took me to SumnerTymn to find Merrilea. You asked her to protect the twins and me." She smiled. "You could have told me sooner, you know."

"Her presence here must be a secret." She sat in silence for a time, shook herself, and got to her feet. "I want to leave as soon as possible. We have a lot to accomplish before I go."

Nomed entered the studio in time to hear the last exchange. "I hope you're not planning to rush off to DerTah, Almiralyn. I told you I'd find Karrew." Sparrow's painting caught his eye. He moved closer. "Wonderful picture of Corvus. Why did he appear on your—"

Almiralyn's expression stopped him. He looked from her to the canvas. "By the power of Emit, I should have known. Karrew is Corvus' shifted form. Why didn't you say so?"

Almiralyn brushed a tear from her cheek and stood up. "I was in shock, and I couldn't think. I have something to tell you. And something to ask."

Sparrow joined them, handed her a clean cloth to dry her tears, and smiled at Nomed. "Brace yourself."

What he saw in the Guardian's face did not prepare him for her next statement.

"I'm resigning as Guardian of Myrrh. Sparrow will take my place."

Stunned, he took a minute to absorb the news. "Have you thought this through? If word gets out you are no longer Guardian and someone with no experience—sorry, Sparrow, but you are untrained—is in charge of Myrrh and the protector of the Evolsefil Crystal and Elcaro's Eye, Nissasa will throw a victory party."

Almiralyn took a deep breath. "Nobody will know I'm not here."

"How do you plan to keep *that* a secret?"

She put an arm around Sparrow. "Because Sparrow is going to shape shift to my likeness."

The blood drained from Sparrow's face. "But we don't know if I can even shift my shape. To fool everyone, I'd need to shape you as Almiralyn, you as Mira, and you as a white bird." Dazed, she shook her head and sank down on a chair.

"You must shift, Sparrow, or the Galactic Guardians won't allow me to leave Myrrh. So Seyes and I are going to help you access your talent."

Nomed laughed. "What a quagmire this is! Is that what you were going to ask me? To help you teach Sparrow to shift?"

She didn't smile. "That and, once we've rescued Karrew, I want you to help me stop Nissasa Rattori and The Mocendi League."

2

DerTah

Wind howled through the Tinga Forest. Waist high ferns whipped from side to side. Rain fell by the buckets full. Mist floated up from the water-logged ground to meet the fog descending from the cloud-laden skies. Esán shivered and huddled closer to Brie in the hollow of a gigantic, moss-covered tree. *Wolloh meant for us to teleport to the seaside village of Atkis. What went wrong? The picture in my head was clear, and yet we ended up in a rainforest.* He thought back to the arena in Shu Chenaro.

One Man, Stebben, Allynae, Gerolyn, and Wolloh stood in individual pools of light, facing away from the arena's center. They had just completed constructing wards to protect Wolloh's land from Nissasa Rattori and his army of traitors.

Wolloh yelled, "Seal and secure!"

The adults turned to face inward. The five pools coalesced into one, enclosing Esán and his companions. It was time. He glanced from one friend to the next. Torgin looked grim, but determined. Ira caught his eye and nodded. Desirol scowled. Beside him, Brie rubbed the Star of Truth on the nape of her neck, her expression puzzled.

"Hold on to me," he commanded. The next thing he knew, they were in a dripping wet rainforest.

Brie nestled closer. *"Do you suppose Nissasa interfered? One Man said he stole the Oracle Stone from WoNa. Who else would have that kind of power?"*

Esán pressed the palms of his hands together and tapped his index fingers against his lips. *"Nissasa?"* He dropped his hands. *"Makes sense."*

Ferns whipped by the wind showered them with drops of cold water. Brie shuddered and adjusted the weather blanket. *"When are you going to tell Des we think the Mindeco made it through the wards?"*

Esán stared out at the torrents of rain. *"When—if we get a break in the weather. Rest while you can."*

She leaned her head on his shoulder and grew quiet. He continued to contemplate the happenings at Shu Chenaro. The last thing he had seen prior to teleporting—Wolloh, the High DiMensioner od DerTah, crumpling to the ground.

Torgin Whalend shivered. After a moon cycle in the Desert of Fera Finnero, the dampness of the Tinga Forest chilled him to the bone. He hunched lower beneath a dripping fern and peered through the mist at his companions. Ira sat by himself beneath the broad leaves of a giant bush, his weather blanket tented over his head and a scowl on his face. Esán and Brie huddled together inside a hollowed tree. They appeared to be quiet. He narrowed summer-green eyes. *I know you're talking. Wish I could use telepathy, then I could be part of the conversation. Ah, well.*

Flicking a raindrop from his brown cheek, he brushed the water from black hair made more curly by the penetrating dampness and frowned. *Where's Desirol?* A glance around deepened the frown. *He's a pain, but we don't want to lose him.*

He sloshed over to Esán and Brie and squatted. "Where'd Des go?"

Esán's blue-eyed gaze swept over mammoth trees to head-high bushes and came to rest on Ira. "Hey, Ira, where's Des?"

The tall boy's scowl deepened. "Don't know, maybe don't care." He tugged at his weather blanket. "Hate this rain. Can't you teleport us someplace dry?"

Esán exchanged glances with Brie. "We can't teleport anywhere."

Ira splashed toward them. "Why not. The Compass of Ostradio will give us directions."

Brie pulled him down beside her. "We think the Mindeco made it through Wolloh's wards and followed us here."

Torgin moaned. "The Mindeco. That's all we need—the most dangerous creature on RewFaar after us again."

No one spoke. His thoughts raced back to the Nesune Ruins in the desert, the place WoNa, the Atrilaasu Oracle, had sent them when the Sebborr and Nissasa's men were closing in on Eissua Oasis. *The Mindeco is more frightening than the death shadow.* Torgin shuddered. The bear-like skull of a head was terrifying. *I still feel the leathery creature's single eye drilling into me...* He wrinkled his nose. *...and I'll never forget the putrid stench of decay wafting from it. Worst of all, it claims Human bodies for its own, and, keeping the memories intact, it destroys the essence of the body's owner. Then, when it's done with it, the creature sheds the body and watches it decompose.*

"Torgin. Torg, wake up." The strain in Ira's tone infiltrated his thoughts.

He blinked. "Sorry. The Mindeco's..." His brow wrinkled. "Did I miss something?"

"Desirol seems to have disappeared." Brie sounded worried. "We called several times, but he didn't answer."

Ira frowned. "Better look for him. If we split up, we'll find him faster."

Esán shook his head. "We stay together. Any of us alone is no match for the Mindeco. At least together, we might have a chance. Grab your packs. When we find Des, we'd better get moving."

Pounding footsteps and a frantic shout brought them to their feet. Desirol burst through the ferns, his eyes wild and fearful. "We have to go," he said between hiccuped gulps of air. "A monster's headed this way. We need to teleport. Fast!"

Torgin blanched. "You mean the Mindeco has found us already?"

Desirol's head snapped in his direction. "The Mindeco is still in the desert, right?"

The companions looked at one another. Esán's gaze stopped on Desirol. "Brie and I think it made it through the wards."

"S-s-so we can't t-teleport, or it will know where we are." The RewFaaran choked. "Wolloh said it left its mark on me. It will find me and take over my body." Panic rode him like a wild horse. He swung around, searching the undergrowth.

"If you had kept your drango tunic, Des…" Ira's unfinished statement brought a flush to the RewFaaran's face.

"I am the son and heir of the Largeen Joram of RewFaar, and I will not swear allegiance to a tribe on another planet."

"I'd have thought staying safe so you could actually become the leader would have overruled your bias." Ira assumed a fighter's stance. "Now, I suppose you want to beat me up."

Torgin looked from one to the other. "We need to get moving. You can fight another time."

Brie nodded her agreement. "Other forest creatures are already moving this way. Our lives depend on our being quiet and not leaving a trail."

Esán gave her a smile of appreciation and turned to Torgin. "Ask the compass the way to the village of Atkis. At least we can head in the right direction."

Torgin gave Desirol a warning look and pulled out the Compass of Ostradio.

"Don't worry, Torg." Ira moved closer. "If he even blinks at it, I'll knock him out."

"You and who else?" Desirol's demeanor dared him to try.

"Stop it." Brie's eyes flashed. "A hideous creature is closing in on us. It will be dark soon. We need to move."

Ira and Desirol continued to glare at each other.

Ignoring them both, Torgin held out the compass. "Show us the way to Atkis."

The arrow spun and stopped. A map rose above the compass and enlarged. Esán studied it. "There are two places marked, the Tinga Forest and Atkis. We need to head south now." Slinging his pack over his shoulder, he began to walk in the direction of the village, Wolloh's intended destination for them.

Torgin tucked the compass beneath his tunic, grabbed his pack and flute, and strode after him. Brie joined Esán. Ira and Desirol scowled at each other and followed.

Drops of water showered down from giant foliage. The ground underfoot trembled. Not far behind them, a creature howled. Silent as hunted mice, the companions moved through the sodden undergrowth.

Determined not to give fear the upper hand, Torgin crept forward, hoping none of them would become prey for whatever hunted them.

Heat dissipated slowly as night laid claim to the Desert of Fera Finnero on the planet of DerTah. In the Fortress of LeCur in its northern reaches, thick stone walls imprisoned the turning's tepid temperature until Fasfro, DerTah's saffron-colored moon, had breached the horizon and sailed high in the sky. Only then, cooled air penetrated the rooms where the Dreela Gidtuss and Dahe Terah, the leader of the Sebborr, met in secret to discuss the war raging along the desert's southern border.

Some distance from the main buildings of LeCur, in a box canyon in the Toelachoc Mountains, moonlight stole over the stone walls and through the metal-latticed windows of a deserted prison. Squares of warm light grew brighter and more defined as Fasfro arced higher overhead. Occasional murky shapes flitted by windows and across the inner courtyard. An aura of misery cloaked the ruins in silence and deterred those who might happen upon it by accident or design from trespassing into its inner chambers.

As though challenging the ghosts of Toelachoc Prison, a kcalo-draped figure adjusted the bundle cradled in his arms, crept forward, and pressed his back against the rough stone wall. A brief pause later, he slipped through an open door and made his way down a long passage. Dark eyes glistened as he paused, trapped for a moment in latticework and moonlight. A quick sprint brought him to a stone staircase that led into the bowels of the prison.

Slowing his pace, he navigated the steep stairs and made his way through the oppressive darkness of the dungeon-like lower level. Undercurrents of violence and death surged around him. He stopped to listen. Neither rodent nor insect made its presence known.

Stepping into a narrow cell, he sat down on a rickety metal cot and settled the swaddled bundle on his knees. A match flared. The stub of a candle sprang to light.

The man pushed his hood back and listened again. Reflected flames sparked in his eyes as he unwrapped the bundle. A dark shape the size of a small baby shuddered beneath his fingers. He bent closer and stroked its feathered back.

"You must stay here until you heal," he crooned softly. "There's food and water and a clean blanket. I fashioned you a perch."

An ebony eye caught the light as a raven's head tipped.

The man carried the injured bird to a rough-hewn branch several inches above the stone floor, knelt, and set it down with great tenderness. Black talons gripped it. The bird steadied itself, ruffled its feathers, and seemed to examine a wing swathed in bandages. Its unwavering eye found the man.

"I slathered it with ointment and splinted it. You should be able to fly when it heals. You must stay here until you're better. If you leave too soon, both you and I will die. Do you understand?"

The raven bobbed its head.

"I'll be back when I can to bring fresh food and water." He stood and blew out the candle. "Cracks in the floors above will let in light when the sun rises." With his hood once more in place, he stepped into the passageway and closed the cell door after him. As silent as a phantom, he merged into the darkness.

The Raven Karrew clung to the makeshift perch and peered after his rescuer. A faint blur of murky white shot past the door. Ghosts of long-dead prisoners flitted into the cell, bringing with them the dank chill of death. Hideous, anguished faces focused and melted away. Withdrawing his attention from his strange cellmates, Karrew ruffled his feathers against the encroaching cold and cast his mind back to the turning of his capture.

Almiralyn's face emerged like an image on the surface of Elcaro's Eye. Her beautiful sapphire eyes gleamed. Her sensitive mouth shaped into an enchanting smile. He could almost feel the gentleness of her touch. How he ached to be near her.

A chill shattered her image and concentrated his thoughts on DerTah. He had rescued the Dansgirl Nichi from the LaTiru, taken her to her family, and lifted into flight above Eissua Oasis headed for Shu Chenaro. Wolloh needed him at the ranch, and yet his heart teased him to return to Myrrh.

Conflicted emotions obscured his awareness of the world around him. Heat searing his wing tips screamed a warning. Too late, he tried to dodge. Fiery talons crushed the breath from his body, dislocating his left wing. Piercing pain pitched him into unconsciousness.

His next clear memory—a cage surrounded by glistening wards and Nissasa Rattori's triumphant eyes peering at him between the bars. Nissasa's torturous reprisals when he refused to answer left him exhausted. His chest bore the wounds of each burning probe. When a soldier entered, whispered a message, and left with Nissasa hurrying after, his body shuddered with relief.

Time drifted by with the slowness of his descent through the Abyss of the Dead with Desirol. He floated in a state of semi-consciousness, where pain was all he knew. The cage being moved and strapped to the back of a rohes, shook him back to wakefulness. A torturous journey jostled him until he almost wished he were dead. Desert heat left him panting and dizzy. The cold of night made him puff up his feathers and crouch lower on his perch.

His physical endurance had faded to almost nothing when the Sebborr surrounding him halted within the gated grounds of a fortress. Once the bustle of setting up camp had ended, a servant moved his cage into a tent and provided him with fresh water and food.

As night's quiet settled over the camp, a cloaked figure slipped into the tent. Gentle hands lifted him from the cage. Skilled fingers explored his injured wing, gripped a dislocated bone, and jerk it into place. Pain dropped him into unconsciousness.

Sometime later, the sounds of a beating heart and the clip-clop of a horse's hooves penetrated his returning awareness. Strong arms cradling him in a warm blanket brought a spark of hope that he was being rescued. Too weak to investigate, he let the rhythmic ride soothe his battered body.

Where am I? Who is my rescuer? What does he know about me? Sidestepping along the perch, like fingers over worry beads, he blinked the unanswerable questions into oblivion and stopped to listen. In order to heal, he needed to rest. Silence, thick and saturated with the violence of another time, pressed in on him. Nothing alive stirred. Tucking his head beneath his uninjured wing, he slept.

Wolloh Espyro lay in the cool quiet of his bedroom at Shu Chenaro, piecing together the past few hours. Setting wards to obscure the departure of the children to safety had left him in an exhausted heap at the center of the arena. Stebben had carried him here, tucked him in bed, and demanded he rest.

He tried to sit up and fell back on the pillows. Fatigue weighed his body like stone. Every joint on his disfigured left side ached. His head throbbed, and his parched throat longed for relief. *I need water.* An arm slid under his shoulders and lifted him enough to sip from an offered glass.

Stebben lowered him and sat down beside him. "How do you feel?"

"More tired than I can ever remember. Wards?"

"We reconstructed them. One Man interwove a spell of deflection throughout. They remain intact—at least for now."

"The children?"

"They teleported. When I searched the village of Atkis, I couldn't find them. We haven't located them yet."

"And Corvus. Has he returned?"

Stebben shook his head.

"I was afraid of that." Wolloh closed his eyes, took in a breath, and released it in a long, soft whoosh. "How long have I been out?"

"It's approaching Tri-Nular. All three moons are almost visible."

A spasm of pain made him grimace. "If I don't rest, I won't be of help to anyone. I need to sleep, my friend. Call me when Lunule hits its zenith."

Stebben studied him for a long moment. "Until the third moon, then. I'll be near if you need anything." The door closed with a whispered click.

Wolloh narrowed his eyes and stared up at the ceiling. *Nissasa Rattori is a dangerous adversary. I'm certain the Mocendi League is behind his betrayal of Lorsedi and Desirol.* A yawn interrupted his thought process. Regrouping, he refocused. *Esán and Brielle can handle most situations. They should be fine.* His lips pursed. *I wish Nomed were here. And where is Corvus?* He yawned again and repositioned his throbbing left hip. *I'll think better when I've slept.* Humming a meditative tune, he drifted into a restless, dream-laden slumber.

Stebben's voice brought him to wakefulness several hours later. "Wolloh, Lunule shines overhead. It is time."

He rubbed his eyes and lay still, ignoring the weariness that made him disinclined to move. "I'll get dressed. Please ask One Man, Gerolyn, and Allynae to meet us in the conference chamber. We have decisions to make."

"Do you need anything before I go?"

Wolloh sat up and pushed the bedding aside. "I'll be fine. Give me a half circle of the chronometer." He reached for his cane and gazed thoughtfully at the crystal knob. When he looked up, Stebben had departed.

Once attired for the coolness of evening, he stood in the quiet room. The simple act of dressing had depleted his energy. He sank down on the bed and rested his head on the knob of his cane. A flash of red flickered at the crystal's center. Wolloh gasped and jerked his head up. With a pain-infused moan, he slumped forward into oblivion.

Soaring high above Shu Chenaro as a DerTahan hawk, One Man assessed the stability of the reconstructed wards surrounding Wolloh's land. Before their restoration, a brief battle had occurred between Lorsedi's soldiers and Nissasa's men. One Man doubled back over the battlefield. *Why did the Sebborr join forces with the traitors and then not involve themselves in the scrimmage?*

Satisfied the wards were solid, he swooped lower in search of Lorsedi or a Pentharian—either Voer or Yaro. The gleam of blue scales brought him into a long glide that ended a short distance from where Voer spoke with a group of soldiers. One Man studied the creature from the planet of ReTaw au Qa. His long braids, multiple piercings, and tattoos made him stand out. But it was his immense height and his lapis blue scales and lizard legs and tail that marked him as alien to this world.

The soldiers dispersed, and Voer joined him. "How's Wolloh?"

"He's resting. We haven't located the children, but we will. I need to see Lorsedi."

The Pentharian led the way to a dugout where the Largeen Joram met with his staff. While Lorsedi completed his meeting, One Man listened to Voer's account of the battle and took stock of his surroundings. Soldiers in combat uniforms worked with trained precision to redeploy equipment and men along the desert border. "RewFaaran troops are certainly well-trained."

Voer studied the confusion in the traitors' camp. "It is unfortunate Nissasa's aspirations created discord."

One Man searched the camp. "I don't see Nissasa anywhere. The Sebborran leader, Dahe Terah, and the Dreela Gidtuss appear to be absent as well."

"Discipline is vital to the warrior. Nissasa's Brigade..." Voer shook his head.

Lorsedi dismissed his staff and waved them over. "The shields fell, One Man. What happened?"

One Man described what had occurred with Wolloh, the children, and Corvus.

The Largeen Joram ran a hand through his flaming red hair. "At least the young people are together. I hope Desirol does nothing...silly. He told me about his behavior at Nesune." He studied One Man's face. "What brings you here?"

"It is vital to have a trained DiMensioner at the front. Gerolyn has volunteered to join you."

Lorsedi's expression went from open interest to stern denial. "It's too dangerous. I can't be worried about her while I'm battling with Nissasa."

"She felt sure you would react this way, but I'll let her speak for herself." He raised his arm and waved.

A DerTahan hawk landed beside them. Gerolyn appeared dressed in desert gear. "I can take care of myself, Lorsedi. We need to keep communications open, and we need to know you are safe. I am the best one to do the job while Wolloh recovers."

One Man drew Voer aside as a heated discussion ensued. "I have to go back. Try to convince Lorsedi to allow Gerolyn to stay. We need to be in touch. I can't keep flying back and forth to make sure he is safe. Too much is happening."

The tall Pentharian observed the two opponents. "I will take care of this, my friend. Go." He strode to Gerolyn's side and looked down at Lorsedi. "Yaro and I will be responsible for Gerolyn's safety. We need her help."

Lorsedi pivoted and walked several steps, paused, and returned. "I will allow it if you, Gerolyn, promise to leave if the risk becomes too high. At the height of battle, the front is no place for a woman."

Gerolyn smiled. "I am not a RewFaaran woman, Lorsedi, but I do promise to leave if it becomes too hazardous for me to stay."

Voer turned and waved. One Man shifted shape and flew back toward the ranch house and the decisions waiting to be made. How to find Esán and his friends topped his list.

3
Myrrh

Henrietta stood in a forest of green stems and leaves. Above her head, sunflowers stretched toward the Myrrhinian sun and bobbed in the gentle autumn breeze. As soon as her feet had touched the ground, the Tropal Portal from The Borderlands whirled back into itself and faded into a faint blur. It had been almost fifteen sun cycles since she had first stepped into it on her way to Idronatti. She remembered the turning Karrew had flown into her home on KcernFensia—the turning that had changed her life forever.

Muggy heat drove her to the open window, where a sea breeze rustled the sheer curtains and fanned her flushed cheeks. "What has happened to my life? Where's the adventure I have always dreamt about? All my training at the Temple of Mahyinaeh didn't prepare me to sit home and do nothing, yet here I am." She flopped down in a chair, bit her lip, and studied her surroundings. Her conclusion—beautiful, elegant, and boring.

An impatient flounce around the room came to a halt beside a table laden with framed family portraits. Her sister's beautiful face smiled back at her. She sighed. "Mairin, where are you? You've been gone far too long. Almiralyn and Allynae are in Myrrh, and I haven't heard a word from them, either. I miss you and your children. I even miss your companion. How is Lanli, anyway?" She faced the room. "I am beginning to hate—"

A raven swooping through the open window silenced her monologue. She ran across the room and threw her arms around the smiling man who had materialized. "Corvus! What brings you to KcernFensia? I have missed you so much. How's Mira? Alli? Do you like Myrrh?"

A deep chuckle shook his chest and made her giggle. He held her at arm's length. "We miss you, too, Henri."

Prancing with delight, she pulled a cord by the door. Within minutes, a young woman entered and set a tray on a table between two chairs. She caught her mistress' eye, smiled, and departed.

Henri sat down on the edge of a chair. "Sit. Tea?"

"I love your special tea." He joined her, accepted a fragile cup, and inhaled the aroma. "You always remember my favorite." He took a sip and placed the cup and saucer on the table.

Henrietta's curiosity exploded into words. "Don't just sit there! Why are you here? I know you didn't make the journey here just to see me."

Corvus sat back and smiled. "To the contrary, I am delighted to see you. It's been far too long. But you're right—I have another reason for this visit. Mira has a request she has asked me to present to you." He grew quiet, his dark eyes searching her face.

"Tell me! I'm all ears."

"Allynae is in love and has, in secret, Joined to SparrowLyn AsTar."

"What! How did he meet her—Gerolyn's daughter—the daughter of the Largeen Joram of RewFaar?"

Corvus rested his hands on his knees and outlined the story as he knew it. When he reached the part where Sparrow discovered her pregnancy, he paused.

Henrietta smoothed a stray strawberry blonde curl away from her face. "She's in Idronatti. He's in Myrrh. Does he know?"

She watched a frown erase the dimple in Corvus' cheek. "Almiralyn can't tell Alli, Henri, because he'll run back to Myrrh and get himself thrown into the Five Towers."

"Then who will look after Sparrow and their baby? How will they manage in Idronatti by themselves?" A delighted smile spread from her mouth to her eyes. "I will. I'll go to Idronatti and watch over them."

Corvus picked up his tea and sipped its fragrant warmth. "Mira was hoping you'd volunteer." A relieved smile deepened the dimple. "There are a couple of drawbacks, Henri."

She ran a dainty finger around the rim of her teacup and considered the ramifications of sun cycles spent on the planet of Thera. She looked at Corvus and shrugged. "The worst thing—time on Thera will impact my longevity—I'll age more rapidly. Of course, I could sit around here and die of boredom while you and Mira are having adventures." She tapped her chin. "My luxurious and lazy lifestyle will end. I can't think that I'll miss it. Life without meaning is not cured by wealth and luxury, but by action."

A walk to the window presented another drawback. She loved the ocean, the smell of it, the feel of sea air against her skin, sailing... She pursed her lips in thought. Mairin, whom she adored, and Lanli had left on a perilous journey, one from which they might not return. Their children, Almiralyn and Allynae, now lived on Myrrh. It seemed everyone she loved had left her behind.

Fingering the silk of the curtain, she conceded KcernFensia was her home, and she would miss it. More important, however, Almiralyn would not ask if it were not essential. She dropped the curtain and turned to find Corvus standing behind her. He took her hands in his.

"Do you still want to come?"

She squeezed his strong fingers. "Tell Mira I'll join her as soon as I have taken care of a few details here."

Corvus flashed a delighted grin. "The babies are due in six Theran moon cycles, and Sparrow will move from her dorm to a new apartment one moon cycle prior to their birth."

Henri blinked, a vision flashed in her mind. "She's having twins!" She closed her eyes and took a deep breath and laughed. "And they are girls, identical twin girls. I can't wait."

He wrapped her in a warm embrace, then stepped back to meet her gaze. "Now perhaps Mira can stop worrying. I have to go." A quick kiss on the cheek and his raven form soared out the window.

She stared after him until she could no longer see a speck of black in the sky. With a fresh cup of tea in hand, she sat for some time, absorbing the seriousness of what she had agreed to. Doubt nudged her to renege. Laughter gurgled up in her throat. "I said yes, and I meant it. Finally, an adventure!"

The soft whir of wings made her set aside her memories. A tiny boy landed on a large leaf. A wide grin encompassed the bottom half of his face. "Welcome to Myrrh. Major Jordett sent me to meet you."

Pulling large, amethyst-rimmed spectacles from her pocket, she perched them on her nose and peered at him.

"You are a Nyti. Am I correct?"

"Yep. I'm Ashor, and you're Henrietta." He hovered in front of her and pointed. "Those make your eyes look huge."

"They make you bigger, too. My friends call me Henri."

"Mine call me Ash. Come on, the Major and Tinpaca Mondago, the RewFaaran captain, are waiting."

Ashor zipped through the tent entrance and hovered near the table. "Henri is here."

Jordett excused himself and stepped outside. Tottering toward him was a diminutive, elderly woman. Perched on her white curls was a wide-brimmed hat. On top, periwinkle flowers danced to the rhythm of her steps. He couldn't help but smile. She was a character, one he found not only entertaining but also knowledgeable and articulate.

"Miss Henrietta, you look quite fetching in your hat. Welcome to Myrrh." He strode toward her and offered his arm.

She took it and gave him a coy smile from under her wide brim. "I love hats, Major. It is good to see you, even if circumstances are not the most favorable."

He refrained from patting her hand and led her into the tent. The Tinpaca and an emerald Pentharian stood as she entered.

"May I present Miss Henrietta Avetlire. Henri, Tinpaca Mondago and Stee."

She held out a hand. "Tinpaca, it's lovely to meet you."

He grasped it between his and smiled. "The pleasure is all mine. Welcome. We hope you have good news for us."

A tip of her head brought her eyes in line with his. "We shall see, Tinpaca. We shall see." Withdrawing her hand, she craned her neck to peer up at the towering Pentharian, touched her heart, and gave him a gracious smile. "Oid eo daizo raa, Stee."

He gazed down at her. The corner of his mouth twitched. Kneeling, he brought his golden eyes in line with her deep violet ones. "Oid eo diazo raa, Miss Henrietta. I honor you as comrade. Zeo a doo." He touched his forehead to hers and returned to standing.

She pushed her spectacles higher on her nose, stood on tiptoes to touch his heart, and smiled at each man. "Let us share information. I am needed in the Dojanacks."

Jordett placed a chair beside him at the table. Everyone settled and looked at Mondago.

With a slight bow of his head, he acknowledged Henrietta. "Please take the lead, Miss Hen—"

She raised a hand. "Call me Henri, or we'll never accomplish anything. Now, this is what I have arranged in Idronatti."

Kieel, the leader of the Terces Wood Nyti, sat on a cross member in the Tinpaca's tent, listening. Soon Jordett would depart for Thera. Envy nudged. *I've never been away from my forest home on Myrrh.* The more he learned about The Borderlands and The City, the more curious he became. His brow wrinkled. *Curiosity can get me into big trouble. Still, seeing beyond the borders of Myrrh...* He grinned with anticipation.

When the discussion ended and Henrietta prepared to depart, Kieel shot out the door and hid in the sunflowers near the portal. He chastised himself for being silly, immature, and irresponsible; and yet he neither left nor changed his mind. *If Jordett's going to Idronatti, so am I.* He wondered if he should tell his granddaughter or ask permission or perhaps give it up—stay in Myrrh and continue to be the staid, excessively tidy, in-control leader he had always been.

If I thought the Major would take me, I'd ask, but if he said yes, he'd assume responsibility for me. He stroked his goatee. *Why am I driven to do this? It is so unlike me.*

Hovering in the shade of a drooping leaf, he watched Jordett say goodbye to Henri and the Tinpaca. The lenses in her spectacles flashed as she looked his direction. He ducked. *Did she see me?*

"Paranoia," Kieel muttered to himself. "She can't know I'm here."

The elder flashed from sight. Kieel gasped when she reappeared some distance from him, well-hidden from the RewFaaran camp, and beckoned.

Curiosity chased Kieel to the out-stretched hand.

Henri lifted him to eye level. "I believe you are intending to follow the Major. Is this so?"

Kieel squared his small shoulders and stared into her magnified eyes. "I know it seems foolish, but I feel compelled." He twirled his walking stick between his fingers, struggling to disperse the obsession that drove him. "If you tell me to stay here, I will."

Her reply was soft and urgent. "Go with him. And, Kieel, stay out of sight. He faces more danger than he knows. Keep your eyes and ears open. He will need your special skills. Here he comes. Take care."

He lifted off her palm. She removed her spectacles, held them in a fisted hand, and vanished.

Major Jordett, dressed in the uniform of the Peoples Plan Protectors of Idronatti, stood near a single lamppost on the outskirts of The Borderlands. He had been absent from Idronatti for over one Myrrhinian moon cycle—just short of three turnings in Theran time. During his time in Myrrh, Almiralyn had taken him to Veersuni to see if Elcaro's Eye would show what was occurring in the city. His journey down the stairway of Retu Erath in the Cavern of Tennisca had left him introspective and quiet. What the fountain had seen fit to share made him even more determined to accomplish the mission he had sketched out for Tinpaca Mondago.

Idronattian born and bred, he had discovered more about himself and life from his time in Myrrh than he had learned during his entire existence in The City. At fourteen, the Induction Counselor assigned him the profession of Law and Order with a parallel path which included training by the PPP. He had enjoyed his studies at the Theran Institute for Diplomacy and Law and excelled in the classes involving interdisciplinary relationships. By his mid-twenties, The PPP had assigned him to a special ancillary branch that gave him mobility within the ranks of both the police force and the military.

What surprised him most about his sojourn to Veersuni was his anger that the traitors from RewFaar had invaded his home. Idronattians were ill-equipped to deal with the challenges now facing them.

Fadin, the Borderlander who had guided him from Antiques by Q to the portal, cleared his throat. "We're settin' up a blockade here, Major. When you're ready t' come back, send Majeska ahead. She'll let us know you're comin' through." He paused, cleared his throat again, and shuffled restless feet. "I kinda need t' go…"

"Thanks, Fadin. Keep your eyes open and let Dom know if he needs to warn Tinpaca Mondago and Almiralyn of trouble." Jordett held out a hand.

The man grasped it. "Be careful, Major." He loped down a quaint cobblestone lane and rounded a curve out of view.

With a final glance at The Borderlands, Jordett jogged a circle around the lamppost. As the ends of his third circle overlapped, he found himself in a small park near the Center for Advanced Healing in the Mid-City District of Idronatti. Grateful for the shade cast by one of the few large trees in the city, he scanned the area. No Idronattians, RewFaarans, or PPP patrollers strolled along the deserted streets. The eerie emptiness kept him immobile. Sweat trickled down his face. Still, he did not move.

Across the street, a gray cat detached itself from the shadows. As his gaze locked onto Majeska's, her ears twitched. She turned and darted between two buildings.

Drying the sweat on his uniform sleeve, he sprinted after her. When he rounded the corner, she sat waiting, her tail whipping through the air. His appearance sent her trotting further down the narrow inter-building pass-through. She paused beside a set of stairs, glanced back, and disappeared into the stairwell. By the time he reached it, she was gone. The basement door gaped open. He ducked through and closed it behind him. Almiralyn's gray cat sat washing her ears halfway down the hall.

Henrietta had arranged for him to meet with two officers from specialized branches of the PPP whom she felt were interested in helping. Their knowledge of Myrrh and the existence of other planets in the solar system would make his job easier.

A quick examination of the hallway informed him there were exits at both ends. His search of the room where Majeska waited was disappointing. Sparse furnishings, a Personal Needs Space, and a closet. He frowned. *Only one door...not great if I need to escape.*

He had just arranged three chairs into a circle when a soft knock announced his first visitor. Easing the door ajar, he studied the brim-shadowed face of a woman. "May I help you?"

"I'm a friend of Sparrow and the twins." She shot a nervous glance down the hall. "Major Jordett?"

He nodded and stepped aside so she could enter. "I'm Jordett."

She removed her cap and lifted speculative eyes. "I'm Anada."

Jordett studied the stern face, the nervous fingers twitching her uniform cap, the reticence he heard in her clipped tone. He understood. They were both at risk—more risk than she could even imagine. He glanced at her uniform. The insignia denoted Unit 11. She was a specialist on Myrrh and The Borderlands. Perhaps she understood more than he guessed.

He pointed at the chairs, took a seat, and relaxed his expression to one of open interest. "We might not have much time. Please tell me why you came."

She sat down on the edge of her chair. "How do I know I can trust you? I prefer not to end up in the Five Towers."

"I understand." He kept his gaze steady. "I want to help Idronatti and its residents. You know I am an officer in the PPP's Diplomatic Division, a liaison between the military and the police branches. My job is to assure that both organizations adhere to the rules of *The Plan.* Like everyone else, when I turned fourteen sun cycles, they adjusted my mind to obscure any memories of Myrrh. For reasons of planetary security, when the PPP promoted me to my current job, they reinstated my memory. That's as much as I'm willing to share until I know you are committed to helping."

She fiddled with her cap, turning it one way and then the other. "Since the RewFaaran Army took over the city, I have felt helpless, Major. Rattori's Brigrade has indoctrinated most of the officers of the PPP. *The Plan* has made us followers. The PPP needs a leader in order to function. Ordinary citizens are staying inside, afraid to come out, afraid of alien soldiers in the streets. When Henrietta found me, I had already decided I had to do something. My friendship with SparrowLyn and Teva taught me what it's like to have friends of my own choosing. I believe it's time for Idronattians to learn how to stand on their own." She held her gaze steady. "Are you shocked?"

He smiled. "Not in the least. I've also discovered individual freedom of late." He leaned closer. "Will you help? It will be dangerous, but it could save this city."

A sharp rap on the door and the quiet squeak of its opening interrupted. A tall, well-built man whose uniform indicated a special military unit strode into the room.

Anada tensed, her expression wary. "Sagus. What are you doing here?"

He scowled. "I might ask you the same question."

Jordett cleared his throat.

The man snapped to attention and saluted. "Lt. Sagus of the PPP Stealth Corps, sir."

"At ease, soldier. Grab a chair and join us."

Anada edged toward the door. "I can't work with him, Major."

Sagus blocked her exit. "I don't want to work with you either."

Jordett looked from one to the other. *Why can't life ever be simple?*

When Henrietta arrived at Nemttachenn Tower, she sighed, inhaled the scents of moss and mulchy earth and pine, and let the sounds of the forest soothe her. *Life in Idronatti left me starved for nature.*

From the shelter of the trees, she assessed the height of the granite tower, surveyed the clearing, and contemplated Nemttachenn's pulsating power. *My life is about to change... I can feel it. Time to find Paisley and the Intersect. Teleporting is fatiguing for this old lady.*

With a purpose to her tottering stride, she crossed to the entrance and paused. A subtle vibration tingled along her left side. Peering through a spell of invisibility, she smiled. *Evolsefil.* The temptation to touch the glistening Prima Crystal almost overwhelmed her. Instead, she studied the players at the chess board across the tower. The translucent giant, she felt certain, was the Sentinel of Myrrh, CheeTrann. The large man was Allynae's friend, Paisley. His ebony face beaming with triumph, he captured a rook, set it beside the board, and leaned back in his chair.

A rumble of frustration echoed through the tower. CheeTrann leaned forward, his eyes squinted in concentration. Paisley seemed to hold his breath. Neither noticed as she walked to the table and stood scrutinizing the board. In unison, they glanced at each other and then turned surprised eyes in her direction.

She donned her spectacles and her most beguiling smile. "I'm Henri. Looks like a close game."

CheeTrann rose like a specter of doom. "You snuck up on us."

She tipped her head back and stared at the bearded face. "You were very involved in your game, so I was quiet. You are rather tall, you know."

He lowered to sitting and shot a sideways look at Paisley. "Can we trust her?"

Paisley nodded. "Yep. This is Almiralyn's Aunt Henrietta. Ashor informed me she was on the way."

"Why didn't you tell me? I could have sent her into oblivion."

Paisley shrugged. "We started a new game. I forgot."

CheeTrann shook his shoulder-length white hair back from his face. "Good to meet you, ma'am. I apologize if I frightened you."

"No harm done. Mind if I watch? I would rather not arrive at the Dojanacks until late evening."

CheeTrann waved a hand. A chair materialized. "Please join us."

Paisley gave her an eager smile. "Ya got any news?"

Henri perched on the seat. "I have just spent time with Major Jordett and Tinpaca Mondago. They asked me to provide you with an update." Both men inclined their heads to listen. Henrietta began with the message she had received to come to Almiralyn's aid.

. . .

The time with CheeTrann and Paisley had passed quickly. They were well-matched opponents, and the game had been close. Paisley's full-lipped mouth pursed in a pout when he lost, then curved into a smile. "Another turning will bring another opportunity."

The Sentinel's laugh of pleasure had echoed off Nemttachenn's walls like the roar of a rushing river.

The ride through the Intersect was quick and easy. She arrived in Meos at middle-night for a reason—Almiralyn had asked her to keep her presence a secret.

The empty square was quiet but for the sound of water tumbling down the rocky fountain at its center. It surprised her that during a war, no guards challenged her sudden appearance. What did not surprise her was the tall, slender woman walking toward her from a dimly lit tunnel.

Almiralyn's wan smile and tired eyes told her much about the state of her niece's emotions. Myrrh's Guardian joined her beside the fountain. They embraced and then contemplated the cascading water.

After a few silent moments, Henrietta glanced up at her niece. "Well, my dear, you called, and I came. Where can we talk?"

Almiralyn linked an arm through hers. "This way, Aunt Henri. Thank you for coming."

They traversed the square and followed the natural tunnel to an arched entryway. Almiralyn pulled a heavy curtain aside. Henrietta preceded her into a beautiful cave where flecks of quartz crystal glistened in salmon walls.

"How lovely, Mira." She sank onto a cushioned bench and sighed. "It has been quite a journey. RewFaaran troops and the PPP were crawling all over Domlenah Midtown Blue. As you know, I've been staying with my friend Deora in the Central Mountains. It was a challenge to return to my apartment. The PPP guarded it. Of course, I couldn't leave Etunir, the crystal you gave me, there. I had to trick one officer into leaving his post. Another one waited inside." She patted her white curls. "It's a good thing I'm quick on my feet."

Almiralyn almost laughed, then sobered. "I have so much to tell you, Aunt Henri."

Henrietta sniffed the air. "What is that tantalizing aroma?" Her stomach gave a hearty growl.

Almiralyn pointed at a small table. "Owae fixed us a meal."

"Oh, my dear, I'm starving. Do you think we could eat while we catch up?" She gave her niece a wistful smile.

This time a laugh eased Almiralyn's expression and brought a sparkle to her eyes. Henri tossed her hat on a bench and crossed to the table. From under her lashes, she noted a touch of color in her niece's face. *Much better. Much, much better.*

4

Der Tah

The lumbering crash of a large animal sent Esán and his friends scrambling between giant ferns and over large, exposed tree roots. Rain pelted through holes in the forest canopy and added the elements of slimy mud and wet moss to their mad dash.

Esán cast his senses ahead. The image of a giant tree formed in his mind. He helped Brie clamber over a wedge-shaped root, took her hand, and ran in its direction. Muffled grunts and groans assured him their friends followed.

The tree came into view. Massive branches stretched away from the gnarly trunk like giant reaching arms. From the lowest, fat tubers covered with lumpy nubs cascaded in a cage-like curtain around it. Snails the size of dinner plates left mucus trails behind as they inched their way over large, thick, spade-shaped leaves. Above them, a rainbow of birds squawked and flapped vividly colored wings in response to their approach.

Brie's drango boots lost traction. Esán steadied her and guided her through a maze of knee-high strangler roots to the base of the dangling tubers. His head tipped back, he tracked the height of the tree until it disappeared above the arch of tangled branches high overhead. *It might be climbable...if we could reach a lower branch.* He doubled over, gripped his knees, and tried to catch his breath.

Brie sucked in air between chattering teeth. "It's s-s-still c-coming."

He straightened and put an arm around her. Torgin, Desirol, and Ira clambered over the stranglers and stood, panting.

"Now what?" Torgin wheezed his question between gulps of air.

Esán straightened. "We need to?" His wards shot up around him. "Run!"

Torgin kicked and shouted as a long, writhing tuber wrapped its nubby length around his body and lifted him into the air. Another snatched Brie and deposited her at the base of the tree. Ira and Desirol sailed through the air and landed in a crumpled pile at her feet. The tubers dropped straight down, buried their tips in the ground, and went rigid.

Esán started toward his friends. "I'll get you out."

Ira's arm shot between the roots. He pointed madly. "Behind you!"

Esán swung around. Hoofed feet thundered closer. A mammoth, boar-like creature exploded from trees and dripping leaves and lunged to a stop, its beady eyes glinting in the dim light.

Esán's mind raced. His first instinct—teleport. *Can't. The Mindeco. Can't leave my friends.* He strengthened his wards.

Snorting and gnashing its teeth, the creature swung its massive head back and forth. Curled tusks protruded on either side of its mouth. A second pair extended like rapiers, and sliced through the ferns and plant growth. Its roar rumbled through the trees and ended in a silence heavy with expectation.

The animal lowered its head and snorted. Esán kept his gaze fixed. Intelligent, tawny eyes stared into his. Nostrils flared. The piggish snout sniffed the wards. A long, pink tongue gave them a tentative lick. Sparks snapped. With a slurping sound, the tongue disappeared. The shields shimmered and steadied.

Esán scanned his memory of Wolloh's book on DerTah. A wave of relief left him shaking. "Ooh. You're a Gothraw." He pointed at his chest. "I'm Esán. I don't want to hurt you."

The tawny eyes questioned.

Esán let the shield fade and held out a hand. The Gothraw sniffed his fingertips and rubbed the four lumps on its forehead against his palm. Taking a cautious step around a rapier, Esán stroked the side of its face. "Do you have a name?"

"Ratcholet." Its telepathic reply was tentative. Its gaze swept beyond him to his trapped companions. *"Ratee Tree bad for Human."*

"Ratee Tree?" Esán gulped down his fear. A passage from the book on DerTah had warned: "Ratee Trees feed on the flesh of mammals."

Ira called out. "What kind of tree?"

The tubers quivered. Large thorns burst from the nubs on their surfaces. Sticky brown sap began to run down the side of the trunk.

Esán sprang into action. "Get into a tight group. I'll try to shield you from here. Be as still as you can."

He attempted to erect wards. A sharp pain knifed through his head. "I c-can't."

"I can help." Brie's mind touch chased the pain away.

He took a relieved breath. *"Visualize a shimmering curtain around you. I'll do what I can from here."*

The tubers shook loose from the ground, whipped through the air, and smashed against the wards. Each blow weakened Brie's ability to hold them steady. Her face grew red with effort. "They're winning."

The Gothraw let out a deep, bellowed howl and leapt forward. Rapier tusks hacked tuber after tuber. Chunks flew in all directions. A loud creak shook the Ratee. It shuddered from its roots to its uppermost branches. The tubers retreated high in the air.

"Run!" Ira grabbed Brie's arm and dragged her away from the tree.

Torgin and Desirol ducked and dodged the snake-like tubers and raced after them. Esán followed. Stumbling through knee-high undergrowth and ankle-deep puddles, they staggered into a huddle well beyond the Ratee and struggled to catch their breath.

The Gothraw sliced one last tuber in two and trotted to their side. A soft rumble preceded the retraction of the long rapiers into sheath-like receptacles.

Brie patted its matted fur. "You're a Gothraw, aren't you? I read about you in Aunt Mira's book."

Torgin frowned. "Is it dangerous?"

Esán nodded. "Oh, it's dangerous, but only when frightened or cornered or if you threaten its young."

The creature licked Brie's arm and emitted a soft purr.

Ira grinned. "It likes you, Brielle."

She smiled and touched a lump on its head. "You're a female, aren't you?"

It nuzzled her cheek.

"How'd you know?" Torgin gave it a tentative pat.

"You can tell because it has four lumps. Three means it's male."

Esán stroked the creature's shaggy side. "It calls itself Ratcholet. It's an herbivore."

Ira touched a pointed ear. "You mean it eats grass and not meat, right?"

The ears turned one way and then the other. The eyes focused on Brie, who smiled. "*She* likes to be called Cho."

"How do you know that?" Torgin demanded. "I'm sure that wasn't in the—"

Desirol shoved Torgin aside and stabbed a finger at Esán's chest. "You led us right to that tree. *You* tried to kill us."

Esán took a step back. "I thought it was safe. I—"

The RewFaaran shoved him. "I'm taking the lead. No one wants to follow someone who almost got us eaten."

Ira shot him a dirty look. "Keep your hands to yourself, Des, or I'll—"

Cho gave an agitated snort, sniffed the air, and galloped away through the undergrowth.

Brie swung around and stared after the departing creature. "We need to move. Something else heads straight for us." She looked at Esán. "You lead. We'll follow."

Desirol glared. "I'm *not* going with him."

"Then stay here." Torgin nodded at Esán. "Let's go."

Taking care to mask his mind, Esán searched the area. Brie sensed something, and it had frightened the Gothraw. As he crept toward Atkis, his thoughts were anything but silent. *Why did I see a dangerous tree instead of a good hiding place? Why couldn't I set up wards around my friends?* A tingle of fear skittered over his scalp. *Who's trying to gain control of my mind?*

Stebben strode into the arena as a DerTahan red hawk swooped over Allynae's head and landed at its center. One Man materialized, pulled his long, wheat-colored hair over his shoulder, and began to redo his braid. He nodded at the Guardian of Myrrh's brother and addressed Stebben. "How's Wolloh? I had a weird feeling he was unwell."

"He was dressing when I left him. We are to meet him in the conference chamber." Stebben walked briskly toward the ranch house. "How did Lorsedi take the news that Gerolyn was joining him at the front?"

One Man flipped the completed braid over his shoulder. "He was none too happy. I left it to Voer to convince him that her presence was important to all of us."

Stebben paused midway to the house, his brow wrinkled in concentration. "Something is wrong. I'm going to check on Wolloh." He teleported to his mentor's door. Urgent need propelled him into the room. Panic almost choked him.

Wolloh lay senseless, half on and half off the bed, his face leached of color. The labored rise and fall of his chest were the only indications he lived.

Stebben knelt beside him. "Wolloh? Wolloh, can you hear me?" He touched the side of his neck. A weak pulse beat a hesitant rhythm against his fingers.

One Man arrived at the door and hurried to his side. Allynae held back.

Stebben kept his voice low. "He was fine when I left—just tired. I've never known him to be ill or indisposed." Worry made the words sticky and thick.

One Man's hand on his shoulder quieted the panic. "We'll figure out what's wrong. Help me move him."

They lifted the limp body and resettled the High DiMensioner on the bed. One Man placed a hand on his forehead. For a long moment, he remained in quiet contemplation. His expression when he looked up was grim. "Whatever holds him so close to death is not something I recognize or know."

Stebben nudged Wolloh's cane from under the bed and grabbed the crystal knob. Blazing heat flooded his veins. A yelp of pain morphed into an extended scream. Like Autumn leaves in a fire, hope withered. Despair squeezed the will to live from his body. The room faded.

The cane, ripped from his rigid fingers, tore the skin from his palm. He fell to his knees, gasping for breath. Strong hands pressed against his temples sent life pulsing through him. His racing heart steadied to a measured beat. His breathing calmed.

The room focused. Hope glinted in his heart. The eyes staring into his belonged to Reader, the man who had saved him from the Mocendi League when he was twelve sun cycles and sent him in search of Wolloh.

Stebben tried to speak and then shook his head. One Man and Allynae helped him to a chair.

Reader looked down at him. "Take a moment to rest, Stebben. We'll be right here."

Quiet settled over the room. Stebben sighed, leaned back in the chair, and closed his eyes. Reader's touch eased the pain in his hands and restored both hope and his will to live. Fatigue weighed his body. Sleep made a furtive approach, wrapped him in its gentleness, and transported him to a deep and tranquil place.

Nissasa Rattori's frigid blue eyes flashed with anger hotter than the sands of DerTah at middle-turning. A contemptuous mask distorting his face, he marched along the line of assembled men and returned to center. His troops remained at attention, their desire to be elsewhere visible in the nervous twitch of their eyes.

Eyes glinting steel, he growled, "Why are you here and not on the other side of those shields? My orders were to kill every one of Lorsedi's men and to bring *him* to me. I provided the opportunity." He pointed at a man. "You, step forward."

An officer complied.

"Explain, now." Nissasa jerked his head at the shimmering curtain.

The soldier started to speak, pressed his lips together, and swallowed. "I failed you, sir."

Rage sent Nissasa into the shape of the DerTahan bearded buzzard. Flames blazed around him. Scissor-sharp talons gripped the man's shoulders, lifted him high above the desert, shook him like a child's toy, and let him fall. The officer plummeted to the ground and lay in a broken heap.

Nissasa shifted and faced his men. "Fail me again, and you will all follow this traitor to his grave." He kicked the mangled body with the toe of his boot, then glared up and down the line. "Get to your posts. When the shields fall again, I want results."

Nissasa glanced at a Sebborr hurrying toward them and frowned. His angry gaze swept down the line of men. "Dismissed."

They scattered, taking their dead comrade with them.

The Sebborr reached his side. "Please, Sajud Rattori, it is very important that you come." He bowed and remained humble and waiting.

The title the Sebborr had bestowed on him sent a thrill of egotistic pride pulsing through Nissasa. Arrogance lifted his chin higher and puffed out his chest. "Lead on, steanpa." He uttered the RewFaaran word for peasant with a touch of disdain.

The Sebborr averted his face and hurried toward a group of tents pitched a good distance from the border. At the entry to one near the center of the encampment, he stepped to one side and bowed.

Nissasa brushed past him, marched into the tent, and came to an abrupt halt. The heat of his smoldering rage reignited. He swung around. "Where is the raven?" The sibilant words hissed between clenched teeth. Clothing, toiletries, anything that came within his reach flew through the air. Anger ricochetted inside his head. Storming to the entry, he found the Sebborran steanpa had gone.

A man in the garb of a high-ranking Sebborr rounded a tent and walked toward him. Shrewd, dark eyes searched his face. "Sajud, what has upset you? How may I help?" DesTel Terah, Dahe's eldest son, made a gracious salaam.

Nissasa seethed. "Where is your father?"

"He has gone home to deal with an important tribal matter, Sajud. He will return as soon as he is able. Until then, I *am* in charge."

Turning on his heels, Nissasa reentered his tent. DesTel remained outside, his expression solemn—*almost* subservient.

Nissasa scowled. "Don't just stand there. Come in."

"As you wish, Sajud Rattori." DesTel entered and surveyed the tent.

"Someone has made a terrible mess. Allow me to send a slave to straighten things for you."

"Someone has stolen my personal property. I want him punished."

"If I do not know what is missing, I cannot assist you, Sajud." DesTel folded his arms and waited.

Nissasa kicked a bar of soap and watched it land near his camp cot. "Someone or something that could help us win this war from my tent. Your father told you about the raven?"

"He did, Sajud. I recall him saying it belonged to the Guardian of Myrrh. It would indeed be a good bargaining chip. I will have all tents searched if that is your wish."

"Do it and send someone to clean up this mess. You're excused."

The Sebborr bowed and left.

Nissasa glowered at his departing figure. "Da'am Sebborr. If I didn't need their help..." He scowled at the tent and its contents. "...and their resources, I'd never have agreed to join forces. Da'am the Mocendi League for putting me in this position." He took a swig from his canteen and screwed the cap back in place. "Can't trust those drabasts, either. Can't trust anybody."

The canteen flew across the tent and rattled to a stop at the feet of a cowering Sebborran slave.

On the Island of Zaltraca off the southern-most tip of Geran Isle, a single cottage overlooked the Sea of Minusa. Wind howled over the high Cliffs of Tymine from morning until night. The sea tumbling against its rocky face sent spray to cover everything in a sticky film. The high-pitched squawk of laridae and the grunt of phalacro blended in a constant chorus that only stilled when the moons of DerTah reached Tri-Nular.

For Coala Renn Whalend, born and raised in Idronatti on the distant planet of Thera, the constant barrage of nature's songs formed a cacophonous symphony. Standing by an open window, she wondered if she would ever return to The City. She thought about her son—his music and the beautiful compositions that flowed from his fingers. *Oh, Torgin, will I ever see you again? I wish I had told you how much I love your music.*

Pushing tousled curls back from her face, she frowned. I didn't want you to think they might assign you a profession that would allow you to develop your genius as a composer. You have too many skills that are useful to Idronatti.

She leaned out the window, absorbing the wildness of the landscape—the total lack of Human presence. *How long have they held me captive? Time moves differently on the planet of DerTah than on Thera, and I have lost track of its passing.*

A gust wuthered by, snatched up the fear fluttering in her belly, and tossed it over the tumultuous sea. She shivered. Clouds amassed along the horizon churned a menacing shade of gray. Bibeed, the woman assigned to care for her, had said a storm was on the way.

In Idronatti, storms were rare. Seasonal transitions were so subtle one barely noticed summer had passed and autumn had begun. Winter left its mark in gentle dustings of snow, followed by brilliant blue skies. She sighed. *I want to go home...to be with my husband and my son.*

Unable to contain her restlessness, she tied on her blue scarf and slipped on a baggy coat. Stepping onto the porch, she stared at the moor-like stretch of land between the cottage and the cliff's edge. When she first arrived, she stayed close to the cottage. The emptiness, the howl of the wind, the fear of what she could not see had terrified her. At Bibeed's urging, she began to explore.

Soon, she discovered a small tool shed half-hidden amidst prickly bushes and rutted track that led away from the cottage and disappeared into a forest of craggy, thick-trunked pines and stubby oaks. One afternoon, she discovered a steep trail leading to an overlook. Navigating it for the first time had terrified her. Now, she relished the challenge of it—the wind tearing at her hair and clothing—the pungent odor of salt spray and sea life at low tide.

She lowered her head and, pressing into the wind, walked to the rocky cliff's edge and down the trail. When she reached the overlook, she sank onto a stone bench and allowed the tactile nature of the environment to strip her agitation away until nothing remained, not even the deepening sense of futility that so often threatened to drown her.

Closing her eyes, she imagined her apartment in Idronatti. Tears pooled as Wilith's handsome face emerged in memory. They overflowed down her cheeks when she thought of Torgin. *I love you both so much.* She wiped her tears on her scarf and stared at the wet splotch.

"I pray you are unharmed, Wilith, and that Torgin has not returned to Idronatti, hoping to rescue me."

Staring at the dark clouds crowding the horizon, she remembered the turning of her unexpected kidnapping, something that never happen in The City. The PPP saw to that and to protecting Idronatti's citizens.

After an uneventful ride from her lab in the Benisuss District to her home in Domlenah Uptown Blue, she stepped onto the Avenue of Trees to find two men in unfamiliar uniforms waiting. The next thing she remembered was waking up in a strange room filled with strange sounds.

A lean man with salt and pepper hair and chiseled features visited once the drug had worn off. He was polite, even deferential. "They will continue to hold you," he had told her, "until Torgin has given Nissasa Rattori the Compass of Ostradio." When she expressed only confusion, he had explained further. "The Guardian of Myrrh gave the compass to your son."

Myrrh had rung a distant bell—one that since then had come into focus. The longer she was away from Idronatti, the more memories emerged and with them a mortifying revelation. She shook her head. *Why didn't I realize it sooner? I developed a chemical spray to inhibit the memories of rats and keep them docile, and the PPP is using it to control the people of Idronatti.*

A large raindrop spattering on the bench beside her brought her to her feet. Struggling against the push and pull of the wind, she trudged up the trail. Bibeed, a frantic warning in her expression, met her halfway, grabbed her arm, and hurried her to the overlook.

"We have to hide, Miss Renn. We have to hide, and fast."

5

Myrrh & Thera

Almiralyn stared at the curve of the ceiling in her quarters. *Why am I not in my bed?* The narrowness of the cushioned bench hugging her to the wall jarred her memory. *Oh yes.* She pushed back the blanket covering her and sat up. An oil lamp glowed on the ledge near the sleeping alcove, where the diminutive shape of her Aunt Henri snuggled beneath a comforter. The chronometer next to it informed her she had slept through the night.

Her guest stirred and pushed up on an elbow. "Good morning, niece." Henrietta yawned and smiled.

Almiralyn shook her head. "You put me to sleep, Aunt Henri. We didn't decide what to do or—"

"Hush, my dear. We both needed to rest. Now, our thinking will be clear and our decisions in keeping with our needs." She sat up and slid to the edge of the alcove. "Where does one freshen up around here?"

"Through there." Almiralyn pointed at a barely noticeable curtain. "I'll find us some breakfast."

As her aunt padded across the cave, a bell tinkled outside the entryway. Almiralyn pulled the curtain aside. "Good morning, Owae. How did you know we were up?"

The ancient DeoNyte smiled. "Your aunt let me know when you began to awaken." She beckoned to a young male holding a laden tray. "Please put that on the table."

Eyes on his burden, he set it down and turned to hurry away. Owae stopped him with a hand on his shoulder. "This is Koos, my new apprentice."

Almiralyn offered her palm. "It is a pleasure to meet you, Koos."

He lowered his eyes, and touching it lightly, skittered into the tunnel.

Owae let the curtain fall into place. "He is very shy and also almost as talented as Elae. When he's grown, he will be a fine healer."

Henrietta reappeared, looking fresh and tidy. "Ah, Owae, it is good to see you. Will you break your evening fast with us?"

The DeoNyte gave Henri a gummy smile. "I would be delighted to join you."

Almiralyn strode down the tunnel. Hydroponic fruit and the grain-like cereal from the DeoNyte food preparation area had left her replete and smiling. Full bellies and a good night's sleep had taken the edge off the decision-making process. Rounding a corner, she arrived at Nomed's quarters and rang the bell.

"Come in, Mira."

She smiled at the use of her nickname and entered. "Good morning, Seyes. I hope you slept well."

A return smile stretched his scarred cheek taut. "I did, and by the looks of you, I'd guess you did, too."

"Aunt Henri worked her magic. I am feeling rested and much more alert. Let me bring you up to date."

They sat opposite each other. She laid out her plan and leaned back to observe his reaction.

"I like it. It considers the needs of Myrrh and your personal needs. Sparrow will be relieved, too. When do you tell her?"

"I am headed there now. Can you be ready to leave in a half circle of the chronometer?"

"I can. You realize the Cycle of Dovi is almost upon us."

"I do. DerTah's three moons will line up between the sun and planet in less than a moon cycle. All portals will shut down, and we risk being stuck until the moons resume their orbits and the sun reappears. The Unfolding presses us to be on our way." She offered her hand. "Thank you, Seyes, for forgiving me and for becoming my ally."

He clasped it. "It's my pleasure. The burden of revenge is heavy. I'm glad to put it to rest. I'll see you at the gateway."

She smiled as she traveled the tunnels to her quarters. *The Unfolding has worked wonders for Seyes Nomed. Hopefully, it will help to save Corvus.*

Kieel had darted through the Tropal Gateway ahead of Jordett and followed Majeska from The Borderlands to Idronatti. Intimidated by the tall buildings and the eerie quiet of the wide streets, he'd hidden in a large tree. *Wonder what the city's like busy? What made me—or Henrietta—think I could help?*

A noise announced Major Jordett's arrival. When Majeska appeared across the street, Kieel shot to a windowsill in the building behind her. He followed Jordett to the room, where he now regarded two PPP officers with a look of exasperation. Keeping out of sight, Kieel waited for Jordett's next move.

Anada and Sagus continued to glower. Jordett looked from one stubborn face to the other and gave an inward sigh. "Idronatti and Thera are in danger. You can help, or you can leave. We have very little time." He sat down and folded his arms across his chest.

Anada glared at Sagus and took a seat. "I want to help. I can forget the past, at least for now, if you can."

The young man chewed on his lower lip, removed his cap, and brushed it against his pant leg. "I guess I can but—"

"No buts." Jordett kept his expression stern. "You can, or you can't. We don't have time to argue. We have to move fast if we want to retake the city."

The lieutenant jerked a chair around and straddled the seat. "I'll help."

Again, Jordett scrutinized one, then the other. "Trust is vital, or we'll fail. Your relationship could put us all in danger and jeopardize the entire mission."

Sagus held out a hand. "The future of Idronatti must take precedence over personal concerns. I can let the past go, Anada."

She gave him a genuine smile. "Me, too." They shook and returned their attention to him.

Satisfied by what he saw, he rested his forearms on his thighs and began. "The information I'm about to share will put you in danger. It has to stay between us, or we are doomed before we start. Clear?"

A touch of fear tinged their expressions as they affirmed their understanding.

By the time he had described events in Myrrh and DerTah, their expressions had changed to incredulous. The PPP taught them about other planets, but not about other life forms. They understood that Rattori's Brigade was from the planet RewFaar, but their emotions fought against it.

Sagus threw his hands in the air. "How are we going to win against troops trained on the planet of warfare? They are..." He stopped and smacked his cap against his leg.

Anada finished his sentence. "...the best in the Inner Universe. But, Sagus, we know our city and our planet. We just have to be smarter and more careful."

Jordett smiled his approval. "My experience with the rebels suggests they are arrogant and, therefore, vulnerable. Let's examine our options. We need more men." He glanced at Anada. "And women. Mondago's soldiers are busy protecting the Demrach and Tropal Gateways. He can spare a couple, but that's it. Who can we trust in the Stealth Corps, Sagus?"

"I am aware of three who have not succumbed to Rattori's Brigade. They may know of others."

"Anada?"

She frowned. "Most of Unit 11 has capitulated. The PPP did not train us to deal with soldiers from off-world. They trained us to put down disturbances in The City and to hunt down anyone living in Idronatti illegally. I know of only two who might help."

Majeska nudged the door open and meowed. Jordett came to his feet and hurriedly crossed the room. The hall was empty, but judging by her behavior, not for long.

When he turned, the two young officers had rearranged the chairs and waited poised for flight. Anada joined him. "I can provide directions to a safe house where we can meet." She glanced at Sagus.

"I'm on your side, Anada. Your secrets are as safe with me as mine will be with you."

She let out a breath. "Thanks, Sagus." Speaking in a whisper, she gave them directions. "I've also contacted a friend in Myrrh. She'll bring a band of Myrrhinians who will help."

Jordett's jaw tightened. "Name?"

"Teva Rivan. She knows Sparrow and the twins."

Sagus slapped his cap on his head. "She's good, Major. Knows how to appear and disappear at the right moment." His eyes held Anada's.

The woman grinned. "She still cares, Sag."

Jordett wanted to roll his eyes. Instead, he ushered them down the hall to the entrance, where Majeska waited. "Out you go. One at a time. We meet tomorrow at the safe house at mid-turning. Be careful. You're important, and so is the mission."

Sagus slipped out first. Anada's gaze followed him, then returned to Jordett. "We'll be fine, sir. Once he sees Teva, bygones will be bygones."

She scanned the pass-through and jogged up the stairs.

Jordett stood deep in thought. *Love does strange things to people.* He sighed. *Wonder how Merrilea is fairing?*

The murmur of voices at the opposite end of the hall triggered his departure.

Kieel felt a tremor of fear as he hovered in the hall near the building exit. He glanced around for Majeska. Her absence made him edgier. A noise at the opposite end of the hall sent him fluttering after the Major, who had slipped out the door, hurried along the pass-through between buildings, and paused at the next street.

The Center for Advanced Healing, a tall, pristine building, stood across the way. An occasional Ria Transport skimmed along the street. The Major adjusted his uniform hat lower on his forehead and walked purposefully toward the front entrance. He glanced at the two PPP patrollers guarding the ramp to the Ria-T plaza and nodded. The patroller at the front entrance snapped to attention and held the door wide. The Major passed inside and disappeared from sight.

Kieel froze in the pass-though. All the strangeness—the Humans and the vehicles—rooted him to the spot. He stared at the Healing Center and shuddered. Gripping his walking stick tighter, he gathered his courage and streaked across the street just as the entrance door swung shut, separating him from the only person he knew in the entire city. Panicked, he dove under the portico and hid in a darkened corner. *How am I going to get inside?* He almost smiled as a woman about the age of Henri exited a vehicle. She leaned on the arm of a man in a brown uniform. On her head was a wide-brimmed hat adorned with a halo of big yellow flowers.

Kieel landed and crawled under a blossom as the man opened the door. Peeking from underneath, he gaped. The reception area was circular with a high, domed ceiling and corridors branching in all directions. He swallowed the dismay that threatened to choke him and forced himself to think.

The woman paused. A voice he recognized sent a wave of relief rolling through him.

"Excuse me, ma'am, you have something on your hat. May I remove it?"

"P-p-lease do."

Fingers closed around him. "There. Your hat is much too lovely to be marred by a dying leaf. May I help you find something?"

The woman gave a timid reply. "My man knows the way. Thank you, Major..."

"Saila, ma'am. Major Saila. Have a good turning."

The rhythm of Jordett's walk told Kieel he was moving away. He pressed his eye to a crack between fingers. The light changed; a door closed. The Major's hand rose to eye level. His fingers uncurled. Kieel stared.

Jordett's expression was quizzical, his tone stern. "What on Thera are you doing here?"

Kieel fluttered to standing. "Henri sent me. I...well...I wanted to help. She told me to stay close to you because I would be needed."

Jordett looked thoughtful. "Henri most often knows what's best. Still, how will we keep you hidden?"

"I could crouch under your hat."

"How about my shirt pocket? You'll have to curl up but—" He frowned. "Something is happening down the corridor. We need to go."

Kieel slipped into his pocket and made himself as small as possible. The heartbeat next to his cheek quickened as the Major stepped into the hall.

Squeezing his knees to his chest and gripping his walking stick in a white-knuckled hand, Kieel prayed he would not be more trouble than he was worth.

In the quiet of the studio, Sparrow studied her painting of Corvus, grateful for her rescue from Vascorrie and worried about his capture on DerTah. Lifting the completed canvas down, she leaned it against the wall and set a clean one on the easel. She hoped to provide Almiralyn with the place where her protector was being held.

Staring at the blank canvas, she let the calmness of the studio—enhanced because she would not be the acting Guardian of Myrrh—envelop her. *I'm so glad Almiralyn talked to the Galactic Guardians and that she's staying here, at least for now. I'm even happier that she'll be teaching me the skills I'll need if events demand her presence elsewhere.* She stirred white and black paint together on her palette and wiped the excess off the brush. A thrill of elation elicited a soft laugh. *Sure hope I can learn to shift shape. Alli, Brie, and Ari can do it. Almiralyn may be right...maybe I can. Wonder what it feels like?*

She blinked. The canvas filled her sight. A vague image formed in her mind. Her brow wrinkled in concentration, she painted a wide swath of pale gray diagonally across the stark white.

Sometime later the sound of footsteps pulled her from what she called her artist's daze—that place where her surroundings faded and only her canvas and her art existed. Pleased that she had completed the painting, she glanced over her shoulder. Myrrh's Guardian stood behind her, sapphire eyes glued to the image. Sparrow dropped her brush in a jar of cleanser and stepped back to examine her work.

Menacing darkness covered the canvas. A single ray of light shot through a hole overhead and pooled around a lone raven on a makeshift perch. Hazy, hate-filled faces gathered around it, their empty eyes staring into the distance. Nothing else could be seen. No hint of place emerged from the dark background.

Sparrow couldn't hide her disappointment. "I tried to discover where he was being held. I'm sorry."

Almiralyn put an arm around her. "It gives me hope, Sparrow. At least he's no longer in a cage. Did you sense wards of any kind?"

Sparrow cast her mind back to her trance-like state. "Not that I remember."

"But you would have painted them had they been there." It was a quiet statement. "And people?"

"Only ghosts." She shivered. "So much anger and sadness—and violence."

Nomed ushered Merrilea into the studio in front of him. She hurried forward. "Seyes said you needed us, Mira."

Nomed tapped his temple. "Got your message."

Almiralyn smiled. "Thank you for coming. Please see what you think of Sparrow's latest painting."

Merrilea looked from the canvas to Sparrow. "Where is that?"

"I'd wager it isn't anywhere on Myrrh." A thoughtful frown stretched Nomed's scar taut.

Almiralyn turned back to the painting. "If you were to guess..."

Realization sparked in his hazel eyes. "I would guess a deserted prison in the Toelachoc Mountains near the Fortress of LeCur. It once housed the most violent criminals on DerTah."

Sparrow grasped Merrilea's hand. "Fortress of LeCur?"

"The capital of Fera Finnero, the home of the Dreela Gidtuss." Nomed smiled.

Sparrow gave him a speculative look. "I wonder if I'll ever see DerTah... and my family?"

Almiralyn gazed at the painting, her thoughts racing. *Can this mean Karrew has escaped?* "But, Seyes, Karrew was with Nissasa at the desert border when we last saw him in the fountain. How did he get to LeCur?"

He shrugged. "We could ask Elcaro's Eye."

A hatless Henrietta joined them, her eyes magnified by large spectacles. "Or you could leave for DerTah and discover the way of it. Standing around theorizing will not provide an answer." She shooed Sparrow, Merrilea, and Nomed out of the entryway. "Off you go. I need to speak with my niece. We'll meet you at the portal."

When they had gone, Almiralyn smiled at her. "You're sure you're ready for this?"

"I'm ready for a new adventure, Mira. Life in Idronatti..." She dropped her spectacles in their pocket and grimaced. "Dreary, to say the least. Had I been able to spend time with Sparrow and the twins—now that would have been a different matter."

"You would—"

"Your instincts were right, Mira. The PPP watched too closely for me to move about freely. Do you have any last-minute instructions?"

"I've spoken with Relevart. He has a plan in place that he'll share when he can. Take care of yourself, Aunt Henri."

Henrietta patted her pocket. "I will. You do the same. We better make this happen, my dear."

They linked arms and stepped into the tunnel, leaving the studio and the painting of the lone raven behind.

6
Der Tah

Several turnings had passed since Karrew regained consciousness in the dark and volatile dungeon. The ghosts of the criminally insane hissed the name of the prison like a mantra, flailed him with their lurid remembrances, and whispered foul-mouthed curses in his ears. "Toelachoc…Toelachoc…Toelachoc Prison." They tormented him non-stop during his waking hours and haunted his dreams when he slept. Had he been stronger, he would have set a ward. Capture and subsequent abuse at Nissasa's hand had left him far too weak to attempt it.

A ghost rushed at him, blew a frigid breath that settled around him like a mist, and puffed into nothing. Hoping to hold on to the heat of the desert and to ward off the night's chill, he ruffled his feathers. When the cold penetrated to his skin, his injuries ached with an agonizing fierceness that left him exhausted.

The tread of soft footfalls propelled him into a corner beneath the metal cot. The cell door creaked open. A figure knelt by his perch. A candle sprung to life, casting its weak light in a small, wavering circle.

Words as soft as a lullaby call to him. "Karrew. Come out. Let me examine your wing."

He stuck his head from beneath the cot and peered up at the man who had rescued him. The feeble light painted shadows across his features, leaving his identity a mystery. Karrew waddled toward him. Each step sent pain cutting into his breast.

The man sat down on the cot and dangled a hand near his feathered side. He tapped it with the tip of his beak, giving permission to be lifted.

Once settled on the man's lap, gentle fingers examined his damaged wing, applied ointment, and re-wrapped it. A sweet-smelling salve soothed the burns on his breast. As the pain eased, he studied what he could see of the man's face. He appeared younger than Allynae by several sun cycles. His dark, wavy hair glinted with touches of auburn, his teeth were even and white. When the candlelight found its way into his eyes, the sadness he saw there made Karrew ache for him.

The man stroked his back. "I'm sorry your wing is taking so long to heal. I know you must shift soon. Be patient, my friend."

Karrew's heart skipped a beat at the man's words. His ebony eye searched the shadowed face.

"Don't worry. I won't tell your secret. No one has guessed that you are more than you seem...not even Nissasa Rattori." He spit the name from his mouth like some foul thing. A look of disgust twisted his profile before he continued. "My father and I must return to the RewFaaran Sajud soon. So far, he has not guessed that we took you from his tent." He bent closer. "My father would never suspect me of stealing you, of going against his wishes. After all, he reminds me often, I owe him my life." He straightened. "He has charged *me* with finding the culprit who absconded with you."

Karrew looked at his wing.

"I put a new ointment on it. If you will allow me to, I will do a healing ritual to help speed your recovery." He removed a small pouch from beneath his kcalo and shook several stones onto his palm.

Karrew nudged them with his beak. The man tossed them into the candlelit circle, picked up one that gleamed different shades of green, and held it to the wing.

> *"Healing stone, please do your best*
> *To repair this wing and heal this breast*
> *Quicken mending, make all right*
> *Help this raven regain its flight."*

The whispered rhyme sent a prickling sensation over Karrew's wing and wounded breast. With the final word, it ceased, and the man set him on the perch.

"If you have need of me, Karrew, just think of me. I will come to you as soon as I'm able. My father and I leave for the border tomorrow." Scooping up the stones, he returned them to their pouch, secured it beneath his robes, and pulled out a small jar. After loosening the lid, he placed it on the ground.

"This is the salve. I have brought extra food. You must shift soon, my friend." He gently touched his breast. "I'm afraid your white feather is gone. Nissasa burned it away. I'm sorry." He blew out the candle. "Take care, Karrew, protector of Almiralyn."

He repositioned his hood, and leaving the cell door ajar, vanished like the ghosts of Toelachoc Prison.

Stebben sat in a comfortable chair, his feet on a footstool, his lap covered with a blanket. Ever since he had grasped the crystal knob of Wolloh's cane, he could not shake the sensation of death clinging to his bones.

Allynae sat near him, his head resting in his hands. Occasionally, he glanced up at Wolloh's bedroom door, then lowered his head once more. He glanced up now and cleared his throat. "What are they doing in there?"

Tucking the blanket tighter, Stebben turned his gaze toward his mentor's room. "That depends on what Relevart and One Man have discovered."

Allynae cracked his knuckles, one after the other. The sharp sound reminded Stebben of fire snapping the tendons in his hands. He grimaced.

Allynae caught his eye and dropped his hands to his lap. "Sorry." He intertwined his fingers. "A nasty habit from boyhood that resurfaces when I'm stressed. I never expected to meet the VarTerel of the Inner Universe. Of course, I didn't foresee the DiMensioner's arrival in Myrrh either. I expected life would be quiet and uneventful. Maybe didn't expect it—*hoped* it. The Unfolding is wreaking havoc with our lives." Another knuckle cracked.

Stebben repositioned his exhausted body, grateful fatigue was all he had to deal with. It could have been worse—like death. Nissasa had meant to kill him. Relevart's unannounced arrival had foiled the RewFaaran's plan.

He thought back to when he was twelve sun cycles, to the time the Mocendi League murdered his parents. He remembered the intergalactic ship where he and his younger sister had been imprisoned. They had taken Chyneria to LaTenge Famele, the women's household on RewFaar. Relevart, whom he had known as Reader, had rescued him. He owed the man. He was certain the opportunity to repay his debt would arise sooner than later.

One Man stepped into the sitting room. "Wolloh's resting and comfortable. Relevart suggests we take a break. He foresees life getting busy soon. I agree. Gerolyn just sent a message from Lorsedi."

Allynae rubbed his palms together and flexed his fingers. "And the message is?"

"Nissasa is on a rampage." One Man's brow furrowed. "Someone has stolen something he values from his tent."

Stebben expressed his satisfaction with a smile. "That's what happens when you hang out with scoundrels."

"There's more. Nissasa infused the Oracles Stone with the ConDra's fire."

Surprise lit Allynae's gray-blue eyes. "How'd Gerolyn find that out?"

One Man pulled up a chair. "I gather that while Nissasa pitched his tantrum, she did a bit of mental snooping. That's about it. The wards are holding. Lorsedi's men are getting restless. Waiting is always the hardest part."

Stebben stared at his unblemished palm, where the fire had stripped it of skin and flesh, and rubbed its healed surface with the tip of a finger. *Thank Ecorus for Relevart.* "I'm certain it was the ConDra's fire that burned my hand. If so, the Oracle Stone can focus it through any crystal mined from the Evolsefil Caverns. We should warn Almiralyn."

Relevart entered the room. "I have already warned her." He closed the door and pulled a chair into their circle. With the wisdom of the ages gleaming in his eyes, he studied each man. A nerve twitched at the corner of Allynae's eye. One Man's expression relaxed. Death fell away from Stebben's bones, and he felt life creeping back into his body.

"Thanks, Relevart. I never expected to be warm again. How is Wolloh? What's next?"

The tall man resettled his rangy body on the chair and stared into the distance. Raising a hand, he whispered a strange syllable and snapped his fingers. A rowan staff appeared in his grasp. He leaned it against his thigh and address his companions.

"It is vital we achieve several goals before the Mocendi League discovers I have left the planet of Persow."

"Can't *you* heal Wolloh?" Allynae asked.

"Unfortunately, only the sacred knife can heal the High DiMensioner." His eyes held Allynae's.

Allynae frowned. "Ari has Efillaeh, and we don't know where she is."

A sudden chill gripped the circle of men. Cold once more skittered over Stebben's bones. He pulled his blanket tighter.

Far from Shu Chenaro in the Tinga Forest, Brie huddled with her friends in the hollow of a huge, dead tree. The rain had ceased, and a steamy mist floated over the ground and trees. She pressed her hand against her stomach to silence its hungry rumble and peered out through the opening. A snake slithering beneath the ferns, snatched a small furry creature in its jaws, swallowed it whole, and curled into a tight coil beneath a rock.

Food and sleep. I could sure use some of both. A soft chorus of snores made her sigh. Torgin and Ira could doze almost anywhere. Desirol, his weather blanket tented over his head, sat across the way, his back pressed against a massive trunk and his head resting on bent knees.

Esán nestled close to her, his eyes distant and his breathing measured. Someone had attempted to control his mind. To foil any further attempts, he had slipped into a deep trance. She had constructed a subtle curtain of energy around him and monitored his breathing. When it was safe, he would emerge. She sighed again.

The Compass of Ostradio had brought them this far. She wanted nothing more than to be out of the Tinga Forest with its giant, carnivorous plants and strange animals. Their conflict with the Ratee Tree still left her trembling when she thought of it. *What else waits to harm us or worse...eat us?* That the tree could have killed her friends made her heart clench.

She glanced around their shelter. The rough inner surface of the tree was pitted and uneven. Different types of moss and lichen had found a home in the damp wood. Although the top of the tree had toppled, something had grown over the opening, allowing only stray rays of light to leak through.

The shriek of a bird sent her gaze darting over the landscape. A flash of blue shot into ferns and other plant growth. Stillness followed its descent. She shivered and pulled her weather blanket closer around her shoulders. *I wonder what happened to Wolloh? He crumpled to the ground as we teleported. Whoever knocked him senseless sent us to a different place than he intended. Now it's up to Esán and the compass to get us to safety.*

Esán's eyes snapped open. The pupils dilated and then shrunk to a normal size. He whispered, "We're being stalked by a ludoc cat."

The Star of Truth sent a sharp, affirmative twinge down her spine. She gripped his hand and swallowed her fear. "Ludocs are the size of a rohes. They have razor sharp canines and long hind legs. They're the swiftest predators on DerTah. If one is after us..." She groaned. "What do we do, Esán?"

"Since we can't get away from it, scaling the inside of this tree is our best solution. Ludoc's are gigantic. With luck, it won't fit in this hollow. I'll get Des. You wake the boys."

He crept through the mist and shook Des awake. A brief argument ensued. Esán pivoted and headed back. Desirol marched after him, muttering under his breath.

She woke Ira. "We're in danger." He sat straighter, elbowed Torgin, and repeated her warning.

Torgin turned pale as Esán joined them and described their adversary. "We are being hunted by a ludoc? I read about those. They're carnivores. What do we do?"

Brie pointed upward. "We climb as high as we can and hope it is an enormous cat."

A low growl immobilized the group.

Esán took charge. "Ira, you're the best climber. You go first. Then Brie, Torgin, and Des. I'll come last and attempt to set a shield."

Ira already searched for hand and toe holds. "I think we can climb this. There are rough patches and indents all over the trunk. Here I go." Grabbing a straggly piece of wood, he placed his foot and began to climb. Brie scrambled after him. The tree's diameter grew narrower the higher they went. Finally, he stopped, braced his back and legs, and pulled her up so she could clasp his thigh. "Hold on. I won't let you fall."

Clambering as close to him as possible, she braced herself against the inner trunk and tried not to think about the bugs living in the rotting wood. Below her, Torgin came to a stop. A growl chased Desirol higher. Esán was invisible below him. Closing her eyes, she stretched her senses outward. The ludoc crouched several trees away, its nose sniffing the air. Brie held her breath as it crept, belly to the ground, toward their hiding place.

Wolloh lay in an unconscious state, suspended between life and death. Dreams pursued him through the fire swamps and boiling mud pits of DerTah, where tiny bugs bit his face until blood poured down his cheeks. His good eye ached from the heat and the blinding light of the sun. His tongue stuck to the roof of his mouth. Heat scalded his lungs with each haggard breath.

As a cool hand touched his forehead, his eyes flew open. He uttered a cry of relief and slipped into a dream where he floated in a cool pool of water, steam rising from his half-submerged body. Beside him, a man held him afloat. He closed his eyes and let the coolness wash over him. Pain eased, and his mind cleared. Again, he opened his eyes.

The man leaned close to his ear. "Nissasa watches and waits. We shall give him what he desires. You must trust me, Wolloh, or all is lost."

Wolloh forced a fragmented reply from his blistered throat.

The man touched his forehead. Life fled.

Relevart gripped his rowan staff and stared down at his favorite student. His emotions hidden, he walked into the sitting room. All eyes turned his direction. He leaned wearily on his staff and shook his head.

One Man rose. Allynae froze in place. Stebben let out a harsh cry that faded into a silence so burdened with disbelief and dismay it threatened to smother them all.

7

Myrrh & Thera & Borderlands

Sparrow and the Guardian of Myrrh watched the great horned owl and a DerTahan dune hawk fly into Nervac Portal and vanish. When the gateway's swirling center returned to its normal filmy oval, Sparrow glanced at the woman beside her. "Are you sorry you stayed in Myrrh?"

Almiralyn's beautiful smile made a momentary appearance. "I believe we made the right choice. Henri and Nomed will make a great team, and I will enjoy training you. Shall we go? Where's Merrilea? I thought she planned to join us here." With a last glance at the portal, she headed toward the center of Meos.

Sparrow hurried after her. "She's with Owae, studying medicinal herbs." She matched the Guardian's long stride. "What will you teach me first?"

"After I check on Wilith Whalend, we're going to Veersuni to re-enforce the shields around Elcaro's Eye. Your first lesson—how to protect yourself and to set wards around other objects or spaces."

They reached the DeoNyte Redael's governing chambers as the door opened and a tall, dark-skinned man in the uniform of a high-ranking PPP official strode into the square, his expression harried.

Sparrow took a moment to catch her breath.

Almiralyn adjusted her direction to intercept him. "Good morning, Wilith. Just the person I wanted to see."

At the sight of the Guardian, the man's agitation increased. "Almiralyn, I cannot remain in Myrrh while my son and wife are in danger on DerTah."

She laid a hand on his arm. "Wilith, I can't let you go to DerTah. Your presence there would create a more difficult situation for everyone. And you wouldn't be any safer than Renn and Torgin. Please be patient."

He rubbed his forehead and sighed. "I am useless. Even my son appears to be more capable than I."

She observed him with a thoughtful expression. "As I recall, you like to read. You're very good at compiling and interpreting facts. Correct?"

He looked curious. "Why?"

"If you are comfortable helping, I have a job for you. One that will further our cause, and one that will use your talents."

The handsome face relaxed into a tentative smile. "I will assist you in any way I can. Doing nothing..." He shrugged. "I need to feel useful."

She linked her arm through his. "Walk with me, and I'll explain what needs to happen next."

Sparrow lagged behind, her thoughts on her upcoming lesson. *I don't know how she knows I have any talent except telepathy and painting.* Worry churned her mind into a whirlpool of 'what ifs' so all-consuming that they arrived at the Cavern of Tennisca before she knew it.

Almiralyn paused, gave her a knowing smile, and looked up at their tall companion. "We are about to descend the Stairway of Retu Erath. Are you prepared to face your greatest fears, Wilith?"

He looked from Almiralyn to the door. "You said Torgin walked the stairway. If he can do it, I can."

"Sparrow and I will go ahead. Please follow. Expect to hear voices and to experience the unexpected. When you arrive at the bottom, you will have gained a different perspective regarding who you are."

"I am not sure..." He rubbed his forehead and, after a moment of struggle, squared his shoulders. "I am ready."

Almiralyn gave him a confident smile. "We'll see you at the bottom." She began her descent.

Sparrow followed. She glanced over her shoulder. Wilith took a hesitant step onto the top stair. Memories of her initiation made her refocus her attention on Almiralyn's back and quicken her pace. Wilith would need time and privacy.

She arrived in the Cave of Canedari, the usual residence of the Evolsefil Crystal, much sooner than she expected. As her mind formulated the question, Almiralyn smiled and answered.

"The stairway was shorter today. You and I did not need to travel its full length. I expect the distance to be much longer for Wilith."

Sparrow looked back at the purple double doors. *I wonder what a PPP official might discover on the Stairway of Retu Erath.*

Wilith Lortin Whalend rarely felt unsure of himself. He was about to become the premier. Selective breeding and years of training had prepared him to ascend to this position. His parents, high level PPP officials, had risen through the ranks to become leaders in their fields. After much testing, the Five Fathers had ordered them joined late in their careers and their lives. Wilith was their only offspring, as Torgin was his. When the PPP selected Coala Renn to be his partner, he had been pleased and proud. Their Joining was one of the happiest moments of his life.

Now standing at the top of the stairway, he felt a tremor of trepidation. What would he discover about himself on this journey? He almost laughed. *This is all nonsense. How can descending a stairway into a cavern be more than a walk in the dark?*

Sobering thoughts cut his laughter short. *The events of the past sun turnings have been outside of my life experience. What I've learned has left me with misgivings about myself and my existence in The City.* He curled his fingers into fists. Sweat soaked his palms. He wiped them on his pant legs and stepped off the landing.

One stair after the other carried him deeper into the quiet cavern.

Nothing assaulted his logical view of life. Confidence replaced his self-doubt. Midway down, he decided, Almiralyn had been teasing him.

Something at the outer fringes of his vision made him pause, his eyes squinting through the darkness. A small light blinked out of sight. *There it is again*. He swallowed his smugness.

"Wilith." A whisper brushed his ear. "Wilith Lortin Whalen." The other ear buzzed with breathy sounds.

He came to a standstill, eyes searching, ears straining to hear. A lifelike image of his father loomed over him. Anger shone in his eyes as he lashed out, one sentence at a time. "Do not disobey the PPP rules again. If you do, we will disown you. You will have no place to go but the Five Towers. That's where they put bad boys who sneak off to Myrrh." His mother's sobs penetrated the walls of her room next door.

An uncontrollable shiver careened through him. His fragile mother had never recovered after that visit from the PPP. Little by little, turning by turning, she diminished. On his fourteenth sun cycle, she did not wake up. He still blamed himself.

The image shifted. His mother sat in a room in The Center for Advanced Healing. The Head Healer shook her head. "We've done everything we can. You have only a short time to prepare yourself and your family." Wilith collapsed on the stairs and covered his face with manicured hands. *All these sun cycles, I thought I was responsible for her death.*

A current of air brought his head up. One after the other, images pelted him: meeting Renn at Mira's cottage when they were children, the realization the PPP would erase all memories of her, anger at the Five Fathers the turning his father celebrated seventy sun cycles and boarded the train to Last Retreat. Emotions crashed over him in waves. At last, the images dissipated. The whispers faded.

Gradually, he stopped shaking. Awareness of his surroundings returned. He glanced up. Double purple doors stood ajar only a few steps away. With the slowness of one wading through water, he descended the remaining stairs and entered the Cave of Canedari, where Almiralyn and Sparrow waited.

He fought to wipe the memories from his eyes, to hide his vulnerability. "I don't...I..." The understanding in their faces made him falter. His guard slipped. Tears streamed down his cheeks.

The Guardian escorted her companions to the Reading Room. Sparrow slipped away and left her alone with Wilith. They had said little since taking seats on the opposite sides of a glossy table in a secluded reading alcove. Wilith's gaze wandered over the elegant vastness of one of the best galactic libraries in the solar system.

He sat back, his expression one of strained amazement. "I never guessed there was a galactic library so close to Idronatti." His finger traced the engraved title on the spine of a book on the shelf next to him. "I've always wanted to read this." He exhaled and placed his hands on the table. "What do you need me to do?"

"Have you recovered from your trip down the stairs?"

"I have much to digest, Almiralyn. It will take time." He pressed the palms of his hands together. "I buried my anger at the Five Fathers so deep I had almost forgotten it. Now I must face it and the ramifications of my return to Idronatti—if I return."

"The Unfolding is impacting your life, Wilith, and the lives of Torgin and Renn. You are not alone. All of us are feeling its effects." She let that sink in before continuing. "Let me explain what I need. Have you heard of the Mocendi League?"

"Only what little the Five Fathers have shared during the past few turnings. I gather it is a group that trains in the Arts of DiMensionery."

"It does, and it uses the Arts to frighten those who are weaker into submitting to its rule. Rattori's Brigade is under its influence. I need you to research the League and its leader, The MasTer. Learn everything you can. Also see if you can find where the League gets its wealth and who finances it. Let me show you the research library."

He gaped. "This isn't all?"

She smiled and preceded him down a flight of stairs to a room with rows of glass cases containing books, manuscripts, and scrolls from all over the Universe. "This is our research area." She handed him a set of keys. "There are three levels. The catalogue is over there. I think you will find its data base very efficient. You'll find notebooks and a mini comp-tab on the table at the end of this aisle."

His astonished expression made her smile. "We use technology, but only where it is truly useful. I'll send a DeoNyte priestess who knows her way around the stacks to assist you. Her name is Elae. Do you have questions?"

"Do you know anything about The MasTer that will help me begin the process?"

The disquiet in her expression gave him the chills. "No one knows much about him. Although the Mocendi live throughout the Inner Universe, The MasTer has never left TreBlaya. Cruelty and destruction are his trademarks. His minions kidnap children with the talent to become DiMensioners, and they are never seen again. As far as anyone knows, no one leaves the ranks of the Mocendi League alive. Death is the only way out. Does that help?"

He gave an absent shake of his head, his attention already elsewhere.

Almiralyn retraced her steps. *The PPP are no longer around to coddle you and make your decisions, Wilith Whalend. It will be interesting to see where The Unfolding takes you.*

Sparrow selected a book, curled up in a chair, and tried to read, while the Guardian conferred with Wilith. A series of yawns made her set it aside. *I'll just rest for a minute.*

A gentle hand shook her awake. Almiralyn smiled down at her. "Have a nice nap?"

She stretched. "I must have. I rarely do that. Where's Wilith?"

"Doing some research for me. Thank you for giving us time alone. His initiation has given him much to ponder."

"I can empathize. Is he alright?"

"He will be."

She crossed the room to the Sanctuary of Veersuni. Zugo, Yookotay's young son, and Elae, the granddaughter of Owae, greeted them at the door.

"I'm sure glad you're here, Almiralyn." Zugo's eager smile made Sparrow grin. "I could use a break and a meal."

Elae laughed. "You're always hungry, Zugo."

"I'm a growing DeoNyte. I need food and lots of it." He gave Almiralyn a respectful smile. "Is there anything you desire?"

She explained that Torgin's father was doing some research for her. "Elae, when you have eaten, please join him and help in any way you can.

You know the research area better than anyone. Zugo, you will return here to guard the fountain. Off you go. Sparrow and I will finish our work in one chron circle."

The young DeoNytes hurried away. Laughter floated back into Veersuni and faded.

The amusement in Almiralyn's expression faded into consternation.. She walked further into the sanctuary, but halted some distance from the alabaster fountain. "Relevart warned me that Nissasa Rattori is using the crystal that was once the Oracle Stone to damage connections to other crystals mined from the Evolsefil Caverns on Tao Spirian."

Sparrow joined her. "Doesn't he realize he's destroying the only means of overseeing all the planets in the Clenaba Rolas Solar System? If his goal is to rule them, that seems foolish."

"The bigger question is why the Mocendi League is allowing him to do it? My sources tell me they are behind his rebellion and control his every move. Clearly, Nissasa doesn't realize his own peril. The MasTer will not tolerate disobedience or disloyalty."

Sparrow fingered a strand of chestnut hair. "Nomed mentioned Nissasa's mother, Roween. Maybe she's clouding the issue for her aggressive son."

A frown furrowed the Guardian's brow. "She is an ambitious woman, more ambitious than Nissasa. I'm glad Wolloh sent her where she is not a danger to others." Energy bristled around her. "Now, Sparrow, your first lesson. The pedestal of Elcaro's Eye houses Vesen, a seven-sided quartz crystal. Its power has been used to construct a complex series of wards around the fountain. Today, you and I are going to add another layer. Since Nissasa doesn't know your energy signature, it will make it more difficult for him to break through the shields."

Sparrow put a hand to her stomach. "Butterflies. I think I'm nervous."

"A little nervousness is not bad. DiMensionery is a serious matter. You must never approach it with a lack of respect or honest intent. Those who manipulate it to their own ends often find themselves without its gifts when they are most needed. When my training was complete, I selected not to join the Order of Esprow. I didn't want the temptation of misusing my power."

"Does that mean you are less capable or that it is less effective when you use it?"

Almiralyn smiled. "No. It simply means I'm not controlled by the rules of the Order. I only use things that allow me to do my job as Myrrh's Guardian. I'm always careful to use DiMensionery for the good of mankind, not for personal gain." She drew her further away from the Eye. "Today we are going to test the depth of your potential. First, I want you to close your eyes and imagine a curtain of light surrounding you."

Sparrow set aside her nervousness and followed the Guardian's instructions. At first, she struggled. Then, with a flash of insight, she understood. Trusting herself as she did when she painted, she pictured an opalescent curtain enclosing her. A tingling sensation rushed over the surface of her skin. Hair on the back of her neck rose and resettled.

The Guardian's voice penetrated her concentration. "Open your eyes, Sparrow."

She gasped. Light encircled her, rose several feet above her head, and extended down into the stone floor of Veersuni.

Almiralyn's eyes sparkled. "You are even more gifted than I imagined. Let the shield go."

Sparrow mentally saw it dissolve. The shield melted away. "I did it! I *really* did it. She shook her head and grinned.

Almiralyn moved to the fountain. "Stand across from me. When I tell you to, I want you to envision a shield of purple flames surrounding Elcaro's Eye. Infuse it with all the love you can muster."

"Why love?"

"Because love is the best defense against evil. Love deflects negativity back to the sender without causing harm."

Sparrow thought about the statement. "I think I understand. We don't want to harm anyone or anything. What if love doesn't work?"

"The power for good comes into play. A choice is made. We inflict harm when it's the only way to stop the progress of evil."

"I feel like I'm in a philosophy class."

Almiralyn regarded her with a teacher's seriousness. "You are: The Philosophy of The Unfolding."

8
Der Tah

Renn Whalend stumbled down the cliff face trail, fighting both the wind and her fright. *Bibeed is afraid. Why? Where is she taking me?* The woman scrabbling ahead of her cast a worried glance over her shoulder. Wind tore at her dress, whipped it between her legs, and ruffled her short hair into spikes. She struggled to move faster. When she reached the bench, she stopped and motioned Renn to hurry.

Renn's too big coat sent her tripping down the last stretch of trail onto the overlook. She skidded to a stop with pebbles flying and her scarf flapping in her face. With an impatient jerk, she righted it and retied the knot.

Bibeed's frantic gaze flew up the trail. "We can't stay here. Please follow." She knelt, picked up a rock from the top of a pile, replaced it at a different angle, and rotated it. A clanking rattle mixed with the cry of the wind and the crashing chorus of waves beating against the cliff. Within moments, the top of a metal ladder appeared and stopped at knee height.

Bibeed swung her body onto it and began to descend. "Hurry, miss. *He* is almost here."

Fear of heights kept Renn still. The panic in Bibeed's wholesome face made her jerk her eyes away from the steep drop to the sea and grab the side rails. She placed her feet on a rung, held her breath, and followed. Partway down, she wondered if they were climbing all the way to Thera. When she finally reached the bottom, she rested her head on a rough metal rung and worked to slow her breathing.

"Please, miss." Bibeed guided her to a rocky ledge as the water retreated to prepare for its next plunging return. She twisted a barnacle-covered rock and listened to the ladder clattering back into its hiding place. Satisfaction lit her eyes. "Come." She urged Renn along the ledge to a grouping of tall, weathered gray stones and helped her to maneuver around the two closest. As they stepped onto a stretch of black sand, Bibeed hiked up her skirt and yelled, "Run, miss, or you'll get soaked!" Without looking back, she dashed toward the cliff face.

Renn grabbed her flapping coat and sprinted, water snapping at her heels like a voracious dog. Bibeed gripped her arm and pulled her into the safety of a protected recess in the towering cliff. Renn brushed strands of hair from her face and studied the woman next to her. "Please tell me what has frightened you. And why we are in danger?"

Bibeed squinted through the fading light of late afternoon. "I'll explain once we're safe." She tapped a rock with the toe of her boot. The back wall of the recess pivoted inward. Ducking through the narrow opening, she motioned Renn to step through. As the wall swung back into place, she whispered, "We're almost there."

Lifting a lantern from a rock enclosure, she adjusted the wick, passed it to Renn, and pulled a small metal box from her apron pocket. She withdrew a tiny stick, which she pressed between the lid and an attached piece of metal. A quick yank ignited the tip. Shielding the flame, she touched it to the wick, made another adjustment, and lowered the glass chimney.

Renn shook her head in astonishment. "How old-fashioned!"

Bibeed shot her a confused look, reclaimed the lantern, and led the way along the passage under the cliff. She rounded a corner and stopped. With the lantern held high, she put a finger to her lips and touched her ear. Renn nodded, straining to hear any sound other than the distant surf and the howl of the wind. Bibeed smiled and dodged beneath an overhang. "We'll be safe in here." She held the lantern higher.

"Oh." Fighting to accept what her eyes were seeing, Renn pulled off her scarf, shook her hair free, and stared.

The partial hull of a wooden ship rested against the rocky wall. Sand and time-smoothed stone formed a floor. Within the curved sides, which remained intact, someone had set up a couple of cots, constructed a table made of sun-bleached boards, fashioned a fire pit, and stacked supplies in a pantry of sorts. She pivoted slowly, absorbing the detail—the wooden deck overhead, the splintered wood where nature's power had torn the aft portion of the boat away, the beautifully carved figure of a woman that lay to one side. "How did it get here?"

Bibeed set the lantern on a keg. Relief had erased the fear from her face. She smiled. "Many sun cycles ago, a sailing ship ran aground on the beach. The story goes it was a Mocendi ship with a crew pressed into service and a cargo of kidnapped youngsters headed for training on the planet of TreBlaya. After the villagers helped the passengers escape, they hitched horses to the hull and maneuvered the boat up the beach to its hiding place under the cliff.

"It took some doin'. What you see is all that remains. They resealed the bulkheads, so it's pretty dry. With a little help, a rockslide dumped stones in front of the opening. The weather and sea did the rest. Ya can't see it from the ocean, and the slide protects it from the wind and rain. You should sit, Miss. You look a bit..." She shrugged.

Renn laughed. "I think bedraggled is an appropriate description." She sank onto a small crate. "Please call me Renn. Tell me why you brought me here."

The woman's pleasant expression hardened. "The Dreela Omudi told me to hide you if he sent word. Seems the Mocendi League are mighty interested in you and your work."

"The Mocendi League?"

"The folk who take the 'Arts' and twist 'em to their own ends. They steal young ones with the gift and train 'em to do bad. Lately, they've gotten stronger. My brother heard they's after our own High DiMensioner and a boy from Myrrh who's got the gift. And they're lookin' for a magic compass."

Renn listened with disbelief. When Bibeed mentioned the compass, all doubt fled. *Torgin has a compass that the RewFaarans and the Mocendi League want. And they both want me.* She didn't need to question why. Her heart thumped an agitated rhythm in her ears. *They want control of my research. More than that, they want to control the Inner Universe.* The enormity of it left her speechless.

On the far side of Fera Finnero, two birds raced from the gateway into the mid-afternoon sky. Shots fired by Nissasa's men careened above them as they dropped behind a dune. They soared through the wind-created troughs until they landed in Human form.

Nomed looked at his elderly companion. "You alright?"

Henrietta flashed him a smile. "I'm exceptional." She smoothed her ruffled curls. "That wasn't a very nice welcome. Now what?"

"You brought Etunir?"

She tapped her pants pocket. "Right here. It should get us through the wards unnoticed. Where's the best place?"

"I think we should avoid Nissasa's troops altogether and go in from the Trinuge side." He gave her a solicitous look. "It's a longer flight. You up to it?"

A tiny smile twitched the corner of her mouth. "I'm betting I'll be less tired than you." She shaped the DerTahan dune hawk and shot into the air.

The great horned owl soared after her, its hazel eyes alive with the delight of flight and the glow of the setting sun.

By the time they approached the border between the desert and Shu Chenaro, night had settled over the land. The golden light from the moon, Fasfro, picked out pitched tents and picketed animals on the sand below. Nomed skirted the camp and winged his way toward the Plains of DoOlb. Beside him, the silver gray dune hawk matched his speed and rhythm.

The cracked and barren plains of DoOlb's outer reaches tempted him to land. *Too close to Nissasa's camp. Too close to the power of the Oracle Stone. Soon we'll cross into the province of Trinuge.* His thoughts strayed to the Dreelas TheLise. *I hope she's surviving Roween Rattori's visit.*

Fasfro's warm glow highlighting the tops of trees welcomed them to the

Dreelas' homeland and lit the way to Shu Chenaro's warded boundary. Swooping lower, he navigated between trees and landed in Human form.

Henrietta materialized beside him, looking fresh and exhilarated. "It's been a while since I've flown any distance. How I love flight."

He smiled. "One of the greatest benefits of shape shifting a bird. Come. We can't linger too long." Picking his way through the overgrowth, he approached the wards and paused. His attention concentrated. He sought anything out of the ordinary—anything that could do them mischief. At last, he held out a hand. "The crystal."

Henrietta placed it on his palm. "You know the workings of Wolloh's mind far better than I do, but be careful."

Nomed knelt and touched the tip of the crystal's termination to the base of the wards. Tiny sparkles of light sprinkled the waist-high rent. He motioned her ahead, ducked through after her, and used the crystal to reweave the wards. When he finished, he assessed them. *Someone besides Wolloh created these. The work is good.*

Henrietta, already in shifted form, perched on a branch above his head, her hawk eyes observing the forest, ready to warn him of danger.

He pocketed the crystal, shifted to the great horned owl, and led her through the forest canopy and into the open sky. Fasfro's saffron orb hovered above them, her warm light mingling with the cool blue of her sister moon as it crested the eastern horizon. Distant stars glistened in the domed heavens.

An unexpected wave of sadness washed over him, dimming the joy of flight and the beauty of the night. Overwhelming loss choking the breath from his lungs almost knocked him from the sky. Banking toward the blue moon, he streaked with the dune hawk toward Shu Chenaro. The ache in his heart told him they were already too late.

Nissasa Rattori threw back his head and laughed a laugh so full of delight that his man servant glanced at him in surprise.

"Don't stare, you fool. Go. Find Des Tel Terah and bring him to me."

The servant shuffled from the tent. Nissasa removed a leather thong attached to a black pouch from around his neck and clutched it to his heart.

"We did it," he whispered. "We sent the High DiMensioner to roast in SeDah."

Tipping the Oracle Stone, which he had renamed Souvitrico, onto his palm, he stared at the fire burning in its depths. Another full-bodied laugh burst from his throat. He held the crystal up to the light. "Ah, WoNa, I imagine you miss your pretty stone." His expression changed to calculating. "But it's mine now. And I have used it to put an end to Wolloh Espyro. Soon your heart will break; soon I will find you, too; and soon you will join your true love in the pits of SeDah." He made a triumphant circuit of the tent. "How do I know that, you ask? I, my dearest WoNa, know because your stone told me your secret."

A noise at the entryway made him whip around, the crystal hidden in the folds of his kcalo. He glared at his servant. "How long have you been there?"

"Only a moment, Sajud."

Nissasa raked a probe through the man's mind and smirked with satisfaction as anguished tears streamed down his face. "It appears I have a guest whom you do not recognize. Send him to me."

The man scurried away. Nissasa replaced the crystal in its drango-lined pouch, glad for the protection it provided. He slipped it beneath his shirt and pivoted to greet his guest. A cold lump settled in the pit of his stomach.

"Hello, Nissasa. It is good to see you." The man facing him wore the purple-lined cape of a Mocendi DiMensioner. He flipped it behind his shoulders and stepped into the tent.

Keeping his expression neutral and his nervousness hidden, Nissasa executed a formal bow. "Vygel Vintrusie. Welcome to DerTah." He straightened and scrutinized his guest. "To what do I owe this unexpected visit?"

"It seems you have acquired something The MasTer covets. I am here to retrieve it."

Nissasa forced his hands to remain at his sides and shielded any thoughts, referencing Souvitrico. "I don't know what you heard but..." He opened a wooden box on his bedside table and held out a small crystal. "I removed this from around WoNadahem Mardree's neck."

Vygel held it up to the light. "This is *not* the Oracle Stone."

"They rescued the Atrilaasu Oracle before I could claim her much coveted crystal." He kept his tone light. "Perhaps another chance will offer itself."

The Mocendi glanced around the tent. "And the Raven Karrew? Where is it?"

Nissasa kept his tone bland. "Someone stole it from my tent while I was busy at the front. We haven't found it, but I will. May I offer you refreshments?"

Vintrusie chose a chair facing the door and lowered his gaunt body onto it. "I suggest you find the Oracle Stone *and* Karrew sooner than later, my friend. Something to drink would be appreciated."

Nissasa pressed his lips together and walked with an unhurried step to the entryway. His servant waited at a respectful distance. Beside him stood DesTel Terah. The heavy-lidded eyes, so like his father's, acknowledged him and then drifted to the tent entrance. Nissasa waved them both forward, sent his man to bring refreshments, and led DesTel into the tent.

The Mocendi looked up with vague interest.

After securing a third chair, Nissasa made introductions. "Vygel Vintrusie...DesTel Terah. DesTel, this is the representative of The Mocendi MasTer from the planet of TreBlaya."

The Mocendi's expression changed to curiosity. "You must be Dahe Terah's son. I had rather hoped to meet your father."

DesTel gave a deferential bow and took his seat. "He is away on tribal business. What brings a Mocendi to Fera Finnero?"

Vintrusie held up the small crystal. "I came for the Oracle Stone, but it appears my information about its whereabouts was incorrect."

Nissasa kept his eyes on the Mocendi, glad he had erased all memories of Souvitrico from the minds of anyone who might have seen him use it on Wolloh's wards. Refreshments arrived and conversation took a more benign route. The Mocendi finished his taccus fruit and wine, pressed a napkin to thin, colorless lips, and placed it carefully on the table the servant had set for them. A vulturine smile transformed his face into that of a predacious animal. He brought hard eyes to rest on DesTel. "Tell me about your brother."

Aware he was being watched, Nissasa remained relaxed. The man's tone had put him on alert. He let his gaze move to DesTel.

"I have four, all of whom are here or at our camp."

The Mocendi appeared ready to pounce. "I wish to meet NeTols."

"He accompanied my father. I'm sorry, sir."

Vintrusie twisted a ring on his middle finger and looked at DesTel from under furrowed brows. "I understand he is not Sebborr by birth, and yet he is your father's favorite. It must be difficult for you."

DesTel's jaw tightened and his eyes held a glint of emotion that was gone as suddenly as it appeared. "He is the youngest—the baby of the family. My parents always doted on him."

The Mocendi stood and shook out the folds of his cape. "I've taken enough of your time. After all, you have a war to fight." He paced to the tent entrance.

Nissasa had risen with him. DesTel rose as the hollow-cheeked Mocendi pivoted in a swirling pool of black and purple fabric. "Please tell your father I am sorry I missed him, DesTel." The cape settled around him. He stepped aside and motioned for the younger man to leave. The Sebborr, a scowl on his face and anger in his long stride, swept from the tent.

Vintrusie watched him round the corner between two tents before returning his attention to Nissasa. "You realize if The MasTer discovers you are being untruthful—"

"I will send word if the Oracle Stone comes into my possession." He nodded in the direction DesTel had taken. "Why are you interested in his brother?"

A wicked smile lit the Mocendi's face. "I am interested in all things, Nissasa Rattori. Take care."

A caustic response sprung to Nissasa's lips, but the man was gone. Marching back to the table, he picked up his wineglass and gulped what remained. A quick mental search told him the Mocendi had left Fero Finnero.

He pulled out the black pouch. "I have things to discover." The crystal cast an orange glow over the surface of his palm. *That da'am Mocendi is so sure of himself—so full of his own importance.* His expression hardened. Wards surrounded him. He prepared to create havoc.

9

Myrrh & Thera & Borderlands

From the pocket of Major Jordett's shirt, Kieel listened to the slap of boot soles on the shiny corridor floor. Afraid to move lest he give himself away, he clutched his walking stick and remained as still as the first light of dawn. A sudden change in direction toppled him from his rigid position. A door shutting sounded like thunder. Kieel stuck his head over the lip of the shirt pocket and tried to get his bearings.

Stairs circled up and down from the spot where the Major stood. *I don't think I understand buildings.*

"Stay down. Surveillance lenses." Jordett's urgent whisper sent him back into hiding.

By tipping his head, Kieel could watch their progress down one flight of stairs after the other. Stealth wrapped the Major's every movement in tense silence.

Their pace slowed. Jordett pressed back in the shadows. Kieel could see his jaw tighten. A door opened. Footfalls moved away from them. When nothing else suggested danger, the Major tapped the pocket. Kieel gripped a handful of fabric and hoisted himself up so he could see.

The Major stood next to a door marked with a series of symbols. He held out his hand. Kieel zipped upward, landed on the palm, and folded his wings. Keeping his growing misgivings about this adventure to himself, he peered through the window. "What now?"

"We need to know the layout of the Ria-T Plaza."

"Ria-T? Is that what the symbols say?"

Jordett nodded. "This is all strange to you, isn't it?"

"I have never ventured beyond the Terces Wood." His wings fluttered open. "I can do some reconnaissance."

Jordett studied him with a doubtful expression. "Don't get caught."

"I won't. What am I looking for?"

"Look for an unguarded exit and the best route to reach it. Barring that, I need to know which exit has the least patrollers posted. Be quick." He cracked open the door. Kieel flew up to the ceiling. Although the sparse lighting afforded him a sense of relative safety, he stayed near the wall, well above eye level. The vast, open space was intimidating. He missed the Terces Wood and its many places to hide.

The parking area turned out to be an underground structure with four levels. At each change in direction, Kieel noted his route and memorized the details that he thought might help the Major. When he had seen everything, he retraced his path with the persnickety exactness for which his people knew him. Across from Jordett's hiding place, he paused in an unlit corner. Nothing in the parking area moved. He made a careful approach to the door, peeked in the top of the window, and tapped it with his walking stick.

The door creaked opened. He darted through and landed on the Major's upturned palm. With meticulous attention to detail, he presented his report. At its conclusion, Jordett gave a low whistle.

"You're good, Kieel. I wish my men were as attentive. Correct me if I missed anything. There are four levels and six exits. The sub-level exit leads to a tunnel that ends at a loading dock and alley. It's not guarded. Level B has a street exit with only one guard." He furrowed his brow in thought. "I'm inclined to do the alley exit, but something doesn't seem right."

Kieel lifted off his palm and hovered. "I agree. Level B feels like a better option. I can guide you through the parking area."

Jordett held open his pocket. "Hop in. We'll see if there's a Drop Car close."

"A what?" Kieel slipped into his hiding place.

"It's a—" The ring of boots against the floor cut off his answer. Jordett crouched beneath the stairs.

Kieel withdrew into the pocket and muttered under his breath. "I hate not knowing what's up."

Above them, the sound of a heavy man descending the stairs changed tenor as he stepped onto the landing and marched to the door of the parking area. Kieel peeked from the pocket. The man's uniformed bulk filled the open door. Strain tightened the muscles of his thick neck. Another uniformed figure sprinted across the parking area. The man stepped out to meet him, leaving the door ajar. A brief conversation changed to an argument.

"I'm telling you, *they* spotted him in the reception area."

"Then where is he? We've searched every floor in the center."

The first man held up a fleshy hand, touched his ear, and listened. Man two clamped his mouth shut and waited.

Jordett slipped from beneath the stairs and moved to the door.

Kieel could feel tension ripple through the muscles beneath the uniform shirt. He gripped his walking stick tighter. *Whatever made me leave the relative safety of Myrrh?*

At the shoppe Antiques by Q, Dom felt uneasy. Something nagged, something that did not bode well for him or for Myrrh. It had been hanging around—a premonition of sorts—for the past two turnings—since he had returned from taking Wilith Whalend to Myrrh.

He had already searched the shoppe several times. He had checked the mirror, the dusty showrooms, the latches on both the front and back doors.

Where's Majeska anyway? He rearranged his desk, took out his crystal paperweight, and positioned it in front of him. *Maybe Almiralyn can tell me what's up.* He reached out to touch it, withdrew his hand, and looked over the top of his spectacles. *There's that nagging again.*

Hobbling into the hall, he stared one direction and then the other. *Nothing.* He cocked his head to listen. He sniffed the air. *Still nothing.* Back at his desk, he studied the paperweight. After a moment's hesitation, he adjusted his spectacles and gazed into its crystal depths. Clouds gathered. Lightning flashed. A crash of thunder shook the paperweight. Angry blue eyes locked onto his. No matter how hard he tried, he could not pull his gaze away. His heart stuttered in his chest. Life's breath hissed from his lungs.

A flash of gray cut across his field of vision. The paperweight crashed to the floor. Light exploded around it. A heart wrenching meow slammed his eardrums. Blinded and bemused, he stumbled backward. When he regained his balance and his vision cleared, Majeska lay in a gray heap on the desktop.

He gathered her up with shaking hands and sank into a chair. "Jeska?" Holding her next to his heart, he moaned, "Oh, Majeska, I am so sorry. You saved me. I—" Sobs of despair shook his shoulders. Tears plunged down his cheeks, drenching her silent, gray face. He pressed his ear to her chest, pulled away, and studied her through his thick lenses.

Amethyst eyes blinked in the light of his lamp. A pink tongue lapped up a tear. Dom started to grin. Majeska wiggled upright, flipped her tail back and forth, and jumped to the floor. Sitting on her hunches, she gave him a round-eyed 'whatever is wrong with you' look.

He threw back his head and laughed. "Thank Emit!" He ran a hand down her silky back. "Good thing cats have a surplus of lives, my friend." He glanced at the shattered paperweight, where it rested against a pile of books at the foot of his desk. "And a darn good thing you came when you did."

Paisley stretched and pushed his chair back from the chess table in Nemttachenn Tower. "Need a break. Ya ever walk in the woods?"

CheeTrann's pellucid form wafted and reformed. His features came into sharper focus. "The tower is my domain. I cannot travel beyond its physical boundaries, my friend. But you should enjoy a breath of fresh air. It has been a long time since I have shared this much time with another. I am happy to rest in the quiet of my tower."

"I won't be gone long." Paisley walked to the entry and stared into the Terces Wood. The Evolsefil Crystal emitted a low hum. The ground began to tremble. CheeTrann arrived by his side, motioned him away from the door, and, with his attention fixed on the Heart of Myrrh, raised a hand. The spell of invisibility melted away. Within Evolsefil, a man stood with his back to the tower's center, his dark hair glowing in the crystal's luminescent light. A slow rotation revealed a bearded profile; one frigid blue eye; a hawk-like nose; thin compressed lips; and finally a second cold blue orb. The mouth formed a frustrated scowl as the glacial gaze swept the tower.

Paisley remained still. The crystal's low hum grew softer. CheeTrann whispered a non-stop series of sounds.

Inside the crystal, the fierce expression on the man's face became a disappointed frown. He made another full rotation. Penetrating eyes explored the granite walls and locked onto Paisley's rigid form. CheeTrann's chanting intensified. The man's image rippled apart and disappeared piece by piece until only the ice-blue eyes stared with such malice Paisley's heart quaked. He clutched his chest. A moan slid past his lips. He felt himself tumbling head over heels. The last thing he saw—the eyes melting like blue candle wax and dripping down the inside of the crystal.

Gradually, he realized he could not see or feel and wondered if he was in his body. Or perhaps he floated free of it to mingle with this twilight nothingness for the rest of eternity. He found it odd that he was not afraid, nor was he worried. Content—the only word that came to mind—was not quite it, but close enough.

The sudden realization he was not alone came as a shock, and yet, he knew an essence other than his own pulsed in the grayness beside him. An attempt to peer into the starless night failed. The effort drained his last remaining strength.

Floating into consciousness some time later, he discovered that his large body lay sprawled on the tower floor. Next to him, CheeTrann regarded him with haunted eyes. Paisley tried to move. Myrrh's Sentinel shook his head and laid a gentle hand upon his brow.

"Be still, my friend. You have journeyed far. Let your body rest."

A word barely formed before it evaporated. He tried again, licked his lips, and with the third try thought he heard it leave his throat to create sound.

The hand pressed lightly. Irresistible sleep immersed him in a dreamless place, where rest healed and endless time passed.

When he opened his eyes, morning light poured in the tower entrance. He yawned, stretched, and struggled to sitting. Birds singing gladdened his heart. The smells of autumn perfumed the air. Life flooded through him. Another yawn squeezed tears from the corners of his eyes. He wiped them dry and stood.

CheeTrann sat at the chess table, his bearded chin resting on his massive chest. Thick, white hair tumbled over his face. Paisley sat down opposite and waited.

When the eyes opened, the specter straightened, his face alive with relief. "You are awake."

"What happened? I was someplace..." Paisley gazed around the tower and shrugged.

"Nissasa Rattori paid us a visit."

"Who? Oh. The man in the crystal." He looked for Evolsefil. "Where is it?"

CheeTrann smiled. "I've hidden it again. And yes, the man in the crystal. What do you remember?"

Paisley touched his chest. "A piercing pain in my heart."

"He tried to kill you. At least he tried to kill whomever he sensed close to the crystal. I took you away, hid you where he could not find you."

"Where was I? It was so peaceful."

"I took you deep into Surazal, death's domain, and kept you there until Nissasa grew tired of searching."

Paisley looked down at his body. "Am I dead then?"

The Sentinel of Myrrh's face softened. "You are very much alive, my friend. I am the one who is dead. My state allowed me to protect you, but now, Nissasa knows you guard Evolsefil. He will not stop looking until you are dead. You must leave Nemttachenn."

"And you, CheeTrann? What of you?"

"He cannot kill me."

"I'm bettin' he can destroy ya."

The specter was quiet.

Paisley picked up his black queen. "I'm not leavin' my post, and I'm not leavin' ya here to fight alone." He placed the queen on the board and began to arrange his pawns.

CheeTrann regarded him through slitted eyes. "I might not save you next time."

Paisley placed his king. "You afraid I'll win?"

A laugh shook the Sentinel's chest. "I can't imagine that happening."

"We shall see. Your move."

Sparrow didn't remember lying down or pulling a blanket up to her chin or closing her eyes. She couldn't recall the moment sleep claimed her. All she knew—a dream, where a game of hide and seek pitched her down long, fiery corridors; into pits of flaming, hungry creatures; and over ground covered with bubbling pools of smoking, hot lava, entangled her.

Hysteria gripped her, squeezing the life from her heart like juice from a plum. Everywhere she looked, icy blue eyes tracked her, watched her, followed her, drilled into hers. Panic sent her tumbling down a steep, lava-encrusted hill. She sprawled at the bottom, a cry for help screaming through her mind. A man's malicious laugh sent a thrill of terror careening through her. Abject fear curled her into a fetal position. Her eyes stared straight ahead, unblinking, unseeing—The laughter echoed again and again and again.

Arms encircled her. "SparrowLyn AsTar, it's Almiralyn. Wake up."

Almiralyn? The name washing over her squelched the flames and quieted the terror. "Almiralyn." Her tongue lapped its familiar ring, rolled it around her mouth.

"Sparrow, open your eyes." Although gentle, the words held a command she dared not disregard.

She forced herself to peek through a small crack between her lids. Relief made her whole body shake. She stared into sapphire eyes and let the sobs escape—let the tears stream—let the Guardian's presence chase away the panic, the hysterical desire to laugh, the icy, icy blue eyes.

The quiet of her quarters soothed her almost as much as Almiralyn's presence. Unable to speak, she relaxed into the Guardian's comforting embrace and gave herself time to anchor in the reality of Human comfort and the safety represented by her companion. When only remnants of the dream flitted through her memory, she sat up and ran trembling hands through her damp hair and interlocked her fingers behind her head. "That was horrid. I have never dreamt like that." Her eyes sought Almiralyn's. "It was a dream, wasn't it?"

Almiralyn frowned. "It was Nissasa. He traced your energy signature. The man is good. So, my dear, are you. I'm impressed by your fortitude. Most would have succumbed. Forgive me for not reminding you to shield yourself."

Sparrow lowered her hands. "How did you know?"

"I had set a part of my mind to guard you. Your telepathic cry for help woke me." She held out a chalice.

Sparrow cupped it in her hands. "I remember when I discovered I was telepathic. One Man and I were following Merrilea behind the waterfall at Demrach Gateway." She took a sip of cool water. "It seemed so natural that I wasn't even surprised." After a deep drink, she crossed to the washstand and splashed water on her face. Patting it dry, she regarded Almiralyn with a new sense of urgency. "I need to paint. I'm not sure what, but..." She hung the towel on a hook. "Do you think it is what Nissasa wants me to do?"

The Guardian came to her feet. "Let's go find out. I'll put shields around us both, and you can see what appears on your canvas. I'm willing to bet we will learn something important."

Submerged in their individual thoughts, they made their way to her studio. Sparrow set about preparing to paint. Almiralyn created a ward-protected area in which to do so. When all was ready, Sparrow picked up her palette and closed her eyes. A vague image formed. She stared at the blank canvas and dipped her brush.

10
Der Tah

Esán scrambled to move backpacks and weather blankets well back in the hollow tree, wedged himself beneath Desirol, and prepared to erect a shield. Not far away, his inner sight picked out a ludoc cat crouched beneath a tree. Its charcoal eyes glistened in the late afternoon light. Pewter gray fur divided into pale gray patches outlined in black blended into shadow. Its arrowhead-shaped head had pointed gray ears topped with black tufts that twitched, picking up sounds Esán knew were far out of Human range. Its extra-long tail curved over its back. The black, tufted tip switched back and forth above its head. Huge nostrils opened and closed. A growl reverberated throughout the clearing.

Two long, lopping strides brought it to the base of the tree. A large paw reached into the hollow, patted around, and snagged a shoulder strap. The backpack toppled out of reach. The gray paw withdrew. A pewter nose squeezed through the opening. Hungry eyes gleamed just below the top arc of the hollow. A frustrated growl shook the tree. The nose withdrew, and the paw returned. Claws raked the lower walls, flinging dirt, dry leaves, and moss into the air.

Ira's agitated exclamation floated down to him. "What's happening? I can't hold on much longer."

Angling his head upward, Esán called softly, "We're like mice trapped in a hole. It's too big to reach us, but it hasn't given up."

The paw swiped the shields. Sparkles of light scattered around it. Another menacing snarl rocked the tree. Once again, the paw retreated.

An image of the ludoc sitting on its haunches staring up at the top of the tree flashed through Esán's mind. The huge cat crouched.

"Hold on, everyone."

The ludoc launched its mighty body into the air, hit the side of the tree, clawed with frantic paws, and plunged to the ground, moss and dead bark raining after it. Speculation gleamed in the dark charcoal eyes. Backing away from the tree, it crouched lower. The immense power of its hind legs rocketed it upward. The tree shuddered beneath its weight. Bared claws found purchase, and the cat began to climb.

Desirol lost his hold and slid downward. "Can't stop!"

Esán let the shields go, jumped to the ground, and rolled to one side. Desirol landed and caught himself halfway to his knees.

Outside the hollow, dead branches crashed to the ground. The tree groaned.

"Alright down there?" Torgin called.

Esán answered with a low-pitched shout. "Good!"

Ira let out a startled exclamation. "Hey. It's reaching in from the top. Not—"

An angry buzzing cut him off. The sound grew louder and more agitated until the tree vibrated with the power of it.

Torgin climbed down beside Desirol. "What's that?" He reached up to help Brie.

Ira scrambled after her. "Hornets bigger than my fist. Run!"

Above them, the ludoc let out an angry howl. The buzzing grew more frantic.

"Quick!" Esán grabbed Brie and ran between ferns. Torgin, Ira, and Desirol tore after them. Ducking beneath a tangle of vines, they huddled together and stared in amazement at the spectacle playing out by the hollow tree.

Hanging by its tail and hind legs from a rotten branch high above the ground, the ludoc swatted at the mottled black and green hornets swarming around it. Splintering wood wrenched the branch lower. The ludoc scrambled to reach the trunk. A loud crack and the cat crashed through dead branches, flipped in the air, and landed on all fours. Hornets streaked toward it. The sound of leather slapping against leather filled the clearing.

Brie gasped. "Look!"

Row upon row of steel-gray scales unrolled from the ludoc's head to its hind quarters until they encased its entire body. A piercing screech shook the clearing. Launching into the air, it unfurled immense, scale-incrusted wings. Wind whipped the tall ferns and flattened fragile plant life against the forest floor. A massive swarm of hornets streaked after it. Around the top of the hollow tree others grouped, their feral buzz less aggressive, their movements less agitated.

Ira gave a nervous laugh. "Its fur changed to leather armor right in front of our eyes. Wow!"

"And it flipped in mid-air and landed on its feet." Desirol shook his head.

Torgin looked dumbfounded. Ira clapped him on the back. "Who woulda thought killer hornets would save us from a killer cat? Right, Torg?"

Brie and Esán exchanged glances.

Desirol caught the look and frowned. "What's up?"

Esán's gaze tracked the disappearing creature. "Ludoc cats don't grow scales and fly."

"Then what was *that*?" Ira demanded.

Brie slipped a hand into Esán's. "I don't remember reading about any creature that changed its coat to armor."

Fear pulsed through the group. Esán swallowed his and looked at his friends. "Of greater concern—those hornets have poison stingers the size of my index finger, and our packs are inside their tree."

Desirol scowled. "So now what?"

Nomed and Henrietta landed in Human form near the raptor center at Shu Chenaro and hurried toward the ranch house. A side door flew open and Allynae waved them forward. He shook the DiMensioner's hand and hugged his aunt.

"I am so glad to see both of you. Thought Almiralyn was coming."

Henri pulled out her spectacles and perched them on her nose. "We decided it would be best if she stayed in Myrrh."

"Safer for all concerned." Nomed ushered Henri into the house. "What's happened to Wolloh? I don't feel his presence."

Allynae's expression grew strained. "I'm sorry, Seyes, he's—"

Nomed choked. "Where is he? Please take me to him."

Henri rested a hand on each man's arm. The next instant, they stood in Wolloh's personal sitting room. A tall, loose-limbed man stood with his back to the door. At the sound of their arrival, he turned and lowered his gaze to rest on Henri's face.

"Miss Henrietta Avetlire." He paused, then smiled. "I knew you would come. We have need of your skills." His attention shifted. "Ah, Seyes, I am so deeply sorry about Wolloh. I know he was like a father to you."

Nomed tried to make coherent sense of the man's words. A sudden heaviness of heart forced him to grab the back of a chair. His knees refused to support him. From some distant place, he saw himself begin a slow-motion fall. Hands caught him, guided him to a chair, and eased him onto it.

Henrietta held a tumbler of water to his lips. "Drink, Seyes. That's it. Better?"

He tried to speak, then nodded. She offered him another sip and rested her small hand on his. Calm spreading through him helped him to regain his focus. He looked up at the tall man. "You're Relevart, Wolloh's mentor."

"Yes. He was my favorite student. I shall miss him." The dark intelligent eyes locked onto his held a warning.

Nomed dropped his face in his hands, gulped a breath, and looked up. "I understand."

"Good. Stebben has had a meal prepared and laid out for us. I suggest we join him."

Henri's eyes widened behind her spectacles. "Ah, Stebben. How is he handling all of this?"

Relevart offered his arm. "Allow me to take you to him, so you can see for yourself."

When they approached the dining room, Stebben beckoned from across the hall. Silently, they followed him beyond an open wooden panel on the far side of the room. The finality of the door sliding shut made Nomed glance over his shoulder.

A hand on his arm urged him along a dimly lit tunnel. Another panel whispered opened. As he crossed the threshold, One Man stepped from the shadows and ushered him to a love seat on which Wolloh's prostrate figure rested.

Nomed sank to his knees and touched the pallid, waxy skin. He bowed his head and let the tears flow. Around him, his friends formed a circle of support. He felt the tingle of wards and knew he could let down his guard. Rising, he faced Relevart. The VarTerel's expression answered the question in his heart.

Relevart surveyed the group. "Even within these wards, circumspection is vital. Please gather closer and listen."

Allynae, Henrietta, Stebben, and One Man slid their arms around each other's waists. Relevart held his rowan staff at the center of their tight group, tapped the crystal's cocooned tip, and whispered,

> *"No one hears from other places,*
> *Dimensions, worlds, or outer spaces*
> *What I am about to share*
> *With those who must be most aware."*

The air in the room crackled. Light streamed around them from the crystal tip of the staff, creating a soft oval on the floor. Relevart nodded. They placed a hand on the rowan shaft and waited, expectancy vibrating around them.

Relevart's essence dimmed and then brightened. "For the moment, we are safe. Listen with care to what I have to tell you. Wolloh rests within a state of near death. Only Efillaeh can save him. And the energy and magic of the raven must wield the sacred knife. Corvus is the only one who can save Wolloh."

Nomed started to speak. Relevart frowned. Nomed nodded his understanding.

Relevart continued, "I will take him to a safe and secret place. Act as though he is dead and buried. Nissasa and the Mocendi League must believe it, or they will find and destroy him." He bowed his head. When he looked up, he frowned and tapped his staff on the floor. "Beware your thoughts and your words. Many follow our story—many who can affect the course of The Unfolding."

The oval of light faded, and the crystal dimmed. Relevart laid a hand on Wolloh's forehead and lifted the staff. Before the third tap, they vanished, leaving Nomed and his companions in a silence heavy with questions.

Nissasa Rattori wiped the sweat from his brow and leaned back in his chair. Fatigue held him in its grasp. Sleep-weighted eyelids fought to stay open. Slumber took him.

Coldness creeping over his body snatched him into wakefulness. Dread left him shaking. His eyes flew open. He jerked upright, searching his tent with a sense of panic. A breeze rustled the tent flap. *Night. It's only the desert's cold.*

Pulling the black pouch containing Souvitrico from under his kcalo, he tipped the crystal onto his palm. Fire orange with a tinge of blue infused its depths with color. A fanatical gleam brightened his eyes. "No one is going to take you away from me. You are mine. You do my bidding. Together, we have ended the life of Wolloh Espyro." He threw back his head and chortled in delight. "Not even a High DiMensioner can withstand *my* power."

He savored the memory of Wolloh crumbling to a heap of mindless matter in his room at Shu Chenaro, of life fleeing his body, of the sudden void where his energy had been. Stebben's blistered palm flashed into view and faded. An image of Almiralyn's gray cat dead in that dreadful shoppe, Antiques by Q, made him hug himself.

"My reach is endless. I have neutralized a crystal in The Borderlands. I know the position of Elcaro's Eye." He pressed the crystal to his lips and held it up to the light. "With your help, I will destroy the wards that protect it. The twins' mother has felt the potency of our united strength. She will never forget my power. Most important of all, I know who guards Evolsefil."

He curled his fingers around Souvitrico and frowned. Frustration replaced his delight. He opened his hand and glowered at the crystal. "Why don't you tell me everything I want to know? Where is Evolsefil? Why is Stebben still alive? And where is that da'am raven, Karrew? I am your master now, not WoNadahem Mardree."

Flouncing from the chair, he made a circuit of the tent. "Where is that Sebborran pig, Dahe Terah? I didn't give him permission to run home and play leader. Soon I will take his place. He will be subservient to me. When he learns I have brought about Wolloh's demise, he will cement himself to my side and my cause. No more vague promises. No more sending his son to meetings as though his time is too precious to waste on a RewFaaran." He grew thoughtful. "I must discover why the Mocendi are interested in NeTols Terah. Who is he if not the blood-born son of Dahe?"

Blistering heat from the crystal scorched his palm. Within its depths, flames blazed around searching, hood-shaded eyes. Pain buckled his knees. A snarl of rage sent chills hurtling over his skin. A hand reached toward him, index finger extended, accusing—damning. The realization that he was in danger paralyzed him. He could not release the stone.

His mother's voice screamed in his mind. "Throw it away. Nissasa, throw the crystal away." A supreme effort sent Souvitrico sailing across the tent and into a pile of clothing.

He stared at his palm. Imprinted where the lines of his life had been, the telltale impression of Souvitrico blazed. "I've been branded—branded by whom?" The answer came to him with a clarity that left him curled into a ball of sheer terror. "The MasTer." *It is only a matter of time before the Mocendi League comes for me.* A sob shook his prone body.

The memory of his mother's warning sent him crawling on hands and knees to where smoke rose from smoldering cloth. Fumbling in the silky folds, he found Souvitrico still glowing and shoved it into its drango-protected pouch. *I have to see my mother. She'll know what to do.* He marched from the tent and raised his arms above his head.

The DerTahan bearded buzzard lifted into flight. Wings blazing, it flew south, its only thought—to find Roween Rattori at the home of the Dreelas TheLise in Trinuge.

Vygel Vintrusie stood on the stoop of the cliff side cottage on ZaltRaca. The MasTer had teleported him to this location with strict instructions to bring Coala Renn Whalend to him unharmed. He shoved aside a touch of annoyance at being summarily removed from Rattori's camp. He thought back to his encounter with the RewFaaran. The name Rattori suited him. He was a rat; a traitor; a conniving, nasty little rodent with no scruples. Loyalty was something Rattori would never understand—something Vintrusie valued above all else.

He would like to have twisted the knife deeper into Rattori's nest of lies, but his loyalty to The MasTer came first. The Mocendi's supreme leader had saved his life and restored him to the full rank of DiMensioner. He shot a grim look around the cottage and thought about the turning many sun cycles ago when Wolloh Espyro had sent him back to TreBlaya, a broken man stripped of power. The MasTer's orders rang a clear and insistent bell in his head. Rattori would have to wait.

He traversed the rough ground between the empty cottage and the cliff. Wind whipped around his bald head and tore at his cape. He pulled it tighter around his gaunt body and paced the cliff edge. Letting his senses roam, he searched for a sign of the woman he sought. Bulging eyes squinted against flying debris, he stepped back from the precipice. *If I am to find her, I need something baring her scent.*

Impatience carried him back to the cottage. A quick search of the lower rooms, including one he felt sure was her bedroom, provided him little of value. He scanned the room again. *I need something personal, something that carries her imprint.* His restless gaze paused on a feather pillow. *Barring that* — He stripped the pillowcase from it and held it to his heart. Eyes closed, he let her essence seep into his consciousness. He sighed and threw the case on the bed. *What a lovely woman. I hope The MasTer will leave her unharmed.*

At the cliff's edge, his instincts directed him to a break in the rocks that concealed a trail. Stooped against the buffeting wind, he followed it to where it ended at an overlook. *I know you came this way, Coala, and you had a companion. Where did you go, pretty lady?*

He stepped closer to the cliff's rugged lip. The power of the roiling sea crashing against the base left him awed. A drop of water hit his bald head.

His bulging eyes scanned the cloud-laden sky, churning with the angry gray of an incoming storm. Large raindrops sprinkled around him in a sparse pattern. The wind increased; lightning tore clouds asunder. Thunder roared. *The overlook is not the place to weather a storm.*

Bending into the wind, he hurried up the trail and fought his way to the cottage. The front door would not budge. Nothing he did would open it. He tried to force the back door. Drenched, angry, and frustrated, he ducked into a battered shed, sank to the ground in a soggy corner, and formed a tent around his cold frame with his cape.

Subtle power even strong than The MasTer's is working against me. The realization left him shaken. *Whoever it is doesn't want me to find Coala Renn Whalend.* Stubborn resolve pressed his lips into a thin line. *Nothing will keep me from finding and taking her to TreBlaya.*

11

Myrrh & Thera

Jordett locked the parking area door. After a quick scan of the hall, he slipped from the stairwell and sprinted to a double set of doors. The touchpad showed the drop car was only two floors down. *Hope it's empty.* He touched the up icon and ducked around the corner. Inside his shirt pocket, he could feel the rigid form of the Nyti Matrés. Kieel had chosen a tough way to be introduced to life in a city.

The doors sliding open revealed the car was empty. Three long strides put him inside. Double doors whooshed shut, and they arrived at Platform II within seconds.

The sudden descent brought a pea-green Kieel scrambling from his pocket. "What was that?" He clutched his stomach and deposited his lunch on the floor. He grimaced, produced a spotless, white hand-cloth, and wiped his mouth. "So sorry. Most unexpected." He hiccuped. "I gather this is a Drop Car."

Jordett tapped his pocket. "It is. Let's go." When Kieel had settled, he surveyed the corridor and made his way to the parking area entrance. The narrow window provided a view of an empty plaza. No soldier or civilians. "I don't like it, Kieel," he whispered. "It's unusual for no one to be around mid-turning. This is a government building and a healing center. There is always activity here. I'm wondering if the sub-level tunnel isn't a better idea."

"It could be a trap, Major, especially since they believe you are in the building."

"You're right. But I have a secret weapon. You can explore the tunnel and report back, so I won't be going in blind." He dodged away from the window into the stairwell. A short time later, he positioned himself in a dark recess across from the sub-level tunnel.

The door was closed. Nothing alerted him to danger. Slipping from shadow to shadow and Ria-T to Ria-T, he traversed the plaza and pressed his back against the wall next to it.

Kieel exited his pocket and hovered on the opposite side. Jordett inched the door open. The Nyti darted away through the gloomy darkness.

Kieel didn't like feeling trapped underground. Rancid un-Myrrh-like smells assailed his nostrils. His nose wrinkled in disgust. The desire to be home almost overcame him. He scolded himself in a stern whisper. "Gotta concentrate. You made the choice to be here."

Flitting a serpentine pattern through the man-made tunnel, he found nothing that alerted him to danger. Midway down, he discovered a recessed door ajar. Peering down from its top edge, he scanned the interior. Nothing moved. On soundless wings, he explored. It contained what he thought were cleaning devices, an array of buckets, and several extra large trash cans. In the corner, he discovered a ceiling grate large enough for a grown Human to enter. Filing the information for future reference, he continued his reconnaissance of the tunnel. When he reached the exit door, he hovered, shook the handle with all his strength, and shot up into the shadows. The windowless door remained closed.

Relieved that nothing alarming occurred, he reversed his search. No sign of a trap sent him back to the plaza door. He tapped on the door with the tip of his walking stick. A brief second later, he tapped again—the prearranged sign he and Jordett had discussed.

The door opened, and the Major stepped into the dark passageway. "Any trouble?"

Kieel landed on his shoulder. "None. It doesn't feel exactly right, but I couldn't find anything to suggest an ambush."

Jordett crept forward. The only sound Kieel could detect was the Major's soft breathing. Tension kept him quiet and poised for flight.

The click of a lock pierced the darkness. Jordett flattened against the wall. Kieel hovered above him, eyes darting from one end of the tunnel to the other.

A feeble light at the far end and the indistinct shuffle of boots on stone alerted them to company.

Kieel floated next to Jordett's ear. "Room halfway down. Ceiling grate."

The Major inched along the wall. The plaza door creaked open. A silhouetted figure slipped inside. The door closed.

Jordett dropped to his knee. Kieel shot into the recess. Nothing moved —not the Major, not the men at either end of the tunnel.

Every muscle in Kieel's body tensed. *I need to create distraction. Is this what Henri foresaw?* Not allowing himself to analyze the situation for more than an instant, he gasped his walking stick, shot down the tunnel, and whacked a squatting soldier. The man swore and grabbed his ear.

Kieel zipped to the other side and swatted him a second time. Straightening, the soldier faced the exit and peered into the darkness. Two silent strides carried Jordett through the recessed doorway. Kieel shot in after him. Booted feet drowned the door's closing click as they raced down the tunnel.

Jordett wedged it shut with a trash can. He pulled a small light from his pocket. A quick search showed a panel with labeled push-tabs on the wall between two shelves. Kieel hovered as Jordett pushed a green one. The grate moved. The Major inched it open until it spanned the width of his hand. Voices outside the door warned of immediate danger. Jordett pivoted and pulled the lid off a trash can. Too full. The next one was almost empty. He climbed inside and beckoned. Kieel whizzed inside and Jordett closed the lid.

"Confusion reigned as the trash container blocking the door crashed against their hiding place. Jordett squatted lower. Kieel fluttered between his chest and his knees. Both froze as the ceiling grate scraped opened.

"I'm betting he went out through this grate. Give me a leg up, and I'll see what I can find."

The sound of shuffling, the grunt of effort. Metal scraping the floor. A second voice. "Give me a hand up. You can go one way. I'll go the other."

Knees hitting metal made a hollow sound that faded into a muted hush.

Jordett lifted the lid enough to let Kieel flutter from the trash can. After a quick investigation of the space, he tapped on the lid. Soundlessly, the Major clambered out, replaced the lid, headed toward the outside door. The hollow sound of knees on metal sent Kieel streaking after him.

At the RewFaaran camp on Myrrh, Tinpaca Mondago paced his tent like a caged cat. *Wonder how Jordett is making out. Wish we could communicate. What's happening on DerTah? I'm blinded by the distances we are from the action.*

He marched to the tent entrance and stepped into the brightness of the Myrrhinian morning. The refreshing coolness of mid-autumn made him long for RewFaar. Sighing, he searched the brilliant blue sky. A silhouetted shape soared above the Terces Wood. Mondago shaded his eyes with a hand. *A vulture and rider. A Pentharian. But who does it carry?*

It reached the camp and landed near his tent. A beautiful woman dismounted. He noted the RewFaaran uniform, the grace with which she moved, the intelligence in the green eyes that studied him. Stee's emerald scales gleamed in the sunlight as he materialized beside her. His lizard-like tail flicked back and forth. Unblinking gold eyes scanned the camp, missing nothing.

Sure glad Voer and his Pentharian team are on my side.

Stee escorted the woman to the tent. "Tinpaca Mondago, may I present Gerolyn AsTar, aunt of the twins, Ari and Brie, and Lorsedi's communications liaison. She has a message from the Largeen Joram."

Lorsedi allowed a woman to carry a message? Tinpaca Mondago stifled his surprise.

Gerolyn flashed a brief, professional smile. "I am pleased to meet you, Tinpaca. Can we speak in private?"

He led the way inside, offered her a chair at the table, and took a seat opposite her. Stee remained by the entrance. His gold eyes held a spark of curiosity.

Mondago maintained a mask of military formality. Gerolyn remained relaxed and at ease. "What is the message, Liaison AsTar?"

Her gracious smile made another appearance. "I'm a civilian, Tinpaca. Please call me Gerolyn." Her expression became serious. "The Largeen Joram has asked me to inform you that Nissasa has left the RewFaaran camp at the border between the desert and Shu Chenaro. Something happened that sent him into his bearded buzzard form. When last seen, he was winging his way toward Trinuge. His men are leaderless. In less than two chron circles, the wards protecting Shu Chenaro will drop, and the Largeen Joram and his men will take Rattori's Brigade by surprise. The Brigade will capitulate. Lorsedi wants you prepared to take possession of the desert end of Demrach Gateway. One of the Pentharian is to return to DerTah with me. He will be our go between."

Mondago liked her no nonsense approach, but he could not shake his ingrained belief that women were ornamental, their sole purpose being to serve and satisfy the RewFaaran male. He struggled to set his bias aside.

She leaned her forearms on the table and pressed elegant hands against the fake wood. "I understand on RewFaar women are..." She appeared to search for the right word.

"We respect our women, but they know their place."

"I am not RewFaaran, Tinpaca. I am KcernFensian, and I trained in the arts of negotiation at the Temple of Mahyinaeh. Lorsedi would not have sent me if he did not feel I could handle any situation." She glanced at Stee's impassive face and back. "I have delivered the message. Now, I must return. The situation in DerTah is urgent. Which Pentharian will you release to come with me?"

Tinpaca turned to Stee. "Send either Yuin or Jeet. I need you here."

The emerald Pentharian gave a slight bow. "Jeet will do this best." He ducked through the entrance.

Gerolyn pushed her chair back from the table. "It has been good meeting you, Tinpaca Mondago. We will see each other again. If you'll excuse me..." She hastened into the Myrrhinian sunlight and mounted onto Stee's vulture back.

Mondago stared after them as they lifted into the air and flew over the forest. "I have to admit she's good." He motioned a young soldier forward. "Send Grantese Tesilend to me. Tell him it's urgent."

Pivoting on his heels, he strode into the tent, extracted a cigar from a box on the table, and gave it an appreciative sniff. A thin, gold lighter ignited the tip. He inhaled and blew out a cloud of smoke. *Life is changing. I wonder if the changes will reach RewFaar?* Another exhale sent a series of smoke rings into the air, where they dissolved one by one. *I wonder...*

Almiralyn remained on guard while Sparrow painted. A forest had gradually taken shape. Hidden beneath a vine and amongst ferns the height of a short man, the children stared as a ludoc cat changed to a flying scale-covered beast. Hornets bigger than a big man's fist swarmed above the small clearing. Hidden some distance away, a singular eye gleamed.

Sparrow cast a frantic look in her direction. "What kind of creature is that?"

"It appears to be a ludoc cat. Ludocs, however, don't have armor. As concerning is the single eye—"

"The Mindeco! Mira, what do we do?" Sparrow sank into a chair and covered her face with her hands.

Almiralyn placed a steadying hand on her shoulder. "At least we know what part of the Tinga Forest they're in. Those hornets are called vespids, and they only live in the southwestern sector. Come. You need to rest. I'll contact DerTah via the fountain and get a message to Henri."

Sparrow cleaned her brushes with shaking hands. "I feel as useless as Wilith was feeling. I want to go to DerTah. How can I help if I am stuck here?"

"You can learn the skills that will keep you safe when the time comes for you to act."

A swift, appraising look was Sparrow's only response. With a sigh, she walked to the entryway and shoved the curtain aside. "You're right, of course. When is my next lesson?"

Almiralyn joined her. "In the morning, we'll begin to refine your telepathic skills and discover what you can do with telekinesis. Right now, turn all your paintings to the wall. We don't want Nissasa to gain the information he can use against us. After that, get some rest. I'll meet you at evening meal. Merrilea and Owae will join us. Yookotay is expecting us in a chron circle plus half. That gives me time to use the fountain."

Sparrow followed her into the tunnel. "Shouldn't I come to help?"

"I'll be fine. Relevart has added his strength to the shields. I doubt Nissasa can break through them, at least for a time." She gave Sparrow a quick hug and took the tunnel to the central square in Meos. From there, she headed for Tennisca. As soon as she had rounded the corner out of view of the square, she teleported to the cavern entrance. The stairway of Retu Erath took her to the double purple doors.

Zugo greeted her with an excited exclamation when she entered Veersuni. "Almiralyn! It's Nissasa. I saw him change."

On the fountain's surface, a flaming bearded buzzard flew away from the RewFaaran camp. The image faded and water fell from the alabaster woman's palms.

Almiralyn looked at Zugo. "What did Elcaro show you before Nissasa appeared?"

"It showed a man on a cliff, and another man in a long cloak exiting a deserted building. Strange ghost-like faces peered after him through barred windows." He handed her a journal. "I wrote everything down."

"Keep watch while I catch up." She carried the journal to a bench, sat down, and began to read. When she completed his account, she joined him at the fountain. "Good work, Zugo. Now, I need more information. You can take a break, or you can stay. It's up to you."

"Will you tell me what you discover?"

She smiled and refrained from ruffling the fur on his head. "Of course. Go on. I imagine you're hungry."

He grinned. "Could use a snack. I'll be right back. Be careful, Almiralyn."

"I promise, Zugo."

He slipped into the Reading Room as she moved to Elcaro's Eye and stared into the rippling water. After checking the wards, she snapped her fingers. The water calmed to a mirror like gloss. A blurred image floated upward from the bottom of the fountain's bowl. It reached the surface and steadied.

Almiralyn leaned closer. "Hello, Aunt Henri. I didn't expect to reach you so soon."

Large violet eyes blinked. Henri settled her spectacles higher on her nose. "Good to see you, niece. Let's catch up while we can. You know Nissasa travels to Trinuge?"

"I wondered which direction he was taking. Isn't his mother at the Dreelas TheLise's home?"

Henri nodded, removed her spectacles, frowned, and returned them to her nose.

Almiralyn kept her thoughts masked. The message in her aunt's gestures sent a warning that implied the seriousness of the situation had increased. They must be discreet, or communicating via Elcaro's Eye could become a liability.

Using a code they had developed before Henri departed for DerTah, she and her aunt exchanged information. Henri confirmed Nissasa had already destroyed Dom's crystal paperweight, discovered Paisley but not Nemttachenn, and tried to kill both Wolloh and Stebben. It concerned her that Corvus was the only one who could save the High DiMensioner. *Nomed and Aunt Henri must find him—and soon.* What surprised her the most—Lorsedi had allowed Gerolyn to join him at the front.

Almiralyn had shared current events in Myrrh and described the picture of the children. The conversation would have sounded like small talk to an outsider. She hoped no one was observing them.

The water in the fountain gurgled and grew quiet. Masking her thoughts, she watched an image focus. Darkness, darker than night, flooded it. Two small sparks of light moved like eyes searching. Two sparks stared straight at her. She did not move—nor breathe—nor think.

Zugo burst into the room and froze. The sparks moved his direction, then darted back. Storm clouds gathered on the water's surface. A whirlpool sucked the sparks into its center. The surface cleared. Water once more trickled over alabaster fingers.

Almiralyn backed away. When she was a safe distance from the fountain, she pointed at the door. Zugo made a silent escape into the Reading Room.

She followed, closing the door behind her. Motioning him to her side, she guided him to a reading alcove near the fireplace.

He peered up at her. "What happened, my lady? You looked like you saw a ghost."

"I don't know what I saw." She stroked the satiny tabletop. "I will return, but I don't think you should. Something or someone is searching. Something extremely powerful. It vanished because another forceful presence took over the fountain. Too many factions are coming into play."

Zugo slumped in his chair, his face a study in frustration. Finally, he sat up and looked her in the eye. "I want to help. How do I stay safe? You need someone guarding the fountain."

"Zugo, this is not a game. It could be dangerous."

"I understand that, but I want to help. My friends are in danger, Almiralyn. If I can't be with them, I need to help them from here."

The young DeoNyte held her gaze. He was on the borderline between child and adult. Could she trust him to make good choices? Could she put him in danger? The steady gaze continued as the boy within the man retreated. The man held himself still, awaiting her decision.

12

Der Tah

Stebben stared out the sitting-room window, thoughts coming and going in no particular order. The morning sun highlighted the green of the taccus trees scattered haphazardly over the landscape and heightened the color of their large, scarlet flowers. Finnero asters sprinkled the area with purple anywhere they took root and prickly pyrus added splashes of yellow-gold here and there between the ranch house and the barn. A lithe desert fox sprinted to its den, breakfast clamped in its jaws. A variety of birds pecked at bugs and seeds, and lizards darted over the hot sand to find shelter in the shade.

It's odd to think that life goes on without Wolloh. The sun rises and sets. Flowers bloom with abundant abandon. His eyes tracked the flight of an orange, spotted cokotpa until it disappeared from sight. Sinking into Wolloh's favorite chair, he felt the worn places that had conformed to his master's crippled body, sighed, and stared at the embers of the morning's fire. *I miss you, Wolloh Espyro.*

Everyone at Shu Chenaro mourned the death of the High DiMensioner. After a quiet funeral, his casket now rested beneath his favorite Cucay Tree in a quiet corner of the ranch. At the reading of the will, the attorney had produced a letter written in Wolloh's hand requesting that everyone remain at the Shu Chenaro for one moon cycle following his death, at which time each would receive a bequeathed gift. Until then, he, Stebben, would take Wolloh's place as master of the ranch.

The request caused a certain amount of consternation that gradually died down as the running of Shu Chenaro reclaimed the attention of one and all.

Stebben straightened at the sound of the door opening. Nomed rounded a second chair. Tired hazel eyes studied him. The shadow of a beard made him seem older, more worn. Disheveled clothing showed his state of mind. Sadness robbed his half smile of warmth.

"How are you holding up, Stebben?" He sank into the chair, leaned back, and shut his eyes.

"I can't remember when I've been this tired." Stebben stifled a yawn. "I barely have the energy to sit here."

Quiet settled over the room. Stebben glanced at the man next to him, yawned, ran a hand from wrist to shoulder, and massaged the muscles of his upper arm.

Nomed opened hazel eyes and blinked against the light from the window. He rolled his head to the side and watched. "Perhaps what I need is coddling at a balneum where I can indulge in hot baths and massages with sweet-smelling oils."

Stebben smiled. "Take me along if you find one and The Unfolding provides an opening."

"Most definitely, my friend." He rubbed the stubble on his chin. "Hmmmm. Suppose I should shave but—"

"Here you are." Henri trundled into the room, spectacles in hand and worry written in wrinkles on her forehead. "Nissasa is heading for Trinuge. Seyes, you must leave at once. TheLise will need you. Stebben, we must prepare to lower the wards. Lorsedi sent Gerolyn to Myrrh to meet with Tinpaca Mondago—" A distracted look smoothed her forehead. She tapped her spectacles on the arm of the chair. "I bet you he didn't expect a RewFaaran to send a woman as a liaison." A studied glance from one man to the other brought her brows up. "What are you sitting there for?"

With more dexterity than Stebben thought possible for a woman her age, she stepped over his extended legs and tapped him on the forehead, and then repeated the gesture with Nomed. His fatigue fled. Energy, like a rush of cool water, gushed through him.

Nomed laughed and came to his feet. "Henri, I don't know what you did, but thank you, my dear. So, Nissasa is on the move. Do we know what prompted such erratic behavior? Generals don't just leave their men during battle."

Henri tottered to the window. "Gerolyn mentioned something about a visit from a Mocendi." She faced them. "The League is closing in. We have to find Corvus and the children before they do, and before the Cycle of Dovi traps us on DerTah."

Nomed rubbed his chin and frowned. "Dovi. I had almost forgotten we were nearing it. If Relevart appears, tell him where I've—" He laughed and shook his head. "Never mind. He'll know, won't he?"

Stebben joined Henri at the window. "Relevart? Where is he? Where—"

Henri gripped his wrist and murmured. "Beware, my friend. Even the walls have ears."

A picture of Relevart fishing him from the Mocendi jump craft so long ago made Stebben pause. "Let us refer to our friend as Reader."

For some time after the strange flying creature disappeared with killer hornets whizzing behind it, Ira and his friends crouched in silence beneath giant ferns. High above them, giant hornets near the nest at the top of the hollow tree swarmed and dispersed repeatedly until, one by one, they settled. Animals returned to foraging, and birds that had grown silent during the chaos began to squawk and twitter.

Ira scanned the sky. "Wonder when the rest'll come back?"

Torgin followed his gaze. "I imagine that depends on how soon they become bored with the chase. I wish we knew what that creature was."

Through squinted eyes, Brie peered up at the tree's splintered top. "I read nothing in Aunt Mira's book on DerTah that resembles it. The ludoc cat—yes. Nothing with leather armor." She dropped her gaze to the hollowed trunk. "Before the rest of the hornets return, we'd better decide how to rescue our things."

Ira spoke up. "What if we just sneak over and grab our stuff and sneak back? They left us alone before. Why would they attack us now?"

Desirol sneered. "Maybe because an enormous paw just turned their nest inside out. I'm not going anywhere near that tree." He shot Esán a belligerent scowl. "So, *leader*, what's the plan?"

Esán ignored the sarcasm. "Since you don't want to go near the tree, Brie and I will put shields around Ira and Torgin. They can sneak over and collect everything."

"You afraid to go over there yourself?" Desirol punched Esán in the arm.

Ira started forward. Esán stopped him with a hard look. "I'm not afraid, Des. If there's a problem, I can react faster from out here."

Desirol put his hands on his hips and thrust his chin forward. "Why don't you just teleport, grab everything, and teleport back?"

"Because," said Brie, "there's a Mindeco out there searching for *you*, Des." She looked at the tree. "We're wasting time. I'll go. Esán, warn me if they're stirring."

"You can't carry everything." Ira clasped her hand. "I'll come, too."

"Thanks. Stay close."

A sheer curtain of light shooting up around them stood the hair on his body on end. He glanced at Brie. She nodded. With the stealth of predators on the prowl, they skulked from fern to big leafed plant to fern and stopped just short of the opening in the tree's trunk.

Brie whispered, "It's clear."

"Esán just talked to you, right? Sure wish I could do that telepathy stuff."

"Who knows, Ira? You might have the gift. Stay here." She tiptoed to the opening and listened. "Come on," she called softly and ducked inside. Working fast, she piled backpacks at the entrance.

Ira shouldered his pack, grabbed two more, and slipped back into the cover of over-sized foliage. Brie followed, her pack already in place and her arms full of weather blankets, canteens, and, most important of all, Torgin's flute.

When they reached the spot where they had left their friends, only Torgin and Esán waited.

Torgin smiled and took the flute. "Thanks. Des took off in a huff."

Ira jammed his blanket into his pack. "Wish we'd left him in the Abyss of the Dead."

Brie gave him a quick hug. "No, you don't. I hate we have to wait around for him again, too. We're close to the edge of the forest. Could be out of it by nightfall. I'd sure love to sleep where I'm not afraid of being eaten."

Esán turned toward the sound of quiet footfalls. "Des."

The subject of their frustration stepped around a gigantic tree and strode toward them. "Needed a moment alone. I think we should go." He pointed at the gap in the forest canopy. Large dark specks formed a cloud above it. "The hornets are returning." He grabbed his pack and his weather blanket. "Thanks for getting my stuff."

Ira exchanged a look of exasperation with Torgin, fell in beside him, and followed Esán and Brie toward Atkis. Desirol trailed behind.

Killer hornets soon became a thing of the past. The tension that had kept Ira and his companions alert and energized began to wane. Torgin's easy stride lagged. Brie leaned more heavily on Esán. Des labored to keep up.

Ira slogged along, feeling as though their trek had lasted an eternity. He began to wonder if the steamy, wet rainforest would ever end. Keeping an eye peeled for Ratee Trees and his ears alert to any sound that might mean danger, he ducked and dodged and scrambled along. The strain of staying vigilant made him grumpy. He kicked a lump of moss, grouched under his breath, and kicked it again. The tip of his finger started to itch, which annoyed him further. Weariness made him stumble. *I need a good night's sleep.*

Up ahead, Brie and Esán forged the way in silence. He knew they talked —used telepathy. A stab of envy almost stopped him in his tracks. He shook himself and stepped over a bulging root.

"Ira?" A high, thin voice whispered in his mind.

He shot a startled glance left, then right.

"Ira."

A chill prickled over his scalp. He rubbed his head and squinted into the musky dusk of the early evening.

"They think they're better than you..."

He froze. "What the—"

"Ira, you have the gift—"

Desirol bumped into him. Anger burning like molten lava roared through his brain.

"Hit him, Ira!"

He swung around and threw a punch. It plowed into the RewFaaran's shoulder and sent him stumbling backward. Almost before he hit the ground, Desirol was on his feet. His fist caught Ira on the chin. The crack of contact—the jerk of his head, the snap of his neck—filled him with rage.

"Again, Ira! Hit him again."

He lunged forward. Knuckles clipped Desirol's nose.

Brie reached for his arm. "Ira, stop."

He shook her hand off and spun around. Esán and Torgin stepped between him and Desirol. Hatred infused the RewFaaran's bloodied face.

The voice in Ira's head stopped. Anger fled like air from a busted balloon. *What just happened?* He sank to the ground and covered his face with trembling hands. When he looked up, four pairs of eyes stared into his.

Brie knelt beside him. "Ira?"

He grasped her hand. "A voice spoke in my head, Brielle. It said my name. It—" He clutched a handful of hair. His eyes rounded in shock. He looked up at Esán. "Was it Nissasa?"

Esán's face was deathly pale. "We're under attack, and I don't think Nissasa has that kind of power."

Ira's stomach lurched. "If not Nissasa, then who?"

The question quivered with dread.

R oween Rattori watched her son's shifted form breach the garden wall and land in a tall tree at the home of the Dreelas TheLise. To say her son's behavior disappointed her was an understatement. However, she realized she was partially to blame because she wanted to control him. She wanted his success to be hers. Taking a moment to organize her thoughts, she sent a telepathic message telling him to stay hidden, threw a shawl over her shoulders, and hurried down the stairs.

It was late afternoon. The household was quiet. TheLise had gone for a ride. Roween shuddered. *How I hate horses. I'm so glad she went alone.* Tissent, the women Lorsedi had selected to accompany them from RewFaar to DerTah, had excused herself after mid-turning meal and left her to her own devices. A grim smile curled her lips. Plotting and planning were easier on one's own.

A footman opened the front door and bowed her through. *Men in menial positions*—she gave him an arrogant smile—*exactly where they belong*—and crossed the courtyard to the garden. Nissasa awaited her beneath the tree where his bearded vulture form had landed. He looked pale and harried. A haunted look made his icy eyes less cool than usual.

"Mother." He kissed her on both cheeks and stepped back.

She surveyed his rumpled appearance and pursed already thin lips into a line of discontent. "Why are you here and not at the desert border where you belong? The future Largeen Joram of RewFaar does not abandon his troops." She snatched his hand and studied his palm. "Now we are in a mess, aren't we? Do you know who branded you?"

"The MasTer." His voice shook.

"And how did The MasTer discover you had the Oracle Stone?"

"I don't know, MaMa."

"Tell me what you have been doing with it."

Hesitant words grew more confident as he laid out what he had done. When he told of Wolloh's death, pride brought the color back to his cheeks. The discovery of who guarded Evolsefil made his blue eyes glow. By the end of his recital, he was no longer a wimpy boy with a hurt hand. He watched her eagerly, almost panting for her approval.

Roween listened with a growing sense of dismay and a level of anger that surprised her. "You used the crystal, you fool. Not only that, but you may have destroyed connections that might be impossible to reweave. How do you expect to control the Inner Universe if you destroy the crystal web? No wonder The MasTer found you. No wonder the Mocendi are after you." She paced away from him, her long skirts swishing around her ankles. At the edge of a small pond, she stopped and glowered at the glassy surface. *Damage control.* She whipped around and marched back to her son.

"You have the crystal with you?"

He hesitated.

"Don't lie to me, Nissasa."

He withdrew a black pouch from beneath his long kcalo. "It's here."

"Give it to me." She held out her hand.

Icy blue eyes returned her stony stare. Mistrust lingered in their depths. "If I give it to you, I am powerless."

"Give it to me now or leave and never insinuate yourself into my presence again."

Nissasa stared. Astonishment, a touch of fear, and then determination exchanged places on his mobile features. "You would refuse to see me, your only son, if I refuse to give you the crystal?"

"*My* son is not a weak-kneed, sniveling little coward. The man before me is. You tell my son I cannot abide cowards and never to present himself in that light again. Tell him it is his responsibility to make Lorsedi Telisnoe sorry he ever passed him over for Largeen Joram—not for proving he was right to do so. Tell him until that time, his mother wants nothing to do with him. Take the crystal and go. Remember, every time you use it, it is a beacon to its whereabouts."

Pivoting on her heels, she marched back the way she had come. The garden gate clicked shut and the front door opened. The same smiling idiot bowed her into the house. She climbed the stairs, stepped into her suite, balled her shawl into a wad, and pitched it across the room. Emotion engulfed her. And how she hated it. *Emotions.* Something she rarely allowed herself to feel. Like a small girl, she flung herself on the bed and buried her head in a pillow and pummeled it with angry fists. When her temper had abated, she rose, straightened the eiderdown, and walked to the mirror over the bureau.

For some time, she observed the woman observing her. *What do you see, lady in the mirror?* Dark hair streaked with gray stuck out around her head in total disarray—close-set, dull blue eyes, a nose too narrow to be pretty, a mouth too thin to be anything but stern. Taller than most women, long-limbed, and lean, she recalled her despised nickname as a child—*Stork.* It had not been her choice. Quick, habitual movements reordered her hair. Soon it lay smooth against her head, center parted and drawn back in a tight bun. With a frown, she noted the two pink splotches on her cheekbones—a sure sign of her emotional outburst.

She gave the mirror an accusatory grimace, arranged her face into its usual expression of haughty disdain, and wandered into her sitting room. Sinking onto an elegantly embroidered chair, she clasped her hands in her lap and closed her eyes. *What on RewFaar were you thinking, Nissasa Rattori? And what are you thinking now?*

Nissasa massaged the brand on his hand and frowned. *My mother called me a coward.* A part of him, the little boy inside—the one who *had* been delicate and sensitive—wanted to cry out, 'but I love you.' The young boy she berated for being sad or caring wanted to run away. The ruthless, self-important man he had become wanted to slap her aging face, to see her cry, to make her sorry she had made him feel small or stupid. He tucked the pouch under his kcalo. *I'll show you what kind of coward I am.*

Hunger gnawed at his belly. Fatigue as deep as the Trinugian Sea threatened to drown him. "Da'am you, MaMa."

He changed shape and lifted into flight. Nestled between two rolling hills near to the Dreelas' home, he discovered a small hamlet. Choosing a sheltered spot near the outskirts, he landed, assumed his Human form, and scanned the landscape. A sign a short distance along the road read, Esccery Inn. An arrow pointed down a winding lane. After a short walk, he arrived in front of a quaint, well-appointed establishment. Early evening had invaded the area. Warm lights glowed in the windows. A uniformed servant bowed and held the front door open.

Nissasa marched through into a small but charming reception area. The man behind the desk widened his eyes. Nissasa glanced down. *Ahhh.* I'm dressed in desert wear in the middle of Trinuge, a province famous for its luscious rain forests and picturesque seaside towns. Removing his kcalo, he draped it over his arm and approached the desk. The man's expression changed to suspicion laced with veiled interest. Nissasa imagined he had never in his narrow, insignificant life seen a RewFaaran uniform.

"I require food and a room." He withdrew a money purse from his pocket and tipped a RewFaar silver coin onto the desk.

The man picked it, flipped it over, and handed it back. "I need real money, sir." His demeanor was polite—careful.

Nissasa pulled a gold coin embossed with the symbol of the House of

Telisnoe from the purse. "I am newly arrived, early for a visit with the Dreelas. Will this cover my needs?"

The man studied the coin and smiled. "It will. May I send someone for your luggage?"

"I sent it ahead."

"And your horse?"

Nissasa's cool eyes grew cooler. "I arrived by unconventional means."

The man smiled a conspiratorial smile. "A DiMensioner."

Ignoring his statement, Nissasa sighed. "I'm tired. Please show me to my room and have food sent up as soon as possible."

The man swiveled a registry toward him and held out a pen.

After a minuscule delay, Nissasa scrawled a semblance of his name.

A small bell rang, and a young woman appeared.

"Show this gentleman to guest suite number one." He stood. "Name's Quipe. Please let me know if you require anything further."

Nissasa gave the man a tepid smile and strode after the young woman. Once in the hall, he allowed his gaze to wander the youthful curves of her body. *I wonder what the game rules are between men and women in Trinuge? After the past few turnings, a bedmate would be pleasant.*

As though aware of his scrutiny, she hurried to a door labeled Suite One and handed him a key. "This is your suite, sir. Enjoy your stay."

The temptation to ask her to join him remained unspoken as she lowered her gaze, slipped around him, and hurried down the hall.

While he awaited his meal, he pondered his mother's behavior. Thinking about her reaction to his accomplishments stoked the embers of his anger. A knock at the door made him put it on hold. He waited until the young server had departed, then pulled out a chair and sat down. *Food and sleep. Then I return to the desert, and the battle I will win.*

"You are already losing the war, Nissasa Rattori."

The telepathic message brought him to his feet. His mental shields slammed into place. *Who in Sedah was that?*

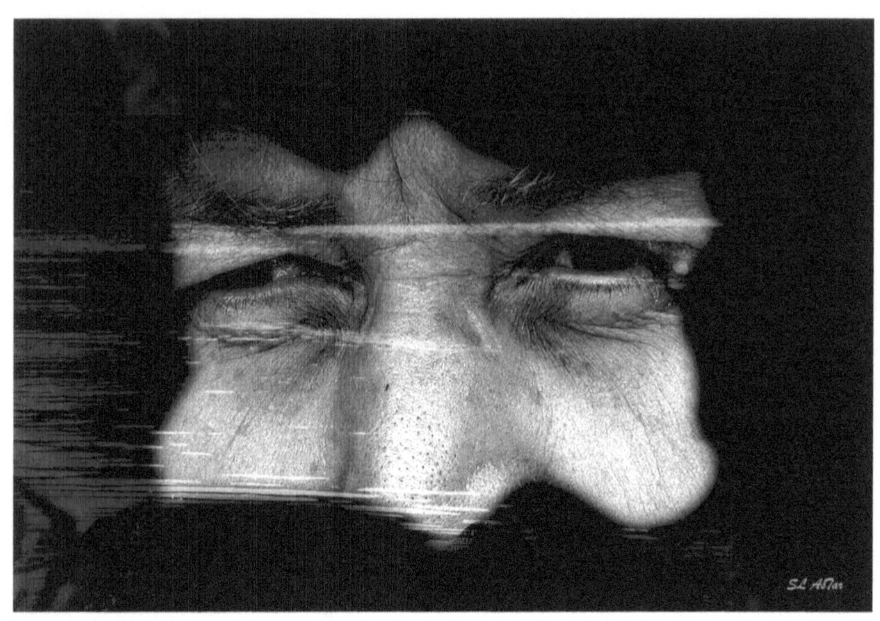

13
Myrrh & Theera

Almiralyn accepted Zugo's offer of help. Learning to conduct himself with circumspection and to make mature decisions would only help him become the adult he had the potential to be. Although he possessed none of the talents that would lend themselves to DiMensionery, he was quick, intelligent, and brave. She reassured herself as she crossed the Reading Room.

I need someone monitoring the fountain. I can't be everywhere at once. Zugo will do a good job. The details in his journal are concise and well organized. He knew not to approach the fountain when the eyes were searching. And I trust him to let me know immediately if something important appears. She hesitated and glanced back at Veersuni. He'll be fine. I gave him a golden citrine crystal from his home caverns. It's programmed to shield him from sight. He promised to wear it whenever he was in the sanctuary.

Satisfied he would be wary, she jogged down the stairs to the Research Library and headed for the section where she had last seen Wilith Whalen. She found him hunched over a parchment, surrounded by piles of books and scrolls. Elae sat next to him, her expression serious and her attention concentrated.

Almiralyn cleared her throat. "Excuse me."

Both jumped. Wilith frowned, rubbed his forehead, and marked the place in the book he had been referencing. "Almiralyn—so sorry. I believe we got lost in the text." He stood and stretched. "I could use a brief respite to clear my head."

Almiralyn nodded. "Let's adjourn to the Reading Room."

Elae pushed her chair back. "A break and food would be nice. I'll fix something and meet you there."

"Please ask one of the other priestesses to prepare the food, Elae. I'd like a full report. You might have seen something Wilith missed."

She nodded and vanished down the corridor of glass cases.

Wilith tapped the parchment he had rolled out on the table. "Elae found this. I think it is important, but there are things that neither of us understands."

Almiralyn slid into Elae's vacant seat and bent over a scroll written in three different languages. Her heartbeat quickened, then slowed. She frowned, struggled to translate a passage from an ancient text, skipped it, and moved on to the next. "This says the Mocendi originated on the rim planet of TreBlaya in the sun cycles before StyLacca, when the destruction of the planet's surface occurred. They were sacerdotal individuals who lived simple, reclusive lives. At some point, they gathered together and formed a sect that began the exploration and study of the mystical arts. Rumors suggested that the Mocendi Sect was instrumental in the destruction that took place on TreBlaya." She paused. "There's a passage that I can't translate. I wish Corvus were here. His training in languages is far greater than mine."

Wilith opened the book he had been referencing when she arrived and flipped back several pages. "It says here that about fifty sun cycles ago, the sect reappeared as the Mocendi League, full-blown and invigorated by the Arts of DiMensionery. The leader is called The MasTer. The title alone engenders fear across the Inner Universe. There is no mention of who he is or where he's from, although it states that he is merciless and cruel beyond imagination."

Elae had joined them as he finished. "Our meal is ready." She glanced at the parchment. "Other than this scroll, I found only one reference to The MasTer, Almiralyn. He is rumored to have the Red Eye of Death. The text says: 'If you make eye contact, death is a long and painful process that begins forthwith.'"

Almiralyn felt a chill of dread. "I must speak with Zugo. I'll join you in the Reading Room."

Hurrying between the glass cases, she hoped her young DeoNyte had not succumbed to the curiosity for which he was so well known. A sideways glance showed her reflection racing beside her, anxiety in every step, fear in the deep blue of her eyes.

From the entrance to Tinpaca Mondago's tent, the emerald Pentharian Stee observed his comrade's approach. Sun bounced off carnelian scales as Jeet zigzagged between tents and glinted on the gold and silver earrings marking his success in battle. On his chest, he bore the tattoos of his birth clan and the initiations that had prepared him for adulthood. He was tall and muscular, with a myriad of finger-thick braids that brushed his waist as he walked. Yellow eyes flecked with orange to match his scales—a rarity amongst his kind—remained focused on his destination.

Around him, RewFaaran soldiers cast curious glances in his direction. Apparently unaware the Pentharian had exceptional hearing, some whispered comments to fellow soldiers. Jeet ignored them.

Stee turned to the Tinpaca. "Jeet has returned from DerTah." He stepped back and motioned his comrade inside.

Mondago stood. "Welcome, Jeet. I hope you have good news. Please take a seat."

Jeet joined him at the table and presented a concise report, which included Lorsedi's plans for securing the Demrach Gateway. Mondago was to ready a select number of men for portal travel. Allynae and Stebben would lower the border shields in exactly one chronometer circle, Myrrhinian time. Mondago made a note.

Jeet continued, "I will scout the DerTahan end of the gateway and return to give the 'go.' With luck, the battle for the portal will give your troops control."

Mondago ordered Grantese Tesilend to select ten men and depart for Demrach Gateway. Stee and Jeet shifted to their vulture forms and flew ahead. The Tinpaca and a small contingent of soldiers remained at camp to guard prisoners and to maintain the security of Tropal Gateway, the portal into The Borderlands.

Stee and Jeet landed near the portal to confer with Yuin. In Pentharian form, they conferred in the low, guttural language of their kind. After explaining the fast-developing situation to Yuin, Stee once again shaped a vulture and took flight. Within a short time, he arrived at the clearing surrounding Nemttachenn Tower and materialized as Pentharian. He strode to the entrance and stared into the dim interior. Paisley and CheeTrann bent over a chessboard made him smile.

The Sentinel looked up. His booming baritone reverberated throughout the tower. "Ah. It is the Pentharian Stee. You have news?"

Paisley grinned. "Hey, Stee. What's happenin'?"

"Tinpaca Mondago asked me to inform you an offensive is about to begin." When he had presented the details, he glanced down at the chessboard. "I do not know this game, only what it is called."

CheeTrann puffed up his chest. "It is a game of battle. One must understand strategy. I do this well." He winked at Paisley.

Stee straightened and tossed a thick braid over his shoulder. "Someday you must teach me."

Both the Sentinel and Paisley walked him to the tower entrance.

"When The Unfolding is complete, I, the protector of Myrrh, will teach you. Until then, may the gods of ReTaw au Qa protect you."

Stee touched his heart, bowed, and caught Paisley's eye. "You take care of each other. And keep Evolsefil safe. I'll return when I have more news."

He shifted and flew above the canopy. His arrival at the portal coincided with Tesilend and his men. Jeet had already flown through the gateway. Tension built in the small clearing. Action was better than waiting. But action brought with it the possibility of death.

Kieel fluttered to the Major's side. Jordett held the loading dock door ajar. Kieel shot through the opening. A quick inspection showed nothing of concern.

"All clear, Major."

Jordett jogged along the dock to the next door. Kieel kept pace in the shadows, his eyes scanning and his ears straining to hear anything alarming. The door was locked. A Ria Van glided into a parking space. Two men jumped out and climbed the ramp. The driver unlocked the door and nodded Jordett through. It locked behind them with a soft clunk.

Immersed in conversation, the men hurried ahead and disappeared into an office. The Major took a right at the next corridor and followed a green line on the floor until they stood opposite an exit. Kieel slipped into his pocket. The major straightened his cap and smoothed his uniform jacket. Taking a breath, he stepped into the open, strolled out the exit into the receding light of late turning, and walked away from the healing center.

Kieel peeked from the pocket, still unable to take in the enormity of the buildings and the river-wide streets. Jordett paused at the corner. A soft feminine voice directed, "Please cross. Stay within the dotted lines." On the far side, he took the first pass-through he came to and jogged to the next avenue. In the shadows near the Ria Train entrance, Majeska waited, her eyes half closed and her tail twitching.

Kieel's heart sank. The twitching tail was a warning. Of what, he did not know. He hoped he'd never find out.

Jordett eyed Majeska, grateful for the warning, but frustrated that he couldn't use the Ria Train. He had to get off the street, *and* he had to find a place to hole up until it was time to meet Anada and Sagus.

The ghost-like shape of Almiralyn's cat trotted across the avenue and along a side street. Keeping her in sight, Jordett strolled along the pristine walkway. He passed no one. Not even a PPP Ria Transport glided by. Another empty block, and Majeska paused. A quick look back and she trotted down the steps to the Ria Train.

Jordett jogged after her and stepped through the official PPP gate to the platform. A sweeping gaze confirmed the station, like the streets, was empty. No patrollers were in evidence. He sank onto a bench and tried not to fidget.

An up-city train whished to a stop. Four patrollers exited and closed in around him.

"You'll need to come with us, Major."

A patroller slipped detention bands on his wrists; another marched him onto the empty train.

"Hold on to the data pole, Major."

When he didn't move, the patroller grabbed his hands and pressed them around the clear pole. His presence on the train was now common knowledge. Every PPP patroller in the city would know within moments where he was.

Buzzers alerted travelers to the imminent departure of the train. A patroller stuck a hand in front of the closure beam. The others marched Jordett onto the platform. Behind them, the door whispered shut, and the Ria Train whistled away up the tunnel.

Across the platform, a deserted down-city train pulled in. Jordett felt a slight nudge and stepped onboard.

He gave his captors a sidelong glance. None of them had touched the clear data poles lining the center of the previous train. Again, they ignored the rule drilled into every Idronattian's head from early childhood. *For the protection and safety of the people, The Plan dictates you must touch the date poles on all Ria Trains.*

While one patrolman blocked the surveillance lens at their end of the car, the others maneuvered him around the poles to one of two seats on the train that the lens only partially covered. The patroller waited for him to sit and took up a position in front of him.

Although Jordett's mind was racing, he kept his thoughts to himself. Recording devices would pick up any conversation. He scanned the length of the car. Emptiness was all that met the eye—emptiness and one small gray shadow crouching in the corner beneath a seat.

Zugo curled up on a bench in Veersuni and read a book about the planet of DerTah. Just because Almiralyn wouldn't allow him to join his friends didn't mean he shouldn't know about it. Besides, he was curious. *My friends are seeing other planets. Sure wish I were with them.*

He squirmed, furrowed his brow, and frowned. A flash of surprise smoothed his forehead. *I'm jealous.* His brows snapped together. *I'm feeling trapped.* He flipped a page and stared at a sketch of a Fire ConDra hovering above rolling dunes. *My friends are seeing different creatures.* A loud, heaving sign floated into Veersuni. *I've lived my entire life in the depths of the Dojanack Caverns.*

Although it was rare for a DeoNyte to venture beyond the boundaries of Meos, rescuing Esán from Seyes Nomed and becoming a part of the fight to save Almiralyn and Myrrh had taken him into other sections of the cavern and eventually into the outer world. *I loved being in the Outside. I loved space and sun and tall grass.* The memory of the wind in his fur made him smile.

He read more about the Desert of Fera Finnero. The information didn't excite him, but the pictures did. *Wonder what it feels like to walk on sand or climb a dune? Sure wish I could see an oasis like Eissua.* The next chapter described the Province of Trinuge. Pictures of the ocean and rain forests intrigued him. He turned the page and began to read about the Tinga Forest. *My friends are there. I understood why the desert would be dangerous for me, but the Tinga?* The sketch of a cat twice the height of a DeoNyte gave him second thoughts. He began to read the description of the ludoc cat.

Almost as though a breeze blew in Veersuni, the fur on his back stirred. He glanced around the sanctuary. Something was different. Anticipation— expectation— His gaze flew to the fountain. Elcaro's eye was silent. The alabaster woman on the fountain's rim gazed at her empty palms. The water's surface gleamed silky smooth in the light from the huge stained-glass window covering one full side of the room.

"Zugo?"

Instinct kept him quiet. He set the book aside, listening intently.

"Zugo." The high-pitched, scratchy voice ignited a desire to know what the fountain portrayed.

"I won't harm you." A series of crackling sounds followed, a short silence, and then, "I can answer your questions about other worlds." Crackle. Snap. "I can show you worlds beyond your wildest imagination." A smothered cough. An enticing silence. "Come to the fountain, young Zugo. Let me look at your face."

Zugo gripped his citrine and took a small step. *One peek won't hurt.* Another step showed him a cloaked figure framed in the rounded white rim of the bowl. Elcaro's Eye zoomed in. Folds of black fell over half-hidden features.

Zugo fought to step back. Paralysis held him rigid. His eyes rounded in disbelief. Fear prickled over the black skin beneath his fur.

"Closer, Zugo. I cannot—" The black folds thrashed one way, and then the other. The image wavered and faded from the edges inward. As though sucked through a funnel toward the bottom of the fountain, it decreased in size until only thin, dry lips trying to form a word were visible. A gurgling gasp choked into silence. The water swirled. Zugo collapsed to his knees.

The sanctuary door burst open. With an exclamation of concern, Almiralyn knelt beside him. "Are you alright?" She helped him to his feet and guided him to a bench. "What happened?"

Zugo's brain scrambled to remember.

"I'm right here, Zugo. You're safe. Can you walk?"

He nodded. She put an arm around him and led him into the Reading Room. Wilith and Elae started forward. A quick shake of her head stopped them. She eased Zugo onto a small sofa and rubbed his freezing fingers.

Grateful for the warmth of her hands, for her presence, to be out of Veersuni, he cleared his throat and exhaled a long, soft breath. "I was reading about DerTah. The sanctuary grew quiet. My instincts told me to stay back. A voice called me forward. Curiosity made me want to peek."

Almiralyn pressed his fingers tighter. "I need to know what you saw."

He squeezed his eyes shut. "It hid in folds of black fabric." He frowned. "Maybe a hood." His eyes opened and found hers. "A pink tongue, colorless lips—perhaps small teeth. The face itself—hazy—weird. I don't know if it was Human, or what made it fade. Was it you?"

"No. I believe the VarTerel came to your aid. Zugo, this is very important. Did you see red eyes?"

He shook his head. "The black folds covered the eyes. What was it? Almiralyn?"

"Let's join Wilith and Elae. I'm sure you could use some food, and we can all discuss what happened. I think you should hear what they have discovered as well."

His fear melted away. His stomach grumbled. "I *could* use a meal."

Almiralyn smiled. "I thought you might."

They joined Wilith and Elae.

"I think food first, and then talk." Almiralyn motioned Zugo to a seat.

He took it gratefully, heaped a plate high, and dug in. He wanted to learn what they had discovered, and he could tell they were eager to hear his story. The thought of the strange image in the fountain almost ruined his appetite. Almost.

14
Der Tah

Vygel Vintrusie crouched beneath his cape in the shack near the Cliffs of Tymine. Rain beat on the battered roof. Howling wind blew through every crack and cranny. His cloak and a warded shield kept him dry. He was cold and hungry, tired and frustrated. If The MasTer had given him just a fraction longer—

A pain shot through his temple. An apology jumped to his lips. He cleared his mind and began a mental search of the cliff side. *I wonder if I should try the doors again...* The pelting rain kept him still. Whoever had interfered would probably be close at hand. He focused. *Where are you, lovely lady?*

His mental probe left him clueless. The beginnings of anger flickered. He piled a few small twigs together, held out his hands, and imagined his fury becoming a small fire. Tiny flames licked at his palms. He stared into the blue-orange light. A dim place came into focus. The inside of a boat rose like a phantom. A grim nod of the head brought him to his feet. *She's in a boat. But where? There's nothing close to here but steep cliffs and pounding water.*

Wind shook the shack. The rickety door flew open. Rain pelted in. He found a large stone and wedged it closed. Shivering in the damp cold, he returned to his corner.

I can do nothing until the storm breaks. Then, Renn Whalend, I will find you.

The wind and rain crooned a lullaby—mesmerizing—hypnotizing— His eyelids grew heavy. A veil enshrouded his mind. He felt himself falling deeper and deeper and deeper.

Pitch black surrounded him. The smell of sulfur made him gag. Scabrous hands tore at his throat. Blistering fingers stripped the skin from his face. His screams echoed back at him, slapping his torn cheeks like a flattened palm. Hideous, featureless creatures flitted through his line of vision. Crackling laughter, silenced by a series of angry clicks, beat his mind to shreds.

"Do I sense a lack of loyalty?" Sparks spit and sputtered.

Panic froze Vintrusie's thoughts.

Rasp, crackle. "The correct answer will save you much pain."

He pushed words through swollen lips. "I am loyal only and always to you, my master."

A charred, black hand grabbed his throat. "Never forget who owns you, Vygel Vintrusie." The hand squeezed a moment longer, then withdrew.

Cough, gurgle. "The VarTerel is abroad." Slurp, crackle. "Bring me the woman and the Oracle Stone. Then I want the young people, the two with potential. They are our link to the past. If he finds them first, I will end your existence." Crackle. Snap. Crackle.

Vintrusie felt himself falling into the blackened pit of TreBlaya—the pit of no return, the place of unending death.

His eyes flew open. He touched his cheek. *Smooth.* He scrambled to his feet, kicked the rock aside, and threw open the door. Rain beat against him, soaked him from head to foot, cooled the fire in his gut. *I must prove my loyalty or die trying.*

Bent against the wind, he made his way to the cliff's edge. The thunder of crashing water, the flash of lightning, and rain pelting down made him wish he was somewhere else. He scolded himself for his lack of discipline and hoped The MasTer had turned his attention elsewhere.

Without warning, he stood in front of an inn, no longer dripping wet. *"A change of plans..."* The MasTer's voice filled his mind. *"Nissasa's ineptitude is about to lose us what we have gained. Take him back to the desert front. Once he's won the battle, bring him to me along with the Oracle Stone. Then you may continue your other errands."*

The voice faded. Vintrusie entered the Esccery Inn and glowered down at the man behind the desk. "I am looking for a friend. I understand he is staying here."

The man started to speak, looked confused, and turned the register for him to read. Vintrusie ran a finger down the list of signatures and stopped at Nissasa's scribble. "Which room?"

"Guest Suite One. Down that corridor."

Vintrusie whipped around, the folds of his DiMensioner's cape swirling around him, and strode toward the hallway.

Henrietta savored the flight over Fera Finnero in her dune hawk form. *How I love the exhilaration of wings against wind, of cool air caressing my feathers, of the freedom of flight!* Nothing matched the sight of the sun setting from high above the planet or DerTah's saffron moon sending rays of light into the sky along the horizon. It was a good time to fly unseen. She kept her personal wards up and impermeable. The fewer who knew she was abroad, the better.

The men had joined Lorsedi at the front to prepare for lowering the shields. They would be busy for a while. It was time she began her search for Corvus. Her first stop—Eissua. She hoped WoNa might be of help.

Her furtive search of Nissasa's camp had confirmed he and the Oracle stone were absent. Once they rescued Corvus, she would find the stone and return it to WoNa. Until then, she could only hope Nissasa would come to his senses and quit unraveling the crystal web.

Below her, the desert transitioned from flat, dry plains to rolling dunes that rose taller and taller the further she traveled. In the distance, the top of a palm tree broke the horizon line. Eissua grew closer with each wing stroke.

The shriek of a Fire ConDra crackled through the silence. Not far ahead, it soared from behind a blood-red dune, its wings flaming, its tongue lashing the air. Sparks showered around her. She landed, shaped her Human form, and removed her spectacles and a small, teal-blue vial from her pocket. With her spectacles in place, she shaded her eyes with a hand and followed the creature's descent. Another shriek shook the desert. More sparks showered around her. Still, she watched. Fiery talons reached toward her. Wing wind buffeted the sands, tore at her hair, plastered her blouse to her body. Still, she waited. Sweat beaded her forehead. She planted her feet more firmly and held up the vial. "ConDra's Fire," she chanted. "Semalf Erutamini!"

The Fire ConDra diminished in size. Tiny claws touched the lip of the vial. Vapor shaped a miniature ConDra. A sucking sound whispered over the dunes. The vapor vanished from talons to tail to flaming breast, from wings to blazing beak, until nothing remained but a faint glow in the corked teal vial.

Henri held up her prize and smiled. "You never know when you'll have need of a Fire ConDra." She returned her spectacles and the vial to a pocket, shifted to a dune hawk, and resumed her flight toward Eissua.

When she crested the final dune and the glistening water of the oasis came into view, she was more than ready to land. As her Human feet touched the sand, she smoothed her wind-blown hair into place and waited. A young girl sprinted to a stop in front of her.

"WoNadahem Mardree welcomes you to Eissua. I'm Nichi. I'll take you to her."

Henri smiled. "A pleasure to meet you, Nichi."

They walked along the edge of the lake to an entrance beneath a rocky outcropping, where a waterfall cascaded and a tall, slender woman waited. Her strange eyes gleamed, one saffron yellow, the other glacier blue. Auburn hair streaked with the dark blue of mourning wreathed around her head as though it were alive. On her shoulder, a small snake flicked its tongue out and in and out and in.

Nichi stopped several feet from the entrance. "I leave you here."

"Thank you, Nichi." Henri continued forward and clasped WoNa's outstretched hand. "It has been a long time, dear friend."

The Atrilaasu Oracle smiled. "It has indeed. Come."

They made themselves comfortable in WoNa's small cave and talked the way old friends do—as though they had seen each other yesterday—not like they had lived on different planets for many sun cycles. Finally, Henri directed the conversation toward her purpose.

"Nomed believes someone imprisoned Corvus in the Toelachoc Mountains. I must go there."

WoNa's snake slithered down her arm and onto her palm. It coiled its tail, stretched its length high, and blinked tiny eyes. "It is telling you I am going with you."

Henri held out her hand. "I know." The snake slipped onto it and flicked its tongue over her palm. "You realize how dangerous it will be for you to leave Eissua?"

"I cannot remain here when Corvus is in need and—" The small snake crawled up her kcalo sleeve and disappeared. "I know the danger. It is no more for me than for you. Let us rest and prepare. Narrtep will take you to your tent. We will leave before the sun rises. Sleep well."

Henri placed a kiss on her forehead. "And you, my friend."

WoNa's protector met her at the cave entrance. "Miss Henri." He bowed low. "The Atrilaasu welcome you to Eissua. It has been many sun cycles."

"It is good to see you, Narrtep. I wish I were here under better circumstances."

He pulled aside the flap of her tent and followed her into its dim confines. "She is determined to accompany you. I must remain here to protect our people." He gave her a look bathed in secrets. "Promise you will watch over her."

"I give you my word."

He bowed again and left. She glanced around the small tent, felt the faint presence of its previous guest, and pulled out her spectacles. Tap, tap, tap sounded softly against her palm. "We will come to you soon, Water ConDria." Tap, tap, tap.

I n the Tinga Forest, Brie caught her breath. *Henri's here in DerTah.* She started to say something, then stopped. The message was private, a secret between them. Besides, her friends had Ira to deal with. His fight with Desirol had left him in shock. Esán talked with him in quiet tones, helping him to understand telepathy and how it worked, and teaching him how to mask his thoughts.

Desirol refused to speak to anyone. He had a swollen nose and a black eye. Brie hoped he wouldn't do anything silly. She hadn't told him the Mindeco was closing in on them. Esán knew, but then he missed little. *I hate to think what might happen if Des wanders off again.*

Torgin sat by himself in the gathering dusk, squinting at the compass face. He frowned, looked up, and beckoned her over.

"Do you think whoever messed around with Esán and Ira's minds could affect the way the compass works?"

She sat next to him. "Why? Is something wrong with it?"

"I don't think so, but it doesn't feel right either." He removed the thong from around his neck and placed the compass on his palm. "Watch. Show the way to Atkis."

Ostradio remained quiet. The needle didn't move. The compass face didn't shift. Without warning, the needle spun counter chronometer-wise, the opposite of normal. It stopped, pointing to where it had begun and nothing else happened.

Brie frowned. "Let's get the others over here—"

A foot kicked Torgin's hand. The compass went flying. Desirol strode after it and picked it up.

"Oh so clumsy, Idronatti boy. Now, what are you going to do?"

Torgin started to rise. Brie held him quiet. "That wasn't necessary, Des. Please give the compass back to Torgin."

"The men of RewFaaran don't take orders from little girls." He clutched the compass in one hand and dragged her to her feet with the other. "From now on, I'm in charge. Give me the Remembering Stone and the sacred knife. Now."

Ira growled, "What the heck, Des, did the Mindeco grab you back there? We've already been through this. Let Brie go. Return the compass to Torgin. And for the love of Thera, grow up."

Desirol started forward, slammed into something invisible, and stopped.

His angry gaze fastened on Esán. "How dare you put a shield around me!" He beat a fist against it, grimaced, and shoved his hand in a pocket.

Esán spoke quietly. "Your behavior would disappoint your father. He wanted you to join us because he knew you would be safer. We're tired of being berated and delayed by you. Either give Torgin the compass, or I will take it from you. Then decide if you want to go back to Shu Chenaro by yourself or join us."

Desirol hid the compass behind his back. "My father needs this compass, and I intend to take it to him."

The compass flew from his hand to Esán's. "The Guardian of Myrrh charged Torgin with keeping it safe. Until that changes," he passed it back to Torgin, "your father will have to wait."

Brie whipped around, eyes searching the darkness between trees. "The Mindeco is here. I can sense it."

Desirol turned deathly pale. "I'm s-s-s-sorry. D-d-don't l-leave me."

Esán motioned everyone into a tight circle. "No one's leaving you. Brie, be ready to set up shields. Torgin, keep the compass handy in case we need it. Ira, same thing with Efillaeh. Keep it ready to use. Surround Des, backs to the center of the circle."

As he finished his instructions, a howl shook the trees and foliage, and the towering Mindeco, his single eye burning in the center of his forehead, burst into the open. A predatory growl rumbled. The bear-like skull lowered. Even in the murky light, he looked terrifying.

Brie felt her friends, right, left and behind her. Fear scented the air. Only Esán remained calm. No one moved as her shields joined with his.

The Mindeco lumbered closer. "Where is the boy called Desirol." Wide nostrils flared. "I smell you, brother of Nissasa. Your body, your mind, your life are mine. Come to me, or your friends die one by one, and you'll *beg* me to take you."

He prowled the perimeter of the shields. Brie shuddered, remembering their last encounter—remembering Yaro. This time, there were no adults to help. She squeezed her eyes shut and concentrated. Huge fists made contact. The shields shuddered with each resounding blow. She struggled to keep her focus. The breath of death showered down on them. Beside her, Esán fought with all his strength. Another blow splintered the shields into nothing. Her temples throbbed from the effort. Esán crumpled to his knees. The Mindeco threw back his head and roared his triumph.

Ira grabbed her arm and dragged, half carried her away from the creature from RewFaar. Torgin pulled Esán to his feet, and they stumbled to circle Desirol. Long, boney fingers plucked him from their midst and held him, dangling like a puppet over their heads.

From somewhere above, a thunderous, high-pitched screech sent leaves cycloning into the air. Branches crashed to the ground as the winged creature from the hornet tree plunged earthward. The Mindeco's single eye bulged. Desirol crashed to a heap on the ground and lay still. Esán and Torgin dragged him behind a tree. Ira helped to lift him into a crevice between two large roots. Brie dropped to her knees next to him.

The mammoth creatures postured, ready for battle, lunged through the air, and met in a tangle of arms and legs. Forest growth flew in all directions. Grunts and growls accompanied their tumbling descent to the ground. Wings lifted the scaled beast above the Mindeco. Talons raked along his lean, leathery arm. Howls of rage shook the trees. The Mindeco crouched, leapt, caught an armor-covered leg, and hauled his enemy from the air. Fists thudding against flesh thundered again and again. The antagonists broke apart. The Mindeco snarled and retreated. Eyes gleaming, his adversary stopped its advance. A conniving expression formed on the angelic face.

Brie cradled an unconscious Desirol in her arms. The Star of Truth blazed a warning. Her heart beat so loudly she couldn't think, as panic built like a geyser in her mind. She glanced at Esán. *"We can't stay here."*

He dropped to his knees and gripped her shoulder. *"Ira, grab Torgin and hold on to me. It's time to teleport."*

The last things Brie heard were the frustrated howls of their enemies.

Nomed pressed owl wings faster. Although he had promised to rejoin Henri after he checked on TheLise, time spent in Wolloh's library had netted him some much-needed information and also a couple of unwanted surprises. One had left him frantic to find his nephew. A passage in a little-known book regarding the planet of TreBlaya had brought to his attention the Astican Davea. The MasTer of the League used the services of an Astican, one with the ability to shift shape. Most often seen in its true form, it was a winged creature with thick, leather scales and a muscular body with taloned feet and hands. Its cherubic face was benign, even beautiful. Its intent was neither.

A Mindeco and an Astican— The children are in grave danger. My promise to help find Corvus will have to wait. Henri is more than capable of taking care of herself. Corvus is a grown man. Esán's need is greater.

He pushed his owl body to maximum speed as he drew closer to the Trinugian border. Thoughts buzzed in his brain—bees in a hive—busy with possibilities. He masked them and kept flying.

It took him from sunset to Tri-Nular to reach TheLise's home in Trinuge. When he arrived, the rounded crest of DerTah's third moon had just risen above the horizon line. He shifted to Human on the balcony outside her personal suite of rooms and peeked in the window. He had no desire to run into Roween Rattori.

Seeing nothing to imply TheLise was within, he prepared to present himself at the front entrance. A brief, whispered thought kept him where he was. TheLise was on the way. He turned and placed his hands on the rough stone of the balcony wall. The Dreelas' ancestral home was a stately old mansion surrounded by beautiful manicured gardens. Beyond them stretched the ocean, its vastness highlighted by three moons. The view was breathtaking. *Why haven't I purchased property near water?*

The quiet opening of a door and the rustle of silk announced TheLise's arrival. He smiled as she joined him. Warmed by the light of three moons, luminous gray eyes flecked with amber gazed back at him. Her dark hair framed a face so lovely it made his heart race. She was almost his height, slender, and lithe. He adored her from the moment they met and had since grown to admire her. Knowing she awaited a compliment, he said, "How are you weathering Roween's visit?"

Her mouth turned down in a pout. Her eyes sparkled with laughter. "You look wonderful, too, Seyes." She rubbed her chin. "Growing a beard?"

He laughed. "You know how beautiful you are. I don't want to spoil you with compliments. I haven't had time to shave. It has been a difficult time."

"Wolloh—"

His quelling look received a nod. He slid an arm around her waist and pressed his cheek to hers. "We need to talk in private."

She leaned her head on his shoulder. "Hang on." A soft whoosh and they stood in a gazebo near the water's edge. Her voice grew low and husky. "Relevart stopped here and told me the news." Tears made her eyes even more stunning. She blinked and brushed a glistening droplet away. "Nissasa was here earlier. One of my gardeners saw him arguing with his mother. He took off in a huff. Roween's maid told mine when she got back to her room, Roween threw a tantrum. Her entire staff has been tiptoeing around ever since." TheLise walked through moonlight and shadow to sit on a bench. "I'm fine. Just bored to tears. So, why are you here?"

He sat beside her. "Nissasa was head this way, and we didn't want to leave you entirely on your own. One Rattori is bad enough. Together, they are deadly."

She slipped a hand into his. "Since he is gone, will you go back to Shu Chenaro?"

"I need to find Esán and his friends. They are in the Tinga with a Mindeco and an Astican are pursuing them."

Her eyes narrowed. "The Mindeco made it through the wards?"

He nodded.

"So Nissasa sent his pet after them. I don't know which is worse, it or the Astican. Do you know who controls the Davea?"

Nomed bent closer and whispered. "The MasTer—"

She gasped, "The leader of the Mocendi League! Nomed, we have to find them and quickly."

"*I* will leave in the morning; you will continue to monitor Roween."

Her sudden quiet lapped against his resolve. She sat straighter. Light from the moon Calegri colored her eyes a cool blue-gray. "Don't leave me here, Seyes. I can help. I need to help. My instincts tell me you're going to need it."

"What about Roween?"

"I'll tell her I have business to take care of in the Cartatt. Tissent will watch her and so will my Major Domo. He is discreet. Both can use telepathy. They'll let us know if she becomes a problem. I can teleport back immediately."

He squeezed her hands. "You almost have me convinced."

She brushed a kiss across his lips. "I'm coming with you. We'll leave at first light. You'll have to sleep in *my* room."

He put an arm around her. "You are a minx, TheLise. I don't suppose you have any food in *your* room."

She laughed. "I ordered it before I joined you on the balcony." Soft light flashed.

Nomed stared at a table set for two. Candles sprung to light. She lifted a silver cover and revealed a Trinugian trout in a bed of steamed sea asparagus. "Fresh caught this afternoon."

He pulled out her chair. "Let's eat and then make plans."

The meal was delicious; the company was delightful. They discussed options. TheLise sent a message to Roween and Tissent, advising them she would be in the Trinugian capital of Cartatt for several turnings. After the meal, she slipped away to meet with her Major Domo and then to confer privately with Tissent.

The suite was now quiet. TheLise had gone to bed. Nomed stretched out on her sofa, staring at the ceiling. *An Astican and a Mindeco...* His errant eyebrow arched, then lowered. *We must find the children first.*

15
Myrrh & Thera

The High-Speed Ria Train shot through the tunnel headed down-city. Jordett would have preferred a District train that stopped every six blocks. A High-Speed gave him limited options for escape. *Only three stops until the Five Towers.*

Air whistled by. Nothing else moved. The four PPP patrollers remained in a tight formation around him, their backs to the surveillance lens. Tension threatened to undo his carefully preserved calm. He forced himself to stare at their backs...to trace the seams of their uniform jackets.

The train rounded a slight bend. The next station flashed by, a blur of PPP patrollers standing equally spaced along the platform. *Two more stops.* The train shot down the tunnel. A patrolman pointed a small device at the lens and clicked, then motioned Jordett to lie on the floor well clear of the doors. Puzzled, he obeyed. The four patrollers joined him. Another station flashed by. *Idronatti Central is next, Idronatti Central and the Five Towers.*

Again, tunnel walls closed around the train. The patrollers hurried to their feet. One pulled him to standing, took off his detention bands, and motioned him to remove his jacket. The patroller peeled off his as well, turned it inside out, and handed it to him. Jordett noted the general's insignia and slipped it on. A hat exchange followed. A general's insignia also decorated the one he put on his head. They then nudged him toward the door between cars. From the corner of his eye, he counted the glowing block markers. *Only ten blocks to the Five Towers.* The train braked and slowed to a crawl. A cloud of white vapor misted the air.

A patroller yanked open the door, stepped between cars, and disappeared. The train inched forward. A second patroller vanished after him. Jordett was next. Fastened to the tunnel wall in front of him were two metal rungs, one at foot level and one at the level of his chest.

"Go." The patroller's directive held a note of urgency.

Jordett grabbed the chest-high bar and jumped from the car. To his left, the first two patrollers clung to identical rungs. The train continued its slow progress until the final patroller hugged the wall. A rush of air announced its return to full speed.

Jordett smashed his hat down on his head and squeezed his eyes shut. A rush of air plastered his uniform to his body. The high whine of the racing train vibrated in his head. Silence, when it arrived, seemed to hold the vibration long after the train had become a speck of black in the long, white tunnel.

Majeska trotted beside the Ria track. Mimicking his captors, Jordett jumped to the ground. In single file, he and the patrollers jogged along the wall to a touch pad. The patroller with the small black box aimed and clicked. A door opened. Another quick jog brought them to a staircase. Still in a single line, they filed up. At the top, they found another touch pad. Point and click. Another door slid open. Like a gray shadow, Majeska slipped out. The patrollers waited, tension radiating in waves off their bodies. A soft meow erased it.

A patroller nudged him forward. Anada grasped his arm, guided him into the back seat of a Ria Transport, and climbed in beside him. A tap on a glass partition between them and the driver set the Ria-T in motion. Jordett glanced out the back window. The patrollers had vanished.

Kieel had kept his head down and wished again he were home surrounded by fellow Nyti. Jordett was in trouble, and there was nothing he could do but wait. The motion of the train, the stop, Jordett moving, the wall pressing into him, the whining cry of air...all left him relieved he'd already lost his lunch.

When the tension holding Jordett rigid eased, Kieel stirred, straining to hear.

Jordett took a moment to gain his bearings. Anada smiled a constrained smile, her eyes uneasy. His gaze darted to the driver and back to her face. "Talk?"

She nodded. "It's Sagus." Removing her cap, she ran fingers through her short, blonde hair. "I'm sorry we had to put you in a sketchy situation, Major. We received information the PPP had seen you enter the Ria Train station and planned to arrest you at your first stop."

"The four patrollers?"

"You'll meet them at the safe house. They're briefed and ready to help us take back the city."

"And the driver of the train?"

"You'll meet him, too."

"Sounds like you've been busy."

"Yes, sir, we have." She handed him a PPP ID card. "Please learn your new sun cycle date and officer code."

He examined it, front and back, and committed the unfamiliar name and information to memory. "General Hedi. I like it." He tucked it in the inside pocket of his jacket. "I'm impressed. My picture, the height and weight, everything looks correct. Whoever did this is very good."

"Yes, sir, I am." A touch of pride echoed in the statement.

Laughter shook his shoulders. *The first since—* Tiny hands pressed against his chest. Kieel's level of impatience was building. He smiled at Anada.

"I have someone I want you to meet."

"Meet?"

Kieel peeked around the edge of his jacket lapel and fluttered out to his palm.

"Oh, my." Astonishment and delight replaced the strain in her expression.

Kieel executed a formal bow. "Kieel, the Matrés of the Terces Wood Nyti, at your service."

She grinned. "I'm Anada. It's a pleasure to meet you, Kieel. I've read about Nyti, but never expected to see one. How do you like Idronatti?"

"I miss my forest."

"I bet you do."

The Ria-T slowed. Anada tapped on a touch screen. "What's happening?"

"RewFaaran soldiers up ahead."

Jordett held his pocket open. Kieel zipped into hiding. "Can we turn?"

"Too close. Too obvious. Better to tough it out and hope."

Anada donned her uniform cap and sat up straighter.

Jordett assumed the posture of a ranking officer. He shot Anada a reassuring look and forced himself to appear relaxed.

Almiralyn listened to Zugo describe what he had seen in the fountain to Wilith Whalend and Elae. The MasTer was closing in. He had read Zugo's mind, but the crystal had kept him from being seen.

Wilith looked puzzled. "What is this fountain? How could this MasTer see Zugo?"

She provided him with a brief history of Elcaro's Eye and pushed back her chair. "I think the best way to explain it is to show you. We'll all go. Stay well back until I give the word. Get out fast if something unusual happens."

She paused at the sanctuary door. "Remember to stay back." She heard Wilith gasp as he followed her into Veersuni. The stained glass window glowed. A snap of her fingers sent vibrant colors flying from the window to the velvet curtains. Captured in the panes of clear glass was the vastness of space. Stars and moons, galaxies and planets sailed past.

Beside her, Wilith stared and shook his head. "I've never seen anything like it." Reverence infused the words. Awe radiated from his dark eyes.

Another snap of her fingers sent the color back to the window. She pointed at the fountain. "That is Elcaro's Eye. It is part of a series of crystals known as the Crystal Laítise, which form a web of connectivity throughout the Inner Universe. I am responsible for the safety of the fountain and the Laítise. Elcaro is an all-seeing, sentient being. It shares what it feels is important. Right now, it's shielded. The fact The MasTer has traced it and attempted to use it emphasizes his power. Stay here."

She moved closer, tested the strength of the wards surrounding the fountain, and commanded it to deflect anything or anyone whose energy she had not embedded in the shields. The water spilling into the bowl ceased. She beckoned her companions into a grouping around the bowl.

Wilith gazed into the fountain. "Will it show us Torgin and Renn?"

Mist rose to the surface, then evaporated, leaving behind a forest with giant trees and foliage. Tiny, in comparison, were five diminutive figures scrambling over huge roots and sloshing through puddles as big as a pond. The fountain zoomed closer. Torgin held a compass in his hand. His companions gathered around him. The image scattered and reformed.

Two women, one blonde and one brunette, sat by a small fire, deep in conversation. The blonde leaned forward. "We can't let them find us, Bibeed. I would rather die than let The MasTer learn my formula."

Wilith gasped. "Renn." His pleading gaze flew to Almiralyn's face. "We have to rescue her before The MasTer finds her." He wrung his hands. "I know her. She will never give them what they want."

The water in the fountain eddied. No image formed. A harsh laugh made the surface quake. Another and another echoed through Veersuni, growing softer and softer until only horrified silence held those at the fountain in its thrall.

Elae's eyes rounded. "Was that The MasTer?"

"Did he hear Torgin's mother?" Zugo demanded.

Wilith wrung his hands again. "Can he trace her? She's not safe. I have to find her."

Almiralyn motioned for silence and led them away from the fountain. After closing the sanctuary door, she preceded them to the opposite end of the Reading Room.

Wilith folded his arms across his chest. "Take me to DerTah."

"Wilith, please don't let The MasTer goad you. You cannot go to DerTah. Esán and the twins will rescue Renn. I need you to finish your research. The more we know about The MasTer, the better our chances of saving our loved ones."

Elae moved to his side and laid her small hand on his arm. Her pale eyes, one blue and one green, searched his face. "I'll work with you non-stop to find out everything we can."

Merrilea walked briskly into the Reading Room. "Sparrow said you needed me. I'd like to help. Research is something I enjoy. Three of us will make things go much faster."

"Four." Almiralyn looked at Zugo. "I'd like you to take a break from Veersuni until I redo the wards."

He started to speak, seemed to change his mind, and nodded.

"Thank you, Zugo. I'll be as quick as I can. Perhaps you could research Trinuge for me? I'd like to learn more about where your friends are."

Zugo's face brightened. "I'd be happy to."

Almiralyn scrutinized Wilith's tired face. "Do you need to rest?"

Rubbing his forehead—an indicator, she realized, of his anxiety level—he produced a weary smile. "I won't rest until Renn, Torgin, and his friends are safe." He watched Elae, Zugo, and Merrilea disappear down the stairs to the research levels and then met Almiralyn's steady gaze. "I give you my word. I won't do anything unless you give me your permission." He strode after his research team, his broad shoulders straighter, his stride purposeful.

Almiralyn understood how hard it had been for him to make that promise. *His wife's and son's predicament terrify him, and he's a very proud man.*

Matching Wilith's sense of purpose, she paced the length of the Reading Room and stepped into Veersuni. She needed answers. Once again, she hoped The MasTer's remained focused elsewhere.

Four uniformed members of Rattori's Brigade and four PPP Patrollers spanned the width of the Avenue of The Lornton in the Benisuss District of Idronatti. Other than their ominous presence, the street was empty and so quiet Jordett could hear Anada's tension building in each breath she took.

"Relax, Anada. Whatever happens, we'll deal with it."

She attempted a smile. The Ria-T slowed to a stop. The windows whispered open. RewFaaran soldiers surrounded the vehicle. PPP patrollers formed a Human blockade. The ranking soldier stepped up to the driver's window on Jordett's side of the Ria-Transport.

"Destination?" he demanded.

Sagus sat as straight as a post. "The Five Towers." His less than respectful reply elicited an arrogant response.

"That would be The Five Towers, *sir*," the RewFaaran growled.

Sagus hesitated. A white-knuckled hand gripped the steering mechanism.

Jordett straightened his general's cap and inched toward the door.

Sagus looked the RewFaaran up and down. "The Five Towers, *sir*." A note of sarcasm penetrated the partition.

"ID," snapped the soldier.

Sagus handed it over.

The RewFaar fumbled, flipped the card in the air, and grinned as it hit the pavement. "Oops. Sorry, PPP garbage. Guess you'll need to get out and pick it up."

In one fluid motion, Jordett opened the door and stepped from the vehicle, his rank and the power it represented wrapping around him like a DiMensioner's cape. His gaze swept from the startled RewFaaran to his equally startled comrades.

He held out his ID. "We are due in a meeting with your superiors. You can clear us through the roadblock now or later. To me, it matters little. Your ranking officer, however, may not appreciate the delay."

The man's lips thinned. He snatched the ID, gave it a cursory glance, and handed it back. "General Hedi, have a good meeting."

"Thank you." Jordett bent to pick up Sagus' card. The RewFaaran's foot jerked back. Jordett glanced up. "I wouldn't if I were you." He straightened and handed Sagus the ID. "Who knows how important we might be?" He ducked into the back seat and closed the door.

The RewFaar held his gaze a long moment. With a mock salute, he waved his men aside. The windows hummed up and the Ria-Transport thrummed into motion. The PPP patrollers separated and moved to opposite curbs. At a moderate speed the Ria-T glided down the empty street. Two blocks, three, a left turn, and the partition lowered.

"Where to?"

Anada answered. "The safe house, and for the love of the Fathers, don't call attention to us."

"I won't. Long or short way?"

"Long, in case we're followed. Keep your eyes open."

She pressed an icon on a touch pad. The partition closed. When she faced Jordett, her eyes were uncertain.

"Do you think they'll follow us?"

"I think they will track us."

Anada smiled. "They can't. We disabled the tack beam so it will lead them away from us."

Jordett felt himself beginning to relax. His companions were young but smart. There was hope—hope that with their help they could take back the city. And then what? If they released the Five Fathers, would they reestablish *The Plan* and the PPP and the subjugation of Idronatti's citizens? The very thought made him wince.

16
Der Tah

One Man, as a red desert hawk, soared above the Demrach Gateway's destination point in the Desert of Fera Finnero, observing the faint spin of the portal. *Not the best place for Mondago's soldiers to land.*

He flew the short distance to the RewFaaran camp. In a wide trough between dunes, wind-formed mounds of sand protected it on two sides. The third opened onto a hard flat area with deep indentations One Man knew to be sand traps. The trough continued in the fourth. Some distance from the center of camp, it intersected with another trough that ended near the portal.

One Man landed on the shaded peak of a tent well-hidden from interested eyes. The camp's position impressed him; the men manning it did not. Nissasa's lack of discipline showed glaringly in his choice of followers.

Projecting his senses in subtle outward circles, he scanned the area.

Twenty men occupied the camp, four of whom were true to Lorsedi. Two were imprisoned near the camp's center. The other two bided their time in their tent. Fourteen men gathered in the shade provided by a large tarp, acting as though it was a holiday. From another tent, two men watched the antics of their comrades. One Man's gentle mind probe told him they were loyal to Nissasa but disgusted with their comrades' lack of discipline. He completed his reconnaissance. No one guarded the perimeter. The end of the trough closest to Demrach Gateway was unattended.

The power of hawk wings carried him into the air. He arrived at the destination point in time to see another hawk exit the spinning vortex into the red DerTahan sky. One Man swooped lower, landed, and shifted at the base of a dune a short distance from the portal.

Jeet materialized beside him and touched his heart. "It is good to see you, father of Esán."

"And you, Jeet. Are Mondago's men ready?"

"We wait only for word from the Largeen Joram."

Using the code he and Gerolyn had developed, One Man informed her via a telepathic message that Mondago awaited Lorsedi's signal. After sharing what he had discovered about Nissasa's men with Jeet, he glanced in the camp's direction. "Either they're playing a game with us, or they're unprepared for battle." He shook his head. "What on DerTah made Nissasa run?"

Jeet gazed down at him, his alien eyes gleaming. "It seems odd that he would leave his men without leadership. This does, however, benefit us."

"Good time for a chat." Gerolyn's message rang like a starting bell in One Man's mind.

"Be there soon." He pointed at the portal.

Jeet leapt into its spinning center. The time differential between planets made his return seem to happen almost before he had disappeared. One by one, Mondago's men leapt free, slid down the side of the dune, caught themselves, and spread out on either side of the gateway. Jeet greeted a well-built man in full battle gear.

"Grantese Tesilend, this is One Man."

The Grantese didn't waste time on formalities. "Tell me what you've observed."

One Man provided a concise report, finishing with his discovery of the four Lorsedi supporters.

"Good work." Tesilend pulled the bill of his cap lower. "One or two men could pull the rest of the traitors into line either direction, Nissasa's or ours. Anyone in the remaining sixteen men stick out as a potential leader?"

One Man cast his thoughts back to the camp. "A couple of guys weren't joining in the festive atmosphere. Both seemed more alert than others." He described their location.

Jeet touched his heart. "With respect, Grantese, may I speak?"

"Of course. Your input is most welcome."

"One Man and I can neutralize the two potential leaders. We can also free the two prisoners."

"*Go.*" Gerolyn's succinct message came through like a war cry.

One Man caught Tesilend's eye. "It's time."

"Good. You two go first. My men and I will circle the camp. We'll wait for a signal from you."

One Man shifted to a hawk and followed Jeet's bird form. The camp came into view. One Man's hawk heart beat faster. Life had not prepared him for battle. He hoped his skills would be of value.

Esán teleported himself and his companions away from the Tinga Forest, leaving the Mindeco and the winged monster behind. He surveyed the rolling hills extending as far as the eye could see. The Mindeco would be on their trail the moment he realized they were gone. A glance at his companions increased his unease. Cradled in Brie's arms, Desirol remained unconscious. Kneeling next to Ira on Brie's opposite side, Torgin clung to the Compass of Ostradio, his eyes darting from it to the rolling hills.

Esán edged closer to Torgin. "Check the compass. If it works, ask it to tell us where we are. Ira, stand guard, while Brie and I will try to wake Desirol."

Ira moved away from the kneeling group.

Brie bent over the RewFaaran. "Des, wake up."

He did not respond.

Esán touched his forehead, jerked his hand back, and frowned. "There's—"

"I know where we are." Torgin held out the compass and pointed southeast. "Atkis is just over those hills." He pointed east. "The ocean is that way." He looped the thong over his head and tucked the compass beneath his shirt. "West is farmland and a river. The compass worked fine. I wonder what interfered with it in the Tinga?" He studied Desirol's prone form. "Why doesn't he wake up? He didn't hit his head when he fell."

Ira stared into the distance and frowned. "He was unconscious before he hit the ground." Almiralyn-blue eyes widened. "That's not good, is it?"

Esán frowned. "The Mindeco left his mark on him in Nesune Ruins and had plenty of time to leave more than his mark in the Tinga. After helping WoNa to restore his memories, I understand his mind as well as I do my own. When I touched his forehead, I felt something alien shifting in his thoughts. If we wake him, it might take root."

"And if we don't?" Brie whispered.

"It could take root anyway, or it could drift—lost and ineffective." He frowned. "I'm not experienced enough to tell."

She appeared to mull over what he had said. "Can we remove it?"

He shook his head. "We don't know how. Corvus would be the best one to pluck it free."

Torgin edged closer. "What's our next move, Esán?"

Ira answered for him. "I say we teleport to the village."

"We can't." Esán rubbed the recent growth of hair on his head. "Not only can the Mindeco follow our energy trail, but now he knows Desirol's energetic signature. I'm surprised he hasn't already found us."

Ira pushed up from his knee and brushed off his pants. "Sounds like we'd better get a move on. I don't want to meet Mindeco again. What do we do with Des? If I weren't sorry for him, I'd say leave him here but…"

Esán climbed to his feet and scanned the dawn sky. "We make a stretcher and carry him. Glad we have a bit of light."

While the boys searched a small stand of trees for fallen branches, Brie cast her senses a short distance outward. Nothing alarmed her. *It's odd that the Mindeco isn't here already.* Sending her mind probe further afield, she tracked their energy trail back to the Tinga Forest. The last whiffs of battle—the enhanced scents of animal sweat and rage and fear—faded into mist and rainforest smells even as she explored the small clearing. No sign of which monster had won or lost remained. *If I didn't know better, I'd think the battle never happened.*

Withdrawing her probe, she inspected every inch of the teleported path she and her friends had taken. *I'm over halfway back. Nothing followed. We're—* A sigh of relief froze in her throat. She stifled the desire to shout and masked her thoughts.

Easing Desirol's still form to the ground, she scrambled up and hurried to where the boys had just finished tying a weather blanket between two long branches. "They've joined forces."

Torgin's whipped around. "Who?" His eyes betrayed immediate understanding.

"The Mindeco and the Astican. That's what the creature calls itself, an Astican."

Esán's pale complexion turned ashen. "An Astican is a Davea creature raised during the Time of StyLacca on the Outer Rim planet of TreBlaya. I'm betting the Mocendi League control it, maybe even The MasTer. We can't hope to fight it *and* the Mindeco."

"Where'd you learn that little tidbit of information?" Ira's gaze flicked over the surrounding hills.

"In a book I found in Wolloh's library. Come on. Let's load up Des and go. We have to hide where we'll be safe from detection by either of the creatures."

Torgin helped Ira lift Desirol onto the makeshift stretcher. "How bad is an Astican?"

"Worse than a Mindeco." Esán threw a weather blanket over the unconscious boy and grabbed his pack.

Ira and Torgin shouldered theirs and lifted the stretcher. "Suggested hiding place?" Ira asked.

Esán frowned. "I wish I knew for sure. Water might be the only place that will work." He took the lead with Brie. A glance at her expression told him she realized the full power of their enemies and that the chances of finding a hiding place were slim.

His gaze glued to Esán and Brie, Torgin slogged through harvested fields, glad for the dimness of dawn but wishing for enough light to find a less treacherous path. His arms already ached from maneuvering the awkward stretcher. Behind him, Ira muttered about the idiocy of RewFaarans and how much he'd like to be somewhere other than DerTah.

Bet there are worse places. Torgin grimaced at the thought. *This adventure is frightening enough. Sure wish we could find my mother and go home.*

Esán held up a hand for a halt and scouted further ahead. Torgin glanced over his shoulder, received a nod from Ira, and lowered the stretcher to the ground. Slipping his pack off, he tried to rub the stiffness from his low back.

Esán retraced his steps and paused by Brie. After a brief conversation, he made his way through loose-packed dirt and dried stalks to the stretcher and jerked his thumb over his shoulder. "Found a track made by wagon wheels, paralleling that row of trees. We're headed roughly southeast toward Atkis. I don't know how long it will take." He glanced at Desirol. "Want me to take a turn?"

Ira rubbed the tip of his finger and kicked a clod of dirt. "Nope. Torgin and I are stronger than you. You could use a bit of your DiMensioner stuff..." He looked hopeful.

Esán sighed. "Wish I could, but we don't want to call our enemies to us, do we?"

Another clod of dirt exploded into bits of dust. "Guess not." Ira glanced down at his drango boots. "If Des had left on the drango tunic and boots WoNa gave him, we wouldn't be in this mess. Hey, what if I exchange clothes with him? Would that mute his energetic signature?"

Brie joined them. "It would, but it would also leave you unprotected."

Ira persisted. "But if it worked, we'd all be safer, right?"

Torgin knelt beside Desirol and pulled back the weather blanket. "I bet we wear the same size boots." He removed one of Desirol's and placed it next to his foot. "See. I'll give him my boots, and Ira can give him his tunic because they're similar in size. That way, we'll still have some protection. What do you think?"

Brie and Esán looked at each other. Esán nodded. "We think it will obscure his signature and buy us some time."

"Wish you two would talk out loud." Torgin pulled off Desirol's second boot and removed his. "It's just rude. Like speaking RewFaaran when you know everyone in the room only speaks Theran."

Ira began to undo the laces on the side of his tunic. "Good job, Torg, on both counts—a good plan and the telepathy thing."

Brie grinned at Ira and knelt to help Torgin put his drango boots on Desirol. "I apologize to both of you. It's just so natural to use telepathy with each other that we forget. There." She patted Desirol's foot and scooted around to give Torgin a quick hug. "Forgiven?"

He laughed and hugged her back. "Of course. I just like knowing what's going on."

Esán joined. "We'll do our best to remember to include you."

Silence reigned as they exchanged Desirol's jacket for Ira's tunic.

The jacket's perfect fit made Ira grin. "I look like a RewFaaran, huh?"

"Right." Torgin stamped his feet. "RewFaaran boots aren't nearly as comfortable as drango hide."

Brie cast a nervous glance over the rolling hills. "We'd better go." She grabbed Esán's hand and trudged down the rutted track.

Ira sobered and squatted to grip the rough wood of the stretcher. "Ready, Torg?"

In unison, they lifted, struggled to get in step, and labored after their friends. Torgin shook his head as he established the cadence and rhythm of Idronatti's exercise march. *Wonder what I'd be doing if I were at home? Composing music, going to the Ed Center, practicing on my keyboard or my flute—* He glanced down. "Hey, where's One Man's flute?"

Esán paused and held it up. "Sorry. Thought you knew I had it."

The moment of panic subsided. "Thanks." He scanned his memories. A clear image of Esán picking it up after he and Ira had finished dressing, a clear image of— "What on Thera..." He halted. The stretcher bumped into his thighs. Ira swore.

"Put the stretcher down, Ira. Esán, Brielle..." He kept his voice low.

When they reached his side, he whispered. "Someone just put a picture in my mind—a tall cliff—me at the edge—me falling. It wasn't *my* memory."

Esán gripped his arm. "What did you do?"

Torgin wrinkled his brow. The furrows deepened. "I blanked my mind and called you."

"What happened to the image?"

"Blinked out like a light. There one moment, gone the next."

Brie squeezed his hand. Esán smiled. "You did great."

Ira looked at Esán. "What's it mean?"

"It means our 'friends' are searching. Our little trick is working, or they wouldn't need to use a probe. Quiet your minds. Stay as close to the trees as you can."

They continued in silence. Torgin held his thoughts in check. He didn't have the talent to use telepathy, but they could use it on him. He shivered and kept marching, marching in RewFaaran boots on the planet of DerTah through the province of Trinuge, marching— He gasped.

"What the—" yelled Ira.

Esán turned, his face blank.

Brie had disappeared.

Henri woke early to the sounds of the waterfall and the quiet giggles of children. She rolled onto her back and stared up at the rounded ceiling of her tent. Brie's essence, though faint, still hung in the air. *My great niece...* Closing her eyes, she let her mind journey. What she discovered made her stiffen. *Mindeco and Astican. Keep your wits about you, girl.*

Shoving the woven blanket to one side, she sat up and allowed her body to find its equilibrium in the vertical world. She stretched and crossed to the washstand. A small hand mirror glowed in the faint light. She held it up, examined lines around her eyes and mouth and the thick white, curly hair sticking out in odd directions. Humor lit her violet eyes. *Ah, life.*

The need to be on the move replaced her morning lassitude. Within a short time, she stood at the center of the tent, dressed in a sand-red kcalo provided by the Atrilaasu.

A soft voice called, "May I come?"

Henri pulled the tent flap to one side to find Nichi holding a tray.

"Mother sent you breakfast." She set it on a small table. "WoNa will be ready by the time you finish. You know our Water ConDria, don't you?"

Henri smiled. "She's my great niece."

Niche's eyes glowed. "Water ConDria saved the Atrilaasu from Fire ConDra. We very happy she on DerTah. You bring her back to us?"

"I will go to her soon. Now I must eat. Thank your mother for me."

The young girl flashed her a smile and departed.

By the time Henri had completed her repast, Narrtep arrived to escort her to WoNa's cave. As they stepped from the tent, he offered his arm and matched his stride to hers. Above them, pale ribbons of color formed random patterns in the sky. The water rippled lavender and gold where the waterfall and plunge pool met. Although the air was moist and cool, Henri could already feel the heat creeping over Eissua Oasis.

At the cave entrance, Narrtep bowed and left her. She walked through the short tunnel and entered the living space. WoNa sat at a table, her distinctive eyes glowing in the lamplight. She inclined her head and offered a hand.

"Good morning, dear friend."

Henri sandwiched it between hers, squeezed it gently, and released it. "It is indeed a glorious morning and an important one. Are you ready to go?"

The Atrilaasu Oracle touched the bare spot on her forehead where the Oracle Stone should have been. "We will find Corvus and bring him to help —" Her eyes seemed to grow larger, more lustrous. A tear leaked from the corner of one, caught the light of the fire, and dripped red-orange down her cheek. Ignoring it, she reached into the neck of her kcalo and withdrew her snake. It writhed between her fingers, then slithered to encircle her wrist.

"I am ready, Henri. I will shape a finnero beetle and ride on your back. When you shift, please land by my hand on the tabletop so I can find you."

Henri shifted. Gray wings flecked with orange lifted her to the designated spot. She sensed the currents of WoNa's change and stretched her neck to observe a small gray and orange beetle land and nestle down in her back feathers. *"Settled?"*

"Yes." WoNa's answer quivered through her head.

"Have you flown before?"

"Yes, some time ago. I am excited and a bit nervous."

"Stay down and hold on."

Henri launched from the table and swooped down the small tunnel into the light of the sun cresting the horizon. She sensed WoNa's nervousness dissolving. Joy flowed from her like ripples in a pond. With the sun behind her, Henri soared higher. The Toelachoc Mountains were on the opposite side of Fera Finnero. With luck, they would arrive before the sun set.

Secure beneath layers of soft, gray feathers, WoNadahem Mardree in beetle form reveled in the powerful contract and release of the dune hawk's back muscles; the whistles and whispers of the wind along the sleek lines of the bird's body; the wha, wha, wha of the wings against the air. Her first flight had been when Wolloh shifted to the osprey and carried her to Nesune Ruins for a retreat, a time of renewal of her vows as the Atrilaasu Oracle, a time for professing her love of her people and of the man who made her heart sing.

Both she and Wolloh had realized their individual responsibilities demanded that they live apart...at least for now. They had promised each other this would not always be so. Each turning, they communicated telepathically. With a regularity that had delighted her, Wolloh appeared at Eissua. Time spent sharing, learning, and practicing their skills enhanced their relationship. Her tiny beetle heart thumped the song of her loneliness.

A disturbance in the sky overhead snapped her from past to present. Henri's hawk form descended and swooped into a shadowy trough between dunes. As Henri's talons hit the sand, WoNa's DerTahan beetle landed beside her. In the same instant, she and Henri materialized side by side.

Henri's hand on her arm kept her quiet. *"Don't move. Fire ConDra."*

Heat washed the dunes, pooled in the trough, and scorched the air. WoNa pressed her eyes shut. Her inner sight picked the Fire ConDra from the red of the sky—one, then two. A third soared in a descending circle above them. Manic shrieks vibrating over the desert loosened sand and sent it cascading down the steep dunes.

"What we need is the Water ConDria." Henri grasped her hand. "If we work together, we can teleport her to us. You have a heart bond. Is it safe to bring her now, or will we endanger her or her companions?"

WoNa bowed her head. Her snake slipped from her wrist to encircle their hands. "It is safe. I'm ready."

The link to Henri's mind washed through hers with the invigorating freshness of dawn. Their memories swam together, like hoco fish heading for their spawning grounds. Immersion into colors, sights, and sounds left WoNa breathless. An unexpected intrusion lurking along the horizon of their connection triggered wards that sprang into place, concealing them— banishing the shadowy form.

Heat blasted hotter, a reminder of their peril. They focused on what they sought.

Brie's abrupt arrival in the desert left her breathless. Blinking against the bright light and the tears flooding her eyes, she strained to see who or what had snatched her away from her friends and Trinuge. Her gaze flashed from WoNa's beloved face to Henri's and fastened on the three Fire ConDra circling overhead.

She raised her arms. The ConDria's form embraced her like a mother's love. Fluid silk caressed her skin. With joy infusing every cell in her body, she pressed massive, watery wings against air and soared upward. The effervescent song of raindrops in the sun spread over the desert. Around her, Fire ConDra circled, flames fanned by the air, lava tongues snapping and crackling in the sudden moisture. Sparks pelted down and fizzled out in the power of water over fire.

Three ConDra formed a blazing line across the sky. Opening her wings, the ConDria began to rotate. Little by little, she wrapped her body in their torrential strength. A ConDra streaked toward her. Faster and faster she spun, a water spout of cyclonic power. Closer and closer it came. Heat sizzled off her whirling form. A missile of fire hit, exploded into tattered burning pieces, and spiraled downward.

The two remaining ConDra screeched a battle cry. The Water ConDria sang a trill of warning notes in reply. A second creature swooped low. The third careened toward her. Unfurling her wings to stop her spin, she hovered, luminous silver-blue eyes locked on its fiery gaze. Blazing talons reached for her. A stream of water spewed from her open beak the instant before she dropped from reach. The third ConDra shot overhead as she swaddled its companion beneath her in the aqueous expanse of her breast and cradled it in folded pinions. Steam blocked the sun. The air sputtered with the hiss and crackle of squelched flames.

Wails of despair beat against the domed sky. The last Fire ConDra fled, leaving the fizzling remains of its companions expiring on the desert floor.

Brie took a moment to relish the cool richness of water, the glory of flight, the freedom and all-encompassing delight of being the Water ConDria. Below her, WoNa held up a hand. Brie's mind filled with the sound of Henri's call to come home. She swept over them, circled, and landed in her Human form.

17
Myrrh & Thera

Sparrow stared at her blank canvas and sighed. *I can't concentrate. I'm worried about the twins and Alli.* She sat down, rested elbows on her knees, and cradled her chin in her hands. The memory of Ari, chin in hands at Almiralyn's kitchen table in the cottage several sun turnings ago, made her wistful for less chaotic times—quiet times with her daughters and Allynae. Another sigh lifted a stray tendril of hair and let it fall. *Almiralyn has been too busy to give me my next lesson in DiMensionery.* Straightening, she rubbed her knees. She had discovered her telepathic abilities when she, Merrilea, and One Man were escaping behind the Demrach Falls on Thera. *So, I know I'm telepathic. What I want to know is if I can shape shift and teleport.*

The urgent emptiness of the canvas called her to paint, to create, to be useful. She shook off her lethargy, forced herself to the easel, and stared unseeing until the whiteness blurred and the cave walls faded. The impulse to sketch sent her rummaging. She found a piece of charcoal, rolled it between her fingers, and studied the pristine rectangle. Acute need directed her hand in swirling movements. Thin beyond anything Human, a figure began to emerge. A skeletal frame, narrow stooped shoulders, an angular, half-hidden profile covered the lower half of the canvas.

Her hand flew to the untouched upper portion of the sketch. The blackened skeleton of an enormous bird of prey began to take shape. Lidless eyes stared. Featherless wings spread wide, its burned beak stretched open in a scream.

The sound of panting and the smells of sulfur and burning flesh snatched her from her artist's daze. She stared at her hand poised mid-stroke and realized the harsh breathing was her own. A movement riveted her attention to the sketch. She gasped.

The image of the bird broke free of the canvas and floated inches from her face. Clutched in its talons, a quartz sphere gleamed. Held rigid by a power she could not control, she stared into its depths. Reflected within, the shattered pieces of what had once been Elcaro's Eye lay strewn throughout a darkened space. A scorched figure sprawled in a smoking heap on the floor.

The charcoal dropping from shaking fingers broke the spell. She dodged backward, tears streaming down her cheeks. The crystal crashed to the floor, rolled to a stop, and with the decimated raptor vaporized in a puff of smoke.

The next instant, she found herself in the Meosian square, her breath coming in rasping gasps. DeoNytes gathered around her.

"Are you alright?" A young female peered up at her.

Sparrow stared blankly at the beautiful face, the white fur, the pale, pale eyes. Frantic to find Almiralyn, she started to speak, perceived the vague image of the Reading Room in her mind, and arrived to find Myrrh's Guardian with her hand on the door to Veersuni.

"Stop!"

Almiralyn's head snapped around. Their eyes met. Sparrow sprinted to her side.

"You can't go in there." Sobs heaved through her body.

Steady arms encircled her, held her close. The scent of roses and lilies calmed her as Almiralyn led her to an alcove and sat beside her.

Sparrow wiped away her tears and stared at her charcoal-smeared fingers. Terror snatched her breath away.

Almiralyn grasped her hands. "I'm here. Tell me what has frightened you. What awakened your talent for teleporting?"

Astonishment replaced the horror. "I teleported. Oh, my." Memories brought a small smile and then a fresh wave of fear. She clung to Almiralyn's hands. "I made a sketch. It was awful...I..." She lowered her eyes and swallowed.

"Describe it, Sparrow."

Struggling to collect her wits, Sparrow gave a description of the dark figure, the scorched bird of prey, and the crystal ball. When she started to explain the image inside it, her throat closed around the words. The harder she tried to speak, the more pressure built in her chest.

Almiralyn placed a finger on her lips.

Sparrow blew out a long breath and remained quiet.

Almiralyn pointed at herself, and then at Sparrow's head. Her eyebrows arched in a question.

Sparrow nodded.

Wards shot up around them both. The gentle tingling of a mind probe alerted Sparrow to the Guardian's presence in her thoughts. It stopped. Almiralyn sat back, her expression solemn. With the wards intact, she pulled Sparrow to her feet and led her into the research area of the Reading Room.

A circuitous route brought them to a large table where Wilith and Elae worked on one side and Zugo and Merrilea on the other.

Zugo glanced up as they rounded the corner. His pale eyes widened. "What's up?"

The prickle of Almiralyn's wards expanding to include those around the table sent chills chasing over Sparrow's body. She rubbed her hands up and down her arms and looked at the Guardian for guidance.

Almiralyn sat beside Zugo and indicated she sit at the head of the table. Expectation gleamed in four pairs of eyes. Almiralyn asked her to describe what had occurred. When she reached the part about the crystal ball, she hesitated. Almiralyn nodded.

She described the scene inside the crystal—Elcaro's Eye shattered, the sprawled figure, smoke rising from its burned body. She glanced from one person to the other and shivered. "The crystal ball crashed to the floor and disappeared in a puff of smoke along with the bird." Her heart quickened. She forced herself to be calm.

Zugo was the first to speak. "What does it mean?"

Almiralyn's reply was quiet. "It means The MasTer would like us to believe he has found where Elcaro's Eye is located. Sparrow's sketch gave him a medium through which he could send the message. What he actually knows is where to find Sparrow."

Wilith frowned. "How did he locate her? He has not found you?"

"Corvus told me that one of the many methods The MasTer uses to gain information is to invade the minds and memories of his minions. Nissasa tried to destroy Sparrow. The MasTer has access to his memories. It's that simple."

Merrilea left her seat and placed her hands on Sparrow's shoulder. "How do we protect her?"

Sparrow touched her friend's finger tips. "I'm a danger to all of you. I should leave." She lowered her hands and stared at the charcoal smudges on her palms.

"Where would you go?" Almiralyn's worried expression heightened Sparrow's apprehension. "Back to Idronatti? Rattori's Brigade would find you."

Elae stroked the tabletop with the tip of her finger. "I believe she is safer here than anywhere else. I have pieced together a theory about The MasTer's arrival in the Inner Universe."

The Guardian's sapphire eyes gleamed with interest. "Please share what you have uncovered."

A tiny flicker of hope ignited in Sparrow's heart. The idea of leaving the Dojanack Caverns chilled her to the bone.

Jordett rested in a quiet bedroom in the safe house. Much to everyone's delight, the journey there had been uneventful. No renegade RewFaaran soldiers followed. Only an occasional PPP patroller policed the streets. Arrival at the building in Upper Domlenah Green happened with no problems. Jordett had heaved a sigh and made a grateful retreat to rest.

Sleep had come easily but was short-lived. His brain woke him with incessant and repetitious dreams of the Five Fathers and Rattori's Brigade joining forces to keep Idronattians from achieving the freedom to become themselves. He threw back the tattered blanket, swung his feet to the floor, and searched for Kieel. The Matrés of the Nyti slept curled up on a much used pillow. Leaving the door ajar, Jordett made his way to the food service space. Anada and Sagus greeted him with a tense smile.

"Did you sleep?" Anada pushed a nouri-pak across the table. "Sorry, we don't have proper food. Shipments from the farmlands ceased with the takeover."

Sagus crumpled his container. "Good thing the PPP stocks plenty of Nouri products, or we'd have rioting to contend with along with everything else." He tossed it down a waste chute. "Do you believe we can regain control of the city and the PPP?"

Jordett finished the last of his drink. "It depends on our resources, men, and weapons. The PPP's response to rousting out the rebels will make a difference. If they see a benefit in ridding Idronatti of Nissasa's men, we have a chance."

"What benefit?" Doubt robbed the younger man's expression of hope.

Anada scrubbed her hair, combed her fingers through it, and leaned toward him. "Sagus, we must believe the PPP wants their control back. Even though they've indoctrinated all Idronattians to conform, to take orders, to be passive, they selected PPP members based on their potential to be a problem. They...we..." She pointed at herself and him. "...might have rebelled against authority. For whatever reason, the Five Fathers realized this and gave us a focus—made us the authority figures. Take you, for example. If you didn't want your power back, would you be here?"

He rocked back in his chair. "No."

"Would any of our recruits?"

A soft knock on the door stalled his response. His booted feet hit the floor with a soft thud as he rocked his chair upright.

Jordett motioned Anada to the door. He pressed his back to the wall behind her. Sagus stepped behind him.

She tapped a knuckle against the door. An answering series of taps and the tension left her neck and shoulders. Pulling the door ajar, she peeked out and opened it wide enough to admit a group of six led by a tall, beautiful brunette with sapphire blue eyes.

Sagus gave a soft gasped. "Teva."

Jordett glanced back. The young man's gaze remained fixed on the woman.

The door clicked shut. Anada hugged her friend. "This is Teva" She turned. "These are friends who want to help us retake the city." She guided Jordett toward the four people by the door.

A brief conversation while they waited for Sagus and Teva gave Jordett the impression they were not ordinary Myrrhinian farmers. The men were hard-muscled and quiet with watchful eyes—the women, lean and athletic with quick intelligence and a keen awareness of their surroundings. He glanced at Anada. *Introductions haven't been made. I wonder why?*

Finally, Teva and Sagus joined the group. Both were smiling, and Sagus had lost his sulky, stubborn expression.

Jordett noted Teva's startling eyes, her lithe length, the angle of her high cheekbones. He sat down and folded his hands on the tabletop. "Do you want to tell me who you are, or shall I guess?"

Teva sat across from him, her expression easy and her posture relaxed. Her companions remained composed and quiet. Intelligent blue eyes studied his face. "I was told you were astute, observant, and forthright. My source was correct."

Sagus' expression morphed from delight to perplexed. Anada looked confused.

Teva address them first. "I apologize for not being honest with you. When you learn who we are and why we're here, you'll understand."

Sagus lowered his eyes. Anada merely nodded.

Teva returned her attention to Jordett. "We all know the importance of keeping secrets. Even our small eavesdropper..." She looked up and held out her hand. "Please join us, Kieel." She waited until the Nyti Matrés landed. "Welcome to our meeting."

He bowed. "I didn't want to interrupt. I hope I may be of service."

She smiled. "I am sure you can. Join the Major while I lay my cards on the table, so to speak."

Jordett almost laughed aloud at the astonishment on Sagus' face as the tiny winged man flew to his shoulder and made himself comfortable. Instead, he cast Teva an inquiring look.

Her expression grew serious. "My companions and I are here at the request of my cousin, Major. Our goal is to help you regain control of the city of Idronatti and to protect Myrrh's connection to Thera."

He waited.

She continued. "Our home planet is KcernFensia."

"And your cousin is?" Jordett felt a thrill of anticipation.

"My cousin is Almiralyn, Guardian of Myrrh."

For the second time, silence reigned. Teva's companions remained expressionless. Sagus gaped. Anada's eyes widened.

Kieel lifted into the air and placed a quick kiss on Teva's cheek. "It is good to have you with us, Teva. I look forward to a chat."

Teva smiled. "I promise we'll find a quiet corner. You must tell me what tempted you away from the Terces Wood."

Jordett observed the exchange with amusement. It had taken him only a moment to process the stunning information. Already more hopeful, he looked from Teva to her five companions. "You're from KcernFensia. Did you train at the temple?"

The man next to Teva put a fisted hand on his heart. "I am called Lenadi. I am a warrior and the brother and protector of Teva Rivan. My comrades Radec and Senar studied with me at the temple. When we were old enough to begin our training as warriors, we went to the Gedosson Academy in EeClarot, the continent of Gedosson's capital. We've also spent time on ReTaw au Qu, learning from the Pentharian." He smiled at the woman next to him. "This is my mate for life, Akeri. She is a warrior/priestess who took her training at the temple with Teva and Falind."

The woman next to Akeri gave a quick affirming nod. "We are here to help."

A brisk but quiet knock brought their discussion to an end. Once again, Anada tapped lightly on the door, listened, and pulled it open. The four patrollers from the Ria Train preceded several others into the room.

Jordett, who preferred order and control, needed to regroup. He stepped to the sidelines to observe introductions and assess his little army. As he scanned the room, he discovered a familiar face, another surprise and not a pleasant one.

Almiralyn's anticipation escalated as Elae shuffled through her written notes, reordered the pages, and prepared to share her discovery. Most of the information the young DeoNyte was about to share would be new to everyone but her. Fresh eyes and new perception could bring to light details that she may have missed.

Elae looked up from her notes. "I'm ready, my lady."

"Please."

Like a storyteller from past ages, she began.

"One hundred sun cycles ago, a cataclysmic explosion shook the expanse beyond the Outer Rim. Des Pencoti, a small solar system at the furthest point from the Inner Universe's Great Central Suns, sustained damage from the backlash, leaving two of its three planets uninhabitable. The third, TreBlaya, emerged from behind its sun unharmed and continued to thrive. About half a centuria later, a group from Beyond the Rim crossed the DéCussate and took refuge in a remote part of the planet known as Los Deeta, the tainted land. According to legend, the gods fought a great battle there. The TreBlayans considered it taboo.

"Several sun cycles passed and nothing was heard from the colony until strange stories began to emerge, stories told by the Trenuh, a tribe that lived near Los Deeta."

"*What* stories?" Zugo demanded.

Elae shot him a patient smile. "I'm getting to that." She consulted her notes and continued. "Members of the tribe reported strange sounds and repugnant smells. One afternoon, they saw smoke filtering through the forest canopy and investigated. Midway to the Los Deeta territory, they found a horribly burned body. Rather than risk a similar death, the Trenuh returned to their village and sent a message to Tal Paci, the governmental seat of the planet's only continent."

She rifled through her notes and pulled out a single sheet. "TreBlaya is tiny. It has only one land mass that wraps part way around its circumference. Water and a scattering of small islands cover the rest of the planet. Technology was nonexistent. The residents were primarily farmers and hunting tribes. Tal Paci would have been much like a village in Old Earth's Europe before the discovery of North America."

Almiralyn caught her eye. "You have been digging, haven't you?"

"Yes." She glanced over a parchment before continuing. "This is the most interesting part. In Tal Paci, there was a religious sect whose leader took his followers to Los Deeta on a mission of mercy from which they never returned. Several moon cycles after their disappearance, two villagers found a burned body and took it to Tal Paci to be examined. Acid rain began to fall before they could make the results public. Everything and everyone on the planet perished. Nothing remained, but a blackened, barren chunk of rock."

Sitting back, she smiled in Wilith's direction. "Wilith discovered the next piece of the story. Would you like to tell them?"

"Thank you, Elae. I would." He tapped several icons on his comp-tab, found what he was looking for, and picked up the thread of the story. "The time of destruction became known as Stylacca. I centered my search around the origin of the group responsible for the annihilation of the inhabitants. Here the story becomes confusing. I found a reference to a group from a penal colony for corrupt users of the principles of SorTechory, a combination of technology and their form of sorcery. Other writings suggest the interlopers were runaways from a rebellion led by someone called The MasTer. Regardless of where they came from, they destroyed cultures by infiltrating, stealing the most talented children, and using SorTechory like an acid blowtorch to obliterate their tracks."

Merrilea pulled her chair up next to Sparrow. "Why is Sparrow safer here than anywhere else?"

"When the acid rain fell on TreBlaya, only a small band of survivors remained—unless you consider a Davea a survivor. The MasTer and his followers lived through the destruction by taking refuge in the bowels of the planet. For many sun cycles, their only companions were the Astican, who became their slaves. One theory suggests the Asticans were once the members of the religious sect, the one that disappeared. But I digress... The MasTer, for reasons I do not yet understand, never leaves TreBlaya."

Curiosity gave Zugo's face an elfin look. "Were the rebels Human?" He shrugged. "Is The MasTer he or she...or it or..."

Wilith massaged his forehead and lowered his hand to his comp-tab. "All the literature refers to him as he. We are, therefore, assuming that he is male. Our research suggests that Humans colonized the planets Beyond the Rim closest to the DéCussate, so it makes sense that he is a descendant of those early explorers. The only other thing we discovered is called The MasTer's

Reach, but we could find nothing about it other than the name. What is important is that The MasTer will not come here. If Sparrow refrains from painting—"

"Wait, I have to paint. I—"

Almiralyn laid a hand on her arm. "We'll figure it out, Sparrow." She held her gaze a moment, then addressed her research team. "You've done excellent work. Keep at it. See if you can confirm The MasTer's home planet and species...and gender. I'm inclined to believe the rebels and those from the penal colony joined forces. They may be from the same planet. Also, see what you can discover about The MasTer's Reach. Elae has a key to the case that holds the oldest and most important manuscripts in this Galactic Library, including EmitEnil. They may have information. Handle them with utmost care; and when you're finished, return them to their climate-controlled cases. Please, Sparrow, come with me."

Almiralyn walked briskly through rows of glass cases, crossed the Reading Room, and paused by the door to Veersuni. She met the alarm in Sparrow's eyes with a look of calm resolve, turned the knob, and stepped into the Sanctuary.

18
Der Tah

In the farmer's field in the Trinugian countryside, Brie flashed from sight. A panicked shout rose in Esán's throat. He choked it down and hurried to join Ira and Torgin, who stared with equal astonishment at the empty spot where Brie had been standing.

"Where'd she go?" Ira demanded. "Did you send her somewhere, Esán?"

"No, I didn't." His clenched fists mirrored the knots forming in his stomach.

Torgin sank cross-legged to the ground beside the stretcher. His warm brown skin had lost its healthy glow. His mouth worked, but no sound came out.

"Brie is with me. Will send her back when I can."

WoNa's telepathic message erased Esán's panic. He scrubbed his head with a hand and blew out a long breath. "WoNa has Brie. She's fine."

"Great." Ira sucked on the tip of his finger. "Now, Brie's on the other side of the planet. By the fathers, I'm tired of surprises. I just want to go home."

Color flooded back into Torgin's face. "You sound like me, Ira. Maybe *you're* the Drotti."

Ira growled and strode down the track.

Esán sighed. "Guess it's up to you and me to carry the stretcher." He placed One Man's flute beside Desirol. "At least, Brie's with WoNa."

Torgin scrambled to his feet. "None of us are safe. I'm not telepathic, but I'm smart enough to know we're all in danger. I just hope my mother's alright wherever she is."

Esán stepped between the makeshift poles at Desirol's head, and together they hoisted the stretcher off the ground. *Not as hard as I thought. I'm getting stronger.* He set a steady pace, his thoughts in a turmoil. *Why did WoNa snatch Brie away? Will she send her back?* Surprise almost made him stop short. *I really miss her.* He searched the track ahead. Ira had vanished behind a group of trees. Anxiety made him pick up his pace.

Torgin groaned. "Warn me the next time you plan to speed up. Can't see Ira, can you?"

"No, but I can feel his presence, so he's not gone." Tightening his grip, he kept on marching. Wolloh had told them to stay together. WoNa must have had a good reason to teleport Brie to the other side of DerTah. *Please send her back soon, WoNa.*

Ira leaned against the trunk of a tall tree and squinted up at the sky. Anger knotted his stomach. Fear for Brie left him muttering under his breath.

"Ira?" WoNa's soft voice eased his agitation.

He sank to the ground and rested his head on the rough bark. His eyes closed. His mind emptied.

"Open your eyes."

Ari yawned and stared at the rolling hills. The sharp pain in her finger ceased. *Where is everyone?* Her eyes widened. *Brielle?*

"Brie is with me, Ari. Take a moment and then—"

Ari ran feminine fingers through her curls. "I remember...Ira. I'm Ira."

She looked down at her body. "Where did my drango tunic go?"

A shout, the sounds of stumbling, a series of sharp barks brought her to her feet in one movement. The world shimmered and steadied.

Ira shook his head. "What a strange—"

"Stand still!" Torgin's alarm echoed over the fields.

Hidden in the trees, Ira made his way back to the track. Midway up the hill, a large dog bound toward his friends, its longish black fur rustling with each step. Esán and Torgin gripped the stretcher and did not move. Ira considered his options. Before he could make up his mind, a man's figure crested the hilltop. He stopped and whistled a series of notes. The dog dropped to its hunches, its tongue hanging out the side of its mouth. The man strode toward the boys. *Friend or foe?* Ira remained silent and watchful in the trees.

Torgin and Esán lowered the stretcher to the ground and edged closer together. The man joined them. Ira strained to hear.

"Looks...you...help."

Esán showed him Desirol. "Our friend is..."

The rest of the conversation was too muffled to hear. When the man whistled for the dog and both headed back the way they had come, Ira sprinted from the trees and arrived panting by his friends.

"Who was that?"

"A farmer who lives near here. Hepler's his name. Where were you, anyway?" Torgin demanded.

Ira scratched his head. "I was..." He looked over his shoulder and frowned.

Esán shot him an understanding smile. "We're just glad you're back. Hepler has offered to take us to Atkis. He's gone for a wagon."

"Says he has errands to run," Torgin muttered. "Hope he leaves that dog behind."

Ira laughed. "You afraid of dogs, Torg?"

"Haven't been around any but Buster." He lowered his gaze.

Ira understood. Almiralyn's dog had been their friend and companion until two Pentharian killed him. Ira touched Efillaeh's jeweled hilt. He still felt guilty that he'd been unable to save him.

A farm wagon drawn by two horses rumbled over the hill and rolled to a stop beside the stretcher. Hepler jumped to the ground. He was older than

Ira expected, weathered and lean. At his brusque command, the dog stayed on the rough wooden seat. A smile lit fading eyes beneath gray, arched brows as he offered a hand. "You must be Ira. Your friends told me you were nearby."

Ira grasped the hand and flinched. Its firm grip took him by surprise. "Thank you for helping, sir."

The man's grin showed good teeth. "No need to call me sir, boy. Let's get your friend loaded in the back."

Settling Desirol took almost no time. Soon, they were on the way. Esán sat on the bench with Hepler and the dog, Shyllee. Torgin sat, an elbow propped on the wagon's side. His distant, sad expression made Ira almost certain he was thinking about Buster. Torgin and Paisley had buried him in the grasslands on Myrrh. Ira sighed. *It seems like such a long time ago, and yet it was only a few moon cycles.*

The jog of the wagon lulled him to sleep. A snore jarred him awake. Torgin caught his eye and grinned. Ira scowled, fought to stay awake, and finally gave in to the rocking motion and the rhythmic clip clop of the horses' hooves along the rough track.

Dreams came and went, faded and earmarked like old-time photos, until he found himself propelled through a series of spinning portals. Flares of color blinded him. A crystal blinked to life and faded. Rushing air tore at his hair and clothing. He slid from the final portal. A tremor of foreboding shook him awake. He straightened and stared. No Torgin. No wagon. Nothing but the cold diamond glitter of stars—nothing but the dark blue sky of a moonless night. His stomach lurched. His head gave a corresponding throb. A wave of nausea left him prone, with his cheek resting on his arm. *Where on DerTah am I?* He moaned and curled into a fetal ball.

"You are safe. Sleep, Ira. Sleep."

The deep voice was warm and calming—hypnotic. Ira's eyes refused to stay open. Sleep overtook him, cradled him, eased the nausea and headache into a distant memory.

Henri observed the wonder of the Water ConDria in her niece's eyes with mild alarm. WoNa expressed the concern in words.

"My dearest Brielle, don't forget the power of changing shape *and* its pitfalls. Neither your aunt nor I wish to lose you to the ConDria."

The thrill drained like a plug pulled. Henri hugged her niece and held her at arm's length. "You don't need to block the joy of it. Just keep your heart attached to your humanness."

"I will, Aunt Henri. I promise." She glanced at the scattered remains of her enemy. "I did that?" She shook her head. "I never remember. At least this time, my shift was conscious."

WoNa reached for her. "Thank you for saving us, blood-bonded daughter."

Brie gripped her hand and pressed it to her heart. "You are welcome, WoNa. What on Thera—I mean DerTah—are you doing here? And how do I return to my friends?" She quickly described what had occurred since the shields were breached.

That a Mindeco and an Astican pursued Brie and her companions worried Henri more than she let her niece know. An even bigger concern was returning Brie to Trinuge. She had drained her energy reserve, and she knew WoNa also needed time to recuperate.

"We can send you back, but not until we've rested."

"And, Brielle," WoNa said, "we can't rest here."

Henri scanned the sky. "You will need to come with us to the Toelachoc Mountains. We're hoping to find Corvus there."

Brie looked from one woman to the other. "My friends will be worried." She tipped her head and gave them a pleading look. "I'm not strong enough to send Esán a telepathic message from this distance."

Henri laughed softly. "And I always thought Ari was the conniving twin."

WoNa squeezed her hand. "I have already alerted Esán. He and I also share a bond. Now, we must go."

"But I have only shaped the Water ConDria. I don't know how to shift to anything else."

WoNa's blind gaze found her face. "Like your Aunt Henri, you will shape the DerTahan dune hawk. She will shift first. Study her shifted form closely; then I will help you change." Her sightless gaze swept over the dunes. "Go, Henri. Danger approaches."

Henri shifted. Brie knelt beside her.

"Hurry, niece."

Slight pressure from WoNa's hand sent Brie into her hawk form. WoNa's beetle appeared on the sand. Henri turned a hawk's eye toward it, picked it up in her beak, and deposited it on her back, where it scuttled beneath gray feathers.

Grateful that the sun had not reached full high, Henri shot along one shaded trough after the other, her senses alert and scanning ahead for trouble—trouble she knew bided its time in the hopes they would let down their guard—trouble she intended to thwart.

Brie's mind buzzed as she followed her aunt in a long, low swoop. *The dune hawk feels claustrophobic after the Water ConDria. I wish—*

"Pay attention, niece. The Sebborr ride this way."

With an effort, Brie masked her thoughts and concentrated on staying close to her aunt. She had no desire to find herself alone in the middle of Fera Finnero with Sebborr near at hand. An image of Dahe Terah's angry face and piercing eyes almost sent her back into Human form. The Sebborran leader had left his mark on her. WoNa had removed it. She had no intention of being caught by him a second time. Expunging him from her thoughts, she focused on her great-aunt and on reaching the Toelachoc Mountains. *I sure hope we find Corvus.*

Following the descending path of the sun, Henri swooped down for a landing. Fatigue accompanied her shift to Human. The desire to be young once more crossed her mind as she materialized, stretched tired muscles, and stared into the distance. Along the horizon, the rounded peaks of the Toelachoc Mountains, washed in the waning light of the sun, glowed a warm carnelian orange. She pushed back her hood. *"At least we're closer."*

Brie alighted nearby and tucked her red curls behind her ears. "I love the

ConDria, but the dune hawk is quite wonderful, too." She rotated slowly, observing the subtle changes occurring in the environment as they drew nearer the mountains. "Where's WoNa? Are those the Toelachocs?"

WoNa's beetle form fluttered to the ground. She appeared with a finger to her lips. "Speak softly. We're quite near LeCur, the capital of Fera Finnero Province and the home of the Dreela Gidtuss. It would never do to alert one of his patrols." She turned toward the mountains. "Yes, those are the Toelachocs. The prison where we believe they hid Corvus is southwest of here."

Brie smiled. "This desert is truly a part of you, isn't it?"

The Oracle's gleaming eyes seemed to see the broad expanse of red sand. "It is my life's blood." She smiled and crooned softly as her small, red serpent slithered onto her shoulder. "Hello, dear one. How did you like the flight?"

It gave several short hisses and a long, whistled sound.

Her laughed response was so soft, Henri caught herself leaning closer.

WoNa held up her hand. The snake bunched the center of its body like a concertina, pushed its tiny tail into her shoulder, and shot forward. It came to rest with its head on the end of her middle finger and its tail twitching back and forth on her wrist. Raising the hand to eye level, she said, "Very few know my small protector's name, but it has asked me to share with you. It is called Tesi."

Tesi's forked tongue flicked out and in. WoNa moved her hand toward Henri and then Brie. Finally, she returned Tesi to her shoulder and spoke in a quiet undertone. "What's our next move, Henri?"

"Rest." She took off her kcalo and spread it on the slanted side of a dune and helped WoNa to sit. With a sigh, Henri lowered her weary body. "Join us, Brielle."

Her niece plopped down next to WoNa. "What do you know about the Toelachoc Prison?"

Henri knit her brow. "Not very much. It's deserted and has been for many sun cycles."

WoNa scooped up a handful of sand and let a slow stream of red granules leak between her palms. "The memories and ghosts of the horror that once existed still linger there. Most are harmless, some are not. As a child, I listened to the older boys telling stories around the oasis fires—gory tales of the brutality of the prisoners and the guards. The prison was not a good place. Men are said to fare better if they chance upon it. Women are told not to wander too close."

"At least there are three of us." Henri settled more comfortably on the kcalo. "We'll stay together. Let's rest before our fatigue scares us into retreating."

Brie curled up with her head in WoNa's lap. Soon, the sound of her soft snores drifted over the sand.

At the Dreelas' estate, Nomed woke early to the sound of TheLise moving around her room. He shoved the bedding aside and sat up. A yawn transitioned into a full-bodied stretch and left him wide awake. Concentrating his attention on the Tinga Forest, he made a telepathic search for Esán and his friends, rubbed his stubbled chin, and frowned.

The bedroom door opened. TheLise stuck her head out. "They aren't there. I checked. Better use the cleansing room and dress. I have a feeling they will need us sooner than we thought."

He hustled through his cleanse, considered shaving, decided it would be a waste of time, and pulled on his clothes. When he walked into the living space, TheLise was completing a conversation with her Major Domo. She shot him a perturbed look. "Tynus has just been telling me that Roween is packing."

"To go where?" Nomed felt the scar on his cheek go taut.

TheLise smiled at her man. "Please."

"She plans to go to Cartatt with the Dreelas, and then join the Largeen Joram at the front."

"Thank you, Tynus." She waved him toward the door. "Don't let *that* woman out of your sight."

Nomed scrutinized a breakfast tray on a table near the sofa. The first bite of buttery pastry reminded him of how hungry he was. He sat down and loaded his plate.

TheLise joined him. "How do we keep her contained if she's running around the planet? Lorsedi will be furious if she shows up in the middle of a battle. What is she thinking?"

"Eat, TheLise." He pushed a chair out with his foot. "We will need all the energy we can muster. As for Roween..." He sipped his steaming vaja and set the mug on the table. "She isn't going anywhere. You will remind her that Lorsedi wanted her out of harm's way. As to your trip—you won't be taking your carriage. Your business is urgent and requires you to teleport. Give a plausible reason you cannot teleport her, like all her luggage. Promise to take her to Cartatt when you return."

She listened, finished her repast, and brushed the crumbs from her hands. "I'll meet you in the gazebo. Take care, no one sees you. You know the Mindeco and the Astican have joined forces?"

"I know. Be quick." He held the door open, shut it after her, and leaned against it, frowning. *Why would they become allies? Why?* His eyebrow arced. *Of course. Nissasa wants Desirol neutralized. The MasTer wants Esán, Brie, and Torgin. Both would like to gain control of the compass and the knife.* He took a quick turn around the room, stopping by the double doors that led outside. A backward glance assured him he had left nothing behind. Exiting onto the balcony, he breathed in the fragrance of morning, shifted, and winged his way to the gazebo. Perching within the leafy branches of a nearby tree, he waited. Acute hearing picked up the sound of TheLise's arrival almost before she appeared. He launched into the air, swooped into the gazebo and landed, his Human eyes resting on her face.

"You look displeased."

Her chin went up. "I dislike stubborn women. I despise Roween Rattori more than just about anyone I have ever encountered. She is manipulative and as shrewd as a fox."

"Did you thwart her efforts to leave?"

"Of course. But she knows something's up, and she won't be satisfied until she discovers what it is."

Nomed glowered. "She is a dumb woman."

"Don't underestimate her, Seyes. She has a minor talent for DiMensionery, and believe me, she knows how to use it. I suggest we depart in the event she snoops around."

Light flared around TheLise. A sleek, Trinugian falcon soared upward, its blue and green wings gleaming in the morning sun. Nomed gazed after her for a moment, shaped the owl, and rose above the trees.

Near to the gazebo, a figure stepped from shadow to sunlight. Roween Rattori shaded her eyes and stared after the disappearing birds. "So you thought to fool me?" She snatched up her full skirt, pivoted on her heels, and stalked back toward the house. Seething with anger, she flung herself through the front door and up the main staircase. At the top, Tissent, her fellow guest and Gerolyn's identical twin, blocked the way. The realization Lorsedi loved Gerolyn more than he had ever loved her increased her fury.

Preparing to shove past her, she snapped, "Out of my way."

Tissent matched her direction, emerald eyes riveted to hers. "You seem upset, Roween. Why don't you come with me? I'll fix you a cup of tea."

Tissent's soft words penetrated her anger, erased her erratic thoughts, and left her feeling dazed. A gentle hand cupped her elbow and guided her to her private rooms. She sank onto a comfortable sofa and yawned. "I don't know what's wrong with me." Her eyelids grew heavy. Another yawn. Grabbing a small pillow, she lay down. The last thing she remembered was Tissent's gentle smile.

The knock on the suite door in the Esccery Inn dragged Nissasa from a deep, disturbing sleep. He thought at first he had dreamt it. A second and much bolder hammering told him it was real and whoever waited on the far side of the door was impatient and none too happy.

Scrambling from the bed, he threw on a robe supplied by the inn and hurried to the door. Easing it ajar, he peeked through the crack. Every drop of blood in his body plummeted to his feet. The door flying open forced him backward. Vygel Vintrusie marched into the suite.

The scathing expression on the Mocendi's gaunt face turned it into an ugly mask. Bulging, watery eyes stared straight into his. "Get dressed. The MasTer sent me to take you back to the desert. I hope you have a good reason for abandoning your men and your command."

Nissasa fought to keep a scowl off his face and suppress the knot of fear in his gut. "It wasn't necessary for *Him* to send you. I have every intention of returning in the morning."

Vintrusie took a menacing step forward. "Get dressed, Rattori. We are leaving now." Boney hands gripped his shoulders and shoved him toward the sleeping chamber. "If you are not out here in five chron clicks, I will teleport you back to Fera Finnero wearing only your skin."

Stumbling toward the bed, Nissasa grabbed his clothes and dressed. A glimpse of his ashen face in the mirror made him gnash his teeth. *How dare Vintrusie treat the future Largeen Joram of RewFaar like an errant schoolboy!* Color flooded back to his cheeks. Forcing a calm he did not feel, he strode into the sitting room.

"I'm ready. But first, I need food. I'm sure you could use refreshments and a moment to catch your breath."

The Mocendi DiMensioner hesitated. "I could use a bite to eat, but then we are off. The MasTer is not a patient creature."

Nissasa pulled a cord beside the door. Within minutes, a faint knock sounded. A young woman entered, learned what they required, and departed.

Vintrusie took a seat at the small dining table. "We must discuss one more thing." He unfastened his cape and let it fall over the back of the chair, surrounding him in the regal purple of its lining.

Nissasa tried not to stare at his cadaverous body. "And what would that be?"

An emaciated hand stretched toward him. "Give me the Oracle Stone, Rattori. Give it to me, or I will take it from you."

"I told you I don't have it. If it comes into my possession, I will turn it over immediately." He curled his branded hand into a fist.

Bloodshot eyes of an indiscriminate color rested on his face. The hand withdrew to pluck fitfully at the purple lining. "Show me your hands."

Nissasa held out an unblemished palm.

"The other one." The protruding eyes narrowed. A crooked nose sniffed the air.

Shoving his hand in his pocket, Nissasa widened the space between them. "Enough, Vygel. You will be the first to know if I find the Oracle Stone."

"I already know. The MasTer sent me to retrieve it. He pulled me away from another important matter to take care of you. If you refuse to honor his wishes, what are your chances for survival? I'd think about that if I were you."

A soft knock ended the conversation. Nissasa opened the door. A servant placed a tray on the table and left.

Vintrusie filled his plate.

Nissasa watched him from hooded eyes and tried to keep his thoughts on the food. The Mocendi made his skin crawl. *What if he can feel the crystal?* He shoved down his growing panic. *I wish I'd given it to my mother.*

19

Myrrh

Almiralyn stood just inside the door to Veersuni, allowing her eyes to adjust and her senses to alert her to danger. Only the soft sound of trickling water, the glow of stained glass, and the scents of cedar and roses filled the room. Elcaro's Eye, serene at the sanctuary's center, gave no sign of disturbance.

"Are you sure we should be here?" Sparrow's hushed tone held a touch of trepidation.

Drawing her further into the sanctuary, Almiralyn whispered, "We have things to accomplish. Stay here."

She crossed the polished stone floor and paused a short distance from the fountain. Nothing occurred to cause her alarm. Water flowed over the alabaster palms of the kneeling statue in an unbroken rhythm—drip, drop, bubbling splash.

She chanted:

"Wards and borders
Shield and secure,
Keep this fountain's
Message pure.

Prohibit those
Who would do ill,
Blind their sight.
Mute their will."

The water ceased to flow. The glass-smooth surface gleamed. A disjointed image drifted upward and floated in a dispersed pattern. Almiralyn called Sparrow to her side and blew across the water. The pieces swirled into place. Sparrow gasped.

An Astican and a Mindeco trotted next to harvested fields. Scaled gray wings unfurled and lifted the Astican into the air. The Mindeco swung his enormous head from side to side, his single eye glued to the rutted track, his wide nostrils opening and closing, opening and closing.

"What is he doing?" Sparrow whispered.

"Seeking an energy trail. I expect the children have passed this way. The Astican is scouting farther up the track."

Almiralyn touched the water with the tip of her finger. The image quivered and resettled.

A wagon drawn by two sway-backed work horses rumbled along beside a single row of trees. Its passengers bumped up and down in rhythm with their ambling gait. An older man drove. Next to him, Esán sat with his arm draped over a black dog, casting an occasional worried glance over his shoulder. In the wagon bed, Torgin sat beside a figure on a stretcher.

With fingers extended, Almiralyn held her hand above the water and brought her thumb and fingertips together. The image zoomed in. Desirol lay unconscious, his fair skin, even paler than usual, highlighted the beginnings of a bruise on his cheek and one swollen black eye.

Sparrow examined the image. "What happened to Desirol, and where are the twins? I don't see them anywhere?"

The image vanished, and a new one snapped into view.

Henri sat beside the Atrilaasu Oracle. Brie slept with her head in

WoNa's lap. Henri pulled out her spectacles and perched them on her nose. Magnified eyes searched the panorama.

"Can she see us?" Sparrow peered into the water.

"I can, SparrowLyn AsTar, and so can the Mocendi leader. Beware. The MasTer's reach is long." Her violet eyes widened. "Danger rides this way. We must depart. Concentrate your power on the other young people."

Sparrow gripped the fountain's rim. "Where is Ar—"

"Ira?" Almiralyn finished the sentence.

WoNa formed a silent word. Henri removed her spectacles and tapped them against her palm. The image dissolved into desert sky and blood red sand. Water's trickled song spilled into Veersuni.

Almiralyn drew Sparrow away from the fountain. "Did you understand WoNa's message?"

The twin's mother looked lost. "No. What did she say?"

"She said Reader."

"What did she mean by reader?"

"It's one name the VarTerel uses. I believe Ira may be with Relevart. We will have to wait for confirmation. At least, we know The MasTer did not snatch him."

"What can we do to help the children?"

"We can impose an illusion between them and their pursuers. I'll need your help."

Sparrow pressed a shaking fist to her chest. "How can I help? I'm so new at this."

Almiralyn laid hands on Sparrow's temples, whispered a series of words, and stepped back, her eyes and voice steady. "What do you see?"

A slow grin of understanding replaced Sparrow's uncertainty. "Another field, a track branching away from the wagon. I'm ready."

Almiralyn taught her the activation Key, and they moved to the fountain. Standing next to each other, fingers intertwined, they placed their free hands on the rim, gazed into the water, and recited,

> *"Tinnottae, Elcaro's Eye,*
> *This illusion let them spy.*
> *Astican and Mindeco,*
> *Take this detour, off you go,*
> *Lose your focus and intent,*
> *Pass into a timeless rent."*

Clouds raced over the surface of the water. The Astican appeared and landed beside its ally. Its guttural description of what it had found made little sense. Almiralyn glanced at Sparrow's confused expression.

The Mindeco growled, "You found them. Lead me to 'em. Remember, Abarax, the RewFaaran boy is mine. The others," he shrugged massive shoulders, "if Nissasa has no need of them, they are yours."

A rasping response left no doubt who carried more power. The Mindeco bobbed his bearish, skeletal head. "The MasTer's will is my will, Abarax."

"It had better be." The Astican wheeled around and trotted down the track.

Almiralyn squeezed Sparrow's hand. The land around the two creatures morphed. Abarax jogged right where the original track remained straight. The Mindeco followed. Time caught them in its net.

Almiralyn released Sparrow's hand. "They will wander until the illusion fades or until something releases them."

"How long until it fades?"

Sitting down on a bench, Almiralyn leaned against the curtained wall. "That depends on how perceptive the creatures are. The moment they start to question their reality, the illusion will begin to lose its strength. Even then, it will take a while. We have bought the young people valuable time. We can only hope they use it well."

Sparrow sank down beside her. "Can we look for Ira?"

"If he is indeed under Relevart's care, they will only find him if the VarTerel wishes it."

"Can we at—"

The smell of smoke penetrated the room. A blackened hand broke the water's surface, charred fingers tasting the air. Wind whipped around the room, flinging drapes in all directions.

Silver-blonde hair flying around her face, Almiralyn dragged Sparrow beneath the bench. Purple engulfed them in fold upon fold of velvet. A muffled howl of frustration began and then came to an abrupt end. The wind ceased. Nothing in the sanctuary moved.

Blood pounded in Almiralyn's ears. Easing her position, she took a quiet breath. Subtle wards surrounded her. Sparrow turned, her expression questioning. Almiralyn gave the tiniest shake of her head.

Until she felt certain they were safe, they dare not move.

The basement room in the safe house buzzed with quiet conversation. Jordett eyed the man across the room, the one man whom he wished elsewhere. Short, squat, and balding, he was quick as the flick of a whip, both mentally and physically. Frequently, he had beaten Jordett in combat training. Over the years, they had often found themselves on opposite sides of an issue. Captain Lavir had never forgiven Jordett for rising above him in rank and position.

Deep-set, light eyes traveled in his direction. Lavir ended his conversation with Sagus and strolled to stand in front of him.

Jordett, a head taller, gave him an expectant look. "What brings you to this meeting, Captain? It doesn't seem to fit your usual style."

"I'm here because I want the control of Idronatti back where it belongs. And you? I heard rumors you were missing. Seems coincidental you would show up now."

Teva walked to Jordett's side. Her beautiful smile encompassed them both. A warm hand rested on his arm. "Is there a problem, Major?"

"I'm not sure. Captain Lavir assures me he is here for the right reasons. My concern is he might have other interests."

Lavir's face flushed red, whether from anger or embarrassment, Jordett couldn't tell.

Teva offered her hand. "I am Teva Rivan, Captain Lavir."

He took her hand. His unwavering gaze met hers. "I am not a spy, not to imply I trust Jordett."

She released his hand. "The Major is in charge of this mission, Captain. If you choose to be a part of it, you will need to accept that and give him your allegiance." She beckoned Lenadi over. "This is Lenadi. If you decide to stay, he would be happy to introduce you to our comrades."

As they walked away, she angled her back to the room. "He's telling the truth. I felt no dissembling when we shook hands. My instincts suggest he will be an asset, but only if you're willing to take the chance."

"And if he leaves?"

"Lenadi will erase his memories of all of us, this..." Her gaze swept the room. "Don't worry about the Captain. Tell me your thoughts regarding what is occurring in Myrrh and what you believe will enable us to regain control of the city."

They talked for some time. She complimented him on his in-depth knowledge regarding Idronatti, the PPP, and the Five Fathers, as well as his understanding of Myrrh's issues. After she shared her thoughts, they convened a meeting.

Feet shuffled as everyone found a seat. Jordett took a head count and cleared his throat. Focused on him were twenty-five men and women, most of whom were younger than himself, plus Lavir and the KcernFensians. He saw fear and excitement. More than that, he saw hope. He cleared his throat.

"To all of you, welcome. To those who don't know me, I am Major Jordett. The plans we are about to initiate put us all in danger. If you have any doubts, it would be best if you leave now."

He made eye contact with the three members he considered possible weak links, including Lavir. No one moved. He continued. "Anything said in this room stays in this room. One unaware slip could bring death to us all." He let that sink in. "I would now like to compliment the team who brought me here. You did a first-rate job. Thank you."

He motioned Sagus and Anada forward. They pinned a set of scaled drawings to the wall and remained standing on either side of them.

Jordett studied the plans of the Five Towers for a moment prior to returning his attention to the group. "We are not using technology for obvious reasons, tracking being at the top of the list. I have had this room swept clean of listening devices. I will outline our plan and then accept suggestions and comments. All your thoughts are important. Please look for weaknesses and strengths so we can maximize our chances for a successful mission."

A tense silence settled over the room.

Shuffling through his notes, he began. "The element of surprise is our greatest advantage. Our intelligence gatherers agree that Nissasa Ratorri's men have no expectation of a counteroffensive. Again, anything said here stays here. We have three primary objectives: 1) to take over the Five Towers; 2) to gain control of the city's transport and communications facilities; and 3) to rid Idronatti of Rattori's Brigade. Sagus, please explain the geography of The Five Towers Compound for our KcernFensian guests."

Sagus stepped to the drawings. "As you can see, the compound surrounds five buildings, each of which contains correctional facilities for The Plan offenders, along with offices for various governmental departments.

"Tower One is the residence of the Five Fathers, their offices, the offices of their staff, and their private quarters. Level-One offenders are processed, reprimanded, and released from this tower within a turning.

"Tower Two houses the PPP Patroller Force. Their offices and labs are within these walls, as well as cells for Level-Two offenders. These perpetrators spend one to eight turnings in confinement.

"Tower Three contains the courts, diplomatic personnel, and legal offices. Cells in this tower house offenders of The Plan for up to one moon cycle.

"Towers Four and Five are the home of the PPP Military. Plan breakers can spend from two to thirteen moon cycles in Four. Repeat offenders go to Tower Five for up to three sun cycles. Those rare individuals sentenced to life are moved to a facility outside the city. PPP and Military personnel are housed beyond the compound walls in a special combined Benisuss and Domlenah District established for their needs. Questions?"

Lenadi raised a hand. "How many PPP and Military are we looking at?"

After casting a sidelong glance at Jordett and receiving a nod of approval, Lavir replaced Sagus at the front of the group. "Grantese Orittra, the commander of Rattori's Brigade, has dispatched most of the military to the Central Mountains and beyond to conquer and hold the outlying territories. From what I could discover, Orittra brought between twenty and thirty soldiers with him to Idronatti. He has stationed PPP patrollers throughout the city. They are under the command of four RewFaarans who inspect their positions regularly."

Jordett interrupted. "How many RewFaarans traveled with the military?"

"None. If the Idronattians do not comply, their families die. Patrollers are under the same threat."

"Thank you. Continue."

"Eight RewFaarans guard the perimeter of the Tower Compound. The remaining men are divided between the towers and the dissemination and transit centers. Orittra is holed up in Tower One in one of the Five Fathers' apartments. That is as much as I know."

Jordett made a note. "Thank you, Captain." He turned to his army. "Thoughts?"

Lavir raised a hand. "What are your plans for the Five Fathers?"

"What do you suggest, Captain?" Jordett kept his expression neutral.

Lavir cleared his throat. "If I'm correct, those gathered here realize our city and our planet have reached a crossroads. We return the Fathers to power and continue under their leadership, or make the changes required to move in a different direction. I would like to see the latter. The people of our city deserve to have control of their lives."

A youngish patroller, one Jordett considered a possible weak link, came to his feet. "Names Davley. I say we execute them. Then we're done with 'em."

Murmured dissent rippled around the room.

Teva stood up. "The best example of your new leadership would be to turn them over to the Galactic Guardians. If that is your choice, I can facilitate it."

Anada oversaw a vote. Only Davley held to the notion of death. Jordett made a mental note to assign him to one of the KcernFensians with instructions to watch him closely.

Anada then put forth the plan to take over city transportation and communications. As she finished, the driver of the Ria Train raised a hand.

"I'm Lt. Cana. The Transit Control Center is well-guarded, but I know a secret way in." He looked sheepish. "Learned about it by accident. I went exploring and found it." He grinned.

Jordett spoke up. "How many men would you need?"

"Two RewFaarans and a patroller, whom I know, man the interior control center. Give me one other patroller who isn't afraid to use his weapon if he has to, and that should do it."

Jordett made a note. "Anyone here know the Dissemination Center?"

A man and woman raised their hands. The woman took the lead. "Holins, sir. I know the DC inside and out." She nodded at the man next to her. "Grodan and I have both worked there. The best way to gain control is to divide and conquer. If we can separate the Grid Keeper from the RewFaaran's, we think he might switch sides. If he does, his men will follow."

Grodan joined her. "He's been upset by the Brigade takeover and unwilling to give them full control of the center. He's working with them, but..." He shrugged. "We'd need at least four others. The Brigade has four soldiers there, and the PPP has another six. It's the RewFaarans we need to bring down. Like Holins, I think the others would fall in line. They're all good men and women."

Again, Jordett made a note. "Let's take a brief break. Sagus, Anada, Lavir, Lenadi, and Teva, please join me at the table."

They gathered in a tight group. Jordett cleared his throat. "I may have misjudged you, Captain. I'll be delighted to be proved wrong."

Lavir's unfaltering gaze met his. "I intend to do exactly that, sir."

Selecting teams began. Jordett glanced from one intent face to the next. *They are all good, even Lavir. I just hope they are good enough.*

Kieel had remained on the Major's shoulder throughout the proceedings. When the teams had been assigned and leaders selected, he landed at Teva's place at the table and sank to sitting beside her hand. She smiled at him.

"Feeling homesick?"

He sighed. "Henri said I could be of use." He plucked a piece of lint from his vest and flicked it away. "But I feel like that lint. Worthless."

"The Major told me about your skills as a scout. We will require them soon. I feel certain there will be a time when only you can save one of us. Keep your eyes open. Learn all you can, trust your instincts, and be ready to act."

"Thank you, my lady." He lifted into the air and hovered next to Captain Lavir. The man looked startled and then curious.

"I have few memories of Myrrh. Although I know I visited there as a boy, I don't believe I ever saw a Nyti."

The tiny, winged man landed on his offered hand and bowed. "Kieel, at your service, sir."

"Good to meet you. The Major tells me you are quite a good scout."

With another bowed, Kieel fluttered up to Jordett's shoulder.

Lavir shook his head. "These sure are strange times." His gaze scanned the room before settling on Jordett. "Thank you, Major, for allowing me to stay. We have had our differences, but I swear to do everything I can to advance our cause." He pulled a mini chronometer from his pocket. "Dawn will come much too soon. I'd better get some sleep."

Kieel watched him depart. When the door closed on the last member of the small resistance, he flew by Jordett's side. "Do you trust him?"

Jordett yawned. "Do you?"

"As much as I trust any of the others." He alighted on a pillow. "Bedtime, Jordy."

Jordett laughed. "Bedtime it is."

Curling up, he closed his tiny eyes. Visions of the Terces Wood infused his dreams—Ashor and Mumshoo, Reana and her dragonfly, his beautiful forest, and the Wood Tiffs. *Will I ever see them again?*

20

DerTah

Allynae and Stebben stood at the center of the arena at Shu Chenaro as the rising sun tinted the sky a warm gold. Gerolyn had sent a message. It was time to raise the shields. Although he and Stebben had rehearsed the process, Allynae's nerves jingled with doubt. *I chose not to become a DiMensioner. What do I think I'm doing?*

Beside him, Stebben maintained a calm and dignified demeanor. His acceptance of his skills and his ability to access them with flawless efficiency were two things Allynae tried to emulate. Almiralyn had told him he was talented. *You shifted to a winged horse, for Emit's sake. Stop negating yourself. It only gets in the way.*

Stebben caught his eye and nodded. They began to chant.

"Shield surrounding ranch and land
Prepare to rise at our command.
Remain intact, do not dissolve,
Hold ready 'til the fights resolve.

Three claps the signal to begin
A fast retreat above the din.
Lift your glimmering, guarding light,
And stay illuminated bright."

Three loud claps reverberated off the walls of the arena. Above them, the wards formed a gleaming, frothy light.

Allynae smiled. "Working with you, Stebben, is a pleasure. What's next?"

"While we await Gerolyn's message, One Man asked me to teach you to teleport. He says you have the talent but resist learning."

The smile on Allynae's face dissolved into a grimace. "I teleported once with Corvus' help." He shrugged. Never managed it on my own."

"Then it is time, my friend. I will be on the other side. You stay here."

Sure hope I can do this. Allynae's apprehension increased as Stebben walked away.

One Man and Jeet, as small desert spiders, hid on the shaded side of the tent where Nissasa's men had imprisoned two of Lorsedi's loyal supporters. Their goal—to alert the men that friends were close and to enlist their aid.

Jeet scurried from sight. One Man followed. The soldiers sat facing the entrance to the tent, hands tied behind them, feet bound to the legs of their camp stools. One Man and Jeet materialized behind them and clamped a hand over their mouths.

"Friends." One Man spoke in an undertone. "No noise. Understood."

Both heads nodded.

"One of us is a Pentharian." He stepped to the entrance, flipped the tent flap closed, and hurried to help Jeet cut their bonds. Within moments, the men were free and rubbing the circulation back into wrists and ankles.

While Jeet guarded the entrance, One Man explained. "We are allies of the Largeen Joram. He sent us to take over the camp. We know you are loyal to Lorsedi."

The taller man looked curious. "How'd you know that?"

The shorter man smiled. "Are you the one they call One Man, the father of the boy The MasTer's after?"

"I am."

"A DiMensioner of sorts," the man told his comrade.

The second man shot Jeet a nervous glance. "Haven't ever met a Pentharian. Heard they'd sided with Myrrh, though." He held out his hand. "Name's Tylest, and this is Rosser. Good to know we aren't alone. What's the plan?"

One Man touched it palm to palm. "Two more supporters of the Largeen Joram are somewhere in camp."

Rosser nodded. "Ya. Frease and Domatee. They were smarter than us and kept their mouths shut."

Quickly, they discussed options for alerting them and for securing the two men who might create problems for the takeover. They decided Tylest and Rosser would stay put until Tesilend's men made their move. One Man would make sure Tesilend knew they weren't the enemy.

Jeet touched One Man's arm. "Time, my friend." He disappeared into the shape of a desert fly and buzzed from the tent.

One Man grinned at the astonished looks on the RewFaarans' faces. "See you in a few." He shifted and buzzed after the Pentharian.

They found Frease and Domatee standing at their tent entrance, watching the antics of their comrades.

Shifting to Human behind them, One Man spoke in an undertone, "Lorsedi Telisnoe sent us. Close the tent flap and turn around."

A short, muscular man flipped the flap into place. Both men turned, their eyes darting from Jeet to One Man.

A hasty explanation later, they were on the move. Frease and Domatee, with desert flies flitting close by, ambled through camp to a tent on the opposite side. Domatee approached first, stuck his head in and called softly, "Need to talk."

A thick-necked man appeared at the entrance. "What?"

Frease looked over his shoulder and back. "Inside. Important."

The man allowed them to enter. The second man rose from his camp stool. "What do you want?"

Two flies buzzed inside. Domatee flipped the tent flap closed. One Man and Jeet materialized behind the two men. In record time, they gagged and trussed them to their cots. Jeet shifted and zipped away to give the signal.

One Man stretched his senses outward. Tesilend's men crept forward between tents.

A traitor rounded a corner and yelled, "Enemy! E-n-e-m-y!"

Chaos erupted. The four loyal RewFaaran's rushed into the fracas. Soldiers met hand to hand. The fighting was intense and brutal. Screams of pain pierced the air, weapons fired, lives ended in pools of blood. The wounded lay still or crawled to the sidelines. Two of Rattori's Brigade fled on horseback, a cloud of dust marking their path across the desert.

One Man flashed into the midst of the battle. Startled soldiers on both sides hesitated. In that momentary pause, he downed the three remaining traitors with a mind probe that toppled them to the ground. A cheer went up. The offensive was over.

Tesilend strode from behind a tent, holding his arm, his face covered with blood. He called a man forward. "Take charge. Set up triage for the wounded on both sides. Have Nissasa's surviving men prepare the dead to be returned to RewFaar for burial."

"Yes, sir."

A man assigned the job of assessing the damage hurried away. As ordered, Jeet shifted and began his patrol of the skies. Orders completed, Grantese sank down on a cot in his tent.

One Man joined him. "Let me see that arm."

Tesilend peeled back the tattered, blood-soaked edges of his sleeve to expose a knife wound on his upper arm. "Not too bad. You'll find a medical kit is in my pack."

One Man found the kit, and with great care, cleansed the wound.

The Grantese flinched. "Burns. How's it look?"

"If you'll allow me to do a touch of healing, it won't be bad at all."

The only reply was a measured glance and nod.

One Man traced the cut with a gentle finger. The bleeding ceased. The edges began to reknit. Time would do the rest.

The man assigned to assess the damage returned as he finished taping the bandage. Tesilend flexed his arm, eased it to his lap, and listened to the report. Only three of his fourteen loyal men were unharmed. Three were dead and eight wounded. Of Nissasa's brigade, two had escaped, three were unhurt, five were dead, and five wounded, two of them seriously.

After the man left, Tesilend sighed, "Good men died today. Good men on both sides."

One Man put a hand on his shoulder. "Rest. I'll help with the wounded and oversee the cleanup. If anything needs your personal attention, I'll wake you."

"Call me in one chron circle," Tesilend called after him.

Walking into the bright light of mid-turning, One Man paused and allowed the sun's heat to penetrate the chill that had gripped him as the battle played out around him. The death of each man—the loss of his place in the scheme of things, the cold emptiness that had once held his spirit— wrung tears from his heart. Thoughts of Wodash od DerTah flashed through his mind. *I'm sure glad I'm not a death shadow. How sad I am for those whose life choices bring them to the place of participating in death's horrors for eternity.*

At the border between Shu Chenaro and the Desert of Fera Finnero, the curtain of protection lifted. Mounted on horseback, fifty loyal RewFaaran soldiers stormed Nissasa's camp. The thunder of hooves, dust, and the clamor of battle filled the air. Confused rebels shouted a warning. Men tumbled from their tents, weapons in hand, incredulous faces turned toward their enemy. Guns fired. Men fell. Like wandering sheep, Lorsedi's men herded the survivors of the assault in to a circle. In less than a quarter circle of the chronometer, the skirmish had ended. Surprise had triumphed.

Voer and Yaro soared above the fray in vulture form, found Nissasa's staff, plucked them up and deposited them at Lorsedi's feet. Lifting again, they swept the perimeter of the encampment, searching for traitors who may have escaped. In the distance, a cloud of dust followed in the slipstream of a fast-moving cavalcade. The Sebborr had deserted the forty men of Rattori's Brigade, taking with them their tents, rohes, and weapons. Nothing else moved on the red sand.

Taking the lead, Voer swooped back the way they had come and landed beside the Largeen Joram. Yaro's golden form appeared beside him. Lorsedi acknowledged their arrival and studied Nissasa's captured troops with forbidding inscrutability.

After he gave orders for the care of the dead and wounded, a contingent of four men left the imprisoning semi-circle. Horses maneuvered to fill the gaps. Nissasa's three ranking officers stood shoulder to shoulder in front of the Largeen Joram. His gaze raked their faces and then traveled to the twenty-three men standing at attention in rows behind them.

"My position as your leader and the Largeen Joram of the planet of RewFaar dictates I have no tolerance for treason in any form. By supporting Nissasa Rattori, you have each one committed treason against the government and leadership of RewFaar. Were we on our home planet, all of you would face The Military Tribunal."

Rattori's Brigade remained at attention, their eyes focused straight ahead. One officer scowled. Two rows back, a soldier sneered. A second clenched fists and muttered under his breath. No one else moved.

Lorsedi gave the two men a calculated look. "You and you, front and center."

Anger laced with hatred suffused the second soldier's face. He launched into a run straight for the Largeen Joram. Voer moved, caught him mid-stride, and held him dangling in the air, feet kicking and fists flailing against nothing.

Unaffected by the man's thrashing, Voer waited, his gaze on Lorsedi. Two loyal soldiers marched forward. The man went limp. Voer set him down between the two and stepped back to his place beside Yaro.

"This man and these officers will be placed in custody awaiting trial. I will give the rest of you the opportunity to pledge your loyalty to the people and governing body of RewFaar one last time. If you don't do so, you will face the Tribunal with your comrades. If you do and break your pledge, you will face a firing squad of your peers."

Rewfaaran soldiers surrounded the four men and escorted them to a guarded tent. One of Nissasa's remaining officers called the roll. Each man stepped forward, repeated the pledge of loyalty, and returned to his place in line. None refused. Following the ceremony, Lorsedi appointed a contingent of his men to remain in Nissasa's camp. The rest were marched to the Shu Chenaro camp and assigned to various tasks.

Voer approved. Nissasa would return to the camp that looked as normal as possible. Voer, Yaro, and Lorsedi were the last to cross the border. Gerolyn met them and, at Lorsedi's request, sent a message to lower the shields. While she concentrated her attention elsewhere, Lorsedi spoke to Voer and Yaro.

"I thank you for your help. Now that we have regained control, I have a request for each of you. Voer, I would like you to remain with me. I appreciate your military training and knowledge. I expect we'll have more to do."

Voer touched his heart. "I am honored to be by your side, Largeen Joram of RewFaar."

"Yaro, find Desirol and his friends and assist them in any way you can. I know Torgin is your heart-brother. Please care for my son as you care for him."

Yaro also touched his heart. "Thank you, Largeen Joram. I will do my best to return Desirol to you unharmed."

Voer and Yaro touched foreheads in the way of the Pentharian. "Be safe, my brother."

"And you, Voer." Yaro vanished and a DerTahan falcon lifted into flight. As he flew deeper into Shu Chenaro, the shields shimmered into place.

Gerolyn joined them. "I know the Key to open a gate in the shields." Her gaze followed Yaro. "Stebben will send him through from the ranch."

Lorsedi's dark eyes searched her face. "What is the word from One Man?"

"They, too, were successful and now hold the gateway. Two men escaped on horseback. He believes they will try to reach Nissasa's camp."

Voer observed them with a slight smile. Gerolyn provided a casualty report and a list of how many traitors were under guard. A request for further instructions concluded her account. The report, delivered with the confidence of one trained to authority, deepened Voer's smile. Lorsedi listened with a reluctance that turned to admiration. The Largeen Joram had met his match in Gerolyn AsTar.

Brie, Henri, and WoNa prepared for flight. Sebborr rode in their direction. Although they did not sense the riders' intent was to find them, they felt the need to be well beyond their reach. Already a slight tremor shook the sand beneath their feet. Brie looked at her companions. She had slept. They had not. The Oracle had dark circles beneath her eyes. Her aunt bristled with energy as she dropped her spectacles into their special pocket and donned her kcalo.

"Shift you two. We must out-fly those men, or we *will* be in a predicament." Her physical body vanished. A dune hawk appeared and cocked its gray head. A violet eye gleamed.

WoNa's beetle fluttered from the slight flash of light accompanying her change and scurried beneath the gray back feathers. The hawk took flight. Brie shifted and soared after her aunt. Side by side, they chased the sun across the sky as it raced to slip behind the Toelachoc Mountains. Below, the dunes gave way to a sand sheet covered with a tessellated mosaic of small stones. As they approached the mountains, dried plants of varying sizes had taken root in larger fractures formed by the sudden rush of water down the mountain slopes during spring storms.

Ahead, a cleft between two red, rocky mountains beckoned. Henri shot toward it. Brie circled back. *No sign of the Sebborr.* She darted after her aunt. A short distance into the partial divide, a fissure wide enough for a horse and rider formed an arched channel to the right. Gliding along it, Brie marveled at the geological beauty of the stone walls, the strata containing stories of the mountains' past. As she neared the end, a flat expanse of dry, cracked ground stretched out to form a box canyon. Framed within the steep walls, a large stone building soaked up the late afternoon sun.

She winged her way to the prison, circled above it, shuddered, and streaked away from the violence emanating from every stone. Swooping to join her aunt and WoNa, she mulled over the Oracle's reference to women not faring well there. Of course, she, WoNa, and her aunt weren't ordinary women. Still, the potency of the emotions she had experienced left her uncertain and wary.

Henri landed a short distance from the gates of Toelachoc Prison. In unison, she and WoNa resumed their Human forms. Brie appeared next to them, her eyes huge and her hand pressed to her heart.

Henrietta tipped her head. "It is not a pleasant place, niece."

WoNa's blind eyes glinted. "Men were tortured here—violence begets violence. We must be cautious, and we must stay together. Women have disappeared from the prison, never to be found again. No one knows what happened to them." She reached for Brie. "You, Brielle, are the most vulnerable. Stay between us." She grew thoughtful. "Do you feel Karrew, Henri?"

"I think so, but I can't be sure." She clasped Brie's hand. "Wards are dangerous to use here. Although they would help to hide us, they would also call the ghosts to us."

"How about an illusion of invisibility?" Brie asked.

WoNa shook her head. "Using any form of DiMensionery increases our danger. As with the death shadow, fear is a magnet. Stay close and look nothing in the eye."

With Brie in between them, the women walked toward the prison. Dried plants and rocky debris made their path an obstacle course. Henri kept her pace easy, steering her companions around larger stones and along what must have once been a narrow roadway. As they approached the gate, sunlight shot through squares of rusted metal lattice work, forming a patchwork of shadow and light on the rough ground.

Henri shaded her eyes and measured the angle of the sun and its distance from the rim of the canyon. "Time is of the essence," she murmured.

WoNa caught her breath. "Wait."

They stopped. Blind eyes opened wider. She tilted her head to one side and then the other.

"What is it, WoNa?" Henri held her impatience in check.

The Oracle exhaled sharply. "It can't be." A hand seemed to hold her heart in her chest. The hand dropped. "I must be wrong." A tear slid down her cheek. "We need to hurry. The air already begins to cool. This is not a place we want to be after the moons rise."

Henri led her companions across the stone floor to a steep stairway and paused. The tingling essence of a recent passing showed someone or something had been here.

"WoNa, we are going down a staircase. It's about the width of a large man with walls on both sides. Brie will be right in front of you."

"The darkness is my friend, Henri. I will be fine. Keep your eyes down, both of you. We are going where men have died in horrible ways. Stay close together. If anything comes near, stop and huddle. The legends say these disembodied spirits dislike—"

A blast of hostile air blew past them. Henri flinched. A faceless figure bolted up the stairs, brushed cool dampness over her body, and disappeared into a gaping hole in the far wall. The barbaric undercurrents in the prison closed around her. Nothing else moved.

One cautious step at a time, she descended the stairs. Alert senses picked up the sounds of Brie and WoNa, the ancient smell of death, the faint screams of the long dead. At the bottom, darkness broken by an occasional weak shaft of light engulfed them. Inch by inch, she shepherded her charges over the rough stone floor. The air, already cold, grew more so the further they went. *We're almost there.*

Something brushed her cheek. A writhing, misty human shape wafted near them, whimpered, and vaporized. Another hovered, empty eye sockets staring. A translucent male figure stepped through a wall and planted his wavering form in her path. Henri came to an abrupt halt.

"Behind me," WoNa whispered.

Henri and Brie obeyed.

The man growled low in his throat, a sound that grew louder as his mouth gaped wider. More apparitions materialized.

WoNa crooned a soft song. Henri strained to catch the words. Brie pressed closer. Hostile expressions grew unsure. The leader snarled. His cohorts echoed the gruesome sound. Hatred etched glowing translucent faces with a ruthlessness that made Henri cringe.

In slow motion, she eased her companions back toward the stairs. A cloud of cold froze her in place. Pulling out her spectacles, she tapped them on her palm. Tap, tap, tap, pause...tap, tap...pause...tap.

WoNa's song picked up its rhythm. Around them, the specters slipped away until only the male figure remained. Vacuous eyes seemed to search their faces. A moan poured from the gaping mouth.

"Water ConDria, come to me." The words wailed like wind in a desert storm. "Come to me, gift of life."

Henri placed a hand on her niece's shoulder. WoNa's snake slithered from beneath her kcalo, hissing a warning.

The apparition floated backward.

The snaked whistled.

With a final windy wail, the figure wavered and faded.

Tesi coiled around WoNa's wrist, eyes glowing like tiny, amber cabochons.

Henri nudged them through the darkness to a cell at the end of the passageway. In the dim light that shot through a hole in the ceiling, an iron lattice door stood open. She drew her companions inside. The faint tingle of its former occupant hung in the air. Behind her, WoNa's snake gave a soft hiss.

"Karrew has been here," WoNa whispered.

"Yes," Henri murmured. She remained near the door while her niece explored the cell.

"He has definitely been here." Brie held up a small black feather. "And there's a perch and a dish of water. Did he fly away?"

WoNa answered. "No. Someone carried him."

Henri gave an urgent shhh. "We need to leave. WoNa shift!"

The small desert beetle flew to her shoulder and scurried into the folds of her hood.

"Niece, hold my hand. Don't let go."

She gripped Brie's hand and pulled her from the cell and down the passage. Ghosts swarmed the stairway. A waterfall of violent animosity cascaded toward them. Henri pressed Brie behind her, her body a shield, her power emanating around them in a sphere of golden light.

From somewhere above, additional power exploded the cloud of doom and sent apparitions darting in all directions. Silence descended, engulfing them, holding them motionless.

Brie whispered closed to her ear. "It's alright. The Star of Truth is tingling."

Henri nodded and crept up the stone stairs.

21

Myrrh

A hush of anticipation hung over Veersuni. Almiralyn peeked between folds of purple velvet. Moonbeams penetrating the stained-glass window and pooling around Elcaro's Eye teased tiny winks of rainbow light from the white alabaster. No water trickled from the statue's hands.

Elbowing the velvet aside, she peered from beneath the bench and eased her body upright. One soundless step at a time, she edged her way forward. Midway to the fountain, she paused. Nothing alarmed her—nothing suggested danger.

Sparrow tiptoed to her side and gripped her hand. Together, they stepped closer. A half-circle of exposed water reflected the light-soaked color of stained glass. Another step brought them to the fountain's rim, the full circumference of the bowl visible and undisturbed.

Sparrow started to speak. Almiralyn gave a tiny shake of her head and waved a hand above the water. A slight tremor dispersed the reflection. An image emerged from the depth of the bowl.

"Hello, ladies." A man's fatigue-lined faced wrung a small gasp from Sparrow.

Relief erased Almiralyn's dread of what she might discover. "Thank you, my friend. I knew it was your interference that saved us from—"

"Do not call attention back to us, my dear. The opposition grows stronger. I have, however, destroyed its hold on Elcaro's Eye and placed several obstacles in its way. Since it may attempt to re-establish its connection to the fountain, use the Eye with care and always with shields in place. *Do not* leave Zugo alone with the fountain."

His expression grew harried. "I have to go. Take care of yourselves."

The imaged flashed from view.

Sparrow turned a quizzical gaze in her direction. "Was that Reader?"

"It was. He appeared more tired than I have ever seen him."

"Can I please ask the fountain to show us the twins?"

The anxiety in her friend's face made Almiralyn bite off a negative response. On the surface, a blurred image fought to focus, faded and returned sharp, clear, and demanding.

A figure draped in the long folds of a kcalo waited half-hidden in shadow at the edge of a fading pattern of lattice work bars. Thin shafts of sunlight tickled the edges of the midnight blue kcalo and gleamed on a tendril of auburn-tinged black hair. Dark lashes rimmed intense brown eyes that stared with concentrated attention at an arched opening in a rough stone wall.

"Who is it?" whispered Sparrow.

Almiralyn kept her eyes fixed on the image in the fountain, a half-smile playing at the corners of her mouth. "With luck, we will soon know. Watch."

Henri's diminutive figure appeared at the top of the stairway. Brie peeked over her shoulder.

Stepping from the beneath the arch, Henrietta withdrew her spectacles and perched them on her nose. Her magnified gaze searched the hall and came to rest on the mysterious stranger. "Ahhh."

"What is it?" Brie murmured.

"We shall see in due course, niece." She walked midway across the space and came to a standstill.

"You are Sebborr, are you not? Should we be afraid?"

Remaining in shadow, he answered. "Tell me who you are, and I will tell you if you should fear me."

Henri smiled. "I am sure you already know who I am, NeTols Terah."

A brief gleam of even white teeth flashed and disappeared. Still, the man did not move.

"You are the aunt of the Guardian of Myrrh. Behind you is the ConDria returned. My father left his mark on her."

Brie stepped from behind her great aunt. "I'm Brielle. Your father?"

"The man who claims me as his son is Dahe Terah."

Brie grimaced and touched the faint scar.

The glint of his smile reappeared. "He will never forgive the Oracle of the Atrilaasu for removing it. But you are not here to discuss my father. Come."

His kcalo swishing softly as he walked, he glided over the silhouetted latticework, rounded a corner, and entered a small room. Light from the only window etched out the shape of a raven.

Almiralyn caught her breath. Her grip on the fountain's rim tightened. She longed to be there, to feel the weight of her friend perched on her arm, and to see herself reflected in his eye.

Sparrow's arm around her shoulders kept her steady. She wiped a tear from her cheek and projected her image through the fountain.

Karrew paced the back of an old wooden chair. A vague feeling he should know who looked down at him nudged. The harder he tried to remember, the more illusive Human thought became. He ruffled his feathers in frustration and sidestepped closer to the window. Whispering breezes teased him to join his brother ravens in flight. He cocked his head. Yearning so deep he could not move flooded his heart. Yearning for— A beloved face flashed into focus. For an instant—an instant—gone.

Henri knelt beside the chair and ran a gentle finger down the raven's back. She shivered. Wildness waited to claim him. He required Efillaeh's power, but Ira was on the opposite side of DerTah. They couldn't get Karrew to him in time. She turned to ask Brie for the Stone of Remembering as WoNa materialized beside them.

"If you use the stone without the knife, you will trap his Human mind in the body of a bird forever."

The Oracle sank onto a rickety cot and ran a gentle finger over the raven's ragged feathers. NeTols slipped soundlessly away.

Henri glanced at WoNa. She gave no sign she had noticed.

"Oh!"

Brie's gasp of surprise pushed the Sebborran from her mind. A sleeping boy had materialized at her niece's feet.

Brie dropped to her knees. "Ira!" She shook him. He groaned and curled into a tighter ball. Another shake. "Ira, it's Brielle. Wake up."

Blue eyes fluttered open. Ira pushed himself up on his forearms and moaned. "Ugh! Feel awful." Scrabbling upright, he dropped his head in his hands and muttered. "I was dreaming about this crazy place, all midnight sky and stars. I couldn't wake up." He tugged at a brown lock of hair. "I can't remember—"

Henri tapped the side of his head.

He blinked. The confusion in his face cleared. "Hi, Henri. Brie. Wow. And WoNa. Where are we?"

Henri used the chair to leverage her body off the floor. "We're in Toelachoc Prison. We're *very* glad to see you."

"Is that Karrew? He doesn't look too good."

He scrambled to his feet, pulling Brie with him. "Hey, Karrew. What's up?"

The raven retreated to the far side of the chair back.

"Gosh, is he afraid?"

WoNa held up an arm. Her snake's urgent hiss cut the air like a surgeon's knife. "Karrew needs Efillaeh and the Remembering Stone now. Henri and I will hold him. Hurry, we have little time."

Henri moved to the chair, lifted the skittish raven, and placed him in

WoNa's lap. Brie tipped the Remembering Stone onto her palm; Ira drew the knife from its scabbard and touched the tip to Karrew's heart. Brie held the stone to his head. The small room grew deathly still.

Almiralyn strained to see what was happening. The dim light obscured Karrew within a circle of bodies. She had read his thoughts and realized they might be too late. Her heart ached at the idea that the man she loved would never regain his Human form or speak or know who she was. A tear splashed on the surface of the water. Ripples rolled to the edges of the bowl. The image ceased to be.

The coolness of the Theran morning swept the last remnants of sleep from Jordett's mind. Seven opposition teams were in place to retake the city and remove Rattori's Brigade from Idronatti. He had assigned KcernFensians, all of whom were telepathic, to the six teams. Kieel would fill the communication gap when needed. At Jordett's signal, Teva would give the order to act. Once the teams had secured The Dissemination and the Transit Centers, the remaining teams would attack the Tower compound. He and his team were the coterie, preparing to secure Tower One. He checked his mini-chron for the time and assured himself his team was ready.

Kieel sat on his shoulder, a tiny yawn distorting his features. He yawned again, shook his head, and climbed to his feet. "I'll scout around." Keeping close to the building, he flew to the rooftop, hovered, and whizzed back to land on Jordett's hand, his usual calm replaced by agitation.

"A huge, black cloud is creeping toward the city."

Jordett tipped his head back. "A storm cloud?" He looked at the trembling Nyti.

"No. Not natural—evil—malevolent—"

Teva interrupted. "The others have seen it, too. It's coming in over Domlenah Blue, headed this way. Lenadi is certain it's The MasTer's Reach."

Her serious expression did nothing to lessen Jordett's sudden wave of apprehension. "I've never heard of The MasTer's Reach."

"Before I explain, I suggest we postpone our offensive until we know for certain what we're dealing with. If indeed it is The Reach, we don't want to give our plans away."

"Tell everyone to pull back to a sheltered position and wait for orders."

While Teva complied, Jordett instructed his team to prepare to move. He led them into the dim expanse of the building's sub-level, gathered them into a huddle, and explained why they had withdrawn.

"Teva will share with us what she knows about The MasTer's Reach."

She nodded. "The Mocendi MasTer cannot leave TreBlaya, or he will perish. He has acquired a crystal from the Evolsefil Caverns, which he uses to delve for information. It does not have far-reaching power; thus, the link it forms to other crystals in the web is weak. Many sun cycles ago, The MasTer discovered an ancient book of demonic craft. Within the text, he learned a way by which he could be on TreBlaya, yet observe happenings throughout the Inner Universe. By burning the flesh from his bones and capturing the smoke and vapor in a container with the ashes, he could collect conscious awareness. Over time, he burned away all but the flesh on his torso and compressed the smoke, vapors, and ash into an air-tight obsidian urn. When he wishes to see beyond the power of the crystal, he releases smoke into a tiny glass vial. One of his minions carries it to a selected spot and breaks it open. The vapor blossoms into a huge cloud. His minions call the cloud The MasTer's Reach."

"Can he do damage via this cloud?"

"If inhaled, the vapors can make you ill, but only in its densest form. If diffused, it is harmless. The most important thing to remember—The MasTer sees, hears, and smells what is happening near the cloud, but he can only use one sense at a time. The vapor also enhances his ability to harvest information from the minds of his minions. He uses the information he gathers via the cloud to assure himself the Mocendi and other underlings do his will."

Jordett glanced out at the sky and back at Almiralyn's cousin. "Can you shape shift?"

Teva vanished and a Theran dove winged its way through the open door.

While Jordett awaited her return, he contemplated the building across the way. The Hall of Life contained all records of The City; the Induction Center, where Idronattians had their memories expunged and their professions assigned; and the Citizens' Depository, containing the childhood memories of every Idronattian. Only the Five Fathers and two high level assistants knew about the vaults. Jordett had found out by accident. His eyes narrowed in thought.

Researchers had discovered early in memory distraction testing that if they destroyed a person's memories, he would become demented. If the memories remained intact, life followed a normal and productive course. He winced. *Productive—the operative word. If we take back...* His jaw tensed. *When we take back Idronatti, do we return the memories, and if so, how? Torgin's mother is the key.*

He searched the sky. *Where are you, Teva?*

Almiralyn wiped her eyes on her sleeve. "I know Karrew will recover. He has to."

Sparrow stared silently into the fountain as Almiralyn gave their overlapping reflections a tenuous smile. "Thank you for letting me cry."

"My mother told me a woman's tears heal the soul. It is better to release them than to choke on the emotions. What now?"

The water swirled their faces into blurred colors, mixing fair and dark, blue and brown until a farm wagon emerged.

On the seat of the wagon, Esán scratched the floppy ears of a black and tan dog and grinned at Torgin, whose fingers skimmed the length of his flute as he played a silent tune. A soft moan from Desirol snapped their attention to where he lay. He stirred, opened his eyes, and stared up at the morning sky. His brow furrowed. Puzzlement registered; a touch of fear followed.

Torgin bent closer. "Desirol, you're safe. We left the Mindeco behind."

Esán climbed over the seat back and knelt beside him. "How do you feel?"

"Odd. Half here, half elsewhere. Caught in between." As he grabbed the side of the wagon and hoisted himself to sitting, a touch of color highlighted his cheekbones. His gaze gravitated to his feet. His hand rubbed the softness of the drango tunic. "What the— Where are my boots and my jacket?"

"We wanted you safe, so Ira exchanged his tunic for your jacket and Torgin traded boots."

Torgin slid the flute into its sheepskin case. "We didn't want the Mindeco to find any of us, including you."

Desirol covered his face with his hands. When he lowered them, his expression was sad. "Thank you. I don't know what to say."

Esán laid a hand on his knee. A tickling sensation made him pull it away. "You said you feel caught in between. What does that mean?"

Worry clouded Desirol's expression. "It's as though I belong to myself, but don't. I can't explain it."

Esán heard Torgin's quick intake of breath and calmed his own growing sense of foreboding. "We shared memories in WoNa's cave. I'd like to do it again."

The RewFaaran scooted backward into the corner of the wagon bed. "The Mindeco got to me, didn't he? Stay back. I can't let him get you, too."

"I won't let the Mindeco hurt me, and we won't let him get you. As soon as we find Ira and Brie, we'll attempt to remove its hold on you. Until then, let me shield your mind so it can't track you."

Dark auburn hair flipped in his face as he jerked his head from one side to the other. "Where are they? Did it get them?"

Torgin told him about Ira's disappearance. Esán explained what happened to Brie.

All the while, the clip-clopped amble of the horses continued. The farmer's soft whistle urged them onward. The wagon crested a rolling hill. Some distance below, a village nestled at the edge of a small wood. Beyond it, the Sea of Trinuge gleamed beneath a cloudless sky.

"Whoa, ladies. Whoa." Strong hands gave a gentle pull and brought the pair to a halt. Repositioning his hat, the farmer shifted to look at his passengers.

"Suggest ya get out here. Sounds like the fewer who see ya, the better. What's the name of the man you're to contact?" He looked from one boy to the next.

Desirol rubbed his brow. "Something Sennd..."

"Well, let me see." The man tapped his lower lip. "If I wanted to escape from Atkis in a boat... You want a boat, correct?"

They nodded.

"I think Gregos Senndi is your man. He owns a ketch called *Melback*. If ya can't locate him, look for Tamosh, his brother. He'll know where ta find him." He scratched his dog's ears. "Best take Shyllee with ya. She'll warn ya if the things following ya get too close."

Torgin's eyes widened. "You'd let us take your dog?"

The farmer laughed. "She's an adventurer at heart and pining away on the farm. Right, Shyllee?"

"Woof."

Esán patted a spot next to him. Shyllee leapt lightly into the wagon bed, her tail wagging furiously. She was a beauty with silky fur, intelligent dark eyes, and a wet, black nose. With a sharp bark, she jumped to the ground, sniffed the air, barked again.

"She says you'd best get going. Take good care of her, and she'll take good care of you." The brim of his hat cast a shadow over his face, but didn't hide the worry registered there. He reached back and brushed his fingers over Desirol's temple. "Hustle. Go straight to the waterfront. Shyllee knows the way. The boat's a forty-four footer, keatwood with green trim. Go."

Desirol touched his temple, frowned, and scrambled to the ground. Torgin flipped the strap on the flute case over his head and settled it across his chest. Dragging his pack, he crawled to the back of the wagon and jumped down. Esán followed. As his feet hit the ground, the farmer gave a low whistle, and the wagon rumbled away.

Desirol stared after it. "We didn't even get to say thank you."

"He knows." Esán headed down the gentle slope. Shyllee dashed ahead, circled back, barked, and trotted toward the sea, her black and tan tail waving like a flag.

Beside the fountain, Sparrow gave a satisfied sigh. "At least all the children are safe."

Almiralyn kept her thoughts to herself.

22
Der Tah

Renn Whalend sat on a large rock, watching the ocean's eternal pitch and roll. Thoughts of Wilith and Torgin churned in her head. The wind whipping her hair around her face made her feel wild and unrestrained—things she had never experienced. Even the fear of being found by the Mocendi DiMensioner couldn't steal her delight at being liberated from Idronatti's life-stifling rules and rigid schedules. The realization that she had contributed to the pathos in the city left her heart aching and her thoughts reeling.

She ran her uniform scarf through her fingers. *The Plan. They should throw whoever thought it up into Tower Five.* Climbing to her feet, she lifted the blue silk above her head. The wind snatched it, flipping it into twisted shapes that reminded her of the life she had left behind, of her work, of the damage she had helped to create. She tossed it high, watched it fly, and gave a laugh of relief as it sailed above the water, tumbled into the trough of a cresting wave, and disappeared in the crashing surf. *Gone. The life I know is gone.*

She climbed down, picked up a handwoven basket, and strolled along the tide line. It was at its lowest point. Bibeed called it the gathering tide. She had taught Renn to collect mussels and crabs from tide pools and rocks and which of the varieties of seaweed were eatable. With a hand made net, Renn learned to catch small, shrimp-like creatures. All were tasty. They ate some cooked, some raw.

"Miss Renn. Miss Renn." Bibeed's shout held a note of alarm.

Renn hurried toward her. The woman grabbed the basket and pulled her to a shelter spot beneath the cliffs. They sprinted to the hidden door. Bibeed fumbled for the catch, found it, and pushed her ahead. The door's soft closing thud left them in darkness.

Renn listened to Bibeed's labored breathing begin to calm as they made their way down the passage and into what Renn had taken to calling the boathome. Although they had only stayed there for a few turnings, it felt like moon cycles.

Bibeed deposited the basket on the table. "Miss Renn, what do you know about the Mocendi?"

"Only what you have shared."

"The MasTer is the Mocendi leader. My brother says he is cruel and greedy and plans to rule the Inner Universe. If The MasTer leaves the planet where he lives, he will die, so he has had to discover different ways to collect information. One way is a black cloud. My brother didn't tell me much. He says the less I know, the safer I'll be. But he told me if I saw a black cloud in an otherwise clear sky, I was to hide you fast." She shivered. "I went to the cottage for supplies while you were out gathering. Don't worry—I was careful." She frowned. "But I saw a black cloud creeping over the forest north of here and headed this way. I'm so glad I got to you first."

"So am I." Renn swore under her breath. She told Bibeed about her scarf. "Sure hope the sea carried it away from here."

Bibeed began sorting through the contents of the basket. "What's done cannot be done. Bet it sank to the bottom." She looked up and smiled. "You did well today, Miss Renn. I'll fix you a splendid dinner."

"What can I do to help?"

"Fetch water from the spring and wash the seaweed. I'll prepare the crabs and mussels."

Renn grabbed a bucket and slipped across the way to the spring. Rapid footsteps and a low voice she didn't recognize made her creep back across the passage.

"You need to leave her and come with me. Being with her could get you killed."

"Shame on you, Cayled. Since when does a Finnaberry forsake someone in trouble? Miss Renn is a babe, Cay. That place she lived taught her nothing about how to survive outside its walls. I won't leave her."

"Bibeed, I'm not askin' ya. Ya need to come now. The MasTer's Reach is searching the cliffs. He's after *her*. You can't be with her when he finds her."

Renn ducked into the cave. Bibeed stood on one side of the table. A sturdy man leaned on the opposite side, his chin jutting out and the muscles of his neck bulging. Bibeed's stance—feet planted apart and hands on hips —showed a stubbornness Renn had only guessed at.

"Please, don't fight over me." She walked to the table and offered her hand. "I'm Coala Renn Whalend."

Bibeed's brother hesitated, then pressed between his large, callused ones. "Cayled Finnaberry, Miss. I mean you no harm. It's just…"

"You want to protect your sister. I understand." She withdrew her hand and looked across the table. "I don't want you hurt because of me, Bibeed. You must go. I'll be fine."

Bibeed's chin jerked up in an excellent imitation of her brother. "I won't leave you, Miss Renn. Cayled can go." She shot him a hard look. "I'm staying."

The man sank onto a camp stool. "Da'am, Bibeed, you're one stubborn woman." He seemed to mull over the situation and heaved a burdened sigh. "Guess I'll just have to stay here and protect the two of ya."

Bibeed grabbed a stool and pushed it toward Renn, then up-ended a wooden box and sat down.

Renn looked from one to the other. "Cayled, why don't you tell us why this cloud bothers you so we understand the danger?"

He rubbed the rough, work-reddened hands of a fisherman down his pant legs. "These be strange times, what with the Mocendi runnin' amuck all over the Inner Universe and their master gettin' greedier and greedier. To add to the mess, Dreela Omudi, the leader of Geran, is jumping in the same boat and puttin' all us simple folks at risk. Rumor has it you're a real smart lady from another planet. It's bein' said The MasTer wants ya for your brain and what it holds. Two turnings ago, an old man came to the village and warned us to watch for The Reach. Told us to hide if it came near." He rubbed his chin and grimaced. "I'm only a simple fisherman, Miss Renn. I love my sister. Nothin' against ya."

A shrug ended what Renn thought might be the longest recital of his life.

"What did the man say about The Reach?"

His brow creased. "Hmmm. Said it be The MasTer's eyes, ears, and nose. It's kinda like one of them dogs they use for findin' stuff."

Renn pressed him further. "Can it hurt us?"

Another frown. "Don't remember him sayin' so. But The MasTer knows what that cloud knows. If it finds you, Mocendi will come runnin'."

Relief lit Bibeed's eyes. "See, Cayled, as long as Miss Renn stays inside, it can't find her."

Cayled gave his sister a sheepish smile. "I'd sure think better if I had a full belly."

Bibeed laughed. "You're a good man, Cay. Go get water while Miss Renn and I fix a meal."

Renn looked from one to the other. "Before you go, Cay, I have a request. Please call me Renn. You are my friends, not my servants."

Cayled pushed back from the table. When he had ducked into the passage, Bibeed sighed. "He's a good man, Mi... Renn. Let's feed him and make a plan."

Bibeed lit the fire beneath the heavy black cooking pot. When Cayled returned, she half filled it with water. Soon, the succulent smell of fish stew wafted through the cave. Renn inhaled. *I sure hope the nose of The MasTer is sniffing elsewhere.*

ight crept over the Toelachoc Mountains, spilling darkness into every crack and cranny. At the prison, it erased the sun ray by ray until only a vague outline glinted in the light of the ascending moon.

Karrew tightened his hold on the chair-back and stared out a small, square window. Human thought circled on the outskirts of his memory. Sudden flashes recalled to mind that Efillaeh and the Stone of Remembering had healed his body. He stretched his injured wing. No pain, only stiffness from lack of use. Hopping lightly to the wooden seat, he peered from first one eye and then the other.

Ira leaned against the far wall, snoring softly. Brie snuggled next to him with her head on his shoulder. WoNa lay on a small cot, breathing the long, low breaths of one deep in dreams. Henri sat at the foot of the cot, her chin resting on her chest.

A feral desire for freedom washed over him. A distant memory stirred. An image struggled to form and quickly fled his ability to remember. Fluttering to the chair back, he curled his talons and clung to it like a lifeline.

He paced from one side to the other, his head bobbing, his mind straining to grasp Human thought. *The knife...the stone...* One eye inspected the Humans who fought to bring him back to himself. *Something's missing... What?*

"Easy, Karrew."

He cocked his head and eyed Henrietta.

"Stay with me, dear friend. Almiralyn would be heartbroken to lose you, and so would I."

Almiralyn. Warmth tingled around his heart.

Henri pulled her spectacles from her pocket, held them to her eyes, and scanned the faces of her companions. *Now why didn't the stone and knife do the deed?* Her gaze came to rest on Ira. "Ahhhh." She stroked Karrew's back. *Why did I not think of that before? I wonder where—*

A male figure appeared in the doorway. Soft light highlighted folds of blue kcalo. He pushed back his hood. Stunningly handsome features etched in Fasfro's golden light almost took her breath away. A warm smile made his good looks even more dazzling.

She stood and motioned him into the passageway.

A grave expression replaced his smile. "I thought the boy would provide the masculine energy needed to help Karrew. I should have stayed, but—"

"You were afraid WoNa would not remember you."

He lowered magnificent, dark eyes. "I didn't want to hurt her."

"She sensed your presence earlier but did not want to hope and be disappointed. I think it is time to end the charade, don't you?"

"What of my fa...Dahe Terah?"

"Time will tell that tale. Wait here. I'll bring her to you. Then we have work to do."

He nodded and paced the moon-painted lattice work.

She tottered back to the cot and bent over WoNa. "My friend, it is time."

The Oracle sat up fully awake. "Someone is here?"

"You have a visitor." Henri led her to the passage and left her captured in the moonlight, facing NeTols Terah.

Torgin, Desirol, and Shyllee clustered behind him as Esán's gaze skimmed over the Atkis waterfront. At his signal, the big dog had led them along a faint trail through a forested area bordering the village on three sides. With trees and brush providing perfect cover, no one noticed them slip into the small graveyard behind the church and down to the alleys of Atkis. Esán had sensed nothing following and hoped Shyllee's calm demeanor suggested, at least for now, that the Mindeco and Astican had lost them.

As he observed villagers bustling about their business, he realized he and his friends would stick out like Idronattians in The Borderlands. The drango tunic, leggings, and boots did not mirror the dress of this seaside village.

Her cold nose into his hand, Shyllee made a sound in her throat. Her tail wagged. She ran down the dirt road and cut two men from the crowd on the main dock. The shorter of the two, broad-shouldered and solidly built, had shoulder-length white hair tied back in a queue. A mustache and beard outlined a full-lipped mouth that curved into a delighted smile as he greeted the happy canine. His companion, taller with the same breadth of shoulder, had longish silver-gray hair tucked behind his ears and a mustache and goatee that were neatly trimmed. His eyes flashed green as he bent to scratch

Shyllee's floppy ears. The shorter man murmured something. He nodded and jogged back along the road.

Ambling at a casual, not-a-care-in-the-world pace, the shorter man followed Shyllee toward the alley. Esán nudged Torgin and Desirol into the shelter of a doorway. He stayed in the open, a flutter of anticipation pulsing in his throat.

Shyllee plopped on her haunches in front of him. The man rounded the corner and ran a blue-eyed gaze from him to the doorway.

"Gregos Senndi. Tell your friends to come out. I've been waitin' for ya. Wolloh sent word he'd be sending ya here." He gave Torgin and Desirol a cursory examination. "Thought there were five."

Esán shared a brief explanation of their reduced number.

A horse-drawn wagon stopped in the alley behind them. Shyllee jumped into the back.

"We'll talk once we've got ya off the streets. Climb aboard and hide under the tarp. I'll let ya know when you're safe to come out."

Esán didn't move. "And your friend is called?"

The man grinned. "He's my brother Tamosh."

"Thanks." Esán scrambled into the back of the wagon. "Come on, you two."

Torgin gave the men a sharp glance, tossed his pack aboard, and climbed on. For once, Desirol followed without arguing. They lay side-by-side and covered themselves with the tarp. The wagon rumbled along. One man or the other answered a yell of recognition or called to a friend. When only the sound of hooves and wagon wheels hitting the dirt disturbed the afternoon quiet, Esán relaxed. Nothing about either man had unnerved him. Shyllee was resting with her nose on her paws. A wide-mouthed yawn ushered Esán into the land of sleep.

Shyllee's bark woke him. Gregos flipped the tarp back. "You're safe, boys."

Esán stretched, clambered down from the wagon bed, and scanned the landscape. The distant village looked like a model in an Education Center lab. Set back in the trees, a tidy cottage faced a small bay, where the elegant lines of a sailboat glowed in the late-turning sunlight.

Torgin and Desirol jumped down beside them. "Where are we?" Torgin glanced around.

"Decided it would be safer to leave from here rather than from the docks in Atkis." Gregos studied the cloudless sky. "Weather feels like it'll hold, so we'll have a bite ta eat, then slip away. We'll sleep on the boat and leave ahead the sunrise. Come in and meet our sister, Marji."

Tamosh smacked the reins and made a clicking noise with his tongue. The horse pulled the wagon toward the back of the house, with Shyllee bounding around it. The aroma of food cooking met them as Gregos ushered them into the cottage.

Torgin grinned. "It smells wonderful in here."

A rosy-cheeked woman came forward, wiping her hands on a flowered apron. She beamed. "Guessed right. Thought you would arrive today. Made a tasty dinner that oughta hold you until tomorrow."

Gregos shot her a questioning look.

A nod and a wink. "Elf loaded the supplies on the boat. Says she's ready to go." Marji seemed to listen. "He's eager to be off." She smoothed her apron and pointed an arthritic finger at Torgin. "You're a talented boy, Torgin. Never doubt that. Esán, welcome carrier of the Seeds of Carsilem." When she got to Desirol, she studied him from head to toe. "Desirol. It only snatched a tiny part of you. If it finds you again—" She shook her head, pulled a small pouch from her pocket, and pressed it into his hand. "Keep this with you all the time. It will diffuse your signature. Take care, young man. Careless ego will get you in more trouble than you can handle."

Shyllee dashed into the room, sending Marji one way and Desirol dodging the other. Tamosh ambled in the backdoor, laughing at his sister as she threw her hand in the air and tossed Shyllee a treat. A boy hesitated in the doorway.

Tamosh waved him into the room. "This is Elf. Helps around the place." He stopped and inhaled a deep breath. "Marji, it smells like the Dreelas' kitchen in here. I'm starved."

She laughed. "Wash up and get yourselves seated."

Evening meal was as merry as it was delicious. Roasted stag surrounded by a variety of root vegetables, fresh baked bread, and fruit braised with butter and honey left Esán replete and smiling from ear to ear. Gregos teased Marji, who responded in kind. While Shyllee gnawed a bone, Tamosh told tall tales that made everyone laugh. A long time had passed since Esán remembered such a joyous meal.

All too soon, Gregos pushed back his chair. "I hate to end this wonderful celebration, but we need to be off. I want us onboard before the light is gone."

Marji wished them a safe journey and shooed them out the door. Gregos and Elf hurried down the path to a wooden dock.

Tamosh gave her a hug. "Take care, Marji. Abarax soars the skies of Trinuge."

She scanned the sunset heavens. "You'd best be off, brother. It won't be long before it discovers they've tricked it and flies this direction. By the time it arrives, I'll be away."

Tamosh gave her a quick kiss on the cheek and whistled for Shyllee. Esán and his friends looked longingly at the cottage as he urged them down the path. Gregos loaded the group, including Shyllee, into a wooden skiff and pushed away from the small dock.

Esán looked back. The cottage glowed fire-red in the last rays of the sun. He gasped as it winked out of sight. *Marji is a lot more than a superb cook.*

Nissasa observed Vygel Vintrusie over a tasty leg of DerTahan chick fowl. Large, yellowed teeth tore at the roasted flesh. Gaunt cheeks puffed with food almost looked healthy. A beak of a nose gave the narrow face a wicked, crafty appearance. Bloodshot eyes half-hidden by lashless lids came to rest on Nissasa's face. Their expression sent a chill creeping over his close-cropped head.

Vintrusie swallowed and tossed the bone on his plate. "The MasTer is very unhappy. The Largeen Joram and his men have secured the border and the gateway. You, Nissasa Rattori, are in disgrace."

Heat flooded Nissasa's cheeks. Once again, he felt like an errant schoolboy. Fear had chased him to hide in his mother's skirts. She had been right to cast him out. Snapping his mind shut, he groped for a plausible reason for leaving the front.

"I was concerned about my mother's health, Vygel. I intended to return sooner, but she needed me."

A sneer stretched thin, colorless lips over his too large teeth. "We can remove that distraction, Nissasa, and will if you allow it to override your judgment again."

Nissasa patted his mouth with a napkin and laid it aside. "On my honor, I will not let her needs supersede The MasTer's."

A sarcastic laugh hit him like a slap in the face. "You have no honor. You live by deceiving others. The MasTer will not tolerate another mistake. If you are foolish enough to do anything else to incur his wrath, I am to bring you to him on TreBlaya."

Before Nissasa could respond, the smell of sulfur penetrated the room. Finger-like pressure gripped his throat. His heartbeat crashed in his ears. Fighting for breath, he struggled to his feet, flung his cravat across the room, and tore at the neck of his shirt. A sudden rush of air into his lungs dropped him back on the chair.

The Mocendi stood sneering down at him. "That was just the preamble to The MasTer's message. The upshot is this: you are to overthrow your father's regime *no matter the cost*." Vygel pursed his lips. "The MasTer has left the matter in my hands. I am to be your adviser and confident." Determination filled his next statement. "*We* will *not* disappoint. Is that clear?"

Nissasa buried his boiling anger beneath a subservient exterior and forced a calm reply. "I will be glad of your help, Vygel."

The Mocendi gave him a hard look. "I'll meet you out front. We will make an inconspicuous departure. You've paid your bill?"

"I'll take care of it and join you." Nissasa lied. With an acid taste in his mouth, he watched the man depart. "I must get back in The MasTer's good graces." A slow smile erased his frown of concentration. "And I know just how to do so."

Masking his thoughts, he crossed to the door, opened it a crack, and peered up and down the hall. Satisfied Vygel was nowhere near, he turned the key and hurried to the bedroom. His reflection in the mirror above the armoire caught his attention. *If I had red hair, I'd look like my father. Then he might have loved me*. A tingle of regret surprised him. He shoved it away and withdrew Souvitrico from its pouch. "I will destroy you, Lorsedi Telisnoe." He stared into the mirror. "And I will find out where Evolsefil is and present it to The MasTer. That should appease his anger."

Touching the mirror with the tip of the crystal, he began to recite,

"Souvitrico, transform this mirror
Into a portal, true and clear,
That I may travel safely to
Evolsefil and claim my due."

Mist overflowed the mirror. The room disappeared. Frothing fog enveloped him, lifted him, transported him.

23

Myrrh

Almiralyn paced a restless circle around Elcaro's Eye, contemplating all it had shared. Her intellect told her to take a break; her heart urged her to discover more about Karrew. Sparrow had stretched out on a bench and drifted into sleep. Veersuni's tranquil atmosphere tempted Almiralyn to do the same. A soft gurgle from the Eye pulled her to the fountain. An image had already captured the surface.

WoNadahem Mardree held out her hands to the figure of a man dappled by a lattice of moonlight and shadow. Her eyes glowed saffron and blue. Her snake coiled on a shoulder, its forked tongue flicking the air.

"Roandee." The name, a whispered prayer, hung between them.

The man took her hands and held them to his heart. A tear glistened on his cheek. "I wanted to come back, to be with you always." Loneliness, desolation, heartbreak drenched his words. He traced every inch of her face with tear-damp eyes. "You look the same—wiser—perhaps sadder. I was afraid when I found you, I would not recognize you. I was afraid *you* would not know me."

"Shhh. How could I ever forget the joy of my life, the young brother who made my heart laugh, my dancing partner, my brave warrior? You were only ten sun cycles when Dahe kidnapped you."

Roandee embraced her, held her with the tenderness of one who thought she might break. The hiss of her snake made him step back. "Ahhhh. Tesi, you remember me. I have missed you, too."

He took her hand and pressed the palm to his cheek. Her fingers explored hungrily—eyes, nose, mouth, the height of his cheekbones and brows, his hair. She smiled. "I imagine the women think you are quite handsome."

His laugh burst forth deep and full and overflowing with life.

WoNa wiped her tears with the back of her hand. "We have little time. Karrew's life hangs in the balance."

They embraced once more. Roandee whispered against her hair. "I have dreamt of you every night since they stole me. They thought, in time, I would forget you. You are my strongest memory of my other life."

"I have only one question, dear brother, and then we must help Karrew."

"And what is that?"

"Did Dahe Terah treat you well?"

"He adopted me as his youngest son and raised me as Sebborr, WoNa. He dotes on me, but only to make sure I owe him my allegiance. I am his tie to you."

"And you have the seer's gift, do you not?"

"Not in the same way you do, but yes, I am an oracle."

She pressed her lips to his palm, then sighed. "We will talk more later. Tri-Nular approaches, the perfect time to help Karrew."

He escorted her into the small room and stayed by her side.

WoNa, wreathed in smiles, took a deep breath. "Henri, Brielle, and Ira, this is my younger brother, Roandee." A tear leaked from her eye. "The Sebborr kidnapped him a lifetime ago."

Henri grinned. "It's about time. Welcome, Roandee. We are glad to have you here for many reasons. Most of all for our dear WoNa."

Ira and Brie touched his palm and then their hearts in the sign of everlasting friendship. Karrew traveled the top rail of the chair, his head bobbing. A deep caw, his first sound since his rescue, rang through the room.

The water rippled. Almiralyn wiped the tears from her eyes. "My dear, dear friend, I am so happy for you." She turned to find Sparrow watching her.

"What did you see? Is Karrew alright? Corvus?"

She explained what had occurred. "It's Corvus' turn next. I only hope it isn't too late." Her focus returned to the fountain.

Sparrow joined her as the water smoothed and a picture floated to the top of the alabaster bowl.

Roandee knelt beside Karrew and whispered, "I am here, my friend. We will make you whole." Lifting the raven with gentle hands, he sat between Henri and WoNa and held him in his lap.

Henri called Ira to her. "It is time to drop the façade, at least for now." She snapped her fingers.

Ari blinked and looked around the cell. "I'm me!" She hugged Brie and Henri and touched WoNa's arm. "I'm so glad you and your brother are reunited. I know how hard it is to be apart for so long."

WoNa smiled. "It is time, my friends."

Brie knelt on one side, Ari, on the other.

Henri bowed her head and chanted,

> *"All is correct and in its place*
> *Balance restored to set the pace*
> *Help us now return from strife*
> *This Human man to his true life."*

For the second time, Brie placed the Stone of Remembering on Karrew's forehead. Ari withdrew the sacred knife and held it up in the light of the three DerTahan moons. The etchings on the blade shimmered with emerald light. Amethysts glowed. She held Efillaeh to Karrew's chest. Cobalt blue light flowed around his head. Purple encircled his body.

Karrew's image filled the fountain. Almiralyn gasped. His mind flew open. His thoughts flowed into hers...

Karrew...Corvus...Karrew...Corvus. Two entities battled for control. Unravelled memories tumbled one after the other in a tumultuous stream. One trembled and another floated to the top. Karrew and Corvus gulped down memories like carrion. A flash of cobalt stopped the feast, pulled a thread from each throat, wove them on the loom of time. Warp and weft, thread by thread, a life took shape. The shuttle flew, picture upon picture upon picture.

The raven's body quaked. A raspy caw and then a word, ill formed and indistinct. The stone grew dark. Efillaeh clattered to the stone floor. All the players stood. Roandee placed the raven on the ground and joined the circle surrounding it.

WoNa recited,

> *"Corvus Karrew Castilym*
> *Come forth and join the ranks of men*
> *Secure your Human heart to thee*
> *Keep Karrew, yet become free."*

Almiralyn gripped Elcaro's rim and repeated the verse under her breath. Her reflection flitted over the water's surface. She started to tremble. The water shook. The picture zoomed in tighter and tighter until only a circle of heads remained.

In unison, the circled companions repeated the verse. With each line, they took a step back. Brie kissed the Remembering Stone and placed it beside the bird. Ari picked up the knife and set it opposite. The raven lifted into flight, soared out the window beneath the stars and the breathtaking beauty of Tri-Nular.

The fountain reversed the zoom. Moonlight washing the exterior of the prison formed on the surface. The twins, followed by Henri, WoNa, and Roandee, burst through the entrance, heads thrown back, to search the empty expanse of desert sky.

Almiralyn sobbed. She sank onto a bench and let the tears fall. *Too late. They were too late. If only...*
Sparrow grabbed her arm and pulled her back to the fountain.

Dark, searching eyes imprisoned a blue moon in their pupils. A dimple flashed, white teeth gleamed. The image pulled out to encompass a man draped in the cool light of Calegri. He mouthed the words, "I love you, Almiralyn Nadrugia."

Water spilled from alabaster palms as Almiralyn's laugh joyful laugh reverberated through Veersuni.

In Idronatti, Jordett stepped from the sub-level, tipped his cap to shade his eyes, stared up at the early morning sky, and wished the Theran dove into sight. He glanced at his mini-chron and back at the rooftops. *Where on Thera are you?*
Anada joined him. "Any sign of Teva?"
"No."
"You worried?"
"Yes."
Anada pointed. "Don't be. Here she comes."
The dove swooped into the pass-through. Teva, elegant and calm, materialized as the dove's talons touched the ground. "Sorry I took so long. The cloud is definitely The MasTer's Reach. A group of Mocendi brought it here. If you want more information, I'll need Kieel's help."
The Nyti Matrés landed on her shoulder. "I'd be pleased to assist."
Jordett adjusted his cap and looked from Kieel to Teva. "First, send a message to the teams to continue to hold tight. I don't want anyone to jump too soon. Let me know when that's done."

Sagus joined the group by the door as Teva moved a short distance away. "Does she have any news?"

Anada filled him in.

He frowned. "Sure wish I could go with her."

Teva joined them. "I do, too, but not for this, Sagus. Kieel is our best bet. I'll help him enter the building where the Mocendi are in hiding. Hopefully, he can find out how many of them there are."

"It would help to know if they have any more Reach ampules, too. Probably impossible..." Sagus shrugged.

"We'll do our best." Teva addressed Kieel. "I'll shift. You ride on my back. Make yourself as small as possible." To Jordett, she said, "Anything else you can think of?"

"Whatever you can discover. Don't put yourselves at risk. Understood, Kieel?"

The Nyti squared his shoulders. "I am always circumspect, Major."

Teva shifted. Kieel mounted the dove's back and wrapped an arm around her neck. In his other hand, he clutched his walking stick.

Jordett watched them grow smaller and smaller. "You'd better be circumspect, my friend."

Kieel refrained from looking down. Although he wasn't afraid of heights, sitting at the top of a tall tree differed from soaring above a city. The dove swooped to a rooftop. Kieel lifted off its back and hovered to one side. Teva appeared, frowning.

"They know someone is here, so listen carefully. The Mocendi are hiding in the uppermost apartment. I'll take you that far and cause a disturbance. When they come out, you slip inside. If I can't return for you, follow the path of the sun for seven blocks. Jordett is on the left. You'll recognize the building. Be careful, Kieel. This is not a game. These men are not above torturing you. Discover what you can and get out. I have cloaked you in an illusion of invisibility. If they sense it, it will dissolve, so stay out of sight."

She dodged through the open door and jogged down the steps to a long hallway. "There are two apartments. You want the one on the right. Ready?"

"Be careful, my lady." He shot to the top of the doorframe.

She slammed the rooftop door, left it flung wide, and pounded up the stairs. The apartment door flew open. Two men ran into the stairwell.

Kieel fluttered to the top of the apartment door and peered inside. Two Mocendi sat across the luxurious blue room, their attention trained on the hallway. Afraid to move, he waited. Jogging footsteps pounded down the stairs. The men reappeared one behind the other.

"I'm telling you, someone shifted up there." The taller of the two scowled over his shoulder. He shoved the door further open and strode into the room.

The second man followed. "You're just looking for trouble, Thorlu. Nobody could have made it through our wards."

Kieel shot to the top of a cornice and squatted low as the door clicked shut. The men gathered around the table, talking in low voices. They were a disparate bunch—tall and short, old and young. Thorlu, the tallest, was handsome, well-dressed, and in his middle cycles. His companion was dumpy, short, and younger than the others. The two remaining men, older and more weathered, listened with frustration etched in deep lines around their eyes and mouths.

"If they've discovered our presence, we need to move faster." The Mocendi seated at the end of the table stood and paced to a window. "I want control of the Five Towers by turning's end. Once we're installed there and the city is ours, we'll reopen the portal the Guardian closed when she arrived in Myrrh." He returned to his seat. A wicked smile lit his face. "Almiralyn's domain will be ours for the taking."

The blood in Kieel's veins turned to ice when he thought about the League controlling his home. Clutching his walking stick with shaking hands, he began to explore the apartment.

At first, he thought his search might be futile. The last sleeping space, however, produced several things of interest. On one end of a chest of drawers, a black lacquer box sat beside its lid. Three small vials, one empty and two containing an amorphous, gray-black vapor, glistened in the dark purple interior. Kieel studied the box. *Can The MasTer see me?* He shot higher, gripped his walking stick tighter, and hovered a moment longer before diving lower for a closer look at the opposite end of the dresser.

Beneath a black cloth, something round—something that emanated evil like the sun emanated warmth—tickled his curiosity. He landed on a chair and stared.

"Come."

The soft word in his mind urged him forward. Fear shivered through his small body. Ignoring it, he fluttered to the dresser, propped his walking stick against the mirror, and dropped to his hands and knees. Revulsion hit him like a tidal wave. He sat back on his heels. Jordett's last statement echoed through his mind: "Don't put yourself at risk."

"There is nothing to fear. It cannot harm you." The caressing words erased Jordett's. He peeked beneath the cloth, saw a vague reflection of his face on the surface of a smoky crystal ball, smelled the odor of burned flesh, and whizzed into the air, his heart pounding so hard he couldn't think. Struggling to keep himself airborne, he pumped terror-weakened wings until he landed, breathless and shaking, on the top of a wardrobe as far away from the chest of drawers as possible.

Numbed fingers plucked at his chest. "Control yourself, Kieel," he scolded. "If you get caught, you will disappoint yourself and everyone else."

Straining to blank his mind and avoid looking at the ball, he fixed his gaze on the box with the vials. *Wish I could take you with me. Can't. So what now?*

The door flew open. The youngest man marched into the room, intense, dark eyes searched floor to ceiling. A frown of annoyance replaced his initial expression of eager expectation. With a disappointed scowl, he marched into the main room. "Nothing. I felt certain—"

"You are imagining things." The voice held a note of impatience. "Now, sit down and let's finish our plans."

A chair creaked. The discussion resumed. Kieel flew to the box with the ampules and lifted one in hands he forced to be steady. Working with efficient speed, he hid it on the top of the wardrobe. He rolled the second one under the dresser. As much as he wanted to smash the crystal ball, he gave it a wide berth, grabbed his walking stick, and returned to the main room.

Hidden behind a large vase of fake blue flowers, he settled down to eavesdrop.

Almiralyn's heartbeat thrummed into an exuberant song. She grabbed Sparrow's hand and pulled her from Veersuni into the Reading Room.

"He's alive! Corvus! Thanks to Emit for this gift." Giggling like a young girl, she hugged Sparrow, stepped back, and grinned. "I have been so afraid of losing him—that he would never know what he means to me." Happiness danced through her entire being. "I wish he were here. At least I know he's back."

Elae entered from the research level, her brow wrinkled in consternation. She hurried toward them, started to say something, hesitated, and smiled at Almiralyn.

"You look happy, Mira." Realization brightened her eyes. She grinned. "Corvus? Is he alright?"

"He is. I'm so relieved, but you seem worried."

Elae held out a scroll. "I think you should see this. I can read some of it, but my TreBlayan is sketchy."

Almiralyn carried it to an alcove, sat down, and unrolled it. Aware only of the information it contained, she barely noticed Sparrow and Elae join her at the table or Wilith, Merrilea, and Zugo arrive.

An unknown word brought her up short. Frowning, she read ahead. Its meaning continued to mystify her. She reread the confusing paragraph. *Ah. Ginori equals origin.* As she continued to read, the room faded. A vision took its place.

On the apex of a huge mound of earth rising high above a dark and barren landscape, the glowing form of a woman raised her voice in a glorious song of creation. As the closing note diminished, she knelt, kissed the ground, and faded from sight. Life stirred. The soft green of new plant growth pushed up through the rich soil. Flowers burst into bloom, covering the mound with color. Saplings sprouted around it and shot upward. Birds took flight. Creatures crawled up the sides of the mound, eyes aglow, tongues licking the air. The sounds of creeks and streams, waterfalls, and oceans infused the air. Wind sang through the branches of full-grown trees, and all life celebrated birth.

Almiralyn continued to read. Time raced forward. The planet of

TreBlaya at the outer edge of the Inner Universe flourished until a rag-tag band of strangers arrived from beyond the DéCussate. Again the text blurred and images flooded her mind.

A towering, black-cloaked form now stood atop the Mound of Ginori. As the setting sun colored the horizon with fiery gold, scrambling figures pushed their way into the gaping mouth of an underground cave at its base. When the last had disappeared, the figure raised clenched fists and started to chant. The mound began to shake; the ground to quake. Blackened fingers uncurled. Acid rain surged from their tips, soaking the landscape and destroying everything in its path. Rancid fumes poisoned the air. The rancid odor of burning flesh wafted over the land.

A deep laugh mingled with the screams of the dying. The figure shifted. A massive bird of prey took flight. Feathers the color of evergreen pressed against the smoldering air. Amber eyes glowed in a mask of red. A wicked beak opened in a screech that toppled the mound to a pile of rubble. Circling wide, it landed near a blazing pit. A figure materialized, tucked a long braid beneath its cloak, and grew to its former size, looming above the land like a demonic fiend. With a hideous laugh, it vanished in a cloud of smoke.

Almiralyn's throat burned as her lungs filled with fresh air. She blinked and brought her gaze to the faces of those who stared at her.

"Merrilea, Wilith, Zugo, I didn't know you had joined us."

Zugo pointed at the scroll. "We want to know what it says, too. Besides, it's time for a break." He grinned. "And a snack."

Wilith laughed. "You sound like Torgin." He sobered. "Could you read the scroll, Almiralyn?"

"It is, in part, the creation myth of TreBlaya." She fought a lingering sense of dislocation and struggled to describe what she had seen.

Elae touched her arm. "Are you alright?"

"Just feeling disoriented." She gave herself a mental shake to cleanse her thoughts of what she had seen and focused back in the present. "Most importance to us is the last section. It states that the planet will be reborn in fire and DosWah will become its master." She shared the second part of her vision.

When she finished, shock held everyone silent.

Sparrow raised a troubled gaze. "The figure in your vision... Was it The Mas—" She shivered.

"I believe, from what I have read and what you have already discovered, that it was indeed The MasTer."

Wilith frowned. "Does that mean The MasTer is DosWah?"

Almiralyn shook her head. "No."

"What is DosWah?" Sparrow asked.

"DosWah is the shadow side of nature." Almiralyn smoothed the curled end of the scroll. "In order to restore balance and abundance to TreBlaya and its solar system, we must re-establish Trilemma—that which integrates DosWah into wholeness."

Merrilea frowned. "Does that mean we must rid the Inner Universe of DosWah?"

Wilith cleared his throat. "My research suggests that ridding the Inner Universe of DosWah is not the goal. Light without shadow or vice versa creates imbalance. Light comes from darkness. From the midst of light, darkness appears. Destroying DosWah is not what's important. It is maintaining a level of balance that allows the Universe to thrive that is vital." His thoughtful gaze took in everyone. "Do we have to defeat The MasTer to restore balance?"

Almiralyn picked up the scroll, reread a section, rolled it up, and set it on the table. "We don't. Others will fight the ultimate battle. We can help by removing as many resources from The MasTer's reach as possible. Rescuing Renn Whalend, protecting the children, and defending Evolsefil, Efillaeh, the Stone of Remembering, and the Compass of Ostradio top the list."

"Is this part of The Unfolding?" Zugo swiveled to look at her.

Almiralyn arched her brows. "We'll only know the answer as The Unfolding continues."

Sparrow tugged at a stray curl. "I'm still not sure I understand what exactly The Unfolding is."

Almiralyn smiled at Elae. "Would you like to explain?"

"I can try." After a pause, she began.

"The ancient texts state that The Unfolding is a revelatory time that magnifies one's weaknesses and tests one's strengths. It is the time that reveals one's talents and helps to develop and refine them. If one cannot withstand the testing of one's strengths—if weakness becomes the ruling factor in a life—that life is at risk. The goal is Individual Trilemma, which is only achieved by weathering life's challenges, successes, and failures with awareness and courage. This is true of all living creatures and of universes, galaxies, solar systems, and planets."

Wilith rubbed his forehead. "Then The Unfolding is ongoing?"

Almiralyn explained. "It is cyclical. A period of testing or unfolding is followed by a period when the Unfolding's lessons are absorbed and integrated."

Elae smiled. "And then the cycle begins again."

The group sat in a thoughtful silence. A priestess arrived with food. Almiralyn couldn't remember the last time she'd eaten. The rush of energy flowing through her body left her smiling to herself. When everyone had eaten, she described what the fountain shared— where Ira and Brie were, and that Corvus had reclaimed his Human life. "Now it's time to discover how Torgin, Esán, and Desirol are doing."

"And Renn? Please, can we check on Renn?" Wilith asked.

"Of course. One thing before we enter Veersuni. Zugo, you must never be alone with the fountain."

The young DeoNyte looked confused. "I thought I was doing a good job."

"It's not about the job you're doing. Reader is concerned for your safety. We don't want the Mocendi get their hands on you."

Zugo shot her an incredulous look. "Through the fountain?"

Elae linked her arm through his. "Reader's concerned, Zugo. That tells me you are important to the outcome of everything that's happening."

"Well...ah...I guess I understand." He brightened. "Let's go see what's up."

Everyone gathered around the fountain. Almiralyn looked from one to the other. "If anything feels strange or threatening, you are to remove yourselves from Veersuni. Do not linger. Understood?"

Four heads bobbed.

Almiralyn snapped her fingers. The water cleared.

Cherubic features ravaged by rage filled the bowl. The Astican's roar flooded Veersuni.

24

Der Tah

Yaro pressed vulture wings against the heat of the desert sky, his warrior's heart torn between the battle he left behind and the gladness he felt at the opportunity to find Torgin. Had he known for certain his heart-brother was safe, the idea of being ordered to leave would have brought much shame. The fact he knew that danger lurked around every turn and that Torgin waded through the midst of it erased any guilt he may have felt. Besides, the Largeen Joram had asked him to protect his son.

The outbuildings of Shu Chenaro came into sight. He swooped over the barn and the raptor center and landed near the arena. Striding to the gate, he arrived in time to see Allynae blur and reappear several feet closer to Stebben. Smiling at his friend's look of astonishment, he strode forward.

Allynae grinned. "Welcome, Yaro. I am learning to teleport and having a small success. What's happening?"

Stebben called out, "Stand here beside me, Yaro. Let's give Alli a dual reason to teleport to my side."

Yaro touched hand to heart. "It will be a pleasure to assist with your lesson, brother of Almiralyn." He greeted Stebben in the ways of ReTaw au Qa and noted the fatigue hanging around him like a cloud. "How can I help?"

"You also stand here beside me, Allynae," Stebben instructed. "Yaro will share his news when you have joined us. Picture yourself here. Concentrate."

Allynae closed his eyes, blurred into faint ribbons of color, and materialized in front of them. His eyes flew open. He looked back to where he had been. "I did it!" A delighted guffaw bounced off the walls of the arena.

Stebben draped an arm over his shoulders. "Now, you can take the three of us to the sitting room."

"Oh, come now, Stebben. I can't teleport that far on my own, let alone with passengers, right Yaro?"

"I have confidence you can do this thing." Yaro linked his arm through Allynae's.

Stebben grinned. "Picture the room and take us there."

Allynae felt his companions willing him to succeed. *I have to do this.* He shut his eyes and pictured Wolloh's study. A deep breath. A silent go. Neither of his friends made a sound. He cracked one eye open, then cast a suspicious look at his teacher. "Did you help me do this?" He waved at the study, where they stood in exactly the spot he had envisioned they would be.

"I did not, my friend. That would not have helped you, only refueled your doubt. Now, do you believe you have the talent?"

Allynae dropped into Wolloh's chair. "I do." He stroked the soft leather. "I do indeed." He smiled at Stebben. "Thank you for your patience. And now, Yaro, do you have any news Gerolyn might have forgotten?"

Yaro switched his tail to one side and sat on the edge of a chair. "It is unlikely that Gerolyn AsTar would forget anything, but I will share what I know."

When they finished discussing the battle news, Stebben sat back and considered the gold Pentharian. "What brings you to the ranch?"

"Lorsedi sent me to find Desirol and the others. Gerolyn suggested you would provide a way through the wards."

Stebben sighed. "Of course. Has she heard anything from Henri?"

The Pentharian pursed red lips, then frowned. "There has only been silence. And what of Nomed? Did he reach Trinuge?"

"He's with TheLise." Allynae grinned. "I believe there's a romance blooming there."

A laugh left Stebben looking less tired. "That romance has been blooming since they met in their teen cycles. Nomed just refuses to admit it. TheLise, of course, loves the intrigue and the game."

Allynae observed the fatigue return. "You've known them a long time?"

"Yes. Wolloh began training TheLise when she was fifteen sun cycles. Davin, later to be known as Seyes Nomed, arrived shortly thereafter. They trained together. They hid in a coffin together at one time." The memory brought a gleam to his eyes.

"Sounds like a good story." Allynae leaned forward.

"Most definitely. The PPP, the Mocendi League, *and* The MasTer wanted Davin. I will share it with you another time." He nodded to Yaro. "You are impatient to be off, am I correct?"

The Pentharian rose from the chair, his formidable height towering over them. "I must find the children."

Stebben, a tall man in Human terms, came to his feet, the top of his head even with Yaro's collar bones. "I still do not detect them in Atkis. I am hoping Gregos spirited them away before they left an impression."

Allynae trailed after them. "Can I help with the wards?"

"You can." Stebben laid a hand on his arm. "Take us to the arena."

Allynae gripped Yaro's wrist and pictured their destination. They arrived in an instant.

Yaro's lizard-like eyes gleamed. "You are good, brother of Almiralyn."

The warmth in the words made Allynae smile.

Stebben strode to the center of the arena. "Yaro, fly south along the Peninsula of Trinuge. You've studied maps of DerTah, correct?"

"I have, Stebben. Atkis is near the tip on the eastern side. I will find it."

"Good. Fly straight up. Allynae and I will open the top of the wards.

Have Esán let us know when you've arrived. Be wary, Yaro. The Astican and the Mindeco have joined forces."

"I will be watchful. What is your next move?"

Allynae listened with interest.

"We await word from Henri. Until then, we must guard Shu Chenaro. The MasTer would see it destroyed."

Yaro touched his heart and bowed his head to each man. "Be brave in battle and true of heart." He vanished into a DerTahan falcon and flew upward.

Allynae and Stebben linked minds and opened an exit. The bird soared through, the exit closed, and Stebben signed to break the link.

For a brief instant, Allynae's mind struggled to readjust, then settled into its normal pattern. He shook his head. "The complexities of DiMensionery—"

Torgin stood on the deck of the sailing vessel, *Melback* with his heart in his throat. He had never been on a boat or near an ocean. Even though they were at anchor, the anxiety that he had shoved away since arriving in DerTah was still present. He swallowed the bitter taste of bile and hoped he wouldn't throw up.

Gregos eyed him with concern.

Torgin gave a tremulous smile and gripped the ropes hanging from what he had learned was a mast. Three steps took him into the cabin. Pausing for a moment to adjust to the oil lamps casting yellow light on keatwood tables and benches, he licked his lips and tried to breathe. Ahead of him, Esán and Desirol looked around with easy interest, asked questions, and responded to the ones Tamosh asked. Torgin swallowed and hoped he would not embarrass himself.

Shyllee press her cold nose against his palm and raised dark, intelligent eyes to his face. *I'm alright. I'll get over this.* Two more steps and he stood in the galley. On the left, the warmth of a wood-burning stove chased the cool night air from the cabin. Opposite, on the right, a table lowered to make into a bed. Next on the right was the head. He wiped his sweaty palms on his pants. The head was a tiny space with a bucket that would be emptied over the side when it was full. *Not even vaguely like a Personal Needs Space.* At the bow of the boat, a keatwood door opened into a V-berth where Gregos and Tamosh slept. Des and Esán had already opted to sleep opposite the stove. Torgin and Elf would sleep in two berths on the hatch level.

Gregos produced a pile of bedrolls and small pillows. "Get some sleep. You're going to need it. Tomorrow, you learn how to be members of the crew. We're up before dawn." He ducked into the V-berth. Tamosh stepped from the head and disappeared after his brother.

Elf grabbed pillows and bedrolls and trundled up the steps to the hatch level. He pulled his berth from the bulkhead and stacked the bedding on top. With his help, Torgin lowered the chart table and seated it into the benches that rounded it on three sides. Elf handed him his bedding, gave him a shy smile, and slipped on deck to stand the first watch.

A few short steps away, Esán and Desirol slept, their soft snores creating a music-like chorus. Uncertain if he was restless or simply not sleepy, Torgin opened the hatch and climbed on deck beneath the three moons of DerTah. Elf, a silent silhouette, stood at the bow. Luminescence played on the water's surface like paint on SparrowLyn's canvas. Phosphorescence caught the moons' light and tossed it around the boat in ever-changing patterns. Torgin, awed by the beauty, felt his fear subside. Fatigue so deep it threatened to drop him on the spot sent him back into the cabin. He used the head, unrolled his bedroll, and stretched out on his back. Shyllee curled up beside him, her head resting on his chest. Absently, he stroked her silky black fur. His last memory—moonlight streaming through the portholes forming patches of light on the keatwood flooring.

Morning came far too early. A hand shook him awake. Esán grinned down at him, excitement radiating like warmth from the stove. "We set sail in a quarter chron cycle. Grab some fruit. Gregos says we can eat more once we're underway." He ducked through the hatch. Torgin glimpsed Tamosh and Gregos already on deck and Shyllee with front paws resting on the railing, her nose sniffing the salty air.

He stowed his bedding in the locker and grabbed a purple fruit he didn't recognize from a small wooden barrel. Elf was nowhere to be seen. Desirol sat at the galley table, his expression blank.

"You all right, Des?"

The RewFaaran continued to stare at nothing. "Just feel strange. I..." He sighed.

Torgin handed him a piece of fruit. "Here. You need food."

"No, Torgin, I need to be rid of the Mindeco. I can sense it in my mind, dark and dangerous and waiting."

Torgin bit into the fruit. "Whoa. Don't know what this is, but I'm all charged up." He savored another bite. "Try it, Des. I bet if you feel better, you won't notice the Mindeco as much."

Desirol bit into the juicy pulp. His eyes rounded. He chewed and swallowed. "That was great! What is it?"

Esán clomped down the steps. "Steero fruit. Corvus brought me some at Shu Chenaro after my assessment with Wolloh. Builds your natural energies. Gregos wants you. We're ready to go."

Des followed him up the steps. Torgin trailed behind. Shyllee greeted them with a bark and a wagging tail.

Torgin stepped on deck and latched the hatch in place. He inhaled the fresh air, gazed at the sea, the lavender sky, a white bird soaring by, and grinned. Last night's fear had receded. Even in the hazy first light of dawn, no fear tugged.

Gregos stood behind the mizzenmast at the helm. Torgin grinned again as he reviewed the terms they had learned last night. Elf and Esán hustled to unlash the mainsail. Tamosh and Desirol conversed on the bow. Torgin guessed they were getting ready to raise the anchor. Shyllee sat at the stern, the wind ruffling her black and tan fur.

Gregos called, "Torgin, join me. I'll show ya how to steer by a compass heading."

Torgin circumvented a pile of coiled line and stepped up beside Gregos at a wooden wheel.

"You're looking better this morning. I've gotta hunch about ya."

"What?"

"I'm betting you're going to love the sea." He caught his brother's eye. "Ho, Tamosh, prepare to haul the anchor." Tamosh gave him a thumbs up. "Esán and Elf will raise the mainsail. We have a light breeze, so we'll ease out of this little bay. Torgin, take the wheel. Use that small island at the mouth of the bay as your heading." He pointed at a compass mounted behind the mast. "Keep the red line centered right here. Don't over adjust. Slight corrections. Understood?"

Torgin swallowed. "Yes, sir. I understand. You won't go far, right?"

The laugh lines around Gregos' eyes crinkled. "I'll be right here, boy. Look alert." He gave Tamosh the signal. The anchor chain rattled and clanked. Desirol guided it down through a small hatch to its storage locker below deck.

"She's free," Tamosh yelled.

Torgin noted the gentle rock and sway.

"Raise the mainsail," Gregos ordered. "Go. Keep her amidships, Elf, until I give the word."

The boys pulled in unison. The sail went up. Torgin eyed the red line and then the small island. The anchor rattled into place on the bow, a breeze billowed the sail, and *Melback* glided through the water.

The compass heading shifted. He turned the wheel, watched the compass adjust back to center, and looked up to see Gregos nodding his approval.

"I'll take the wheel." They exchanged places." Elf, ya got the lines? Good. We're sailing close to the wind, so stay alert." He addressed Torgin. "I understand you're good at math."

"Yes, sir."

Tamosh ducked into the cabin with Shyllee at his heels and tossed a pair of gloves in a bucket.

"Good. Tamosh is going to teach ya to navigate."

A thrill of excitement made Torgin grin. "You mean he'll teach me to read charts?"

"And to use a sexton and to help set a course that'll keep us outta trouble. Are ya interested?"

"Yes, sir, I am."

Tamosh poked his head out. "Come along then. We'll get started."

When Torgin reached the cabin, Tamosh had already spread a chart on the table. The lesson began. Torgin could only marvel at his good fortune.

Corvus faced the group in the door to the prison. They had risked their lives to save his. The saffron moon slipped halfway below the horizon. Middle-night approached. Middle-night at Toelachoc Prison could prove deadly for the living, especially the women.

He smiled as the red-haired twins launched toward him.

"Corvus! Corvus! It is you. We're so glad to see you again." They planted a kiss on each cheek.

He held them at arm's length. "Ari and Brie! It is good to see you *both*." He let them go and gathered Henri in his arms. "Thank you, Henrietta, for everything."

She smiled up at him, her violet eyes gleaming. "It was close, dear boy. Never scare us like that again."

"I promise." He took WoNa's hands. "Thank you, Atrilaasu Oracle, for leaving your haven to save me. I plan to repay the favor."

She lowered her extraordinary eyes. Her snake hissed.

He leaned closer and whispered, "Soon." Then he turned to the man who waited half in shadow. "How can I ever thank you enough for rescuing me, for caring for my wounds? I owe you, my friend."

Roandee shook his offered hand. "You owe me nothing, Corvus Karrew Castilym." He put an arm around WoNa. "I have the thing I have wanted most in the Universe." Concern clouded the handsome face. "You must leave." He touched WoNa's cheek. "I cannot go with you, dearest sister. For now, I must continue my charade. To do otherwise will bring harm to us all." He hugged her and whispered, "I'll visit you soon."

Tears spilled from her eyes as he strode toward the Cliffs of Toelachoc, kcalo swishing and darkness closing around him. She seemed to listen. Tesi gave a long, shrill whistle. The Oracle held out her hands. "Form a circle. We'll teleport beyond the mountains. I'll place an image in your minds. Make haste! Calegri reaches its zenith."

Low, agonizing moans rising in volume from within the prison walls ignited a rapid response. Shoulder to shoulder in a tight circle, all but Corvus closed their eyes. The Oracle recited a songline. Cold night air swirled around them.

The last thing Corvus saw was Toelachoc Prison, outlined in cool blue.

The moons and prison vanished. Dim light and the soft splash of water replaced them. Brie broke the circle and looked around. "I know where we are."

"The Temple of Nesune," Ari completed the thought.

The twins laughed.

Corvus guided WoNa to a bench beside the HeLew od Metis.

Tesi gave an extended hiss.

Henri pulled out her spectacles. "I have always wanted to visit the temple. Thank you, WoNa."

The Oracle smiled. "We needed to shelter for the night. Our enemies will watch for us at Eissua. I believe doing the unexpected is essential to foiling their plans. Please remember to stay on the walkway. The Abyss of the Dead is a most unpleasant place." She sighed. "I need to rest."

Brie unrolled her sleeping mat and laid it at WoNa's feet. "You can have my mat."

WoNa lay flat on her back, crossed her arms over her chest, and dropped into an immediate and deep sleep.

Ari looked down at her and whispered. "Wow, that was fast."

Brie linked her arm through her twin's. "Let's see what Aunt Henri and Corvus are up to."

They crossed to the Statues of Sinnttee, where their aunt knelt in front of the goddess Tutsasseen, cupped her hands to catch water from the quartz crystal bowl, and drank. Removing her spectacles, she held them beneath the stream of water. The lavender frames turned to violet, and the lenses thinned. Henri dried them and perched them on her nose.

"Ahhhhh. The Goddess of Wisdom—her gifts are many."

"What happened?" Ari demanded. "Can you see better?"

Henri took them off and tapped her chin. "Let's just say I can see differently, with more discernment—with the gift of wisdom." The spectacles disappeared into a hidden pocket in her kcalo. "And you, Corvus, what did Sorttince have to share?"

His response was somber. "I saw a vision, one I hope will come to pass. You'd better rest, Henri. Dawn will arrive all too soon."

Ari wheedled, "Come on, Corvus, tell us about your vision."

His dimple deepened. "It's good to have you back, Ari. My vision is just that—mine—private and personal."

Brie laughed at her twin's disappointed expression. "Let's get some sleep."

Ari flounced over to her pack and grabbed the mat. Henri had already materialized one for herself and lay on her side, staring at the statues. Corvus sat with his back against a bench, his eyes tracing the intricate pattern of the HeLew od Metis. Brie doubted he'd sleep much. She laid down next to her twin.

Ari squeezed her hand. "It's nice to be me for a change. Wonder how long I've got?" She yawned. "Love you, Brielle."

"Love you, too, Ari."

Soft breathing was her only answer. She studied the selenite faces of the statues, each one so unique in its own way. Manitullie, the god of youth and young adulthood, stared down at her. Corvus caught her eye and smiled. She moved nearer to her sister and closed her eyes. Dreams came quickly.

Corvus sat in the quiet of Nesune and reviewed his return to the world of men. As much as he loved his Karrew form, he felt a reluctance to return to it. He knew in his heart it was safe. The statue's vision had shown him flying in raven form. *Flying to the one I love.*

He blanked his mind and listened. Water trickled from the four bowls of Sinnttee, an occasional soft snore floated aloft, the easy breathing of sleep... nothing alarming. Restless energy left him wide awake. He got to his feet and made an agitated patrol of the area.

WoNa slept with the abandon of one who fears little. Henri, too, seemed unbothered. He stared down at the twins. They slept nose to nose, their fingers intertwined. Red curls intermingled and fell over fair, freckled cheeks. He bent and brushed a curl aside. *Enjoy your time together.* Straightening, he sighed. *I fear it will be short.*

Deep longing bubbled to the surface of his thoughts. *I'll come to you soon, love of my life.* He eased onto the end of a bench and fixed his gaze on the face of Sorttince. Ebony eyes stared back at him. *Introspection.* He slipped to the floor and sat cross-legged. With eyes closed, he slowed his breathing. It was time to discover what he had missed during his absence.

25

Myrrh

The Astican had fire in his eyes. Bared teeth ground together. The rosebud mouth burst open in a roar of denial that sent water sloshing against the fountain's sides.

Zugo started to speak. Almiralyn clamped a hand on his and shook her head. Staring in horror at the creature's image, no one else moved. A new picture formed.

The Mindeco, Rikell, backed away from the furious Davea. "What's made *you* so angry?"

The features twisted into a caricature of a child throwing a tantrum. "They have tricked us, imbecile."

The Mindeco glowered. "Tricked? What do you mean tricked—"

"The children never came this way, Rikell."

Rikell flinched at the sneered use of his name and watched Abarax rocket upward encased in a bolt of lightning, the motion of its great wings sweeping the dried dirt into small tornadoes of dust and debris.

Spitting and coughing, the Mindeco dropped to all fours and lumbered down a track. A strange flicker caught his eye. He sat back on his haunches and scanned the surrounding fields. They flickered, solidified, and then began to break apart. The sound of ocean surf made him glance over his shoulder. The fields were gone. He balanced on a ledge high above the sea. Standing slowly, he pressed his chest into the cliff and clung to the rough surface. His eye traced the height of the face. A shudder shook the entire length of his body.

Like a mammoth bird, the Astican swooped from the sky. Its cherubic features almost belied the rage in its eyes. "We're on the wrong side of the peninsula." It hovered above the cliff and roared, "I am Abarax, Astican of the Fire Pits of TreBlaya. I will find who did this. And I will send them to burn for eternity." With a low growl, it flew over the land toward Atkis.

Rikell, Mindeco of RewFaar, began the search for a way up the cliff.

Almiralyn waved her hand above the fountain. The water swirled into a new image.

Abarax's frustration and its fear that the children would escape over water pressed it to fly faster. It reached the opposite side of the Trinugian peninsula and the village of Atkis as the sun's light faded. Hidden in descending darkness, it prowled the streets, peeked in windows, listened to the whispers of men. Nothing suggested the children had been there, or how they might have arrived unseen.

Disappointment carried it to the crown of a nearby hill, where it folded its wings and marched back and forth. Rage boiling up from its innards spilled into the night. *Do I return for the Mindeco or leave the imbecile to his fate?* It paused and stared out to sea. *If the children have reached water and moved beyond my reach...* A howl formed in its throat. Choking it down, Abarax narrowed cherub-blue eyes and muttered under its breath. "I can't cross the smallest puddle in this form without incurring agonizing pain." It wet rosebud lips with the tip of its candy-pink tongue. "I can do so in a different shape, but I'll need a partner."

Exasperation fueled its flight back the way it had come. Everything in its makeup balked at accepting help from the Mindeco. The witless incapability of the creature to understand the magnitude of The MasTer's dream and the importance of the Human children to its success tempted it to turn back. The need for an emissary who could help it cross over water kept it on course.

At long last, it reached the high cliffs on the opposite shore and scoured them for its quarry. Fasfro's saffron light picked out the pathetic creature sitting on the ledge, legs dangling, long fingers gripping the rock-strewn edge to keep from falling.

Abarax swooped, taloned feet extended, gripped Rikell's shoulders, and lifted him kicking and screaming into the air. One look down and the Mindeco ceased his battle for what amounted to instant death and allowed the Davea to carry him inland over fields and hills.

Everyone gathered around the fountain saw the thoughts of the two creatures. Almiralyn scanned their faces and their emotional responses: Wilith's disbelief, Merrilea's fear of what was to come, Zugo's desire to be with his friends, Sparrow's concern for the children. Only Elae seemed unworried. Simple curiosity and the intuitive knowledge that The Unfolding would take care of the outcome were all that Almiralyn could detect.

Bursting with information, Kieel ran a mental list to make certain he remembered everything. Below him, the Mocendi preparing to take a break refocused his attention. The youngest had excused himself to fix a snack. No one seemed interested in leaving the apartment.

Patience. If you let yourself fret, you'll make a mistake. Patience. Scrunching lower, he waited for an opportunity to retreat to the top of the cornice.

Food arrived, and the group dispersed long enough to use the Personal Needs Space. They stacked plates with succulent treats and settled down to eat. Kieel's stomach growled. *Sure could use some proper food.* He shot upward. A tiny cloud of dust accompanied his touch down on the cornice nearest the door. Stifling a sneeze, he made himself as small as possible.

The Mocendi spoke little during their meal. The eldest man made a frequent scan of the room, frowned, and kept eating.

Kieel fretted. *Calm down and watch for your chance to leave.*

A disturbance in the hall started with a muffled expletive and grew louder and more angry. Thorlu wiped his mouth, threw his napkin on the table, and crossed to the door. The moment it opened, Kieel bolted through and crouched low on the door frame.

Two young men gave Thorlu a sheepish look. He glowered. "Take yourselves outside and get a bit of fresh air. Check out the roof, and don't interrupt us again."

"Yes, sir. We apologize. We—"

His comrade grabbed him by the arm and hurried him toward the stairs at the end of the hall. "Shut up. You'll get us in more trouble."

As Thorlu withdrew into the apartment, Kieel darted after the young men. With a sigh of relief, he arrived on the rooftop, and, hidden behind a vent, eavesdropped.

"By The MasTer's Reach, what made you pick a fight down there? You almost got us in real trouble. Those four are pretty nasty when riled."

"You picked the fight, not me. What made *you* do it?"

They looked at each other. At the same instant, understanding dawned on their faces. They sprinted down the stairs. Teva materialized, the rooftop door swung shut, and the lock clicked into place. "Hurry, Kieel. We only have moments."

She shifted to the dove. He mounted and wrapped an arm around her neck. They soared skyward until Kieel could no longer see which building they left behind. Banking in a wide circle, the dove carried them from one side of the city to the other. When it finally landed, they were in a park beneath a small bridge. Teva materialized and held out a hand.

Kieel touched down and tapped the palm with his walking stick. "I have learned more than I expected. We need—"

The crunch of gravel spun him around. Teva swore under her breath as a man stepped free of the trees.

"Teva Rivan. What a pleasure! It always surprises me how much you resemble your dear cousin." His tone was pleasant. The weapon in his hand was not.

"Hello, Thorlu Tangorra. Imagine meeting you here." Teva sounded calm and contained.

Kieel kept his fear in check.

Thorlu advanced forward. "Don't move, little man. It would be a shame to end the life of your lovely companion."

"I'm surprised you would pick on someone so much smaller than you, but then..." Teva's fingers curled around Kieel's legs. A quick flick of her wrist sent him hurtling upward. His wings caught the air, and he whizzed into foliage and branches, well-hidden amongst autumn-colored leaves.

Below, Thorlu hadn't moved. Teva's hand dropped to her side. Their eyes locked.

"Put the weapon away, Thorlu. Or are you afraid to pit your skills against mine?"

The blond Mocendi hesitated, appearing to struggle with some internal desire. His eyes never leaving Teva's face, he slid the weapon into a pocket. "I want the little man. I've never met a Nyti. He is one, correct?" His tone remained pleasant.

Teva remained immobile, but alert.

A sudden blur and Thorlu arrived by her side, his powerful hand gripping her upper arm. His nostrils flared only inches from hers. Arrogant eyes flashed with anger. "If you don't want her hurt, little man, you'd better show yourself."

"He's not a fool, Thorlu." A sweet smile curved her lips but left her eyes sapphire cool. "I suggest you remove your hand. It would be too bad to lose the use of it."

A cruel laugh and a tighter grip—the only response she received—made Kieel cringe. *I want to help. How?*

"Patience."

The telepathic voice was male, but not Thorlu's. Kieel crouched lower and peeked between leaves. Nothing moved. Not even the sparrow in the tree opposite continued its search for bugs. Life stood still.

Cruelty thinned Thorlu's full lips. "Brave words for a priestess."

Teva's smile vanished; her eyes hardened and narrowed.

The Mocendi's cry of pain pierced the air. He jerked his hand away from her arm and stared at the swathe of red blisters on the palm. "You little—" His other hand flew up and a bolt of sizzling light barely missed her cheek.

She dodged to one side. Thorlu lunged. She vanished and reappeared, gazing down at him from the bridge over the stream.

The Mocendi launched into the air and landed on the deserted bridge.

A mental probe stabbed through the trees. Kieel, his thoughts hidden, did not move. Thorlu picked up a pebble and pitched it into the stream.

"I'll find you, Teva Rivan. And when I do..." Only silence and empty air remained as The MasTer's Mocendi vanished.

Kieel scanned the park. *Do I move?*

"Patience." The masculine voice sounded once more in Kieel's mind.

The sparrow flew to a branch below him and gazed up at him from a single eye.

"Follow."

Kieel gripped his walking stick, doubts shouting in his mind. *What if it is an enemy? What if it's a trap?*

The sparrow chirped and soared upward.

Gathering his courage, he followed the small bird from tree to tree until it flew into the open and over the street. Kieel landed beneath a bench and examined the familiar building across the way. Relief made him giddy. "Calm down," he muttered. *If the enemy is watching—* He pursed his lips. *I'm little with wings. They'd be looking up.*

A patroller approached, paused at the corner, and glanced his direction. His heart skipped. *I know her.* Something fell from her hand. She set a bag on the curb and searched the ground. Without giving himself time to think, he dove in. A small object plunked in beside him, a hand gripped the bag, and the patroller's boots hit the street. She strode down the block and hesitated by the pass-through. He shot from the bag and flew in the door midway down. Once in the sub-level, he flew straight to Jordett and collapsed on the table, panting from an adrenaline rush that left him shaking.

The Major let out a breath. "Anada found you. Thank goodness."

Kieel laid his walking stick on the table and pressed his palms together. "Teva?"

Lenadi entered the room. "Teva is fine. She'll join us when she can. You did well, Kieel."

Kieel's questioning frown transformed into a smile. "You were the sparrow."

"I was. I am never far from Teva. For a moment, I thought you wouldn't follow me.

"I almost didn't."

The KcernFensian smiled. "You've had quite an adventure. How're you doing?"

Kieel sighed. "I'm fine, just thirsty, hungry, and exhausted. Lots to tell."

Jordett motioned a patroller forward. "Find something for our scout to eat. Bring water as well."

The patroller gave Kieel an interested look.

Kieel winked. The man grinned and hurried away.

Jeet walked from the Demrach Gateway into the Terces Wood. Overhead, dim rays of Myrrhinian sunlight filtered through the clouds and canopy. A breeze brushed his cheek. He breathed in the crispness of autumn, grateful for a reprieve from the desert heat.

Yuin, his ruby-red comrade, stepped into the clearing. "Oia lala di. It is good to see you, my comrade."

They touched foreheads and spoke in undertones for a short time. When they were done, Yuin conferred with two RewFaaran soldiers. The three merged back into concealment amongst fern and trees.

Jeet shaped a panther and trotted down the path, reviewing the events on DerTah as he made his way to meet with Mondago. The battle for the gateway was bloody, though short. The Tinpaca had lost good men.

At the edge of camp, Jeet resumed his natural form, announced himself to the soldier on guard, and walked toward the Tinpaca's tent, tail twitching and orange scales gleaming. He wondered as he passed soldiers, who continued to regard him with wary interest, if they realized how strange *they* looked to him. The thought made him ponder the variety of the Inner Universe.

A flash of emerald green at the entrance to Mondago's tent ended his musings.

"I'm glad you are unharmed, my brother." Stee followed him inside but remained near enough to the entrance to intercept problems.

Mondago sat with a cloud of cigar smoke dissipating around him. "Good to see you, Jeet. Join me. Stee?"

Stee touched his heart. "I prefer to keep watch."

The Tinpaca nodded. "What have you to report, Jeet?"

"Your men now control the gateway, but at a high cost." Jeet gave a brief description of the battle and finished with a tally of Mondago's troops. "Three dead and seven wounded. The remaining three are unharmed. Tesilend sustained a minor wound to the upper arm that One Man partially healed."

"And Nissasa's Brigade?"

Jeet reviewed the count. "Two escaped, three are unhurt, five are dead, and five are wounded, two of them seriously. One Man received word from Lorsedi that his troops secured the border. A good turning's work for everyone."

Mondago stared at the tip of his smoldering cigar. "Paid for with the blood of good men." He snubbed it out. "Any orders?"

"Hold the portals at this end. I'm to return and support Tesilend unless you require my services here."

"Go. Ask One Man to inform Lorsedi we've heard nothing from Jordett."

Jeet stood. "I will, sir. When the Major contacts you, send either Stee or Yuin through the portal. I will keep you informed as to any changes in DerTah."

The Tinpaca walked him to the edge of the trees. "Thank you, Jeet. May your turnings be long."

Jeet bowed. "And yours." He shifted to panther and padded through the forest shadows, enjoying the coolness until the portal came into view. Shaping his natural form, he made his farewells to Yuin and leapt into the shimmering vortex. The DerTahan heat hit him like a shock wave.

In vulture form, Stee soared over the Terces Wood, senses alert to changes in the forest below. As the sun dipped the edge of its blazing orb behind the Dojanack Mountains, he landed at Nemttachenn Tower, his Pentharian nostrils inhaling the invigorating freshness of autumn. Through an opening in the canopy, he observed a V of birds silhouetted against the first tinted clouds of dusk. The clearing seemed untouched by the events of the past several moon cycles.

A low rumble shattered the illusion of peace. Nemttachenn quaked on its foundation. Stee vanished. A falcon streaked upward. It perched on the ramparts, then swooped on soundless wings, following the descent of the interior staircase. Midway down, it came to rest, its raptor eyes searching.

At the center of the tower, Paisley stared transfixed at the fully visible Evolsefil Crystal. CheeTrann was nowhere to be seen. Again, the tower shook. Small stones tumbled down the stairs and rolled to a stop amidst scattered chess pieces.

Evolsefil began to hum. Within its crystalline center, the filmy shape of a male figure clutched something in his hand. Greedy, ice-blue eyes scoured the tower and came to rest on Paisley's inert form. The gossamer man stepped free of Evolsefil and waved a hand.

Paisley's eyes glazed over. His knees gave way. He collapsed in a heap at the tower's center.

The man knelt beside him and held a glowing fire-red crystal above his head. Paisley trembled and cried out. The apparition's cruel mouth twitched into a wicked smile.

Behind him, CheeTrann materialized, almost as tall as the tower. A black and amber jar appeared at his feet, its lid gleaming beside it. "Nissasa Rattori!"

The figure whirled around. Its glacial gaze traveled the enormous height of the Sentinel.

CheeTrann rumbled.

> *"Nissasa's essence come to me*
> *Into this vessel that you see*
> *Trapped within until the time*
> *I reverse this holding rhyme.*

As the Sentinel of Nemttachenn chanted, the quintessential being of Nissasa Rattori flowed into the jar.

"Lid!" CheeTrann ordered.

Stee flashed into his Pentharian form, grabbed the lid, and secured it in place.

CheeTrann shrunk to his normal size. "It is good to see you, Pentharian of ReTaw au Qa."

"And you, Sentinel of Myrrh."

Paisley moaned and pointed.

Inside the Evolsefil Crystal, an image of Nissasa's immobile physical form stood in the middle of a room. A gaunt, bald man in the purple-lined cape of a Mocendi DiMensioner snapped boney fingers in front of his lifeless eyes. The man circled the room, stopped in front of an armoire mirror, and stared. Whipping around, he grabbed Nissasa's right hand and uncurled the fisted fingers. Imprinted on the palm, the scarred impression of the Oracle Stone glowed red.

CheeTrann motioned Stee and Paisley away from the tower's center and faded.

The Mocendi paled. His mouth shaped the words, "The MasTer is always right."

Evolsefil's golden threads began to vibrate, diffusing the image until only the man's bulging eyes remained. The hum ceased. The threads stilled. The eyes melted into golden nuggets that exploded in a flash of light.

CheeTrann reappeared and spun a spell of invisibility around the crystal heart of Myrrh, whispered a chant to secure and bind it, and faced his companions.

"It is safe to come out."

Stee emerged, rubbing the jewel in his ear. "Another player. Do you know who?"

CheeTrann looked thoughtful. "One of The MasTer's personal Mocendi." He shrugged his massive shoulders.

Paisley stared at the jar. "Is Nissasa Rattori truly in there?"

"That which enlivens his body now resides in the charnockite jar. His physical body is wherever he was at the time he last used the Oracle Stone."

"Will he ever be whole again?" Stee asked.

"Only when the body and the quintessential being reunite. One of you must take the vessel to Almiralyn. Tell her what it contains. Tell her the Oracle Stone infused with ConDra's Fire is contained within. She will know what must be done."

Paisley folded his arms across his chest. "I can't leave you alone, CheeTrann."

Stee picked up the jar. "We can travel via the Intersect and be back before the moon rises."

CheeTrann began to grow faint. "Go. I will guard Evolsefil."

Paisley pressed full lips together and led the way to the Intersect entrance. At the bottom of the steps, he spoke the Key.

Stee grinned as they shot through the starlit sky. When they reached the Dojanack entrance to Meos, he glanced back. The stars in the Intersect had disappeared. Like a current of cold water, foreboding skimmed the surface of his emerald scales.

26

DerTah

Nomed and TheLise arrived in Atkis at middle-night. They assumed their Human forms and hiked through the woods to the small church on the outskirts of the village. From there they made their way to the only inn. Their arrival caused a flurry of activity that would have resulted in the eviction of a less important guest from the best rooms had TheLise not interfered.

At her behest, the innkeeper bowed them into a shabby suite, consisting of a cramped salon and sleeping space. "How," he asked, "could the Dreelas not send word ahead?"

Her assurance that she was not unhappy with him for the delay in finding accommodations or the rustic condition of the rooms only slightly assuaged his concern. Nomed noted the impatience beginning to creep into TheLise's expression. With a polite smile, he ushered the man into the hall and asked a few searching questions about strangers or strange happenings in the village. When nothing was forthcoming, he slipped him a gold coin, gave instructions for a meal and wine, and sent him scurrying down the hall.

TheLise met his return with a baleful expression.

He collapsed onto the chair next to hers. "Don't look daggers at me, Dreelas. I told you to stay home and take care of Roween."

The corner of her mouth twitched, but the vexation she was feeling kept it from manifesting into a smile. "I'm tired; Esán and friends aren't anywhere in the village; and I would love a glass of *good* Trinugian wine."

He looked at her with a you-poor-thing expression and relaxed back in his chair.

She bit her bottom lip. "Oh, Seyes, stop looking at me that way. You know me far too well. Did you order that ghastly man to bring food and drink?"

"Actually, I asked him rather nicely, in the hopes that he would provide us his best of each." He moved to the door. "We shall see if it worked."

Without waiting for the man to knock, Nomed pulled it wide. The innkeeper followed by two young men entered, one with a food laden tray, the other with a decanter of claret and two glasses.

A small table was laid and the young men bowed themselves from the room. The innkeeper hovered only long enough to ask if anything else was desired prior to slipping into the hall and shutting the door.

Nomed poured wine, inhaled its aroma, and handed TheLise a glass. "This should improve your mood, my dear."

She sniffed, sipped, and sighed. "Divine. Who would have thought a place of this ilk would have my favorite wine?"

"There isn't an inn in Trinuge that does not crave your patronage. I imagine the innkeeper stocked this in the unlikely event of your arrival on his doorstep." He held up his glass. "To you, my dear."

The food proved to be almost as good as the wine. TheLise relaxed and smiled. "Now all I need is a good night's sleep, and I'll be ready to go." She studied the room. "Can you stand another night on a sofa?"

"Long years of hiding and exploring, have given me the gift of sleep almost anywhere. You take the bed. I am happy to—"

A timid knock raised his eyebrow. A young boy waited in the hall twisting the corner of his jacket and looking as though he would like to bolt.

Nomed assumed a pleasant expression. "Yes?"

"I'm here to tell the Dreelas what I saw today."

"Come in." TheLise bathed the boy in a radiant smile. "What is your name, young man?"

"Tymn, my lady."

She set her glass on the table. "What is it you wish to share, Tymn?"

A frightened gaze flicked to the window. "This afternoon I saw a black dog lead Gregos Senndi into the alley. Didn't know the dog, so I followed. He met three boys a bit older 'an me. The dog sniffed my scent so I took myself off. Later, I saw a very scary creature prowling through town." He balled his hands in to fists and swallowed.

TheLise leaned closer. "Can you describe what you saw?"

He wiped his palms on the seat of his breeches. "Face was mostly in shadow, but it had the looked o' them baby angels ya see in church books. When I sneaked out back to get a better look..." A shiver shook his sturdy frame.

Nomed put a hand on his shoulder. "It's alright, Tymn. We won't let it hurt you. Go on."

"It sniffed the air and ran for the trees. It was big and had wings and smelled like a struck match tip. I hid fast and didn't tell anyone until the 'Keep' asked for you, my lady."

After several questions that netted little, Nomed said, almost as an afterthought, "Did it say anything?"

The boy's eye grew round. "Yes, sir. 'Abarax will return.' Does that mean it will come back to Atkis."

TheLise pressed a silver verlis into his hand. "Perhaps. If it does, hide and don't come out until it is gone. Understood?"

Tymn nodded and shoved the verlis in his pocket. "Thank you, Dreelas. Sir."

Nomed held the door ajar. The boy sidled through, trotted down the hallway, and clomped down the back stairs. Nomed returned to his seat and raised his eyebrow. "Astican?"

"Yes. I wonder where the Mindeco was?"

"Can't imagine. Hiding in the woods perhaps. You know the Astican were created from the burned flesh of a Human. Did you know water is their nemesis?"

"I didn't. And Abarax? Its or his name?"

"Most definitely *its* name. Astican are androgynous." Nomed grinned. "As so often is the case, knowing the proper name gives us a small amount of power over it."

TheLise yawned. "I can't think." She crossed to the tiny sleeping space off the salon and returned with a pillow and a much-used blanket. "Sleep well, Seyes. I feel certain tomorrow will be another adventure."

Nomed made a quiet circuit of the room, locking the door and one window. *Tomorrow we need to find Gregos Senndi and his brother.* Tymn had told them the brothers carried cargo throughout the Sea of Trinuge. *Find them, and we'll find Esán and his friends. The Unfolding escalates. Mindeco and Astican...* He shook his head. *Hopefully the water will slow them down.*

Plopping onto the couch, he sneezed as the dust resettled, spread the blanket over his tired body, and fell asleep almost before his head touched the lumpy pillow.

Henri lay in the quiet of Nesune Ruins listening to the sound of water and the soft snores of her companions. Corvus sat across from her, his chest rising and falling with the rhythm of his slow, even breathing. Beneath closed lids, his eyes jerked from side to side. His capture and healing had left their mark. Time to understand their impact would have to wait. His skills and the sacred knife and Remembering Stone were needed at Eissua. She doubted that he and the twins would be together in one place for much longer.

Grumbling to herself about the pains of aging, she used a bench to stabilize her ascent to standing. With a wave of her hand, the sleeping mat vanished. She smoothed her hair and looked at the twins, who even in sleep, radiated their delight at being together. Too soon, Ari would have to assume the form of Ira. They continued to be safer with her in that guise.

WoNa stirred. Tesi uncoiled its length from around her heart and slithered to her shoulder as she sat up and stretched.

"Good morning, Henri. I hope you slept well."

"Old bones don't appreciate stone floors but—"

WoNa put a finger to her lips. *"Wake the girls and Corvus. We have company approaching."*

Corvus shook the girls awake and hurried them to an alcove hidden behind the statues. Henri grabbed WoNa's sleeping mat and her hand. A glance back showed her an archway forming at the far end of the walkway.

"Blank your minds." WoNa's message was clear. Silence but for the faint trickle of water settled over the ruins

Corvus eyed the tall, lanky man striding along the white stone walkway. In his left hand, he held a rowan walking stick, the top of which glowed. Behind him the archway shrunk to the size of a small coin and squeezed into nothing.

"You can come out, Protector of Almiralyn," he called. "I won't harm you or your charges."

Corvus stepped from behind the statue Ceeconni and circumvented the HeLew od Metis.

The man smiled. "It is good to see you Corvus Karrew Castilym. You had me worried."

"I had me worried. It is good to be in your presence, Relevart, Doyen of Time. What brings you to Nesune?"

The older man straightened the slight stoop of his shoulders and rubbed his low back. "The time has come to raise the dead. We must be quick. The MasTer amasses his Mocendi from throughout the Inner Universe. It will take the combined powers of many to blunt their attack."

Henri and WoNa joined them. Ari and Brie held back, arms linked and identical faces questioning.

Relevart greeted the women with a charming smile. "Miss Henrietta, WoNadahem Mardree, the gift of you both in the same place is breathtaking."

Henri, placed her spectacles on her nose and looked him up and down. A laugh glinted in her magnified eyes. "It is a delight to be in the presence of the VarTerel."

WoNa offered her hand. "Thank goodness you have come."

He squeezed it and turned his attention to the twins.

"Come here, young ladies, and let me get a better look at you."

Ari, hands on her hips, stared up at him. "You're Wolloh's teacher. I've wanted to meet you."

"You're Ari, and I'm very happy to meet you. Hello, Brielle." His eyes gleamed. "Wolloh told me he had awakened your talents. They grow stronger. Do you notice anything different?"

Longing crept into Brie's expression. "I feel as though every cell in my body is changing to accommodate a person I don't know. Sometimes I'm so clear it leaves me breathless, others I am dazed and..." She bit her lip. "I know I can do things, but I'm afraid to try for fear I won't have the understanding to control the power."

Relevart placed a hand on her shoulder. "Patience, my dear. You are wise to move with caution. Your instincts are good. Let them guide you. Now, we must be gone from here. Join me in a circle."

Corvus stepped in between the twins. A picture flashed in his mind. The next instant they stood in the deep caverns of Eissua Oasis. Oil lamps placed around the space caught their shadows and tossed them up the walls. At the center, so close to death that it seemed to enshroud him, Wolloh reclined on a cot. A kcalo the color of the moon Calegri draped his still body. His blue-gray face showed no signs of life.

WoNa knelt by his head and rested a hand on his heart. Her startling eyes lifted to Relevart's face. He knelt opposite and placed a hand over hers.

"We are in time, WoNa, but we must work faster than either you or I would like." He became all business. "Brielle, at his head with the Stone of Remembering. Ari, please give Efillaeh to Corvus. His bloodline combined with the magic of Raven makes him the only one who can safely wield it."

Ari handed it hilt first and seemed at a loss.

Relevart smiled. "Your personal power is strong, young woman. Kneel at Wolloh's feet. Twin energy will balance his field as we work. Corvus, opposite Henrietta. Ari, hold his ankles. Brie, place the stone upon his brow. Corvus, your role is clear. Begin."

In the far distance, thunder rumbled. Flashes of purple light jumped from the knife to the reclining man. His back arched. His mouth rounded, emitting a deep gurgling groan. He hit the cot with a resounding smack. Corvus touched Efillaeh's tip to his forehead just below the Remembering Stone and drew it downward, outlining his aristocratic nose, the distorted curve of his mouth, his chin and neck. He traced a line from his breastbone and heart to his navel. Without lifting the tip of the knife, he continued its journey over the abdomen down the length of Wolloh's right leg, tapped the sole of his foot, transferred the knife to his left hand, tapped the left foot, and traced the leg to just below his navel.

The memory of Torgin kneeling beside Yaro, this same knife clutched in his hand, formed and dissolved. Corvus knelt and placed the tip of the knife between the two ribs.

> *"Efillaeh, the sacred blade,*
> *Pierce into the hidden glade*
> *Of time, no time, of in between*
> *Repair the life behind the screen.*
>
> *Open veins and open heart*
> *Open mind and all restart*
> *Refill the shell that has been hollow*
> *Return to life this man called Wolloh."*

With the final word, he drove the knife into the High DiMensioner's heart.

Time as Wolloh Espyro understood it ceased the moment Relevart touched his forehead and ushered him to this place. Constant twilight wrapped the world in which he wandered, a sole occupant stranded between now and then—life and death. In rare moments, he thought he sensed the presence of another. So fleeting were they that he filed them away in a mental folder labeled imagination, a folder packed with odd things like color and sound and taste and touch.

Concrete thought in this dimension felt like a diaphanous piece of silk tumbling in the wind. He would have found it almost impossible and immeasurably exhausting to describe the endless terrain through which he roamed. He stopped his treadmill pacing and gazed ahead. A vague memory took shape. *Wolloh the Wanderer. Have I always prowled the inner expanses of my psyche?* An irrevocable aspect of who he had once been whispered, *"Not so."*

The endless, silent trek continued—passing no time, arriving no place, losing more and more of himself with each step. One small spot in his heart refused to give in, refused to let go of the final threads holding him to time. So absorbed had he become in holding them firmly in hand, he almost missed the subtle changes occurring around him: cobalt blue creeping into his mind, purple washing over the surface of his skin, a tingling sensation trembling through his limbs. Again, he stopped.

Pressure on his brow opened a spigot of memories that poured into his mind with such force he fell to the ground, rolled onto his back, and immersed himself in each and every one—his mother's gentle face, his father's sadness when he, Laurent Davead Zuill DeLongeer, was banned from Roahymn, his escape on the planet of Persow, Stebben, Shu Chenaro, his mentor and training, and WoNa—memories of a lifetime encapsulated in an instant.

The vague and far off sound of chanting enlivened his belief that he had not ceased to be. A name filtered by distance floated through the expanse of in-between. Pain sliced through his heart. Pain beyond anything he had ever experienced opened veins and arteries, pounded through his body, and ended with his first deep, lung expanding breath since Relevart's touch.

Lead-heavy lids fought his need to see. When at last he won the battle, tears flowed down his cheeks. She knelt beside him, her lovely face too thin from worry, her exquisite, blind eyes overflowing with love. Slender fingers cradled his crippled hand.

Words refused to form. She touched his lips and whispered, "Rest. We will be here when you wake."

Relevart laid a hand on his forehead. "Sleep, Wolloh."

His gaze trailed from the VarTerel to the group at his feet. Red-haired twins, one on either side of Corvus, watched him with expectant smiles. He let his eyelids win. With a sigh, he slipped into a gentle, dreamless sleep.

E sán stood on *Melback's* deck beside Tamosh, inhaling sea air and grinning. *This is where I belong.* He almost laughed out loud from the sheer joy of water and moonlight and the cool wind ruffling his short hair. The first glimpse of the sea had left him speechless. His heart still sang with the delight of it. A yearning rooted deep and long hidden burst open like a blossoming rose. He had spent his life land-locked. Never had he expected to feel this level of love, wonder, and fascination for the sea.

He leaned on the aft railing and watched moonlight dance in the sailboat's wake. Atkis had long since passed from sight below the horizon. The boat skimmed Eschems Strait toward an anchorage on the far side of Bockettle Island. Tamosh told him they would spend at least a turning there, resting and training for the next leg.

He returned to the helm. Tamosh smiled down at him. "You look as though you have come home."

"I feel like the sea is part of me. I don't know why. I was raised in a mountain village on Thera."

Tamosh shot him an interested look. "You don't feel Theran to me."

Esán stared up at the moons and wondered where in the vastness of the Inner Universe his true home was. "My father and mother are from Tao Spirian, but I have never been there." The wind sprinkled the words over the sea.

"Ahhhhh. Now that would explain it. You have the sea in your veins. Tao Spirian is a world composed mostly of water. Myriads of islands cover its surface. The population is small and growing smaller. It is said that a man bearing dual Seeds of Carsilem will save the planet and its folk."

Esán's heartbeat quickened. "How do you know so much about Tao Spirian?"

"I love to learn. I spent the greater part of my life traveling from one library to another, here and abroad. Gregos thinks I am addled, but..." He shrugged. "I met a man in the library in TiCeed in the province of Geran who suggested I read up on Tao Spirian."

"Who was the man?"

"DerTah's High DiMensioner, Wolloh Espyro."

Gregos climbed on deck with Elf at his heels. "We'll take over. Go get some sleep."

Tamosh patted Esán on the back. "Go on."

Esán descended the two steps to the upper cabin and stood for a moment deep in thought. Behind him, Tamosh updated Gregos on the heading and the distance they'd traveled. The murmur of voices trailed off until only the sound of the wind and the slosh of the water against the boat could be heard. Tired, yet exhilarated, he stretched out on his berth.

Tamosh knows the High DiMensioner. It sure is a small Universe.

He yawned and rolled onto his side. With the rocking of the boat and slapping of the lines against the mast singing a lullaby, he drifted into dreaming.

The Astican set the Mindeco on the ground at the outskirts of Atkis and landed beside him.

Rikell rubbed his shoulders and shot it a nasty sneer. "Thought you didn't need me. But then, some say the Astican are afraid of water."

Abarax growled. "Not afraid. Water scalds the flesh from our bones when we are in this form. Don't worry, I'll shift and be right by your side." It sniffed the air. "I picked up the faint scent of the children earlier. They were in an alley near here. Didn't find another trace. We need to discover where they went, *and* we need a small, fast boat and the knowledge of how to use it. Let's find you a victim. What do you need?"

"A reprobate with the know-how to do the job, and a private place to take him over unobserved."

Abarax moved from one tree to the next with Rikell skulking behind. Midway through the village, it paused. The smell of stale ale and food permeated the air.

"Stay put, Mindeco. Be back as soon as I can. Don't let anyone see you, or we'll have panic to contend with."

Its shift was instantaneous. On rat feet, it scurried in the half-closed door of a bar and under a table, nose twitching. A foot wedged the inner door open. The rat sprinted through. Concealed beneath a low wooden bench, it probed the minds of the clientele.

A smallish man with a greedy gleam in his eye leaned on the end of the bar, a tankard in hand. The rat dodged from barroom to kitchen. The perfect victim had been found. After returning to its natural form, Abarax found Rikell hidden beneath a rickety staircase behind a pile of empty barrels and crouched beside him.

"Found our man. One of the best sailors in town. Also one of the most unpopular. Seems he's a bit of a skinflint. Name's Brubger. His boat is *Possession*. He's headed down to the dock later to check on her. You can take him there."

"How do you plan to be on the boat when you can't stand water?"

"I'm about to become your pet monkey. Don't make me shift on the water."

"And if I do?"

"I won't die alone."

Rikell kept his thoughts well-concealed as he followed the Astican's monkey form to the harbor. *Possession*, the only vessel tied to a dock some distance from the main waterfront, turned out to be a small, sleek single master with a keatwood deck and trim. Brubger might be stingy in other ways but not when it came to his boat.

While Abarax climbed to the top of a stack of boxes and barrels, ready to give the signal when Brubger appeared, Rikell wedged his large body behind a pile of fishing net and blown-glass floats. The Astican's close proximity made him edgy. The business of taking over a body needed his complete concentration. A wrong move could destroy the important neuro connections in the brain which would link him to the memories of the man. If he was to sail this boat, he'd need every memory he could acquire.

A small barrel rattled, toppled, and rolled to a stop. A short, sturdy man swore and dodged around it. He smoothed thinning, dark hair away from an unpleasant face and cast a cautious look over his shoulder. Close-set eyes narrowed. Pulling out a parchment packet, he peeked inside. A soft, gleeful guffaw accompanied its return to his pocket. With a cheerful whistle, he continued along the dock.

Rikell did a quick survey of the area. *All clear.* Stepping behind Brubger, he wrapped an arm around him, covered his mouth and nose with a hand, and pulled him hard against his chest. The man went limp.

Rikell steeled himself for immersion into the body. The initial pain of shrinking to Human size always left him gasping. He gulped a mouthful of air, shoved his protruding jaw against the man's occipital bone, and extended his neck forward. Everything blurred. Momentary confusion—the merge was complete.

He took a tentative step on rubbery legs, ran a hand through sparse hair, and blinked eyes that fought to focus. His new legs steadied. His mind cleared. He threw back his head and laughed. *A Human body!* Walking briskly toward the sailboat, he savored the taut-muscled power of his new acquisition. Pulling the packet from his pocket, he studied the bill of sale for a small farm. Memories told the rest of the tale. Brubger was a cheat and a scoundrel.

Possession nudged the jetty with her bow. A thrill ran through Rikell as he stopped to absorb the beauty of the small craft. Brubger adored her.

Abarax jumped aboard and stared at him from the top of the small cabin. For the briefest of moments, Rikell considered tossing the creature overboard. *"I won't die alone"* thrummed in his mind. With a shrug, he climbed onboard and began to acquaint himself with Brubger's personality and his boat.

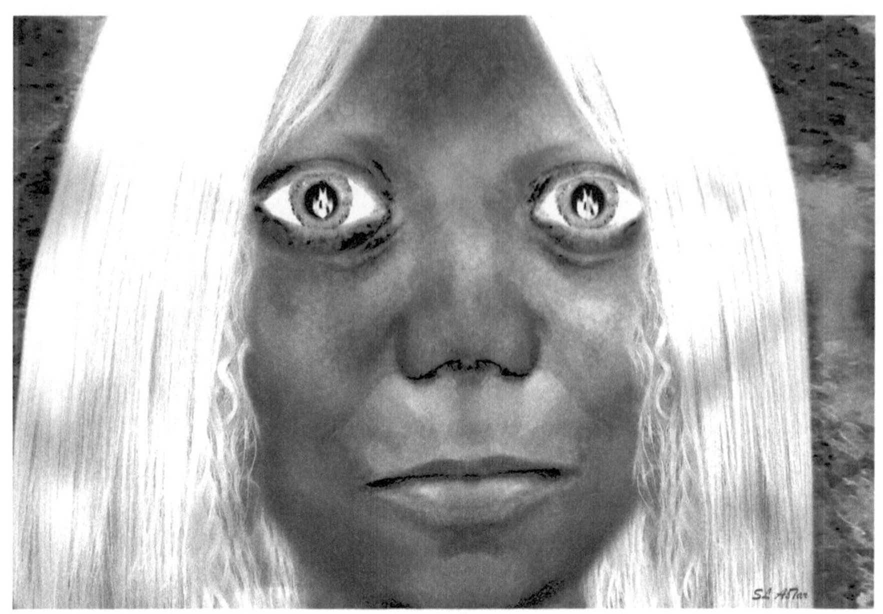

27
Myrrh

Stee and Paisley sat in a small room off the conference chamber in Meos. A young DeoNyte had met them at the Intersect entrance and taken them to Yookotay. The Redael had sent his assistant, Sitrio, to fetch Almiralyn. At Stee's urging, Yookotay had gone to seal the Intersect entrance. Now they waited.

Paisley tugged at his mustache. "What was the awful darkness in the Intersect? Do you think it followed us?"

Stee gazed at the charnockite jar sitting in the middle of the table. "I don't believe it had anything to do with us until we used the Intersect. It may have something to do with the jar's contents."

He stood as the Guardian of Myrrh entered the room. Paisley lumbered to his feet and flashed her a shy smile.

Almiralyn returned his smile with one that included them both. "Hello,

Paisley. Stee. I understand you've had quite an adventure." She relaxed into a chair. "Please sit and tell me what happened."

Stee signaled Paisley to begin.

"CheeTrann and I were playing chess. Evolsefil began t' hum and the invisibility charm t' fade. Before I could move, Nemttachenn started t' shake, the chess pieces flew t' the ground, and CheeTrann vanished. Things grew quiet. I started t' pick up the pieces. Something made me stare at the crystal. Nissasa's ice-blue eyes stared into mine. My instincts shouted danger, but I couldn't move. I think I might have stopped breathing."

Stee picked up the narrative from his entrance into the tower and finished with the darkness in the Intersect.

Almiralyn ran a finger around the lid of the jar. Her serious expression spoke volumes. "I can read Nissasa's essence. He is a servant, albeit against his will, of The MasTer. It's too bad his mother's greed placed him in jeopardy. He is not too bright and didn't tell The MasTer's emissary he possessed WoNa's Oracle Stone. A choice that I believe may precipitate his undoing." She glanced again at the jar. "He has infused the stone with the ConDra's fire and renamed it Souvitrico."

Paisley looked confused. "Isn't the stone in the jar?"

Almiralyn nodded. "It is."

He gave her a quizzical look. "Can you retrieve it?"

Her sapphire eyes narrowed as she gazed at the jar. "Only Nissasa can retrieve it."

"You mean we gotta find his body and bring it here?" Paisley rubbed his stubbly chin.

Stee grunted. "How long does he have before his body begins to decompose?"

"With the help of Vygel Vintrusie, The MasTer's Mocendi, maybe half a moon cycle. We must alert Nomed and TheLise, since they are the closest to his position. If they can get him to Shu Chenaro, One Man can take the jar there and help to reconnect Nissasa's essence with his body."

"What about the Intersect? Can we use it?" Stee asked.

"The cloud you saw is what the Mocendi call The MasTer's Reach." She shared a quick explanation and concluded with the supposition that it would dissipate in time. "My question is who released The Reach in the Intersect? Did Nissasa have an ampule with him? Was the cloud able to escape between the molecules of the jar? Or is there a Mocendi we are unaware of in Myrrh? We need the advice of Wolloh or Relevart. You can't use the Intersect until we discover the answers and are certain it's safe."

Stee fingered a dark green braid. "But we can leave via more conventional means, correct?"

She glanced from him to Paisley. "*You* can."

He smiled. "It would not be good to worry Tinpaca Mondago. He has enough to concern him. I will shape a vulture, and Paisley can ride on my back to Nemttachenn."

Paisley choked. "I'm too big. Never flown before. Might fall off..."

Stee touched a fisted hand to his heart. "My vulture form is strong and powerful. I will not let you fall."

Almiralyn stood. "I have a better idea. Sitrio will take you both to the Nervac Gateway. You can make the dimensional jump to DerTah, fill in One Man, and tell him I require his presence. The less we use telepathy between dimensions, the safer we are. When you're done, you can return through the portal to Nemttachenn."

Paisley stared at her. "You mean—me—to DerTah—another world."

Almiralyn's gaze remained steady. Her beautiful eyes held the hint of a smile.

He stopped sputtering. "Of course, my lady. Your will is my will."

She strode from the room and returned with Sitrio. "Lorsedi's men guard the gateway. Tell them I sent you. Be careful and stay alert. It appears The MasTer's influence grows stronger by the turning."

She flashed from view.

Paisley sighed. "I like her better as Mira."

Sitrio escorted them to the portal, taught them the Key for DerTah, and stepped back.

Stee put a hand on Paisley's arm. "Are you ready?"

"Ah, what's it like, flying between dimensions?"

"Like nothing else in the Universe. On three, run and jump into the vortex. Ready?"

Paisley clenched his fists. "Ready."

Stee counted.

Velvet blackness engulfed Paisley, stifling sensation and sight. He gulped a soundless breath and blinked against the darkness. The next instant vibrant bands of color—greens, yellows, reds, and blues—streaked past him on all sides. Like a Ria Train, he shot forward. Currents of air tugged at his hair and clothing. A small circle of white light appeared in the distance and grew bigger and bigger. Increased speed cannoned him toward it, blasted him through it, and dumped him in red-orange sand under a burgundy sky studded with stars. On the far horizon, the crested curve of a saffron moon washed the desert sands with a warm glow. The chill in the air sent gooseflesh skipping over his skin.

Stee's lizard-like eyes observed him with interest. "How was your first jump?"

"My what? Oh...jump." He grinned. "My heart's pounding like a smithy's hammer. It was good." He laughed. "It was great!"

Stee climbed to his feet and offered a hand. Paisley gripped it. He arrived at standing as two soldiers appeared, drawn weapons glowing in the moon's light. Their expressions were cold and grim.

Stee took the lead. "Almiralyn sent us with a message for One Man. I am Stee. My companion is Paisley. You know my comrade, Jeet."

The two conferred, lowered their weapons, and motioned them to follow.

The trek over the sand left Paisley panting and trailing behind. *Sure hope we get there soon.* He mopped the beginnings of sweat from his brow and picked up his pace. As he rounded a dune, tents silhouetted against firelight and moonbeams came into view. His escort stopped to speak with a soldier, who looked them up and down. The portal guards plodded back the way they had come. The new man shepherded them through the camp to a tent bearing the flag of RewFaar.

"Wait here." He ducked inside. Voices murmured. He reappeared. "The Grantese will see you."

Stee preceded Paisley. Jeet and the Grantese both rose.

Tesilend greeted them with a hearty hello. "You have news?" He indicated two camp stools. "Please take a seat."

Stee flipped his tail to one side and sat. "I thought One Man was with you."

The Grantese nodded. "He's on patrol. We're expecting him any time now." He smiled at Paisley. "Jeet tells me this is your first time off Myrrh. How'd you like your first jump?"

Paisley felt his cheeks grow warm. He swallowed his natural shyness and answered. "Never experienced anythin' like it. Hope t' do it again."

Tesilend grew serious. "I have no doubt you will. What brings you to DerTah?"

Stee began to describe what had occurred in the tower. Paisley's attention wandered. *I'm on another planet—in the desert—in a RewFaaran camp.* He pinched his arm to wake himself up from the unbelievable dream. *I'm really here.*

Jordett excused himself for a few moments of private thought. Kieel had eaten his fill, then proceeded to provide details regarding The MasTer's plan for Thera. He continued to be amazed at the small man's ability to assimilate detail, analyze it, distill it down to the essentials, and present it.

Mocendi were being amassed from throughout the Inner Universe. They would take up positions on Thera with the largest contingent in Idronatti. As soon as they established control, the portal Almiralyn had shut down upon her arrival in Myrrh—one with an anchor point in her garden and a destination point in the inner sanctum of the Five Towers—would be reopened. Once Mocendi controlled both dimensions, Thera's surface would be prepared for The MasTer and the League. All life would be destroyed. The centralized position of Clenaba Rolas, Thera's solar system, would provide the Mocendi with access to a majority of galaxies in the Inner Universe. That and the wealth of information stored within Myrrh's geological composition and its Galactic Library would give The MasTer a strangle hold that would be almost impossible to break.

Jordett tried unsuccessfully to suppress a shiver. *Well, that's for the future. What matters now is removing Nissasa's Brigade from power. Once this objective is accomplished, the next will be to shore up the city against a Mocendi attack. Don't know quite how to go about that, but I imagine the KcernFensians will.*

Teva's appearance at his side ended his inner discourse and his solitude.

"Sorry to interrupt, but we need a decision. Do we call off the offensive and reschedule or proceed."

Jordett reviewed his teams and the plan they had laid out. "We have seven teams and seven objectives." He ticked them off on his fingers. "Team 1...secure and lock down the Dissemination Center. Team 2...secure the Transit Center. Team 3...secure the perimeter of the Five Towers. Team 4, secure Tower One and find the Five Fathers. Teams 5, 6, and 7...secure Towers Two through Five. All teams but number 7 have a KcernFensian leader. Kieel will fill the gap as our go between."

Teva nodded her approval.

Jordett squared his shoulders. "We go as planned. Give the signal to take up positions and await the go." He studied her face as she made telepathic contact with the team leaders. The resemblance to Almiralyn was uncanny. *Give her blonde hair and brows and lighten her complexion—*

She caught his eye. "Done."

Walking into the sub-level, Jordett motioned his two patrollers to join them. "It's time. Tower One is our objective. Once the perimeter is secured, move in. It's full light, so take care. Kieel took a quick look around. Guards have been posted at all entrances. Other than that, we don't know for certain what we're going to find inside the compound."

The patrollers gathered their equipment, slipped from the sub-level, and took up their assigned positions. Jordett, Kieel, and Teva left last.

The streets surrounding the Five Towers had been constructed like the spokes of a wheel. Six streets intersected with Tower Avenue, the street that encircled the compound. Two of the spokes housed the Transit and Dissemination Centers. Seven teams skulked the length of the mid-block pass-throughs that brought them to the avenue and their assigned vantage points. Leaders checked in. Team 1 was given the order to go. No one else would move until the Dissemination Center was secure.

Sweat trickled down the back of Jordett's neck. The waiting was the hardest, the waiting *and* the not knowing.

Teva closed her eyes. "I'm receiving a vague image from Falind. They've bypassed the exterior guard and entered the building. I can't see. She must be occupied. Wait. They've reached the control center. Holins enters and hands the Grid Keeper a note. He follows her into the corridor. Sagus is talking to him. A RewFaaran steps into the hall. Grodan snaps to attention. Falind attacks from behind." Teva frowned. "Lost the connection."

Jordett shook his head. "How do you do that?"

"It took long sun cycles of practice."

"I thought you had the gift naturally."

"One of the first things you learn is that a gift has to be tamed, trained, and honed to perfection or it's worthless. Hold on." Her eyebrows bridged her nose, her eyes closed in concentration. Air whistled from her mouth in a satisfied exhale. "It's done. They have control. The Grid Keeper is onboard and his men with Grodan are off to secure the exterior of the building."

"Alright, Teams 2 and 3, go." Jordett turned to his small group. "We're next."

"They're away." Teva grinned.

Jordett looked up at the Theran sky. *Sure hope they're as successful.*

Almiralyn materialized in the Cave of Canedari and stared at the spot usually occupied by Evolsefil. The Unfolding moved toward its conclusion. She and her comrades had much to accomplish in order to prepare the way for the crystal's return. She hurried down the Hall of Priestesses and entered the Reading Room. Wilith, Zugo, and Merrilea gathered in a group at the far end. Sparrow and Elae, at her request, had remained with Elcaro's Eye.

Zugo sprinted the length of the room. "What happened, Almiralyn? Why did my father send for you?"

She indicated Veersuni. "Please ask Sparrow and Elae to join us."

Wilith shook his head as Zugo dashed into the sanctuary. "The exuberance of youth is exhausting."

Merrilea's sad, gray eyes followed the young DeoNyte. "Esán was ill for so long I had almost forgotten." She sighed. "I wonder how he is—where he is?"

Sparrow and Elae entered the Reading Room with Zugo urging them to hurry. They clustered around Almiralyn. After a quick explanation of Stee and Paisley's visit, she finished with a statement. "We need more information."

Wilith and Elae said in unison, "I'll go."

Merrilea met Almiralyn's steady gaze. "I want to see what the fountain has to share, but I'm close to something, something that might help Renn. I'd like to continue my research."

Zugo's silence and stubborn expression spoke louder than words.

Almiralyn kept her face neutral. "I believe Zugo and Sparrow should come with me. I'll check in with you when I can."

Elae hurried from the room. Wilith and Merrilea, deep in conversation, followed at a slower pace.

Zugo relaxed and grinned. "Thanks, Almiralyn. I promise not to be in the way."

"You aren't in the way. If I tell you to leave, don't question. Just go."

He ran ahead. Sparrow walked beside her.

"You're quiet, Sparrow. Is something amiss?"

"Nothing I can put my finger on. While you were gone, something about the fountain changed. I checked the wards and they seemed solid." She shrugged. "I don't know—"

"Help m—" Zugo's terror-saturated yell tore throughout the Reading Room.

Almiralyn gripped Sparrow's arm. "Shields now." Her own shot up around her.

The scene in Veersuni sent shock waves racing through her body.

Singed velvet curtains hung limp and smoking. The stained-glass window glowed red. The fountain's bowl bore the blackened prints of a hand. On the floor beside it, a crumpled heap of scorched white fur lay half in and half out of a pool of bloodied water.

Sparrow gasped.

Almiralyn's warning glance silenced her. *I need your help.* She hoped her telepathic message was clear.

Sparrow stepped up beside her and grasped her hand. *Protect Z.*

Almiralyn nodded. Together they wrapped the injured body of Yookotay's son in a blanket of light. It rose above the floor and floated toward them. Slow, steady backward steps took them into the Reading Room. They lowered the unconscious DeoNyte to the floor.

Almiralyn touched Sparrow's arm. *"Get Merrilea."*

Sparrow sprinted for the research level.

One long stride carried Almiralyn to the sanctuary door. She closed and sealed it. Nothing would be able to leave or enter from any entrance including the fountain. If The MasTer's essence still infused Elcaro's Eye, he would be trapped.

Kneeling beside Zugo, she laid a hand on his matted side. A lift and fall, so shallow it was almost imperceptible, eased her fear.

Merrilea with Sparrow, Wilith, and Elae burst into the room. Merrilea knelt, her eyes on Zugo. "You moved him?"

"Telekinesis. He has not been physically touched."

Merrilea ran gentle fingers over his body. "No broken bones, at least not that I can feel. Roll him onto his back. Gently."

Merrilea pressed her lips together. Almiralyn heard Sparrow's cry of dismay. Wilith made no sound, only put an arm around the twins' mother.

"Oh, Zugo." Elae's eyes brimmed with tears.

The fur had been burned from his chest. The wrist and palm of one hand blazed red with burned flesh and blisters. His face, contorted into a grimace of pain, looked gray.

Almiralyn allowed herself a moment of anger, then focused. "Elae, take Merrilea with you and prepare Ephos, our healing room. Ask for assistance from the high priestess. Wilith will bring Zugo there as soon as you're ready. Sparrow, stay with him. I will tell Yookotay what has happened and bring Owae. No one approaches Veersuni."

One thought teleported her to Yookotay's chambers in Meos. A worried Owae waited for her with medicine bag in hand. The ancient healer led her straight to the ReDael.

Yookotay's expression told little of his feelings as he listened to Almiralyn's description of his son's injuries. When she was done, he sent the young female outside his door to find Zugo's mother, closed the door, and faced her. "Will he live?"

"I believe so. His hand is burned badly. Efillaeh can heal it once Ari returns to Myrrh."

"And when might that be?" His pale eyes searched her face.

"I don't know, Yookotay. I am so sorry. I should have kept him by me."

The ReDael sighed. "He knew he was not to be in Veersuni alone, and yet he chose to ignore it. Life's lessons are not always easy. What can I do to help with Veersuni?"

"Have you heard anything from One Man? I need him here."

"I will see what I can discover."

A DeoNyte female swept into the room. Silky white fur framed delicate features. "Zugo?"

"Lisseta." Yookotay put an arm around her. In a grave tone, he shared Almiralyn's news. "The Guardian will take you to him. He'll remain in Canedari's Ephos room until he is healed. I'll have your things brought to you."

The soft, blue eyes that met Almiralyn's were calm. "Please, my lady, take me to my son." She held out her hand.

Almiralyn took it and slid an arm around Owae's waist. Both women exclaimed as Yookotay's chamber disappeared and the walls of the Cave of Canedari closed in around them. Almiralyn led the way through the double doors to the Hall of Priestesses. Elae ushered the two women into Ephos.

Sparrow stepped into the hall and closed the door. Concern deepened the fine lines around her eyes. "He hasn't regained consciousness. Owae and Merrilea don't know why. Do you think you can help?"

"That will depend on what transpired at the fountain."

"What do we *do* about Veersuni?"

"I've sent a message to One Man. When he gets here, we'll decide the best course to follow. Right now, we need Zugo to wake up and tell us what happened."

The door opened. Elae stepped into the hall with Wilith. Her face was drawn and worried. "He's awake but refuses to open his eyes. I think he might calm down if he hears your voice, Almiralyn. Wilith and I are going to continue our research. The more we know, the better our chances of putting a stop to The MasTer."

"Thank you. Don't discount the importance of even the tiniest detail."

Their receding footsteps escorted her into the room. Sparrow stationed herself just inside the door. Lisseta stood at the foot of the bed, watching Owae and Merrilea minister to her son. They stepped aside as Almiralyn approached.

Zugo lay on white sheets. The burns on his hand and chest had been cleansed. He tossed and turned and muttered.

"He refuses to open his eyes," Lisseta whispered. "I don't understand what he is saying."

"I believe he's speaking TreBlayan. Owae, Merrilea, and Lisseta, please leave us. I'll call if I need anything. Sparrow, please stay."

Lisseta paused by the door. "Take care of him, Almiralyn. He is our only child."

"I promise. Wait outside."

When the door closed, she beckoned Sparrow forward and spoke in an undertone. "Secure your wards. Be prepared to put an additional shield around me if I need one." She took a moment to shield herself and turned back to the bed. "Zugo, it's Almiralyn. Can you hear me?"

The tossing ceased. Pale eyes flew open. The dilated pupils encircled reflected fire. The mouth twisted into a malicious grin.

Almiralyn motioned Sparrow back and made a slow circuit of the bed.

Zugo's fiery gaze followed her every move. Jumbled TreBlayan spilled from cracked lips. The tirade paused. Zugo thrashed his head from side to side, stopped, and looked straight at her. "Help me." The words were clear and desperate.

Almiralyn put a finger to her lips.

The wicked grin returned. The fire in his eyes grew brighter. A howl of pain ripped through Ephos. His body went flaccid. Consciousness fled.

Nestled in a small circle of burned fur, the tiniest spark of light blinked and was gone. An examination of the area showed her a tiny zigzagged arrow protruding from his temple. She beckoned Sparrow to her side.

Sparrow frowned. *"What do we do?"*

"Remove it. Very carefully." Almiralyn loosened a thread from the hem of her shirt and pulled it free. Forming a loop at one end, she tied a slip knot and whispered,

> *"This thread is strong and will not burn*
> *It carries nothing that can be learned*
> *Make it fast to lightning bolt*
> *Like a feather let it molt."*

The thread hovered above the tiny protrusion. She looped it over the end of the zigzag and pulled it tight. A gentle tug—nothing. With the second, the thread grew taut. The zigzag resisted. She continued to pull. A slight movement... She jerked the thread. The zigzag shot free, flashed bright white, and vanished.

Zugo groaned. Blood-shot eyes fluttered open. Fire no longer blazed in his pupils. He licked his dry lips. A spasmed cough became a moan of pain.

Almiralyn moved closer. "Zugo?"

He took a shaky breath. "I'm so sorry, Almiralyn. I..."

"Shhhh." She laid a cool hand on his brow.

His eyes closed.

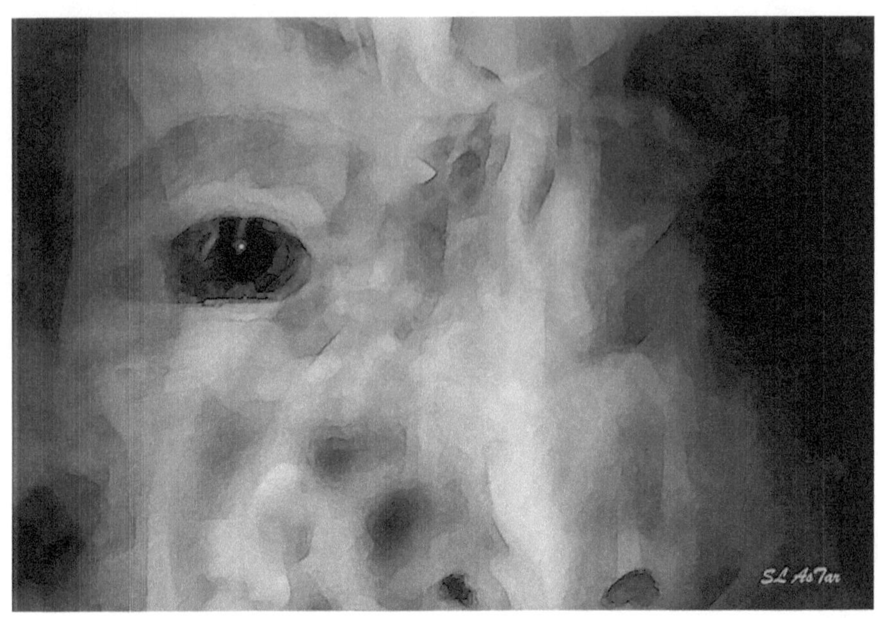

28

DerTah

The whispered breeze of an exhaled breath woke Wolloh from a deep and restful sleep. He opened his eyes to a sight which made his heart leap. WoNa slept beside him. Hungry for the sight of her, he propped his head on an elbow and drank in her beauty—the wild, red hair, the high cheekbones, the child-like innocence of her face in repose.

She rolled from her back to her side. A smile spread from her lips to her magnificent eyes. "You're awake."

"I am, dear WoNa." He took her hand and kissed the palm before touching it to his disfigured cheek.

Gentle fingers searched the terrain of his face—touched his chin, his forehead, his feathered eyebrow—and came to rest on his hair.

Her dreamy smile clung to sleep. She yawned and sat up. "They tell me your hair has turned pure white. I wish I could see." Her finger trailed over his ear to his shoulder and came to rest.

He sat and pulled her to him. "I'm not surprised. I have been wandering in Surazal, where the living rarely go."

She nestled closer. "What was Surazal like?"

"Bleak and dreary and deathly quiet. Even the tread of my feet was silent. I seemed to walk forever. In rare moments, I thought you might be near."

Footsteps and the tap of a walking staff stopped by his resting place. "She only left your side to search for Karrew." Relevart gazed down at him. "You are looking well. How do you feel?"

Wolloh savored cool inhaled air and smiled. "I feel good. Thank you for bringing me back."

"I had lots of help."

WoNa turned in his arms and pressed a hand to his heart. "Corvus worked his particular magic."

"Ahhhhh. I remember. The time of reawakening carried much pain." He looked at his mentor. "I am whole?"

"I believe you will discover you are better than whole."

"My hair is white?"

Relevart tapped the crystal within the intertwining rowan. The leaves withdrew, the crystal gleamed. He held it out for him to see. A reflection shimmered into focus. "You have fully integrated the osprey."

Wolloh glanced at his crippled hand.

"The physical damage will always be a reminder of that younger, less mature self. You will discover changes in your inner being and the powers you steward in this life." Once again, he touched the crystal. Rowan sprigs encapsulated it. "I understand you would like time with WoNa, but others are eager to see you."

Relevart guided WoNa to a chair. Wolloh sat on the edge of the cot. A giggle in the outer cave preceded Brie and Ari. Corvus and Henri followed. Soon, the underground cavern echoed with good cheer. Wolloh absorbed the sense of wellbeing overflowing around him with a bemused smile. The twins stayed close together, starting and finishing each other's sentences. Corvus conferred with Relevart. Henri and WoNa lavished attention on him until he thought he would drown in it. He was relieved when Relevart rapped his staff on the floor and drew the attention his direction.

"Although we would like to forget what is occurring outside these walls, we cannot." He moved to WoNa's side and laid a hand on her shoulder. "I fear, WoNadahem Mardree, that The Unfolding demands we each fulfill our destinies, and that means we must leave you."

Tesi appeared at the neck of her kcalo and hissed a series of short staccato sounds. WoNa smiled. "We must do what we must do. Tesi reminds me it is time I return my attention to the Atrilaasu and the needs of the tribe."

Relevart faced the twins.

Brie's brown eyes filled with tears. "It's time, isn't it?"

"It is."

Ari hugged her. "Love you, sis." She stepped back, shook her red curls back from her face, and bent to plant a kiss on WoNa's cheek.

Ira straightened and ran a hand over short brown hair. He looked from one person to the next until his startling blue eyes came to rest on Wolloh. "You're back."

"I am." He smiled. "Thank you."

Relevart held his staff high. Within the rowan cocoon, the Froetise Crystal glowed. He rapped on the ground one time. Ira and Brie vanished. He looked at Corvus. "I send you where you are most needed. Take care." Another brisk tap and Corvus flashed from sight.

Henri peered at him over her spectacles. "You have a job for me, I presume."

"I do, Henrietta. Do not despair. Your adventures are not yet over." He bowed and touched the crystal to her cheek. She melted away.

Nodding at Wolloh, he said, "We must go as well."

Wolloh squeezed WoNa's hand. "I'll return when I can."

A clipped rap, rap, rap faded. He stood beside Relevart in the vastness of Mittkeer.

Esán lay on his narrow berth. Gusting wind rocked *Melback*, pushing her one way, then the other. The calm in between settled her into a gentle sway; the gust rebuilding set her rocking again. He loved the sounds of the wind and the rippled slap of water against the hull. A sense of power he had never experienced quickened the blood in his veins. His heart throbbed to the rhythm of the tides. For the first time in his life, he felt whole and truly alive. A sigh akin to an ocean breeze whispered through him.

Another gust of wind set the boat dancing on her anchor chain. He put his hands behind his head and stared out the porthole. Silhouetted landscape slid by one way, hesitated, and reversed. Lunule, DerTah's crescent moon, framed momentarily in the porthole's roundness, delighted him. He smiled to himself and contemplated his time onboard *Melback*.

After leaving Atkis, Gregos had taken them on a circuitous route that lasted the full turning. Training had begun the moment the sun peaked the horizon and continued long after they had dropped anchor behind Bockettle Island where, Tamosh explained, *Melback* was well-hidden, but they could detect an approaching vessel from the watch-perch at the top of the mainmast.

Gregos' exacting expectations left the inexperienced crew of *Melback* exhausted, elated, and sore. Esán had never seen Torgin so happy. His time with Tamosh learning to navigate left him simmering with excitement. Even Desirol seemed to forget the Mindeco and immersed himself in learning new skills.

A wind gust grabbed the sailboat and swung her to port. Esán smiled. *Starboard, port, aft, stern, bow—the terminology seems familiar and comforting. The only thing that would make the time better...Brielle's presence on board.* He caught the thought and held it close. *Why do I miss her so much?* Closing his eyes, he called up her image and sighed.

A hand touched his arm. His eyes flew open and widened.

"Hi." Brie, grinning down at him, made his heart sing.

Ira stood behind her, examining his new surroundings. "Never been on a boat. What's she called?"

The door to the V-berth swung open. The boat's captain stepped into the galley with Tamosh yawning behind him. "She's *Melback*. 'Bout time ya got here. I'm Gregos. This is my brother Tamosh. You?"

"Ira, sir."

"I'm Brielle AsTar." Brie offered a hand, her expression quizzical. "But you already knew that."

He placed his palm on hers. "I did, young lady. Wolloh told me you were a smart one. Good to have ya both aboard."

Shyllee's excited bark broke his commanding gaze. Brie blinked.

The dog's wagging tail and sniffing nose announced her interest in the new arrivals. Ira held out a hand. Shyllee sat and offered a black and tan paw.

Ira grinned and shook it. "Great dog."

Brie knelt and received a lick on the cheek. Laughing, she scratched the dog's ears, ran a hand over her back, and gave her a quick hug.

Torgin stuck his head in the upper hatch. "What's all the— Brie! Ira!" He clattered down the steps. "How'd you two get here?"

Gregos cleared his throat. "Torgin Whalend, ya've got the watch. Ya'd best get back to doin' your job, boy."

"Yes, sir." Color tinted his brown cheeks as he did an about face and ducked out the hatch to rejoin Elf, his watch partner.

Gregos waved Tamosh back to the V-berth. "Esán will help ya settle in. Best get some sleep. We set sail with the rising sun." The door closed behind him.

On the berth above Esán, Desirol yawned and ogled the new arrivals. "Where'd you two come from?"

"Brie'll tell ya." Ira rubbed Shyllee's head. "Come on, girl, let's go talk to Torgin."

Shyllee dashed ahead of him through the open hatch.

Esán patted his bedroll. "Sit down, Brielle, and tell us where you went. We want to hear everything."

Torgin returned to his post on deck, glad the winds had grown quiet, and watched two moons slip from one cloud to the next. Tri-Nular had passed with Fasfro's disappearance below the horizon, its warm glow diminishing as Calegri's blue light cooled the sky. *How did Brie and Ira get here? What's happening on Thera? He frowned. Where is my father, and how is Mother coping?* Shyllee's cold nose nuzzling his hand reminded him of Buster. He rubbed her ears and let the sad memory fade. She sat, her eyes bright and her ears alert.

Ira walked up beside them. "This is some craft. I've only seen a sailboat in a book. What's she like underway?"

Torgin grinned. "She's amazing. Sailing is unlike anything I have ever experienced." He explained what he'd been learning. "Gregos is a taskmaster.

When he gives an order, he expects an immediate response. Tamosh is demanding too, but less brusque." He shrugged. "Tell me what happened to you. One minute you were next to me, and the next you were gone."

"Relevart teleported me to a place called Mittkeer." Ira shivered. "Made me pretty sick. When he sent me to Toelachoc Prison, I felt better."

Torgin looked up a rope ladder that stretched from the top of the railing all the way to the watch-perch. Elf waved and gave him an all-clear sign. "I have to do a deck-check." He patted Shyllee's head. "Stay, Shyllee. Come on, Ira. I'll teach you a few things; then you can tell me all about the prison."

Brie lay on Torgin's bedroll, her head spinning. Gregos' palm on hers had left her with all the information she would need to be part of the *Melback's* crew and more. She had experienced mind links with Wolloh and WoNa. Both had been subtle. Perhaps because Gregos was a stranger, she felt taken aback. A deep breath calmed her racing thoughts. Reviewing the information he'd shared—chart reading, sailing skills, including how to anchor, which sails to use for what type of wind, how to tack, how to come about—left her silent and sober. *Why do I need to know so much?*

She pulled the blanket up under her chin and tried to sleep. When her eyes remained wide open and her thoughts continued their chaotic tumble, she made her way to the hatch. Torgin and Ira stood by the mizzen-mast, discussing how the compass worked. The boy name Elf looked down at her from his perch near the top of the mast. She smiled and waved. He nodded and returned his attention to the sea. A gentle mind touch left her thoughtful. A Mocendi had damaged Elf's vocal cords when he refused to become a disciple of The MasTer. Gregos and Tamosh had rescued him and given him a home.

Esán came up behind her. "Time for the watch to change." He called softly over his shoulder. "Let's go, Des. We're up."

Brie glanced in Desirol's direction. "How's he doing?"

"When he's busy, he's alright; when he isn't, he withdraws. The Mindeco's pull is pretty strong." Esán sighed. "I only hope Rikell isn't as aware of Des as Des is of Rikell."

A mutter of frustration preceded the subject of their conversation up the galley steps. "Lost my boot. Found it." He smoothed his borrowed tunic. "Feel better when I have 'em on. They seem to ground me."

Shyllee met Esán as he stepped on the deck. "Hey, girl, you gonna take the watch with me?" Tail wagging, she settled on her favorite seat at the stern. Esán stuck his head in the cabin. "Come on, Des, Torgin and Elf are waiting. Brie, you can have my bed."

She tugged at a curl. "Mind if I tag along?"

He grinned his delight and took her hand. "It's Des' turn on the watch-perch, so I can show you around."

They made the exchange. Torgin hugged her. "Ira told me everything." A yawn left his eyes watering. "Gotta get some rest."

Elf descended from the watch-perch, nodded to Desirol, and crossed the deck. He smiled at Brie. *"I am glad—"*

Shyllee's growl rumbled through the night.

Elf's sad dark eyes swung from Brie's face to sweep the sea. An image filled her mind. A small sailboat prepared to round the end of the island.

Esán spun around, his eyes squinting into the darkness. He gave Elf a push. "Go tell—"

"He already did." Gregos and Tamosh stepped out into the pale light of Lunule's creamy crescent.

Nomed tossed and turned on the uncomfortable couch in the inn and forced himself to surface from a troubled sleep. Dreams sent him swooping in owl form over one narrow ocean strait after the other in pursuit of what he thought was a boat carrying Esán. A glimpse of his slender nephew standing on the deck of a two-masted sailing vessel tempted him to follow, but no matter how fast he flew, he could never quite catch up.

He threw the tattered blanket aside, pushed his tired body to sitting, and stiffened. A sleeping man sprawled in the only chair in the room, his chin on his chest, dark hair falling around his face. Nomed relaxed. *Well, well...*

Corvus yawned and shook his hair back, exposing a dimple in the right cheek that deepened when he spoke. "Good morning, DiMensioner."

Nomed rubbed his stubbled chin. "It appears *you* slept well. It is good to see you safe and Human."

"It is good to be so. I am pressed for time. Can we awaken TheLise?"

"No need." She glided into the room.

Nomed glanced down at his rumpled clothing and shook his head. She looked well-rested and elegant, not at all like she had slept in a lousy bed fully dressed.

"Good morning to you both." Her smiling gaze flitted past him to their visitor. "I am glad to see you looking so well, Corvus. What brings you to Atkis? Have you seen—"

Corvus laid a finger on his lips and nodded. "All is well. Help me shield the room. I have news to share."

Wards shimmered into place. TheLise sat down next to Nomed. Corvus drew his chair closer and recounted his initial rescue, of WoNa and Roandee, of his own return to Human, and finally of Wolloh's return from Surazal, the land of the dead.

TheLise smiled. "Quite a story. I particularly like the last chapter."

Nomed leaned closer. "So, why are you here? Certainly, not just as the carrier of news."

"I'm here to share one more story." He gave them the gist of Nissasa's latest adventure. "Relevart would like you to find Nissasa's body and take it to Shu Chenaro. One Man will bring the jar with his essence to you, by which time I hope to have found Esán and his friends. I'll bring them to you there."

Nomed left the sofa and walked to the window. When he turned, he didn't hide his discontent. "I am unsure that I will trust you or anyone else with the rescuing of my nephew. He and his companions are pivotal to The Unfolding and, therefore, important to The MasTer. How can you hope to save them by yourself?"

"I won't be alone. Yaro is on his way here. Seyes, you and TheLise are the best ones to find Nissasa. He is in Trinuge. And he is with a Mocendi named Vygel Vintrusie."

Nomed's eyebrow shot up. "Vygel? I thought a DiMensioner of Esprow stripped him of his power."

"Word has it that The MasTer reinstated him and made him one of his personal guard."

Speculation gleamed in TheLise's gray eyes. "Relevart could have sent you, but he chose us?"

Corvus nodded.

Nomed frowned as she joined him. "What? Do you think I'm selfish to want my nephew safe, that I'm neglecting my duty if I don't care about Nissasa Rattori?"

"No, Seyes, I don't on either count. What I know is that something important made the VarTerel choose us. This is not about Nissasa. This is about Vygel Vintrusie; this is about defeating The MasTer at his own game."

Nomed fought his desire to be the one to find Esán. A part of him wanted—no, needed—to rescue him, to prove to his nephew and to himself that he had changed. He realized the old Seyes would have remained fixed on his own needs. Sitting down opposite Corvus, he looked him straight in the eye. "Promise you will find Esán and do everything in your power to keep him safe. Promise—"

TheLise leaned down and kissed his cheek. He swallowed, waited for her to sit beside him, and returned his attention to Corvus, whose intent gaze had never left his face. "Well?"

"I promise, Seyes, to do my best to find Esán and friends and keep them safe. I promise to die before I let any harm come to them." He held out his hand.

Nomed took it and smiled his crooked smile. "Please, Corvus, don't die. Almiralyn would never forgive me."

Corvus remained in the room for some time after Nomed and TheLise departed for the Dreelas' estates. Efillaeh had done its work well, but he continued to recuperate from his injuries at Nissasa's hand. The place on his chest—the spot where the single white feather had been in his raven form—ached with stubborn persistence. He pressed a hand to it. *I wonder if it will ever truly heal.*

Setting such thoughts aside, he paced the room, considering his arrival in Atkis. Before seeking Nomed and TheLise, he had done some exploring. The back streets and alleys on the land side of the village bumped up against a small forest that thinned into the fields and rolling hills of the peninsula. A well-kept main street ran the length of the village. Paralleling the waterfront, a rougher lane culminated in a series of workshops, warehouses, and shanties. The stench of the Mindeco and the Astican hung in the back alleys and along the far end of the dock.

He cast his senses outward. *Yaro will arrive soon. What form will he take?*

From between the drawn curtains, he studied the street below. Early morning activities had begun: a farmer delivered supplies to the inn, a young boy tacked up a note on the notice board across the way, fishermen exchanged quips as they made their way to the harbor, and a harried-looking man gestured and questioned his way up the street. He hurried to join a man exiting the inn. Corvus tuned in to the conversation.

"Have you seen Brubger?"

"Nope. Not since last night at the bar. You checked his boat? He's always aboard her by this time."

"*Possession* is gone. I was supposed to be on her this morning. Now I'm stuck in Atkis." Their conversation faded as they moved further up the street.

The curtain fell back into place. Corvus strode from the room, found his way to the back alley, and stood for a moment in the shadows of morning. He had considered never shape shifting again. His time trapped in raven form had been terrifying. Memories of his humanness slipping away—of the raven becoming all he knew—unnerved him.

"Oid eo daizo raa, Corvus, protector of Almiralyn." Yaro regarded him from beneath a wooden staircase on the opposite side of the alley.

Assuring himself that no one watched, Corvus crossed to the Pentharian. "Oid eo daizo raa, Yaro. It is good to see you. We need to talk. The Dreelas reserved a room in the inn for me. We can speak in private there."

Yaro bowed his elegant head, shifted into the form of a fly, and landed on his shoulder.

Corvus retraced his steps to the dingy suite at the inn.

The Pentharian materialized and glanced around. "This does not look like a place the Dreelas would appreciate."

Corvus smiled. "That is a story I will let her share. Please take a seat and tell me what's happening at the border."

They exchanged information. Yaro provided an account of the battle and Lorsedi's orders to find and protect Desirol and his friends. Corvus gave a brief description of the events that had brought him to Atkis. He shared the conversation he had heard earlier. "I believe the Mindeco has taken a new body."

Yaro traced a tattoo on his hand. "It appears we must learn of this Brubger and his *Possession*."

Corvus nodded. "I believe the docks are the best place to begin."

R ikell sat at *Possession's stern*, a hand on the tiller. Glad for the intermittent light of two full moons and the sea's gentle chop, he had followed the shoreline. Brubger's excellent memory assured him he was on course. The man's knowledge of the boat and the area around Atkis was exceptional. He had been obsessive regarding just about everything, including sailing. Detailed charts for the entire Sea of Trinuge, all the way from Atkis to Geran, lined one wall in the cabin. Better yet, he had memorized those that pertained to his home territory.

Rikell ran a hand through thinning hair and smiled. He loved his new body and his new persona. Brubger's conniving, selfish character fed his most primitive urges. Unlike the loyal soldier Nissasa forced him to take over in the desert, Brubger's personality complimented his own. He had gladly shed the soldier's body when he received the order to chase the children across Fera Finnero.

The lines slapped, and the sails luffed. He frowned and adjusted his heading. The winds were picking up. *Don't like the idea of sailing in stormy weather.*

Brubger's memory suggested the closest anchorage was behind Bockettle Island. A gust sent *Possession* skimming along. *Hope I didn't bypass Melback.* He glanced up at the thickening cloud cover and sudden darkness shrouding the shoreline. No other boats had caught his attention. *Almost feels as though Possession is sailing the Sea of Trinuge alone.*

He thought about Abarax hiding in the cabin, his small monkey's body shaking with fear. Brubger's face produced a nasty smile. The Astican had remained on deck until they left the harbor in Atkis. The smile grew more evil. All that water chased him below. *Now he's trembling like a babe in the corner of his berth.*

Rikell reviewed Brubger's fastidious chart in his head, adjusted their course, and pulled open the hatch.

Keeping the sarcasm out of his voice, he called, "How's it going, Abarax? Care to join me on deck?"

A book soared across the cabin and slammed into the wall. "I'm keeping track, Mindeco. When I shift, you'll wish you'd treated me better."

"Ah, poor Astican. I won't tease any more." Rikell withdrew and returned to the tiller. *It won't be long before I can drop anchor and rest. If my calculations are correct and the wind holds, I'll reach Bockettle in three quarters of a chron circle.* The wind howled. *Possession* lost her heading. Rikell made a quick change. *Unless the wind blows us off course.*

29
Myrrh & Thera

One Man arrived in the Dojanack Caverns to the news that Zugo was badly burned; Almiralyn watched over him in Ephos; and Veersuni contained something evil and dangerous. He now stood at the top of the Stairway of Retu Erath. The Cavern of Tennisca opened up like a giant mouth, calling him to enter. Descending provided a sense of solitude, solitude that he missed after fifteen years alone at Timreh Pass, solitude that he relished.

A breath tickled his cheek. "Fly, One Man."

Another breath, another voice. "Fly, One Man. Almiralyn waits."

A breeze of whispers lifted him into heron flight, infused his mind with visions, and grew quiet. He swooped through open purple doors and materialized in the Cave of Canedari, the cave where he had met Esán for the first time. Clear memories captured him. Needle-sharp and poignant, they pierced his heart. A panel in the floor slid open. He heard the rush of water beneath his feet.

The Lake of Rorret boomed, "The Unfolding careens toward completion. Do not linger long in your memories, Somay Efre of Tao Spirian."

The doors to the Hall of Priestesses opened. Light shot across the floor. The panel whooshed shut. Almiralyn's elongated shadow bathed his feet. He strode forward and took her offered hands.

Solemn eyes met his. "Thank you for coming, One Man. I need you and your skills."

He kissed her cheek. "Rorret sent a message."

"I heard. Let's make haste."

They hurried down the hall, exchanging news as they went. Sparrow met them in the Reading Room and held up a small, handmade book. "Wilith found this beneath a pile of old parchments. He believes it might be important."

The book bore a simple title engraved on a battered, black leather cover: *El Stroma*.

Almiralyn grew pensive. "I only know of one El Stroma." She passed it to One Man.

Brow creased in concentration, he skimmed through the pages of spiderweb script. "El Stroma is a planet in the Outer Universe just beyond the DéCussate." Flipping to the first page, he read, "It is the Time of Ending on the planet of El Stroma. Most have fled or died. Acid rain falls in torrents. I write this brief history hoping someday the planet's former beauty will return."

Sparrow said, "It sounds like what happened on TreBlaya. Do you—"

Veersuni's door rattled. Smoke trickled beneath it and crept over the Reading Room floor. One Man met Almiralyn's gaze.

"We have work to do." He crossed to a shelf, slipped the slender book between two of similar size, and rejoined the women. Stepping between them, he grasped their hands. "Individual wards in place." Almiralyn's glowed, his wards shimmered into place, and Sparrow's encircled her. "Good. Now, one around the three of us." One Man closed his eyes, took a breath, and opened them. "Good. Let's explore from here. Do not let go of my hands. Keep your intent masked."

One Man allowed his senses to ripple outward, beyond the door, through smoke hanging in the air. The smell of sulfur and burning flesh pervaded the sanctuary. Hatred gushed from Elcaro's Eye. A searching, malevolent presence fought to lose itself from the fountain's grip. He ended his mental exploration and opened his eyes. Almiralyn looked grim—Sparrow terrified.

The twin's mother shuddered. "Is that who I think it is?"

The Guardian nodded. "The essence of The MasTer has become trapped in the fountain."

One Man contemplated the door. "Should we send him where he belongs?"

Almiralyn answered, "We have to send him back. We know we can't destroy him via the Eye, and we need the fountain clear so we can use it."

Sparrow looked unsure. "How do we know he'll go?"

"Because," One Man explained, "our strength combined with the wards around the Eye will be difficult for him to resist. I suggest we enter Veersuni and see what we can do to free the fountain of its guest. Once inside, form a circle around it and hold hands." He looked at the two women. "Don't let go until I give you the word. Almiralyn, take the lead."

Almiralyn braced herself and opened the door. Smoke billowed around her. One Man's firm grasp kept her steady. She glanced back. Sparrow's dark eyes were enormous, her face devoid of color, her mouth set in a resolute line.

Acid smoke brought burning tears to Almiralyn's eyes. She blinked them away and traversed a floor covered with burned bits of velvet. Black smudges on the window's surface obscured its rich colors and created odd patterns on the sanctuary walls. At the center of the disorder, Elcaro's Eye gleamed alabaster white as though refusing to be affected by the filth trapped inside it.

She paused and looked back. Two pairs of eyes urged her on. Once in place around the glistening bowl, Sparrow reached for her hand—closing the circle—locking the danger inside.

A high-pitched howl of anger shook the Eye. Water splashed and rolled. A single large wave emptied the bowl, exposing the tip of the Vesen crystal, and then plunged back into the fountain with the force of a miniature storm surge. Wind ripped around Veersuni, tearing at hair and clothing, flinging flame-tattered curtains one way and then the other, and slapping scorched pieces of velvet against bodies, windows, and walls. Another shriek of rage ended in a dense, smothering silence.

Elcaro's Eye grew calm. A long hiss of air sent bubbles skittering over the surface. Sparrow gasped and shook her soot-covered hair back from her face. Her expression grew calculating. Flames flared in her eyes. Almiralyn squeezed her hand. Their eyes met. One moment, The MasTer's essence stared back; the next, Sparrow reclaimed her mind.

One Man blew across the water's surface. A ravaged face emerged. Red eyes began to glow.

"Look at me." One Man's telepathic message exacted immediate obedience.

Three pairs of eyes locked gazes above the fountain. Almiralyn began to chant.

"Elcaro's Eye rid your bowl
Of all that does not play a role
In this realm of Veersuni,
Release it, never more to see."

A burned and blackened landscape formed on the Eye's surface, a blazing pit of fire at its center. The water began to boil. The filmy outline of a shrouded figure formed and hovered in the rising steam. Vapors swirled, dispersing the image until only a hood draped head remained framed in a circle of flames. Pale lips moved. Words flew like tiny blackbirds into Veersuni and evaporated, unheard. The mouth rounded in a scream of disappointment. The image melted away.

Water trickled from the statue's open palms and dripped into the pristine bowl. "Rebuild the wards," One man instructed.

They worked together until multi-layered shields enclosed the fountain. He released Sparrow's hand.

Almiralyn put an arm around her shoulders. "You did well, SparrowLyn."

A wan smile brightened Sparrow's tired face. "I sent him back."

One Man grinned. "You sure did." He touched her forehead and frowned.

"What?" she demanded.

"I'm not sure. May I do a mind link?"

Her hand shot out and grabbed a fluttering speck of black from the air. The word "no" appeared on her palm. She rubbed it on her pants, stared at the faint smudge, and back at One Man. "Yes. Find out what he did."

One Man clasped her hands and closed his eyes. When he opened them, his expression was sober.

"What do you remember about the twins?"

"The twins? I remember every—" She swallowed. "Everything except what they look like."

Jordett looked up at the Theran sun blazing overhead. This was one of those times he wished for lousy weather. Clouds and rain would hide their movements better than bright sunlight. He glanced at his mini-chron. *Mid-turning. Wanted this done by now.*

Teva joined him. "Got a report from Senar that the Transit Center is ours. Quick and clean. No one hurt. The battle for the perimeter continues. Two men are down, one is ours. Davley, I think. Hold on." She seemed to listen. "They wounded Lavir, but not badly. So far, Nissasa's men are holding steady. Wait—" More listening. A small smile. "Akeri did a mind sweep. Two RewFaarans are here because Nissasa's blackmailing them, not because they care if he becomes the Largeen Joram. She amplified their doubts. We'll see if that helps."

Jordett removed his cap. "We need a distraction that will provide our team the opportunity to enter the compound. If we can take Tower One and capture Orittra, then we have leverage. The leader of the Brigade in our hands would facilitate a much quicker takeover. Thoughts?"

Teva held up a finger, nodded, and turned her attention back to him.

"Lenadi will take care of a distraction. Lavir told him about a side gate used only by the Five Fathers."

Jordett nodded. "I know it. Tell Lenadi it's a go."

When she gave him the sign that all was in place and had informed the other team leaders of their plans, he led his team to the street opposite the gate. Gunfire echoed through the quiet of Idronatti. The muted spit of RewFaaran weapons answered. Jordett and his team sprinted to the compound wall. Teva gave the all-clear. Jordett tried the gate. Locked. The touch pad gleamed in the sun. He took a chance and tapped in an emergency code. A muffled click generated a rush of relief and a grim smile.

Using the gate as a shield, he scanned the area. Nothing. His two men dodged inside. Teva followed. He wedged the gate open and joined her in a recessed doorway in the side of Tower One. His two men squatted behind bushes on either side of the gate. The pounding rhythm of running feet pressed them lower. He pushed Teva behind him. A shot rang out. The running ceased. *Hope that wasn't one of ours.*

Teva whispered, "It wasn't."

He glanced over his shoulder. She shrugged.

Love your gifts. He heard her soft laugh and pointed at the door. *What's on the other side?*

"Two patrollers."

Motioning her out of sight, he waved his men to either side of the recess, assumed a harassed demeanor, and knocked.

A square in the door opened. Narrowed eyes peered at them. "Who's there?"

"Colonel Saila. Open up. I've got a message for Orittra."

The face disappeared. Another took its place.

Jordett radiated impatience and power. "We got trouble. Let us in."

A shot fired close at hand. "Move it."

The square slammed shut—a pause—the door opened a crack.

Jordett gave it a shove. A patroller stumbled backward. The other, caught by surprise, stared. The next minute gave Jordett control of the door and the side gate. A brief discussion with the patrollers also gained him two additional men. Teva's mind touch assured him they were trustworthy. After giving them instructions to let no one else in the tower, he led the way toward the third-floor offices where Orittra and two staff members were meeting.

Bypassing the Drop Car, Jordett led the way upstairs with Teva next and his two men bringing up the rear. Sidling beneath the small surveillance lens, he jogged up the first flight and stopped short of the door. *Safe?*

Teva squeezed his shoulder, their prearranged signal. On the second floor, her response was the same. Her hand on the back of his neck stopped him several steps below the third story landing. "One guard down the hall—RewFaaran."

He started to move. Pressure from her hand stopped him. He half turned.

She mouthed one word that made his heart stutter. "Mocendi."

Finger on his lips, he pointed his men down the steps. When they reached the second-floor landing, Teva motioned them to hold on to her. She gave almost silent instructions. "Don't think. Hold on to me. Don't move."

Jordett fought to keep his mind in check. It wanted to react, to warn, to regroup, and to plan. Teva held his gaze. His mind went blank.

Thorlu Tangorra scanned the corridor in Tower One. Without knocking, he marched into the third-floor office of Grantese Orittra. A quick mind touch crumpled Orittra's two companions to the floor. Thorlu glared down at the astonished RewFaaran. "It appears, Orittra, that you have trouble pounding at your gates. And yet, I find you hiding here. Your behavior would not impress Nissasa or The MasTer."

The man blanched. "I w-w-was m-meeting with my staff to make some decisions." His gaze darted to the two unconscious soldiers as he came to his feet.

Thorlu shoved him back in his chair. "I didn't come to argue with you. I'm here to inform you The MasTer has sent orders to escalate the takeover of Idronatti and to warn you he will not tolerate mistakes."

"Of course. Yes. I..." Orittra shut his mouth.

"Good, man. If you have nothing of value to say..." Thorlu grew still.

Somewhere within the Five Towers compound, a weapon fired. He rounded on Orittra. "When I return from squelching this minor rebellion, I plan to visit the Five Fathers. Since you're responsible for their continued imprisonment, I will introduce you. It is time they, and you, know what The MasTer has in store for them." He pivoted and marched from the room.

Teleporting to the foyer on the ground floor, he executed a mental sweep of the area. Nothing out of the ordinary came to his attention. From the shadows beside a tall window, he surveyed the inner compound courtyard. PPP patrollers and two RewFaaran soldiers guarded the main gate. Everything else was quiet.

Flipping his cape behind his shoulders, he stepped through the front door and paused. Another scan uncovered nothing of concern. Business as usual, that was all.

A sneer of frustration morphed to a speculative frown as he re-entered the main foyer.

"Hello, Thorlu." Teva Rivan walked toward him. "What brings you to the Five Towers?"

"I should ask the same of you." He glanced around. "Is your little man with you? I'd still like to ask him a few questions."

"I'm sure you would."

Teva's beautiful smile almost melted his anger; her words fueled it. He held up a bandaged hand. "I owe you one, my dear. It seems your handy work takes time to heal."

"I warned you to remove your hand, did I not?" She stopped a short distance from him.

A sound behind him made him glance over his shoulder. "Lenadi. On guard, are you?" He moved to keep both KcernFensians in his line of vision. "So what now?"

A shield shimmered up around him. Good, had it been his, but it wasn't.

"You can't hope to keep me trapped in shields this flimsy." He attempted to push through and stopped. Two more KcernFensians appeared in the foyer. The realization he might be in over his depths dawned. Arrogance negated it. Masking his thoughts, he prepared to teleport. Nothing happened. Keeping his expression bland, he tried again.

Hauteur straightened his spine. "If you do not let me go, The MasTer will make you pay more than you can imagine."

His shields trembled. Heat infused his body. The room and the KcernFensians disappeared.

After Teva flashed from view, Jordett guided his team back up the steps. At his command, his men entered the hall and disarmed the guard. Grantese Orittra noted their arrival in his office with a distracted nod. When he realized the visitors were not under his command, he calmly laid his weapon on the table and folded his arms across his chest. Jordett's men secured the unconscious soldiers and then took up positions on either side of the door.

Jordett sat down opposite Orittra. "I need two things from you: The Five Fathers' whereabouts and control of the Five Towers."

The RewFaaran Grantese straightened a stylus, folded his hands on the table, and pressed his lips into a firm line. The non-responsive demeanor continued until Teva materialized at Jordett's side. Astonishment dropped Orittra's mouth open.

Teva gave him a polite nod. "A word in private, Colonel?"

Jordett followed her into the hall. "If you will you give Lenadi command of the tower teams, he has discovered a way to take the compound and the towers."

Jordett didn't hesitate. "Give the word."

After several tense moments, she relaxed. "Done."

"Mocendi?"

"We created an illusion that everything was per usual. Thorlu fell for it. He is a smart man and a powerful Mocendi, but he has an enormous ego." She frowned. "We're certain someone monitoring his actions extricated him from our combined shields. I gather Orittra is not talking."

"Resistance is part of his training."

Her face set in stern lines. He knew the look. Almiralyn had worn it on several recent occasions. "You have an idea?"

"I can do a bit of snooping in Orittra's mind." She grew quiet, listened, and gave a grim nod. "Lenadi's plan is in place." An air of authority cloaked her like the Mocendi's cape. "I'll need your two men."

Jordett motioned them into the room and followed.

Teva walked around the table. "Please, gentlemen, I will need your help to keep the Grantese in his chair."

Orittra's expression did not change. "You will get nothing I do not want you to know."

She looked down at him. "You have a choice. You can answer the colonel's questions, or I will do a mind probe."

Lips pressed together, he stared straight ahead.

The men on either side held him in place. Teva pressed the palm of her left hand to his forehead. The only sound in the room was Orittra's labored breathing.

Almiralyn observed Sparrow with a sympathetic eye. She could only imagine how hard it must be to realize someone had removed the visual memories of your loved ones. The face of Corvus formed in her mind.

"Sparrow, One Man, and I can give you mental pictures of the twins. You continue to possess enough memory that we can add the layers you need to recall your girls."

A soft knock interrupted. A young priestess stuck her head in the room. "I have urgent word from Dom."

Almiralyn waved her into the sanctuary. "Tell us."

"He used a piece of his crystal to relay this message: "Four Mocendi meeting in shoppe. Plan to use mirror portal to enter Myrrh. Goals: to destroy the RewFaaran camp, to take over the Demrach Gateway, to enter DerTah and gain control of the desert portal.

"Thank you. Keep monitoring happenings in Idronatti."

"Yes, my lady." With a nod to Sparrow and One Man, the young woman exited and closed the sanctuary door.

Almiralyn moved to the fountain. A snap of her fingers brought the flow of water to a standstill. Color enlivened its surface. A TreeOm perched near the top of a tall birch tree came into focus. It dissolved and the leader of the Wood Tiff's round face appeared.

"Yes, my lady. What can I do for you?"

"Tibin, I need you to send a Nyti to warn Mondago of four Mocendi headed his way. Tell him to clear the camp. Tell him I'll hide the forest portal."

The Wood Tiff's usually merry countenance grew serious. "Mocendi. Oh, dear. I'll send Reana. The Tiffs will hide the soldiers. Don't worry."

"Thank you, Tibin. Let me know if you need help." She waved her hand and the Wood Tiff vanished. "Sparrow and One Man, I need your help." As she spoke, the Demrach Gateway emerged in Elcaro's Eye. She held out her hands. "Form a closed circle and concentrate on the portal. At my command, see it grow to the size of a repoc. Hold it at that size while I transport it. Are you ready?"

Hands gripped hers. Energy coursed through her. She focused on her intent. The portal began to swirl. At her command, it reversed its spin and began to shrink. "Now. Hold it steady." Concentrating her will, she levitated the coin-sized portal, carried it through the Terces Wood to the center of the Grove of Mehloc, and recited a poetic command.

> *"Secure and hold this portal here*
> *Within the hemlock till all's clear*
> *Obscure its presence deep inside*
> *Where only ancient secrets hide."*

Three sharp claps and the water flowed once more. She sank onto a bench and lifted tired eyes to the pattern of colors in Veersuni's stained glass window.

Kieel yawned, trying to shake the exhaustion threatening to drown him. The things he'd seen and experienced would forever give him nightmares. Pools of blood, faces gone lifeless, the terror in young men's eyes as death came to take them overshadowed everything else in his memories. He shuddered. Death in the Terces Wood—animals killing other animals for food or to protect their young or in defense of their lives seemed less horrifying. Humans killing Humans brought home an awful truth: in certain circumstances, he was capable of killing.

It took every ounce of discipline he possessed not to run and hide. He did his duty—carried messages for Lenadi from one end of the compound to the other, fetched help, even held the hand of a dying man. A blood stain on his pants made him cringe. As hard as he tried, he could not rub it into oblivion. He suppressed the desire to sob.

Jordett's Oppositional Force, or JOF, the name given to the group who fought to regain control of the city, took control of the Five Towers. Both sides paid high prices. The KcernFensian, Radec, died protecting Anada. Of the Idronattians, five were dead, including Davley. The enemy wounded several others, Sagus seriously.

Seven RewFaarans were under lock and key in Tower Four, four were dead, and three were under guard in the infirmary in Tower Five. A small group remained at large in the city. Jordett met with those PPP patrollers and military assigned to the Towers by Orittra and offered them the opportunity to join JOF. A positive result allowed him to deploy three additional groups. Two departed to capture the remaining RewFaarans. The third covertly spread the word that Idronatti was under the control of the PPP. It was vital the Mocendi and The MasTer believe Nissasa's Brigade continued to hold the city.

Kieel stifled another yawn and noted the worry on Jordett's face. Teva's probe of Orittra's mind provided a minimal amount of information, but nothing regarding The Five Fathers. Either Orittra was good at evading the probe, or he didn't know their whereabouts. Their personal staff, she discovered, imprisoned in a cell in Tower Four, but of the five leaders there was no sign.

Jordett glanced his way. "Kieel, join us."

Stifling yet another yawn, he flew to the table where the major sat with Teva, Lenadi, Anada, and Lavir, who sported a sling and a bandage on his cheek.

Teva's understanding expression warmed him. "You look tired, Kieel."

He touched down in front of her and noted the fatigue in her eyes. "It has been a rather difficult turning."

Jordett smiled. "It's about to become more so. I need you to return to Myrrh and tell Mondago what happened here."

Fatigue vanished, leaving him invigorated and happier than he cared to admit. "Myrrh? You want me to go to Myrrh?" He wiped the grin from his face. "I don't know the way. How will I get there?"

A gray shadow moved from under Anada's chair and leapt into her lap. Amethyst eyes blinked at him.

"Majeska!" He fluttered forward, stroked her nose, and looked at Jordett. "When do we leave?"

"As soon as we've talked."

Everyone else stood. They had their assignments. Kieel almost tap danced on the tabletop. *And I have mine.*

30
Der Tah

While Yaro's mourning dove shape perched in a tree at the edge of Atkis Harbor, Corvus discovered all he could about Brubger and *Possession*, talked to the master sailor about potential places to anchor, and learned more about Gregos and Tamosh. What he heard about the brothers eased his apprehension to a small degree.

When information ceased to add to his knowledge, he left the waterfront and strode to the stone church near the village outskirts.

Behind an ancient mausoleum, Yaro shifted to his natural form. "Our charges travel toward the southeast coast of Trinuge. It sounds like the shortest and least dangerous route."

Corvus nodded. *"Soprano Narrows."* The two words, like the softest zephyr, rustling through his thoughts, left him frowning. His mind, still recovering from his long stay in raven form, failed to reveal the reason for his unease. He picked up a small pebble and rolled it between his palms. *Why does the name sound an alarm?*

Tossing the pebble aside, he glanced up to find Yaro regarding him with a question in his alien eyes. "You are worried about…"

"I suggest you shift again, and I'll take us back to the harbor. We have to discover as much as we can about Soprano Narrows."

A short time later, he strode from the trees and headed for the master sailor's small, cluttered office. The man shared valuable knowledge regarding the Narrows and provided a sketched chart, which Corvus slipped into his pocket. Urgency directing his path, he returned to the churchyard.

Yaro materialized; then flashed from sight. Alert for trouble, Corvus did an immediate about face.

A man in a purple-lined cape stepped onto the path from behind a gnarled and ancient tree. "So, Corvus *Karrew* Castilym, you have recovered from your…" A dangerous smile twisted his handsome features. "…adventure?" He glanced around. "Come out, Pentharian. I know you're there."

Corvus kept his mind masked and his demeanor easy. "Hello, Thorlu. Isn't Atkis a bit banal for your tastes?"

"Like you, it's not the village that interests me."

"So, what prompted you to leave the Pits of TreBlaya?"

"Much more than I have time to share." He took a step forward.

Corvus flicked an invisible speck of dust from his black tunic. "I wouldn't press your luck, Thorlu."

"Oh, I won't." He began to withdraw a hand from beneath his calf length cape, yelped in pain, and collapsed to the ground.

Yaro appeared and nudged the fabric enshrouded body with a toe. "I used my stunning agent. You know this man?"

"From a long time ago." Corvus knelt by Thorlu's side. "Hold on to me."

The instant Yaro touched his shoulder, Corvus teleported them inside the mausoleum. Settling the Mocendi on the stone lid of a crypt, he imprisoned him with a binding rhyme, one he hoped would contain him for at least a turning or two.

Yaro observed his actions with interest. "You, too, are a DiMensioner?"

Corvus finished his task and led the way outdoors. "My talents are of another lineage, though some resemble the Arts of DiMensionery. We must hurry. I suggest you shape a raven."

The next instant Corvus soared into the air, encased in the body of Karrew for the first time since his healing. The sheer delight of flying left him breathless. His fear of shifting melted into the recesses of his mind.

Nomed and TheLise reached her home by late afternoon. They had shifted to DerTahan hawks and flew rather than teleporting, thus obscuring their thoughts in the wildness of nature. Neither wanted to alert Vygel Vintrusie of their approach.

They arrived in TheLise's personal suite to find Tissent, Gerolyn AsTar's twin, waiting with a message from, in her words, "a person you both know well." She delivered it, told them she would continue to keep Roween under control, and left them to discuss its contents and what to do next.

"Vygel and Nissasa are at Esccery Inn. Make Haste." TheLise patted her short hair into place. "We have work to do."

Nomed agreed with some misgivings. "Vygel Vintrusie is The MasTer's personal Mocendi and imbued with more power than any other of his chosen minions. He is also loyal beyond belief. We must tread with care, or we'll lose Nissasa before we begin the search."

At TheLise's request, her groom saddled two horses and brought them around to the side door. They rode in silence the short distance to the forested-grounds of the inn. Hidden within the trees, Nomed examined the rustic charm of the building, the welcome it exuded, and the bustle outside the front door. Since he had stayed there, he knew the general layout.

"I'm betting he's in a suite on the ground floor. I could shift and fly closer."

"We can't use DiMensionery, Seyes, or we *will* alert Vygel. I suggest we ride up to the inn and go inside. I will explain to Quipe, the Innkeeper, we are there to pay a visit to my house guest's son. My excuse—his mother is unwell. You have kindly escorted me. I will make small talk while you discover his room number. Then I will make the acquaintance of Vygel Vintrusie."

"I don't like it, TheLise."

"Do you have a better idea?"

"No."

Her minx of a smile almost made him laugh. "Alright, but keep your wits about you. Vygel is every bit as smart as you and much nastier."

They rode from the trees up the drive. At the entrance, Nomed helped the Dreelas to dismount, instructed the stable boy to keep their horses close at hand, and escorted her into the reception area. Innkeeper Quipe sprang to his feet and hurried to meet her. TheLise explained her mission and gave the man Nissasa's name.

Quipe blanched and stuttered, "DiMensioner Telisnoe's friend has instructed me to allow no one into his rooms. I am so sorry, Dreela TheLise."

Her expression innocent, she linked her arm through his and walked with him toward the desk. "Friend? His mother assured me he was here on his own."

Quipe grew even paler. "It appears Telisnoe is ill. His friend is attending him until he recovers."

TheLise motioned him to sit. While he rounded the counter, she flipped casually through the guest book, caught Nomed's eye, and, leaving it open, moved to the opposite end of the counter across from the Innkeeper's desk. "I cannot tell his MaMa he's ill and unable to visit her without at least checking to see if he needs anything."

"I will let DiMensioner Vintrusie know you called, and that if he requires anything—"

With all the dignity of her station, TheLise held up a gloved hand to stop the effusive flow. "I understand your predicament. Please send word when Nissasa is receiving guests." She joined Nomed, who struggled to keep his expression gracious, and together they left the inn.

Once outside, he chuckled, "Poor man. He almost had a heart attack. I believe he made the right choice. You are much less frightening than a Mocendi DiMensioner."

TheLise laughed and shook her head. "Did you get the room number?"

He smiled. "Ground floor, Suite One. I've stayed there."

The stable boy brought their horses and received a handsome tip from Nomed and a gracious smile from his Dreelas. Once beyond view of the inn, they cut back through the woods, tied their horses to a bush, and slipped back inside via a side door. The empty hallway led straight to Suite One. Nomed remained out of sight. TheLise knocked. When no one answered by the fourth knock, he motioned her away, turned the knob, and pushed the door open. The smell of urine and feces wafted into the hallway.

Covering her nose with a hand, TheLise entered and walked toward the bedroom. Again, Nomed motioned her aside, pushed the door ajar, and with an exclamation of disgust, stepped inside. Nissasa Rattori lay on the bed, fully dressed in a pool of his own bodily fluids. There was no sign of Vygel Vintrusie.

Nomed felt for a pulse in his neck and turned to the waiting Dreelas. "He's alive, but not for much longer unless we get him some care."

TheLise became all business. "It appears he became excess baggage. I can't believe they left him to die." She pulled a bell cord by the bedroom door. "We have to transport him to my house, Seyes. Teleporting will kill him. One Man will have to bring his essence to us."

A maid appeared at the door, choked, and covered her mouth.

"I want Innkeeper Quipe now."

The girl bobbed a curtsy and trotted down the hall. Within minutes, Nomed observed Quipe hurrying toward Nissasa's room. Moving aside, he prepared to watch the Dreela of Trinuge in action.

TheLise greeted the man with a wintry smile. "I cannot believe this has occurred in an inn in my province. I hold you responsible, Quipe. You will send word to the undertaker that you have need of a hearse. Tell him a friend of mine has passed. Have him park at the side door. You, personally, will bring clean blankets to wrap Nissasa in. No one is to know he lives. As far as you are concerned, I am taking him home to have him prepared for burial. Am I clear?"

"Yes, Dreelas TheLise, very clear." Quipe bowed himself from the room and hustled away.

"A hearse. How clever, my dear." Nomed waved a hand in Nissasa's direction. "Aren't we going to clean him up first?"

TheLise met his gaze, her expression hard. "No. Roween Rattori needs to see what her meddling has brought to her son. She will clean him up; she will attend to his every need until we rejoin his body and quintessence."

Nomed tipped a make-believe hat. "I'll get the horses, my lady." He hurried along the hall, musing to himself. *There is nothing more deadly than a Dreelas' scorn.*

Aboard *Melback*, Esán found Brie's hand as her eyes found his. The pursuing boat contained the Mindeco, and they both knew it. They also realized the second energy signature belonged to the Astican. Esán started to speak.

Gregos put a finger to his lips and motioned everyone below deck. The hatch whispered shut. He pitched his voice low. "Sound carries over water, so please keep it down. We don't want them to discover we're here. Keep your thoughts masked. Since our enemies won't recognize Elf's energy signature, he will be our scout."

Ira looked Gregos in the eye. "You sure know a lot."

"Marji's an excellent teacher and taught us well. We're not DiMensioners, but Tamosh and I have enough talent to help in a jam."

Torgin whispered, "What now?"

Gregos chewed his bottom lip. "We've got options."

"You're kidding, right?" Desirol's statement, though quiet, sounded like a shout. "We have to leave right now! The Mindeco will find us—all of us— and he'll take me—and—"

Gregos' blue eyes turned steely. "Settle down, young man. *Melback*, and you, are my responsibility. Elf, show us the name of the boat and who's aboard."

In rapid succession, Esán received mental pictures of the name *Possession* on the bow of the small, sleek sailboat, a stocky, middle-aged man at the tiller, and a monkey cowering in the corner of a bunk.

Tamosh fingered the earring in his left ear. "Brubger. Glad it wasn't someone we liked."

Gregos frowned. "What my brother means is that Brubger is a mean man."

Elf touched his arm and held his gaze for a long moment.

The Captain's grim expression eased. "They don't know we're here—at least not yet. By the time they round the end of the island, we won't be. This is what we practiced for. In a quarter chron, we need to be underway.

No noise. Elf, help Ira with the anchor. Tamosh and Torgin, find us a route Brubger would avoid at all costs. Brie, with me at the helm. Des and Esán, man the sails. Shyllee, you've got the watch." He opened the hatch. "Go!"

Desirol held back. "I'm t-t-too t-tired. I can't—"

Gregos raised his bushy brows. "I'll tell ya when you're tired, boy." The brows came together over the bridge of his nose. He squinted knowing eyes. "Or scared. Now go."

Melback's crew went to work. Esán expected to hear the clank of the anchor chain or the soft click of the lines against the mast. Not one sound disturbed the night quiet.

Torgin studied the rudimentary chart Tamosh spread on the table. Like others he had seen, it contained notes and symbols in the margins to show hazards or safe places to anchor. Staring at the rough sketch of Eschems Strait and Marauder Passage, the expanse between Aksala Island and the primary coast of Trinuge, he frowned. Nothing suggested another way to go unless they backtracked.

Tamosh donned a pair of silver-rimmed spectacles, then removed them to rub his eyes. "Sure wish I had more detail on this chart. Gregos told me a passage cuts through Aksala, but I've never sailed it."

Torgin fingered the thong around his neck. "Maybe this can help." He withdrew the Compass of Ostradio from inside his shirt and offered it to Tamosh. "Almiralyn gave it to me."

His spectacles in place, the man studied the device in his hand. He gave a low whistle. "No need to explain, young friend. Never expected to see Ostradio, let alone hold it." He handed it back. "How's it work?"

Torgin balanced it on his palm. "Show me the passage across Aksala Island."

The needle jumped and began to spin. It came to a stop pointing northeast. A chart rose above the compass face and enlarged to an easily readable size. *Melback's* position glowed green. A red dot showed *Possession,* the vessel in pursuit of them; and a blue line indicated a thin, rocky passage listed as Soprano Narrows.

"Not the Narrows." Tamosh swore under his breath. "Can you make it bigger?"

Torgin touched the name. The image zoomed in until every detail of the Narrows was clear.

"Ask if there's a safer way." The compass remained static and the chart visible. "For sure, Brubger won't want to follow us—no sane man would," he muttered.

Why's Tamosh so reluctant? Torgin squinted and looked closer. The passage appeared to be narrow and rocky, with some tricky currents, but surely by an experienced sailor could navigate it. Otherwise, Ostradio would not have shown it as a viable route.

Brie watched her friends make silent haste, readying the boat to weigh the anchor. The heartening presence of Gregos beside her calmed her growing sense of foreboding. She had grown to trust him.

He beckoned her closer. "I need ya to put an illusion of invisibility around *Melback*."

She swallowed. "I don't know how."

He gave her an encouraging pat on the back. "Sure ya do. Think what Wolloh would do."

Trying to recall the times others had created an illusion in her presence left her drawing a blank. *Wolloh? Not that I remember... WoNa! WoNa put an illusion around Eissua Oasis.* She closed her eyes and tried to remember what the Oracle had done. Finally, she whispered a simple rhyme and envisioned the boat enveloped in a filmy curtain that reflected the surrounding area like a mirror.

> *"Hide Melback from prying eyes,*
> *From anyone who seeks or spies.*
> *Illusion, wrap us in your charm*
> *That none may frighten or alarm."*

"Brie, open your eyes." Gregos gave her a pat on the back and a smile. "Elf says it's in place. See, ya know how, girl."

Before she could reply, Ira turned and held two thumbs up. The anchor was aboard and secured. Gregos signaled Esán and Des to raise the sail and prepare to slip away from Bockettle Island, leaving the Mindeco and Astican behind.

The gusting wind calmed to a brisk breeze that caught *Melback's* sails and sent her slipping soundlessly through the water. Clouds swallowed the crescent moon, leaving the anchorage in the deep shadow of pre-dawn as *Possession* rounded the end of the island, sailing straight for them.

Gregos steered *Melback* into the Strait of Eschems and adjusted her heading toward Trinuge's southern coast. Elf looked back. A picture flashed in Brie's mind—Brubger sniffing the air like the Mindeco that possessed his body. He picked up a spyglass, scanned the anchorage, and tossed it aside in disgust. Sniffing again, he called to the Astican.

Gregos swore. "Can't see us, but we're upwind. Da'am, he's got our scent. Elf, get Tamosh. And bring the chart of Eschems."

Tamosh climbed on deck with Torgin close behind, the compass map hovering above Ostradio's face.

A quick conference left both men grim. Brie sensed nothing but trepidation in Elf's mind. She watched Tamosh take the wheel and Gregos gather his crew together in a tight huddle.

Concern laced his forthcoming explanation. "Torgin's compass shows only one way to lose *Possession*—Soprano Narrows. Not where I'd go by choice. Brubger lost a boat to the rocks in the Narrows. Almost died. Sure wish I could say it was different, but the Narrows is our best hope."

Desirol's dark eyes darted to the shadowy shape of Bockettle Island and back to Gregos. "What's so bad Narrows?"

"It's narrow and rocky. The waters are unlike any I've ever experienced. The one time I sailed it, I was about your age. Almost didn't make it. Dumb luck is all that saved me." He peered back through the muted light of dawn and then at his crew. "Esán and Ira, do a sweep of the deck. Make sure everything is secure. Torgin and Desirol, I need ya below. Stow everything ya can. Take Shyllee with ya. Elf, do your magic. I need to know when it's slack tide. Pray it's sooner than later. Brie, females have a better chance of making it through the Narrows than men. Memorize everything Ostradio knows about the Narrows and get back up here. We'll be at the entrance in half a chron circle."

Shyllee rose to her feet, wagged her tail, and padded after the boys as everyone scurried to carry out their assignments. Brie settled at the table in the cabin, the compass glowing in her hands. *Soprano Narrows*. The Star of Truth shot a warning current over her skin.

Henri found herself in a dim passageway. The faint aroma of cooked shellfish hung in the air. An opening up ahead flickered, suggesting a fire. She sat her spectacles on her nose and peered through the crystal lenses. Her unobtrusive scan picked out three individuals. A smile played at the corners of her mouth. Relevart had sent her to Geran, the Island of ZaltRaca, unless she was mistaken.

A man appeared in the opening, a shotgun raised. He wore the look of a harried watch dog. Suspicion and a touch of fear lit his eyes.

Henri raised her hands. "Please don't shoot. I'm a harmless old lady."

Two women crowded behind him. The darker of the two call out. "What's your name?"

"Henrietta. I'm sorry to intrude, but—" She paused. *Will they even know of the VarTerel?* "Relevart sent me."

The man clutched the gun tighter. "Don't know any Relevart."

"Lower the gun, Cay." The dark woman edged around him. "I know of Relevart. He's the VarTerel of the Inner Universe." She walked to Henri and offered an arm. "Please, Henrietta, come in."

Henri stepped from beneath a low overhang and stared in surprise and delight. What she assumed would be a cave was instead the inside of an older sailing vessel. She removed her spectacles and smiled at a slender blonde woman whose summer green eyes held intelligence and caution. "Hello, Renn Whalend. I am Henrietta. My friends call me Henri."

The caution did not fade. "You are the mysterious woman who lives across the hall from Torgin's friends, Ari and Brie. Are you a friend or an enemy?"

Cayled gripped the shotgun, ready to raise it. Bibeed's face, so like her brother's, did not lose its welcoming expression.

"It is my hope you will consider me a friend. Relevart thought I might help, or I wouldn't be here."

Welcome changed to worry on Bibeed's face. "Are they here? Have they found us?"

Henri sank onto a stool. "Please, may we sit? I will answer as many questions as I can."

Cayled laid the shotgun on the table and sat down across from her. Bibeed and Renn pulled up stools on either side of him. Henri smiled to herself. *Guess I'm on trial.*

Renn liked Henrietta but worried she was missing something important—something she would regret later. Still, the elderly woman had answered all their questions. Even Cayled's natural suspicion faded by the end of their discussion. Bibeed had never doubted Henri's authenticity. Renn sat by the fire, watching them prepare breakfast as though they had known each other for many sun cycles.

She stirred the coals in the fire pit with a stick. *At least Wilith is safe in Myrrh. And Torgin—* Henri had told her he sailed to her rescue, he and his friends. They were in the Sea of Trinuge. Their journey would take them around the Cape of Trinuge, along the coast of TheDa, and across the Triple Moon Strait. What she needed was a map.

Henri glanced up and smiled. The next thing Renn knew, Cayled joined her, unfolded an old, faded map of DerTah, and smoothed it out on the table. Fascinated by his knowledge of the solar system, she listened closely. Her scientific mind wanted to ask how the moons affected the tides; how the planet's shorter orbit of the sun impacted the growing season; how DerTah responded during the Cycle of Dovi, the time every thirteen sun cycles when the planet's moons and sun lined up.

She and Cayled were deep in conversation when Henri snatched her purple rimmed specs from her pocket and perched them on her nose. Her magnified eyes scanned the boathome, then stared at the rocks overhead. Frowning, she motioned Renn and Cayled to join them.

"The MasTer's Reach searches. A Mocendi of great strength flies within it. He is using the eyes and ears of his master to seek you out, Renn. Listen carefully. Bibeed and Cayled, I am leaving Renn in your care. Keep her hidden until her son and his friends arrive. Do not leave this cavern until you're certain nothing hunts the cliffs and beaches."

Renn folded her arms across her chest. "And you?"

Henri met her gaze with cool violet eyes. "I am about to become you. But I will need your help. To successfully fool the Mocendi DiMensioner, I must fully become your likeness, so you and I must share a mind link."

"Which means?" Renn felt a spark of curiosity.

"It means that for a moment we need to mingle our thoughts and memories. I must gain enough of your scientific knowledge to fool the Mocendi and The MasTer, but not enough for them to use the information. I will take nothing from you, only impressions."

Renn hesitated. "How can I let someone else take my place?"

Henri removed her spectacles and put them in a hidden pocket in her shirt. "You have a son and a husband. You are vital to the independence of Idronatti's citizens. Without you and your research, what the PPP has done cannot be undone."

"And if they discover you are not me?"

"If that bridge appears, I'll figure out a way to cross. Now, let's get to work. I must be in the cottage before the black cloud arrives."

Still, Renn delayed. Bibeed whispered, "The longer you wait, the bigger risk for Henri. Let her save you, Renn."

Henri offered her hands. Renn clasped them. Memories flowed from one woman to the other, thoughts, feelings, images interwove. Renn gasped as the connection broke, leaving her alone in her own mind.

Henri released her hands. "Thank you. I am honored to share a bond with you. Now, I must shape your likeness. Is there anything I need to add besides what I see? A birth mark, a mole, a scar that's hidden?"

"I have a butterfly shaped birthmark." She touched the side of her left thigh. "It's about the size of the end of my little finger."

The elderly woman began to shift. Renn gasped. Blonde hair, green eyes, a serious mouth replaced the soft white curls, violet eyes, and lightly lined cheeks. Age spots melted away. Renn could only stare at her identical twin. Feeling somewhat taken aback, she reached out and touched a strand of blonde hair. "My goodness, you look just like me." She shook off her sense of non-reality and became serious. "If you're going to fool them, we'd better change clothes. Women in Idronatti never wear pants. Also, my clothing carries my smell and energy and that should help you."

Bibeed shooed the astonished Cayled out the door. "Don't wander far."

They made the exchange. Renn removed a small locket clasped it around Henri's neck. "It has a picture of Wilith and Torgin, old-fashioned, I know, but I love it. Bring it back to me, Henrietta."

Henri touched it, kissed her cheek, and vanished.

Renn stared at the empty spot. *Please be careful, Henrietta.*

Henri arrived at the top of the Cliffs of Tymine as the MasTer's Reach topped the trees on the far side of a field of erika flowers that edged a forest of thick-trunked pines and wind-blown gambelii oaks. The black cloud hovered. She could feel the senses of The MasTer first stretching to catch a scent, then listening, then straining to see in the brighter atmosphere of DerTah. Wrapping Bibeed's baggy coat around her limber younger body, she moved with ghost-like invisibility to the cottage, slipped in the front door, and hurried to the room Renn had described as hers.

Black vapor covered the window. She smelled the scent of burning flesh. The door flew open. The gaunt figure of a man blocked her exit. Bulging, bloodshot eyes swept from her blonde head to her toes. A mind probe lacerated her thoughts.

"Coala Renn Whalend, we meet at last." The voice, as disfigured as the man, was lacking in anything warm or humane.

Henri held herself still. Outside the wind scattered The MasTer's Reach. Opposite, the man lost a vestige of his power. With effort, he fought to regain it.

She did not move. "Since you know my name, it would be polite to share yours."

The bulging eyes blinked. A triumphant smile, more chilling than the raw cold of a winter wind, twisted thin, bloodless lips. "Vygel. Vygel Vintrusie."

31
Myrrh & Thera

The quiet of Veersuni soothed Sparrow's overwrought nerves despite her ongoing indecision. Almiralyn dozed on a bench, recuperating from transferring the Demrach Gateway to the Grove of Mehloc. Color from the stained-glass window hovered in front of her, patterning her with red and blue and gold. One Man, hands clasped behind his back, gazed out the cleared glass at the magnificence of the star-sprinkled sky.

Sparrow pulled a small leather pouch from her pocket and fingered the round objects inside. Her mind resumed its incessant, worried buzz. The MasTer had stolen her visual memories of the twins. Mocendi had invaded Myrrh. It felt like Allynae had been gone for many moon cycles. The twins were on a boat somewhere in the Trinugian Sea on DerTah. She let out a heavy sigh and decided.

As she joined One Man in front of the window, she let her gaze follow the path of a shooting star. "Beautiful, isn't it?"

Esán's father smiled down at her. "More vast and beautiful than we even begin to imagine."

She held out the pouch. "I want you to take these."

He tipped the contents onto his palm. "The Tabagie's eyes. You're certain, Sparrow?"

"You have far greater need than I, One Man. Please take them and use them to save our children."

He tucked the pouch in his pocket. "Thank you, SparrowLyn AsTar. I am honored by your trust."

For a time, they remained silent. Sparrow thought about the creature that Wolloh had sent to warn them. It had delivered its message and begun to fade when it told her to keep its eyes. If added to fire, it had explained, they would bring the Tabagie back to aid her. She touched her heart. *Thank you, Tabagie.*

Across the room, Almiralyn sat up. Nimble fingers flicked her hair into a braid. "I think it's time to share some memories, don't you?"

One Man escorted Sparrow to the bench. "We do."

With her friends, each holding a hand, Sparrow closed her eyes. Relief made her light-headed as identical faces, red curls, a sprinkling of freckles, and dark brown eyes enlivened the faded remembrances she had kept.

When they had finished, she turned to Almiralyn. "The MasTer knows what the twins look like. That can't be good."

The Guardian didn't mince words. "He already knew what they felt like. It's his minions that their likeness will help. All we can do, Sparrow, is hope he is too busy to pass along the information." She stood up. "Let's discover how TheLise and Nomed are doing and see if we can keep his focus elsewhere."

Almiralyn waved a hand above the fountain. The dripping water calmed. One Man moved to her side.

Sparrow ignored a growing reluctance to use the fountain and placed her hands on its cool, rounded rim. A blurred image steadied.

A funeral wagon waited at the back door of a mansion. Accompanying it were Seyes Nomed and the Dreelas TheLise. Solemn servants removed a swaddled body and carried it into the house. Nomed and TheLise followed.

The scene changed. The body lay on a bed. A tall, dark-haired woman stared down at it. When she turned to regard her hostess, her narrow, homely face wore an accusatory scowl. "What did you do to my son? Why is he so..." She wrinkled her nose and cough into a hanky. "Why does he smell?"

TheLise looked from Nissasa to his mother. "Your friends in the Mocendi League left him to die, Roween."

"They wouldn't do that. He is important, a DiMensioner, the future Largeen Joram of—" She caught sight of Nomed's arced brow, clamped her mouth shut, and redirected their attention. "What's wrong with him? He's hardly breathing."

"He used Souvitrico to discover the whereabouts of the Evolsefil Crystal. His essential life quintessence is being stored in a charnockite jar on another planet. A certain level of power is required to keep his body alive until we reunite it with his essence. It appears The MasTer decided Nissasa had ceased to be useful. The Mocendi protecting the body is gone. Had Seyes and I not found him, he would be dead."

Roween bristled with rage. "This is all your fault, Dreelas."

TheLise replied in an icy tone. "No, Roween Rattori, this is *your* fault. Had you not craved power, your son would not be in this situation. I suggest you clean him up. When he is ready, Seyes and I will do what we can to preserve his physical body." She started to leave, but paused. "If you are wise, you will not call attention to Nissasa's presence here. We brought his body in a hearse. It would be best if everyone thought he died. Also, please remain in your quarters until Nissasa is back on his feet." She strode from the room.

Roween grimaced at the silent body of her son. "How could you have been so *foolish*?" She crossed to the bell rope and pulled. Her personal maid appeared.

"I didn't ring for you."

The woman curtsied. "The Dreelas' staff are all busy, my lady."

Roween's eyes glinted with hatred. "Get me water, clothes, and several towels."

The maid hurried to the door.

Roween called after her, "Bring me one of your dresses and an apron and find a change of clothes for my son."

The maid disappeared. Roween stormed around the room. "I will make you sorry, TheLise of Trinuge."

Water trickling from alabaster palms dispersed the image into foaming flecks of color. Sparrow looked at her companions. "Will Nissasa's essence withstand teleporting?"

One Man gathered his long hair over his shoulder. "No. I believe it will manage a portal jump, but teleporting can disturb delicate molecules. I'll have to carry it overland."

Almiralyn calculated travel time from the desert portal to Shu Chenaro. "That will take too long."

Sparrow gazed into the Eye, and then back at her friends. "Allynae can take you, One Man. He can shape the flying horse. You will be there in no time."

"Of course. What a great idea! I'll send Gerolyn a coded message to bring him to the desert portal." He kissed Sparrow lightly on the cheek. "You've done good work today. Try not to worry about the twins. They have many powerful protectors watching over them." He patted his pocket. "Including the Tabagie."

Almiralyn walked him to the door of Veersuni. "Yookotay has the jar, and you know the rhyme of release and re-entry. Take care and send us word as soon as you can."

Her expression when she returned to the fountain was speculative. "I think we should check on the twins, don't you?"

Sparrow took up her position by Elcaro's Eye. "Indeed, I do."

Almiralyn took a deliberate breath.

"Elcaro's Eye, your knowledge share;
Show us how the children fare.
Help us understand their fate,
And where their adversaries wait."

The water churned into effervescent colors that slowly began to coalesce.

Kieel limited his conversation with Jordett to the details most important for Mondago to hear. When they finished, night had settled over the city. He bid farewell and darted out the door after the Guardian of Myrrh's gray cat.

Majeska padded from shadow to shadow through the eerie streets of the deserted city, occasionally sniffing the air or dodging into a darkened doorway as a PPP Ria Transport skimmed past. Jordett had ordered patrols to continue. PPP military in RewFaaran uniforms also made the rounds. Anyone paying attention would assume that Nissasa's Brigade controlled Idronatti.

Kieel flitted above Majeska, below the first-floor windows of the buildings lining their route. They had gone a substantial distance when his guide stopped in an alley across from the tallest building in Idronatti. The Sun Spire glowed ruby red in the diffused shafts of light that shot up from the ground, bathing its magnificent height in a warm wash. The Sun Spire, Jordett had warned him, was the danger point.

Kieel flew across the shimmering moat surrounding the Spire and zipped from bush to flower to bush in the gardens bordering it. He landed in a tree close to the drawbridge Majeska would use to cross to the drop car on the exterior of the building and scanned the area for his guide. A twig snapped. A hand snatched him from the branch and held him in the light.

"Well, well, well. What have we here? I'd say it's the Nyti Thorlu told us about."

Kieel stared at a face of one of the Mocendi's young henchmen. He tried to wiggle free. The man laughed. "Spunky, aren't you? Don't think I'm gonna let you go. You're my meal ticket, little man. I bring you back, and I get a leg up to the next apprentice level."

Kieel forced a calm he did not feel and let curiosity creep into his question. "Are you a Mocendi?"

The man lifted him to eye level. "So you talk, too. Hey, they said you know stuff we should know." Cunning lit his eyes. "How about you answer *my* questions? I might even consider letting you go. What do you say?"

An arrow of gray fur slammed into the man's chest. Arms flung wide, he stumbled backward, loosed his grip on Kieel, and let out a howl of frustration as his 'meal ticket' zipped over his head.

The man's pounding footsteps and heavy breathing pursued Kieel as he whizzed after Majeska into the open door of the drop car. The man thrust his arm between the door and the jam. A buzzer blared. Majeska gave a sharp meow. Kieel drew his small sword, gathered his full strength, and stabbed the hand.

With a startled cry, the man yanked it back. The door closed; the car shot upward. Kieel pressed the three numbers Jordett had drawn for him. The car came to a stop. The doors opened on a long, white corridor.

Majeska sprinted and leapt into the roiling mist covering the far end. The car lurched. Kieel dodged through closing doors, shot down the hall, and dove after her. The next instant, he hovered beside a street lamp. From across the way, Majeska gave a clipped meow and sprinted down a dimly lit lane.

A thud behind him warned Kieel to move. He glanced back. Adrenaline pounded through him. The exclamation "By The MasTer's Reach" chased him as he bolted after Majeska. Midway down the lane, a door opened. Majeska shot in. Kieel followed. The door closed. Feet pounding on the pavement echoed through the night.

A tall man with longish dark hair and an unblinking eye emerged from the darkness and offered his hand. "Fadin's the name."

Majeska purred.

Kieel touched down on the extended palm. "Kieel, Matrés of the Terces Wood Nyti, at your service."

Fadin winked at Majeska. "Formal, isn't he?" His good eye, the one that blinked, looked back at Kieel. "Once we get that wanna-be Mocendi under lock and key, you'll be safe t' go. Won't be long. Mirror's still in the shoppe. Jeska here knows the way."

A soft tap on the door stopped his chatter. He cracked it open.

"All clear."

Fadin opened the door and held up his hand. "Kieel, meet Saaul."

Kieel bowed. "Hello, Saaul."

"Howdy." Saaul grinned. "Haven't seen a Nyti since I was a youngster. Sure wish my kids, Tima and Tansy, could meet you, Kieel. When things are calmer, come visit us."

Majeska meowed and trotted down the lane.

Fadin grinned. "The lady's gettin' impatient. Best get underway."

"Thank you." Kieel chased after her, afraid to let her out of his sight.

Dom met them at the door to Antiques by Q. "Hey, Jeska. Kieel. Best keep movin'. Mirror's waitin'. Take care. Four Mocendi used it a short time ago. Only three came back."

When they arrived in the sunflower patch, Kieel wanted to shout for joy. Instead, he landed by Majeska, where she crouched beneath a tall sunflower and peeked between broad green leaves. The RewFaaran camp looked to be deserted and every bit as eerie as Idronatti's empty streets. Forest sounds... the chirp of birds, the buzz of insects, and the chatter of animals...were absent. Not even the trees of the Terces Wood whispered in the autumn breeze. Kieel longed for his walking stick and sword.

Majeska skulked away from the camp and into the trees beyond the sunflower field. Kieel followed, zipping from one shaded spot to the next. When he reached the trees, he paused. Ashor darted into view and beckoned. On the far side of the camp, the young Nyti fluttered to a branch and pointed. Kieel's heart convulsed in his chest. Reana, his only granddaughter, hovered inside a small cage in front of a tent. A Mocendi DiMensioner stood with his back to her. Pivoting on a heel, he put his face close to the bars, and narrowed his eyes.

"You *will* tell me what you know."

She folded her arms across her chest and pressed her lips tight.

The Mocendi scowled and stalked into the tent.

Kieel glanced at Ashor. "I recognize him from Idronatti. If we're going to rescue Reana, we'll need help. Take me to Tinpaca Mondago."

He took one last look at his granddaughter. *Don't lose your temper, girl.* Holding his fear for her safety in check, he followed Ashor into the Terces Wood.

Almiralyn and Sparrow stood side by side, their attention fixed on the image forming in Elcaro's Eye.

Sparrow leaned closer. "There's something there, but I can't make it out."

Almiralyn waved her hand above the water and smiled. "A spell of invisibility? Brie is growing by leaps and bounds."

On the fountain's surface, a dim outline appeared. Sparrow gasped and gazed at a two-masted sailing vessel gliding through the mists of early morning. "My dear Brielle…"

The image pulled out to show calm water reflecting the muted shoreline like a looking glass. An occasional bird soared overhead. Too close for comfort, a smaller boat gave chase.

The fountain zoomed in. A stocky, white-haired man stood at the wheel of the larger craft. The hatch opened. Red curls flared in the early morning light.

Almiralyn squeezed Sparrow's hand. "And here's our girl."

Climbing on deck with Shyllee close behind, Brie let her gaze wander from the boat's captain to the watch perch where Elf sat and finally to the dog settling at her favorite spot in the stern. The information gleaned from Ostradio surged through her thoughts. *None appeared that intimidating. Why are Gregos and Tamosh so afraid of it?*

Gregos beckoned her forward. "Ya learned everything about the Narrows already?"

"Yes, but I still don't know the reason it's so frightening to experienced sailors."

He favored her with a wry smile. "Let's hope ya never discover the reason. No use me tellin' ya and callin' forth a problem." He licked his lower lip and glanced over his shoulder.

Brie's gaze followed his. "How soon before we reach the mouth?"

"All too soon, my dear." He stepped aside. "Take the helm. Let's see what ya've learned."

By the time they were closing in on the Narrows, Gregos had put her through her paces and drilled her on every conceivable emergency. "Wolloh was correct. Ya sure are one smart girl."

Tamosh joined them and trained his glass on *Possession*. "Something strange going on back there, Gregos. Brubger is heading for the shore at that bit of a cove where we sometimes anchor."

Gregos took the glass, studied the smaller boat, and passed it to Esán. "What do you make of that, boy?"

"Don't know, sir, but I can find out."

"Well, don't just stand there. Go!"

Esán handed the glass to Brie and shifted to his kestrel form.

Brie tracked him as he flew shoreward and then cut south, staying close to the shoreline but well-camouflaged by the trees. As *Possession* edged into the small, semi-enclosed anchorage, she lost sight of him. The next thing she knew, he materialized beside her.

"Brubger tossed a bag connected to a long line over a branch hanging just short of the water. When I tried to see into it, I met with a block. My guess—the Astican is on land."

Gregos muttered a few choice words under his breath. "Everyone to their stations. If I yell for ya to clear the deck, I mean it. Don't stop to look or listen. Get yourselves below and cover your ears! Elf, at the bow. Warn me of trouble." He glanced at Brie, who had taken up her position at his side. "We have a slack tide in less than a quarter circle. The entrance to the Narrows should be smooth sailin'. Then it'll pick up speed. I'll stay close as long as I can. Torgin, keep the compass handy. Tamosh, ya've got the watch."

Melback made a graceful, easy turn into a narrow passage. Midway through, it opened into Soruch, the widest part of the Narrows, and then became even narrower. Brie gazed into the distance. Tides on DerTah could be complex, depending on the interaction of its three moons. *Melback* had a finite amount of time to reach the far end before the unbridled power of the tide flushed her back to Eschems Strait.

Agitation radiating from Gregos washed over her. Behind them, Tamosh scanned one shoreline and then the other. At the bow, Elf trained his attention on the water. In the distance, she sensed the Mindeco struggling with Brubger's resistance to entering the Narrows and prayed the man would win the battle. She could not feel the Astican.

Melback crept forward with the shore so close on either side that Brie could almost reach out and touch it. With unerring skill, Gregos navigated the tight corner into Soruch, where he had told her DiMensionery did not work. Inch by inch, she watched the spell of invisibility peel away until *Melback* became visible again. The morning breeze, which had supported their journey since first light, ceased. The sea lay slick and still, not one ripple in any direction. *Melback* stopped, becalmed—unmoving. Anticipation engulfed the Narrows.

Brie flinched as the Star of Truth sent a stabbing pain up her neck. Her gaze bounced from shore to shore and back to the open expanse of water. A single high note shredded the thick silence and scattered it over the sailboat like tiny ice crystals.

"Clear the deck!"

Gregos' command sent everyone but Brie, Torgin, and Tamosh racing for the hatch. The clatter of scrambling feet as they descended into the cabin mingled with a second operatic note. Gregos gripped the wheel. Determination etched every line of his body.

Torgin clung to Brie's arm, his eyes huge and his breath coming in quick gasps. He gulped and pointed. "Look!"

Circling *Melback*, reflected on the water's surface, open-mouthed female faces spewed musical notes into the air. Half notes, whole notes, quarter notes formed and burst, vibrating the morning with their high-pitched verve. Repeatedly, notes soared upward. Time and again, their sound pelted *Melback* and her crew. More and more demanding in its tone, the song began to take on form.

"Desirol, Tamosh, Esán...Ira, Gregos, Torgin..." The names rose, trembled in the air, and crashed into the water.

An outer ring of male figures began to emerge. Mounted on spuming stallions of the sea, they carried glistening bows fitted with silver arrows that glimmered in the sun's light. Gregos swore and motioned Torgin to the deck. Flashes of silver arced over the boat and evaporated as they hit the shore.

At the stern, Tamosh collapsed, unconscious. The spy glass rolled from limp fingers. Water soaked his shirt and pooled around his shoulders.

Gregos motioned Brie to the wheel. Grabbing his brother under the arms, he dragged him to the hatch. Esán and Desirol wrestled him below. Gregos staggered back to her side. The twang of bow strings merged with the notes exploding. The boat rocked in time to the mesmerizing rhythm.

An arrow rushed past Brie's cheek. Gregos toppled to the deck, water drenching his clothing and showering her with gleaming droplets.

She caught her breath and clutched the wheel. The fluid coolness of the

Water ConDria flowed over her, infused her with wonder. Laughing for joy, she shook tendrils of silvery hair away from her face.

"Brielle, no!"

Something about the voice intrigued her. She shook her head—tried to remember.

"Brie, don't shift." Ira gripped her shoulders. His blue eyes turned to brown. Red hair tumbled around a feminine, freckled face. "Brie, it's me... Ari."

Brie stared at the familiar face, shook her head again. *Ohhhh. Ari!*

The silky coolness receded, leaving her soaked in the warmth of her twin's hug. Ari held her at arm's length. "You can't go. We have a boat to save."

The seductive song transitioned to angry shrieks. Arrows pelted the boat. Fluid faces contorted as water-colored eyes closed to slits. Mouths rounded. Spouts of water plummeted the deck. The boat pitched. Liquid fists sent rhythmic quakes through wooden bulkheads.

Brie struggled to find a solution somewhere in what she had learned. Ari's arms around her waist kept her on her feet. Her hands on the wheel steadied her.

All the lessons came rushing back. Brie looked at Torgin's pale face. "Are you with me?"

He nodded.

"Help Ari take Gregos below, and then—"

The shrill cry of a beast of prey showered down on them. Torgin and Ari, rooted to the spot, stared at the far side of Soruch, where the Narrows tapered to its slimmest point. Abarax, Astican of TreBlaya, hovered above the trees.

Brie shoved fear to the back of her mind. "Get Gregos below."

Amidst the clamor of soprano voices mixed with the Astican's primitive cries, they half-dragged, half-carried Gregos to the hatch. Esán and Torgin pulled him to the safety of the cabin.

Ari hurried back to her side and clasped her hand. "Now what?"

In the sanctuary of Veersuni, the image in the fountain dispersed, leaving the water devoid of anything but the gentle drop, drip, drop from alabaster palms.

Sparrow cried out in dismay. Frantic brown eyes found Almiralyn's. "Make it show us more. It can't leave us like this. I can't..." Tears for her daughters tumbled down her cheeks.

Almiralyn took her hand. "I'm sorry. I can't *make* it do anything. The fountain tells us what we *need* to know, not what we *want* to know."

A tear dropped from Sparrow's chin. Ripples rolled into stillness. The water grew calm, a mirror gleaming in the depth of the Caverns of Tennisca. From the very bottom of the bowl, a faint image floated upward. Bobbing and weaving as though caught in a tidal current, it arrived, steadied, and came into focus.

Below deck on *Melback*, Torgin looked at the prostrate figures of Gregos and Tamosh. Still as death, Desirol sprawled on a berth, his eyes open and staring. Elf sat with his back to the bulkhead, hands pressed over his ears.

Only Esán seemed unaffected by the chaos above. He sat at the chart table with One Man's flute in his hands. "Torgin, you are the only one who can save us."

"What can *I* do if the Mindeco is out there, ready to jump aboard? What if..." Torgin clamped his mouth shut, inhaled through his nose, and blew out through his mouth. "I haven't been so afraid—" A wry laugh cut him short. "—since I got on the boat in Atkis."

"You're much different from the boy who came to Myrrh a few moon cycles ago." Esán held out the flute. "My father gave this to you for a reason. He understood your power, Torgin. Go and work your magic."

Something—the tilt of Esán's head, his tone, the confidence in his eyes —compelled Torgin to reach for the flute. He held it in shaking hands and listened to the song of the Narrows, to water slapping the deck, to the cry of the Astican. His uncertainty melted away. Inspiration blossomed in his musician's heart.

Esán pulled the hatch open. Torgin climbed on deck, walked to the helm, faced the bow, and played one high, sustained note. The frenzied shrieking ceased. Water stopped pounding the deck. Ocean eyes widened. Mouths closed. Archers lowered their bows and reined in their aqueous mounts.

At the far end of Soruch, the Astican hovered, his cries silenced and his gaze fixed on *Melback*.

Torgin inhaled and lifted One Man's gift to his lips. Solitary notes floated into the Trinugian sky, building gradually, creating ethereal musical images: oceans made of light, liquid mornings and fluid moons, phosphorescence dancing in the wake of a fast moving-boat. So exquisite was the melody, so elegant the chorus, so heartfelt the song that the boat's rocking settled into a gentle cadence. Each note brought a quivering response from the sopranos of the Narrows. Fingers of water drummed in hypnotic counterpoint against *Melback's* wooden sides.

Abarax trumpeted an aggressive cry. Torgin hesitated. Singing sopranos urged him on, sang the melody, matching the flute's iridescent tones. Voices and instrument merged in a song so beautiful tears fell from the cloudless sky. Water frothed and roiled around archers, reforming their ranks to create protective shields at the sailboat's bow and stern. Torgin picked up the tempo. Smooth as silk, *Melback* slipped through the sea. Closer and closer she came to the tapered beginning of the last stretch of inland waters.

The Astican soared upward, its cherubic features glowing with predatory delight, its winged shadow casting darkness over the shores. Arrows of water arcing toward it elicited a howl of alarm and sent it fleeing inland. At last, they could see the breadth of the Sea of Trinuge, wide and glistening in the stark light of middle-turning. The archers at the bow formed lines along the shores. Archers at the stern surged forward, their power propelling *Melback* from the Narrows into the wide expanse of ocean.

Torgin lowered his flute and faced the Narrows. The sopranos sang a final note and melted into the sea. The army of archers raised their bows, shot one last arrow into the heavens, and vanished.

He turned to find his companions gathered on the deck. Ari and Brie threw their arms around him, their eyes gleaming with pride. Gregos and Tamosh, still dazed, patted him on the back, thanking him for saving their *Melback*. Elf gave him a shy nod. Esán stood in the open hatchway, a knowing smile on his face. Shyllee scrambled up from where she had crouched low against the stern and ran to sit at his feet. The only one not present was Desirol.

Torgin didn't miss him. Wonder overflowed in his heart. His entire body thrummed with the power of music. For the first time in his life, he knew his purpose in the universe.

A shout of terror from the cabin ended the moment. Esán scrambled below, followed by Gregos and Tamosh. Torgin handed the flute to Ari and followed. Desirol stood in the lower cabin. Triumph glistened in half-crazed eyes. In one hand, he held a small, broken ampule and in the other, a piece of gleaming quartz.

32

Der Tah

One Man sat in a tent on the outskirts of the RewFaaran camp near the desert portal, waiting for Gerolyn and Allynae to arrive. A meeting with Grantese Tesilend, Paisley, and Stee had left all concerned, quiet and thoughtful.

With the Demrach portal inoperable, traveling to Myrrh was limited to the DeoNyte capital of Meos or NaiDisbo Canyon in the Dojanack Mountains. Stee felt a responsibility to rejoin Mondago. Paisley wanted to return to Nemttachenn. Tesilend worried over the safety of his commander and the men under Mondago's command.

One Man thought back to one of his mother's teachings: *Only time takes us where we need to go.* A difficult childhood had prepared him to care for himself; the Seed of Carsilem had honed his skills. *My mother gave me the name of Somay. I believe it is time to embrace it.* The idea took root. He smiled.

Tossing the entrance flap aside, he took stock of his surroundings—the RewFaaran camp—the desert dunes. Two DerTahan hawks made a lazy circle and landed in the late turning sun. Gerolyn walked briskly toward him. Allynae materialized, stood for a moment looking lost, and followed. Once inside the tent, One Man explained his decision to be known as Somay.

Gerolyn's lovely smile warmed him. "What does it mean in Tao Spirian?"

"Just before my mother died, she told me it means Spirit Sun. When I became known as One Man during my time in the Dojanack Mountains, I left my true name behind, knowing the time would come for me to reclaim it."

Allynae grinned. "I'm glad the time has come."

Gerolyn kissed his cheek. "Welcome, Somay, Spirit Sun of Tao Spirian." She became all business. "I can't stay. Tell me what's happening in Myrrh, and what you know of Sparrow, the twins, and Desirol. Lorsedi is waiting for news."

Somay presented a concise but clear picture of the issues that had arisen. Throughout, she remained unemotional. When he finished, she shook her head.

"He will not be happy." She touched the black and amber jar. "Can you make Nissasa whole again?"

"Only time will tell. How is Lorsedi taking it?"

The entrance flap flipped to the side. Heat penetrated the tent. "He refuses to discuss it." With that, she was gone.

Allynae cleared his throat. "How is Sparrow handling all this?"

"You'll find her changed, Alli. Her gifts are opening more every turning. She is terrified for you and the twins, but she grows stronger and more confident with each training session."

"I sure miss her." He sighed. "When do we leave?"

"As soon as Fasfro clears the horizon. We have a detour to make."

"A detour?" Allynae stroked his mustache. "Where to?"

"Eissua Oasis. We need to consult with WoNa about the Oracle Stone—how to remove it from the jar and protect it until we can return it to her."

Five knuckles cracked. "I've only shaped Starfire once. Hope I can do it again."

Somay smiled. "I have every confidence you'll do fine."

Two chron circles later, Allynae and Somay bid their farewells to Tesilend and walked to a spot between dunes where they were hidden from the camp. Somay carried the charnockite jar tucked under an arm. Allynae carried his resurgent self-doubt.

He raised stormy blue eyes to the night sky and tried to remember how he had shifted shape when WoNa had needed to escape Nissasa and the Sebborr. Taking a deep breath, he shut his eyes and imagined the stars flowing from the heavens into his body. When he peeked beneath half-open lids, Somay's encouraging smile left him battling insecurity once again. He thought about Brie and her shift to the ConDria, about Ari and her ability to become Ira Raast. Finally, he let go of all thought, raised his arms to the sky, and whispered, "Starfire, come."

An absence of sound, light, color; then an overwhelming flood of sensory stimuli brought a cry to his lips. A whinny filled the night. He stamped a hoof and shook a midnight mane. Somay's weight settled on his back. Extending his mighty wings, he flicked his long tail and launched into the air.

Nothing in his life had prepared him for Starfire's immense power. Since his first change to the magnificent winged creature, he had dreamt nightly of becoming it again. A thrill of wonder coursed through his Human awareness. Hanging tight to his humanity, he prepared to enjoy the flight to Eissua.

WoNa waited at the entrance to her cave. Water plunging over the outcropping behind her served as a background for the deep whaaa, whaaa of Starfire's massive wings. The Atrilaasu Dansmen's murmur of wonder told her he had crested the desert trees at the far end of the oasis. Air rustling her kcalo informed her the midnight stallion had landed in front of her.

Somay slid to the ground. "It is good to see you, WoNa."

She nodded, stroked Starfire's jowls, blew in one nostril and then the other, and stepped back.

The horse vanished into the man. "Hello, WoNadahem Mardree." Momentary loss infused his whispered greeting.

"Welcome to Eissua, Shaper of Starfire." She led them into the cave and sat down. "Please share my table."

While they settled, she ran a hand over the jar Somay had placed in front of her. The ConDra's Fire with Nissasa's cool essence moved in a swirling pattern over the black and amber surface. The rhythmic pulse of the Oracle Stone tingled against her palm. When the scrape and creak of chairs ceased, she folded her hands in her lap.

"Nissasa's essence weakens. The weaker it becomes, the stronger the ConDra's fire within the Oracle Stone. Only the ConDria breath can cool the fire and remove the stone from the jar." She placed a reddish-brown pouch on the table. "This is made from the heart of the drango. Brielle must put the stone inside and bring it to me. Together, we will remove the fire. Now, you must go."

Allynae walked from the darkness of WoNa's cave into the cool light of DerTah's blue moon. WoNa and Somay emerged behind him.

The oracle paused. "Your true name has great power, Somay. It is good you reclaim it."

Somay bowed his head. "Thank you, WoNadahem."

She reached for Allynae. He took her hand. She moved to his side, whispered the name that changed him to stars and moonlight, and touched his cheek. With a shuddering breath, the power of Starfire enclosed him. Somay mounted and grasped his mane. Hooves sending a shower of sand around him, Starfire galloped the length of the oasis, unfurled his wings, and leapt into the heavens.

Below him, the desert sped by. Above, the night sky embraced him. Joy propelled him onward until he reached the border of Shu Chenaro. The wards parting to allow them through framed Wolloh's home as it crested the horizon. Clinging to one more moment of flight, he circled over the ranch.

With a touch of sadness, he landed at the center of the arena and folded his wings.

Stebben walked from the ranch house, a broad grin overshadowing the fatigue in his step. "What a marvel you are, Starfire. I can understand Brie's excitement." He accepted the jar from Somay. "Welcome, One Man."

Somay dismounted. "Please, I am Somay, fully myself and proud to be so."

Stebben smiled. "It is time, Somay. Wolloh wi...would be pleased."

Starfire pawed the ground and snorted. Allynae materialized before he had even thought to change. A wave of wistfulness twisted his smile.

Somay clapped him on the back. "Well, done, Allynae. What a grand ride!" He sobered. "I think food is in order, don't you, Stebben? And I can't imagine you aren't starving, Alli."

The statement elicited a rumbling growl from Allynae's stomach. He laughed. "Would love something to eat. Have you heard from Nomed, Stebben?"

Seated around a small table in Stebben's private quarters, Allynae and his companions enjoyed good food, pleasant conversation, and a glass of Wolloh's excellent port. Nomed had informed Stebben Nissasa was safe but unable to travel. Allynae smiled to himself at the thought of 'Starfire' in flight again. Chairs scraping the floor yanked him from his daydream to find Somay and Stebben halfway to standing. Shields shot up around them. Somay put a finger to his lips. The lights dimmed. A portal opened at the room's center. Wolloh stepped through, his black hair with its stripe of white shining in the portal's brilliance.

Stebben started forward. Somay caught his arm and kept him at his side. Grabbing a goblet, he tossed it. The High DiMensioner did not flinch as the goblet passed through him and shattered against the wall. The portal vanished; the man melted into nothing.

Allynae frowned and shook his head. "Was that a hologram?"

Stebben nodded and collapsed in a chair. "How did you know it wasn't Wolloh?"

Somay poured some port in a glass and handed it to him. "Almiralyn told me Wolloh's hair has turned white. Had I not known that..." He shrugged. "The Mocendi have discovered a way to breach the wards around Shu Chenaro. Finish your port, Stebben. We have work to do."

Stebben set the glass on the table, put a hand on Somay's arm, and touched Allynae's shoulder. The next instant, they were in the arena. Somay's face was grim as he motioned them into a circle.

Allynae squelched his ever-present uncertainty and listened to Somay's instructions.

Corvus soared above the strait of Eschems, his alarm escalating. He and Yaro had discovered *Possession* in a semi-enclosed anchorage south of Soprano Narrows. Below them, Brubger stood on the deck, an ampule in one hand, a quartz crystal in the other. With Yaro circling above, Corvus streaked toward the boat.

Brubger's small, beady eyes tracked his progress. A fiendish grin curved his stingy mouth. He held the ampule above his head and snapped it in two. Black smoke enveloped him and sent him flashing from Mindeco to Brubger and back to Mindeco. Brubger's body shuddered and fell to the deck. The flesh melted from the bones. A bloodied skeleton crumbled to fine dust and scattered over *Possession's* deck.

The Mindeco roared and vanished. Corvus landed to the last strains of riotous laughter, and a boat emptied of all but lingering fingers of black vapor that slithered around his neck and squeezed. Above him, Yaro shifted from raven mid-flight, swooped over the deck, gripped his shoulders with vulture talons, and carried him away from *Possession*.

On a small, stone-littered beach, the Pentharian set him down, coughing and gasping for breath. As he recovered, Corvus noted the set of Yaro's jaw and the dangerous glint in his eye. The Mindeco had almost killed him in the Nesune Ruins. Within minutes, they were in raven form and streaking through the air, hoping to find *Melback* before the unthinkable took place.

The mouth of the Narrows lured them onward. They shot along the first stretch, arrived at Soruch, saw nothing, and continued. Near the end of the narrowest section, the sounds of voice and flute rang out and grew silent. Hovering over the trees, the Astican howled in frustration. Heading out to sea away from the Astican, *Melback's* sail billowed in the wind. A scream of terror followed in its wake.

Corvus swooped toward the boat and landed with Yaro at his heels to find the twins, a boy he didn't know, and a dog at the helm.

"Corvus. Below." Brie's fearful message sent him through the open hatch. The scene that met his eyes sent his heart to the pit of his stomach. Desirol, cornered by the Senndi brothers, Torgin, and Esán, glanced crazily from one to the other. In his hands, Desirol held the broken ampule and the small crystal. His eyes widened as Corvus and Yaro descended into the cabin.

Torgin gasped, "How—"

Gregos growled over his shoulder. "Don't just stand there, Pentharian, help us restrain him."

Yaro disappeared. A small, brown bat sunk sharp teeth into Desirol's neck. The boy cried out and toppled. Tamosh and Gregos eased him onto a berth. Gregos made room for Corvus. Tamosh left to assist the twins at the helm.

Corvus placed a hand on Desirol's forehead. "How long?"

Gregos answered. "Not very. The Mindeco took him moments before ya arrived." He peered down at the unconscious boy. "The creature appeared out of nowhere."

Brie scrambled down the steps, holding the pouch with the Remembering Stone in her hand. "You need this, Corvus."

At the mention of his name, Gregos nodded his approval. "The protector of Almiralyn. Glad t' have ya onboard."

Corvus accepted the pouch. "I'm glad to be here. Thank you, Brielle." He slipped the blue ribbon over Desirol's head and rested the pouch above his heart. "The Mindeco can only take over fully if Desirol forgets who he is. The stone will help him hold on to his memories." He straightened. "This will be a dangerous time for all of us. If the Mindeco gains control, there is no way to save Desirol. If he leaves the boy's body, it will..." An image of Brubger rose in his mind. "It will not be pleasant, and no one on this boat will be safe."

Yaro reappeared on the outer deck and stuck his head in the cabin. "Come, Torgin, my brother. Let us give Corvus and Desirol some room. You can introduce me to your friends."

Torgin climbed on deck.

Gregos paused before following. "Our sister Marji gave him a special pouch to protect him."

Corvus studied the unconscious boy. "I wondered what I was feeling. She's a powerful woman."

Gregos nodded. "Ay, she's a good one." He stepped aside to make room for Ari to join them and hurried on deck.

His focus on Desirol, Corvus listened to Ari's description of the Soprano Narrows. Her joy at being with her sister in her true form radiating around her made him smile. He had gotten the measure of Gregos, Tamosh, and Elf and liked what he discovered. Elf intrigued him.

Desirol groaned. Dark eyes opened, searched his face, and widened in horror. Pushing himself to sitting, he grabbed Corvus' arm.

"The Mindeco got me, didn't he? I can feel him." He licked dried lips. "He's strong—a-angry. I don't know if I c-can fight him. I..." Shaking fingers, fumbled with the blue velvet pouch at his neck. "What?"

"Brie has lent you the Remembering Stone. Keep it on your person at all times. Understood?"

His grip on the pouch tightened. A crafty expression flitted over his pale features. He clutched a handful of auburn hair and fought for composure. A full-bodied shudder left him hugging himself and sent the Mindeco back in hiding.

"Why am I still here? Why hasn't it taken me over?"

Corvus rested firm hands on the boy's shoulders. "You wear a drango tunic and boots. They keep it at bay. Marji gave you a special pouch. The Remembering Stone hangs around your neck. *You* have control, Desirol. Friends surround you, and all of us will help you fight the Mindeco."

Tamosh blocked the light flooding in through the open the hatch. "Black cloud in the sky."

Desirol choked back a sob. "The MasTer."

Corvus came to his feet. "Ari, shift. Now." He tapped the top of her head.

Ira frowned back at him. "Ahhh, hi, Corvus."

"Hello, Ira." He beckoned Esán to his side. "You're with me. Brie and Ira are with Desirol. Your job—keep him calm."

He emerged on deck to find the crew of *Melback* at their assigned stations, with Gregos at the wheel and Tamosh managing a full set of sails. He scanned the sky. Hovering over the end of the Narrows, a cloud of black billowed around the Davea's winged form.

Esán gasped. "If the Astican can fly over water…"

As the words formed, the creature launched over the Sea of Trinuge. Corvus and Gregos exchanged glances. *Melback* could never out sail The MasTer's Reach.

Henri schooled her expression to one of fearful expectation, kept her personal thoughts well-masked, and allowed Renn-like fear to play beneath the surface. Vygel had neither said anything since introducing himself, nor had he removed his piercing gaze from her face. A mind probe made her eyes water. She remained silent.

He cleared his throat. "I'd ask where you've been hiding, but don't imagine you would share." He watched her closely.

She lowered her eyes and studied the pattern in the braided rug by the bed.

A boney finger lifted her chin. Acid breath brushed her cheek. For an instant, they were eye to eye, and then he stepped back, leaving her with a pounding heart and a yearning for fresh air in her lungs.

"It seems your son is determined to rescue you. Rather than disappoint him, you will remain here until he comes. You will stay in this cottage. If you should try to leave, you will regret it." He fastened a slender black bracelet around her wrist. "This will tell me where you are at all times. Take care, Renn Whalend."

Henri frowned at the space where he had stood and murmured, "Can't say I'm not glad you're gone." Crossing to the window, she withdrew her spectacles from their hidden pocket and inspected the black bracelet. A frown of distaste accompanied her close perusal. *I believe I am imprisoned by The MasTer's burned flesh, the Reach solidified.*

"Miss Renn." Bibeed peered through the bedroom window. "The door wouldn't budge. Are you alright?"

Henri motioned her back and, with the careful use of telekinesis, slid the window open. Crisp autumn air wafted through the room, removing the stale smell of smoke and decay left behind by Vygel. "Bibeed, you shouldn't be here. If the Mocendi discovers you, I cannot guarantee your safety."

"We needed to know you're alright. If I hadn't come, R... Henri would have."

Henri shared what had occurred since her departure from the boathome. "You must warn Torgin and his friends."

"What about you?"

"I can take care of myself."

Bibeed hesitated. "Come with me."

Henri held up her wrist. "I'm being monitored. My presence would endanger all of you. Go, Bibeed. Do *not* come back to the cottage until this is over."

With stooped shoulders and a heavy step, Bibeed made her way through the field of purple and pink erika blooms. Henri waited until she disappeared down the cliff trail, and then she closed the window and explored the cottage. Small and cozy, it would at least be a comfortable prison. She built a fire in the fieldstone fireplace and sank into an overstuffed chair. Her gaze fixed on the flickering flames, she ordered her thoughts and sighed.

Unexpected fatigue weighted her lids. An alarm sounded in the part of her brain that was deeply hidden. Her eyes flew open. Relevart stared down at her.

Swallowing her desire to give the VarTerel a welcoming smile, she let a touch of panic creep into her voice. "Who are you? Another Mocendi?"

The man continued to stare at her.

"If you're looking for Vygel Vintrusie, he's not here."

Relevart faded. "Oh, but he is, Renn Whalend." Vygel, too, faded.

Henri released her grip on the arms of the chair and ran her hands over silky blonde hair and along the sides of her neck until the palms touched and the fingers intertwined.

I said I wanted adventure, didn't I.

33
Myrrh

Almiralyn and Sparrow watched transfixed as Elcaro's Eye painted a new picture on the water's surface.

Melback raced through the water. Not far behind, engulfed in the black vapor known as The MasTer's Reach, the Astican steadily closed the gap between them. Esán knew the sailboat could not outdistance her pursuer. Gregos had said there was nowhere close to hide. The Compass of Ostradio showed the same thing. *The Astican has trapped us in a vast stretch of open ocean.* He chose not to speculate as to the outcome if Abarax overtook *Melback*.

He shaded his eyes and watched Yaro's vulture form circling above.

"Help us!" Brie's panicked cry exploded from below deck.

Esán rushed to the cabin. Desirol, his face contorted into a hideous mask, straddled Ira's sprawled body. His fist slammed into his friend's nose. Ira yelped. Blood spurted. Desirol pulled his arm back.

"Desirol, stop." Brie knelt above them on a berth, a bruise blooming on her cheek.

He looked up, lowered his fist, and sagged. Ira pushed him off and rolled aside. "By the Fathers, Des. Did ya have to hit me?"

Corvus flashing into sight brought Desirol to his feet, eyes wild and hands working to remove the drango tunic. *"Esán, get Yaro."*

Esán shifted to his kestrel form, streaked through the hatch, and into the sky. His wings pressing against the cool sea air, he soared ahead of the vulture, hovered, and dove. The enormous bird dropped like a stone. The moment its talons touched the deck, Yaro appeared, took one look in the cabin, and vanished. By the time Esán arrived on *Melback*, Desirol lay unconscious.

"Tie him up and lock him in the V-berth." Gregos was adamant. "Can't fight him and the Astican at the same time. And that beast is closing fast." He brushed past Esán and returned to the helm.

No one spoke. Corvus tied Desirol hand and foot. Yaro carried him to the V-berth and locked the door. As a safeguard, Corvus sealed it with a powerful ward.

Ira, cloth to nose, mumbled, "Will Efillaeh help Des?"

Corvus sighed. "I'm afraid it will only make matters worse. Use it on your broken nose and join us on deck." He motioned Esán ahead of him.

A glance aft made Esán cringe. Even at a distance, jubilation shone from the Astican's eyes. Its scaled wings pressed harder. The gap decreased rapidly. Above, on the watch perch, Elf used his talent to fill the sails. *Melback* shot forward.

Brie scrambled on deck and went straight to Corvus. "If water could penetrate the vapor, would it stop him?"

"I believe it might."

The stench of burned flesh washed over the boat. Abarax swooped, snatched Elf from his high perch and tossed him into the sea. Yaro shifted to the vulture, picked the flailing boy up by the shoulders, and deposited him on deck. Again Abarax swooped, clawed feet ready to claim another prize. Gregos spun the wheel. The booms swept over the deck. Sails snapped in the wind. *Melback* shuddered with the sudden course change.

Esán reached for Brielle. His hand found only emptiness. Frantic not to lose sight of her, he shaded his eyes and gazed after her shifted form. Soaring upward, the Water ConDria intersected the path of their enemy. Vapor sizzled against her shimmering body. The Astican shrieked and hurtled higher; the cloud reforming around it. She circled, whipped her wings through the darkness, and hovered, gleaming in the Trinugian sun. The creature howled and dove toward her. She held steady. An instant prior to impact, she plunged into the sea.

Abarax fought to stop its plummeting descent. Black vapor billowed around it. Like a balloon, it lifted him—carried him high above the churning water.

Oblivious to the Astican, Esán ran to the rail and searched the water's surface. "Brielle. Brielle, come back to me. ConDria, free yourself from the sea!"

Corvus joined in. Ira, Yaro and Torgin, Gregos and Tamosh picked up the call. Shyllee added her bark. Elf closed his eyes and held his arms open and pleading.

Again they called, and then again.

Water surged and roiled beyond the bow. *Melback* rocked and rolled. The ConDria broke the surface, her song filling the air. Watery wings carried her skyward. She peaked, hovered, and plunged, an arrow of shimmering silver, straight toward the sea. Inches above the surface, she swept up and over *Melback*, turning the sails to catch the wind.

The Astican shot toward them, cherubic blue eyes fastened on the ConDria.

Esán's frantic gaze darted from one to the other. The ConDria shrilled a trail of notes.

"Look." Elf's excited message drowned Esán's fear in a pool of wonder. Off the bow, where the ConDria had risen from the sea, a portal's translucent spin caught the light. *Melback* careened through. The ConDria streaked overhead. The portal vanished, leaving the Astican trapped on the far side.

Melback floated, suspended in an expanse of white. Silence enshrouded boat and crew. The ConDria had vanished. Esán peered ahead into the blinding light. Ira and Torgin crept to his side. Icy cold crept over their skin. Glacial wind tugged at their hair. The light hummed, flared, and vanished.

Torgin caught his breath and grabbed Esán's arm. Ira breathed, "What the... Wow."

Melback sailed between the walls of a deep fiord, ice sculpted walls rising high on both sides. Crystallized flakes of snow fell from a gray sky to melt on the surface of a pewter sea.

"Where are we?" Torgin whispered.

Ira shivered. "More important, where's Brie?"

Esán scanned the sky, caught his breath, and pointed.

High overhead, a glistening silver-blue bird caught an updraft and soared, looping and arcing and swooping in the cold light. Its gradual descent held the group in a state of rapt amazement.

Ira hugged himself against the chill. "That's our Brie. Isn't she beautiful?"

Torgin exhaled a frosty cloud and smiled.

Esán could only stare, mesmerized by the exquisite grace of his best friend. Love burst from his heart. *Brielle AsTar, I love you!*

The ConDria swooped over *Melback*, spread her magnificent wings wide, and floated in a flurry of falling snow.

Esán reached into her mind. *"Come home, Brielle."*

She circled a final time, materialized beside them at the bow, and, eyes shining with happiness, reached for Esán's hand.

Gregos' command ended the moment. "Crew One, man your posts. We have a boat to sail. Torgin, bring that compass. Crew Two, better get some rest."

"Back to business." Ira grinned and made his way to his post.

Esán hugged Brie. "Go rest. Later, I want to know what it's like to be one with the sea."

Watching her walk away left him feeling bereft and alone. Staring over the cold, gray sea, he contemplated what had just occurred. Neither the compass nor the charts Tamosh had drawn showed a portal. Gregos certainly didn't know one existed. Until Brie emerged from the Sea of Trinuge, there had only been a wide expanse of water. *Does she have the power to create one, or does some unknown source of power exist beneath the sea?*

Almiralyn heard Sparrow gasp and gripped her hand. Brie's battle with the Astican left them breathless. When the portal opened and closed, leaving the Astican behind, they both cheered.

Sparrow studied the ice-sculpted mountains. "Do you know where they are? They're safe, aren't they?"

Almiralyn smiled. "I believe they may be in the TheDa Mountains. We shall see. At least, their enemies don't know where they are. I'm so glad Corvus and Yaro found them in time."

"What of Desirol? Can you remove the Mindeco without killing him?"

"Relevart is the only one who knows the answer to that question." She dipped a finger in the water. The surface rippled into calmness. "Please check on Zugo while I continue to work?"

Sparrow slipped from the sanctuary.

Almiralyn made a circuit of the room. The MasTer's invasion of Elcaro's Eye had left Veersuni feeling unfamiliar and unclean. With her back to the stained-glass window, she envisioned the sanctuary's return to its former peaceful, nurturing environment. When at last it embraced her with gentle tranquility, she waved her hand above the fountain. An image appeared and solidified. The interior of Nemttachenn came into focus.

At the tower's center, a Mocendi DiMensioner, his low rank marked by the plain black lining in his cape, made a slow rotation. Restless eyes scanned the rounded space, tracked the stone staircase spiraling up and out of sight, and paused at the spot where Evolsefil rested in its cloak of invisibility. He reached out, ran his hand over the cool, smooth stone, and frowned. Flipping one side of his cape behind his shoulder, he mounted the stairs and began the long climb. At the top, he gazed over the forest canopy in all directions, his expression puzzled. Shifting to a bright orange bird, he flew over the trees toward the land where Almiralyn's cottage sat hidden by the powers of DiMensionery, the acreage where the RewFaaran camp now stood.

The image cleared, and another formed. A large cage hung outside a tent. An older, more senior member of the Mocendi League attempted to catch a caged Nyti.

Like a frenzied hummingbird, Reana zipped away from the large hand, tiny wings blurring as she dodged from side to side, top to bottom. The man attempted to freeze her frantic motion with a rhyme of immobility and failed. A muttered list of profane expletives accompanied the slamming of the small door. As he fumbled with the lock, the orange bird landed atop the cage and set it in motion. A sharp bump to the older man's elbow sent the lock flying. Without hesitating, Reana threw the catch on the door and whizzed out of reach. Her dragonfly flashed to her side.

The older Mocendi snatched the bird from the top of the cage and held it at eye level. "You just cost me a hostage and a source of information. If you are back to report nothing, you'd better take yourself elsewhere. And if I ever see you shaping a bright orange bird again while you are here to spy, I will strip you of your rank and dump you in the Death Pits of TreBlaya." He pitched the bird into the air and marched into the tent.

The image vanished in a swirl of color; a new one took its place.

Kieel sat in the TreeOm of Tibin, the leader of the Wood Tiffs, reporting to Tinpaca Mondago. Worry creased his brow. Periodically, his gaze flicked to the round window behind the Tinpaca. He gave himself a mental shake. Still, he could not dispel the image of Reana in the cage. *My granddaughter's safety depends on my ability to do my job.*

"Is that all?" Mondago nudged.

"Almost, sir." Precisely and to the point, he completed his report. "Jordett has control of the Five Towers and the city. He expects the Mocendi to try something soon. He has the five KcernFensians to help him counteract whatever they attempt."

Mondago rolled a cigar between his finger and thumb, inhaled its scent, and returned it to his shirt pocket. "I am impressed, Kieel. You have a head for detail. It's a pleasure to have you on our side."

A dragonfly buzzed into view and hovered.

Kieel fluttered into the air. "Thank you, sir. Could I have a moment?"

"Of course."

Kieel shot through the open window. Reana flew into his arms and rested her head on his shoulder. He hugged her close. When she stepped back, she wore a serious smile.

"Grandy, I'll tell you everything, but first I have news for the Tinpaca."

Kieel led the way inside.

Mondago held up a palm. She landed. "I owe you a thank you, Reana. Your excellent diversion kept me and my men from being trapped by the Mocendi."

Kieel flew to her side. "A diversion?"

Reana shrugged. "Me and some friends made a bunch of noise, attracted the Mocendi's attention, and led him away from the camp." She grinned. "Mondago and his soldiers got away."

He frowned. "Is that how the Mocendi caught you?"

"No, Grandy, that was later. I had the watch. I got distracted and ended up in that cage." She bit her lip. "Tinpaca, those are wicked men. Her tiny nostrils flared. "And more are coming. Once the Mocendi take over Idronatti, they will prepare Thera for The MasTer. Their next step will be to take over Myrrh. Only two Mocendi are looking for you and the Crystal. They have a trap set in case you or your men decide to snoop around. The older man called it a ward net. Said if someone touches it, it'll hurt 'em bad."

Mondago's brow furrowed. "Do you know what it looks like?"

Reana shook her head.

He looked at Kieel. "Will you look around and figure out what this net is? I'll send Yuin, the Pentharian, with you."

"I'll go, but I don't want Reana involved."

Reana folded her arms and screwed her face into a stubborn mask. "If I don't go with you, Grandy, I'll go by myself. Ashor and Mumshoo will help me."

Mondago cleared his throat. "Reana, I have a more important job for you. I need you and your friends to carry messages to my men and back. Can I count on you to organize this?"

The stubborn expression melted into a grin. "Yes, sir. We will be ready to work once I get everyone together."

He smiled. "I knew I could count on you. Let me know when you've assembled your team."

She gave Kieel a quick kiss on the cheek and flew out the window.

Mondago watched her go as a red moth fluttered to his hand. "You know Yuin, Kieel. Be careful, both of you. Don't get caught. Don't take chances. Get back here as quickly as possible."

The moth fluttered out the window. Kieel thanked the Tinpaca for distracting Reana and darted after it.

The song of dripping water filled Veersuni. Almiralyn heaved a sigh of relief. *Reana is safe for the moment. A ward net... Hmmm.*
"Elcaro, show me the ward-net."

A blur of muted blues and greens appeared and melted away. On the surface, the RewFaaran camp formed. Barely visible to the naked eye, spiderweb-thin strands wove a fence around the perimeter. While she watched, a small bird flew into the net and dropped to the ground, immobile. She projected her senses through the fountain and examined the inert body. The heart pulsed with a slow, stuttering beat. It would recover. She withdrew and snapped her fingers. Water resumed its journey from palms to bowl.

When Sparrow arrived at Ephos, she found Merrilea and Owae in the hall, discussing Zugo's care. Fatigue magnified the lines in the elder's face. Merrilea's shoulders drooped, and her smile seemed forced. Sparrow caught Merrilea's eye and touched Owae's arm. "You both need to rest. I'll stay with Zugo."

Quick to accept her offer, Merrilea put an arm around Owae and guided her down the hall.

Sparrow entered the healing room to find Lisseta asleep in a chair and Zugo snoring softly. Singed white fur framed the young DeoNyte's face and continued over his shoulders. She flinched at the sight of his blistered chest and hand.

The snoring stopped. Pale blue eyes regarded her with a moment of confusion; then lit with recognition. "Sparrow." His voice cracked. "Thirsty."

She slid an arm under his shoulders and held a cup of water to his lips. When she eased him back, he seemed to sleep. His breathing slowed and then quickened. His eyes fluttered open and sought her face.

"The MasTer...he got in my head. Something strange—" Pain creased his brow. He stifled a moan and clenched his teeth together. When the wave had passed, he attempted a small smile. "Sorry."

"Don't be sorry. Burns aren't fun. You were saying something about The MasTer."

"At first, I experienced only anger and hatred." His brow wrinkled. "I know this sounds silly, but his attention faltered. He felt different." Zugo gulped in a breath. "Vulnerable, softer, more—" He flinched and stifled a groan.

Sparrow bent closer. "Zugo, I'm going to find Owae. You need something to help with the..."

He grabbed her hand. "Almiralyn."

"I promise to tell her."

His grip went slack.

Owae entered as she turned to go, her bare feet silent on the stone floor. She made a quick examination of her patient and began to prepare a draught for his pain. "Thank you for the break, Sparrow. Tell Almiralyn that Merrilea has returned to her research."

"I will." Sparrow hurried down the hall and paused at the Reading Room door. Zugo's information about The MasTer and Owae's comment about research rekindled her interest in the book Wilith had found.

"Now, where did One Man put it?" A memory of him sliding it between two similar books directed her gazed to a shelf across the room. A quick search left her empty-handed. Frowning, she ran a finger over the titled spines, stopped at a small gap between two slender volumes, and eased them further apart. Tucked as far back as possible, she found the small, leather-bound journal. She cast her mind back to One Man's actions earlier. *I know he didn't hide it. I remember it lined up with the books on either side.*

More intrigued than ever, she curled up in the corner of a big chair near the fireplace and examined the battered cover and its title, *El Stroma*. She pondered the excerpt One Man had shared: "It is the Time of Ending on the planet of El Stroma. Most have fled or died. Acid rain falls in torrents. I write this brief history hoping someday the planet may be returned to its former beauty." The picture it conjured up made her shiver.

Flipping the tattered pages, she studied the strange alphabet and the spidery script shaping the letters. One word appeared repeatedly. She traced its unfamiliar contours with her fingertip. *I wonder if it is a name...perhaps the name of the person who wrote the journal?* With a sigh, she closed the book and pressed it between her hands. *I'll never be able to decipher this.*

A painting on the wall opposite caught her eye. The impulse to return the journal to the shelf flickered and died. *Of course. Why didn't I think of that sooner?*

Clutching the journal to her chest, she teleported.

Almiralyn contemplated the cascade of drops from the statue's palms, turmoil seething through her thoughts. The desire to rid Myrrh of the Mocendi almost overpowered her common sense. Relevart had told her to stay in the caverns. Discarding her restlessness like an old coat, she went in search of the High Priestess of the Caves of Canedari. After sharing the latest news, she asked her to send a message to Tibin, asking him to warn Mondago and the creatures and small folk of the Terces Wood to stay clear of the RewFaaran camp until she let them know it was safe.

This errand complete, she considered her next move. *With Sparrow's help, I can use the ward-net to make the Mocendi's lives miserable.* Fully expecting to find Allynae's companion ensconced with Owae, Merrilea, and Lisseta, she hurried to the healing room. Merrilea's absence made sense; Sparrow's aroused her curiosity.

She left after a brief discussion with Owae about Zugo's condition. The young DeoNyte was holding his own, but the burns inflicted by The MasTer were slow to heal. In the Cave of Canedari, she stopped and gazed at the spot where Evolsefil usually stood. *If I were Sparrow, where...* She laughed. "I'd be painting."

Teleporting to the studio entrance, she sent a telepathic message. *"May I come in?"*

The curtain whipped aside. "Mira, thank the Fathers you're here. Come and see."

A large canvas dominated the space. Next to it, propped up against a jar, was the journal Wilith had found. Almiralyn positioned herself in front of the painting, taking in every detail.

Divided into panels, it depicted three different scenes. A dawn of a new turning, a woman cradling two newborns, the world overflowing with color and life. Panel two showed a transition to fear and uncertainty. A different woman hid two small children in her long skirts. Overhead, the clouds churned. Smoke tinted the landscape shades of gray. In panel three, dead bodies littered the ground. The sky glowed red; the countryside lay barren and black beneath a pounding rain. Most arresting, however, was a young woman standing amid the chaos, wielding an acid torch. Hatred, scorn, and malice distorted the lovely face. Her muscular body was slender and well proportioned. Long, dark hair caught up in a braid hung over one shoulder. Gleaming against her bloodied tunic was an open silver locket. The picture inside showed a boy of perhaps three, his eyes bright with intelligence.

"It's the story in the journal." Sparrow regarded her painting with a puzzled expression and shared her conversation with Zugo. "What do you think it all means, Mira?"

Almiralyn studied the woman on the canvas. Her mind traveled back over the past moon cycles, dissecting her dealings with the Mocendi League and its leader. She recalled a momentary appearance of a braid in the fountain and the misty figure that rose from Elcaro's Eye, its head bowed, its arms held out in supplication. "Do you know who she might be?"

Sparrow shook her head. Excitement replaced her puzzled examination of her artwork. "Whoever she is, she's important to The MasTer and the League."

Almiralyn picked up the journal and laid a hand on her arm.

Wilith, Merrilea, and Elae looked up in surprise as they materialized by their table in the research area.

Elae noted the book in her hand. "You read it?"

"No, Sparrow painted it. Before we show you the painting, she will share a brief conversation she had with Zugo."

When Sparrow finished, Almiralyn waved a hand, and the painting appeared.

Everyone crowded around the canvas. Wilith cleared his throat. "Is she related to The MasTer?"

"She could be his daughter," Merrilea said. "Or his wife."

Wilith rubbed his forehead. "He wouldn't allow his wife or daughter to become involved in a revolution."

"Why wouldn't they be involved?" Sparrow asked.

"Because women don't fight…" His voice trailed off as Almiralyn, Sparrow, and Merrilea all shot him a quelling look.

Elae, oblivious to the conversation, scrutinized the painting. "Who is the boy in the locket?"

Almiralyn studied the small portrait. "That is the important question, isn't it?"

In Veersuni, the kneeling statue gazed into the bowl of Elcaro's Eye from glistening sapphire eyes. A single drop slipped from her palms. The water formed rippled circles and grew still.

Wolloh walked at Relevart's side through endless space. Constellations came and went; Nebula bloomed and faded; stars died and new ones birthed; galaxies whirled by; and still, his mentor continued the unbroken rhythm of his long stride. It occurred to Wolloh to wonder why the VarTerel brought him to Mittkeer. The question formed and faded; the walk through All Time and No Time proceeded.

The sound of cascading water whispered through the sanctuary. A knowing smile touched the lips of the alabaster statue, then resettled into its usual serene expression.

Relevart strode through the Land of Time, his mind centered on the need to make several important decisions. Mittkeer provided a place to think and plan, while losing none of that human commodity—time.

Froetise kept him apprised of events beyond the boundaries. The MasTer *had guessed* that he, Relevart, had left Persow, that Wolloh lived, that Evolsefil was hidden somewhere in the Terces Wood. He *assumed* that Renn Whalend was his prisoner, that Nissasa had died, that he was winning one battle after the other, that Thera and Myrrh would soon be his. He mustered his Mocendi for the final battle, reveling in his power and already celebrating the success of his plans for the future.

Relevart cast a sideways glance at his former student. Wolloh had been a challenge to train—a worthwhile challenge, but a challenge nonetheless. Confident Wolloh was worthy of participating in this auspicious moment, he smiled to himself. *The balance of power in the Universe shifts. The Unfolding's conclusion draws near.*

Bilar, the constellation of justice and balance, created a swathe of radiance across the endless expanse of Mittkeer. Relevart faced his companion.

Wolloh stopped beside him. His intense, single-eyed gaze regarded him. "I gather it is time to inform me of your plans."

Relevart studied his features—the handsome right side, the disfigured left. "Do you remember your youthful dreams?"

"Do you mean my desire to achieve the rank of VarTerel? My choices shattered that dream a long time ago. Ah, youth. A time of assured thinking: I am the best, the strongest, the smartest, I don't have to listen, I *am* invincible." Nostalgia shaped his smile, stretching the left side of his mouth to accommodate it.

Relevart placed his staff between them. "That arrogant young man exists only in memory, Wolloh Espyro. Your life's journey has taught you more than you can imagine." He began to chant,

> *"Froetise, divide this staff in two.*
> *Make both solid through and true.*
> *Replicate your crystal power*
> *Before which evil's minions cower."*

The rowan staff blurred and split down the center. Two shafts nestled together beneath the gleam of Froetise. Relevart gripped one in each hand.

> *"One power for good and all;*
> *Two shafts to avert the fall.*
> *Standing together or apart,*
> *They thwart those wielding The MasTer's art.*

A loud crack melted into the vastness of Mittkeer. Two staffs crackled with power. A gust of wind caught them—tossed them upward. A flash of light engulfed them. From the afterglow, four towering figures emerged, staffs in the hands of two. Matching step for step, they marched forward and, in unison, halted a short distance in front of Relevart and Wolloh.

A single voice boomed. "We, the Galactic Guardians, command the VarTerel of the Inner Universe to step forward."

Relevart complied.

The figure touched the tip of the staff's encased crystal to his forehead. "From this moment forth, you will be known as Avlin Enus, the Universal VarTerel. Your role is to correct the wrongs of those who claim the Universe as their own. You will find and nurture a partnership which will bring balance to the Cosmos. If you agree, Avlin Enus, to accept these additional responsibilities, take this staff as the symbol of your office."

Relevart bowed and accepted the staff. Adrenaline rushed through his body. His arms stretched wide. His heartbeat thrummed so deep he thought his chest would explode. The crystal tip of the staff burst into dazzling light that bathed him, cleansed him, and left him pulsating with power. His head throbbed as the blinding light faded but left behind visual clarity and acute mental awareness.

Wolloh observed the proceedings with a growing sense of expectancy. When the Guardian faced him and lifted the second staff, he found he could not breathe.

"Wolloh Espyro, High DiMensioner od DerTah, are you prepared to fight for the good of the Inner Universe from this moment forward and for all time?"

Oxygen gushed into his lungs. "I am."

"Welcome, VarTerel of the Inner Universe. Avlin Enus will serve as your mentor. Listen to him well." He touched Wolloh's disfigured cheek. "We leave that which you have created as a reminder and a lesson that is visible to all." The man held out the staff. "Accept this staff, known henceforth as Vinredi, as a symbol of your new office."

Wolloh took it. Power careened through every fiber of his body. Searing heat doubled him over. A blaze of light blinded him. Thunder rumbled across Mittkeer. When he straightened and his vision cleared, the Guardians had vanished, and a solemn Avlin Enus regarded him.

"How do you feel?"

Wolloh breathed. "Grateful to you for your trust, Avlin Enus. And grateful for the opportunity to serve."

The new Universal VarTerel smiled. "I will continue to be known as Relevart until The Unfolding releases me to pursue another course. Now, Wolloh Espyro, VarTerel of the Inner Universe, you have a lot to learn in a short time. Hold on to me and raise Vinredi. Your training is about to begin."

34
Der Tah

After the wards around Shu Chenaro were rebuilt and recoded, Somay sat astride Starfire with the charnockite jar wrapped in a canvas carry bag attached to his chest. Clutching a fistful of mane, he peered down at the Tinga Forest. The impressive size of the trees and foliage brought to mind ludoc cats, gothraw, and insects twice the size of his hand. *Wouldn't mind seeing it someday.* He glanced ahead where the Sea of Trinuge glowed with the approach of morning. Soon it would be time to land.

Slouched over the jar to streamline his body in the wind, Somay pondered his life's journey. The Seed of Carsilem pressed him to be on the move. The Unfolding rushed ahead. He swam in the backwash instead of at the forefront. The urge to act, to find his son, to rid the Inner Universe of the Mocendi League made him chafe against the need to assist with the rejoining of Nissasa's physical body and his quintessence.

When the Dreelas' estate came into view, Starfire began a circled descent to search for a place to land unobserved. A small clearing in the trees bordering the manicured gardens surrounding the house opened up below them. As Starfire's hooves touched the ground, he furled his wings and snorted softly.

Somay jumped to the ground.

Starfire looked back at him. His ears twitched. He shook his starlit head, pawed the ground, and shifted. Allynae looked grim. "Trouble on the way."

Somay slipped deeper into the trees. Allynae ducked behind a large leafy bush. A tall, angular woman rushed down the path, her homely face made more unattractive by a disappointed sneer. She knelt and studied the ground. Stood up and scanned the sky. "I saw you. I know you're here."

Seyes Nomed ambled into the clearing. "I can assure you, Roween, there is no one here except you...and me, of course." Almost eye to eye with her, he drawled, "I'm curious. The Dreela requested you remain in your rooms." He perused the clearing. "And yet you are here." His hazel eyes glinted with steely light.

Roween's chin jutted out, and her eyes flashed. "I am the LaChett of the Largeen Joram of RewFaar. No one tells me what to do." She flung herself down the path, tripped on her long skirt, and flounced like an angry child into the house.

Nomed kept his gaze fixed on her back until the slamming door hid her from view. He whispered over his shoulder. "The solarium is straight ahead on the right. Meet me there. I'll make sure she's under control, and then we will join TheLise."

Allynae stepped from behind the bush and brushed the dirt from his knees. "What an unpleasant woman."

Somay handed him the canvas carry bag and lifted the jar free. "I'm guessing we haven't seen the last of her." He looked toward the house. "Nomed's on his way to the solarium. Shall we?"

A short time later, Somay placed the jar on a table in the small, private sitting room where TheLise greeted them with a smile and the positive acknowledgement of Somay's decision to reclaim his birth name. "You have always been Somay to me." Her Dreelas' demeanor cloaked her. "Nissasa's body has almost reached the limits of its endurance. The sooner we reunite it with his quintessence, the better. Did WoNa tell you what to do with Souvitrico, the Oracle Stone?"

Somay related her instructions.

Nomed frowned. "Of course, Brie is not within reach. It seems nothing about these turnings is easy." He held the door open.

TheLise swept through. "I suggest we hurry. Roween is having tea with Tissent, who will do her best to keep her occupied."

Roween's rooms were close at hand. Somay crossed to the bed and studied the pale face of Nissasa Rattori. Hollowed cheeks gave him a haggard appearance. It had been several turnings since his body had received any type of nourishment. His skin was waxy and longing for hydration.

Allynae stood at the foot of the bed. "How do we do this? We need to be quick."

Somay placed the jar between Nissasa's ankles and moved to the head of the bed. He taught the rhyme of release and re-entry and then gave simple instructions. "Do not touch the body. We're here to watch, not participate. Should one of us touch him before his is fully back, it could destroy his ability to return to wholeness. TheLise, remove the lid."

She broke the seal, set the charnockite lid aside, and stepped away from the bed. Together, they began to chant,

> *"The goal is to this man, make whole,*
> *Quintessence, ignite Nissasa's soul.*
> *Rejoin, remake, replenish, retether,*
> *Essence and body, merge back together."*

A translucent gray mist poured over the lip of the jar and rolled in waves over the entire body. As it reached the head, the chest rose, the lips yawned wide, and the mist began to flow up nostrils and into the gapping mouth.

The door flew open. Roween Rattori marched straight to the bed and threw herself across her son's body, dispersing the remaining mist. She glared up at Somay. "How dare you touch my son without my permission!"

Nissasa's eyes flew open. His maddened gaze fixed on his mother. Grabbing her arms, he shoved her to her knees and sat up. Wild eyes found the jar. Scrambling to the foot of the bed, he gathered it in his arms and began to rock, back and forth and back and forth.

Somay stepped into his line of vision. "Nissasa, look at me."

Cold blue eyes blinked.

"If you try to retrieve Souvitrico, you will sustain permanent damage to your hand."

Roween shoved him aside. "You lie. You want the crystal for yourself." She plunged a hand in the jar. A DerTah shattering scream pierced the air. Tears spilled down her face. A choked sob ended as Somay caught and supported her limp body.

Nissasa grew deathly still and stared at his mother with bewildered alarm. Allynae removed the jar from his shaking arms and knelt beside Roween as Somay lowered her to the floor. TheLise pulled her hand free and released it with a gasp of horror.

Shock silenced everyone in the room. Flames licked the surface of the fingers and palm of Roween's right hand. A web of sizzling red traveled over the surface midway up her arm, turning the flesh to black. While they watched, the fingers withered, leaving only blackened bones.

Behind them, sitting on the edge of the bed, Nissasa began to sob. "MaMa. I want my MaMa." The grown man had returned as a child.

Torgin stood with the adults on *Melback,* studying the chart suspended above the compass face. The portal had deposited them near the coast of TheDa, a mountainous province across the Sea of Minusa from Geran and the Isle of ZaltRaca. He measured the distance in his mind—ten DerTahan elims—just short of eight Theran miles. *We're closer, Mother, but it feels like a world away.* He glanced at the icy shoreline. *Without the ConDria's portal, we'd still be on the opposite side of the planet.*

Gregos put a hand on his shoulder. "Amazing compass, boy. You and Tamosh check Natlaki Bay for the best anchorage. I've got the wheel. Elf, go find yourself a sweater and man the watch perch. Esán, you're with Corvus and Yaro in the cabin."

The needle on the Compass of Ostradio spun and stopped. A new, more detailed chart rose above the face and enlarged. Torgin and Tamosh studied the two best places to drop anchor. The one to the right of the fiord's entrance appeared the most promising. A chain of islands sheltered it from winds off the Sea of Minusa.

Gregos gave him a pat on the back. "Good work. Go below and see what your friends are doing. Grab us each a sweater and get back here."

Below deck, Torgin slid onto a seat at the chart table next to Ira. Desirol sat between Corvus and Yaro, with Shyllee at his feet. Brie and Esán sat on the opposite berth. He gave the RewFaaran a searching look. "How are you doing, Des?"

"I'm still here. Guess that means I'm holding my own." He clamped his mouth closed and swallowed. His fists balled at his sides.

Shyllee lifted her head and growled. Desirol's tension faded. He sighed and reached down to scratch the dog's ears.

Corvus sketched out their plan. "Brie and Esán, you will come with me to scout the situation on ZaltRaca. Yaro will stay on the boat to help Desirol keep the Mindeco in line. In the morning, *Melback* will set sail for the island. Torgin, your job is to help Tamosh plot a safe course through the turbulent waters of the Sea of Minusa. I will keep in touch telepathically with Ira and Elf." He turned a serious face to Desirol.

"Keep busy and keep your wits about you. Don't take off the drango tunic or boots, and keep the Remembering Stone and Marji's pouch with you at all times. Shyllee will help you monitor the Mindeco. If he gets too strong, Yaro will use stunning serum to calm you both. As soon as we rescue Torgin's mother, we'll find the VarTerel. Right now, your job is to stay calm. Understood?"

"Yes, sir." He looked at Ira. "Sorry, I broke your nose."

Ira patted the knife. "Efillaeh took care of it."

Elf appeared in the open hatch.

Corvus looked up and smiled. "Good, Elf, come in. Torgin, you'd better take a sweater up to Gregos. Des, go with him and get some fresh air. Esán and Brie, I'll join you shortly."

Desirol and Shyllee climbed on deck and took a seat at the stern. Torgin pulled Brie and Esán to one side. "Promise you'll find my mother and keep her safe."

Brie planted a kiss on his cheek. "We promise to do our best."

Esán met his gaze. "You take care of *Melback*. I expect we're going to need her."

Below deck, Ira folded his arms and chewed on his bottom lip. Everyone had an important job but him, even Des—control the Mindeco. He'd used telepathy, a little, not enough to feel confident that he could use it in a crisis. *Ah well, Elf is great at it.*

Yaro, his lizard eyes glowing in the subdued light, observed him from across the table. Ira squirmed and stared at a snake tattoo on his cheek.

The Pentharian touched the coiled Reptile. "I hatched under Nep Rin Tese, the sign of the serpent, an honor few receive."

"Aren't others…" Ira swallowed. "…*hatched* under the sign?"

"It is a sign that is rare in our heavens. We will not see it again from another twenty plus sun cycles."

Ira wanted to ask more questions, but Corvus finished giving Elf instructions and sat next to him.

"I have a job for you, Ira. One I'm hoping you never have to perform. This is important. Listen carefully. If the Mindeco should decide to shed Desirol's body, you are the only one onboard who has the power to stop him and to save Desirol's life."

A thrill of dread tightened Ira's throat. "What do I have to do?"

"You must take Efillaeh and insert the blade beneath the occipital bone." He pressed a spot on Ira's neck between the top of the spine and the base of the skull. "It has to be exact. An error will set Rikell free and turn him on you. Yaro can help, Ira, but you are the keeper of the sacred knife. You must be the one to wield it. Show me where you would insert it in me." He lifted his hair and presented the back of his neck.

Ira ran his finger along the bottom edge of his skull, found a soft spot beneath it, and pressed.

Corvus faced him. "Good. Take Desirol aside and find the exact spot. Don't tell him why. The Mindeco is aware enough to understand. If you use the knife on Desirol for any other reason, Rikell will take control. One more thing… Once you insert the knife, keep it there until I give you a sign." He turned to Yaro. "If this happens, you know what's needed."

"I do, Corvus. The sun rides the horizon. You must go. Ira and I will take care of *Melback* and her crew."

Corvus and Yaro touched palms, then foreheads. Corvus climbed on deck and called Brie and Esán to him. Ira arrived in time to see three laridae lift into the air and soar over the fiord, pale orange wings catching the light of the late turning sun.

The laridae, a type of gull inhabiting the shorelines of Trinuge, had a streamlined body and sleek wings that caught the air and sent Esán soaring after his companions. He missed the keen mind and exceptional eyesight of the kestrel, but realized it was important not to attract unwanted attention.

The flight over the Sea of Minusa proved challenging. Wind currents stirred the air into swirling eddies and tossed him one way and then the other. Releasing his need for control, he allowed the instincts of the laridae to take over, flew to Brie's side, and matched his wing stroke to hers.

The sea slid by; the sun dipped lower in the sky. Still, they kept flying. *How much longer?* The fatigue of a long flight left him straining to keep up. He forced his mind to concentrate on other things.

Relevart had told Corvus the Mocendi held Renn Whalend prisoner on ZaltRaca, a large island off the southern coast of Geran. Gregos' description: "windblown and sparsely populated." On the north side closest to the Geranian mainland, several small fishing villages littered the coastline. The southern side of the island boasted weather-carved rock formations, windy cliffs, and treacherous seas. Few made their homes in the south. It was on this shore that they would begin their search.

"Look alert."

Corvus' command snapped him to attention. A land mass crested the horizon. Even from this distance, Esán picked out the hint of a black haze hanging over it. Corvus had chosen correctly. If the Reach watched, Torgin's mother must be somewhere near.

The closer they came, the more forbidding the haze appeared. Soon he could pick out the shape of phalacro lining the cliffs, their long, black necks stretching, their sharp, black eyes peering. Corvus swooped lower. Esán held a position off his right wingtip and Brie off his left. He swept east of the bulk of the phalacro beyond the outer edge of the haze and landed on a towering rock formation. Small waves caressed its base. A single phalacro circled nearby.

"Stay." Corvus dove low above the water, skated over the surface, and landed. A quick motion of his head and he lifted into the air, something silver wiggling in his beak. He dropped it in front of them. *"Eat."*

Brie nudged it with her beak.

Corvus tore it into pieces and swallowed one whole.

Brie gulped her piece, ruffled her feathers, and squawked.

Esán tossed a morsel in the air, his attention on the phalacro, winging its way back toward the haze. Corvus caught the piece of fish, swallowed it, and swooped over the sea. Brie followed. Esán circled and shot after his companions. *Nothing seems to be other than it appears, nothing except The MasTer's Reach and the flock of phalacro at his command.*

Brie swooped behind Corvus. A sandy beach, tall cliffs, and fields of scrubby plants covered with purplish flowers flowed by beneath her. A grove of stocky, wind-blown oaks closed in around her. Ahead, Corvus materialized and waved her down. Esán landed beside her and shifted. The sun's light faded and left them in the night quiet of the woods.

Corvus touched her arm and whispered, "Over there. See it?"

She squinted through the hazy darkness. Light glowed in the windows of a small cottage. Waves battering the cliff face beyond it chorused with the screech of seabirds. The faint glimmer of stars penetrating the dispersing Reach was the only other light. The world felt dark and threatening.

She stifled a shiver. "I see."

He put an arm around her shoulders. "You know the plan. Esán and I will be close by."

Shifting to a miniature DerTahan night owl, she flew across the field to a small, dilapidated shed and landed. Unease held her motionless. Her knowledge of Torgin's mother made her the right person to affirm Renn's presence, but... She swiveled her tiny head and listened. Acute hearing picked up the muted hum of wards. Her mind blank, she tracked them as high as the eaves of the cottage. Soaring upward, she landed on the peak of the sod roof and surveyed the surrounding area. Nothing moved. Only the telltale odor of burned flesh hinted that the Reach had hovered above.

The roof, she discovered, had two chimneys. Perched on the rim of the one not in use, she peered over the edge, jumped in, and caught herself inches above the grate. Sticking to the shadows, she swooped through a kitchen, down a dim hallway, and landed on the mantle in the living room. Her head tilted to one side, she studied a woman resembling Renn Whalend curled up in a chair by the fire. Something triggered an alarm. Owl's eyes blinked and focused on the slow rise of her hand.

With a finger on her lips, the woman shook her head. An array of images flooded Brie's mind. *"Go."* The urgent command sent her flying back the way she had come. The chimney's dark shadow embraced her. Tension and a touch of fear held her immobile on the roof's ridge. Alarm set her in motion. She flew downwind of the cottage, past the rickety shed, and over the field bordering the cliffs. Zig-zagging between trees, she landed on the rough-barked branch of a squat pine some distance from where her companions hid. A phalacro swooped overhead. A second seabird circled and flew west.

Water, wind, the rustling of branches rubbing together were the only sounds Brie could detect. Her silent owl wings pressed against the air, carried her to a tree under which Esán and Corvus rested, and slowed her descent. In human form, she landed between them and sank to the ground. With her hands clasping theirs, she closed her eyes and relayed the shared images: Renn Whalend in the hull of a wrecked ship, the two people with her, a cave entrance at the bottom of the cliff, the gaunt face of a Mocendi DiMensioner.

Corvus murmured under his breath. "Henrietta Avetlire, what game is Relevart playing?"

Esán whispered, "Do you know the Mocendi?"

"He's The MasTer's right hand. If he's in charge here, Henri is in more danger than she realizes. We need to get Renn to safety. Henri is good, but…"

Brie frowned. "We can't leave her here alone."

Corvus squeezed her hand. "We'll come back for her. Right now, Renn is our focus. Relevart knows what he's doing, Brie. Let's find the cave entrance."

A circuitous route brought them to the base of the Cliffs of Tymine. Henri's picture left little doubt which rock to press. The stone door swung inward. Esán led the way inside. Corvus closed the door behind them. Dense darkness pressed them into a tight stationary group. A gruff voice barked, "Move, and I'll shoot."

Corvus squeezed Brie's arm. She called out. "I'm Brielle AsTar, a friend of Torgin's. My friends are Esán Efre and Corvus Castilym, the Guardian of Myrrh's protector."

A lantern at the end of the passage etched out a sturdy man aiming a shotgun. "Let the girl come back, Cay."

Corvus released her arm. Brie walked up to a dark-haired woman, who motioned her under a low overhang. "In there."

Renn Whalend stood beside a plank table. A smile of relief replaced the fear of a second before. "Brie. It is you. Where's Torgin? Is he here?"

"Torgin isn't with us. If my friends can come in, we'll tell you everything you want to know, Citiwoman Whalend."

A mix of emotions—relief, disappointment, the return of fear—appeared and were gone in an instant. "Please call me Renn. It's alright, Bibeed. Bring them back."

Soon, they gathered around the table. Brie listened to Corvus and Esán answer a barrage of questions. Her mind wandered to the cottage at the top of the cliffs. *What is Aunt Henri doing? Is she safe? What if...*

35
Myrrh

Almiralyn and Sparrow had left Merrilea, Wilith, and Elae to continue their hunt for proof of The MasTer's identity.

At the door to Veersuni, Almiralyn paused. "Be careful. Drawing The MasTer's attention to our search for answers will only cause problems. If we can discover his motivation—why he is so angry—perhaps we can find an end to this battle of wills."

Sparrow rubbed a splatter of gold paint on her hand. "I believe the pictures in the locket are the key."

Almiralyn stepped over the threshold and breathed in the tranquility of Veersuni. At her behest, the High Priestess had ordered the sanctuary cleared of all signs of the recent tempest. She crossed to the fountain, gazed at the rippling water, and sorted through her tumultuous thoughts. Events were ongoing. The Unfolding raced toward its climax. Intermingled within its currents, a galactic game intensified. The mystery of The MasTer rose to the forefront. A question that would provide information without raising suspicion slowly took shape. Quiet but curious, Sparrow waited beside her.

The window's patchwork pattern reformed on the fountain's surface. Dripping water merged the irregular shapes one into another. Drop by drop, a picture began to form. A hush settled over Veersuni. Almiralyn blinked back tears.

Sparrow whispered, "Who?"

The beautiful woman in the fountain shot a furtive glance over her shoulder. "We have little time, Almiralyn. The game you play is full of danger. Tread with care. Learn what you can of TreBlayan birth-mates. Your father and I love you and Allynae." The image faded.

Almiralyn cried out in dismay, "Don't go. I—"

The song of dripping water whispered through Veersuni. Elcaro's Eye had shown her what she needed to know.

Sparrow guided her from the sanctuary and sat beside her in a reading alcove. "Was that your mother? You look so much like her."

Almiralyn brushed her tears away. "You just met Mairin Nadrugia. I was fifteen sun cycles when she and my father, at the request of the Galactic Guardians, left on a secret and very dangerous mission. We've heard nothing from them until now."

"That must have been difficult."

"I'd been in training at the temple for three sun cycles, so I wasn't living at home. Alli had a harder time. He was only ten. We were told they had died. I never believed it."

Sparrow hugged her. "Perhaps The Unfolding will bring them home."

"Perhaps it will." Almiralyn lost herself in the memory of her mother's face, of the last time she had seen her in person, of the inner knowing that she and her father lived. With a sigh, she pushed back her chair. "It's clear my parents' mission continues. So does ours. Please ask Wilith to research TreBlayan birth-mates, then rejoin me in Veersuni."

As Sparrow disappeared into the research level of the Galactic Library, Almiralyn stared into space, her thoughts refusing to let go of the image of her mother. It occurred to her it might have been a fraud, a trap to lead her down a wrong path. Her memory re-examined her mother's features, the silver-blonde hair, the eyes that glowed the deep blue of the sapphire. The tone of her voice held a quality hard to copy, one that Almiralyn knew well. Certain that Elcaro's Eye had shown her truth, she entered Veersuni and went straight to the fountain.

A soft snap of her fingers stopped the flowing water and calmed the surface. As though she flew above her land, a panorama of Myrrh's beauty flowed over the water. Grazing in a gulch deep in the foothills, Gemlucky, her black stallion, kept watch over her small herd of horses and the pony Tam. Behind them, the late-turning sun enriched the salmon, red, and black of the Dojanack Mountains. Mount Niar, the only crystal peak, glistened, reflecting the light and the surrounding beauty. *How I love these mountains.*

She smiled as the fountain panned across the brown and gold of the Grasslands in autumn. The Terces Wood flowed by, bringing with it memories of the crisp dampness of fall. Nemttachenn Tower rose above the forest canopy, its granite walls glowing in the sun. Then the fountain closed in on her acreage and held steady. Almost undetectable, the ward-web hung, draped like a spider's silky web, around the RewFaaran camp.

Sparrow slipped into the sanctuary and tiptoed to her side. "I delivered the message, Mira."

Almiralyn, her attention fixed on the fountain, nodded and traced a symbol in the air above the shimmering image. Thread by thread, the web began to unravel. A slender strand floated upward. She circled her finger and, with a twist of her wrist, signaled it to wind into a ball. Sparrow, quick to follow her example, grinned as her ball of energy began to grow.

When they had dismantled the entire force field, Almiralyn motioned the balls to the center of the fountain and merged them together. Mimicking a knitter, she created a blanket of energy big enough to engulf only the tents occupied by the Mocendi and then let it fall. Anchoring it to the ground with a whispered word, she instructed the new ward to keep the Mocendi trapped inside. Next, she instructed it to respond with a loud hum whenever anything touched it.

"Secure and seal," she whispered.

"Secure and seal." Sparrow grinned.

On the water's surface, a man, anger infusing pallid cheeks with red, marched from a tent. Striding forward, he ran into the wards and jumped back as a loud humming exploded in the clearing. Again and again, he tried to undo the damage. Over and over, he failed. A fisted hand beat the air. "I will undo this, and then I plan to find you, whoever you are." He marched back into his tent and flipped the entrance flap into place.

Water flowed, expressing delight with each droplet that fell.

Almiralyn sighed. "I need a break and a quick nap. I'll meet you in the Reading Room in two chron circles?"

Sparrow pressed her hands against her lower back. "I think a nap and a snack are in order for me, too."

They left Veersuni, walked to the Cave of Canedari, and paused in the silent emptiness before teleporting to their own quarters. Almiralyn stretched out in her sleep alcove and watched the quartz crystal embedded in the salmon walls twinkle in the light of her small oil lamp. Silencing her brain's need to question, organize, and plan, she rolled on her side and slept.

The Five Towers in Idronatti had been hard won. Jordett and the KcernFensians had sustained losses they could ill afford. Only a few of Nissasa's Brigade remained at large in the city. Where the RewFaarans had imprisoned the Five Fathers remained a mystery. Jordett had released the PPP officers who had chosen not to follow Orittra and the Mocendi and assigned them to positions of leadership. No one contested the Major's right to command.

The moon sailing overhead signaled the end of the long turning. Fatigue forced Jordett to bed down in an apartment in Tower One. The chronometer alarm ringing woke him up feeling, if not refreshed, at least better. Splashing water on his face, he toweled it dry, glanced at the chronometer next to the bed, and hurried from the room. Two floors down, the KcernFensian contingent gathered around a table. Radec's death was marked by the quiet grieving that enshrouded them.

Teva pulled out the chair beside her. "We've just returned from patrolling the city. The Mocendi are withdrawing. We, the supposed leaders of Nissasa's Brigade, have received a message that we are to hold the city until their return."

Jordett tapped the tip of his stylus on the table. "Very interesting. There is something occurring elsewhere that is more urgent. Question. How do they travel between planets besides via portals?"

Teva glanced at Lenadi. He nodded and began.

"The information we have received suggests that the League has a central command ship that houses the Mocendi. Children, whom they kidnapped because of their potential, are incarcerated and trained there. This ship remains in orbit around TreBlaya. They use a second ship equipped to jump from planet to planet and from galaxy to galaxy for travel. It can also transit the Inner Universe via a series of worm holes. When it is on a mission away from TreBlaya, a jump craft remains docked to the command ship. The MasTer and his Davea, the Astican, inhabit the planet. We believe The MasTer receives visitors in a chamber built within his residence. None of us have traveled there. But we know of those who have."

"I am assuming Almiralyn knows this information. What she may not know is that the Mocendi are focusing elsewhere, perhaps DerTah. Can you get word to her?"

Teva answered. "Lenadi has already sent a message to Dom."

Jordett taped a note into his mini-compu. "Excellent. Let's continue working on our plans for Idronatti."

At Antiques by Q, Dom shoved a battered hat on his head and shuffled to the cellar door. The largest piece of his broken crystal paperweight continued to connect him to Myrrh. His close call with death made him leery of using it. He preferred to deliver a message in person.

Muttering to himself about the indignities of growing old, he gripped the hand railing and limped downstairs. The mirror leaned against a dingy stone wall. Mist swirled on the cracked surface and tumbled to the cellar floor. A couple Mocendi had used it a turning ago. The caretaker of the mirror since its creation, Dom knew it well. For a long moment, he scrutinized it. When nothing set off an alarm, he pressed his palm against the glass. The print formed a fist. The index finger extended and drew a large keyhole.

He knew Almiralyn created the portal based on Old Earth's *Through the*

Looking Glass, her mother's favorite book. He pushed his spectacles higher. *Here I go.* Grabbing hold of his hat, he leapt. Sunflowers and quiet met him at the other end, quiet so intense, he ducked out of sight and listened.

A bright-eyed Nyti landed beside him and whispered, "Hey, Dom."

"Ashor, what's up? I gotta get a message to Almiralyn."

The tiny boy frowned. "Can't go to the Dojanacks. Almiralyn says no Intersect until further notice. I can take it to Tibin, and he'll see she gets it."

After sharing the message, Dom jerked his thumb toward the RewFaaran camp. "Feels pretty strange here. What's going on?"

Ashor grinned. "Almiralyn trapped a Mocendi in the camp with wards. They make a racket every time something touches them. The man is furious. Mondago's men captured another Mocendi and have him tucked away, waiting to be questioned."

Dom pulled on his whiskers. "Wonder if they were goin' wherever the other Mocendi are off to. Pretty frustratin' to be trapped here, huh?" He resettled his hat. "Best get back. You take that message straight t' Tibin."

He arrived back in the cellar and shuffled toward the steps. Footfalls overhead backed him up. Dodging under the staircase, he made himself as small as possible and waited. The cellar door opened, boots clattered on the wooden treads. A black caped figure pressed a hand to the mirror, watched the keyhole appear, and jumped.

Dom considered the portal. Curiosity tempted him to follow. Ignoring it, he forced his achy body up the stairs, swearing as he went. "Place is like a racetrack. Best find somewhere safe t' hide. Hate not knowin' what's up." He tripped. His hat tumbled to the bottom of the steps. With a muttered expletive, he began a shambling, frustrated descent and froze.

A black caped figure materialized in front of the mirror, picked up his hat, and held it out. "I believe this belongs to you."

Dom made no move to retrieve it. "May I help you?"

The young Mocendi flashed to the step below him. "You can tell me who set the wards in Myrrh."

"Actually, I don't know. Don't live there, you see. Live here." He snatched the hat, scrambled up the last three steps, and stumbled into the hallway.

The Mocendi arrived first. His hand shot out. Dom winced and tried to pull away. The grip tightened. Antiques by Q vanished.

Almiralyn woke with a start. *What was I dreaming?* She closed her eyes, made herself relax, and let her mind wander back through her dreamscape.

Devastation wrought by acid rain stretched around her in all directions. Charred plains, blackened mountains, trees burned to the ground. The carcasses of animals and birds littered the landscape. Once fertile farmland lay scorched and pitted. Small villages resembling heaps of trash overflowed with people's lives—their homes, possessions, and bodies. Horror choked her. This ravaged world was Myrrh.

She sat up, fighting back despair. Shaking hands made it hard to dress. Her reflection in the oval mirror over the washstand stared back at her. *Control yourself, Almiralyn. It was a dream.* She gripped the edge of the basin and took a deep breath. When she raised her gaze to the mirror, the panic in her eyes had subsided.

Braiding her hair calmed her further. *I have to find out who The MasTer is before he reeks more havoc throughout the Inner Universe.*

Picturing Veersuni, she teleported. The serenity of the sanctuary relaxed her need to rush, shushed her mind's twists and turns, and erased her fear. Panic solves nothing, it seemed to say. Panic is a destroyer of successful resolution.

Breathing in the faint scent of roses and lavender, she walked to the fountain, where water flowed over carved fingers and merged into the tiny wavelets traveling in endless circles. Not sure where to begin, Almiralyn cleared her mind. The water stilled. A midnight sky focused.

Wolloh Espyro stood in the middle of Mittkeer, his staff, a duplicate of Relevart's, held high, and the olive green of his good eye gleaming. He flashed from view and reappeared in the research area of the Galactic Library in Myrrh. At a table littered with books, scrolls, and manuscripts, Wilith, Merrilea, and Elae sat suspended in time. Hurrying forward, Wolloh searched through the materials, picked up the TreBlayan journal and vanished, leaving them to return to their research.

A continuous blur of color raced over the water's surface so fast, Almiralyn clutched the fountain's rim. Its sudden halt jarred through her body like the unexpected braking of a Ria Train. Hazy colors refashioned themselves into an image far removed from the Dojanack Cavern's on Myrrh.

Sun peeked between cumulus mounds of pearly white that drifted apart to show farmland and mountains below. Nestled in the foothills bordering the mountains, the faint image of a cottage grew more substantial.

The door flew open. A tall, white-haired man strolled into the intermittent sunshine, stretched his long arms wide, and laughed a laugh so deep and rich and charged with elation that the foothills tossed the joyous sound to the mountains, and the mountains to the sky. Laughter rolling onward formed a series of echoes, a chorus of delight that left the turning brighter and brighter.

Wolloh's sudden appearance at the bottom of the porch steps, one hand holding his staff and the other hidden in the folds of his calf-length black coat, ended unfettered joy. A serious Relevart regarded him from beneath bushy, white brows. "Well, how did it go?"

Wolloh withdrew his hand and held up the journal of *El Stroma*. Relevart's long fingers wrapped around it, caressed it, pressed it to his heart. He held it out and stared as though transfixed at the tattered black cover and two words comprising the title. Flipping to the first page, he began to read, pronouncing the strange words with knowledgeable ease.

Surprise registered on Wolloh's face. "Where did you learn to speak the language of the Eleo Preda? I thought it died after El Stroma's demise."

Relevart waved him into the cottage. "I've always known it. When I was very young, I remember my parents telling me never to speak it." A frown creased his brow. "Now, let us discover what we can learn about El Stroma."

Wolloh limped up the stairs and into the cottage.

The water trembled. The rim of the bowl framed Relevart's face. He murmured a phrase under his breath. Time fell away, erasing the years, the fine lines, the white hair. A small boy's frightened visage steadied. Almiralyn's hand went to her heart. The boy portrayed in the silver locket in Sparrow's painting stared up at her.

The water's return to its continuous drip, drop, drip erased the image.

Too stunned to think, Almiralyn sank onto a bench. Elcaro's recent revelations left her head and heart spinning—first her mother and now the discovery that the VarTerel came from El Stroma—the revelation that something connected him to the young woman in the painting and possibly to the Mocendi MasTer.

She massaged the lines on the palms of her hand, allowing her mind time to process the pieces of the universal puzzle being revealed within The Unfolding. The memory of Wolloh's new staff raised her brows. "I believe we have a new VarTerel." Her brow furrowed. "Does that mean Relevart's status has changed as well?"

A throat cleared. She glanced up. Sparrow stood beside her. "I thought I'd find you here. What was that about Relevart?"

Almiralyn pressed her palms together and struggled to put her thoughts in order. Sparrow's expression as she described her dream and what the fountain had revealed grew more and more incredulous.

"It never occurred to me the boy might be Relevart." She approached Elcaro and ran a finger over the carved alabaster braid circling the rim of the bowl. "The fountain's very much like you, Mira. Sometimes it seems almost alive. I wonder what other secrets it knows?"

Almiralyn joined her. "It knows things we will never know. Let's see if our research team has uncovered anything that will help with our mystery." She touched the statue's upturned palms, linked arms with Sparrow, and strolled from the sanctuary.

The fountain's watery song whispered through Veersuni as the effects of The Unfolding wove worlds, galaxies, and lives together on its undulating surface.

36
Der Tah & Persow

Brie's mind dodged her attempts to focus on the conversation at the table in the boathome. The cottage at the top of the cliff kept intruding. She couldn't forget her Aunt Henri or the bracelet that monitored her every move, or that she waited alone in the cottage, not knowing what might happen next. Agitation drove her from her seat. Aimless intent carried her from the table to the pantry to the fire pit, where a pot of soup simmered. The overhang beckoned. A glance over her shoulder assured her she was unobserved.

Ducking under the uneven edge, she trailed her fingers along the stone wall and made her way down the passage. When she reached the secret door, she searched for the rock that would trigger the mechanism to open it. Stymied, she sagged against the wall. A fleeting memory of her escape with Zugo from Seyes Nomed in the Cavern of Tennisca re-ignited her resolve. Placing her hands on the solid rock, she took a breath, watched the molecules rearrange, and walked through into the sheltered outer recess. A shift to the laridae and she flew to the cottage, landed on the sod roof, and listened intently.

Cool air ruffled her feathers as she considered her next shift. *Life has certainly become more interesting in the past few moon cycles.* She shifted. A gray wanderer moth fluttered down the chimney, along the hall, and into the living room, where it landed on the mantle.

The fire had died down. Aunt Henri slept wrapped in a threadbare quilt. She had shaped Renn Whalend to perfection. Tired beyond recent memory, Brie shaped a tiny mouse, curled up behind a tin mug of dried flowers, and slipped into dreaming.

The crackle of the fire woke her. Renn's summer green eyes gazed at her through crystal lenses. *"Better come and eat while you can."* She rested a hand on the mantle. Brie's mouse scampered onto the palm. Fingers curled around her. In the kitchen, Renn set her on the table. *"I'm not sure how close they're watching. It seems clear..."*

Brie materialized. "I couldn't leave you here alone."

Renn shoved a bowl of mush and a chunk of bread her way. *"Eat. Then we'll decide what to do. Corvus will be here any minute. He's not too happy with you."*

Corvus noticed Brie slip away from the table and almost stopped her. Aware of her intention and that *Melback* would not leave Natlaki Bay prior to sunrise, he let her go. He felt certain Vygel would not remove Renn from the cottage until he had her, the compass, and probably Torgin, *to help keep his mother in line. His eyes narrowed. The Mocendi know the sacred knife is on the boat, along with Desirol. Vygel doesn't know what happened to Melback.*

He turned his attention to Esán, where he slept by the fire pit. Brie's return to the cottage had left him ready to rush after her. Only Corvus' promise to bring her back had calmed him enough that, with help, he slept.

Frowning, Corvus scrutinized the dark purple circles rimming the boy's eyes. His skin looked dull and paler; his cheeks hollow. The disease that had gone into remission when he arrived in Myrrh raised its ugly head once again. This time, only a trip to Tao Spirian would save him.

Corvus sighed and set off down the roughed-out passage to the entrance. The twist of a rock swung it inward. Stepping out under the slim curve of Lunule, DerTah's pearlescent moon, he scanned the sky. *Somewhere up there a Mocendi ship orbits the planet. If Vygel is onboard, he will have finite opportunities to check on Renn.*

Shaping a pale orange laridae, he soared into the night, paralleled the cliff face, shot upward over the field of erika, and landed above the wards on the roof. Far to the east, pale light edged the horizon. Below in the cottage, he sensed two bodies. Vygel's energy signature tainted the wards. He ruffled his feathers and side-stepped to the western lip of the chimney.

A phalacro landed on the peak of the roof. Its black head swung his direction. Calculation infused its brain. Corvus ran a wing feather through his beak and pecked at a small mite on his breast. The phalacro's vigilance relaxed. Corvus flew over the fields and dove over the cliff. His shift to a small bat was instantaneous. Back at the house, he discovered the phalacro gone and zipped down the chimney.

Torgin lay on his side on Elf's berth, using an arm for a pillow. The anchorage he and Tamosh found was calm but for occasional gusts of freezing wind. The boat, anchored between the shore and a small island, floated in calm waters. In the cabin, the small wood-burning stove took the edge off TheDa's wintry cold.

Cozy, warm, and a wee bit sleepy, Torgin found it easy to forget the drama of the past few turnings until he glanced at Desirol. The RewFaaran sat on the lower berth opposite the stove, leaning against the bulkhead, a hand on Shyllee's head, terrified of sleeping. Torgin could empathize—if the Mindeco waited inside him, he wouldn't sleep either. Never far from Desirol's side, Ira snored softly on the upper berth.

Gregos glanced up from where he, Yaro, and Tamosh sat at the chart table, poring over rough sketches of the route the compass had proposed for the next turning's journey. "Better sleep, boy. Morning's on the way. Sailing the Sea of Minusa isn't gonna be a picnic."

Glad it was Elf up on the watch perch and not him, Torgin closed his eyes. He drifted into a light doze, jerked himself awake with a snore, and dropped off again. A hand shaking him awake startled him from a dream of Astican and Mindeco. He stared up into Ira's deep blue eyes.

"We're underway in half a chron circle. Gregos wants you with him at the helm. Tamosh left breakfast in the galley. Des was up all night. Yaro put him to sleep, and now he's scouting ahead. Shyllee'll bark when Des wakes. I put a set of oilskins on the chart table. See ya outside."

Torgin ate, donned the rain wear, and clambered on deck to find Gregos at the wheel and the boat underway. "Sorry, Captain. I didn't mean to oversleep."

"Must've needed it. Get out that compass, boy. Keep me on track."

As *Melback* nosed her way from behind the islands, the wind filled her sails and sent her gliding through the water toward the mouth of Natlaki Bay. Clouds hanging heavily over the Sea of Minusa hinted at the potential of rain.

Melback creaked and groaned as her smooth passage ended in waves as high as the Captain was tall. Gregos muttered under his breath and called out. "Safety lines! Hang on. Comin' about." The main boom swung from starboard to port. The sails billowed. The boat shuddered and stabilized. Huge raindrops splattered the deck. Gregos swore. "Just what we need—wind and rain." He yelled up at the watch perch, "Elf, look alive up there!"

Torgin had learned that beneath the surface of the Sea of Minusa, currents surged and boiled, creating eddy pools that could sink a boat in no time. When he had asked Tamosh if they were stable enough to chart, he'd frowned and shaken his head. *I wonder...* "Ostradio, show me the currents in the Sea of Minusa." The arrow spun and stopped. A chart rose above the face. Current patterns swirled and shifted. A red dot showed *Melback's* position. Straight ahead, a huge eddy swirled below the surface.

"Captain, we're headed for an eddy pool." He held out the compass.

Gregos' mustache drooped around a frowning mouth. "Heads up. Changing course," he bellowed.

He spun the wheel. Tamosh trimmed the sails. *Melback* zagged starboard, rode the crest of a wave, and dropped into a trough. Water breaking over the bow gushed over the deck. Torgin slid all the way to the hatch, righted himself, and brushed rain and sea from his eyes. Scanning the water off the port side, he noted a different texture on the surface, a place where the waves changed shape and foam spiraled.

Tamosh gave him a broad smile. "Good job, Torgin."

Gregos clapped him on the back. "Saved our hides, boy. Keep your eye on that compass."

Rain slowed to a drizzle. The roll and pitch of the waves eased, and *Melback* and her crew settled into a routine. Torgin had once again saved the turning. He no longer felt as if he didn't belong, that he was dead weight. *I might not read minds or change shapes, but...* He smiled to himself. *I have my own talents and skills.*

Somay sat on the balcony of his room at TheLise's home. Beyond the garden, the Sea of Trinuge merged into DerTah's only ocean, the VerDeas. Somewhere out there, Esán struggled to hold his illness in check. Somay felt the tug, the battle his son waged. The Unfolding was the only thing preventing him from taking Esán to Tao Spirian. His future and the future of the Inner Universe depended on his full participation in the events to come.

Refocusing his attention, Somay reviewed the results of yesterday's activities. He and TheLise had done what they could for Roween's arm and hand. The fingers were beyond repair. The wrist and lower arm would take time and Efillaeh to heal them. After making her as comfortable as possible, they had left her in her maid's care. Her interference with the uniting of Nissasa's body and his quintessence had left him with the mental capacity of a child of five. Not even the sacred knife could undo the damage. *Too bad. The man, when removed from his mother's influence, might have had potential; the child will never grow up.*

Unannounced, Allynae strode onto the balcony. "I can't stand just sitting here. The twins, Esán, Torgin, and Desirol are all up to their ears in trouble; and here we are in TheLise's lovely home, doing nothing." He slouched in a chair and cracked his knuckles, one by one.

Before Somay could respond, the Dreelas knocked, pushed the door open, and walked onto the balcony. Nomed accompanied her and perched on the stone balustrade surrounding it. TheLise remained standing, her beautiful eyes resting on Somay. He noted the flecks of amber swimming in the pewter gray, the enticing curve of her mouth, the warm honey-tan of her skin. *No wonder Nomed is smitten.*

She shot Nomed a coy look and sat down beside him. "Somay, we need a plan. We can't stay here while The MasTer embroils the young people in his deadly games. It is time to find them and do our best to help."

Somay caught the rise and fall of Nomed's infamous brow. *Relationships —Tianna, my lifemate, how I miss you.* He clamped down on his wayward thoughts. "Alli and I were discussing the same thing. I suggest we find out what we can prior to making plans. Do you have a crystal, TheLise? One that will connect us with Almiralyn? When I left, Elae had found a journal entitled *El Stroma* in the research area. I am hoping they have deciphered its contents. I feel certain it has something to do with The MasTer."

TheLise conducted them along one hallway after the other until she came to a door near the solarium. A narrow staircase took them to another labyrinth of narrower, less elegant corridors. She unlocked a nondescript door, ushered them inside a dark room, and relocked it. A snap of her fingers illuminated several small oil lamps. A tall, clear crystal claimed the center of the room like a queen on a throne. Allynae whistled. "That's a beauty, TheLise."

"Wolloh gave it to me when I attained the rank of DiMensioner. It's from the Evolsefil Caverns and connects to the crystal web. I apologize for the lengthy walk, but I thought it best not to teleport. Who knows who may watch our every move? The room has powerful wards. Nomed and Wolloh are the only ones, other than myself, who know about the crystal or this space. I suggest we put up individual wards before I contact Almiralyn via Elcaro's Eye."

Somay created his shields and waited while his companions followed suit. The accumulated power surrounding the table left him wondering if they had just created a beacon.

TheLise expected his concern. "This room has an insulated ceiling and walls, Somay. Nothing goes out, nothing comes in. We probably don't need our wards, but I prefer to be cautious."

Nomed's scar stretched with his smile. "My lady thinks of everything."

Somay lowered his gaze to the crystal, wishing for even a fleeting glimpse of Esán's mother.

Henri, her Renn face displaying surprise and a touch of nervousness, kept her thoughts focused on the man in front of her. Vygel had flashed into sight an instant after Brielle vanished. Her bowl and mug remained on the table.

He picked up the mug and sniffed the rim. "You've had company. How nice." Bulging eyes bored into hers. The mug hung from one boney finger. "Who?"

When she refused to answer, he let it fall. The sound of it shattering made her jump. A rough hand gripped her arm, guided her to the living room, and pushed her into a chair. Towering over her, he snarled, "Answer me, Renn Whalend."

His questions and probing continued. Henri observed him from beneath Renn's long dark lashes, her concentration complete. He discovered nothing she did not want him to know. His intelligence was not the issue. He simply saw what he expected to see and found what he expected to find. The man lacked imagination. But then, she doubted The MasTer encouraged the Mocendi to think, only to obey.

For the third time, he paced the room and returned, his expression menacing. "Tell me who was here, Renn. If you refuse to tell me, when I get my hands on Torgin, I will make him miserable."

She let a hint of panic scurry through her thoughts. "The woman assigned to look after me is the only person—"

Blue-veined hands gripped the arms of the chair. "Why did you return to the cottage?"

She touched Renn's locket, where it lay hidden beneath her shirt. "I left something here that is important to me."

He leaned closer. "What's so important, Renn Whalend? Show me."

She drew in a shaky breath, withdrew the locket, and let it rest over her heart.

A boney finger caressed it, traced the line of the chain, touched her throat. Sour breath brushed her neck. A desire to slap his hand away froze her into stillness.

Finally, he straightened. "Why did the woman caring for you leave you alone?"

"I wanted her safe, so I sent her away."

Vygel sank into a chair and drummed restless fingers on a side table. "The MasTer is becoming impatient. Tell me where your son is and how soon he will arrive."

Henri kept Renn's expression impassive. "How would *I* know that? You've kept me locked away here."

Two long strides brought him back to her chair. "Someone visited you here. Two dirty bowls, two dirty mugs..." He paced to the fireplace and back. "If you don't start talking, I'll take you to someone who will make you answer me."

Henri continued to study Renn's hands.

Vygel yanked her to her feet and growled. "The MasTer will not appreciate your lack of cooperation."

Flipping blonde hair from her face with a jerk of her head, Henri snatched her arm from his grip. "Don't touch me again, Vygel Vintrusie. If The MasTer wanted the truth beaten out of me, *you* would have done it already. I have information the League needs. I will be more likely to share if I am treated well." She breathed in and resumed her tirade. "Your people kidnapped me and brought me here against my will. I have no idea where my family is. I want to return to my home, something I feel is unlikely. *And* I am confronted by you regularly. To say that I am angry, distraught, afraid is an understatement. What else do you want to know?"

Vygel's thin lips twisted into a speculative smile. "You are a surprising woman, Renn Whalend. I did not realize you had so much..." His smile grew wider. "Fire. Well, I have things to do. Don't go anywhere while I am gone." A wicked laugh rattled from his throat as he disappeared.

Corvus materialized. "Good work, Renn."

Henri collapsed in her chair. "You heard?"

His dimple deepened. "I did."

Almiralyn's aunt straighten Renn's blue uniform skirt and sighed. "He is the most fatiguing man. Why are you here?"

He started to speak.

Her hand flew up. "Don't tell me anything that he can pick from my brain. I have enough to keep under wraps."

He winked. "Brielle, come out. Esán is frantic with worry."

Brie appeared beside her great aunt. "Tell him I'm fine. I'm not going back, Corvus. Aunt Henri needs me."

Henri folded her arms. "Stubborn. Just like your Aunt Mira. I'm fine."

Corvus studied Brie and then Henri. "She may be right, Henri. If Vygel takes you elsewhere, it wouldn't be a bad thing to have a secret weapon."

Brie perched on the arm of the chair. "You mean you'll let me stay?"

"I will, but—" The hair on the back of his neck rose.

Brie's hand flew to the Star of Truth. She vanished.

Renn's expression registered alarm.

Corvus mouth the words, "Be careful." He, too, disappeared.

For Wolloh, returning to Relevart's cabin in the foothills of Persow felt like coming home. Nothing about it had changed. He smiled as he remembered how arrogant he was as a young man. *Well, almost nothing.* Wolloh gazed at the fire while Relevart perused the El Stroman journal and thought back over his own metamorphosis from Laurent Davead Zuill DeLongeer, citizen of the planet of Roahymn, to the VarTerel of the Inner Universe. He felt sure his mentor also reviewed his life story, otherwise, why send him on a 'training travel' to retrieve the journal?

Relevart lowered the journal to his knees. His head relaxed back. Only his quiet breathing, the intermittent crackle of the fire, and the creaks and groans endemic to the cabin mingled with the silence. Wolloh thought perhaps he slept until his head rolled to the side and dark, wise eyes misted with tears came to rest on his face.

"I've always known I was not from Persow. I didn't realize I might not be from this solar system or the Inner Universe. My travels have taken me many places, Wolloh, but I have never gone beyond the DéCussate Zone into the Outer Universe."

Setting the journal on the small table between their chairs, he crossed to a bookshelf, removed several thick books, and reached into a crevice in the cabin wall. He returned to his chair, carrying a small, plain wooden box, which he continued to hold.

"At twelve sun cycles, my Persowan mother took me to visit an old, old woman who lived in the mountains near here. I remember her as tiny and frail, with white hair and piercing eyes as dark as a raven's wing.

Leaving my mother to rest from our long walk, the old woman led me to a mountain cave, where we sat by a crystal-clear pool. She gave me this box." He withdrew a tiny key on a long, silvery chain from around his neck. "And this key. When she tried to explain in her thick accent, I shook my head in confusion. She switched to Eleo Predian. I understood every word. She told me not to open the box, but to hide it somewhere safe. I'd know when to look inside."

He touched the journal. "The time has come." The key turning seemed louder than such a small lock should warrant.

Wolloh leaned closer.

Relevart lifted the lid and caught his breath. The box contained two items: an oval, silver, and moonstone locket minus its chain and a much-handled piece of parchment. His expression unreadable, he picked up the locket, pressed the tiny catch, and examined the contents. Sudden moisture brightened his eyes. For a moment, he stared into the fire, and then he snapped the locket shut, slipped it onto the chain with the key, and tucked it beneath his shirt. With a sigh, he unfolded the parchment and read it, first in Eleo Predian and then in DerTahan.

> *"Two held in one, two intertwined.*
> *Last representatives of their own kind.*
> *Two torn asunder and worlds apart*
> *Age and grow and mature in their heart.*
>
> *The time draws near to play their role*
> *Rejoin together, return to whole,*
> *Two held in one, uniting what's true,*
> *Planet El Stroma created anew."*

Wolloh accepted the parchment and compared the spidery script to the handwriting in the journal. "The same person who wrote the journal wrote the poem. What does the journal tell you?"

Once again, Relevart stared into the fire. "A midwife in her middle years recorded the story of the last effort to save the Eleo Preda from extinction. The politics of the time were complex. The RomPeer and his followers chose genocide to obliterate a people whose life span was longer and whose spiritual beliefs ran counter to those of the 'true' people, the Pheet Adole."

His mobile features hardened. His gaze grew distant. "More must wait until a later time. We are needed."

Relevart replaced the poem in the box, returned it to its hiding place, and picked up the journal. "This will be much safer in the library in Myrrh." Holding it aloft, he murmured a series of words. It vanished. A wave of his upraised hand sent a pile of objects in the corner of the room sailing to one side.

Wolloh handed him his staff and followed him into Mittkeer. Momentary confusion left him bemused. He gripped his staff. His mind cleared. Relevart raised Froetise. Mittkeer became a blur of stars and sky.

37

Myrrh

With a sense of disappointment, Almiralyn returned to Veersuni. Wilith, Elae, and Merrilea had found nothing on birth-mates. Torgin's father was quick to assure her the search had just begun. He felt certain they would turn up something soon.

The need to paint had taken Sparrow to her studio, leaving Almiralyn a much-needed moment of quiet. She stretched out on a bench and let her mind wander. *The Dojanack Caverns are wonderful, but they are not my home. I miss the cottage. I yearn to walk in the autumn sunlight, to inhale the scents of the Terces Wood, and to hear the birds singing and crickets calling.* She sighed. *My training at the temple prepared me to be in the thick of things.* Her brows drew together, then relaxed. *Myrrh, my chosen responsibility, must come first.*

A gentle knock ended her solitude. She opened the door to find an anxious DeoNyte priestess on the threshold.

"A message came from Teva via Dom via Tibin. The Mocendi are withdrawing from Idronatti. Teva believes something important is happening elsewhere. Ashor also mentioned that after Dom returned to the shoppe, a Mocendi came through the portal and returned almost immediately. He's worried something may have happened to Dom."

"Thank you, Traeh. I'll see what I can discover. Let me know if you hear anything else."

The priestess nodded and withdrew. Almiralyn took up her position by the fountain. Before she could ask about Dom, the water steadied and TheLise's face emerged on the surface.

"Almiralyn, it is good to see you."

"And you, TheLise."

The fountain zoomed out to show Nomed, Allynae, and Somay. Nomed spoke first. "Hello, Mira. We thought we should share news and decide what is the most important next step."

When they had exchanged information and developed a general plan, Almiralyn returned to her bench. Her gaze fixed on the stained-glass window, she reviewed what she had learned. Allynae's reaction to their mother's appearance in the fountain was as she had expected—relief, frustration, a longing to have seen her. Nomed's narrative regarding Roween's interference with the rejoining of Nissasa's body and quintessence aroused her pity for the man who would be forever a child. Her description of the journal, Sparrow's painting, and what Relevart had shared in the fountain had left everyone thoughtful. She had shared that she believed the Galactic Guardians had awarded Wolloh the rank of VarTerel and had finished with the message from Dom and Ashor's concern.

Her information about the whereabouts of the children had given them what they needed to make plans. Somay's concern for Esán's health was worrisome. The boy would need all his strength for what lay ahead.

Silence in Elcaro's Eye roused her from her thoughts. Hurrying to the fountain, she saw Dom, bound hand and foot, in a room furnished in various shades of blue. Across an impressive desk, a good-looking, blond Mocendi reclined in a leather chair.

Thorlu Tangorra, how did you extricate yourself from Corvus's bonds so soon?

Thorlu's studied gaze rested on Dom. "You are in an unenviable position, Dominee. As the guardian of the mirror portal, you know your way around Myrrh. You know Almiralyn. I am more than certain you know the whereabouts of the Evolsefil Crystal." The studied gaze changed to a stone-hard stare. "Tell me what I need to know, or I'll rip it from your mind piece by piece."

Dom grimaced. "My life has been a mixture of delights and regrets, but I'd rather not end it as a madman. I know everything you need to know and will share it happily." He held up his hands. "I'm too old and too tired to fight you. Untie me, and we can talk like men with a common cause." His face twisted in pain. "You don't have to dig, Thorlu."

The Mocendi glared down at him. "You do anything stupid—"

"I betrayed Almiralyn once. Why should I worry about doin' it again?"

Thorlu untied the knots that bound his hands. "Your feet stay tied." He sat on the edge of the desk. "Talk."

Dom rubbed his wrists and picked up his hat, where Thorlu had it had thrown on the floor at his feet. He worked the battered brim with arthritic fingers. "What do you want first?"

"Where is Almiralyn?"

He played a spot on the brim, back and forth and back and forth. "She's in Myrrh."

"Don't play games, Dom. Where in Myrrh?"

Dom seemed to contemplate the question. Again, he fidgeted with the hat.

Thorlu yanked it from his fingers and tossed it out of reach. "Answer my question, old man, or I'll start harvesting."

Dom peered over his spectacles and licked a white powder from his palm. "Get yourself another snitch, Th-th..." His body convulsed, fluid gurgled in his throat. He pitched forward, a motionless heap beneath the toppled chair.

Almiralyn gripped the fountain. "Dom, what have you done?"

Thorlu jerked the door open and ordered a young, low-ranking Mocendi into the room. "Cut him loose, and wake him up."

The younger man knelt, cut the ropes at Dom's ankles, and pushed the chair aside. Fingers fumbled for his pulse. The man shook his head. "Dead."

Thorlu kicked the prone figure. "Leave him. We have more important things to do." A flash of light left Dom's body alone in the room. The image faded.

Almiralyn calmed herself. "Teva." Her cousin's face rose to the fountain's surface. Without exchanging a word, Almiralyn placed an image of Dom in her head. Teva nodded and was gone.

The image in the fountain blurred and steadied

Teva and Lenadi arrived in the apartment in Domlenah Uptown Blue to find it empty but for Dom's sprawled body. Lenadi picked up the discarded hat. Teva checked for a pulse. When she found none, she opened Dom's mouth and inhaled. A stringent odor assailed her nostrils. With a nod, the three arrived in the infirmary in Tower Five.

Lenadi inspected the brim of the hat. White powder coated his fingers. "Think I'll have this tested." He nodded to Jordett as he left.

The Major rested a hand on the bed railing. "Is he dead?"

Teva looked down at the wrinkled bluish skin, sunken eyes, and unmoving chest. "To the untrained eye, he looks dead. He appears to have no pulse, nor can I detect a heartbeat. What gives me hope is that I smelled a hint of timatie on his breath."

"Timatie?"

Teva eyed the old man. "It's an herbal mixture that creates the appearance of death."

"How long will he remain unconscious?"

"It depends on the strength of the dose. If it was too strong, he may never wake up. Lenadi has taken a sample to the lab for testing. Hopefully, he only took enough to keep him unconscious for a few hours. Time will provide the answer." She walked to the door. "Others will care for Dom. We have work to do."

Jordett looked at the still figure. "Don't die on us, old man."

A cascade of droplets broke the image into pieces. Almiralyn inwardly thanked her cousin and snapped her fingers. A new picture began a slow ascent from the bottom of the bowl.

Ira stood on the deck of *Melback*. His turn at the helm had been uneventful. Although the sky's cloud cover remained an oppressive blanket overhead, the storm had dissipated. Ostradio's current chart showed the swirl of eddy pools behind them. Optimism blossomed. Gregos thought they would make it to ZaltRaca by mid-turning on the morrow. Ira could hardly wait to walk on solid ground again.

Des emerged from the cabin with Shyllee at his heels. The RewFaaran claimed he had been fighting sea sickness. Ira thought it was more likely fear. Who wouldn't be afraid if they carried Rikell, the Mindeco, inside them?

"Des. How ya feeling?" Ira patted Shyllee's head. "Hey, girl."

"Alright. The Mindeco is quiet, so I don't have to fight so hard." He gazed ahead. "How much longer?"

"We'll be there tomorrow. Where are Torgin and Yaro?"

"They're studying the compass and sketching charts for Gregos and Tamosh." He shaded his eyes and looked up at the watch perch. "I think Elf likes it up there."

"Strangeness." Elf's message held a tinge of fright.

Ira tipped his head back, caught his breath, and whispered, "Get the Captain." He scanned the sky. "Fast."

Overhead, the clouds had turned a strange color. Gray tinged with scarlet surged and seethed into a circular pattern that became more and more opaque.

Tamosh followed his brother on deck. "Another portal?"

Gregos countered, "Not a good sign. We've nowhere to hide, and I doubt we'll like what's up there. Elf," he called, "get yourself down here."

Elf began a scrambled descent, paused, listened, and scrambled faster.

The word *'Mocendi'* screamed in Ira's mind. "The Mocendi are up there."

Yaro's Pentharian eyes flashed to the sky and back. "I'll shape a vulture, take two boys, and come back. Hurry." He shifted. Torgin climbed on his back and reached for Des.

The RewFaaran cowered away and started to shake. "Can't. Ira go."

Ira put an arm around his shoulder. "Won't leave you, Des."

Gregos gave Yaro a sharp slap on the side. "Go"

The vulture shot into the air. Ira gave Desirol a sideways glance, then watched its ascent. Torgin, flattened against its neck, was almost invisible.

The water in Elcaro's Eye refocused on the living room in the cottage on ZaltRaca, where Henri assumed the demeanor of Renn Whalend.

Corvus' spider form clung to a web in the dark corner of the room. Below, Brie's presence was undetectable. Renn faced a haughty Vygel Vintrusie. The gaunt angles of his face thinned into a sneer.

"We have located *Melback*. Soon your son and his friends will be in our hands. The MasTer has sent me to bring you to him. Do you know what that means?"

Renn pressed trembling lips together and shook her head.

"It means that you will never see Idronatti again."

She stepped back, widening the gap between them.

His longer stride brought him to her side. A hand gripped her arm.

The spider dropped on a silken thread. Corvus materialized and stared at the emptied room. Almiralyn's niece and her aunt were beyond his reach.

A quick scan showed the wards around the cottage were no longer in place. He threw open a window, shaped a laridae, and streaked over the erika field and down to the beach. Landing in the middle of a group of chatting gulls, he searched the sky, cliffs, and beach for anything or anyone suspicious. When nothing triggered an alarm, he flew to the recess, shielded his presence, and teleported to the boathome.

Cayled and Bibeed gave a surprised gasp.

Torgin's mother's hand went to her throat. "Oh, dear. Corvus."

Esán's stool fell with a muffled crash as he came to his feet. "What's wrong?" He stood stock still, his concentration total. "They're gone. Both of them, Brie and Henri. Where?"

Corvus answered, "Vygel took them."

Esán rounded the end of the table. "Don't just stand there, Corvus. We have to go after them."

"When we know their location, we will. Now, we have to warn *Melback's* crew the Mocendi are on the way. Cayled and Bibeed, I am entrusting Renn to your care. Do not leave here. Renn, I will do my best to bring Torgin. Barring that, I'll be back to get you."

He put a hand on Esán's shoulder. Gambelii oaks and thick-trunked pines took the place of the cave. "You alright, Esán?"

"Yes." His anger exploded. "Why did you let Vintrusie take them?"

Corvus sighed. "I wasn't quick enough. Let's not make that mistake again. I need to send a message to Elf and Ira." He shut his eyes, found their minds, and returned his attention to Esán.

"We'll leave here as ravens. Vygel knew that someone watched Torgin's mother. I don't know what their plan—"

"Vygel is gone. I'm teleporting. No one is here to sense our departure."

"If anyone *is* still—"

"My friends are on that boat." Esán stepped beyond his reach. "You fly."

He flashed from sight. Corvus shook his head in frustration. "Not the best time to behave like an adolescent, Esán." Shaping Karrew, he teleported.

Curiosity pressed Almiralyn closer as a new picture formed on the crystal clear water.

The crew of *Melback* clustered together as a rush of air hit the deck. Clouds parted. Like a mouth opening wide, a scarlet and black orifice spun into view. An ear-splitting roar pierced the air. The sails flapped, lines licked the masts, the wheel spun. *Melback* jerked and plunged. Crew and dog scrambled to stay upright. Shyllee's frantic bark joined the chaos. The boat tipped from starboard to port as Esán materialized and grabbed Ira's arm. The stentorian sound roared louder. *Melback* bucked, and torn from the sea, rose into the vast vortex.

A profound silence blanketed the Sea of Minusa. The two-masted vessel reappeared, suspended in the gaping mouth. Clouds spiraled into the portal's center. Wind and sound exploding hurtled the sailboat seaward. Two men leapt from the deck. The portal vanished. *Melback* slammed the water with a shattering crack. Gregos and Tamosh plunged feet first into the sea.

Almiralyn fought to slow her hammering heart and inhaled air into lungs emptied by her shout of denial. The door to Veersuni flew open. A frantic Sparrow ran to the fountain and stared.

On the Eye's surface, a raven swept over Gregos and Tamosh clinging to the splintered stern of the sailboat. Carved on it in bold block letters was the name Melback.

"I just painted a vortex with a boat rising into its center. The children were onboard. Then the boat reappeared with no children. Oh, Almiralyn, I was hoping I was wrong. What now, and what about Torgin?"

Like the blink of an eye, the fountain cleared, and a different image snapped into view.

Almiralyn fought to slow her hammering heart and inhaled air into lungs emptied by her shout of denial. The door to Veersuni flew open. A frantic Sparrow ran to the fountain and stared.

On the Eye's surface, a raven swept over Gregos and Tamosh clinging to the splintered stern of the sailboat. Carved on it in bold block letters was the name Melback.

"I just painted a vortex with a boat rising into its center. The children were onboard. Then the boat reappeared with no children. Oh, Almiralyn, I was hoping I was wrong. What now, and what about Torgin?"

Like the blink of an eye, the fountain cleared, and a different image snapped into view.

Yaro shaped the vulture and soared back the way he had come. The Sea of Minusa came into view, its surface sparkling with the diamond light of the mid-turning sun. Swooping lower, he scanned the spot where he had last seen *Melback*. In a swath of debris, he spotted two men and the raven Karrew clinging to the wreckage. Tamosh oozed blood from a cut on his head. Gregos cradled an arm next to his chest. Close by, Yaro's sharp eye picked out Torgin's flute in its sheepskin case, rolling up and down with the waves. Swooping, he caught the strap in his talons and flew over what remained of the stern.

Karrew soared upward and plucked the flute from his grasp. Yaro felt the raven land on his back; then Corvus' added weight.

"Tamosh, grab hold of Gregos with one hand and Yaro's leg with the other," Corvus yelled.

Yaro hovered lower and lower until fingers gripped his leg. The world blurred. When it refocused, the brothers lay on a beach next to a panting Corvus.

Yaro appeared and smiled down at him. "You did well, my friend. We are many to teleport all at once."

"They helped, or we wouldn't have made it in one jump." Corvus crawled to the side of the brothers, made a quick examination, and climbed to his feet. "Helping me to teleport all of us took its toll. Both are unconscious. Fortunately, I can manage a short distance on my own, especially with you smaller, Yaro. We don't want to frighten Renn and her friends." Corvus repositioned the flute across his back and squatted between the brothers.

Yaro shifted to a small moth. The beach vanished. From his perch on the end of Torgin's flute, he observed the reactions of the Humans as his comrades materialized next to them in a boat inside a cave.

Corvus straightened as Cayled surged to his feet, shotgun in hand. Bibeed gasped. Only Renn remained still, her eyes searching Corvus' face.

"Where is Torgin?"

"It's a long story." He acknowledged Bibeed and Cayled with a nod.

Renn's expression did not change. "I expect to hear it. First, who are your friends?"

Tamosh had regained consciousness and pushed himself to sitting. He brushed wet hair from his face. "I'm Tamosh, and this is my brother, Gregos." He gave him a shake.

Gregos gasped in pain and struggled upright. Corvus and Tamosh helped him to a stool. When he had caught his breath, Corvus examined his arm.

"Nothing is broken. I believe keeping it immobilized for a couple of turnings will make all the difference."

Gregos managed a relieved smile. "Thank you, Corvus."

Bibeed clucked worriedly under her breath and gathered the materials needed for a sling and to cleanse Tamosh's cheek.

Once the men sat snuggled in blankets and Bibeed had rinsed their clothes laid them out by the fire to dry, Tamosh explained their role in Torgin's story. When he finished, he nodded at Corvus. "I believe Corvus has someone else for you to meet."

Corvus placed the flute case on the table. "What do you know of the Pentharian?"

Bibeed frowned. "I've heard that they fight for the Guardian of Myrrh."

Renn looked puzzled.

Cayled laid a hand on the stock of his shotgun. Leeriness lurked in his eye. "They be warriors, mercenaries. Not to be trusted by honest men."

"They are," Corvus countered in a neutral tone, "warriors who are renowned throughout the solar system for their skill and their integrity. I need your word, Cayled, that you will not shoot my comrade."

Cayled removed his hand from the stock. "You have my word."

The small moth fluttered to the ground. Yaro materialized in its place, his long braids cascading down his back, his golden scales glinting in the fire's light, his lizard tail twitching back and forth.

Bibeed's hand flew to her mouth. Cayled controlled the reflex to reach for the shotgun. Renn's eyes widened.

Yaro gazed down at her. "I am Yaro, the heart-brother of Torgin. I am honored to meet you, Renn Whalend." He touched his hand to his heart and bowed his head.

She walked around the table and looked up at his formidable height. "Torgin's heart-brother?"

He explained. "In my culture, we honor a heart-brother as family. Torgin is my brother. He has asked me to take care of you in his stead."

Bibeed let out a breath. "Well, I never." She pushed a sturdy box toward him. "Welcome, Yaro. Do sit down so I can look ya in the eye."

Yaro placed the box next to Renn's stool. Corvus joined them. Cayled kept his shotgun close but began to lose the wariness. Bibeed set steaming bowls of fish soup in front of everyone and took her place at the table. "I believe we are ready to hear your story."

Yaro, Gregos, and Tamosh took turns. Renn listened, her expression filled with wonder as she learned about her son's bravery, his gifts, and how much he had grown since she had last seen him. At the tale's conclusion, she looked from one to the other. "How can I thank you for taking care of Torgin?"

Corvus held her gaze. "By returning to Idronatti and helping your people reclaim their lives."

"But what of my son? I can't leave DerTah without him." For the first time, fear sparked in her eyes.

Yaro knelt beside her and placed the flute case in her hands. "Torgin asked me to give you his flute and to tell you he loves you. He knew, Renn, that he was going where we cannot follow. You and I must put our trust in Wolloh and Relevart to keep him safe. Corvus' words are true. I must take you to Almiralyn and to the father of Torgin. Idronatti and Thera need your skills."

Renn stared at the sheepskin case. "I wish I knew more of Wolloh and Relevart." She looked from Yaro to Corvus. "You trust these men to take care of my son?"

Corvus answered, "They are more honorable and better equipped than anyone else in the Inner Universe to protect Torgin."

The image melted into the calm stillness of water.

A deep voice reverberated through the sanctuary of Veersuni. "I am flattered, Corvus."

Sparrow yelped in surprise and jerked around. Almiralyn shot a knowing glance over her shoulder and turned.

Relevart smiled a complacent smile. "It is a pleasure to see you, too."

Almiralyn tipped her head and studied the tall, rangy man. "You have changed, Relevart."

"That I have, my dear. The Galactic Guardians have awarded me the rank of the Universal VarTerel. In that capacity, I am asking for your service, Almiralyn Nadrugia." His dark eyes came to rest on Sparrow. "And yours, SparrowLyn AsTar. Come." Leading them into the Reading Room, he closed the door and tapped it with the tip of Froetise. "In case," he murmured, "just in case." He continued toward the far end of the room, his power radiating around him.

Sparrow's mind raced as she hurried to keep up with his lengthy stride. *How can I possibly help?*

When he reached the fireplace, he faced the women. "Mira, you will accompany me. SparrowLyn, you will take on the role of Guardian of Myrrh."

Panic opened Sparrow's mouth and shut it without a sound.

Relevart's eyebrows shot up. "You are more prepared than you realize, my dear." He touched the glowing tip of Froetise to the center of her forehead.

A tingling current raced over her scalp. One synapse at a time, it transited her brain until every cell vibrated. Her sight blurred and then grew more acute than she could ever remember. Her ears picked up every sound. Scents—different bodies, the fire, the mustiness of old books—almost overwhelmed her. She gasped for breath like one who had barely escaped drowning. "Wh-what did you do?"

"I woke you up, my dear. Now, let's see you shape shift."

The shifts were instantaneous. Almiralyn, Mira, the white bird flashed like the blips on a compu-screen. Again, she gulped in a mouthful of air.

"Now, Sparrow. Make each shift on your own." The Universal VarTerel's command brooked no discussion.

One at a time, she did as instructed, then grinned. "I did it."

Almiralyn hugged her. "You did, and beautifully, I might add."

Relevart drew them down beside him on a couch. "No one must know you're not the Guardian of Myrrh, Sparrow. No one. Not even Merrilea or Yookotay. Elae may guess, but she will keep your secret. Check the fountain often, but do *not* ask it questions that will give you away. If possible, I will send someone to aid you." He pulled Almiralyn to her feet. "I suggest you give Sparrow the key to the research cabinets."

Almiralyn placed a small crystal key on her palm. "Keep it safe for me, SparrowLyn AsTar."

Relevart tapped his staff and, with Myrrh's Guardian, vanished.

Sparrow, alone in a way she had never known, experienced a sudden sense of paralysis. *I am the Guardian of Myrrh.* Lifting her chin, she said it again out loud. "I am the Guardian of Myrrh." The power behind the title transmuted her inability to act. Giddy with relief, she slipped the key in her pocket, shaped Almiralyn, and descended the steps into the research area.

<h1 style="text-align:center">38</h1>

Der Tah & TreBlaya

Torgin examined the celestial chart floating above the compass face. He, Wolloh, and Wodash had two stops to make prior to meeting Relevart in Mittkeer. Torgin glanced at his companions, then at the stars and night-blue sky extending endlessly in all directions. *It's like we're inside a globe of stars. How will we ever locate anyone?*

Wolloh touched his arm. "Stop dreaming, boy. Put the compass away."

Torgin shoved the compass beneath his tunic as Wodash's icy fingers gripped his shoulder. He could not suppress a shiver, but realized with a jolt of surprise that the death shadow no longer engendered fear, just pity.

Wolloh held Vinredi aloft. "Shu Chenaro."

The sky blurred into taccus trees and red desert. Wolloh's home glowed in the gold and salmon light of early dawn. A door flew open. Stebben strode toward them, his expression elated. Wolloh's pronounced limp carried him forward. They embraced. Wolloh teleported them to his sitting room, where he leaned his staff against the wall and settled in his favorite chair.

"I have missed this chair, this room, and you, Stebben. Please sit. Torgin, pull up the footstool and join us. Wodash, stay close."

They exchanged updates. Stebben and Gerolyn were in touch daily. The borders of Shu Chenaro and the desert portal were under Lorsedi's control. The Largeen Joram had returned Nissasa's men to RewFaar to appear before The Military Tribunal. No sign of the Sebborr since their timely departure, soon after Nissasa's defection, left many questions unanswered. Lorsedi was certain that with Wolloh presumed dead, they would reappear. Gerolyn had shape shifted and flown to their camp. Dahe Terah had hopes of taking Shu Chenaro for his own.

When Wolloh had finished, he stared into the distance. A sigh escaped his deformed mouth. "As much as I want you with me, Stebben, I cannot leave Shu Chenaro or DerTah without a High DiMensioner's presence."

Surprise gleamed in Stebben's dark eyes. "You mean—"

"I mean that before we depart, I will initiate you to the rank of High DiMensioner. You will then, with every ounce of stealth you can manage, seek NeTols Terah, WoNa's younger brother, and bring him here. He is as gifted as WoNa. You will need his help. Tell him it is my will and the will of the Universal VarTerel. TheLise will also remain on DerTah. Don't hesitate to call on her or on WoNa if necessary. Beware the Dreelum Gidtuss and Thaer. They are both hungry for power and willing to sacrifice much to get it."

He motioned Stebben to his feet, grasped his staff, and rose. "Torgin and Wodash, stand and bear witness."

Torgin took his place, his heart pounding with happiness for the man next to him.

Wolloh's face glowed with pride as he began. "Are you, Stebben Stol, willing and able to accept the responsibilities of the rank of High DiMensioner?"

"I am."

Touching the tip of his staff to Stebben's forehead, Wolloh raised him to the second highest ranking in the Order of Esprow. "You have been due for this honor for some time. Congratulations. Relevart has reprogramed the crystal in my cane for you. Use it with discretion. We would stay to celebrate, but The Unfolding speeds on. Take care, my friend."

Torgin felt Wolloh's light touch and found himself in a small room, where several people gathered around a tall, shimmering crystal.

Nomed sensed tension building. Allynae cracked his knuckles with a frequency that shouted his agitation. TheLise's humor had become more edgy. Somay withdrew to the quiet of his inner being. Nomed arched his brow. We're all tired of inaction. *If we don't decide on a plan soon, one of us is bound to come unglued.* He rubbed his scar. *I want to go where I can protect my nephew. Not—*

Wolloh's appearance with Torgin and Wodash, of all things, cut his silent rantings short and intensified the atmosphere in the room. Allynae gaped. Somay emerged from his contemplative state with a long sigh. TheLise, the first to recover, planted a kiss on Wolloh's smooth cheek.

"I understand felicitations are in order. What's it like being a VarTerel?"

Wolloh angled his good eye to her. "I'll let you know once I find out." His chin lifted, bringing his full face into view. "Relevart sent me to meet with you. He is now the Universal VarTerel. I am making the following requests on his behalf. Nomed and Somay, you will accompany me. TheLise, you will remain on DerTah to oversee the planet's welfare. Stebben is prepared to work with you. Also, WoNa's younger brother may prove to be of help."

TheLise's enthusiastic smile melted into a momentary pout. Shaking herself, she said, "You know I want to go wherever you are going, but I understand DerTah is a prize. I'm the best person to protect it."

Wolloh's proud smile washed over her. "Thank you, my dear. I knew we could count on you. Allynae, I require you to return to the Dojanack Caverns." His good eye traveled the group. "The information I am about to share is confidential. It must stay in this room. Almiralyn is no longer in Myrrh. Sparrow has taken her place and assumed her persona. She is feeling very much alone. Abandoned to her fate, if you would. She is well-equipped to handle most things, but your presence, Allynae, will give her confidence and provide her with the guidance she requires. You will leave as soon as we finish our business here."

A knuckle cracked. "I have only one question, Wolloh. What about our daughters?"

Nomed laid a hand on his shoulder. "I promise to bring them back to you, Alli. All of us will do our best to protect them." Hazel eyes found the death shadow. "Even Wodash, correct?"

The death shadow's face grew pensive and sad. "In another life, I had a daughter. I will protect yours, brother of Almiralyn, far better than I protected my own."

Allynae looked somewhat taken aback. "Thank you, Wodash od DerTah." He put an arm around Torgin's shoulders. "Please take care of this young man."

Wodash responded with a slight bow of his head.

Once again, Wolloh's attention shifted and refocused. "Somay, Nomed, and Relevart call. We must go. Torgin, stand on my right; Wodash, on my left. Please hold on to my staff."

Nomed fought a moment of befuddlement as the room blurred into starlight. Mittkeer opened up before him. Memories of his first visit flooded his thoughts. Wanted by the PPP, he escaped to the Central Mountains, used the portal, and ended up in Fera Finnero. The Mocendi League knew of his talent and would have made him their own. Relevart found him first. A shortcut through Mittkeer had brought them to Shu Chenaro, where he had met Wolloh Espyro and TheLise for the first time.

He glanced up to find Wolloh observing him. The new VarTerel lifted his staff. The small crystal cocooned at the tip began to glow. With a nod, he turned and limped through the star-studded space.

Nomed trained his eyes on the crystal and followed. *Mittkeer. Memories. Time stands still, but only until we emerge wherever The Unfolding takes us.*

Henri rubbed the wrist where the black bracelet had been and surveyed her new surroundings. Well-hidden ceiling-lights illuminated the cubicle's pale tan walls. She sat on the only furniture, a cot. A tiny Personal Needs Space took up one corner. A constant mechanical hum made her skin crawl. Surveillance cams followed her every move. She searched for a door but could not find one.

Aware of the constant probing of her mind, she infused her thoughts with Renn's memories, those that would give her captors enough, but not too much, information. The strain of maintaining compartmentalized recall made her head ache and robbed her of the alertness she required to *be* Renn Whalend. Fatigue urged her to rest. She refrained. Sleeping increased her vulnerability. Until ample time had passed to assure Renn's safe arrival in Myrrh, she must remain vigilant.

A small moth the color of the brown blanket on the cot landed beside her. The mattress compressed. An invisible hand touched hers. Whispered words brushed her cheek. "Sleep. I'll watch your mind." The mattress resumed its normal firm flatness.

Hesitant to give in, but more tired than she cared to admit, Henri stretched out on the cot.

Brie sat on the floor with a hand resting on her aunt's shoulder. She considered reshaping the moth. Keeping a hold on her humanness meant she must have time in her own body. She wiggled her foot and smiled. Gregos had been right. She knew how to make things invisible, including herself.

A probe penetrating her aunt's mind focused her on the job at hand. With a deftness that surprised her, Brie kept Henri Avetlire separate and hidden. Only Renn's memories floated in the almost limitless expanse of her aunt's mind. Feeling like a voyeur, Brie observed the emotional story of Renn's life—dislike of having her memories erased at her Time of Induction, delight in her assigned profession, love of Wilith, sadness when she learned the PPP would allow them only one child, joy when Torgin was born, fear when she awoke in the cottage on ZaltRaca—all these combined to create a picture of Torgin's mother.

Brie's vigil made her realize she, too, must hide memories of her aunt deep in her mind. *One slip...* She shivered. *From now on, I will only see you as Coala Renn Whalend.*

A panel in the opposite wall slid open. Brie squeezed Renn's shoulder and shifted.

Renn stretched and opened her eyes. Vygel Vintrusie stared down at her.

"It is good that you rested." His grim smile chilled her. "It is time to get to work, Renn Whalend."

She sat up and tucked sleep-tangled blonde hair behind her ears. He motioned her through the door and guided her along a narrow companionway ending at a wall of windows. Symbols entered on a touchpad opened a door. He waved her ahead.

Although the lab appeared to be a replica of the one she frequented in Idronatti, she realized the technology used was superior to anything she had seen on Thera.

Vygel cleared his throat. "When we arrive in TreBlaya, The MasTer expects a sample of the serum you were working on in Idronatti."

Renn frowned. "I was working on several projects, Vygel."

"He is interested in two: the spray you created to control the citizens of Idronatti and the serum you developed to regenerate damaged Human tissue. You should find everything you require here. If not, ring the bell at your compu-center. I suggest you get to work. We will leave for TreBlaya soon." He smiled an emotionless smile. "Someone will guide you back to your quarters when you are through. They will serve your Mid-turning meal here. Remember, if you play games, Torgin will pay."

"You have Torgin?"

The soft swish of the door closing left her question unanswered.

Her breath caught in her throat. *"Torgin..."* A shaking hand fluttered to her heart.

Forcing a calm she did not feel, she wandered the lab, testing her knowledge of the equipment setup for her use. In the supply closet, she inventoried the supplies lining the shelves. The information she had selected from Renn's mind gave her a fair understanding of what it required to create the formula for the spray—she had purposely chosen an earlier version of the research—but she had little information regarding the serum.

Pursing her lips in thought, she picked up a small comp-tab and a stylus and returned to the supply closet, the only place she could not detect surveillance cams. "Brie," she whispered.

Her niece appeared in the furthest corner from the door.

With a finger to her lips, Renn motioned her to the floor. "Listen closely. We will sleep in shifts. I will monitor your mind as you monitored mine. Good work. You'd better eat here at mid-turning. I'll keep what I can for you from the other meals. Stay as far from me as possible when Vygel is present. What he lacks in imagination, he makes up for in diligence. Speaking of which..."

Brie vanished. A small black fly shot upward. Vygel blocked the doorway, bulging eyes searching. Renn gave him a frustrated scowl and held up a stylus. "Dropped it. What can I do for you?"

Wishing that Renn's younger body was more real than illusion, she leveraged her weight to accommodate an arthritic knee and got to her feet.

Eyes narrowed, Vygel took a step closer. "Are you injured?"

Renn rubbed her knee and grimaced. "I fell on the cliff trail down to the lookout at the cottage. It doesn't bother me unless I move wrong." She picked up her comp-tab, made a couple of notes, and moved past him into the lab. "This laboratory is remarkable. I must assemble what I need and familiarize myself with the equipment before I begin, but it looks promising." She sat down at her compu-center.

Vygel's continued presence raised the hair on the back of her neck. The door slid shut. She let out a breath and touched the locket at her throat. *I hope you're safe, Renn Whalend.*

Corvus sat in the boathome's quiet with sleep eluding him like the ghosts in Toelachoc Prison. Yaro stood guard at the tunnel entrance. Renn and Bibeed slept on the two cots. The men, wrapped in blankets, slept on the ground. He rested his elbows on the table and tapped his lips with his index fingers. *Why am I so edgy?*

The tingle of shifting energy raced over his skin. Yaro materialized beside him. Relevart and Almiralyn stepped into the dim light of the dying fire.

Corvus realized, without remembering the action to get him there, that he had risen. Adrenalin pounded through his veins. He couldn't tear his gaze from the woman who had claimed his heart. The dimple in his cheek deepened. Still, he could not move.

Relevart grinned. "Well, young man, are you going to embrace her, or just stand there gawking?"

Almiralyn's laugh of delight freed him. He rounded the table, caught her in his arms, and whispered, "I have missed you more than I can say."

She rested her head on his shoulder. "I was so afraid you wouldn't ever come back to me."

He wiped the tears from her cheeks and kissed her gently.

The quiet tap of Relevart's staff broke the spell.

She intertwined her fingers in his and smiled. "Thank you, Relevart, for giving us a moment. I believe you have business with..." She glanced around to find an audience flashing grins of understanding.

After everyone took a seat at the table and introduced themselves, the Universal VarTerel called the meeting to order. "Gregos and Tamosh, you will take Renn and Yaro to the portal in DoOlb." He handed them a money pouch. "Part of this is to be used to pay for a boat named *SeaBella*. She is waiting for you in the fishing village of Metto Bay and is a vessel similar to *Melback*. Use the remaining coin to stock her for a trip to the portal on the DoOlbian shore and to pay the wages of a crew member to take Elf's place until he's rescued." His attention shifted to Renn and Yaro. "The portal takes you to the desert. The desert gateway will carry you to Myrrh." He glanced around. "Questions?"

Gregos pocketed the pouch. "Thank you, Relevart. I promise we'll get Renn and Yaro to the portal safely."

"Thaer, the Dreela of DoOlb," Relevart cautioned, "is in league with Gidtuss and Dahe Terah to gain control of DerTah. They do not realize The MasTer intends to turn the planet into a Mocendi stronghold. Be careful. Expect the portal to be guarded. I provided weapons similar to the ones that went down with *Melback*. You'll find them in a locker in the forward berth."

Cayled cleared his throat. "And what of Omudi, Dreela of Geran? Where is his allegiance?"

Relevart turned his intense gaze on Bibeed and Cayled. "Omudi was content to help Nissasa win the leadership of RewFaar by providing a hiding place for Renn. He has no interest in involving himself with Thaer and Gidtuss."

"What of Torgin?" Renn asked. "Yaro told me he is with a man called Wolloh."

"Your son has an important part to play in what's coming. You, Renn Whalend and Wilith, are instrumental in what happens to the citizens of Idronatti and the planet of Thera. Focus your attention there. We will focus ours on the safety of Torgin and his friends." He grasped his staff and stood. "Corvus, Almiralyn, we must be off."

Renn hurried to Corvus' side and held out the flute. "Please take this to Torgin. Tell him I am *very* proud of him." A tear glistened in the corner of her eye.

Corvus slung the strap over his shoulder. "I'll deliver it and the message." He squeezed Almiralyn's hand.

Relevart's light touch transported them. Stars sprinkled the night sky; nausea tore through his body.

Allynae shaped a Dertahan red hawk and flew toward Shu Chenaro. He yearned to be with those going to rescue his daughters. *If I were more confident in my skills in DiMensionery...* He soared higher to avoid the giant trees of the Tinga Forest and watched a large purple and gold bird break through the canopy. Having no desire to encounter it firsthand, he streaked toward the Trinugian border.

The wards protecting Shu Chenaro crested the horizon. Each wing stroke carried him closer to his companion. The heaviness in his heart at leaving his daughters behind began to lighten. *Sparrow needs me. Overseeing Myrrh can be challenging. Since I know Mira better than anyone but Corvus, I'm the best one to help her sustain the illusion that she is Almiralyn.*

Allowing what awaited him to draw him onward, he concentrated on reaching the ranch. At the outer edge of the shields protecting Shu Chenaro, he landed and assumed his Human shape. As much as he liked to think he was mastering telepathy, he continued to find it difficult to use when he was in a shape other than Human. He masked his thoughts and sent Stebben a quick message. The wards shimmered and thinned. He stepped through, shifted, and continued his flight.

Two red hawks, soaring side by side, raced toward him. A Fire ConDra blazed past them, intersected their path, banked, and shot higher. A warning whispered through his mind.

Dropping to the ground, he shifted, crouched in the shade of a taccus tree, and watched a dust devil gather speed and size. Wind torqued it upward and swept it, spinning over the ground. Another gust added strength and rotation; a third heaved it aloft just as the Fire ConDra swooped, talons extended. Dust engulfed it, smothered its fire, and carried it higher. An abrupt decrease in spin and speed released the flameless body to fall earthward. Impact left it dazed and broken. Two men materialized. A kcalo-draped figure pulled a knife and slit the ConDra's throat, ending its existence and its agony.

Stebben and his companion sprinted to Allynae's side, caught him by the arms and teleported to the raptor center at the ranch.

The Sebborran flashed a wide, brilliant smile. "That was close."

Stebben clapped his companion on the back. "The dust devil was a great idea, one I intend to keep in my arsenal." He caught Allynae's eye. "Good to see you, Alli. This is Roandee, WoNa's brother. Roandee, meet Almiralyn's brother, Allynae."

Esán regained consciousness with the worst headache of his life. His stomach churned, his throat burned from the dry heaves that shook his body. He squeezed his eyes shut and rubbed his temples. An image—*Melback*. The flash of recall knotted his stomach for different reasons: the sucking sound of *Melback* pulling free of the ocean, *Melback* rising into the air, dizziness claiming her captain and crew. Like fluid through a sieve, more images poured in. A blond man with a bandaged hand who forced them to watch a huge V-Screen on a pristine wall, where *Melback* plummeted back toward the sea and Gregos and Tamosh disappeared below the surface of the water. Darkness infused his thoughts, darkness so thick and vile he knew he would not live. He gasped for air, felt it whoosh into his lungs, felt its almost *silent* exhale. Straining to hear, he held his next breath. Not one sound suggested his friends were near.

I ra rolled onto his side and vomited. The stench stimulated another wave of nausea. He closed his eyes, forced the bile back down his throat, and eased himself to sitting. Dizziness almost toppled him, even though pitch-black erased the features of his prison so thoroughly that his palm in front of his face was invisible. Raising his hand, he envisioned a finger pointed at the bridge of his nose, imagined himself watching it move toward him. His eyes crossed. The dizziness fled. He dropped his face in his hands. No sound wrapped him in a cocoon. No sound held him in oblivion. *Where are my friends? Shyllee? Gregos?* The image of the captain and his brother hurtling toward the sea—*Melback* crashing into the water—he moaned and vomited again.

E lf swallowed his nausea and forced himself to be still. He knew where he was. Vygel Vintrusie had ordered his vocal cords cut on this ship. He had escaped. *They* wouldn't allow him to do it again. He knew his fate. Worse than death—cast into the pits on TreBlaya. He knew others who wouldn't bend to the League were thrown in to the TreBlayan fire pit to burn for eternity. A spark of panic ignited. He snuffed it out. *I still live. I will live. I still live. I will live.* The mantra calmed him, erased his fear. *This time, I am not alone.* A smile curved his silent lips. The skills of DiMensionery came to him naturally. Brie had cloaked *Melback*. He reached out and touched Shyllee's soft fur. An illusion of invisibility hid her presence.

D esirol felt nothing, not his eyes blinking, not his arms or legs moving, not the breath entering and exiting his lungs. He could not sense the Mindeco fighting for control or the fear the creature triggered every time he gained another foothold. Juxtaposed against the total lack of sensory perception throughout his body, his ears magnified every sound. The tick, click, buzz of some type of machinery close at hand echoed down his ear canal and boomed against his eardrums. So loud—so loud he thought he would go crazy. So loud. And all he could do was listen—listen to the repetitive tick, click, buzz.

B rie pondered Vygel's discussion with her aunt and frowned. *Torgin...a prisoner? Maybe I can* search the ship and find him. Buzzing around the lab, she had discovered several hooded vents. Some sucked stale air from the lab while others blew fresh air in. A cursory exploration beyond one of the fresh air vents had left her curious and thoughtful. Can I use the air ducts to see if Vygel's tell*ing the truth?*

Mid-turning meal arrived on time. Her aunt smuggled most of it in to her in the supply closet and paused on the pretext of continuing to inventory what the shelves held. From her dim corner, Brie explained her intention.

Renn's face grew more and more solemn. "If you get lost or caught, there is nothing I can do to help."

"I will be very careful. I promise."

"This ship is massive, Brie. How will you know where to start?"

"I'll begin here at the lab and work my way outward."

Her aunt gripped her arm. "You will report to me once every chron circle. Agreed?"

Brie felt a rush of relief. "Agreed."

Footfalls in the lab sent her into bug form. Her aunt returned to her list.

Vygel leaned against the doorjamb, his expression bland.

Brie shot through a vent and waited to be sure her aunt was safe.

The Mocendi ran a hand over his bald head. "Tell me, Renn. What progress have you made?"

"Really, Vygel. I have just begun to educate myself. Go away and let me work."

A haughty glare was his only reply. The Mocendi vanished.

39

Myrrh

Sparrow descended the stairs into the research area of the Reading Room library, a jumble of thoughts chasing around and around in her brain. A sideways glance left her mind blank and her progress at a standstill. Sapphire blue eyes stared back at her; a silver-blonde hair fell in a long, thick braid well past her waist. Almiralyn's mystified expression made her glance behind her. Confusion changed to a smile of delight.

I really did it. I shaped Almiralyn. She tossed the braid over her shoulder with a movement she had seen the Guardian do often, stood taller, and let her eyes travel the length of the tall, slender body. *I mustn't forget who I am.* Eyes glued to the reflection, she repeated to herself, "I am the Guardian of Myrrh. I am Almiralyn Nadrugia."

As she walked down the aisle, the mental image of a stone box made her pause and peer into the nearest case. She examined the rows of books and the stacks of manuscripts lining the shelves. Excitement fluttered in her stomach. A rough, reddish-brown corner protruded from beneath a pile of scrolls. Almiralyn's key unlocked the door. Carefully moving the scrolls to one side, she uncovered a stone box about the size of a book. It bore signs of mistreatment: a chipped corner, a crack running down the right side, and the scorched evidence of fire. On the smoke-blackened surface, she could barely make out a single engraved symbol.

Giddy with excitement, she made a quick search of the books on the top shelf of the cabinet. On tiptoe, she lifted down a large tome entitled *Universal Symbology* and thumbed through it. "It has to be here," she muttered. When she reached the last page, she shut the book, hugged it to her chest, and frowned. "Maybe I missed it."

Placing the book on the bottom shelf, she tapped the cover and opened it at random. "Ahhh."

She smiled at the clear sketch of the symbol. Printed beneath it were two words: *Rimu Minthum* and, beneath them, *The Eye of the Gods*. A concise explanation of its origin followed.

After replacing the book on the shelf, she carried the box to a nearby table. The pounding of her heart accompanied eager fingers as she explored the rough thickness of the edges. An indent, so small she almost missed it, caught at her nail. Closer examination showed her nothing unusual. She sat back and shut her eyes. Allowing her artist's instincts to guide her, she ran the tip of her smallest finger over the spot, felt a minuscule change, and pressed. A gap split the left edge. With her heart beating even louder, she wedged her fingers in the opening. Gentle leverage allowed her to pry the top away from the bottom. The box gave a muffled crack. The lid came free, exposing a dark blue bag.

Eager fingers plucked it free, eased the drawstring opening, and tipped a clear crystal into her hand. Domed on one side and flat on the other, it magnified fine lines on her palm. She raised to eye level. *What are you?* Slipping it back into the protective bag, she returned it to the rounded hollow in the stone box and repositioned the engraved lid on top. A soft clap and the box returned to the way she had found it. She cradled it in her arms and hurried to the area that Wilith, Merrilea, and Elae had set up for research.

She arrived as Elae held the journal aloft. "I thought we had lost this. I wonder where it— Hello, Almiralyn, you look excited."

Sparrow placed her treasure on the table, reminded herself that she represented Myrrh's Guardian, and picked up the journal. "I'm delighted this is back. Relevart sent Wolloh to retrieve it as part of his training for VarTerel. If I am not mistaken, I believe I may have found something that can help us translate it." She laid it next to the box and motioned them closer.

Everyone gathered around.

Wilith contemplated the symbol. "I've seen that somewhere. Where was it?" He began to search through a pile of manuscripts.

Merrilea picked up the journal, flipped through the pages, and smiled. "Here." She held it out. "I wish we could read this."

A sketch of the symbol nestled in spidery script on the last page.

Elae's heart skipped a beat. "I know what this is. A book on ancient tools of translation described it and how to use it." As she talked, she sorted a stack of research materials, discovered what she was looking for, and began to read.

"The Rimu Minthum, the Eye of the Gods, was created on the planet of Tao Spirian in the early part of Cos vi Drey circa 31 1 31. Used to translate arcane texts, it became known as the Scholars' Kristl. A disagreement between two groups of distinguished academics resulted in its disappearance. Although the Kristl resurfaced for a short time, no one has seen it for over one centuria. It was last known to be encased within a stone box transported from beyond the Outer Rim."

She looked up. "Can you open the box, Almiralyn?"

"I did once. I'll try again."

Moving her fingers over the left edge, she found the minuscule indent and pressed. The box opened with its muffled crack. She set the top aside and tipped the stone onto her palm.

Merrilea exclaimed, "It's beautiful. How does it work?"

Elae set the book aside and picked up the journal. "The book says to place the Kristl's flat side over the text you wish to translate." She put it on the first line of text in the journal. A glow illuminated the script beneath.

Words spiraled up from the page into the crystal center, one by one, until it could hold no more.

She placed the flat side on a clean sheet of paper and moved it across the page. A translation in the same spidery script formed in its wake.

Wilith yawned. "This will take some time. I need a break."

Elae arranged paper and the Kristl so she could continue. "I'm too excited to take a break."

Merrilea pulled her chair closer. "Elae and I can begin the translation. We'll call if we discover anything important."

Wilith caught the Guardian's eye. "Perhaps we can pay a visit to the fountain?"

Elae glanced up as they retreated along the corridor of cases. She frowned. *Almiralyn seems different.* The Kristl hummed beneath her fingers, summoning her back to the task at hand.

Wilith stared into the fireplace in the Reading Room. Almiralyn's last report suggested Torgin had escaped the fate of his friends and Renn was safe, but nothing more. *So where is my son? What has happened to Renn?* He rubbed his forehead and frowned. The Guardian had excused herself and recommended he rest until her return. *How can I rest when I don't know what's happening?*

The desire to know more carried him halfway to the sanctuary. *What am I doing?* He glared at the door. *I do not need permission to learn about my family.* Before he could change his mind, he walked briskly into Veersuni.

The serenity of the sanctuary eased his uncertainty and soothed his sense of urgency. He stared thoughtfully at the new pattern in the stained-glass window. *I wonder if it is always changing, like life since my arrival in Myrrh?*

Crossing to the fountain, he watched the water flow from the statue's upturned palms and the surface ripple in response to each drop. Unsure how to begin, he dipped his index finger, rubbed the wetness between his finger and thumb, and whispered, "Coala Renn Whalend, where are you?"

The water ceased flowing; the ripples stilled. A flash of light skittered over the surface, creating an image in its wake.

A Pentharian, three men, and a woman sat with Renn around a rough-hewn table in the battered remains of a ship's hull.

From the descriptions Almiralyn shared, he recognized the Senndi brothers and the woman Bibeed, who cared for his companion. He guessed the gold Pentharian must be Yaro, his son's heart-brother. The third man he did not know.

The shorter of the two brothers stood and offered his hand. "Well, Cayled, if you're sure, we'd be honored to have ya crew for us."

The man grinned. "That's it then. We can leave. Best way to cross ZaltRaca is by horse and wagon. Neighbor through the woods has one we can borrow. I'll head over to get it. Meet ya up at the cottage in two chron circles. Bibeed can come with me and stay with our friends."

Bibeed's face flushed red. "You aren't leaving me behind, Cay. Where Renn goes, I go. The VarTerel charged me with her safety."

Cayled shot her a stubborn look. "It's too dangerous, Bibeed."

She folded her arms across her chest. "I'm going, Cay. I can help."

Renn put an arm around her shoulder. "We will take care of each other. We both go."

Tamosh's green eyes glowed with a hint of humor. He glanced at Gregos, who grinned at Cayled. "It is pointless, my friend, to fight the will of a woman."

Gregos slapped Cay on the back. "Don't worry. *SeaBella* will accommodate us all. Besides, there's always room for an excellent cook."

Bibeed gave Cayled a quick hug. "I'll be fine."

He gave her a begrudging smile and then grimaced at Gregos. "Seems I'm outnumbered. Let's make plans."

Gregos frowned. "I don't think ya should go alone to get the wagon. We can't be sure the Mocendi didn't leave someone behind."

Yaro fingered the jewel in his earlobe. "I also do not believe it is wise to leave from the cottage. I can carry you, Cayled, and Gregos to your friend. You can arrange for the wagon. I will then make trips to bring Renn and Bibeed and Tamosh."

Cayled grinned, his rancor forgotten. "You mean we get to fly?"

Yaro smiled at his enthusiasm. "I will shape a vulture. It will be much quicker. And safer for Renn Whalend."

Wilith watched Renn's slow smile broaden and wished he were there to share her excitement. The image swept across the surface. Colors blurred together and reformed.

Renn listened to Yaro's last-minute instructions, watched him shift to a vulture, and with Bibeed's help, mounted. Gold vulture eyes peered back at them and blinked. The enormous head swung forward, and the creature launched into the air.

"Yeeikes!" Bibeed threw her head back and chortled with delight.

Renn gasped as the beach fell away below them. She scanned the night sky, noted the swath of the stars overhead, and caught her breath at the beauty of golden moonlight highlighting the trees of the woods beneath her. Torgin had flown with Yaro as she was now; Torgin, who was terrified of heights. A laugh of amazement danced away on the wind that tangled its cool fingers in her hair and made her eyes water.

Too soon, the big vulture swooped lower and landed in a field behind a large, shadowy structure. Giggling like a schoolgirl, Bibeed slid to the ground and threw her arms around her brother. Renn stood alone, staring up at the heavens.

Yaro materialized beside her. "You look happy, Renn Whalend."

She laid a hand on his tattooed arm. "Thank you, Yaro. I will never forget the beauty of that ride."

Torgin's heart-brother bowed his head. A golden-brown braid brushed her cheek. Awe flooded her thoughts. *I am so glad about this adventure.*

Gregos joined them. "The wagon's ready, Yaro. We'll follow the main track to the coast. Get that brother of mine and meet us along the way." He linked his arm through Renn's and guided her into the dim interior of the roughly constructed building.

For a moment, she stood still, inhaling the scents of life in a barn: hay and horses, the faint smells of manure, mildew, and aging wood. A cat rubbed against her ankle. A cow mooed. Her first time in Mira's barn burst into memory. Astonishment left her grinning.

Wilith watched the image fade with a touch of envy. *Renn has experienced in a few turnings more than I have in my lifetime.*

Profound silence gripped the sanctuary. A new picture merging into wholeness one constellation at a time side-tracked his discontent.

A midnight sky stretched in all directions. Torgin listened intently to a man Wilith assumed was the new VarTerel. Seyes Nomed, Somay, and a hideous creature that made his skin crawl waited nearby.

Torgin withdrew a compass from beneath his tunic and whispered a question. As the needle spun and stopped, the VarTerel raised his staff, and the group vanished. Elcaro's Eye grew quiet.

Wilith sighed. *Torgin is so grown up. Renn is preparing for another adventure. With luck, she will be in Myrrh soon. With luck—* A nagging fear stirred in his gut. *Is there such a thing as luck during The Unfolding?*

Jordett gazed from an open window over the city of Idronatti. The light of mid-morning glowed on the tall, gray buildings lining the streets surrounding the Five Towers. The air smelled fresh after a light rainfall at dawn. People were returning to their scheduled lives, their routines re-established by the blow of the whistle that segmented their turnings into exercise, work or school, mealtimes, and sleep.

Below, as in all districts, citizens marched along the pristine streets, afraid to look either right or left. Many of them had not left their apartments since the Mocendi arrived.

Jordett's men found all but one of Nissasa's traitors. No Mocendi had fallen into Jordett's Oppositional Force, JOF's net. That The MasTer's DiMensioners had withdrawn from Idronatti and left Nissasa's Brigade in charge made him edgy. He felt certain that something important was about to happen, something involving the twins and their friends.

Teva joined him. "We've had word from Myrrh. The journal Almiralyn told us about is being translated." Her sapphire eyes sparkled. "We'll know more about The MasTer soon."

"Any news on the Mocendi's destination?"

She pursed her lips and shook her head. "We believe their traveling ship is circling DerTah, which is worrisome. They could gather everyone onboard for a return to TreBlaya. On a positive note, we've received word that Wolloh is the VarTerel of the Inner Universe and Relevart is now the Universal VarTerel. Since they've vanished, we believe they are traveling through Mittkeer."

"Mittkeer?"

"The place of All time and No time, the place from which the VarTerels travel through time and dimension."

"Time travel. Jumping from dimension to dimension..." Jordett scratched the stubble on his chin. "Life has become one constant revelation since I first met Henrietta and the twins." He grew quiet, his thoughts in turmoil. "What's your next move?"

Teva looked past him to the city beyond. "We are committed to helping you assist the people of Idronatti. As soon as Renn and Wilith Whalend return, we hope to develop a program to help Idronattians begin to take control of their lives. Right now, we're in a holding pattern. Anything that changes outward appearances here will alert The MasTer. We can do little except maintain the calm in the city." She sighed. "I will be gone for a couple of turnings. Lenadi goes with me. Akeri will be your right hand until we return."

He frowned. "Trouble?"

"Lorsedi's men have detained two Mocendi in Myrrh. Once we've learned what we can of The MasTer's plan, we will remove them from the game. I checked on Dom on my way here. He's still unconscious. Falind is overseeing the infirmary and the care of the wounded. She'll keep her eye on him. I'll update Akeri on our progress so she can keep you informed."

Jordett nodded. "Any news on the Five Fathers?"

"We're certain they're somewhere in this compound. Senar and Lavir are searching the lower levels."

She flashed from sight, leaving him staring out the window. A whistle blew. The streets grew quiet. Morning exercise was over. The people of Idronatti worked, learned, and listened for the next whistle.

How will they manage when whistles no longer define their turnings? Life is full of decisions from what to wear to whether to exercise. What will happen when their professions are no longer chosen for them? He sighed. *What would I do?*

Veersuni echoed with Wilith's retreating footsteps and the soft close of the door. Elcaro's Eye glowed in the light from the window. Drops of water played a game of chase on the fountain's surface. Its song grew still, the water motionless. An image formed.

A man's narrow, pointed features came into focus. Beady black eyes scanned a room, where four men slept on cots lining the walls. His expression twisted into an angry frown. Again, his eyes swept over the room's occupants. *The Mocendi MasTer and his DiMensioners have betrayed us into believing the entire planet of Thera and Myrrh would be ours, that we would no longer be answerable to the Galactic Guardians.*

Soru, the man's second in command, jerked awake. Close-set brown eyes darted around the space. "Anyone come to see us, Viennoc?"

Viennoc shook his head. "We have enough food for two turnings. I don't expect anyone before then."

Soru swung his feet to the floor and rubbed exhausted eyes. "How'd they discover this room? We're the only ones who know it exists." He gave the other Fathers a surreptitious glance. "Which one told 'em?"

The speed with which an older man with hunched shoulders and gray hair shot to his feet belied his fragile appearance. He lifted a clenched fist. "What makes you think one of us would snitch? Perhaps it was you."

Soru launched to standing, an ugly scowl on his face. "You little weasel—"

Viennoc cut him short. "Enough."

Blood rushed to Soru's cheeks. "Don't—"

"Now, Soru. If we start to fight amongst ourselves, we will be in real trouble."

Jarel dropped his fists. "Viennoc is right. If we don't work together, we may never leave here." He sank onto his cot and tugged at a straggly, gray mustache as Nema and Gnitsy, the remaining Fathers, chorused, "What's all the racket?"

Nema stretched long, lean limbs and crossed to a table. He pulled out a chair and lowered onto it. "Suggest you two stop yelling, and we figure a way out."

Gnitsy hauled his rotund body off his cot. Folds of fat jiggled as he waddled to the table. His balding head gleamed in the muted light. Dull brown eyes peered from beneath drooping lids. "Seems like we're stuck. We know how to get in. Never thought about a *way* to get out."

Jarel and Soru sat down on opposite sides of the table. Viennoc observed his comrades in silence. The realization that he disliked them was not a new one. It was, however, exacerbated by several turnings spent in close proximity. He cleared his throat. "Nema, you helped to design this hid-y-hole. How do we get out?"

Nema shot him a dirty look. "I created it to keep prisoners in. Unless someone opens the door from the outside, we aren't going anywhere."

The heaving power of Gnitsy's mass sent the table flying and the Fathers scrabbling backward. Chairs crashed to the floor and expletives filled the air. "I'll get us outta here."

An uproar ensued. Nema grabbed for his arm and missed.

Soru shouted, "No, Gnitsy!"

Jarel folded his arms and muttered about the stupidity of fat men.

Gnitsy shoved him aside, lunged for the door, slammed a shoulder into it, and howled in pain. Clutching it with a meaty hand, he rounded on Nema. "What's the da'am door made of, you fool?"

Nema slapped his flabby cheek. "I designed this lock-up to keep prisoners in, not to let them escape. The door is steel, you big fool. I'm betting you broke your shoulder."

Viennoc righted his chair and observed his colleagues from beneath raised brows. *Why the Galactic Guardians saddled me with you four is beyond me.* He folded his arms across his chest and prepared to wait for the chaos to settle.

Elcaro's Eye scattered the image and resumed its drip, drop, drip.

40

Der Tah & Beyond

Brie didn't enjoy shifting to anything smaller than a moth. Bugs, unlike mammals, seemed disconnected from her humanness, so as she crawled through the open weave of the mesh vent cover, she shifted to a mouse and eavesdropped on Vygel's conversation with her aunt. When the Mocendi vanished, she shifted to the moth and continued to explore the ventilation system.

The round shaft was about the circumference of her Human thigh. A brown tube covered with tiny filaments quivering in the light flow of air stretched along the bottom. Flying into the slight breeze, she searched for its source. Its flow and the sound of water drew her around a sweeping curve that ended at a round, covered vent. Near its bottom edge, she found a spot of light, shifted to a small beetle, crawled through, and scurried down the wall.

Concealing herself in the shadows behind thick foliage, she changed to

Human. Cupped hands smothered an astonished gasp as she took in the beauty of her surroundings.

Lush green with patches of bright color filled the space. Plants and trees grew in every direction. Butterflies flitted from one flower to the other. Jewel-colored hummingbirds whizzed past, their wings a blur. An occasional bee buzzed by. A waterfall tumbled over dark rocks into a pool surrounded by a garden.

In the shape of a butterfly, she fluttered from flower to flower. The circular space rose several stories high and appeared to be almost as big around as the Five Towers' compound in Idronatti. At the ground level, camouflaged by taller plant growth, shelved structures covered with a variety of smaller plants followed the curve of the walls. Bark-covered paths meandered through the space like trails in the Terces Wood.

The more Brie explored, the more astounded she became. The space teemed with life. From floor to ceiling, plants thrived. Beehives throughout provided a means of pollination. Each level of the round space provided a home for different plant species. Fish swam in the pool. A variety of birds nested in the trees. A beetle scurried over a mound of dark rocks. Thick brown roots climbed the walls and disappeared into vents. The space lived and breathed.

A door opened below, and a uniformed figure entered, checked a series of icons on a screen, and began a circuit.

Brie shifted and shot through the mesh vent cover and flew toward the lab. Midway, she passed a branch in the shaft. The urge to see more tempted her down its length. At the end of the shaft, the rancid odor of vomit wafted through the vent. The space beyond was dark. The Star of Truth throbbed a warning and then a tingle of recognition.

Crawling through the mesh screen, she remained hidden beneath the cover. Darkness as thick as molasses left her blind. A low moan alerted her to someone close by. A ceiling light began to glow. She froze in place. The door opened. A man entered and crossed to the cot beneath the vent. He shook a boy who lay there in a tight fetal position.

Ira moaned again. The man helped him to sit up. He sipped from an offered cup and watched the man clean the floor and set a bucket where he could reach it.

"Your stomach should settle soon. Try to rest."

He left. The door slid shut. The light dimmed. Ira stretched out and stared into the blackness.

Brie's thoughts churned. *Ira is here, which means the Mocendi found Melback. Is the rest of the crew here?*

She wanted to tell Ira she was close by, sensed someone monitoring his thoughts. One slip could give her away. During her quick search of the room, she discovered surveillance lenses in all corners.

Darting back through the mesh cover, she followed the shaft beyond the lab and soon discovered two more cells. Esán slept in the first one. Elf sat on the floor in the second, his head resting on his bent knees. An invisible Shyllee had almost given her away. She found no sign of Desirol or Torgin. *Before I look for them, I'd better check in with Renn.*

When she arrived at the lab, bursting with news, Renn Whalend, aka Aunt Henri, was nowhere to be found.

Misgivings kept Yaro, in laridae form, perched in a tree overlooking the tidy farm where he had delivered the women to Gregos and Cayled. Impatient to return for Tamosh but unwilling to leave without making sure Renn was safe, he made himself remain still and watchful.

The barn doors swung wide and a large cargo wagon rumbled out under Calegri's cool, blue light. Cayled sat next to Gregos on the high bench, reins in hand, guiding two broad-backed farm horses down the track between fields.

Swooping low, Yaro scanned the deep cargo bed and its stacks of boxes and barrels. Only when he felt satisfied Torgin's mother and her companion were well-hidden, did he bank away toward the Cliffs of Tymine.

He glided to a stop on the beach below the cliffs and shifted. Tamosh dodged free of the shadowed recess outside the door to the cave and jogged across the sand, unease in his face and Cayled's shotgun clutched in his hand.

"After you left, a phalacro landed and shifted to a Mocendi. Seemed agitated. A small vortex formed overhead. He vanished into it."

Yaro gazed up at the heavens. "Do you think he saw us leave?"

A quick shake of the head. "No. Seemed pretty self-absorbed. He sent a mental probe along the cliff face, but..." He shrugged. "I watched him from a concealed recess a short distance down the beach. He found nothing."

"You took a big chance, my friend."

Tamosh's gaze flicked over the cliffs. "Our sister taught us a few things. One is how to blend in with our environment. Came in handy tonight. Let's go."

Yaro studied the intense face. "Can you blend in with my feathers?"

"I can and will."

"It is good." Yaro shifted.

Soon Tamosh's weight pressed against his vulture back. Powerful wings carried them upward.

Tamosh looked down at the cliffs, fields, and woods and grinned. Nothing could spoil his pleasure as the world glided beneath him. *I've dreamt of flying, of stretching my wings and soaring.* He laughed to himself. *This is the next best thing.*

All too soon, trees fell away into rocky, windblown fields. Beyond them, he could pick out the dark outline of a barn and a farmhouse tucked in a copse of the trees. As they flew closer, he tensed. Flames licking at the dry wood sent smoke billowing from the barn's loft window.

Yaro swooped into the cover of the trees and shifted. "This is the farm of Cayled's neighbors. We discover why their barn is in flames.

Tamosh loaded the shotgun as Yaro shaped a small, brown bat and shot away toward the burning structure. Bending low, Tamosh dodged through the field to a tall hedgerow paralleling the side of the darkened house. Nothing stirred. A woman's frightened scream broke the night silence. The sound of running feet, furniture upending, and a man's hoarse cry sent the bat through an open window. Tamosh dashed toward the house. Bounding onto a small porch, he pressed his back against the rough siding near the window and listened. A floorboard creaked. A man swore. The farmhouse grew quiet again.

Yaro appeared at the window and motioned him inside. With his rifle cocked and ready, Tamosh ducked through the doorway. A man sprawled at

Yaro's feet. A woman stood opposite, her terrified gaze fastened on the imposing Pentharian.

Tamosh lowered the rifle and stepped forward. "We are friends. You met my brother, Gregos Senndi, earlier today with Cayled Finnaberry. I'm Tamosh Senndi. I believe you know Yaro. We were on our way to join them when we saw the fire in your barn."

The woman hugged herself and suppressed a shiver. "I'm Janis. My husband Frith loaned his wagon to Cayled and his sister. They hadn't been gone long when two men burst through the door." She choked back a sob and spoke through chattering teeth. "They t-took Frith. I d-don't know w-where he is. This man came back and tried to f-force me—" Sobs shook her shoulders.

Yaro's red lips formed a thin line, his eyes held a coldness that made Tamosh shudder. The Pentharian picked up the unconscious man and dumped him on the couch. "Tie him up. He has much to explain. I will find Frith. Keep the house dark in case there are others around." A hawk shot out the window.

Janis gasped. "I'd never met a Pentharian until he brought Gregos to meet Frith. I never expected him to change shape so fast." She swallowed, shook her head, and glanced at the unconscious man. "I'll get rope." The words were firm and clear.

While she was gone, Tamosh searched the man's pockets. He withdrew a small ampule of black vapor wrapped in a soft cloth and held it up in the dim light, then slipped it in his pocket. The man on the couch moaned. Janis dumped a rope at his feet. With her help, Tamosh secured him in a chair.

The front door opened and closed with a soft thud. Janis gripped his arm. Yaro entered carrying a soot covered man and lowered him on to the couch. "Your companion lives, Janis. I found him trapped beneath an old wagon. The other man is dead."

Tamosh arched his brows over question-filled eyes.

Yaro smiled. "I believe our farmer got to him first."

"Frith." Janis knelt and brushed his hair back from his face. "Frith, open your eyes. It's Janis. Please look at me."

Tamosh withdrew the ampule from his pocket and offered it to Yaro. He jerked a thumb toward the man in the chair. "Found this on him."

Yaro fingered the tiny glass vial and handed it back. "The MasTer's Reach. We must destroy it, though I don't understand how it is done."

"Marji told us to break it in a large body of water." Tamosh slipped it back in his pocket. "Why are they after us?"

Janis spoke over her shoulder. "They're hunting a boy with a compass and a girl with the Star of Truth. Seemed pretty sure they're with Cayled and Gregos."

Frith coughed a harsh, raspy cough and stared up at his companion. "How…"

She moved aside. "You know Yaro. This is Tamosh, the brother of Gregos."

The farmer pushed himself to sitting and noted the man in the chair. "The other one?"

Yaro smiled. "You did well, my friend. He will bother you no longer. What do we do with this one? It is vital that Tamosh and I leave to warn our friends they are being pursued."

Frith cleared his throat. "Omudi, the Dreela of Geran, is offering a reward for anything regarding the League. I'll send a message to TiCeed. The reward will help us with a new barn."

Tamosh stroked his beard. "I believe that is good. This man is an errand boy, not a DiMensioner. I feel nothing to suggest he has the gift, and Relevart told us the Mocendi have withdrawn."

Yaro nodded. "Ask Omudi to provide the Dreelas TheLise with any information that could help the VarTerel."

Frith pulled a wrinkled hand-cloth from his pocket and wiped the soot from his face. "We'll make sure he gets the message." Glancing at his wife, he pointed at the prisoner. "What do we do with him until we turn him over to the Dreela?"

"If you will bring me a cup, Janis, I will leave serum for you to put in his water." Yaro tapped his pointed tooth. "It will keep him unconscious."

They said their goodbyes, and Tamosh once again experienced the elation of flight. Fingering the ampule in his pocket sobered him. *I have to destroy this somewhere safe.*

Allynae enjoyed his short time with Stebben and Roandee. He liked and trusted Stebben. Once he got past Roandee's startling good looks, he found that WoNa's younger brother intrigued him. The dust devil had been his work.

Flying high above Shu Chenaro, Allynae forced himself to keep his thoughts focused on the present. Although still protected by the shields, awareness was essential. Ahead, he could make out the border. Tents lined both sides. Men patrolled and guards were posted in both camps. *Too bad about Nissasa. Didn't like him, but wouldn't have wished his fate on anybody.*

Swooping lower, he stretched his talons earthward. Human feet touched sand. Of all the Arts of DiMensionery, shape shifting had become his favorite. He loved the gift of flight and marveled at the power and the cunning of the red hawk. Given a choice, however, shaping Starfire... He had no words to describe that most breathtaking experience.

The soft crunch of feet on sand alerted him to the approach of a soldier.

"Your name and your business."

"Allynae Nadrugia, brother of the Guardian of Myrrh, here to confer with Lorsedi Telisnoe."

Suspicious eyes studied him. "Can't let you through, sir, unless you can prove your identity."

Gerolyn ducked under a tent line. "Hello, Allynae. Lorsedi is waiting to hear your news." She nodded to the soldier. "Thank you. I will take him from here."

The man frowned, shrugged, and walked away.

Gerolyn's gaze followed his retreating figure. "Men from RewFaar have a difficult time with women in authority. Change is coming. It will be more difficult for some planets than for others."

She escorted him through the camp to Lorsedi's tent. The man on duty nodded them in. The Largeen Joram of RewFaar and the Pentharian Voer stood as they entered.

Lorsedi motioned them to the table. "We are eager for news. How are my sons?"

Allynae shared the happenings in Trinuge. Lorsedi's face remained expressionless as he learned his oldest son would be a five-year-old for the rest of his life. Desirol's possession by the Mindeco and the measures put into place to protect him, and then his subsequent kidnapping by the

Mocendi brought the Largeen Joram to his feet. He paced to the tent entrance and back to Allynae.

"You tell me the Mindeco has Desirol and that he is beyond our reach. How do we remove the creature without killing him? How do we rescue him and his friends?" Anger tinted his fair complexion. "Yaro has failed me."

Voer's alien face maintained its perpetual calm. "We have only lost a battle, Lorsedi. The war has yet to be won."

Allynae sat straighter. "Wolloh and Relevart have gathered a group to pursue the Mocendi and to rescue the children. If I did not trust them to bring back my girls, your granddaughters, I would not be here. Nor would I be on my way to Myrrh. Yaro continues to do his part as directed by the VarTerel. All is not lost, Lorsedi." He scooted his stool back and stood. "I must leave. Stebben is now a High DiMensioner and with TheLise's help will oversee the safety of DerTah. They will be in touch."

The Largeen Joram rose, military bearing eclipsing his anger. "My regards to Myrrh's Guardian. I hope to meet her someday."

Gerolyn walked him to the edge of the camp. "It frustrates Lorsedi that he is here and not with Wolloh. I do not blame him." She sighed. "Please take care of SparrowLyn. Tell her I am proud of her, Allynae."

His brows arched. "You know?"

She smiled. "I am her mother. When she is uneasy, I feel it. I've let Grantese Tesilend know you are on the way. Paisley and Stee wish to return to Myrrh with you."

"Thank you for everything, Gerolyn. I promise to take good care of your daughter."

His shift was instantaneous. Hawk wings carried him toward the gateway camp. Paisley, Stee, and Jeet awaited his arrival in the Grantese's tent, where they exchanged news. Jeet led the way between dunes. They paused as the faint spin of the vortex came into view. Two RewFaaran soldiers motioned them forward.

Stee and Paisley took the gateway to Naidisbo Canyon. From there, Stee would carry Paisley to Nemttachenn Tower and then find Mondago and his men. Jeet spoke with the guards, made his farewells, and returned to camp.

Stee and Paisley jumped first. Allynae watched them go. He murmured the Key for the Dojanack Caverns, felt the silence embrace him, saw the flash of vibrant colors, and arrived on the outskirts of Meos.

Sitrio, Yookotay's right hand, stepped from the shadows. "Your sister is most anxious to see you. She is in her quarters."

Knowing that Sparrow had taken Almiralyn's place, Allynae thanked him and strode down the tunnel, his heart leaping with joy at the thought of seeing his companion, of inhaling the sweet scent of her, of holding her close at last.

Henri sat across the desk from a good-looking, blond Mocendi who had introduced himself as Thorlu Tangorra. The moment the attendant ushered her into his presence, she sensed intelligence that outstripped Vygel's and a shrewdness and cunning Vintrusie did not possess. Danger sizzled in the space. Danger for her, for Brie, and for Renn Whalend.

Drawing on Renn's intelligence and her own gifts and training, she buried Henri Avetlire even deeper and waited, hands folded in her lap and eyes alert and interested.

Thorlu rounded the desk and sat on the edge next to her chair. "Where is your son?"

Her gaze flew to Vygel as he entered the space and back to Thorlu. "I thought he was here, on your ship."

"We believe he was with you and your friends on ZaltRaca. Tell me what their plans are." The calm words were almost soothing.

Renn wanted to shiver but kept herself still. "The woman who cared for me is the only person I know on the island."

"What about the brothers who owned the ship that was bringing Torgin to you? When did you meet them?"

She squeezed her hands tighter together and let confusion reign in her mind. "Torgin left Idronatti several moon cycles ago. He has not contacted me since, nor have I seen him. When I last heard about his whereabouts, he was in a desert." She shot an accusing look in Vygel's direction. "You had me kidnapped and taken to the cottage on ZaltRaca. I have no information to share."

Thorlu walked back around the desk and sat down. "There are ways to make you talk, Renn."

She studied the handsome face, the calculating gray-green eyes.

"Someone has monitored my every thought since I arrived here, which should tell you I don't have any information to share."

His brows shot up.

"Yes, Thorlu, I sensed your mind probes. In case you are unaware, my experiment deals with how to control minds. The brain is one of my specialties. I am aware when someone is fooling with mine." She paused, took a breath, and placed her hands palms down on the desk. Her unwavering gaze on Thorlu, she continued. "I'm glad Torgin is not on this ship. If I knew where he was, I would not tell you. You can pick whatever you want from my brain, so you already know as much as I do about my son."

A probe stung her mind. She held her gaze steady. The probe withdrew.

Thorlu directed Vygel. "Take her back to the lab. She has work to do." He gave her a malicious smile. "As soon as we capture your son, Renn Whalend, we will take you to The MasTer. We shall see how *he* deals with you."

Vygel grabbed her arm and yanked her to her feet. She glared at his hand. "I have no choice but to go with you, Vygel." Her gaze fastened on his bulging eyes. "You don't need to drag me."

His eyes bulged more than usual. His thin-lipped mouth worked, but no words formed. Thorlu laughed and held the door open. "At least you are entertaining, Renn."

In the quiet, empty the lab, Brie paced the floor in the storage closet. *Where are you, Renn?*

Her answer came with the almost silent shish, shish of the door. Shifting, she flew into the lab.

The figure of Renn Whalend sank into a chair and gave the tiniest shake of her head. Pulling blonde hair back from her face, she interlaced her fingers behind her head and closed her eyes. When she finally opened them, she picked up her comp-tab and walked to the storage closet.

Brie followed and landed in her favorite dark corner, waiting for a sign that it was safe to shift to Human. When it didn't come, she reined in her impatience and stayed where she was. Renn came and went several times before she walked back to the corner and nodded.

Brie materialized and mouthed, "Can we talk?"

Renn's smile looked tired. "It seems we have both had adventures today. Tell me what you discovered."

After she described what she called the plantitarium, Brie told her about finding Ira, Esán, Elf, and Shyllee. "I didn't locate Desirol, and I couldn't find Torgin anywhere. Where were you? I was so scared."

Renn's summer green eyes held an expression Brie did not recognize. "They found *Melback*, Brie. Torgin was not on the ship. I don't know about Desirol. I hope Yaro is on his guard, because I believe he and the brothers are being pursued." The expression heightened. "We have a new enemy onboard. His name is Thorlu Tangorra; he is much more clever than Vygel. It is vital that you stay out of his way."

Her expression, Brie realized, was fear, something she had never seen on her aunt's face.

41

Myrrh & Der Tah

Kieel sat on a large sunflower, soaking up the Myrrhinian sunshine. Even after several turnings, his body still held the chill of his time in Idronatti—his time in battle. Images of blood and death haunted his turnings and pursued him through his dreams at night. As hard as he tried, he could not erase the horror.

Below him, the gateway began to spin, announcing guests from The Borderlands. Darting to a patch of shade, he observed Teva and Lenadi exit the Tropal Gateway. The soft whir of wings brought him to eye level.

Teva smiled. "Hello. I was hoping we would see you."

His smile felt strained. "Mondago sent me to guide you to him. He suggested I show you where the older Mocendi is on the way. Hey, Lenadi."

"Good to see you, Kieel."

Flitting from leaf to leaf, he led them the short distance to Almiralyn's acreage. A momentary pang twisted his stomach. He missed the Guardian's cottage, her barn, and her pond. He missed her.

Skirting the edge of the camp well away from Almiralyn's trap, Kieel landed in a thicket opposite the Mocendi's tent and waited for the KcernFensians. The wards shimmered faintly in the sun.

Teva joined him, put a finger to her lips, and patted her shoulder. When he landed, she spoke a soft phrase. A section of the wards about the size of a door melted away. Lenadi approached the rear of the tent. Teva followed. Kieel glanced back. The wards reformed. A tingle of fear—*I'm trapped inside.*

The KcernFensians separated. One to the left and one to the right, they circled the tent.

A man strode through the entrance, his eyes searching. "I suggest you show yourself. I know you're here."

Teva motioned Kieel to the top of the tent and stepped into view. "Hello, Émil. It has been a long time."

From his perch, Kieel noted the slight stoop of the man's shoulders. His graying hair looked steely in the sun. His light eyes glinted beneath heavy lids. A broad nose beaked over a full-lipped mouth. Nothing about the face was pleasant. Cruelty etched it like a mask. Kieel's chill intensified.

The man's demeanor radiated rage, but his words were controlled. "Teva Rivan. When did we last meet? Ah, yes. I remember. We were in KcernFensia, at the temple. As I recall, you ousted me from the training program." A sneer of distaste distorted his unpleasant features. "What brings you to Myrrh? Your dear cousin?"

"It seems, Émil, that I need to ask *you* a few questions."

His smile grew wicked. "And if I don't feel inclined to share?"

"I believe you know the answer to that. Tell me what I need to know, and I will put in a good word with the Galactic Guardians."

The smile slipped. "You are serious, aren't you?" Wards shot up around him. "As you see, Cousin of Almiralyn, I didn't need you or your training program."

A bolt of lightning flew from his hand toward her heart, hit an invisible wall, and disintegrated. A second aimed at her head rebounded back in his direction. His wards quivered with the impact, began to break down, and strengthened anew.

The malicious smile returned. "We seem to be at a draw. You won't get answers from me. But I believe you will undo the wards that trap me in this tent." He advanced toward her.

Their wards crackled as they touched. The man stumbled back, his face contorted with pain.

Teva did not move. "Lenadi, please join me."

Her protector walked to her side. Ropes composed of light slithered through Émil's wards and bound him hand and foot. The wards dissolved. Lenadi caught the man as he crumpled and carried him inside.

Teva whispered a quiet phrase. Almiralyn's trap melted away. She caught Kieel's eye. "Inform Tinpaca Mondago that we have the Mocendi and that he and his men can return to their camp. Tell him to bring their prisoner with them. We'll question him here." She ducked into the tent.

Kieel zipped between trees. The Wood Tiffs had hidden Mondago and his men in a grove of large, trunked, weathered Tirips Trees close to Nemttachenn Tower. Tirips Trees carried magic in their core. Known to protect good from evil, they also trapped those with malicious intent.

Dodging between two gray branches, Kieel landed amongst the silvery leaves. Reana, Ashor, and Mumshoo patrolled the grove. His granddaughter touched down beside him.

"Hi, Grandy. What brings you here?"

"Teva sent me. I have a message for the Tinpaca. Any trouble?"

"Only the Mocendi. He is one angry Human."

He gave her a quick hug. "I'd better deliver my message. Take care of yourself."

"You, too, Grandy."

He flew down to a makeshift camp at the center of the grove. Mondago and Tibin sat in conversation. The contrast between the distinguished, well-muscled RewFaaran officer and the short roundness of the Wood Tiff with his big head and his jiggly belly made Kieel smile and consider the unlikelihood of this meeting. *The Unfolding has changed all our lives and continues to do so.*

Tibin waved. "Hey, Kieel."

Mondago offered his palm.

Kieel landed. "Teva sent a message, Tinpaca."

The Tinpaca called over his personal staff. Stee, who had just returned from DerTah, and Yuin joined them. Kieel regarded the emerald and ruby red Pentharian with a touch of awe. It amazed him that these creatures from another planet would come to the rescue of Myrrh.

Mondago settled on a stump. "Please, Kieel, share Teva's message."

Kieel began, "The Mocendi—"

A man's shout cut him short. Tinpaca and his staff shot to their feet. Stee and Yuin exchanged looks. Three frightened Nyti streaked from the trees.

Reana hovered in front of Mondago, wings a blur, her eyes too big for her face. "That horrid Mocendi has Tibin's mate and their baby."

"A soldier tried to protect them. He's hurt pretty bad," a very pale Ashor added.

"The Mocendi can't escape the Tirips Trees' magic, but he's threatening to kill Sibine unless you set him free, Tinpaca." Mumshoo twisted his top hat between shaking fingers.

Kieel's heart trembled in his chest. The man's scream had reminded him of Idronatti and the battle for the Five Towers. He fought for breath. *The Mocendi has Tibin's mate and baby. The Mocendi has Sibine and Adin—*

Allynae paused outside Almiralyn's quarters and rang the bell. His sister's voice bade him enter. A tinge of disappointment kept him still. He laughed to himself and entered the Guardian's quarters. Sparrow stood at the center of the space. Chestnut hair falling in soft curls framed her beautiful face. Dark eyes overflowing with love met his. Two long strides carried him to her. Her arms encircled his neck as he picked her up and held her to him. He set her down. She took his face between her hands and kissed him until he knew his heartbeat echoed throughout the caverns. When she finally stepped back, they stared at each other and grinned like two teenagers.

He pulled her down beside him on a bench. "I have missed you—"

She brushed his lips with a gentle kiss and smiled. "I missed you, too. I have so much—"

Almiralyn appeared in her place. Sapphire blue eyes held his gaze. The bell at the entrance chimed, and a voice penetrated the curtain. "Almiralyn, may I come in?"

Almiralyn moved further down the bench, gave him a mischievous grin, and answered, "Of course."

Elae entered, waving a piece of paper. "Welcome back, Alli."

"Good to see you, Elae." He grinned. Her attention had already made a swift shift to Almiralyn. He leaned back to watch his companion's performance.

"Elae, please sit down and tell us why you are so excited. Is it the translation?"

"Mira, we found it. We discovered what birth-mates are."

Almiralyn smiled. "Please tell us everything."

Elae composed herself, checked her notes, and began.

"Floree Galeenite, a birther on the planet of El Stroma during the wars that ended in the pogrom of the Eleo Preda, wrote the journal. She tells the story of an attempt by an Eleo Predian rebel group to save their culture and their people.

"El Stroma, a planet about the size of Tao Spirian, had two major continents and a scattering of islands. Although there were smaller island tribes, the populace on the continents was divided into the Eleo Preda and the Pheet Adole.

"At first, the two dominant cultures managed to co-exist by maintaining separate communities on separate continents. The Eleo Preda were a gentle people. Agriculture was their life. They farmed and protected the land and the wildlife existing there. They considered themselves the stewards of the continent of El QuilTran. The Pheet Adole had built an industrialized nation. They lived in small, squalid towns and in the two principal cities on the continent of El SyrTundi.

"Time passed. The RomPeer, leader of the Pheet Adole, and his council became greedy. They wanted more land, and they coveted the longevity of the Eleo Preda. Politics had become complicated, and wealthy families engaged in battles with one another. The RomPeer had to find a solution or play mediator. He preferred to spend his time bringing the Eleo Preda to heel.

"In order to insure the family lines of the aristocracy continued and that wealthy households refrained from warring against one another, the

RomPeer's medical researchers developed the practice of Protariflee. When the young of the wealthy reached puberty, their eggs and sperm were harvested and handpicked samples frozen for a later time. Because of their longevity, Eleo Predian women were kidnapped and impregnated with fertilized eggs, one male and one female from distinct family lines, the hope being that the Eleo Preda gene for long life would pass on to the birth-mates. The babies were born and placed in the care of host mothers. Once the families of origin reclaimed their babies, the host mothers disappeared.

"The premise for Protariflee appears to be the belief that gestating in the same womb created a closeness that, like twins, would last throughout the birth-mates lifetimes."

Elae reviewed her notes.

Allynae tugged his mustache. "Did the families have other babies?"

"The cost for Protariflee was high. Families could pay for another birth-mated offspring, but most did not. The birth-mated child was their first child and their heir."

Almiralyn looked thoughtful. "How did the Eleo Preda respond?"

"The elders of the Eleo Preda realized they did not have the means to fight the Pheet Adole. Anticipating the potential end of their people, they enlisted the aid of a group of young activists. Two infiltrated the Protariflee Center and received the training required to perform Protariflee procedures. They then helped to smuggle four talented Eleo Preda into the lab and put their training to use. Following the selection process, they froze and stored the chosen eggs and sperm.

"One activist, a young woman named Jaradee, volunteered to be the host and at the appointed time, they transferred the embryos. Someone at the center leaked word to the RomPeer, and a search ensued. A small group of rebels bent on protecting Jaradee and the precious children she carried in her womb helped her and Floree, her birther, to escape. After the babies were born, Jaradee and Floree worked together to keep them safe. When the children were three, the RomPeer's men discovered their hiding place. The women decided they would have a better chance of survival if they separated.

"Floree smuggled the boy, Rethdun, to a small town on the edge of the space field where, with rebel help, she booked passage aboard a universal jump craft. When they eventually landed on Persow, Floree found a young couple who pledged to raise Rethdun as their own. After the boy's twelfth birth celebration, Floree returned to El Stroma in search of Jaradee and the girl they had named Rayn.

"During her absence, the rebellion continued to grow. Careful questions produced scant information. Jaradee and Rayn were caught on their way to El QuilTran. Their enemies murdered Jaradee. Before her captors could turn her over to the RomPeer, the activists rescued Rayn. When the trail turned cold, Floree returned to Persow. Six sun cycles later, she received word from El Stroma that a young female activist had emerged and become the RomPeer's prime target. The informant told her the girl called herself Rayn."

Elae set her notes aside. "That's as far as we've gotten."

Allynae reviewed the facts. Realization straightened his spine. His gaze fastened on the visage of his sister. Her mouth formed an "O."

"So, Relevart, the boy in the locket, is the young woman's birth-mate. Did she survive the war? And what of their relationship to The MasTer?"

Elae yawned. "We were making mistakes, so we took a break. After we've rested, we have several more entries to translate. Hopefully, they will tell us if she survived and what connects her and Relevart to The MasTer." She stifled another yawn. "If you don't mind, I think I'll take a nap. Merrilea's in her quarters. Wilith is in the Reading Room reviewing my translated sections. We plan to return to work in a couple of chron circles." She yawned again and departed.

Sparrow materialized. "Allynae, who do you think she is? Do you think Almiralyn knows?"

He smiled and clasped her hands. "Maybe. She's usually ahead of the curve in matters such as these. What it means—only Emit knows." He kissed her fingers one by one and gathered her into his arms.

She studied his face. "I missed you so much. I can't even remember how I survived all those years we were apart." They teleported to her personal quarters.

He laughed. "Wolloh told me your talents had matured." He held her closer.

She relaxed against his chest and sighed. "Safe at last."

He inhaled the fragrance of her hair and matched her sigh. The intrigue surrounding The MasTer and its impact on The Unfolding would give them little leisure to enjoy each other. *Now* was the only time they had.

From somewhere dark and deep, Dom noticed the needle dripping cool liquid into his veins. The timatie he had taken made his brain sluggish. He hoped the Mocendi had left him for dead. The needle suggested, however, that he was somewhere besides the floor of the room in Domlenah Blue.

Unwilling to open his eyes to the discovery that he was a prisoner, he allowed himself to drift in the dreary world between sleep and consciousness. A sudden weight on his mid-section bounced him to wakefulness. A small tongue licked his cheek. He peered from beneath a lid. Majeska's amethyst eyes stared into his. He ran a hand along her back.

"Hope this means I'm safe, Jeska."

A rumbling purr teased a small smile to his dry lips.

A door opening followed by footsteps suggested company. Jordett picked up Majeska, rubbed her tummy, and placed her back on the bed.

"Hi, old man. You had us worried."

Dom licked his lips. "How long?"

Jordett plumbed a pillow and slipped it behind his head. "About three turnings. We weren't sure you'd come back."

"Took a healthy dose. Didn't want to betray Almiralyn a second time. She might not have given me another chance. Thorlu is a thoroughly dangerous man, Jordett. Does Almiralyn know?"

"I believe she met him as a younger woman. She has a strong dislike of him. I suggest you rest. I'll get word to her you're awake."

Dom ran a hand over Majeska's silky side. "I know I'm bein' cranky, but I'd rest better in the shoppe."

Jordett motioned a nurse in a PPP uniform to join them. "Take a couple of turnings to rest, my friend. This is Naya. She'll take care of you."

Dom tried not to stare at the beautiful woman smiling at him. Time was when he would have made a play for her. Instead, he returned her smile and decided a couple of turnings basking in the warmth of her dusky beauty would be just fine. He always had liked dark hair and bright chestnut eyes. Her skin was tawny and her figure...

Jordett caught his eye and winked. "I'll check on you later. Rest."

Naya adjusted his blanket. "I'll bring you some broth in a bit. Right now, I think you should follow the Major's orders."

She dimmed the lights and stepped into the adjoining room.

Majeska snuggled closer to his side and purred. Glad for her company, he thought back to his encounter with Thorlu. There was an Old Earth saying that he'd read in a book of ancient quotes: "Handsome is as handsome does." Thorlu's good looks could be deceiving. He sure hoped Almiralyn and her companions kept their wits about them. The Mocendi exuded danger, like a wild boar after prey.

Naya slipped into the room and added something to the fluid dripping into his veins.

A yawn left him feeling lazy. His eyes struggled to stay open. The last thing he remembered—Naya's fingers on his wrist and her lovely smile when she saw him watching her.

A young PPP officer met Jordett as he exited the infirmary. Lavir and Senar needed him. Setting aside his desire to find Akeri and learn if she had word from Teva, he took a Drop Car to the lower level. Lavir's triumphant smile suggested success, but he said little. Jordett followed him through a maze of underground passageways until they arrived in an obscure area of the tower. Lavir motioned him through a doorway. Senar sat in front of several V-Screens observing four men engaged in an argument and a fifth sitting on the sidelines.

Lavir grinned. "Viennoc looks pretty fed up. I always felt the Fathers were a mismatched bunch, but..." He shook his head.

Jordett pulled up a chair. Senar touched the replay icon. Learning their group dynamic would be essential to handling the Five Fathers of Idronatti.

The Sanctuary of Veersuni glowed in the light from the stained-glass window. The alabaster woman on Elcaro's rim seemed to stiffen. Water ceased to spill from her palms. Reflected color tinted her eyes blue and her braided hair silver-blonde. The water caught her image and tossed it over the fountain's surface. A picture somersaulted upward and flipped into place.

A tall, cadaverous figure in a full-length, purple cape paced a cheerless room. In an arched recess on an carved obsidian pedestal, a quartz crystal orb rejected the gloominess and glowed. Black velvet curtains draped the walls and enclosed a single four-poster bed. Opposite in another curtained recess, a swag of royal purple adorned a simple but elegant obsidian throne. To one side, framed by a tall, gothic-style window, stood a ebony table with a matching high-backed chair. The polished onyx floor shimmered like black ice in the cool light from a hidden source.

The figure paused in its repeated back and forth. A gulped breath shook its body. A series of rasping coughs lingered in the space, their harsh chorus sounding again and again.

An Astican entered the room and offered a black goblet.

The figure sipped. The coughing eased. It appeared to study the creature's cherubic features.

"When I sent for you, I expected you to return immediately." The accusatory statement rattled up from somewhere deep and dry. "What took you so long?"

The figure's prolonged bout of coughing held the Astican quiet. When at last the hacking abated, Abarax dropped to one knee and bowed its head. "I came as soon as I received word, MasTer." It lifted blue eyes to the hood-enshrouded head, hoping to glimpse the face. "I wish only to please."

In a swirl of purple, the tall figure pivoted and crossed to the crystal orb. A single finger tapped it before the figure traversed the room to the throne. The swish of fabric brushing the floor ceased; the figure lowered onto the seat. "I have a job for you, one only you can do."

The Astican remained on its knee, its eyes tracking The MasTer's every move, its thoughts racing.

The hood cast the now half-hidden face into shadow. "*They* are about to discover my secret, Abarax."

Cherubic eyes blinked. Its expression unreadable, the Davea lowered his head further.

"Come here, Astican, and stand before me." A coughing fit left The MasTer gasping for air.

The creature rose, scaled wings folded against its back, and stood in front of its master.

"You can atone for your tardiness, Abarax." The harried flick of a hand sent folds of velvet to cover a scarred ankle. "I will forgive you, make you my right hand, give you my favor even above Vygel and Thorlu. Would you like that?"

The Astican again bowed its head, hiding its expression, hiding the malicious delight that sprang to its eyes. "My wish is to serve in any way that will please you."

The figure stood and drew a curved black sword from a scabbard attached to the throne. The razor-sharp edges gleamed. A red stone sparked in the hilt.

"You, Abarax, must swear to tell no one what I am about to share. No one or you will die by this blade. Do you swear?"

Cherub-blue eyes lifted to gaze at the purple enshrouded figure. "I swear, my master, to keep your secret for eternity and beyond."

"Swear that you will do my bidding. Swear that should you fail again, you will drive this sword through your own heart." A cough rattled through the room.

Abarax waited for the quiet to return. "I swear to do your bidding. Should I fail, I swear to drive your sword through my heart." The monumental truth of what it had done left it weak-kneed but elated. Containing its emotions, it waited for the revelation that would give it more power than the top Mocendi, the two men who had belittled it and its kind since they were children.

The purple cape pooled on the floor. A rawboned man in a loose-fitting, black robe glared down at the Astican. Limp hair of an indiscriminate color framed a haggard face. Withered skin hung flaccid on skeletal cheek bones. Irises tinged with red glowed in deep-set sockets.

Abarax quelled its desire to gasp, to gape, to stare. The male figure wavered. A woman solidified in his place.

Long, graying hair caught up in a braid cascaded over one shoulder. Her face, like that of her male counterpart, reflected a life ravaged by pain and trauma. A hint of her former beauty lingered beneath the scars and wrinkles and sagging skin. Age-creased lips formed a wistful line beneath a once elegant nose. Eyes as black as ebony that gleamed with the understanding of the galaxies in all their evil and their goodness outweighed everything else.

Medium height in her loose, black robe, The MasTer leaned wearily on the sword. "I am too tired to maintain the masquerade. I have misused my body until it now betrays my every desire. Shifting has become too great a task for it to bear. You, Abarax, will be my contact with the outside world. Only you will communicate with me and for me." A spasm of hacking coughs shook her cadaverous frame.

Abarax held itself still, kept its face blank, and prayed she could not see the shockwave quaking through it.

A sad smile softened the once lovely face. "I've shocked you. How can The MasTer be a woman...especially a woman who is so ruthless; who controls a band of intelligent, talented, and evil men; and who conceives of such diabolical and hard-hearted plans? Women, Abarax, must be strong or die. *I* survived."

The Astican bowed its head in humble acknowledgement of her words.

The image in the fountain somersaulted to the bottom of the bowl. Color no longer tinted the kneeling statue. Water dripped from her palms, filling Veersuni with the secrets within its trembling song.

42
DerTah & Beyond

Brie didn't sleep. Concern for her friends haunted her, and the Star of Truth's stinging kept her on edge and alert. *What is it trying to tell me?*

She hitched a ride on Renn's shoulder to the lab. After buzzing into the vent, she followed the shaft to the plantitarium, her favorite place to escape. Behind the plant growth and a safe distance from the door, she shifted to her Human form and inhaled the fresh air.

Exploring it had made her more and more curious. She had discovered the brown tubes in the bottom of the shafts formed a root system that extended ship-wide. The tan walls formed a membrane that absorbed oxygen and nutrients. By accident, she discovered waist-high towers placed equidistant around the vast space that produced rain.

The entrance door opened. Startled, she tripped backward and hit the wall. The plantitarium vanished. She froze in place, senses reeling. When nothing alarmed her, she exhaled a relieved breath and slowly turned. Her mouth rounded in a silent exclamation of surprise. The space into which she had tumbled was large enough to hold several people. The curved walls were windowless and had no doors. Roots from vents lining the inner wall crept over the surface, covering it with a vein-like pattern. Where they touched the floor, the surface looked like moss.

When she extended her arms to the sides, her fingertips were twice her arm's length from the walls. A considerable distance above her head, the space narrowed and the outer wall arched toward the interior wall. She estimated the length of the space was over four times her height. At the far end, different edible plants surrounded a small pool.

Struggling to absorb what she was seeing and to keep her thoughts masked, she wrapped a curl round and round her finger. The Star tingled.

A soft 'shh' sounded in her mind. Elf stepped through the wall. Beside him, Shyllee appeared, her long tongue hanging from one side of her mouth.

Elf grinned.

Brie threw her arms around him. *"Safe to talk?"*

He held her away from him and listened intently. *"Safe."*

Her head filled with images of Elf as a young boy hiding in this space, building the pool, and planting the garden. She saw Elf stealing a material from the ship stores that absorbed waste, purified it, and distributed it for fertilizer in the gardens beyond the walls.

His hands on her shoulders tensed. *"We have to save Ira and Esán."*

The Star of Truth sent an answering stab of pain down her neck.

Esán felt like Wolloh's 'bug' under a microscope. The High DiMensioner's scrutiny, however, had been benign compared to Thorlu's. Although the Mocendi's pleasant expression remained unchanging, Esán knew the enemy behind the smile crouched, ready to pounce.

A mind probe buzzing in his brain magnified the headache he couldn't seem to get rid of and left him cranky and disconcerted. Tested, scanned, and analyzed nonstop, he felt like a torture victim. A resistant and silent prisoner, he had done his best to tuck information that might be dangerous to others away in the outer regions of his mind. Behind a blank face, trivial thoughts drifted and faded.

Thorlu tapped a V-screen set in his desktop. "The results of your health scan show you have a rare disease that they can only heal on Tao Spirian. Your tests suggest it *was* in remission." The pleasant expression morphed to shrewd. "I have a proposal. Answer my questions, and I'll take you to Tao Spirian."

Allowing nothing but disinterest to show on his face, Esán remained quiet.

The Mocendi walked around the desk. Cold eyes searched his face. "It would be a shame to destroy your mind, bearer of dual Seeds of Carsilem. You know I can peel away your memories like the petals from a flower's bud. Where are Torgin and Almiralyn's niece? Where are they headed? How do they plan to get there?"

Esán pressed his lips together. A small moment of triumph blazed. *Brie is safe.*

Thorlu's rapacious smile flashed wider. "Ah. Brie."

Kicking himself for his lack of control, Esán stared at a small bug crawling on his hand. A minuscule tingle touched his mind.

Thorlu gripped the arms of Esán's chair and yanked it around to face him. "I can and will make your life miserable, Esán Efre."

Esán shrugged. "You already have, sir."

The boy vanished. Thorlu howled in frustration as Vygel rushed into the room, saw the vacated chair, and smirked.

"Well, well. It seems he got the better of you, Thorlu Tangorra. Why am I not surprised?"

Thorlu rounded the desk and grabbed the front of Vygel's tunic. "Find him and confine the others where they cannot escape."

Vintrusie yanked his tunic free. "You are *not* my superior. I take orders only from The MasTer." A churlish look accompanied the obsessive smoothing of his tunic and the frenetic rearranging of his cape. "You know I hate to be touched, Thorlu." His awkward gait carried him beyond the door.

Thorlu hissed. "I detest you, Vygel Vintrusie. I promise to take your place as The MasTer's right hand." He returned to his chair and drummed his fingers against the table. Only one boy had ever escaped from the ship, Elf, and they had recaptured him. Malice contorted his handsome features. *"And they've locked him in a security cell, which is sure to win The MasTer's favor. The dual Seeds of Carsilem make Esán another candidate for escape.* The drumming on the desk became more intense.

If I were a boy, where would I hide on a big ship?

Yaro and Tamosh left Frith's farm with a rifle and plenty of ammunition under the bench seat of the wagon. When they reached the fishing village of Metto, Tamosh accompanied Gregos and Cayled to find *SeaBella*. In the shape of a golden dog of indiscernible breed, Yaro stayed close to Renn and Bibeed until they boarded the new boat. Only then did he dare shift and fly back to assure no one had followed.

With the women safe on SeaBella, he set off to explore. The carved poles outside each village home piqued his interest, especially when he discovered they represented many of the same things the tattoos in his culture symbolized. He spent time with the village elder, who exhibited neither surprise nor fear when he materialized in his true form. The old man reminded him of his mother's brother, the Pentharian ancient-one who had trained him in the arts of warfare.

Sad to leave his new acquaintance but glad to remove Renn from ZaltRaca, he stood on the deck of the new vessel, listening to the mid-turning song of the village women as the sailboat pulled away from the wooden docks.

Gregos and Tamosh, thrilled with *SeaBella*, grinned as she glided out into Geran's southern passage. Cayled went to work recoiling the dock lines. Bibeed headed for the galley.

Only Renn lacked the spark of excitement that ignited the energy and spirit of her companions. She sat at the stern, staring back at the shore with such sadness Yaro thought her heart must be breaking.

"You are sorry to leave ZaltRaca, Renn Whalend?"

She sighed. "Even though I was a prisoner there, I felt free for the first time in my life. I will miss that and the sea and the wind and DerTah's three moons." She caught a teardrop on the tip of her finger and watched it shimmer in the sun. A quick movement sent it to merge with the salty sea. "At least I can leave one small piece of me behind—a part of the ocean I have grown to love."

"Of course, I hate to leave without Torgin." She stared up at the sky. "But my heart tells me he is safe." Her eyes, so like her son's, regarded him. "How safe are we, Yaro? Do you think the League's men follow?"

"If I wanted your son and Brie, I would send several men, not just the two we discovered at the farm. Until you are in the care of Myrrh's Guardian, we are still in danger, Renn. Until then, we must be vigilant."

Renn's gaze returned to the sea.

Gregos beckoned him from the helm. "Do you think they'll pursue us, Yaro?"

"I believe the Mocendi will guess our destination and, therefore, we are likely to encounter trouble at the portal. Which does not mean one of them won't follow us."

Yaro looked back. ZaltRaca slowly vanished below the horizon. He shifted to a laridae and flew aft. The calm sea reflected the pale orange of the DerTahan sky. A scattering of clouds drifted high overhead. DerTah's saffron moon would soon rise in the east. *Almost time to find a safe haven.*

The silhouetted shape of a boat sailed from Southern Geran Passage between ZaltRaca and the mainland and into the strait. Yaro swooped back to *SeaBella* and landed beside Gregos.

"A fishing trawler pulled out of the passage. It could be nothing, or—"

"Could be something." Gregos squared his shoulders. "Sure could use that compass about now. Tamosh," he called, "I need your charts. Good thing he's traveled Tri-Moon." He squinted up at the watch perch. "Cayled, keep your eyes open up there."

Cayled acknowledged the order with a wave.

Tamosh climbed on deck. "We're exposed until we reach the far shore. We've got the wind and the tide in our favor. Once we reach the shore, there's a small cove that'll give us shelter for the night."

Gregos nibbled his mustache. "But will it hide us from the enemy?"

Tamosh frowned. "Only if they don't know we're there. The bottleneck entrance is the only exit."

Yaro looked at Renn. "Better go below, Renn Whalen."

With a longing glance at the Isle of ZaltRaca, she crossed to the hatch.

Yaro watched her climb below. *I will do my best, heart-brother, to protect your mother.*

Almiralyn shook the cobwebs from her brain. Her first trip to Mittkeer had been during her girlhood training on KcernFensia; she had forgotten the confusion that accompanied her entrance into the Land of Time. The warmth of Corvus' hand in hers helped her regain her equilibrium.

She surveyed the starscape and smiled up at the VarTerel. "Mittkeer always takes my breath away."

"It is beautiful, isn't it?" Relevart's eyes narrowed. "We must go. Wolloh and his team are on their way."

Matching her stride to his, she noted his regal bearing, the assurance in his step, and his unerring ability to navigate with nothing but the sameness of the star-studded sky to guide him. She also noted the watchfulness wrapping around him like a cloak.

Unease prickled over her skin. *Only a VarTerel and his chosen can enter Mittkeer. Why am I so jumpy?* The eerie silence reminded her she walked through All Time and No Time. She rubbed chilled hands up and down her arms. *I haven't left Myrrh since I arrived in the Terces Wood many sun cycles ago. No wonder I'm anxious.*

Corvus glanced at her. His dimple deepened. His dark eyes gleamed. This was his first time in Mittkeer.

She returned his smile and remembered her first time.

She awoke to the knowledge the last turning of her girlhood sun cycles had arrived. After a meeting to discuss her new role, the High Priestess of Mahyinaeh and her acolytes had initiated her into womanhood.

Anticipation drove her from bed. After dressing with particular care, she studied herself in the mirror. The pink highlighting her cheekbones intensified the sapphire blue of her eyes. Her long, silver-blonde hair floated around her like a veil. Her simple blue robe hid her feminine curves and gave her the appearance of a demure young girl. She smiled. Everything would change this turning.

A knock announced the most important person in her life. Corvus gazed down at her, the dimple in his cheek deepening, the corners of his mouth rebelling against the serious expression he demanded they maintain.

He offered his arm. "It is time, Almiralyn."

Nervousness and excitement brought a girlish giggle to her lips. She stifled it, placed her hand on the elegant sleeve of his tunic, and walked by his side. Feeling suddenly shy, she watched him from beneath her dark lashes. *I'm the only one in the temple with a protector. I know my role as Guardian of Myrrh is important, but—*

Their arrival at the Temple entry stayed her questions. Corvus released her arm and stepped back. She knew he waited as she followed a young novice into the pristine beauty of the sanctuary reception area. She also knew he would be there when she stepped again into the sunlight.

Her interview had been pleasant and thought-provoking. The reports from her mentors of the past several moon cycles of training brought her praise and the reminder to be humble in the face of her talents. The novice then escorted her to the initiation hall to join the eight other young women who waited. They greeted each other with solemn expressions and suppressed excitement. This turning was the end of the first stage of their contest against themselves. More training awaited them. This turning, however, they celebrated leaving their childhood behind.

The simple temple ceremony left her teary-eyed as she placed her lighted candle at the base of a tall quartz crystal and repeated the oath of SegoSond.

> *"I pledge to honor the path of right,*
> *Equality instead of might,*
> *To honor diversity in all life;*
> *To promote peace where there is strife."*

Nine girls had made their pledge and followed the High Priestess to the transition room. After bathing in the cleansing waters, they braided their hair, pinned it in an elegant bun, and dressed in attire depicting their new station within the temple.

Almiralyn emerged to meet Karrew in a gown that matched her

sapphire blue eyes and modestly accentuated her natural curves. His expression told her she looked beautiful. Next to him stood a man she had met only once, the VarTerel of the Inner Universe. He offered a hand. The moment his weathered palm touched hers, the temple vanished, and she stood within a vast globe of stars and sky, her head spinning and her heart pounding.

Relevart smiled down at her. "The time will come, Almiralyn, when you will travel Mittkeer to meet your destiny."

They stood side by side in the intense silence, the glow from the crystal tip of his rowan wood staff in a soft pool around them. He squeezed her hand. The stars blurred; the Temple came into focus.

She glanced at the VarTerel and wondered if this was the time of which he had spoken. The muscle at the corner of his mouth twitched. He picked up his pace. Almiralyn wished she could see what he saw. His lips quirked. Her head filled with Wolloh's face. The new VarTerel and his companions had reached Mittkeer.

The transition into All Time and No Time steeped Torgin in anticipation. A surreptitious peek at Wolloh, Nomed, Wodash, and Somay filled him with awe. In the normal world, their power was formidable; in Mittkeer, it felt overpowering.

Wolloh glanced his direction and smiled. "We are a talented group. I include you in that statement, young Torgin. I wish I'd seen you in action in Soprano Narrows. You must play your flute for me sometime."

Warmth flooded Torgin's cheeks. His hand moved to grip the flute. The hand dropped. "My flute went down with *Melback*, sir." He cast Somay an apologetic look. "I know I promised to return it to you, and now I cannot."

Somay put an arm around his shoulders. "I'll carve you a new one when this is over."

Wolloh's good eye stared beyond the group. "Relevart has arrived. We need the compass, Torgin. Ask it to show us the way to Mittkeer's center."

Torgin held the compass so all could see and repeated Wolloh's instructions. The needle spun in a golden blur and stopped.

Wolloh peered at the night sky. "And so it is." With his staff illuminating the way, he limped forward. Somay and Seyes walked behind him. Torgin tucked the compass beneath his tunic and looked up to find Wodash next to him.

"I promised to take care of you. Walk with me through this Land of Time."

With a touch of surprise, Torgin fell in step beside the creature who had frozen him in the Tower of Nemttachenn, the creature who had haunted his nightmares for moon cycles afterward. *He smiled to himself. Like me, Wodash has changed. Is this, too, part of The Unfolding?*

Wolloh glanced back and favored him with a knowing smile.

Brie let relief flood her tiny body. Esán had understood and followed. She exited the vent at the back of the plantitarium and shifted. The instant Esán materialized beside her, she grabbed his hand and stepped through the wall, drawing him after her. She grinned at his look of total astonishment as he knelt to hug Shyllee.

"How did you find this?" he whispered. His eyes explored it inch by inch, paused on the pool and garden, and traced the roots on the wall to the vents above.

"I fell through the wall by accident. Elf found the space when he was training to be a Mocendi. He set it up in case he ever needed a place to hide. When they destroyed his vocal cords and sentenced him to the pit, this is where he hid."

"Where is Elf?"

"He's rescuing Ira." Brie tilted her head. "He plans to construct an illusion that will make the guards think Ira is still in his cell. When Ira is safe, Elf plans to find Desirol."

"Mask." Elf's message brought their conversation to an end. Esán's face went blank. Brie dropped a curtain around her thoughts. Neither moved.

Time passed. A drop of sweat beaded on Brie's brow, ran down her nose, and dripped onto her chin. A soft tap, tap sounded. Shyllee's tail wagged.

Esán mouthed, "Ira."

Brie stepped through the wall.

A wild-eyed Ira gaped at her. The plantitarium door opened. She grabbed his arm and pulled him after her into the hidden space.

Esán touched a finger to his lips and then his temple and shook his head. Ira nodded.

They huddled together, barely breathing. Shyllee sat with her head cocked to one side and her ears alert.

"Relax." The message wasn't from Elf.

Esán pressed his mouth shut. Brie tightened her grip on Ira's arm. She pointed at herself and the vents on the wall. Shifting, she crawled through the mesh. At the ground level, some distance below, Thorlu Tangorra stood with Vygel Vintrusie. His gray-green eyes searched. A probe scanned the lower level, slid over a butterfly, and moved on, leaving a fading image of Esán behind.

Fear that staying together in a small space made them a huge target sent her darting back through the vent and into Human form. She quickly mimed a plan, muffled Shyllee's presence with an invisibility charm, and in bug form shot through the mesh with Ira and Esán following. The moment they emerged into the plantitarium, they shifted to butterflies and dispersed in different directions.

Brie felt Thorlu's probe brush by her and fluttered lower. The probe moved up to the next level. She hoped Esán and Ira had followed her example.

Vygel paced the perimeter of the space. A less intense scan made a furtive sweep. Thorlu swung around. "Don't interfere with my probe, Vintrusie." The tension between the two Mocendi beat like a drum.

Vygel's ugly face grew uglier. "I am The MasTer's Mocendi. I outrank you. Don't mess with mine."

Thorlu turned his back, completed his scan, and marched from the chamber.

Vygel stood in the silence for some time, scanning the space. "The lab tech said the boy came in here. There's nowhere to hide. He must have been seeing things." With a glance from the floor to the distant ceiling, he strode into the companionway. The door swished shut.

Remembering Renn's warning regarding Thorlu, Brie fluttered from flower to flower until she reached the shadows of the bigger plants. When significant time had passed, she flew to the wall, changed into a small bug, and crawled through the vent. Shyllee sniffing her Human hand reminded her to remove the illusion. The space grew suddenly crowded as Esán, Ira, and her Aunt Henri materialized.

Ira shot a nervous glance at the elderly woman. "H-how'd you know where to find us? What about Torgin's mother?"

Henrietta tapped her spectacles against her palm. "A dupligram of Renn is resting in her quarters."

Esán looked puzzled. "A dupligram?"

Henri sighed, "A dupligram is a double. Corvus taught me to create one when I was much younger."

Ira opened his mouth to speak.

Henri shook her head. "No time. The Mocendi gather. I counted over thirty aboard the ship already. And Thorlu has Elf. We're in danger, but Elf most of all. You must rescue him. Thorlu plans to use him to find you. Elf also knows that I have taken Renn's place. His gifts are many and powerful." She sagged. "I can't maintain the dupligram much longer."

"Where is he?" Esán asked.

"Thorlu trapped him in dragonfly form and has him in a glass box in his quarters." She tapped her spectacles against Brie's forehead and disappeared.

Brie stared at the spot where she had stood. "She put directions in my head. Thorlu's quarters are on the opposite side of the plantitarium."

Esán grew thoughtful. "What's the best shape to take us there?"

Ira grimaced. "Definitely not a dragonfly."

"I'll rescue Elf." Brie kept her tone firm. "Thorlu knows your energy signatures. He doesn't know mine."

Ira looked unconvinced.

Esán started to protest. "You can't..."

"Wolloh unlocked my abilities for a reason. I can rescue Elf; I can fool Thorlu. Your job is to get him out of his quarters. I'll need time to learn the makeup of the ward and alter it as well as that of the glass box."

Brie didn't give them time to argue. She shifted and crawled through the vent. Perched on a broad leaf near the door to the plantitarium, she reviewed her plan. She knew the risk she took. She also knew Elf would die to keep them safe.

43
Myrrh

Kieel swallowed his fear and focused on his long-time friend.

Tibin's ruddy complexion paled. "Sibine and Adin—i-i-n d-d-danger—" He choked and staggered to his feet. "Please help them, Tinpaca Mondago. Please—"

"We will get them back, Tibin." The Tinpaca placed a steadying hand on his shoulder. "Kieel, we'll need the Guardian's cousin to help. Please bring her here. Reana, you and your team hide in the trees near the Mocendi and keep watch. I want reports every quarter chron on what he's doing. Don't get caught. Stee, see if either you or Yuin can get close enough to use your numbing agent?"

Kieel fluttered to Tibin's shoulder. The Wood Tiff's whole body trembled. "We'll get them back, Tibin."

He streaked between trees. Teva would know what to do. Within sight of the camp, he landed and surveyed the area. Nothing suggested danger.

Teva ducked from the Mocendi's tent. Her gaze fastened on his. *"Stay."* She said something over her shoulder and walked his direction. *"Let's go."*

At the tree line, she shifted. A small bird followed him through the woods to the Tinpaca's camp. Mondago and two soldiers came to their feet as she materialized across from them.

Kieel hovered nearby, observing the RewFaarans' astonished expressions with a small smile. Teva was every bit as lovely and as powerful as Almiralyn.

She touched a hand to her heart. "Tinpaca Mondago, it is a pleasure to meet you. Major Jordett sends his regards. I will make a full report, but first..." She knelt in front of Tibin. As though repositioning a wayward curl, her fingertips brushed his forehead. His eyes rounded. "Fear is a disabler you can ill afford, Tibin. We will need your help to rescue your family."

She straightened. "Tinpaca, I understand you have a man injured. Let's discuss what must be done."

Mondago pressed his lips together, fingered the cigar in his pocket, sighed, and gave her a rueful smile. "It is rare for a RewFaaran to deal with women in positions of authority. I have met two in as many turnings. Forgive me for taking a moment to adjust my thinking. A group of Nyti watched the Mocendi from a safe distance. Voer and Yuin have gone to see if they could get close enough to use their stunning—"

Stee exited the trees, his alien face grim and his tail twitching. Golden eyes came to rest on Teva. He touched his heart, then offered his palm. "Oid eo daizo raa, cousin of Almiralyn."

"Oid eo daizo raa, Stee." Her palm touched his. "Tell us what you have discovered."

"Wards surround the Mocendi and his captives. Your man is outside the shields, Tinpaca, but too close for us to remove him unseen."

Mondago turned to Teva. "I bow to your expertise."

The two soldiers exchanged surprised looks.

Teva inclined her head. "Tinpaca, I believe a distraction would be helpful. It is vital that you and your men return to camp. Maybe this could be done with chaos? Also, while I am here, I will reposition the Demrach Gateway nearer Almiralyn's land, which will allow you to communicate more easily with DerTah. Right now, I need two of your men and Stee with me."

The Tinpaca addressed the two soldiers. "Asdall, you organize the return to camp." He nodded to the other man. "You're with me."

Teva nodded her understanding and graced Asdall with a smile. "My protector and comrade will remove the Mocendi who is at your camp from Myrrh. Please introduce yourself should his return precede mine."

The RewFaaran kept his face blank, glanced at the Tinpaca, and left.

Teva returned her attention to the Wood Tiff. "Tibin, you and Kieel will carry a message to the apprentice Mocendi. He is called Endes. Tell him we have contacted Almiralyn. Tell him she is the only one who can release him from the grove. I will be close by."

Reana whizzed from the trees. "He's becoming more agitated. I think he's scared."

Teva bent down to bring her eyes level with Tibin's. "You must be steady and courageous. Sibine and Adin need to know that you are unafraid."

Tibin squared his shoulders. "I will do my best, Teva."

She straightened. The aura of a warrior settled around her. Her beautiful face became more chiseled, her eyes cold and hard. Stee moved to her side. Mondago and his man exchanged glances.

Kieel shivered. *War knows no boundaries. War turns even the most peaceful souls to warriors when it threatens those they love.*

Paisley stood alone in the Terces Wood, inhaling the cool air of late autumn. *One chron circle ago, I breathed desert dryness and saw nothing but sand in all directions. I've jumped dimensions and visited another planet.* Amazement broadened his grin. "Ya."

Stee had dropped him within walking distance of Nemttachenn and departed for the RewFaarans' temporary camp. Paisley grinned. *Never knew how much I'd love flyin'.*

Fallen leaves crackling beneath his feet reminded him again that he had traveled far. He picked up his pace and soon stared up at the rounded-height of Nemttachenn, gleaming and gray in the afternoon sun. He shook his head. *It was night in the desert when I jumped into the gateway. Life's sure changed.*

At the tower entrance he paused, felt the subtle tingle of Evolsefil's presence, and stepped into the dark interior. A soft blue light wafted up from the tower floor. Dark eyes twinkled in the dim light. A white mustache drooping around a big, welcoming smile materialized below a beak of a nose. CheeTrann stepped free of the light, his feet planted wide apart and his huge fists resting on his hips.

"It is good ta see ya, Paisley James Tobinette. I've been lonely, something I haven't experienced in many aeons. Finding a good friend is rare."

Paisley grinned. "I've missed ya, too. And I've missed our games of chess." He crossed to the table and lowered his large body onto a chair. "So much has happened."

CheeTrann sat down and peered at the tower entrance. "I believe we have company about to arrive on our doorstep. Your stories will have—"

"Let me go. You have no right—" The explosion of anger ended in a snarl.

CheeTrann's presence filled the tower. Paisley launched his body to standing. A man's stocky figure darkened the entrance; a second taller figure stepped into view.

"Who trespasses within my domain?" Nemttachenn shook with the power of CheeTrann's voice.

The taller man shoved his companion through the entrance. "I am Lenadi, brother of Teva Rivan. I bring you a Mocendi, Protector of Myrrh. The Guardians await his arrival."

The Mocendi stumbled to his knees in a puddle of black and purple.

The second man continued to block the entrance. "Teva asked me to remove this man from Myrrh. She suggested the Sentinel in Nemttachenn might help."

CheeTrann peered down from his immense height. "Prove you are who you say you are."

"Teva remembers meeting you soon after Almiralyn arrived in Myrrh. You gave her a very special gift."

"That I did." He loomed bigger. The kneeling Mocendi cringed and hunched lower. The tower trembled. A vortex opened in the floor. CheeTrann's voice boomed. "Mocendi, should you see The MasTer again, tell him Myrrh will *never* be his."

The portal yawned wider. The Mocendi struggled to stand. Lenadi waved a hand. The Mocendi toppled forward into the swirling colors, his cape opening like wings fighting to fly as he plummeted. A howl of dismay clipped short by the loud clap of thunder accompanying the closure of the vortex melted into nothing.

Lenadi bowed his head. "Thank you, Sentinel of Myrrh. Teva will want to know where you sent him."

CheeTrann resumed his normal size and picked up a chess piece. "The Galactic Guardians will chart his course. He will not be returning to Myrrh, Thera, or DerTah anytime soon." He sniffed the air. "Evil still walks the Land of Myrrh."

Lenadi crossed to the table. "We have also captured an apprentice Mocendi whom I know would love to make your acquaintance."

CheeTrann placed the queen on the board. "Tell Teva Rivan to bring him herself. It has been too long since her last visit."

Lenadi bowed and vanished.

Paisley sank into his chair. "Life is too full o' people comin' and goin.' Will it ever be normal again?"

CheeTrann sat and picked up a pawn. "Normal? Ha. Life, my friend, is an adventure. The best *you* can do is live it one turning at a time." He put the pawn in its place and grinned. "And play an occasional game of chess."

Sparrow smiled at Allynae's image in the mirror and then watched herself shift to Almiralyn.

He shook his head. "I would never have believed it without seeing you make the change. Your illusion is so perfect."

She fingered her blonde braid. "When Relevart touched my head, and I shifted..." Almiralyn's laugh filled the room. "He gave me no choice, Alli."

His arms encircled her waist.

She turned and kissed his cheek. "We have work to do. Don't forget that I am your sister. The minute we leave this room, I am the Guardian of Myrrh. Until I return here, I must embrace my role totally."

Stepping away, he gave her one last appraising look. "You never cease to amaze me. Walk or teleport."

"I'm too eager to hear what the team has discovered." She laid a hand on his arm. Canedari came into focus. Hurrying through the double doors into the Hall of Priestesses, she led the way to the research area. Excitement palpating the space raised the hair on the back of her neck.

Eyes gleaming, Elae held up the journal. "We've completed the translation."

Wilith rose and pulled out a chair. "I can't believe the resources available to you here."

Merrilea's bemused smile broadened. "Almiralyn, you'll never guess what we've discovered."

Sparrow sat down, reminded herself what her role was, and said, "Who wants to begin?"

Allynae lounged in a chair opposite, taking in the excitement bubbling around the table. Almiralyn's research team was bursting with eagerness to share. Papers littered the table. The screen on Wilith's mini-comp glowed.

Wilith took the lead. "I uncovered a mention, but little new information, regarding birth-mates from my search of the library's techno-files on the Outer Universe. Although little has been recorded about the vastness beyond the Rim, El Stroma's proximity to the DéCussate makes it one of the few planets on which historians have gathered information. The one new piece of information I found suggests that although the Pheet Adole developed Protariflee on El Stroma, the practice may have transited the DéCussate. Prior to the acid rains that destroyed life on the planet, El Stromans fled their home. I am following a couple of leads. If I find anything, I will let you know."

Almiralyn nodded. "Thank you, Wilith." Her gaze switched to Elae, who squirmed in her chair like an excited child. "I think you should go next, Elae."

The young DeoNyte tried to calm her excitement. "Merrilea's the one who uncovered the truth..."

Esán's aunt laughed. "But you're the better storyteller, Elae. Please don't keep Almiralyn waiting."

Allynae held his breath. *Are we about to find out who The MasTer is?*

Zugo peeked from between the new curtains in Veersuni. Water trickled into Elcaro's bowl, erasing the image of a moment ago. He pushed the curtain aside with his uninjured hand and walked to the fountain. Pain throbbing in his chest and hand made him stagger. He steadied himself on the alabaster rim. The reflection of his blistered chest and singed fur made him cringe.

Elcaro's Eye had called him from his dreams. Ignoring Almiralyn's warning not to be alone with the fountain, he had sneaked away from his mother and Owae. He had tiptoed into Veersuni as Abarax offered The MasTer something for his cough. When Zugo realized whose image occupied the fountain, he hid behind the curtains and eavesdropped.

To the quiet sound of rippling water, he reviewed the conversation and its startling revelation. *The MasTer is a woman. I have to find Almiralyn.* The thumping beat of his heart sent a wave of pain shooting through him. Gasping, he sank onto a bench and fought the fatigue threatening to overwhelm him.

Closing his eyes, he forced his breathing to normalize. When the pain subsided, he rose unsteadily and made his way to the door. A brief rest. His hand found the handle. The weight of wood proved to be a challenge. An aching breath shook his body. He pulled the door open and stumbled through. Vague images melted into nothing as the room went dark.

"Zugo. Zugo, wake up."

Do I know that voice?

"Zugo, it's Elae."

Elae. Ahhhhh.

A small hand gripped his. The heaviness left his body. A shooting pain almost sent him back into unconsciousness. Someone lifted his head. Warm liquid slipped between his lips, slid down his parched throat. The pain grew easier to bear. He inhaled and opened his eyes.

Elae's anxious gaze searched his face. "Oh, Zugo, what are you doing out of bed?" She handed a small cup to Owae.

"Almiralyn," he whispered. "I need—"

"I'm here, Zugo."

Like an angel, she appeared at the foot of the sofa. Allynae stepped into his line of vision and helped him to sit. Vaguely, he realized that Wilith Whalend and Merrilea were there, as well. He steadied his breathing.

"I snuck into Veersuni. The MasTer and a winged creature... I hid behind the curtains." He stopped to catch his breath, to search his mind. A yawn distracted him.

Almiralyn knelt beside him. "What did you learn, Zugo?"

He gripped her hand. "The MasTer—she's a woman."

"Did you discover who she is?"

His eyelids grew heavier and heavier. He couldn't think. Someone lifted him. Allynae's rugged features focused momentarily, and then he could no longer fight the healing herbs.

When Almiralyn and her team returned to the research area, their concern for Zugo melted into palpable expectation. Elae flipped through her notes. Wilith tapped his comp-tab, squinted at its contents, and tapped it again. Merrilea calmly awaited Allynae's return.

Almiralyn traced Ari's infinity sign on the shiny surface of the table and let her mind, Sparrow's mind, wrap around the news. *The MasTer is a woman. I wonder if Relevart knows? Of course he does.*

Allynae's arrival interrupted her thoughts. He dropped into a chair. "So, Elae, I'm betting you already knew The MasTer was a woman. Did you find out who *she* is, where *she's* from? Tell us everything."

Elae glanced at Wilith and Merrilea. Both wore tired but elated smiles. Her startling eyes came to rest on Almiralyn. "Do you want the entire story or just who she is?"

"I would appreciate knowing what you know."

Placing her four-fingered hand on the cover of the journal, Elae began her story. "As you know, the war on El Stroma was hard fought. It soon became clear that the Pheet Adole were winning. The people of the continent of El QuilTran did not have a chance against the industrialized war machine of the RomPeer.

"Around this time, a male rebel, The MasTer, begins to appear in the writings. Under *his* leadership, the rebels grew angrier and more evil-intentioned. If the Eleo Preda could no longer make El Stroma their home, then no one would. They smuggled Eleo Predian survivors aboard ships headed for the Inner Universe. As soon as they were safely underway, the rebels went to work, turning the RomPeer's technology against him. Acid rain began to fall. Life on the planet ceased to exist. The remaining rebels, including their leader, escaped on a small ship, which deposited them on the planet of TreBlaya."

"Wait!" Allynae came to his feet and paced the length of the table and back. "We know the rebel leader was Rayn. We know the rebel leader destroyed TreBlaya and made it the headquarters of the Mocendi League. Could Rayn be The MasTer?"

Sparrow wanted to shift to herself, contained the urge, and said in Almiralyn's voice, "If so, Relevart, the boy in her locket, is her birth-mate."

The silence in the Reading Room sizzled.

44
Der Tah & Beyond

Sudden fatigue weighted Esán's body. The encounter with Thorlu had taken its toll. The illness that had almost killed him on Thera stirred. Remission had been short-lived. Ignoring his desire to rest, he rubbed his throbbing head. *Brie needs me to think.*

Ira cleared his throat. "You're sick again, huh?"

"Just tired." He sighed. "Elf might not make it if we don't create a distraction. There's an alarm on Thorlu's desk. If he's got one, there have to be others."

Ira thumped him on the back. "Genius. I saw one near the console in the plantitarium when we were hiding." He shifted.

Esán ignored his growing sense of lassitude, followed Ira's example, and crawled after him from their hideout. In butterfly form, they flitted from leaf to leaf. When nothing indicated danger, they materialized behind a bush near the console.

Ira whispered, "You keep watch. I'll see what I can discover." He crept into the open. The sound of an alarm sent him dashing back. "What on Thera!"

Esán gripped his arm. "Hide."

The door swished open. Three men in the black-lined capes of apprentice Mocendi marched into the space.

Esán shifted and fluttered after Ira's gold and orange butterfly. Passing it as it dropped into a crevice, he flitted further up the side of the waterfall. Hidden beneath a broad-leafed bush, he waited and listened.

A skinny apprentice scanned the space. "Why didn't someone notice the illusion in the boy's cell sooner? Now we'll never find him."

An older, stockier man growled, "Spread out. He has to be here."

Esán felt his energy leaking away. *Sure hope the Mocendi give up before I lose control of this shape.* He fluttered deeper into shadows. *At least Brie has her distraction.*

Ahigh-pitched, pulsating whistle shattered Thorlu's concentration. "What in SeDah—"

The purple lining of his cape tossing light like a prism, he strode around his desk and glared at a dragonfly trapped in a tall, glass box. "Is this your doing, Troms el Shiv?" He pronounced Elf's true name as though spitting something distasteful from his mouth.

Vygel marched into the room. "Ira Raast has escaped. It seems we have now *misplaced* them all. Our brethren are frantic."

Thorlu's eyes narrowed. "The young people are not their responsibility, Vygel. They're ours. And we have not lost them all." He stalked over to the glass box. "Your friends, Elf? Where are they?"

The dragonfly darted one direction and then another. Thorlu leaned closer.

"If The MasTer didn't want you for himself, I'd rip your mind to pieces." He stormed to the door. "Don't just stand there, Vygel. We now have two boys to find and secure. The MasTer grows impatient."

From a vent on the wall, Brie watched the dragonfly's opalescent wings glimmer teal blue in the soft light. It angled toward the door.

Tiny Human eyes stared after the disappearing Mocendi. Its wings beat faster.

Brie flashed into sight. Concentrating her attention on the ward surrounding the box, she memorized its molecular makeup and visualized a tear the size of her hand. When it appeared, she committed the structure of the glass to memory.

A second alarm sounded. Her fist shot through the ward and penetrated the glass barrier. A dragonfly identical to Elf's shot upward from her open hand. Elf's landed on her palm. Curling her fingers around it, she withdrew her hand, returned the molecules of the box to their original pattern, reknit the tear in the shields, and vanished as Thorlu stormed into the space.

Henri returned to her quarters, dissolved her dupligram of Renn, and assumed her likeness. Thoughts of Esán accompanied her on her walk to the lab. Their first encounter had been in the Holistic Healing Center in Idronatti. She and the twins were helping a young boy return to The Borderlands. Her hand pressed against her breastbone. *I ended up in the Center with heart palpitations. Esán was there, too.* She lowered the hand. His powerful presence had enticed her to explore. She found him in the final throws of the disease she helped to put into remission. *Now it's reinfecting his system like an arachnid weaving its web. And this time I can do little.*

She entered the lab and hurried to her workstation. Renn's orderly mind had provided her with all the information she required to fulfill The MasTer's requests *and* to do some experiments of her own. Holding a small tube of colorless liquid up to the multi-spectrum light, she observed a subtle change, one that made her nod in satisfaction. *If I can refine this, it might help—* A noise behind her made her jump.

"Hello, Renn. You seem pleased with yourself. I gather your little nap left you revitalized."

Renn cast an irritated glance in Vygel's direction and began entering the information in her data repository. "I do my best thinking when I am at rest. You should try it, Vygel."

He leaned awkwardly on the counter. "We can't find your son's friends,

Renn. It seems they have escaped from their security cells. Would you care to speculate on how they managed it and where they are?"

"One moment, please." She continued to enter data. When she finished, she glared at him. "Really, Vygel, if you are suggesting I helped them to escape…" She shook her head and returned to her work.

"You are more than you seem, Renn Whalend. I find you fascinating." He edged closer.

His boney hand stroking her arm sent a chill up her spine. "You're not the only one on this ship who likes research, Renn Whalen." He fingered a strand of her hair. "I have conceived a small experiment. I think they will come out of hiding to protect *you*."

She sighed and stepped beyond reach. "Vygel, I have work to do. Please allow me to do it."

He sidled nearer. Long fingers dug into the flesh of her arm. He pulled her to him. Bulging, bloodshot eyes roamed her face, her hair…

She wanted to slap his ugly face.

Shish, shish. The door opened and closed. For a moment, Thorlu remained still; then he flipped his cape over his shoulders, where it hung in rich, rippling folds, and gazed at his fellow Mocendi from half-closed eyes.

"Renn has work to complete before we leave for TreBlaya, and yet I find you indulging your personal needs instead of allowing her to finish. I cannot imagine The MasTer would approve."

Vygel's grip tightened. "I intend to use her for bait to bring those children out of hiding."

Thorlu almost purred. "What makes you think they'll come out for her?"

"She's their friend's mother."

Cool eyes moved from her face to her captor's. "In case you haven't noticed, Vygel, we are not dealing with ordinary young people. They are intelligent and perceptive. Obviously smarter than you. Would you come out of hiding if you knew The MasTer wanted Renn alive and unharmed, even if one of his chosen Mocendi threatened to harm her?"

Vygel's Adam's apple bobbed. Uncertainty bristled. The grip on her arm eased. Renn noted Thorlu's bland expression. He knew exactly how far to push Vygel. She forced herself to remain quiet.

Torgin walked next to Wolloh through the endless night sky. He glanced at the compass in his hand. The needle pointed straight ahead. Wolloh's limped stride did not falter. Behind them, Somay and Nomed matched the new VarTerel's pace, their footfalls soundless. Wodash floated beside him, his glacial cold wafting around his almost formless body. Torgin couldn't suppress a shiver.

In the far distance, a tiny glow caught his eye. Unlike the myriad of stars, it appeared to move along the same trajectory they traveled. *Wonder if Wolloh—*

"I see it, young Torgin. Your eye is good." Wolloh spoke the soft words from the deformed side of his mouth.

Torgin noted the stretch and pull of the scars, the strange working of distorted lips. A wave of pride produced a thoughtful smile. His fear of the High DiMensioner had transitioned to respect for the man who, despite his great power, humbly acknowledged the youthful arrogance that had led to his disfigurement. Torgin glance at Wodash. The realization that the glacial creature had become his friend and protector added to his sense of self-confidence.

The distant glow edged nearer. Within the crystal tip of Wolloh's staff, a soft radiance stretched toward it. Opposite ends of a pale path glowed. With each step, the gap between grew smaller. At last, the ends touched, blended, formed one glowing pathway through the night-scape.

Torgin whispered, "It's him, is it not?"

Wolloh's step did not falter. "It is."

The words faded. The path stretched ahead. Cocooned in silence, they continued.

Torgin sighed. He longed for the missing flute, for the beauty of its music, and wondered what it would sound like in the vastness of Mittkeer.

Tamosh huddled with Yaro and Gregos on *SeaBella*. The sun hovered above the trees on the shoreline, painting the landscape in jewel colors. Dusk would soon begin to cloak the end of the turning in warm gold and pale orange. Some distance behind them, the fishing trawler kept pace. She hadn't closed the gap, but she hadn't fallen back either.

Gregos chewed his bottom lip, a sign that he worried. "We need to anchor before we lose the little light that's left. Don't want 'em to notice us duck through the bottleneck. Don't want 'em to find it either."

Tamosh withdrew the ampule from his shirt pocket. "Marji said when this breaks beneath the water, it gives off a mist that hangs in the air. Cayled and I can row the dinghy out to the strait's center. I'll break the ampule. As soon as the mist rises, you can slip into the cove. We'll catch up."

Gregos looked the length of the vessel. "She's a big girl to handle alone."

"I can help." Bibeed joined them. "I've been sailing since I was small. Renn can help Yaro."

"I need Yaro to do some snooping. We need to know how many're on that boat." Gregos stepped aside. "Take the wheel, Bibeed. Show us what ya can do."

Bibeed grinned. "I've been dying to see how she handles."

"Yo, Cayled. Come on down," Gregos called. "Tamosh, get the dinghy ready to launch. Yaro, shape a seabird and do some snooping. Get back here fast as ya can."

A laridae soared upward, light from the setting sun tinting it a rich salmon. From his place at the stern, Tamosh followed its ascent with a touch of envy.

Renn peeked through the hatch. Gregos waved her forward. "Stay close to Bibeed and do what she tells ya. She's pretty darn good."

Cayled grinned as he crossed the deck to join Tamosh. "She's better'n I am."

They got busy lowering the dinghy and climbing aboard. Gregos leaned over the side. "Not much light left. Ya best make it fast as ya can."

Tamosh pushed off. Cayled began to row. *SeaBella's* sail caught the wind, and she began to pull away.

Tamosh answered Cayled's unspoken question. "I do not know what will happen when I break the ampule. Be prepared to row like a Mindeco is at your back. Ready?"

Cayled gripped the oars. "Ready."

Tamosh knelt at the stern and tested the wind direction. "Keep her into the wind. I'll tell you when to go." The ampule felt warm to the touch. The closer he moved to the sea, the hotter it got. Scalding heat crawled over his fingers. He plunged the ampule beneath the water, snapped it in two, and let the pieces go. An anguished feminine face rose to the surface. Its mouth shaped a scream. Water bubbled it into oblivion. Steam misted upward and spread.

"Go, Cayled."

The dinghy shot forward. Cayled hit his rowing stride—dip, pull, lift, forward, dip, pull, lift, forward. Roiling water chased them, caught them, gurgled around them. Steam smelling of burnt flesh wafted higher. Bobbing like a cork in a pan of boiling liquid, the dinghy pitched and rolled. Ocean bubbled over the side. Tamosh began to bail.

The boat lurched upward. Cayled lost his grip on the oars, swore as one jumped its lock and splashed overboard. Grabbing the other one, he wielded it like a canoe paddle against the frothing current.

The narrow entrance to the cove appeared at the edge of the mist. Tamosh growled his frustration and looked over his shoulder. A foggy curtain obscured the shore and *SeaBella*. The dinghy gave another violent lurch. Cayled pitched overboard. The small boat bounced ahead, leaving him hidden by the thickening mist and the roiling sea.

Oarless and alone, Tamosh gripped the bulwark. Waves heaved it shoreward. Rocks loomed, ready to snag it, break it, send it to the bottom. He cast a frantic look behind him. A vulture dropped through the mist and rose with Cayled clinging to its legs, flew to the top of a cliff, set him down, and swooped toward the dinghy.

Tamosh crouched lower. Mountainous jagged rocks rushed closer. Talons gripped his shoulders and lifted. The wooden boat slammed against the shore, gave a loud crack, and splintered into pieces. Tamosh clutched the roughness of Yaro's vulture legs and thanked Emit for his life.

On the cliff top, Cayled caught him as Yaro lowered him to the ground. They laughed with relief and clapped each other on the back. The Pentharian materialized, a quizzical expression making his alien features look almost Human.

"That was too close, brother of Gregos, yet you laugh."

Tamosh grinned at the tall off-worlder. "Gratitude that we still live, Yaro, that makes us giddy. Marji didn't tell me breaking the ampule would create a tsunami. Thank you for coming to our rescue."

"You sure have great timing, Yaro." Cayled shook water from his hair. "What did you discover about the trawler?"

"Two men who are not used to the sea and a rough-looking sailor are onboard."

Cayled wrung out his shirt. "What do ya mean—not used to the sea?"

Yaro's red lips parted in a grin, showing strong white teeth. "Their stomachs could not keep down their meal."

Cayled laughed.

Tamosh gazed over Triple Moon Strait. Mist enshrouded the shoreline. The sun had taken its light and fled below the tree-covered hills. The rising moon tinted the horizon gold. He would have enjoyed the view if he hadn't been worried about Gregos and *SeaBella*. As it was, he wanted to find his brother. Yaro met his gaze and shifted.

Brie materialized in the hide y-hole and opened her hand. The dragonfly lifted into the air and shifted shape. Elf smiled at her.

"Thanks, Brielle."

She grinned. "You're welcome. Wonder if Thorlu discovered the decoy?"

Elf shook his head. *"Not yet."*

Ira flashed into view. "Hey. Good to see you two." He rubbed Shyllee's head. "Where's Esán?"

The Star of Truth burned a warning. Brie clutched his arm. "I thought he was with you."

"He was until those Mocendi guys invaded the plantitarium. We split up. You know he's sick again?"

Brie paled. Elf put a finger to his lips. His eyes glazed over, then cleared.

"He's by the waterfall in Human form, too sick to make it here on his own. We'll need to help him."

Ira looked from Brie to Elf. "Can't you two teleport him here?"

Elf shook his head. *"The entire ship is watching for us. If we teleport as a group, our energy signature will give us away. The only thing keeping us safe in here is the roots making up the walls act like a buffer."*

Brie focused her intention on Esán. "I think he can walk with help. I'll go. Be ready to assist if I need you." She didn't wait for a reply but shifted and crawled through the mesh vent. Unable to discern anyone within the boundaries of the plantitarium, she shaped a butterfly and made her way to the waterfall. Hidden by a border of shrubs, she found Esán. His already pale cheeks looked even paler. The purple smudges beneath his eye that had all but disappeared were back. Shallow breathing hardly moved his chest.

Brie fought her rising panic and brushed his short hair with her fingertips. His eyelids fluttered open. A weak smile tugged at his mouth.

"Knew you'd come."

"Can you walk?"

"Depends on how far." He struggled to sitting.

"The wall is a couple of city blocks as the raven flies. I can support you."

He nodded. "Better move. Company on the way."

She helped him to his feet and slipped an arm around his waist. Halting to allow him time to catch his breath or to manage a wave of pain slowed their progress. Halfway to their hiding place, Elf appeared, picked him up, and strode toward the hide y-hole. Brie trotted after them, her senses alert for trouble. Elf and Esán stepped through the wall.

The plantitarium door opening sent her into butterfly form. Thorlu entered with Renn Whalend in tow.

With a look of bewildered astonishment, Renn rotated slowly. "This is..." She shook her head. "Where? How? This is truly unexpected, Thorlu. Did you do this?"

"No. This is the work of The MasTer. When he escaped from El Stroma, he brought plant samples with him. At first they filled a small portion of the space." Thorlu glanced around. "Now we have a paradise." Moving to her side, he guided her to revolving shelves on which smaller plants grew. "You asked about herbs. This is where you will find them. You must, however, have a gardener with you."

A uniformed man entered and joined them. "You called me, sir." He spoke with deference, his heavy accent softening the words.

"I did, Teola. This is Renn Whalend. Please assist her. When you are done, escort her back to Research Lab One." He crossed to the door and paused. A hard stare left Renn shaken. "Don't let her out of your sight. Get her to tell you where the missing young people are hiding, and I will reward your efforts." He flashed his charming smile and vanished.

Renn saw the man beside her tense. Gentle eyes found hers. "It would be best if you told me what he wants to hear. Thorlu is a hard man." He held up a hand. Two fingertips were missing. "I have disappointed him before."

Renn controlled a shudder. "I'm sorry to put you at odds with him again, but I know nothing of the children, except they are onboard and missing."

A gentle smile washed her with warmth and understanding. "And you wouldn't tell if you did. It is not your way. These children... What are they to you?"

"They are my son's best friends." She moved to a row of plants. "I need a small amount of winter cress, laverian, and monel leaf. Do any of these grow here?"

He rotated the shelves, extracted samples of each, and placed them in small containers. "Thorlu will not give up. You can tell him later, or you can tell me now." He held up his hand. "And save my fingers."

Renn tipped her head. "You're good, Teola. I'd be tempted if I knew anything. Please take me back to the lab."

The door slid aside, and he ushered her through. He said no more about the children but questioned her about life in Idronatti. She felt no mind probes until he had left her in the lab. Placing the three containers at her workstation, she focused her thoughts on her notes. When the probes withdrew, she nibbled a few bits from the lunch tray and wandered into the supply closet.

Brie materialized. "That was weird."

"It was weird and, therefore, quite disconcerting. I'm not sure what he gleaned from the conversation, but be on guard." She held out a small vial. "Give this to Esán. It will ease his pain. Tell Ira to use Efillaeh as well. We can't cure him, but we can make him more comfortable. Go. Teola has returned to the lab."

She picked up a small box and strolled to her station.

Teola smiled down at her. "Do you always talk to yourself, Renn Whalend?"

"Yes. It helps me clarify my thoughts. Did you need something?"

"I'm just here to observe." He continued to smile.

She sighed and began to gather the ingredients for the spray that would give The MasTer control of the Inner Universe.

Gregos worked the sails and shouted instructions to Bibeed and Renn. When he glanced over his shoulder to check on his brother, his heart jolted. Mist and sea churned around the small dinghy. It bounced one way and then the other on the turbulent water. He tore his gaze away and scanned the shoreline. The cove opening came into view. Tamosh and Cayled were on their own.

Working to keep the boat on course took all his concentration. Bibeed proved an able sailor, but still... *SeaBella* was an unknown.

"Coming about," he hollered.

The booms swung across. The sails luffed, filled with wind, and sent *SeaBella* gliding through the bottleneck into a beautiful cove lit by the last rays of the descending sun.

He had briefed the women on what had to be done to anchor safely. He couldn't have asked for a better crew. Before he knew it, they dropped the anchor and set it; lashed sails in place, and *SeaBella* glowed golden in the fading light.

Darkness settled over the cove. Bibeed went below to fix a meal. Renn stayed at his side.

"Tamosh and Cay will find us, won't they?"

He put an arm around her shoulder. "They'd better."

She stared through the encroaching night. "They weren't that far behind."

He forced a smile. "Looked like The MasTer's Reach gave 'em trouble they didn't expect. What's important is that the bad guys sailed right on by. That's why we can light a lantern to guide our boys home. Keep your eyes peeled. If ya see something, give a soft whistle."

Renn sighed. "I have never learned how to whistle."

Gregos turned her to face him. "Guess it's about time ya learned." He pursed his lips and whistled a soft tune.

She rewarded him with a delighted laugh and puckered her lips. Nothing came out. Again and again, she tried to make a sound.

"Lick your lips, Renn, and keep your tongue back."

A small shrill sound brought with it a girlish giggle. She gave him a hug and tried again. When the whistle trilled louder, she grinned. "I have to show Bibeed."

He watched her descend into the cabin. Her innocence and spontaneity charmed him. Tamosh whispered through his thoughts. *Where are ya, brother?*

Renn climbed part way on deck, whistled, and grinned. "Dinner's ready."

He joined the women and sat staring at his bowl. Bibeed patted his hand. "He's alright, Gregos. I'd know if something happened to Cay. You'd know if Tamosh was in trouble. Now quit staring at your food and eat it."

The boat rocked with a sudden shift in weight. Gregos jumped to his feet. "Into the V-berth," he said in an undertone.

"No need to panic." Tamosh stuck his head in the open hatch and waved. He clambered down with Cayled and Yaro close behind.

Bibeed threw her hands up in delight and enfolded her brother in a bear hug. "Good thing ya came back."

Gregos raised a brow. "Thought ya knew he was alright."

She put her hands on her hips and favored him with a shattering look. "He's here, isn't he?"

Renn held out a hand to Yaro. "I'm so glad you are safe."

He touched her palm and then his heart. "I, too, am glad, Renn Whalend."

Bibeed set bowls of food on the table. "Let's eat, and you can tell us your adventures."

Gregos listened to his brother's tale with a knowing smile. When he was done, he gave him a pat on the back. "Like I always say, Tamosh... When it ain't your time, it ain't your time." He winked. "You did good work today."

45
Myrrh

Tibin stepped from the trees into the small clearing where Endes, the apprentice Mocendi, slumped on a stump. Sibine sat at his feet with Adin in her lap. Sprawled to one side, the wounded soldier moaned in pain.

Endes lunged to standing, dragging Sibine with him. Adin whimpered. Sibine rocked him gently, her brown eyes never straying from Tibin's face.

The apprentice sputtered, "W-where is the Tinpaca? If I am not set free, they both die."

Tibin swallowed his fear and made himself appear relaxed. "We've sent word to the Guardian of Myrrh. She's the only one who can release you from the grove. She will be here soon."

Endes clutched Sibine's shoulder. "I want my freedom now."

Tibin forced a steady reply. "Sibine has done nothing to you. The grove only imprisons those with evil intent. Let her go, and you might discover that releasing her and Adin would set you free."

An ugly scowl hardened the young man's jaw. "Don't expect me to believe your silly fairytales." He grabbed Adin, climbed up on the stump, and held him above his head. "If you want your son to live, make the Tinpaca set me free. Bring the Tinpaca or—"

The sound of men laughing, the scuffle of feet, the noisy disassembling of makeshift tents filled the copse of trees.

"What's all that racket?" He jumped down and shoved Adin at Sibine.

Cradling her sobbing child, she sank onto the stump and hummed a quiet tune.

Endes growled. "Stop that noise."

Adin cried louder.

Eyes huge, Sibine gazed at the angry man. "He will quiet down if you stop yelling."

Endes brought a hand up, ready to strike.

Tinpaca Mondago walked from the trees. "I wouldn't harm them if I were you."

Swinging around to face him, Endes scanned the woods. "What's all the noise?"

"My men are returning to camp. It appears your master has left Myrrh."

Endes' scowl wavered. "You lie. He would never leave me behind."

Mondago shrugged. "He did not leave of his own free will. You, however, are much smarter." He nodded at Sibine. "You hide behind the vulnerable...a mother and child."

Pride stiffened the man's spine. "I am smarter. So you just bring that Guardian woman here or... Wait." Doubt crept into his tone. "You aren't playing with me, are you?" He yanked Sibine to her feet. "If you are, she pays."

Tibin started forward. "Don't touch—"

The Tinpaca's hand on his shoulder stopped him. "It would be foolhardy for me to play with a desperate man."

"Desperate. What makes you think *I* am desperate?"

Tibin looked up at the tall RewFaaran Tinpaca. Danger radiated around him, and yet his voice remained calm and his demeanor steady. Tibin looked back at Sibine, searching for fear in her eyes. He found none, only a calm expression and her trust-filled eyes on his face.

Mondago cleared his throat. "Since it is clear you are not desperate, it would do much for your situation with the Guardian if you were to release the Wood Tiffs and allow me to help my wounded man."

Endes pushed Sibine down on the stump. "The Tiffs stay with me until the Guardian has freed me and escorted me safely from Myrrh." He glanced at the injured soldier. "Don't touch him. He deserves to suffer for his attack against a member of the Mocendi League."

A shrug and a sad smile accompanied the Tinpaca's reply. "Have it your way."

Tibin gasped.

Teva materialized, a cord of light in her upraised hand. Transfixed, the apprentice watched it whirling above her head. With a snap of her wrist, she sent it flying. For a split second, it hovered over him. His shields shimmered into nothing. The rope dropped, tightened around him, and held him immobile. His face contorted with rage. He tried to speak, but no sound passed between his puckered lips.

Mondago strode forward and picked up Sibine and Adin. A soldier hurried into the clearing and knelt beside his fallen comrade.

By the time Tibin realized what had happened, it was over. Mondago put Sibine and Adin down beside him. The RewFaaran tickled the baby's foot. "He sure is a handsome little Tiff."

Sibine handed Adin to Tibin and placed a kiss on Mondago's cheek. "Thank you, Tinpaca."

"Your mate has had a bad turning, Sibine. I suggest you take him home." He straightened.

She glanced at Tibin. "I'll do that."

Tibin offered his hand. "Thank you, sir."

Mondago shook it. "You're welcome. I'd better check on my man."

Sibine took Adin. "Teva may need help."

Tibin approached the immobile Endes. "What now, Teva?"

"Our young Mocendi is about to depart Myrrh. Take your family home and tell the Wood Tiffs to remain alert. The Unfolding is not over, so I can't guarantee there won't be more trouble in Myrrh."

Kieel flitted from a tree branch where he had watched the drama unfold. "Well done, Teva."

She touched her shoulder. "Join me and you can help take our guest to the tower." The three vanished.

Tibin shook his head, put an arm around Sibine, and gazed at their son. "I've never been so frightened in my life, Sib. Not even when a Pentharian bit Fen."

She kissed his cheek. "You were so brave, Tibin." Adin gurgled. Sibine pinched his toe. "We are so proud of you, aren't we, Adin?"

Tibin walked with his family through the trees of the Terces Wood. *I wonder if I will ever feel safe again.*

In her quarters, Sparrow nestled next to Allynae, watching him sleep. She studied his rugged features, the silver highlights in his dark hair, the mustache that was looking like the real thing, the stubble on his chin. *It seems like forever since we've been together.* She snuggled closer, savoring how safe and confident he made her feel.

His stormy blue eyes opened, searched her face, and lit with a smile. Pushing up on one elbow, he kissed the tip of her nose and brushed a strand of hair from her cheek. "You look beautiful, all sleep-tousled and full of dreaming. How long have you been awake?"

"Not long. My mind started to chatter about The MasTer's gender and identity." She rolled onto her side. "I'm sure Relevart knows about The MasTer, aren't you?"

He pulled her to him and kissed her hair. "Since he let Mira know he is Rayn's birth-mate, he must have guessed she is The MasTer—but we can't know that for sure."

Sparrow squirmed in his arms and sat up. "We have to get word to them."

He groaned. "Are you suggesting we go back to Veersuni and use the fountain?"

She climbed over his sprawled body and stood up. "I am." She tossed him his trousers and slipped into the DeoNyte version of a Personal Needs Space.

When she emerged ready to go, Allynae sat on the side of the bed, fastening his boots. "We could have waited a little longer, you know."

Ignoring his teasing smile, she kissed him and pulled him to his feet. "It's time to go see what we can discover."

He gazed down at her, his brows raised in a question. "Haven't you forgotten something, Guardian of Myrrh?"

"Oh." She shifted and grinned. "Better?"

He tugged Almiralyn's long braid. "I like you better as Sparrow, but..." He clasped her hand.

She closed her eyes, pictured The Reading Room, and focused on her intent.

He laughed softly and held open the door to Veersuni. "After you."

She moved past him into the empty sanctuary. The tranquility of the sacred space embraced her. The sound of the fountain's song drew her forward and then grew silent. Her reflection, overlapped by Allynae's, smiled up at her, then both dissolved.

Middle-night blue and glistening stars flooded the fountain. A path of light sliced the image into two sections. At opposite ends, crystals glowed atop two rowan staffs. Two men held them high. A light flashed. The staffs, now only inches apart, cast their light over a diverse group.

Almiralyn and Corvus stood on either side of Relevart. Surrounding Wolloh were Torgin, Somay, and Nomed. Wodash od DerTah hovered nearby.

The Universal VarTerel gazed from one face to the next. "Together at last. The end draws near. We have a goodly distance to travel in this land of no time." He motioned Torgin to his side. "We need the compass, boy. The Mocendi ship prepares to depart DerTah for TreBlaya. It is vital that we arrive there before it. Ask it the way."

Torgin held out the compass. "Ostradio, show us the way to the planet of TreBlaya."

The needles spun, and the face glowed. A chart of the heavens formed and hovered. Constellations marked a path like signposts in a vast sea of stars. Relevart and Wolloh exchanged nods. The chart melted away and the compass face ceased to glow.

"Thank you, boy. Keep the compass close to your heart. It will tell you if we go off course." His voice grew more serious. "Others try to enter Mittkeer, so be vigilant, all of you. Wolloh and I will take the lead. Wodash, be our rear guard. Alert me to any changes, no matter how small. Stay in a tight group. Almiralyn and Corvus protect Torgin and Ostradio. Somay and Nomed, be prepared to contain us within an illusion of invisibility if Wolloh or I give a sign."

The group reassembled and began its trek through Mittkeer.

The water in the fountain rippled. Relevart's face focused. *"SparrowLyn and Allynae, keep your recent discoveries close. The time has not yet come to share. Do not stray far from Elcaro's Eye."* Again, ripples ruffled the surface. Again, it stilled.

Brie passed through the hid-y-hole wall and knelt beside Esán, who lay curled up on the mossy floor. Ira knelt across from her. Elf remained standing, his expression concentrated, his gaze distant. Shyllee sat at his feet.

Pulling Henri's vial from beneath her drango tunic, Brie brushed her fingertips over Esán's brow.

He moaned and struggled to push up on one elbow. "Where?"

"You're safe. Elf brought you here while I went to see Aunt Henri. She sent you this." She showed him the vial.

Ira helped him to sitting.

Esán uncapped the tiny bottle, took a sniff, and drank its contents. He heaved a heavy sigh. "I don't know what she put in it, but I feel less tired already."

"She said Ira should use Efillaeh, too. It won't heal you, Esán, but it should slow the disease's progress."

Shyllee growled and inched closer to Elf, her hackles rising and her teeth bared.

He gripped her collar. *"Be still."* His message, a shout in their heads, stopped all movement, all thought.

A low hum vibrated the air in the space.

Brie's eyes widened. Esán grabbed her arm.

Ira gasped. *"What on Thera!"*

Elf pressed his lips together. *"The ship's engines..."* He closed his eyes.

When they opened, Brie saw first fear and then resignation. A wave of trepidation washed over her. *"The ship is leaving for TreBlaya, isn't it?"*

He sank to the floor and buried his face in Shyllee's silky fur.

A breeze blew through Veersuni, stirring the curtains. Color from the window flew to hover above the fountain, where Almiralyn's features faded, leaving Sparrow's stricken expression captured in stained glass richness. Allynae's arm around her did nothing to ease her sudden and deep sense of dread.

In the Terces Wood, Nemttachenn rose gray and majestic in the autumn light. Kieel gulped. Teleporting always made his stomach feel queasy. He fluttered to a branch and observed the antics of Teva's prisoner. Like a marionette, Endes danced and capered around the clearing, trying to break free. Teva yanked him to a standstill, his anger reflected in eyes filled with fire and face flushed a bright crimson.

Kieel sniffed the air, savored the invigorating coolness, and rejoiced at being in *his* Terces Wood.

Teva inhaled and focused her sapphire gaze on Endes. "I love autumn, don't you?"

His nostrils flared as he struggled to break free.

"I'm assuming your fight to be free means you are ready to leave Myrrh. Please, Kieel, lead the way."

Kieel shot through the entrance to find CheeTrann and Paisley waiting at the tower's center. Behind him, Endes growled and swore his way into Nemttachenn. His startled gaze picked Myrrh's Sentinel from the dimness. His mouth dropped open.

CheeTrann loomed over him. "Shut your mouth, boy. Didn't your mother teach you it's rude to stare?" He grinned at Teva.

She smiled up at him. "Hello, Sentinel of Myrrh. It has been too long since we last met."

Delight gleamed in his eyes. "I agree, Teva Rivan. I don't believe you have made the acquaintance of Paisley James Tobinette, my friend and competitor."

"Hello, Paisley James."

A self-conscious smile tipped Paisley's mustache at an odd angle. "You look like Almiralyn." His dark skin glowed with the infusion of blood in his cheeks.

CheeTrann laughed and slapped him on the back. "An astute observation, Pais."

Teva's captive struggled and spit disjointed syllables into the air.

A deep rumble shook the tower. "Your guest seems impatient to be away from Myrrh, Teva."

Endes tried again to squirm free of her hold. She caught Kieel's eye and winked.

The man's sputterings turned into speech. "You will be sorry you treated me with such disrespect." He glared. "The MasTer will exact revenge for your treatment of one of his Mocendi."

CheeTrann stroked his white beard. "First, boy, you are not a Mocendi, you are an apprentice. Second, I see no reason the Mocendi League would show an interest in someone with so little talent." The ground began to tremble as the vortex spun into view. "Third, I doubt you will ever see The MasTer again."

The next instant, Endes plunged into the vortex, and it swirled closed. Teva smoothed her chestnut hair back from her face and gazed at the two men. "I sense he will not find life easy where he has gone."

CheeTrann's features hardened. "By the time the Guardians rescue him, he will do anything they require."

A flash of light introduced Lenadi into the group. "Trouble, Teva. They need us in Mittkeer. Relevart asks that you, CheeTrann, help us reach the place of All Time and No Time."

CheeTrann frowned, faded, and refocused. "The Unfolding races ahead. Kieel will inform Mondago of your change in plans. I will return the Demrach Gateway to its new position. Hold on to each other. Do not let go until Relevart tells you to do so."

Teva and Lenadi embraced.

Kieel alighted on the staircase. The Sentinel raised a hand.

"Open, Mittkeer. Admit these souls
To help The Unfolding achieve its goals.
Take them to the VarTerel
Within the realm that you guard well."

A fissure the height of a tall man opened within the confines of Nemttachenn. Stars shone bright in the dark and distant sky.

"Nava Dec," CheeTrann called.

A wave of star-speckled blue poured through the slit, swaddled Teva and Lenadi from head to foot, and receded, taking them with it. The edges of the fissure merged.

CheeTrann lowered his hand. "I have only done that once before, so I hope they end up where Relevart needs them." He sat down at the table, his expression troubled.

Paisley sat across from him.

Kieel landed on the edge of the table and studied both men. The distant look in their eyes puzzled him.

His wings fluttered. "What do you see?"

CheeTrann picked up a knight. "The players gather in the Land of No Time. Only Emit understands the strategies and desires of all the participants."

Paisley nodded, his expression both solemn and sad.

Both remained entrenched in their own thoughts.

Kieel zipped from the tower and headed for Mondago's camp. The Tinpaca and Jordett needed to know what happened. *Dare I return to Idronatti?* The thought left him quivering with dread.

Jordett and Lavir left the Five Fathers locked in their underground cell and hurried to Orittra's office. Akeri glanced up from her comp-tab. "Please help yourselves to a nouri-drink."

Orittra nodded a welcome. He had made the decision to help reestablish calm in Idronatti.

Jordett returned his nod. "Glad you decided to join us. I'm sure Lorsedi will appreciate your loyalty."

He had the grace to blush. Jordett smiled to himself, grabbed a slender tube of green fluid, and sat down opposite Akeri. Lavir pulled a chair out and sat beside him.

Akeri did not wait to be asked to begin. "Almiralyn sent word from Myrrh. The Mocendi ship has left for TreBlaya. Torgin is not onboard. We have also learned that Renn continues her trip to DoOlb under the care of Yaro and the Senndi brothers. Thus far, they have encountered no problems. Shu Chenaro and the desert gateway remain secure. TheLise reports that all is quiet in Trinuge. Much to her delight, Lorsedi ordered a contingent of men to escort Roween and Nissasa to RewFaar, leaving her free to do the VarTerels' bidding. When the men return, they will bring Chyneria Stol to visit with Stebben at the ranch and to await word regarding her son, Desirol. Stebben, Roandee, and WoNa have been alerted that the end draws near. Falind asked me to inform you that Dom and Majeska have returned to Antiques by Q." She glanced at her comp-tab. "I believe those are the main details."

Jordett set his empty tube on the table. "Did Almiralyn give you any orders for us?"

"Keep Idronatti as stable as you can. For the moment, she feels the Mocendi are focused elsewhere. Falind has been experimenting with the drug used to control the city's residents. She believes it is better to continue its use unaltered. When Renn and Wilith return, Falind will help her establish a schedule for its gradual withdrawal, while Wilith works with you to develop a plan for reeducating the populace."

Lavir leaned back in his chair. "It's amazing to think that the Galactic Guardians would select men like the Five Fathers to build and care for a city of people. What made the Fathers take a jog down the wrong road?"

Akeri pushed her chair back. "Even the best men are tripped up by the lure of power and wealth. If you'll excuse me, it's time to patrol the city." She pushed her chair in. "I'll report in when we're back, Major."

Jordett smiled at the bemused look on Lavir's face as the door closed behind her. Akeri's sultry beauty was highlighted by lustrous, dark hair and startling emerald-green eyes. She exuded self-confidence and personal power. "She's lovely, isn't she?"

Lavir said, more to himself than his commanding officer, "Too bad she's joined to Lenadi."

Jordett let his thoughts follow their natural course. *I miss Merrilea. Hope she's missing me.*

In Veersuni, glowing snippets of color flew back to the stained-glass window. Sparrow clung to Allynae, feeling numb and disoriented. "Alli, our daughters…" She couldn't force her tumultuous thoughts into words. He hugged her closer. "They're on the way to a solar system on the Outer Rim." His chin rested on her head. "Aunt Henri is with them."

"And Wolloh and Relevart are on the way there, too." She sniffed. "Why doesn't that make me feel better?"

He kissed her lightly. "Because the outcome is unknown. It would help if you assured yourself they were alright."

The water in the fountain turned cloudy and then cleared. Sparrow gasped as a huge mushroom-shaped ship came into focus.

El Aperdisa, the Mocendi ship, left its orbit around DerTah and sailed as gracefully as a swan on a lake through the vastness of space. Its metallic blue surface glowed with the vibrance of a living thing. The upper section, the mushroom cap, rotated at a constant rate. Propulsion units driving it from orbit flared at the base of the smooth lower cylindrical section. The 'cap' spun faster. Elcaro zoomed out. DerTah floated in the distance. The ship's edges began to blur. DerTah grew smaller still. A white light engulfed the ship and died into the darkness of space. El Aperdisa had vanished.

Sparrow trembled from head to foot. Ari and Brie were on that ship. The reality of it left her fighting for breath. Allynae's strong arms scooped her up. Stubble against her cheek, the whisper of his breathing, the steady rhythm of his heartbeat calmed her.

He lowered her to a bench and sat beside her, his arms protecting, loving, soothing. Still, the sobs came. The fear that she might never see her girls again threatened to drown her.

A hiccuped attempt to quell the flood of emotions quaked through her. "I'm not Almiralyn, Alli. I don't know how to do this."

He handed her a handkerchief. "What makes you think she would react any differently? The girls are her nieces. She loves them, too. Almiralyn is as Human as you are." He gave her a lopsided grin. "And as female."

Sparrow dried her tears and blew her nose. "Now what do we do?"

"What Relevart told us to do—stay close to the fountain."

She leaned on his shoulder. "Let's hope it shows us something soon."

46
DerTah

Thorlu and Vygel gazed at a massive screen and watched DerTah grow smaller. Behind them, a group of their colleagues chatted. They sounded nervous. A return to TreBlaya was a rare thing. Unless one incurred The MasTer's wrath, one could go a lifetime without returning or seeing him. As long as you did his bidding and sent a stream of recruits for training, your currency account reflected The MasTer's approval.

Thorlu had often wondered where the bottomless well of wealth came from. When he'd asked Vygel, the man had been vague. Thorlu continued to be curious.

Vygel fussed with his cape and glanced back at their colleagues. "Hate groups."

Thorlu scanned the crowd. "This one is particularly unsavory. They're not The MasTer's usual type. Have you told them why he summoned them to TreBlaya?"

"Not my job, Thorlu. Yours." Bulging eyes stared at the screen. "I hate DerTah and the Clenaba Rolas solar system. Vygel's toothy smile held a touch of vindictiveness. It's time to let Renn know she is about to meet her destiny."

Thorlu kept his gaze on the screen. "As I seem to recall, Renn does not return your affection, Vygel. Perhaps it would be best if you allowed her to complete her work for The MasTer."

Vygel shot him a dark look. "You take care of your business, Thorlu. I'll look after mine." Pivoting, he marched from the space.

Someone snickered. "Tangorra, why are we here? We've got things to attend to. Can't waste time running to TreBlaya and back."

The group fell silent, all eyes turned his direction. He smiled down at them, a smile so gracious it would melt the frosting on a cake. Few had met him, and few knew what hid behind the smile or the polite tone.

"The MasTer has summoned you to perform a task for him. When he is ready, I'm sure he will share. A word of caution: He is a man of little patience. I am sure you know that above all else, he values and rewards loyalty. Do not let him know your discontent. He is The MasTer. He pays you, clothes you, and educated you. You are who and where you are because he took you in."

Thorlu strode through the small crowd to the door. The men cleared a path as he approached, their faces stony. In the passageway, he paused.

Someone said, "Didn't take us in. Kidnapped us. Made us do his bidding."

A man replied. "I'm not complaining. Look where we are. We're rich, powerful, and feared. Without The MasTer, we'd be nothing."

Thorlu made his way to the lab. He had a feeling Renn Whalend might appreciate his help.

Esán leaned against the wall, reveling in the life flowing through his body. Ira's treatment with Efillaeh and Henri's concoction had left him feeling *almost* good. At least his disease slept. He knew when it returned and took over his body, he might not recover. Hugging himself, he smiled. *Now is all that matters. I'm alive and alert, and I intend to stay this way. We're on the way to TreBlaya. My instincts tell me I'm going to need all the strength I can muster.*

Sitting on the floor with his arms around Shyllee, Elf let his fear go. A return to TreBlaya did not mean instant death. He had powerful friends. He glanced at Esán, glad that his color was better. Energy pulsed through him. Elf hoped his new friend would manage the trip and whatever awaited them at the other end. Brie would help him, and Brie had more power than she realized. Shyllee licked his face. He wiped his sleeve across his cheek and hugged her warm friendliness. *Besides, I have Relevart's dog. You won't let the Mocendi hurt me, will you, girl?*

Brie sat next to Esán, her hand in his. She sensed the return of his energy and almost cried with relief. He moved closer and put his arm around her shoulder. In that instant, she felt warm and safe and another emotion that surprised her—loved. She felt loved by the boy who had claimed her heart. *If—no, when—we make it out of this mess, perhaps...* His blue eyes shifted from a fixed stare at nothing to rest on her face. She saw it there, the love he, too, had discovered. She leaned her head on his shoulder and savored the moment.

Ira tried to nap. Desirol—his face, the Mindeco, its struggle to take over his friend—haunted him. He opened his eyes and stared at the curve of the ceiling. *Desirol is in danger. I sense it in every fiber of my body.* Beneath his drango tunic, he fingered the hilt of the sacred knife. *Corvus charged me with his care. If the Mindeco sheds his body, Efillaeh is the one thing that can save him.* Shrugging his need for sleep aside, he sat up. *If anyone knows where Des might be on this ship, it's Elf.* Elf looked up and nodded.

Desirol lay in a drugged stupor. Whenever he began to the surface, someone sent him plummeting back to where he and the Mindeco walked side by side. The tall, gangly creature never looked his direction, only stared straight ahead and muttered strange, sinister words. Desirol kept his gaze on the featureless ground, kept his attention fixed on keeping himself intact. He wished his friends would find him. He sighed. Like him, they might be drugged. The Mindeco growled. Desirol kept walking, kept his eyes down, kept his hand on the Remembering Stone in it's velvet pouch.

Henrietta Avetlire, as Coala Renn Whalend, worked in the lab not too distant from the room where Desirol lay in a drug-induced sleep. She could feel the boy's struggle and wished she had the means to help.

The sound of the laboratory door's soft shish, shish sent all traces of Henri into hiding. Vygel's awkward gait carried him to her workstation. Something about his manner, the look on his face, made her inwardly recoil.

He picked up a flask, swirled the contents, and watched it resettle before returning it to the counter. "I hope you are close to completing your work, Renn. We have left our orbit around DerTah. Our next stop will be TreBlaya." He sniffed and inched closer. His hand hovered near her cheek, then lowered. "The MasTer is an exacting individual."

Steeling herself, Renn held a flinch in check. "If I am to finish before we reach TreBlaya, Vygel, I need uninterrupted work time." She took a deep breath. "Which means, please go away."

The gawky man bristled but said nothing. He gazed down at her for a moment longer, wheeled around, and marched from the lab.

Renn picked up a test tube and studied its contents. The door opened. Thorlu strode to the station and smiled down at her.

With a sigh, she replaced a test tube in its holder and shot her visitor an irritated look. "If you came to tell me we are on the way to TreBlaya, I know. I also know I need to accomplish the tasks assigned to me. This lab has been as busy as the Avenue of Trees during morning exercise. I can't get anything done. Please tell me why you are here so I can get back to work."

"Poor, Renn. I gather Vygel stopped by. I believe he has a crush on you, my dear." He scrutinized her station. "Teola gave me a list of the herbs you requested. I am assuming you used them in the serum to regenerate Human tissue."

"All but the winter cress. I used it to make a headache remedy for myself. I can show you what's left if you'd like."

He took a step nearer. His breath stirred the hair on the top of her head. Fingers, like a vice grip, tipped her chin up. "Never lie to me, Renn. I can protect you better than anyone on this ship. If you lie, it will make me disinclined to do so." He released her chin.

She didn't move. "If I do what I am asked, why would I need protection from you or anyone else?"

"I believe you have guessed that Torgin is not on the ship. You will never see either your companion or your son again. You are a beautiful woman, and you are fair game. I can guarantee that once The MasTer no longer needs you, you *will* need my protection."

With the grace and power of a big cat, he strode to the door. Renn sank onto her stool. A part of her wanted to scream in frustration, a part to wilt with despair, and another to stop the facade of the docile Idronattian. *Where is all this leading? Time and TreBlaya hold the answers.*

Brie watched Ira with interest as he gathered his friends around him in a tight huddle. Agitation made his blue eyes dart from one person to the next.

"Des is in trouble. I feel it right here, all turning long." Splayed fingers pressed against his belly. "I can't sleep because I dream of him. He's always in my thoughts. We *have* to find him."

Elf put an arm around his shoulders. *"Your talents mature, Ira Raast. I've sensed him and Rikell, too. The Mindeco is tired of being confined in a body he has no control over. Better to drop it and take another."*

Brie slipped a hand into Esán's and looked at Elf. "Do you know where they're keeping him?"

He nodded. *"The infirmary down the hall from Renn Whalend's lab. The Mocendi are keeping him drugged to control the Mindeco."*

Esán pursed his lips in thought. "I bet Renn can make a drug that will keep the Mindeco quiet."

"I'll go find out." Brie prepared to shift. "You make a plan while I see if Renn has any suggestions. If something happens and I don't make it back, rescue him without me."

Esán stayed her with a hand on her wrist. "Check with the Star of Truth. If it says you're safe, fine. If not, I'll go."

Brie concentrated on the star. A strange vibration running through the ship mingled with a sharp tingle down her spine. Her gaze flew to Elf.

"Our first jump. We'll make three before we reach TreBlaya." He touched the Star on her neck. *"You'd better hurry. If you need help, I'll be close by."*

She shifted and crawled through the vent into the plantitarium. Zipping to the ventilation shaft, she arrived at the lab and crawled into the storage space. Below her, Renn waited in the shadows. Brie changed to Human.

Renn put a finger to her lips, then whispered, "I am watched non-stop." She handed her a small bottle. "For De—"

A pain shot up Brie's neck. Renn whipped around. Thorlu stood in the doorway.

"Ah. You must be Brie, Esán's friend. I wouldn't disappear if I were you, Miss AsTar, or Renn will pay." He held her gaze for a long moment, then glanced up at the mesh vent. "I've wondered how you were staying hidden. You'll have to give me a tour when you take me to your friends." A devious look momentarily morphed the handsome face. The smile that followed raised the hair on the back of Brie's neck.

"You, Brie, are going to be my secret weapon." The smile widened. "You—"

An alarm blared, lights flashed off, then on, then off. The alarm blared again. Brie shifted, shot through the vent, and headed away from the plantitarium. Inside the cell that had served as Esán's prison, she materialized.

Elf appeared beside her and clasped her hand. The next instant they stood in a cargo bay, and the next they arrived amidst box-lined shelves in the silence following another blast of the alarm. The lights flashed on.

Brie peeked through a rectangular window at Desirol, where he lay on a bed in a narrow space. Beside him, a screen lit up and equipment attached to the bed began to buzz and hum. An attendant hastened into the room, checked Desirol's pulse, scanned him with a hand-held body scanner, and bustled away. Another man hurried in, pushed buttons on a touch screen, checked readouts on the equipment, nodded his satisfaction, and left.

The door slid open a third time to admit Thorlu.

Brie glanced up at Elf. *His face looked as blank as his mind felt.*

Yaro, in the shifted form of a laridae, circled the small cove where *SeaBella* lay at anchor and her crew slept. Swooping over Triple Moon Strait, he discovered the fishing trawler further up the strait in a curve in the shoreline that provided a small amount of protection. Landing on the mast, he observed two men standing on the deck below.

The stockier man, a smoker with yellow-stained fingers, took a puff and looked bored. The other scratched his stubble covered chin and ranted.

"How could we have lost them? It's a strait, for The MasTer's sake. When I hired you, you told me you knew it like the back of your hand."

A cloud of smoke preceded the stocky man's reply. "Musta missed it in that mist. Seen nothing like it 'round here. Wasn't willin' to risk my boat." He took a final drag and flipped the butt over the side. "Now, ya can either stay up here and gripe, or ya can rest. I'll see ya at dawn." He disappeared below.

A third man joined his comrade on deck. "Don't worry about that idiot." He jerked a thumb in the direction the boat's captain had gone. "When we've captured the kids, we make him pay, big time."

"Think they got the trap set?"

"Ya. Wished they'd left a Mocendi though. The kids are supposed to be pretty powerful."

"We'll handle it. Besides, we got help at the portal." He stretched. "Better rest up."

Yaro flew inland and made his way back to *SeaBella*, where Gregos and Tamosh awaited him on deck.

"Well?" Gregos demanded.

Yaro described the men on the boat and repeated their conversation.

Gregos chewed the tip of his mustache. "Trouble in the ranks. Good for us, bad for them. Sure wish we knew what kinda trap."

Tamosh mused, "Interesting that they expect to find the young ones aboard. We ought to use that to our advantage. If we can create a distraction that pulls the focus to us, maybe Yaro can sneak Renn into the portal before they notice."

Gregos yawned. "Suggest we get some sleep. Hard to plan until we see the lay of the land, so ta speak." Another yawn carried him below deck.

Yaro looked down at Tamosh. "Worried?"

He shrugged. "Would be stupid not to be. Glad you're with us, Yaro."

Yaro inclined his head. "Sleep well, Tamosh. Tomorrow will arrive too soon."

Tamosh slipped below. Night's quiet cradled *SeaBella*. Yaro stared up at the heavens. A deep longing for ReTaw au Qa flooded his heart. He missed the swampland and Mangal trees, the hummocks and myriad of creatures that lived there. He missed his own kind. Stretching out on the deck, he whispered, "I have a promise to fulfill. When Renn Whalend is safe, I must find my heart-brother. Only when The Unfolding is complete..." He yawned and, with the skill born of long cycles of grabbing rest on the fly, he slept.

47

Myrrh

Sparrow woke with a start. The tomb-quiet of Veersuni and Allynae, finger to lips, kept her silent. She raised a questioning brow. His gaze swung to a soot-colored mist wafting above the fountain. Evil pervaded the sanctuary.

Shivering, she slipped a hand into his. In unison, they moved soundlessly toward Elcaro's Eye. Halfway there, they hesitated, tense and straining to hear.

As though blown by the wind, the mist thinned. The water, as still as a stagnant pool, seemed to wait. Sparrow and Allynae took a cautious step forward.

The image of a pristine canvas came into focus on the surface. A silhouetted woman raised a brush and began to paint. Allynae whispered, "You."

Sparrow, eyes glued to the water, nodded.

Quick brush strokes brought an angelic face to completion. The artist's silhouette misted into nothing. On the canvas, cherub blue eyes blinked.

A hacking cough, a raspy voice… "What do you see?" More coughing.

Large, scaled hands tore the canvas to pieces. Trembling water erased the image. An older woman huddled in folds of deep purple wavered into focus. A tall, winged creature handed her a goblet from which she sipped.

The coughing eased. She lowered the goblet to her lap. "If all is clear above, we will fly today, Abarax." Her harsh voice quaked with fatigue.

The creature bowed. "The ship has not yet returned and the sun hides behind a curtain of clouds, my master."

She sipped again from the goblet and set it aside. "Let us go while my strength holds." Her cape slipped from her shoulders. She took his offered hand and descended the two steps to the floor. "Ring the bell. Make sure everyone has obeyed and hidden from sight." A cough wracked her emaciated body. "I want no one to see me."

Abarax crossed to a tasseled pull and yanked, once, twice, three times. Deep, muffled chimes sounded the warning. The Astican scooped the woman up in leather-scaled arms and carried her down a long corridor. Midway, he stepped through Gothic arched doors onto a balcony and helped her to stand.

For a time, she rested pale, withered hands on a black stone balustrade. Sunken eyes scanned a long dead landscape. "It looks the way I feel." Exhaustion weighted the words as much as it weighted her body. Fleshless arms wide, she drew one deep, wrenching breath and shifted. An eagle-like bird with deep green plumage soared upward.

The Astican unfurled scaled wings and lifted into flight with its responsibility—keep The MasTer safe—uppermost in its mind.

Barren hills and dried riverbeds stretched below them. Nothing moved; nothing lived. Where lush forests had once thrived, charred trees strewn by blasts of wind decayed on heat-blistered ground. Rancid odors rose in plumes of acid steam from jagged cracks scarring the surface. An immense pit gaped wide. Fire blazed. Smoke billowed upward.

The MasTer banked in a wide arc. Strong galee wings carried her to the balcony, where she landed and collapsed in a heap. The shift to Human left her gasping and coughing. Abarax carried her back to her chambers, laid her on a single fourposter bed, and helped her to drink from a goblet.

"Wake me when the ship arrives."

It bowed and pulled the black drapes closed around her bed. Her guardian and her conspirator sat upon her throne and watched.

Its face once more filled the fountain's bowl. Hatred, malice, loathing shone in its cherubic eyes. Its gaze traveled to the shrouded bed. Pity and compassion made a fleeting appearance. A greedy glint registered and stayed.

The image dissolved, leaving behind the hint of a mist wafting above the surface. Water droplets cascaded into the bowl.

Sparrow wiped a tear from her cheek. "She has done horrid things to worlds and people, but..." She stared at the water. "We've read so much about her; yet I never expected to see her." She looked at Allynae. "Why do you think she wants the children?"

Allynae scratched his chin. "She wants Efillaeh and the compass and the Remembering Stone."

"But the Mocendi could have stolen those and taken them to her. I understand she has a personal desire to bring Elf to heel, but why the others? Why Esán? The Seeds of Carsilem? He has no sacred object to give her. I understand Torgin. His presence gives The MasTer control over his mother. Desirol might give her power over my father and RewFaar's leadership. Why the twins? They are Lorsedi's granddaughters, but I doubt he would put his planet at risk for them."

"I don't know the answer, Sparrow. Everything about this is troublesome, but we don't have enough facts."

Pacing to the window, she studied the abstract pattern. *Why, why, why?* Measured steps carried her back to the fountain. "Esán and the twins, especially Brielle, have the potential to train DiMensioners. What has The MasTer to gain by having them in her physical presence?"

Elcaro's Eye grew still, riveting their attention on the bowl. Muted colors splattered over the surface and coalesced into tangled auburn hair, framing a fair-skinned face sprinkled with freckles.

Sparrow saw in the face a resemblance to her father, Lorsedi Telisnoe, a resemblance that reminded her the boy was her half-brother. "It's Desirol, Alli."

"Looks like they're drugging him. I imagine that's keeping the Mindeco under control."

Sparrow grabbed his hand and pointed.

Desirol moaned and curled his fingers around the Remembering Stone. His eyes opened. A blond man looked down at him. Desirol frowned and murmured, "Do I know you?"

The man smiled. "We met once. How do you feel?"

"Drugged." He didn't know why, but the handsome face put him on guard.

"We don't want that creature inside you to take control. Drugging you controls it." The lights dimmed and brightened. His jaw tensed. "I am here for a reason, Desirol. Your friends may try to rescue you. If they do, you are to ring your attendant's call button. They can't protect you, but *we* can. You mustn't leave here, or the Mindeco will win the battle. Do you understand?"

Desirol discerned an undercurrent of dishonesty in his manner but nodded. "I understand."

An alarm sounded three short blasts.

The attendant bustled into the room. "What's going—"

Thorlu's expression stopped him. "Double dose of the drug. Don't leave him unattended." Pivoting on his heels, he strode toward the door.

The attendant shot a dark look at Thorlu's disappearing back and then moved to Desirol's side. "Double dose could kill you." His fingers flashed over the touch screen. "A single dose is enough. I'll be back to check on you. As soon as it starts to wear off, I'll give you another." He touched the screen again.

Desirol flinched. The ceiling blurred. He fell down, down, down to where the Mindeco waited, his single eye so dark and so deep that Desirol thought he would drown.

The water in the fountain bubbled into stillness. A new image took shape.

Brie stared through the rectangular window at the receding back of Thorlu's blond head. Everything about the handsome Mocendi made her uneasy. She pressed further in the darkness next to Elf. *"Why does the alarm keep going off?"*

"Esán and Ira. They'll be here soon."

The thought finished. The boys appeared in the cramped space.

Ira grinned. "Espionage at its finest. Now what?"

Renn Whalend entered the room. Her hand flew over the screen. The buzz and hum of the equipment ceased. She peered around as though waiting.

Ira started to move. Elf's hand on his shoulder held him still. The hatred on his face stopped everyone.

Again, the door slid open. Vygel Vintrusie crossed to the table and looked first at Desirol, and then at Renn.

"I suggest you end your silly game. The MasTer has summoned us. The jump to TreBlaya is imminent."

Renn vanished into Thorlu's tall handsomeness. Fury burned in his eyes. "We would have all the young people in our grasp if you weren't a fool."

Vygel shrugged. "They're not going anywhere. They can't get off the ship. We'll find them when we need them."

"What makes you think they will come out of hiding because The MasTer has summoned them?"

Another shrug. "He is more powerful than us. He'll find them, and we'll capture them."

Thorlu flashed him a scornful look. "And that makes us appear ineffective. The MasTer dislikes inefficiency." He bared his teeth and hissed, "I want those young people in my hands before we reach orbit around TreBlaya."

The ship's hum grew louder. Vygel sneered. "Too late, Tangorra. We made the final jump. We're home."

A uniformed man entered. "We have attained orbit. The MasTer awaits your report." He did not wait for a reply.

Vygel glanced at Desirol. "Better hook him back up. Wouldn't want that Mindeco loosed on the ship." A malicious grin showed off his abundance of irregular, yellowed teeth. Flipping his cape as he turned, he strode from the room.

Loathing contorted Thorlu's features. He pressed the call button. The attendant, who bustled to his aid, listened to his instructions, and left.

Brie focused on the attendant as he moved a series of icons around the screen. Equipment hummed back into action. Desirol moaned, then settled deeper into his drug-induced sleep. Lights softened; the attendant left.

Around her, Brie could feel the tension growing. Would Thorlu be back? Elf relaxed. A small smile wiped negative emotions clean. In their midst, Aunt Henri materialized, large spectacles perched on her nose. Without a pause, she marched into the infirmary.

"Brie, you memorized how to detach Desirol. Do it now. Elf, stand at his head. Ira, take his feet. Esán and Brie, opposite me." She took her place, hands resting on Desirol's arm.

Everyone hurried to their position. Brie reversed what the attendant had done. The mechanical hum stopped. She stepped to the bed and unfastened the straps at his wrists and ankles.

Henri nodded. "Good girl. We teleport to Shyllee. Go."

They arrived in an instant and lay Desirol on the floor.

Henri handed Brie a small jar. "This is for Des. It won't knock him out, but it will calm the Mindeco." She removed her spectacles and tapped her palm. "We're in orbit around TreBlaya. You must stay hidden until Relevart calls." Another tap and she was gone.

Her disappearance left unspoken questions in its wake, yet no one seemed inclined to speak. Ira sat by Desirol's head. Brie could feel his relief. Des was here. Esán slid to the floor next to her and leaned his head on her shoulder. Elf sat on a rock at the edge of the small pool, Shyllee at his feet.

Anticipation kept Brie's mind in turmoil. *TreBlaya. We're orbiting a planet on the Outer Rim. Where is Torgin? Is Yaro with him? And Mother and Father? Will I ever see them again?* She regarded her companions. *At least we're together—for now.*

Drops of water scattered the image and filled Veersuni with the soft sound of Elcaro's Eye at rest.

Allynae led Sparrow to a bench and put his arm around her.

"Hard to imagine that our daughters are at the Outer Rim."

Sparrow found it hard to express in words all the emotions that seethed inside her: fear of what was to come, hope that Relevart would reach the twins in time, dismay that Thorlu had discovered Brie.

A soft knock on the door sent her into Almiralyn's form. She moved from the shelter and safety of Allynae's embrace. He shook his head and mouthed, "You're amazing."

She pulled her long braid over her shoulder, glanced at the color, and hid her surprise at how easily she shifted. "Come in."

Elae hurried into Veersuni. "Merrilea translated another manuscript that references El Stroma. We think what she found is important." Her gaze strayed to the fountain. "Shall I bring her here, or would you prefer to go to the research area?"

Allynae saw his companion hesitate and spoke up. "I'll stay here and mind the fountain, Mira. You can tell me what's up later."

"Thank you, Alli. Lead the way, Elae."

He watched them go with a touch of misgiving that seemed to accompany every instance when Sparrow moved beyond his line of vision, especially when she had assumed Almiralyn's form. Chastising himself for being a silly fool, he relaxed against the wall and studied the fountain. He remembered its arrival in Myrrh—the turning he, Karrew, and Almiralyn, as excited as a small child, had stepped from the Demrach Gateway into the Terces Wood for the first time. She and her protector had taken a flying tour of her new domain and returned, bubbling with delight. That night, she had restored the fountain to its full size in the cottage sanctuary. *How she loves that cottage. I know she yearns to return there.*

He sat up and cracked his knuckles one by one. *There it is again—that tiny, nagging nudge.*

Silence in Veersuni roused him from his thoughts. A sense of time in abeyance carried him to the fountain. Mirror-still, the water reflected the heavens. A group gathered with Wolloh and Relevart around two embracing figures swaddled in sky and stars. Relevart waved a hand. A man and a woman stepped free.

Well, I'll be. Teva and Lenadi. Haven't seen you in sun cycles.

Pleasant memories of their youth on KcernFensia of training together at the Temple of Mahyinaeh made him smile. Teva and Almiralyn had been nearly inseparable. He and Lenadi had been fast friends since childhood. When he was ten sun cycles and his parents left and did not return, Allynae knew he would not have managed without Lenadi's support. A touch of envy reared its head. He shoved it away. *My place is at Sparrow's side.*

Relevart's voice infiltrated his thoughts.

"El Aperdisa has reached TreBlaya. The children are safe, as is Henrietta. Torgin and the compass have brought us to our destination. We can be on the planet in an instant. I suggest we take a moment to rest." He glanced beyond the group, said something to Wolloh, and raised a shimmer ward around his companions.

The fountain shifted its focal point. As always, Allynae found himself fascinated by the intimate perspective Elcaro provided of those who appeared on the water's surface.

Torgin sat at the edge of the group and pulled his flute from the case. Corvus had returned it to him and given him the message from his mother. He ran his fingers over the silvery smoothness. *I sure hope she's alright.*

Afraid to make a sound in the strange atmosphere of Mittkeer, he positioned the flute and pantomimed a melody that had been haunting him since his arrival. In his head, he heard it begin with a single low note that reached for the next and then the next until, threaded together, they flooded his mind and carried him away on the wings of their beauty. He lowered it and sighed. *I might have lost it forever. Thank you, Yaro, for saving it and Corvus for returning it.*

A staff nudging his foot made him jump. He scrambled to his feet.

Relevart regarded him. "It has an amazing sound. And you, Torgin, are an extraordinarily gifted musician." He laid a hand on his shoulder. "A time will come when you must play it for everyone you hold dear. Be vigilant, Torgin. If you miss the moment, it will not come again."

The Universal VarTerel ran a finger down the flute's length and turned to speak with Teva and Lenadi.

Somay joined him as he slipped the flute into its case. "You and your talent changed an ordinary branch from a Tirips Tree into an instrument of rare beauty and power. I am so glad I made it and gave it to you up there in the Dojanack Mountains. You were so young then." He smiled. "A mere boy. Now you are a young man." Pride glowed in his eyes. "I am proud to know you."

Torgin felt the heat of a blush warm his face. "Thank you, sir. I love it."

Elcaro, like a camera's lens, traveled over the assembled group and stopped on Seyes Nomed.

Nomed stared at the vastness of Mittkeer. *I wonder if we've traveled any distance in this strange place. Time, no time...* He rubbed the diagonal scar on his cheek and glanced at Almiralyn. *Life is strange. The woman whom I hated all my life has become a valued friend. Because of her, I realized revenge is a huge and unrewarding burden.* His gaze moved to Somay. *I reclaimed my relationship with my brother and met my nephew.* Wodash floated into his line of vision. *I've seen a death shadow move beyond hatred and begin reclaiming himself.* Thoughts of TheLise teased a smile to his lips. *She is a minx, but I love her.* The admission left him reeling.

Somay rolled the Tabagie's eyes through his fingers one way and then the other, his thoughts following the course they so often followed these turnings. *Is Esán managing? Has the disease progressed too far? Will I be able to get him to Tao Spirian in time?* He returned the eyes to his pocket. A wistful smile—a sigh of loneliness—a longing for his life-mate, Tianna. She awaited them on Tao Spirian. Her concern for their son, her desire to meet Esán, to get to know him, to tell him why she had left intermingled with his thoughts from morning until night. Mixed with that, her love for him, her mate, her true love plucked at his heartstrings, calling him home. His Seed of Carsilem thrummed and hummed and whispered his destiny. *The time draws near; the time draws near; the time...*

The statue on the fountain's rim glistened in the light from the window. Water flowed into her open palms and spilled into the alabaster bowl.

Lost in thought, Allynae sank onto a bench. Elcaro had shared intimate moments in the lives of people who had become his friends. Their insights inspired him to examine the changes he had experienced. *I have embraced my personal power. DiMensionery no longer makes me edgy. I use my training and my gifts with confidence. My heart has found its home in the love of a woman. I have met my daughters. I am a lucky man.*

The serenity of the sanctuary embraced him. He yawned and considered napping. The door to Veersuni opened, removing the option. Almiralyn, with Wilith looming behind her, beckoned him to join her. The fountain's drop, drip, drop followed him from the sanctuary.

48

Der Tah & Beyond

Elf gazed in wonder at his friends. Exhaustion had won the battle, and they slept. He remained vigilant. He wanted nothing to happen to them. Friends were something he had never expected to have again—except Gregos, Tamosh, and Marji, of course. A small smile tugged into being. He allowed it a moment of freedom before returning his attention to what was happening aboard the ship.

He loved everything about El Aperdisa, everything except the Mocendi. El Aperdisa lived. For whatever reason, The MasTer had created a small kingdom aboard her, one rich in all things that would bring a world to life, from the smallest to the largest. The place that fascinated him most, the cryogenics vault, contained the eggs and sperm of every animal and bird that had lived on El Stroma. As much as he hated The MasTer and his irrationality, he loved him for the magnificence of El Aperdisa.

Shyllee raised her head and listened. Beautiful, wise eyes regarded him.

You know the balance of power is about to shift, don't you girl? Her ears lifted. Her head tipped. She pushed up on her haunches.

Ira sprawled close. Elf shook his shoulder.

He blinked and jerked to sitting. "Trouble?"

"Soon. Wake the others."

Esán woke at the first shake. Brie snuggled closer, then woke with a start when he touched her forehead. They left Des to his drugged dreams.

Esán pulled Brie to her feet. Stepping backward to give her more room, he tripped over Desirol's sleeping form, gave a gasp of surprise, and fell backward through the wall.

Elf started forward. Brie's hand shot through the barrier. Esán's hand clutched hers. He stepped back into the hide y-hole, his alarmed expression speaking volumes.

Henrietta Avetlire felt Esán's fall through the wall like someone had dowsed her with a bucket of cold water. She came to her feet and wrapped her fingers around her spectacles. *The masquerade is over.* Dropping Renn's form, she teleported. Her arrival in the secret room coincided with Esán's reentry.

"He looked right at me." His voice shook. "He saw me disappear. We have to leave now."

"Let's not panic." Henri kept her voice soft. "We have plans to make. Please listen closely."

Abarax glared at the two Mocendi whose incredulous expressions made his heart sing. Neither Thorlu nor Vygel believed it had access to The MasTer, and they did not.

"He has instructed me to tell you, Vygel, to bring Renn Whalend to the conference room here at El Soasi with the return of the sun when the third bell chimes. Thorlu, he expects to see the children shortly thereafter. You will bring them. Do you have questions for The MasTer?"

Neither man spoke.

Abarax touched the screen. It went blank. A caped figure stepped from the shadows.

"You did well, Abarax. I believe their response was all you could have hoped for."

"It was, my master."

"Clear the way. I wish to return to my chambers."

Abarax strode down the long, empty hall, checking for others of its kind. Only Astican lived on the planet's surface. Only Astican could withstand the heat and decay. Although the atmosphere on TreBlaya was similar to that of other inhabited planets of the Inner Universe, the destruction on its surface had created a layer of ash and acid not breathable by Humans. El Soasi, The MasTer's residence, built on a mountainside above the contamination, was contained within a domed structure connected to an oxygenation plant. The plant cleaned, recycled, and cooled the air. Abarax and his kind could breathe on both levels.

Assured the staff remained in absentia, it escorted The MasTer to her room, helped her to prepare for bed, and took its place on the throne. El Soasi had become its domain. Heady with the power rushing through it, it stifled the desire to shout in triumph and grinned a vindictive grin. *Thorlu and Vygel will suffer at my hands as I have suffered at theirs.*

Thorlu strode from the room with Vygel on his heels. In his private quarters, he wheeled to confront his companion. "Do you know what is going on?"

"I am as surprised as you." Vygel lowered his gawkiness onto a chair by the dining table.

Thorlu paced. "Do you believe that creature, or is it lying?" He did an about-face and retraced his steps. "Has it imprisoned The MasTer or worse?"

Vygel pushed a chair with his foot. "Stop that infernal pacing and sit down. We don't have time to waste. If we can't find those wretched children, both of us will suffer."

Glaring down at The MasTer's Mocendi gave Thorlu a moment of satisfaction. "The entire crew and all our League brothers are scouring the ship for them. We need to make certain The MasTer is unharmed."

Vygel shot him a dubious look. "And we do this how? El Soasi is well guarded. How do you propose to bypass the Astican at the entrance?"

Thorlu rotated the ring on his middle finger. The MasTer had given it to him as a reward for his service. Vygel wore an identical one. With them, they could gain access to El Soasi via one of two balcony doors. *The danger would be if Abarax had stationed Astican at both secondary entrances.*

A buzzer sounded. A young technician appeared on the ID screen. Tightening his jaw, Thorlu touched open. The man entered.

"We may have a lead on the children. A boy appeared in the plantitarium, looked straight at me, and vanished. I can show you where."

Vygel came to his feet and touched the man's arm. They vanished.

Muttering a string of obscenities, Thorlu teleported and arrived by the door. On the opposite side of the plant-filled space, Vygel and the technician prowled through bushes. Thorlu flashed to their side and joined the hunt. They found nothing to suggest anyone had been there. Above their heads, five round vents lined a root-covered wall. Around them, bushes covered with small orange flowers thrived.

Vygel peered through the bushes. "Are you positive you saw someone up here?"

The man looked crestfallen. "Of course, I'm sure. I'd never bother you if I weren't."

The MasTer's Mocendi gave him an awkward pat on the back. "Perhaps this wasn't the place. Let's go back to the door and confirm the direction you were looking. Thorlu will stay here and mark the spot." He ushered the man ahead of him down a manicured path.

Thorlu waited until they were halfway across the plantitarium before he turned to contemplate the wall. The technician saw Ira, and now Esán. *Too many coincidences...*

Focusing his intent, he sent a probe through the wall. Nothing registered. Then he heard it—the smallest intake of breath. He stepped through the wall. A circle of five young people, an elderly woman, and a dog surrounded him. For the second time, wards he had not created shot up around him.

A mist, muffling the sights and sounds of morning, hung over the small cove where *SeaBella* lay at anchor. Yaro climbed on deck and sniffed the damp air. He savored the scents of low tide. They reminded him of the swamps of ReTaw au Qa.

Today *SeaBella* would reach the DoOlbian shoreline closest to the portal. Yaro's warrior instincts shouted...*warning, caution, take care!* Footsteps behind him announced the boat's captain.

Gregos snorted. "Dislike the feel of the turning. Don't like the mist or the low tide." His frown deepened. "I'm tempted not to leave the cove." He scanned the misty shore. "Tamosh is preparing the weapons. Sure glad Cayled and Bibeed can both handle a rifle."

Yaro empathized with the man's gruffness. "I believe, Captain, that I should go on a reconnaissance flight. Something's not right."

Gregos cast a black look at the mist. "Agreed. I'll set a watch schedule and keep Renn outta sight. Get back fast as ya can. I'm not moving *SeaBella* until I'm sure what lies ahead." He offered Yaro his palm. "Be safe."

Yaro placed his on top of it. "You, as well. Take care of Renn Whalend." His shift to laridae carried him skyward. Streaking away from the shore, he began to explore.

A short distance from the cove, the mountains of TheDa softened into rolling hills that flowed into a wide expanse of flat, grassy land dotted here and there with small farms and villages. When he reached the capital city of Inev, he veered east toward the shoreline and followed it north to a river basin, where hills sprinkled with wildflowers and ancient, squatty evergreens rolled north to the arid plains that bordered the desert of Fera Finnero.

The portal's translucence came into view at the edge of a grove of trees in a shallow valley, a chron circle's march from the shore. Landing at the top of a tree, he surveyed the surrounding countryside. His eyes picked out nothing unusual; his instincts told him differently. He could sense the Mocendi League's energy signature, but they were supposed to have left DerTah.

As a forest fox, he trotted closer. Still, the world appeared normal. He shifted to a small songbird and flitted from tree to tree. Perched within an arm's length of the portal, he followed his warrior's instincts and waited. As the DerTahan sun had reached its zenith, the air next to the portal wavered. A man carrying a rifle stepped into view.

The man paused, shouldered his gun, and scanned the landscape. Rangy and tall with a swarthy complexion and close-set dark eyes, he wore the tattered garb of a tribe Yaro knew as the Spanilmen. Their reputation as aggressive fighters and barbarians with a lust of blood and death was well known.

The man called out, "All clear."

Three more Spanilmen stepped into sight. One glanced over his shoulder.

"Illusion's holding. Didn't believe it would. Guess the Mocendi know a thing or two."

The first Spanilman began issuing orders. "Jak, take a horse and check the landing. See if the boat's close. Git back here fast." He pointed at a second man. "You, Deth, head up valley. See what you can find for a morning meal. Ket and me, we'll stay here in case we git some company."

Jak and Deth lopped away in opposite directions. Their companions stepped back through the illusion.

Yaro soared high overhead, flew well beyond the portal, and winged his way back through the trees. The men, their campsite, and their horses and wagon were visible on this side of the illusion.

Wasting no more time, he shifted to the laridae's faster form and streaked straight for the shore in search of the fishing trawler. At the landing, a rickety dock bobbed up and down with the incoming tide. Not far offshore, the trawler with its dinghy tied off the starboard side had dropped anchor. Reinforcements had arrived.

Winging his way north, Yaro searched for a place to anchor beyond the landing, one that would allow them to approach the portal from the backside. He spotted two places with potential. With his internal compass as a guide, he headed back to *SeaBella*.

The sun had begun its descent toward the horizon when he landed by the helm.

Gregos clambered on deck to greet him. "Took ya long enough."

Yaro lowered himself onto a bench. "There was much to learn."

Tamosh appeared in the hatch. "Do you two want to come down?"

Gregos waved him on deck. Cayled, Bibeed, and Renn followed. Yaro gave them time to arrange themselves comfortably. At a signal from Gregos, he began to describe what he had learned. When he finished, no one spoke. All eyes went to Gregos.

The captain bit his bottom lip. "I'm thinkin' ya have a plan, Yaro. Spit it out."

Yaro looked from Gregos to Tamosh. "How much did your sister teach you about DiMensionery?"

The instant Thorlu stepped through the plantitarium wall, Henri gave the sign. The children circled the startled Mocendi. Wards created by their combined power shimmered into place. Thorlu could not move. Cool, gray-green eyes scanned the group. "And Renn Whalend is where?" His gaze fastened on Henri. "Of course, Henrietta Avetlire, you took her place. I should have guessed."

Henri shrugged. "People see what they expect to see, Thorlu."

He struggled against the wards. "You will, of course, let me go."

"I think not. We haven't decided what to do with you, but..." She smiled. "Letting you go is not an option."

Muffled voices penetrated the wall. "Thorlu, stop playing games. Where are you?"

Thorlu opened his mouth. Henri tapped her palm with her spectacles. He shut it.

Shyllee growled.

Elf pointed. *"Vygel's examining the wall."*

"Tangorra, if you are in there, you'd better answer." The rap of knuckles — silence—another set of raps.

Henri muttered under her breath.

The slap of a flattened palm, an angry outburst, and a fisted hand appeared. Elf and Ira pulled Vygel Vintrusie into the space.

Henri tapped her spectacles. "Expand the wards."

The luminescent curtain reformed, trapping the two most powerful Mocendi in the Inner Universe.

Henri felt their combined power beating against the barrier. "Concentrate. We are strong enough."

Ira groaned. "I can't...I"

Henri looked at Brie. "It's time, niece."

Brie touched Ira's temple. Ari gasped and focused her attention. The wards strengthened.

Vygel gaped. "We've had both twins the whole time." His bulging eyes raked Henri's face. "I don't believe we've met."

"Allow me," Thorlu purred. "May I present the aunt of the Guardian of Myrrh and the great-aunt of our twins, Henrietta Avetlire."

Vygel's brows shot up. "No Renn?"

Thorlu shook his head.

Vygel pressed his colorless lips into a thin line. "It is time to stop playing games. Release us, or you will be sorry you interfered with The MasTer's Mocendi." With renewed energy, he fought the wards.

Thorlu closed his eyes and intensified his power. The wards trembled.

Henri called out, "Hold on."

Shyllee barked, then barked again. The hide y-hole disappeared. Tail wagging, she dashed toward a man emerging from the middle-night sky.

Relevart knelt and rubbed her ears. "Hello, girl." He straightened and held his staff high.

"Henrietta, it is good to see you. Hello, children. You can relax. I've got them."

Next to Brie, Esán sagged. She slipped an arm around him.

Thorlu marched forward and came to an abrupt halt. "You can't keep us against our will, Relevart."

Vygel remained quiet, his eyes resting on the figure of a man limping to Relevart's side. He murmured, "Wolloh Espyro. I should have known."

Wolloh met Vygel's indignant gaze with a disfigured smile. "Vygel Vintrusie, you're looking better than the last time we met."

The Mocendi struck the wards with a fist and growled. "I will win the battle this time, Espyro."

"We shall see." Wolloh planted his staff next to Relevart's.

A distant rumble brought a glint to Thorlu's eye. "Free us, VarTerel, or you will die at the hand of The MasTer."

Lightning tore the heavens in two and sent thunder reverberating across Mittkeer. Thorlu and Vygel fought harder. The wards wavered.

Relevart raised his staff. "Esán and Brie, on either side of Wolloh. Henri and Ari, join me. Elf in the middle. Desirol behind Elf. Shyllee, guard Desirol."

Henri took her place, pulled her spectacle from a pocket, and perched them on her nose. Billowing smoke rolled through the Land of No Time. Wings beating the smoke into nothing carried a band of Astican through the stars and blue-black sky.

The leader commanded, "Release The MasTer's Mocendi."

Relevart aimed the full power of Froetise at the wards, reinforcing their strength. "Take them if you can."

Seven Astican circled and then landed. Cherub-blue eyes scanned the line. The leader's laugh boomed. "VarTerel, you and your feeble group cannot hope to withstand the onslaught of my kind. We have destroyed many a VarTerel before you. And we will end your life here in your domain."

It unfurled massive wings. "Let the Mocendi go, and we will leave the children unharmed."

Relevart did not waver. "You will not harm what The MasTer deems important."

Wolloh's staff shot light into the night. A veil of stars and sky lifted. Almiralyn, with Corvus on one side and Somay on the other, formed a line behind Desirol. Torgin stepped in behind the Guardian with Nomed, Lenadi, and Teva behind him. At the back, Wodash od DerTah awaited his destiny.

The leader frowned. "The fight has become unfair. Give us the Mocendi. And we shall see who wins."

Relevart's steady gaze never faltered. "I will free the Mocendi to fight with two of my men. If my men win, Thorlu and Vygel are mine to punish, as the Order of Esprow demands. If the Mocendi win, we will not visit TreBlaya."

The leader took a step forward. "If The MasTer's Mocendi win, the children are ours."

"So be it." Relevart released the wards.

Thorlu and Vygel strode to the side of the Astican, their capes flaring. Ill will gleamed in their eyes.

Thorlu raised a scarred hand. "Teva Rivan, when I win, you will pay."

Vygel snarled, "Prepare for battle, fool."

Corvus and Somay strode to meet them. Sparks scattered around the four as their wards disintegrated and their DiMensioner's power fled.

Thorlu retreated. "You did not say that we must fight without our power, VarTerel."

Relevart shrugged. "Are you afraid, Thorlu Tangorra, to fight man to man?"

Fury in his eye, Thorlu held up his hand. "I wish to choose my weapon."

Relevart nodded.

A rapier materialized and glinted in the starlit atmosphere of Mittkeer. Corvus stepped forward, wielding a raven-black saber. Vygel, poised and ready to fight, sliced the air with the sharp-pointed blade of an épée.

Somay's eyes gleamed. "Looks like a toothpick I mighta whittled." The solid haft of a broadsword materialized in his hands. He hefted it with ease, sliced the air one direction and then the other, and grinned. "Now that's a blade!"

Vygel gaped. Bulging eyes flicked from the delicate slenderness of his weapon to the breadth and length of his opponent's. He licked pale, thin lips. "I c-c-can't fight that."

The VarTerel lifted his staff. "You made your choice, Mocendi. En garde!"

Somay took a menacing step. Vygel yelped and danced backward. The sound of metal on metal pierced the endless night.

Henri watched, her heart in her throat. Beside her, Wolloh and Relevart held the power of DiMensionery at bay.

Thorlu and Corvus fought with the prowess and concentration of trained warriors. Blade against blade, they parried one blow after the other. A slight hesitation impeded Thorlu's timing. Quick as a raven, Corvus lunged, plowed into his side, and knocked him flat on the star-sprinkled blue. Straddling the Mocendi's chest, he pressed the black blade to his throat. Thorlu froze. His eyes narrowed.

Vygel let out a squeak of dismay as the tip of Somay's weapon sliced a gash in his cheek. He inhaled a haggard breath, wiped blood from the cut, and attempted to dodge Somay's advance-lunge. His daintier épée bounced off the sturdiness of the broadsword and flipped into the air. With the agility of an athlete, Somay pivoted, caught it on the edge of his blade, and sent it flying out of reach. A quick side-step took him behind the shaken Mocendi. His arm encircling Vygel's neck left the man gasping for breath. With a foot jammed into the back of his leg, Somay forced him to his knees. Yelping like a wounded dog, Vygel struggled to stand.

Somay tightened his grip. "Be still or *die*."

Vygel Vintrusie, The MasTer's Mocendi, sagged. Behind him, the Astican muttered amongst themselves. Their leader growled over its shoulder. "Quiet, fools. Hold formation." It fixed its gaze on Relevart. "Release them. You have proven your power. We will take them and leave."

Relevart's expression remained grim. "Corvus, Somay, bring the Mocendi to me and step away."

Thorlu scrambled to his feet, smoothed his crumpled clothing, and stood tall and proud. Hard eyes glared above his firm jaw. A bruise forming beneath one eye was the only sign of battle. Vygel stepped to his side, blood smearing his face and dripping from a gash on his arm.

The Universal VarTerel hefted his staff. "You have defamed the statutes of the Arts of DiMensionery. As dictated by the Universal Order of Esprow and the Galactic Guardians of the Fourth Galaxy from the great Central Suns, the punishment for this offense demands banishment from your time period." He stepped back and pointed his staff at their mid-sections. "Witnesses, one and all, hear and remember." His words filled the vastness of Mittkeer.

> *"Banned and banished, send them to*
> *A time with lessons hard and true,*
> *Where challenges will redefine*
> *Twix good and evil in their mind."*

Light flashed from the end of the rowan staff. Vygel and Thorlu cannoned backward through Mittkeer. Shouts of anger and dismay faded as they grew smaller and smaller and vanished from sight.

Relevart addressed the Astican. "Your Mocendi did not win the battle as you expected. Return to TreBlaya. Tell The MasTer what has occurred and that we wish to visit in peace."

The leader unfurled its wings. "We will take you to The MasTer in pieces, VarTerel."

Seven Astican lifted into the night, calling to each other in a chorus of strident shrieks. One dropped, talons extended and cherub eyes projecting its fury.

Henri whispered, "ConDria, rise."

49

Myrrh & Der Tah

When Allynae joined Almiralyn in the Reading Room, excitement brightened her smile. Beside her, Wilith looked stunned. She offered a hand. "I have a lot to tell you and SparrowLyn. Wilith, please keep an eye on the fountain. Merrilea is resting and Elae is checking on Zugo. We won't be long."

The next instant, they arrived in his companion's quarters. Almiralyn's blonde beauty melted into Sparrow's brunette loveliness. Allynae brushed a stray chestnut tendril from her face, gathered her in his arms, and sighed. "Someday, it will just be us—you and me—with no need for Mira to intrude into our rare moments together." He held her at arm's length and grinned.

She stood on tiptoe and kissed him before pulling him down beside her on a cushioned bench. "Alli, you will never guess what Merrilea discovered. I am still trying to come to grips with what it means. I wish Almiralyn was here to help. She always knows how to untangle the mysterious. I'm an artist. My brain doesn't—"

He gathered her hands in his. "Why don't you just tell me what you learned? I can't help unless I understand what's up."

She took a long, calming breath and began.

"Merrilea found several pages regarding the disbanding and escape of the Eleo Preda from El Stroma. Some facts are pretty sketchy, but here goes. By the time Rayn, the activist leader, realized she and her followers could not survive the onslaught from across the sea, only three thousand Eleo Preda could make the journey beyond the DéCussate to the Inner Universe. A Pheet Adolean traitor packed the people aboard three slave ships headed for three different galaxies. Rayn and her followers remained behind. Their goal —to destroy the continent of El SyrTundi and the Pheet Adole. We already know they escaped in a small craft that took them to TreBlaya. What we have now discovered is that one of the slave ships brought refugees to our galaxy, and specifically to Clenaba Rolas, our solar system." She grew quiet.

Allynae frowned. "Is that all?"

Sparrow leaned forward, her brown eyes boring into his. "In Clenaba Rolas, three planets accepted Eleo Predian refugees. Alli. Roahymn, Tao Spirian, and..." She inhaled. "KcernFensia." Her exhaled breath brushed his cheeks.

"KcernFensia. Where did they settle?"

"In a rural area."

"Which continent?"

"I'm not sure. Merrilea said it was a small village surrounded by farmland." She furrowed her brow in concentration. "She called it Caleso."

"Caleso." He came to his feet and traversed the cave and back. "Sparrow, what do you know about Gerolyn's background?"

"Very little. I had always thought she was from Myrrh until Almiralyn told us differently. What about *your* family? Where are they from?"

He sat down and plucked at his mustache. "I need a chron circle in the research area. If what you have shared means what I think it means..."

Two long strides carried him to the entrance. He paused with his hand on the heavy curtain. "Well, are you coming?"

She laughed. "I'll come, but I must shape Almiralyn first."

"That's fine. I like my sister too. Let's go." He grinned, watched her shift, and offered his arm. "I suggest we walk to Tennisca like regular people. I could use some exercise and some time to think."

Allynae urged Almiralyn down the tunnel, his thoughts reviewing what she had shared and the ramifications if his conclusions were correct.

Wilith stared into Elcaro's Eye and muttered to himself. "Almiralyn told me to *watch* the fountain. I want to see Renn and Torgin." He frowned and rubbed his forehead. Years of following the rules warred with his desire to make his own choices.

Gripping the fountain's rim, he stared at the black of his hand resting on the pristine white of the alabaster bowl. *Black and white... My entire world is based on black and white, with no shades of gray.* His somber reflection stared up at him. A prominent forehead, wide nose, dark eyes, and full-lipped mouth set him apart from many of his co-PPP officials. *Why has it never occurred to me to trace my heritage, to search for my ancestral roots?* Again, he massaged his forehead. *I have access to the best library in this solar system.* A smile erased the serious official on the water's surface. A face filled with charm and intelligence gazed back at him, a face that reminded him of Torgin, of his son, whose summer green eyes were so like Renn's. His heart ached to see them both, to hold Renn, and to let Torgin know he loved his music.

He glanced back at the sanctuary door. *Almiralyn didn't say I could not ask Elcaro a question.* He squared his broad shoulders and stared into the rippling water. "Show me Renn Whalend and the Pentharian Yaro."

Rhythmic dripping from the statue's palms continued, then gradually ceased. A glimmer of light flashed at the bottom of the bowl. The sound of wind and rain filled the sanctuary.

In a small cove, rain drops pock-marked the water with tiny circles. Wind tossed small white caps over the surface, where a sailboat danced on its anchor chain.

The storm hit without warning. A deluge pounded the cabin and deck.

Wind howled overhead and changed direction on a whim. Small white-capped waves rocked *SeaBella*, carrying her one way and then the other.

In the galley, Renn fought to keep from throwing up. She swallowed the rising bile, threw an arm out to catch herself as the boat rolled, and cast an imploring gaze upward.

Bibeed slid onto the bench beside her and offered a tin mug. "Here. Drink this. It should help."

Renn gulped down the bitter fluid and shuddered. "What was that?"

Bibeed laughed. "Bitters and honey with a touch of my secret ingredient. Your stomach'll settle soon." She glanced at a porthole and frowned. "This storm is not caused by nature. Cove's pretty well protected. So, why's the wind blowing us around?"

Gregos clambered down the two stairs between the upper and lower cabins. "If not nature, then what?"

Yaro loomed behind him. "Or who? Is The MasTer's Reach stirring things up?"

Tamosh's head appeared above the dividing partition. "Maybe some vapor bubbled to the top."

Bibeed squinted and wrinkled her brow. "It's almost like the storm is protecting us. SeaBella is invisible from above and from the cove's entrance. Like a smoke screen." She grinned. "Or a storm screen."

Gregos caught Tamosh's eye. "Marji. Wondered how long she could stay away."

Renn frowned. "Marji?"

A rosy-cheeked woman with curly salt and pepper hair materialized in the galley. Her hazel eyes sparkled with good humor. Her wide smile wiped the chill from the cabin like a warm summer breeze. "Hello, Renn. I'm Marji Senndi." She nodded to Bibeed and Cayled. "Nice to meet you, Bibeed and Cay." Hands on hips, she gazed up at Yaro. "Haven't had the pleasure of meeting a Pentharian." She tapped her bottom lip with a finger. Triumph brightened her smile. "Oid eo daizo raa, Yaro."

The golden Pentharian bowed his head and touched his heart. "Oid eo daizo raa, Marji Senndi. I am honored to know you."

Gregos gave a huff of impatience.

She looked him in the eye. "Calm yourself, Greg. Relevart sent me. Nice boat, by the way." She smiled up at Tamosh. "Good work with the Reach. Now, I've news to share and plans to discuss." She sat on the bench and scooched in next to Bibeed.

The men squirmed around the table and sat down. Yaro remained standing.

Gregos regarded his sister. "Well, woman, Relevart must be pretty worried or ya'd still be keeping' an eye on Atkis."

The rain, which had grown less intense, suddenly beat down with a vengeance. A gust of wind rocked the boat. Renn paled.

Tamosh caught himself before he pitched off the end of the bench. "Why the storm?"

Marji waved a hand. The wind ceased its howling and the beat of the rain turned to a gentle patter. "A man at the portal had one of The MasTer's ampules. The storm's making sure The Reach didn't find you."

Gregos slapped his knee. "Knew it was your work. Besides The Reach, why'd Relevart send ya?"

"The Mocendi informed The MasTer that Renn is not in TreBlaya. The VarTerels are concerned about her journey to Myrrh. It's our job to get her there, and to keep the Mocendi confused about her whereabouts while we do."

Tamosh pulled at his goatee. "Do the men at the portal know?"

Marji shook her head. "They still believe that they're lookin' for a boy and a girl."

Renn peered around Bibeed. "How can you help, Marji?"

"I am what Trinugians call a Derrea. I see the future. Wolloh helped me to develop my skills in DiMensionery." She held up a hand and wiggled her fingers. They disappeared. "My particular gift is illusion." Her hand reappeared with rings on every finger. She blew on her hand, and the rings vanished. She smiled at Renn's look of astonishment.

Gregos jerked a thumb toward Yaro. "He went to look around. I'm bettin' between the two o' ya, there's a good plan."

A small smile brightened Marji's face. "Yaro, we need a place to anchor beyond the portal. What did you discover?"

"There are two such places within walking or flying distance." He described the situation.

Marji placed the palms of her hands together, intertwined her fingers, and gazed into the distance.

Dripping water broke the picture into pieces, leaving Wilith wishing for more.

In the research area, Sparrow and Allynae studied a map of KcernFensia. She had returned to her natural form. Merrilea rested in her quarters, Elae had gone to visit with Zugo, and Wilith stood watch in Veersuni. She sighed. Shifting shapes left her mentally and physically drained.

Allynae glanced up and put an arm around her. "You're doing a good job as Guardian, Sparrow. I know it's tiring, but it won't be for much longer."

The absent tap of his stylus drew her attention back to the map. "Which of the three continents did the Eleo Preda make their home?"

He smoothed the map and pointed. "At the time they arrived, if my dates are correct, DosKaram was the least populated continent on the planet. The number of refugees that arrived in KcernFensia was just over a harshad. One harshad and twenty, as I recall. At the request of the High Priestess of the Temple of Mahyinaeh, the government offered the refugees land along the southwestern coast with the caveat that they use their exceptional agricultural skills to develop it. Most of them accepted the offer. A small group petitioned for permission to farm on EeClarot, our largest continent. Again the High Priestess interceded. Four families took up residence in a coastal town called Caleso."

Sparrow thumbed through a book of birth records that lay beside the map. "You asked me if I knew Mother's family history. Are you thinking what I am thinking?"

"That your mother might be part Eleo Predian? The idea has occurred to me."

"How can we find her? We don't have her real name. She took AsTar from Standin when we moved to his farm in the Central Mountains."

Sparrow sat down next to him. His hand rested on a record book of births on the KcernFensian mainland. A name caught her eye. "Alli, let me see the ledger." She ran a finger down the page and frowned. *What was that name?*

Allynae looked over her shoulder. "What have you found?"

"Not sure." She sat back and closed her eyes. A memory surfaced.

The chair in Mira's kitchen faced the window. Sun poured in and patterned the floor with light. Karrew sat on his perch, grooming his feathers. Majeska curled up in her lap while her mother braided her hair. She was ten, bright-eyed, and torn between sadness and excitement. Her father was taking them to Thera to live in the Central Mountains. She loved Myrrh. "I don't want to live on Thera. I want to stay with Mira." Her mother kissed the top of her head, whispered a word in her ear, and tapped her forehead. "I put a secret in your mind. When you need it, it will surface." Two turnings later, they left Myrrh.

She examined the list again. One word jumped at her, one word—her mother's whispered secret.

Allynae's steady gaze calmed her sudden agitation. "It's alright, Sparrow. I'm here."

She drew an invisible line beneath a name. "My mother's surname is Dakarai."

Allynae read from a list entitled Eleo Predian Refugee Births. "Gerolyn Eleebanna Dakarai & Tissent Xan Dakarai born to Edina Eleebanna Dakarai and Xander Abadi Dakarai in the Eleo Predian colony of Caleso on the Continent of EeCarlot, KcernFensia." He held her close. "Your grandparents are full-blooded Eleo Preda, so is your mother. Our daughters are half."

She squirmed in his arms and cupped his stubbled chin in her hands. "Is that why The MasTer wants Ari and Brie?"

He gripped her shoulders and pulled her to him. His kiss left her breathless but did not erase the question.

"Well?"

"Sparrow, I don't know why she wants the girls. My best guess is that their heritage has something to do with it."

"And your heritage? What do you know about your ancestry? Have you ever met your grandparents?"

"Timon Clarot Nadrugia was my grandfather's name. It's KcernFensian. Our family goes back to the original colonists."

Sparrow frowned. "If your father was Timon Clarot, where did your middle name come from?"

It was Allynae's turn to frown. "I'm sure Walerain is a family name."

She walked to a case of birth ledgers and pulled two. "I'll look at one while you skim through the other." Lowering them to the table, she resumed her seat.

Allynae shrugged. "I don't mind looking, but we have other things to research."

Sparrow flipped through the pages in her ledger. "I don't expect any surprises, but I want to be sure for the girls." She began the laborious work of reading every name and date.

The soft patter of bare feet penetrated her concentration. With only seconds to spare, she assumed the Guardian's shape. Elae rounded the corner.

"Wilith would appreciate it if you joined him in Veersuni, Almiralyn. He's seen something that concerns him."

Slipping her notes between the pages of the ledger, she pushed back her chair and stretched. "Alli, want to stay or take a break?"

"I could use a different focus." He marked his place and followed her along the corridor of glass cases. "What do you suppose Wilith has seen?"

Almiralyn climbed the stairs to the Reading Room. "We're about to find out."

As they traversed the room, Wilith pulled open the door. "The fountain has grown quiet, but maybe it will show more to you, Mira." He stepped aside.

A chorus of howls echoed through Veersuni. A sonorous stream of notes erased them. Wilith hurried to the fountain. A Water ConDria hovered in front of a skyscape of middle-night stars.

Brielle's shift to the ConDria sent a chill of dread through Esán. He turned to Relevart. "She can't fight them all. We have to help her."

Bushy brows slammed together. "What do you suggest, boy?"

Ari joined them. "We need another ConDria."

Elf pointed. Seven Astican flew in an ever-decreasing circle around Brie. Relevart raised his staff and whistled a series of notes.

Dropping below the Astican, the ConDria swooped and glided over the group gathered around the VarTerel. Drops of water rained from her outstretched wings. Where they touched, changes began. Esán caught his breath as fluid coolness coursed over his body. Ari's yelp of delight preceded her shift. Elf pressed aqueous wings against the air and followed in the ConDria's wake. More water droplets fell.

Almiralyn began to shift. Teva ran forward, her face lifted. A drop ran down her cheek. The heavens echoed with the ConDrias' cries.

Seven Astican hovered, faces filled with hate. Brie streaked for the leader. It flew to meet her, inhaled, puckered its rosebud lips, and blew. Folding her wings, she plummeted through the glittering darkness of Mittkeer. A blast of scorching flames blazed past her into limitless time.

Esán raced straight for the Astican's back. Brie soared along its line of trajectory, aiming for its belly. Water enveloped it. A shriek of shock and pain shook Mittkeer. The screams grew louder, diminished to gurgling, and ceased. A final gurgle sent the creature plunging into forever with no remembrance that it had ever been.

Henri observed the battle, entranced by the beauty of six magnificent ConDria. On either side of her, Wolloh and Relevart focused their combined power to keep them in flight. A fluid beak clamped around the throat of an Astican. Water poured down its scaled chest. A cry of pain ended in a smothered silence. Another Astican fled in the tear's direction, the form of a small bird replacing the enormous body. Nomed shifted. The great horned owl swooped into action, caught the bird in its talons, and crushed its tiny bones. Somay's blue heron joined the fray. Bodies of brown and shimmering blue wove in and out, dodging, dipping, and banking to avoid collisions or to close in tighter. Karrew ascended into their midst, his sharp beak finding its mark.

Three Astican attempted to escape certain death. Owl and heron blocked their retreat. Two ConDria closed in from behind. A panicked backward glance sent one Astican into the shape of a blackbird. Fear hurtled it toward the tear. The long beak of the heron snapped shut around it. The tiny body fell into the abyss of sky and stars.

Wings of water wrapped the others in an embrace of death. A chorus of shrieks sliced the air. Two Astican shriveled and vanished. Only two remained to continue the fight.

A ConDria faltered, swooped lower, and landed. Esán collapsed at Wolloh's feet. Somay flew to his side, returned to Human form, and knelt beside him.

Above, two ConDria cut between the remaining Astican, trapping one within their fluid wings. Twisting and thrashing, it struggled against wave upon wave of water until its shrieks ceased and it dissolved into nothing. The last of the seven streaked toward the tear. The raven and the great horned owl gave chase.

Relevart raised his staff. "Let it go."

Nomed and Corvus materialized beside him. Froetise glowed at the tip of his staff. A shaft of light shot after the escaping Astican, sliced its wingtip as it exited Mittkeer, and, like a welder's torch, mended the rent in the fabric of time.

Three ConDria touched down and shifted. Brie ran to Esán's side. Almiralyn shook the water from her hair and hugged her cousin. Lenadi, who had remained at Desirol's side, joined them. Elf materialized, a broad grin on his face.

One ConDria remained in flight.

Henri leaned down and tapped Brie's shoulder. "We'll care for Esán. This is your only opportunity to fly with Ari."

Brie's instantaneous shift left Henri brushing dampness from her face and hair. The Water ConDria soared upward.

Esán regained consciousness, and Somay assisted him to sitting. Torgin and Elf moved to Desirol's side. Everyone gazed upward.

Henri lifted spectacles to her eyes and followed the two ConDrias in their joyous cavorting. "Another gift of The Unfolding."

Relevart smiled, his eyes never leaving the shimmering creatures. "And there is much, much more to come."

That Ari could shape a ConDria had never crossed Brie's mind. The fact that Relevart held her twin to the shape and gave them time to share the experience of water and flight filled her with exhilaration.

Ari's fluid blue eyes met hers with so much love, understanding, and wonder that Brie thought she might burst. In tandem, they created shimmering loops and circles. Brie burst into song. Ari's alto voice harmonized perfectly with her twin's sweet soprano. Below them, Torgin pulled out his flute and began to play. A melody of pure joy accompanied them as they soared around each other in interweaving patterns. Wing tip to wing tip, they rocketed straight up, made a loop, and side-by-side nosedived through the star-spangled night of Mittkeer. Flying in opposite directions, they soared in a wide arc, met at the top center, and swooped lower. The deep, swishing wha wha wha of their powerful wings filled the air. Wind whipped their companions' hair and garments and brought looks of astonished delight to their faces.

Relevart raised his staff. Torgin played a final trembling note. As the ConDrias landed, wings wafting and wide, Ari and Brie flashed free of their shifted forms. Tears streaming down their faces, they fell into each other's arms.

Ari wiped shimmering droplets from her cheek. "Now I understand why you love the ConDria so much." She threw her arms around Relevart. "Thank you!"

Surprise brightened his eyes. "You are most welcome, Arienh."

Brie knelt and grasped Esán's hand. "Are you alright?"

His smile, though weak, warmed her. "I'm just tired." He squeezed her hand. "The ConDria is wonderful."

A sharp bark cut through Mittkeer. A growl followed. Desirol stumbled forward. "I can't hold it...I..."

Lenadi reached his side first and put an arm around his waist. Desirol clung to him, gasping. Relevart touched his temple. Everyone gathered around as Lenadi lowered him to the ground.

Fear for her friend throbbed in Brie's chest.

Trembling drops spilling into the water erased the image. Four pairs of eyes remained fixed on the alabaster bowl.

Alli released a deep, noisy breath. "Weren't our girls gorgeous? What a treat for Ari to shape a ConDria."

Elae's gaze lifted to Almiralyn's face. "I knew something was different about you."

Sparrow materialized. "Merrilea is in Ephos. Please fetch her, Elae, then I'll explain."

Elae nodded and hurried from Veersuni.

Wilith sank onto a bench, folded his hands, and stared at the floor.

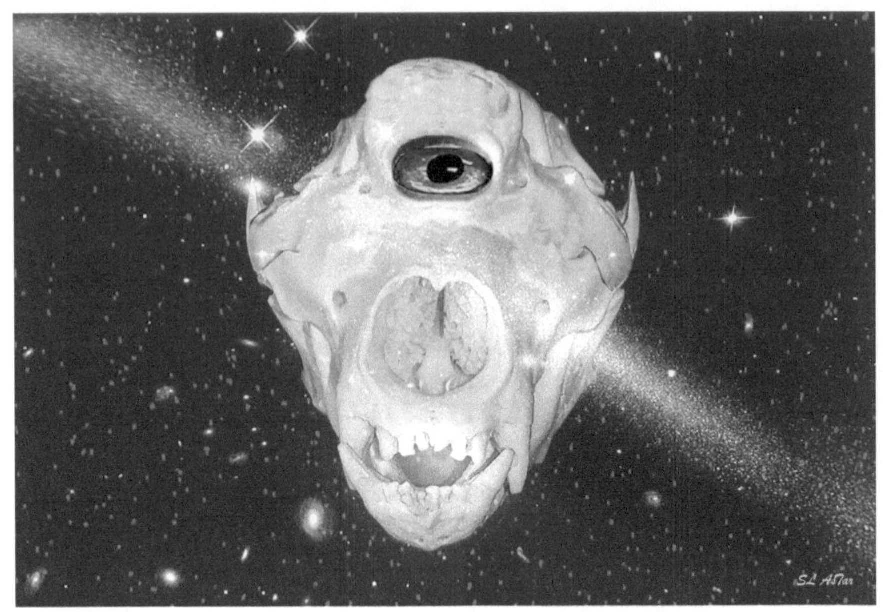

50
DerTah

Yaro stood the watch on the deck of *SeaBella*. From the stern, he observed the three moons of DerTah. *Tri-Nular, DerTahan's call it, when all three light the heavens.* His gaze traveled the arc from the pearly crescent in the east to the glacier blue Calegri at its zenith to Fasfro's' saffron yellow orb where it kissed the western horizon. Surrounding them, stars glistened. With the end of Marji's storm, the world had regained its calm beauty.

Marji—an interesting woman. The plan they had developed satisfied his warrior instincts and used her gifts in ways she could embrace. They would leave at first light, an illusion of invisibility cloaking their journey. In the meantime, all was quiet aboard *SeaBella*. Sleep had come easily. He needed little and thus he stood the watch that would take them to dawn.

The slow passing of time gave his mind time to question. *What is happening in the desert? Is Voer still with the Largeen Joram? Stee, Jeet, Yuin, where are you and what adventures enrich your lives? Heart-brother, are you safe?*

The hatch slid open, and Marji climbed on deck. She smiled. "You're a noisy thinker, Yaro." She shut the hatch.

"I try to see the future, Marji Senndi. It has been too long since I have been with my comrades. I worry about my heart-brother. I am ready for this Unfolding to achieve its goal. My home calls."

She joined him and leaned on the railing. "Your clan awaits your return. If I understand correctly, few are hatched under Nep Rin Tese, the sign of the serpent, and even fewer carry the wisdom of the water snake as you do." She paused and tipped her head to see him better. "At your next hatching ceremony, it will be time for you to assume your duties as a Nep Rin Tese Venerat. How do you feel about leaving your life as a warrior behind?"

Yaro met her questioning gaze. "I am a good fighter, but I have never embraced it with the zeal of my comrades." He tracked the descent of Calegri and thought about the role he would soon play. "My heart is more gentle. Although I will miss my warrior brothers, I look forward to the solitude of the Venerat, to the time when I may serve my clan in a new way."

Marji nodded and raised her eyes to the heavens. "Lunule rises high. Soon it will be time to wake everyone." She offered her palm. "I am honored to fight by your side, Yaro."

He took her small hand between his. "Een dimo a den, Marji Senndi. The honor is mine." He bowed his head and pressed her palm to his heart.

Gregos, clearing his throat, made them both turn.

Marji grinned. "Morning, brother."

"Mornin', Marji. Mornin', Yaro. Time to get to work. Bibeed put some breakfast on the table in the galley. Soon as ya've eaten, we'll set sail."

Marji smiled at Yaro and climbed below.

"Your sister is a good woman."

Gregos stared after her. "Lucky ta have her aboard. Ya ready?"

With a chorus of good mornings, Tamosh, Cayled, and Bibeed clambered on deck.

Yaro shaped a laridae, soared through the bottleneck, and explored the strait. Nothing raised an alarm. He swooped back into the cove and materialized next to Gregos.

Marji and Renn sat at the stern. Bibeed manned the watch perch.

Tamosh and Cayled were ready to haul the anchor and hoist the sails. At a sign from Gregos, Marji stood and recited:

"Illusion surround us; hide us from sight.
Until I release you, conceal our might.
Nothing sees in, yet we can see out
To follow our heading with nary a doubt."

With the raising of her arms, a filmy curtain hugged *SeaBella*, formed a dome overhead, and faded into invisibility. She lowered her arms. "It's done."

Gregos shouted orders. Chain rattled and disappeared below deck, and Tamosh secured the anchor for sea travel. The sails caught the wind, sending the boat gliding through the water and into Triple Moon Strait.

Solemn and watchful, Renn sat in the stern with her hands clasped in her lap.

Yaro joined her. "You are quite somber, Renn Whalen."

She stared at her hands. "They are heading into danger because of me." Her gaze lifted to his face. "I wish it were not so."

"It is their choice to protect you. Like me, it is an honor."

"But, Yaro, what if someone gets hurt or..." She shuddered. "Dies? How will I live with that?"

"Be *now*, Renn Whalen. Living in the future steals from this beautiful moment, and it will not come again."

She sighed and tipped her chin up to catch the wind in her face.

He stared ahead, trying to follow his own advice.

A grim-faced Abarax marched along the corridor, leather wingtips dragging on the black ice floor. The MasTer would dislike its news. It paused at her door and stroked rosebud lips with a talon claw. Gathering its courage, it knocked.

A harsh voice called out. "Enter, Abarax."

Inside The MasTer's room, it again paused, awaiting her command. It watched her from beneath thick, long lashes, sitting on her throne, staring at her hand.

"When I was young, my hands were smooth-skinned and strong, not a mass of veins, wrinkles, and aching joints." She gripped a mirror with clumsy fingers, lifted it, and frowned at the reflection. "Once upon a time on the planet of El Stroma, I was beautiful. So beautiful, in fact, that the RomPeer coveted me for his personal harem."

Unbidden, Abarax took a step forward. "How did you escape him, my master?"

She laid the mirror aside and raised sunken eyes to its visage. "I, Abarax, became a man—learned to fight, to make decisions, to take what I wanted like a man. You are the only one who knows my true gender." She pursed wrinkled lips. "Unless the Guardian of Myrrh has discovered it."

Accusation saturated the room, soaked into the black curtains, hovered in the space between them. Abarax froze. Cherubic eyes did not blink. The inhale and exhale of its breath made no sound.

A long, dry cough wracked her body. Abarax did not move. She sagged against the back of the throne, sucking in shallow breaths. Another bout of coughing brought blood to her lips. She wiped it away on the sleeve of her robe and struggled to remain upright.

"You don't look happy, Astican. Tell me what makes you quake before you have even made your report."

It bowed. "I hardly know where to begin."

Another tortuous cough left her gasping. Abarax filled her chalice. "Drink, MasTer." Its head remained bowed until she set the goblet beside her.

A cruel gleam lit her eyes. "Tell me of your friends, Thorlu and Vygel. Have they found the children?"

"Thorlu and Vygel are gone, MasTer." It strove to hide its delight.

"*Gone*? What on TreBlaya do you mean by *gone*?"

"As you instructed, I sent seven Astican into Mittkeer to intercept the VarTerels."

Her hand went to her throat. "VarTerels-s-s?" The final 's' hissed through the room.

Abarax cringed at her tone. "We have learned that the Galactic Guardians raised Relevart to the level of Universal VarTerel and Wolloh

Espyro to VarTerel of the Inner Universe. They are both here—in Mittkeer."
It rushed on. "The children captured Thorlu and Vygel. The VarTerels
teleported them into the Land of All Time and No Time."

She smacked the arm of the throne. The goblet clattered to the floor.
"And your band of Astican—" A cough cut her question short.

It waited until she regained her composure. "Only one Astican returned
from Mittkeer, MasTer. It told me Relevart banished Thorlu and Vygel to
another time. All the Astican, except the one that returned, are dead."

Using the arms of the throne, she pushed to standing, eyes riveted to his
face. "We still have Renn Whalen?"

It took several steps back and kept its eyes on the floor. "It appears we
never had her. An elderly woman took her place."

Rasping breath changed to a yowl of fury. El Soasi rocked on its
foundations. Abarax dropped to one knee and covered its head. When quiet
returned, it peeked from beneath its lids.

A steel-hard gaze bored into it. "You will bring the VarTerels to me. And
the children. And the elderly woman. You will do so with such speed that I
will hardly miss your absence. You will—"

A cough ripped up from her guts, bringing with it blood that dripped
down her chin and spattered the front of her robe. She touched it, stared at
her bloodied fingers, and back at Abarax. "Bring me Relevart." A gurgling
sound choked the breath from her tired body. She slipped to the floor,
unconscious.

Relevart knelt beside Desirol's prone body. "The time has come to rid
the boy of the Mindeco." He looked at Esán. "We need your power
to join with ours. Do you have the strength?"

"I do, Relevart." Somay helped him to his feet and put a supporting arm
around his shoulders.

"Once we remove him from the body, the Mindeco will first seek a new
one to inhabit." He waved the death shadow forward. "This is your time,
Wodash od DerTah. If you overpower the Mindeco to save the life of this
boy, your stay in the land of death will end."

Wodash hovered closer. "And will my family forgive me?"

"You will be with your wife and daughter, but only if they open their hearts to you."

The death shadow seemed to grow smaller. His sad expression transitioned to utter hopelessness.

Torgin looked at the devastated face. "When we first met, Wodash, I could not see beyond my fear of you. Now I am not afraid. I see you as a friend. Your wife and daughter will not turn you away." He touched his heart. "I feel the truth of this."

A spark of hope returned to the death shadow's pallid face.

Desirol moaned. Relevart placed a hand on his shoulder. "Almiralyn, on his heart's side; Teva, opposite. Arienh and Elf, at his head with Henrietta. Have Efillaeh ready. Torgin and Esán, at his feet with Brie between you. When we help him stand, he will face you. Place your left hands on his heart. Wolloh, behind Brielle. Corvus, protect Almiralyn. Lenadi, join Teva. Nomed and Somay, with me at his back. Shyllee, heel."

Everyone moved to their assigned positions.

"We are forming a wall through which Rikell cannot pass. When I give the word, Somay and Nomed will help Desirol stand. If the Mindeco tries to exit his body before I call him forth, Arienh, you will insert Efillaeh at the base of the occipital and keep it there. When I tell you to remove it, step into line with Somay. Those of us at the back will form an exit tunnel. The moment the Mindeco steps free. Almiralyn and Teva will close the gap behind him, blocking his retreat. Wodash, be ready."

Relevart released Desirol's shoulder and stepped away.

Desirol tried to hold his fear in check. His mind told him he fought a losing battle. His heart, the Remembering Stone, and Marji's pouch reminded him he could—would—win.

The Mindeco surfaced, squeezed the air from his windpipe, and gripped the blue velvet pouch. His eyes flew open. A tortured exhale hissed through Mittkeer. Relevart tapped Desirol's chest. The beast retreated. Somay and Nomed hoisted Desirol to his feet and held him steady. A circle of bodies closed around him. Hands pressed against his chest.

Again, the creature stirred. Its fists beat against his ribcage. Desirol felt his jaw tense and protrude. His mouth opened in a scream that was not his. His brain throbbed. Tears streamed from unblinking eyes. The creature stilled. Then an explosion of movement jerked and twitched and pitched him from side to side. The muffled sound of Relevart's voice, a sharp sting at the back of his neck, and the battle came to an abrupt halt.

Desirol blinked. Brie, Esán, and Torgin filled his line of vision. Wolloh stood behind them. The tiniest hope flared. The Mindeco rebelled; then grew quiet. Desirol knew it waited for its chance.

The words of the Universal VarTerel began as a whisper and grew louder. One by one, voices added their strength.

> *"Mindeco from Trutore, RewFaar*
> *Release this boy without a scar.*
> *With healthy body and mind secure,*
> *Leave him healed, alive, and pure."*

The sacred knife withdrew. Desirol gasped. Piercing pain crumpled him to his knees. A stabbing explosion out the back of his head left him shattered and shaking. The pounding in his brain blurred his vision. Bodies encircled him, caught him as the world went black.

Ari had removed Efillaeh and backed away. When the Mindeco burst into Mittkeer, her first instinct was to run. Her second—to freeze. His single eye frantically searched, Ari felt sure, for another body. He lumbered forward, his gaze fixed on Relevart. His massive bear jowls opened in an ear-slitting howl. He crouched. Relevart held his ground. The Mindeco lunged. At the last instant, Relevart stepped aside.

Wodash od DerTah caught the Mindeco in a two-armed embrace. Cold, white eyes peered into the single dark eye of his salvation. Rikell's enormous fists plummeting the frigid body came away covered with frost, then ice, and finally shattered into shards that melted as they hit the blue of Mittkeer. His struggle to break away froze him bone by bone until only his head remained mobile. He thrust his pointed jawbones into the neck of the death shadow. Two creatures flashed in and out of each other, in and out of time, into focus and out. Relevart and Wolloh lifted their staffs. A ball of light formed over the heads of the battling creatures. A word from the VarTerels and it enveloped the Mindeco and death shadow in bright white light. Blinded watchers covered their eyes. Another word and the light faded. Ari peeked between her fingers. Gentle rain fell to the ground in a crystal, clear pool. The shape of a kneeling man solidified. Sad eyes moved from one face to the other and came to rest on Relevart. A heavy sigh shook the man's body. "Thank you."

The Universal VarTerel touched the tip of his staff to the water. The pool shrank and disappeared, taking the man with it.

Ari clutched the sacred knife, found she had forgotten to breathe, and inhaled a huge gulp of air. She gazed up at Relevart. "Where is the Mindeco?"

"I returned him to the Trutore Mountains on RewFaar. He will not remember his time here."

Ari sighed, studied the sacred blade, and slipped it into its sheath.

Brie clasped Desirol's hand and examined the pale face. A subtle brain scan showed nothing. Neither Desirol nor the Mindeco remained.

"I can't feel him at all." She moved to make room at Desirol's side.

Relevart knelt and laid a hand on his heart. "Desirol is here, but we must help him return." He removed the Remembering Stone and handed it to Brie. Marji's pouch went into his pocket. "Elf, what do you see?"

"Writhing black cords searching for a place to attach."

Relevart nodded. "His attachments to the past. Everyone but Arienh and Elf form a circle around him. Ari, Elf will tell you where the cords are; you will cut them away."

Brie slipped her hand into Esán's. Henri and Almiralyn joined them. Elf drew Ari down next to him. Methodically, they moved around the still body. He pointed. She cut. Small snake-like cords appeared, hit the star-speckled atmosphere of Mittkeer, and vanished. At last, he helped Ari to her feet.

"We're done." Ari slipped Efillaeh into its scabbard.

Relevart motioned Elf into the circle. "Ari and Brie, you carry the imprint of Desirol's family. Please hold the Remembering Stone together. Blank your minds. It will find what it needs to return."

Brie tipped the stone into her palm. Ari covered it with hers.

Relevart tapped their hands with Froetise. "Torgin, please put the compass on his heart." He waited until it was done. "Twins, when I tell you to, place the stone on his head and step away. Esán, you know his mind better than anyone else. Kneel and place your hands on either side of his head. You will know when to open your mind to his." He took Marji's pouch from his pocket, set it at Desirol's feet, and nodded. Brie placed the Remembering Stone at the center of his forehead and joined the circle.

Wolloh limped to stand at Desirol's side, opposite Relevart. They began to recite,

> *"Compass of Os-tra-dio*
> *Help this boy return to whole*
> *With the stone, please guide him hither*
> *Do not allow his soul to wither.*
>
> *Shape a path of memories*
> *That tie him back to his stories.*
> *Return him to us filled with life,*
> *Leaving behind his recent strife."*

The compass needle began to spin, a blur of gold above the face. The Remembering Stone glowed. Tendrils of cobalt blue light encircled Desirol, traveled up Esán's arms, and spun a web around his head.

Esán's labored breath, the only sound in Mittkeer, made Brie wish she could take his place. Nothing else moved. All eyes were fixed on Desirol Telisnoe. Wolloh and Relevart laid their staffs on either side of him. The crystals in their tips gave off a slight glow.

Esán's breathing slowed. The blue light faded. His eyelids fluttered open in a wide-eyed stare.

Brie started forward. Relevart shook his head. She remained in the circle.

Desirol's first hint that he had not died—a subtle tingling in his chest —brought with it a tiny spark of hope. He attempted to compose a thought around this sensation. It faded from his consciousness. Something touched his forehead. A vague memory of a similar event misted into nothing. Slight pressure on the side of his head sent a jolt of energy coursing through him. The familiar touch ended any doubt that he lived. His heart thumped. Blood pulsed through his veins.

Memories leaked into his mind like water into an empty glass—the gentle face of a woman with chestnut hair and a beautiful smile... *Maman!* A man with flaming red hair... *Papa!* Icy blue eyes sent goosebumps racing over his skin. *Nissasa.* Memories flowed faster, poured one after the other until he felt as though he were swimming in a sea of people and events. *Wolloh, Relevart, the twins, Torgin, Shyllee, Elf, Esán...* He caught his breath. *Esán!* He focused his attention on his arms, laughed with delight when they moved, wrapped his fingers around slender wrists, heard a quick intake of breath. His eyes opened to an upside-down face hovering above him. "Esán." He exhaled a long breath and let his arms fall to his sides.

The hands moved from his head. The sound of shuffling... He laughed. *I can hear!*

Esán's face came into focus, right side up. "Welcome back, Des."

He wanted to sit. His line of vision filled with Wolloh's odd face. Again, he laughed. *Not odd—beautiful.*

"Lie still, young friend. The Mindeco is gone, but he took his toll. Let your body and mind catch up with each other."

Wolloh moved away. The twins took his place. He furrowed his brow. How to tell them apart? Memory filled the gap.

He whispered, "Say something."

One twin gave him an impish grin. "You sure scared us."

The deep voice made him smile. "You're Ari. I know by your voice." A wave of pride surged. "I remembered."

She laughed.

Brie leaned down and kissed his cheek. "I'm glad you're back."

Torgin appeared next to Esán. "Hello." He held up the compass. "Ostradio helped to bring you back. Guess you can hold it whenever you want now."

Relevart loomed over him. "Help him stand. We are about to have company. Don't leave his side. Wolloh, beside me. Everyone else behind us and stay close."

Desirol struggled to sitting. Torgin and Esán hoisted him to his feet. A rush of blood to his head made him stagger forward. Strong arms caught him. He glanced from side to side. Corvus and Nomed held him steady.

I am surrounded by friends and the Mindeco is gone. I am safe for the first time— He gasped.

The curved, black blade of a sword sliced through the middle-night sky.

51
Myrrh

Allynae put his arm around Sparrow. "I'm so sorry. I didn't mean to reveal your secret."

She sighed. "I'm actually glad. I'm not very good at artifice and very uncomfortable with deceiving people I care about."

Merrilea entered Veersuni ahead of Elae. "You need me, Sparrow?"

Wilith moved to make room on his bench.

Sparrow stepped away from Allynae. "Please sit down, and I'll explain."

Merrilea looked puzzled. "Explain?"

Almiralyn appeared in Sparrow's place. Sparrow reappeared. "Relevart took Almiralyn with him to help the children. He asked me to take her place and not to tell anyone except Alli. I am asking you to keep my secret. I apologize for not trusting you."

Elae gave her a quick hug. "You're doing a good job."

Merrilea frowned. "When will Almiralyn be back?"

Wilith stared into space. "The question is, will she be back at all?"

Allynae cleared his throat. "Something's happening in the fountain."

Sparrow hurried to his side. Wilith, Merrilea, and Elae gathered around the bowl.

An aerial view of a coastline slid by on the water's surface. Inland, a large town, reflected light from the late morning sun and tossed it skyward. Beyond it, the shoreline curved into a shallow bay where a fishing trawler sat at anchor. A rickety dock with a dinghy suggested the occupants of the boat had gone ashore. Further still, the fountain zoomed in on a small cove and steadied.

Wilith leaned closer. "Where—"

"Look." Elae pointed.

As though a curtain was being drawn, *SeaBella* slowly inched into view.

On shore, a woman with salt and pepper hair lowered her arms. "There you go."

A laridae swooped in for a landing and Yaro appeared. "They're all at the portal, except the captain of the fishing trawler. He's onboard his boat."

Gregos Senndi put an arm around the woman. "You're sure you want to do this, Marji? We can figure another way."

"Of course, I'm sure." Marji's bright laugh eased the tension, suffocating the group. Bibeed grinned. Renn lost the nervous expression she had worn as *SeaBella* became fully visible. Cayled remained somber. Yaro studied Marji with a slight curve to his lips.

Tamosh hugged her. "Good girl, sis."

Gregos scrutinized the tall Pentharian. "You're sure you can fly through the illusion, Yaro?"

"I watched four men walk in and out of it. We'll be fine."

Marji regarded her brothers. "Don't get yourselves shot. I expect you both to be healthy and alive when I see you next."

Gregos checked his rifle. "We won't start trouble unless they do. Six of them. Three of us." He shrugged. "We can take 'em."

Bibeed set the butt of her air rifle on the ground. "Four of us." She patted a pouch at her waist. "Yaro gave me darts dipped in his stun serum. Besides, I'm a great shot."

Cayled managed a small grin. "She's better then great, Gregos. Wouldn't leave her behind if I was you."

Gregos gave her an appraising look. "Do ya shoot as well as ya sail?"

She shouldered her rifle. "Better."

He looked at Yaro. "Your serum… It'll knock 'em out for how long?"

"A turning plus, Captain."

Gregos grinned. "Good. Bring Marji back safe, ya hear?"

"I'll bring her as soon as I can. Be vigilant, my friend. We won't make the run for the portal until you have their complete attention. Give us time to reach the other side of the illusion." He nodded to the women. "You had better make your farewells."

Renn hugged the brothers and Cayled. "Thank you for everything. Please be careful."

Bibeed caught her up in a big hug. "Take care of yourself, Renn Whalend. Don't forget us."

Renn brushed a tear from her cheek. "I will never forget you."

Gregos chambered a cartridge. "Let's get this done."

Yaro shaped a vulture. Gregos and Tamosh helped Renn and then Marji to climb on his back.

A soft coolness settled around him.

Cayled shook his head. "Marji, you're something else. Can't see ya at all."

On Elcaro's surface, the group grew smaller. Landscape took over the image.

As though seen through Yaro's eyes, treetops came into view. Nestled amongst them, three small tents surrounded a campfire, where a man sat on an upturned bucket cleaning his weapon. Another knelt nearby, washing out an iron kettle in a narrow stream. The men from the boat sat on a dead tree trunk in deep conversation. The remaining two stood watch.

Yaro's vulture form landed on the top of the hill opposite the portal; the women dismounted. He materialized beside them. "Tell your brothers we're in place, Marji."

Her eyes narrowed. "It's done. They're on the move." She inclined her head, her concentration complete.

Yaro's tail switched back and forth. He squinted into the distance. "I wish I could see what you see, sister of Gregos."

A picture flashed in his mind. Beside him, Renn gasped. "I see them."

Marji nodded.

The image on the fountain became indistinct. At the center, a small circle of green began to spread and to sharpen.

Gregos came into focus, then Tamosh, Bibeed, and Cayled. Leaving Tamosh hidden in a copse of trees, Gregos and the others crept up the side of a ridge and spread out near the top. Below, six men went about the various tasks required to run a well-ordered camp. Gregos' goal—to draw them into the woods and away from the portal. He figured they'd leave two men on guard. Bibeed caught his eye and pointed upward. He raised a hand in response. With the skill of someone much younger and lighter, she climbed a tree, found a sturdy branch, and disappeared into autumn golds and reds.

At his signal, Cayled let out a muffled yell and scrambled down the ridge toward the small cove. In camp, the men grouped together. Two trotted away, seeking who caused the yell. From the trees where Tamosh hid, a gunshot echoed through the morning. The remaining men grew more agitated. Two grabbed weapons and skulked toward the copse of trees.

Once they were behind him, Gregos crept closer to the camp. The MasTer's men stood guard on either side of the portal, their attention fixed on the woods. Circumventing the gateway, Gregos worked his way around to the front side. The snap of a twig shouted a warning. In one movement, he swung around, plowed into his assailant, and sent him crashing to the ground. Gregos ducked the butt of a rifle. His fist connected with the man's chin. A blow to the shoulder knocked Gregos sideways. The man lunged, caught Gregos around the hips, and sent them head over heels down an incline. The muffled sound of fists finding their mark mixed with their grunts and groans. Gregos landed a blow to the man's windpipe. He went limp beneath him. A shadow fell across them. The muzzle of a rifle nestled at the base of Gregos' skull.

His assailant growled, "Don't even breathe."

A shot fired. The man's hand flew to his neck. He groaned and toppled, unmoving.

Water in the fountain frothed blood red, eradicating the image. Sparrow snapped her fingers. A new picture gradually formed.

Renn's eyes grew round in a face gone pale. "Not..."

Marji shook her head. "Let's go, Yaro. No time to waste."

The moment the Pentharian's vulture flashed into being, Marji urged Renn forward. "Hurry. We got company."

The tall Spanilman Yaro had described as the leader lumbered up the hillside, eyes squinted, intently searching.

Scrambling onto his back, Renn settled between Yaro's wings and reached back for Marji. Their hands clasped.

"Don't move. I know you're there."

Renn's frantic gaze fastened on the rifle pointed in their direction.

Marji called softly. "You're still invisible, Yaro. Go!" Her grip released.

Yaro lifted into the air and flew straight for the portal.

Below, Marji became visible and sprinted for cover. The man captured her in his sights. She vanished as two shots fired simultaneously. He jerked sideways and fell. She appeared behind a tree, her gaze glued to the portal. Around it, the illusion shimmered and vanished. Renn and Yaro were safely on their way.

In Veersuni, Allynae watched Yaro and Renn become visible as they entered the portal. Flashes of color streaked the water's surface. The image went to black.

Wilith gripped the rim with trembling hands. "Does this mean she made it?" He looked at Sparrow. "Please tell me she is safe."

Sparrow laid a hand on his. "They made it into the portal. Nothing suggests they didn't make it to Fera Finnero."

Frowning, Wilith rubbed his forehead. "It will show us more. I know it will. It has to."

The door to Veersuni flew open. Across the fountain from him, Merrilea broke into a wide smile. Allynae's mustache tilted around a lopsided grin.

Wilith glanced over his shoulder, pivoted, and took an awkward step forward. The next instant, Renn was in his arms, her head pressed against his chest, her breath warming his heart. "Oh, Wilith, I thought I would never see you again." She hugged him harder and then smiled up at him. "Aren't you going to say anything?"

"I..." He glanced around and realized the others had slipped away. She stood on tiptoe, placed her hands on his damp cheeks, and kissed him. Surprised, he smiled down at her. "You've changed."

She laughed, "So have you. Sparrow has promised us time to catch up later. Come and meet Torgin's heart-brother." She pulled him toward the door.

He stopped her, lifted her to eye level, and kissed her one more time.

Sparrow led the exit from Veersuni. Yaro gazed over the heads of his companions and smiled. Voer bowed, hand on heart. The two Humans with them turned. Her mother waved and linked arms with a tall, dignified man in a RewFaaran uniform. Nervousness fluttering in the pit of her stomach, Sparrow reached for Allynae. He took her hand. With him by her side, she made the longest walk of her life and stopped a short distance from her parents.

Her mother looked so different—more self-assured—glowing with happiness. Gerolyn opened her arms. "It is wonderful to see you."

They hugged. Gerolyn held her at arm's length. "The role of Guardian of Myrrh suits you."

Sparrow laughed. "It's only until The Unfolding is complete, Mother. What made you come to Myrrh?"

Gerolyn motioned Lorsedi Telisnoe to join them. Sparrow tensed. Allynae rested a hand on her back. His presence gave her courage to gaze up at the chiseled features, the red hair, the brown eyes so like the twin's.

"Hello, SparrowLyn, it is a pleasure to meet you at last. You are every bit as lovely as your mother said you were." His deeply accented voice carried assurance and authority.

Sparrow offered her hand. "I am glad to meet you, Lorsedi."

He took it between his strong ones. "SparrowLyn, I hope that when

The Unfolding reaches its conclusion, we can spend time together." He released her hand as Wilith and Renn emerged from Veersuni and traversed the length of the room to where Voer and Yaro talked in quiet voices.

Sparrow caught Elae's eye. The young priestess slipped into Veersuni and closed the door.

Yaro smiled at Renn and acknowledged Wilith with the bow of his head. "I am honored to meet the father of Torgin and mate of Renn Whalend."

Wilith, looking slightly taken aback, held out his hand, palm up. "I do not know how to greet you in your language, but I intend to learn. Thank you for your care of my companion and my son."

Sparrow introduced Merrilea to Gerolyn and Lorsedi, spoke briefly to Voer and felt a sense of relief when Elae appeared in the sanctuary doorway. She addressed the group gathered around her. "I believe they need us in Veersuni."

She slipped her hand into Allynae's and led the way. Once inside, everyone gathered around the fountain. She studied each face. It was a large group and a diverse one. Her instincts told her those who needed to be present were. She gazed into the bowl. The glitter of stars appeared on the glassy surface.

The light from Relevart's staff glinted off the black blade, slicing through the fabric of Mittkeer. Behind the VarTerels and Henrietta, Brie's grip on Esán's hand tightened. Somay remained close to his son's side. Next to her, Torgin clutched the flute case. Elf stood next to him with a protective arm around Ari. Corvus and Nomed continued to support Desirol. Almiralyn, Teva, and Lenadi formed a rear guard. Shyllee sat at Relevart's feet, ears twitching. No one made a sound.

The sky parted. An Astican stepped through, the sword held high, a ruby in the hilt glinting in the subdued light. "I, Abarax, come to you at the request of The MasTer. I mean you no harm." It lowered the sword.

Brie observed its cherubic features, muscled chest, and thick neck. Its scales glowed with a silvery sheen. Abarax continued to be the most impressive Astican she had seen.

Relevart broke the intense silence that had permeated Mittkeer after the Astican's pronouncement. "We will join you in El Soasi on TreBlaya but will not accompany you through the slashed opening. Were we to do so, it would trap us on TreBlaya for all time."

Abarax scowled. "And you will join us, how?"

"By the means available only to a VarTerel. Go. Tell The MasTer we want a guarantee of safety for our entire party. When we receive this, we will join you at a place of your choosing."

"*I* guarantee your safety, VarTerel. *I* speak for The MasTer."

Froetise dimmed, and then brightened. Relevart looked over his shoulder. "Brie. Star?"

Brie touched the Star of Truth. It felt warm but sent no warning pain down her back. She leaned forward and whispered, "It remains quiet."

Wolloh spoke quietly, "I believe it speaks the truth."

Relevart pursed his lips. "Hmm. We will accept your word, Abarax. Do not consider breaking it. We are a powerful group."

It inclined its head. "When shall I tell The MasTer you will arrive?"

"I will mend the slash after you depart. Set a beacon to guide us safely into El Soasi. We will come directly."

The Astican retreated. Relevart and Wolloh repaired the long slice in the sky, leaving no sign of the encroachment into the sacrosanct domain of Mittkeer. With the ambience of peace and calm restored, Relevart turned to Torgin.

"The compass, boy. Ask it to show us the doorway into El Soasi on the planet of TreBlaya."

Torgin withdrew Ostradio and repeated Relevart's request. The needle remained stationary. He frowned, held the compass in a vertical position, and asked again. The needle spun and stopped, pointing down.

Relevart placed his staff in front of Torgin. The heavens thinned, exposing a dimly lit room. From the center, the Soasi beacon, a small, squat crystal, beamed a shaft of light at the portal opening.

Leaving the tip of his staff pointing into Mittkeer, Relevart sidestepped the beam and entered the room. Nomed, Corvus, Somay, and Lenadi spread out behind him. Almiralyn and Teva followed. Brie and her friends remained in Mittkeer with Wolloh and Henri.

Abarax stepped from the shadows. With his appearance, the beacon faded, and a hidden light source warmed the room. "Invite the others to join us. I have given my word. You are safe in The MasTer's home."

Relevart motioned them inside. The wall solidified behind them.

Elcaro's Eye grew quiet.

Renn looked up at Wilith. "Will it show us more?"

He pinched the bridge of his nose and sighed. "If it chooses."

Renn gasped. "Look."

A pale, sunken face peered from the interior of a quartz sphere. The eyes blinked. The face vanished, leaving the surface blank. A new scene emerged and zoomed out to show a room enshrouded in black curtains, an alcove where a crystal sphere sat on a black pedestal, a single bed encircled by drapes, a table and chair in front of a Gothic window. One final sweeping pan ended on a black throne. A tall figure concealed within the folds of a deep purple cape reclined against the back, features hidden in shadow.

Veersuni's quiet deepened as Elcaro showed Relevart waiting in a long, dim corridor with his staff in hand and Shyllee by his side. The murmur of the Astican's voice and a soft rasping reply penetrated into the hall.

Kneeling, the VarTerel scratched the dog's ears. "Stay close and alert. I don't want to be surprised." He straightened.

Abarax appeared and motioned him inside. "The MasTer will see you now."

"Will you be joining us?"

It shook its head. "I will, however, be close by should my master have need of me." Its blue-eyed gaze held his for one long moment.

Relevart stepped across the threshold and paused. "On guard, girl."

The faint scent of smoke wafted up his nostrils. Profound hopelessness washed over him. Tightening his grip on his staff, he walked deeper into the room.

A tall male figure, enshrouded in the folds of a dark robe, rose from a throne as he approached. "At last, Relevart. I have waited a lifetime to—" A long rattling cough shook the man's body. He picked up a goblet from the arm of the throne and sipped its contents. A final hacking spasm, another sip, and he sank onto the seat and set the goblet beside him.

Relevart observed the trembling in his hands and noted the supreme effort it took him to maintain his façade. "You are wearing yourself out."

The MasTer came to his feet. "You know?"

Relevart raised his bushy brows. "How could I not know? We—"

The figure shuddered from head to foot and shifted shapes. The vein-webbed hand of an old woman slipped from beneath the cape. A tremor shook it as it shoved the hood back. Withered cheeks wet with tears; dark, sunken eyes and a winkle-puckered mouth emerged in the dim light. Gray hair hung in a thin braid over her shoulder. A spasm of coughing left a smear of blood on her hand.

Relevart leaned his staff against the throne and scooped her up in his arms.

She touched his cheek. "I never expected to find you." Another rattling cough shook her emaciated body. "I have done horrible things because I thought they murdered you."

"Shhh." He laid her on the bed, adjusted her pillows, and sat beside her. "I have friends with me who can help you regain some of your strength."

Hopefulness lit the ravaged face. "If they can give me even a short time —" A cough scattered the hope like chaff in the wind.

He wiped the blood from her hand and chin. "I'll ask Abarax to bring them."

Clinging to his hand, she whispered, "Please." She licked her lips. "How much do you know?"

"Let me bring Henri and the twin's, and we'll see if we can make you more comfortable."

"And the boy with dual seeds. I need—"

Abarax strode into the room. He gazed from his master's hand resting in Relevart's to her face. "He has not hurt you?"

A feeble shake of her head stopped him. "Do as he asks." She closed her eyes and whispered, "Hurry."

Relevart gave the Astican instructions and walked him to the door. Within minutes, Henri joined him. From a distance, she studied the frail woman on the bed.

"I wondered if you knew."

He sighed. "I have always known she lived. Sparrow's painting provided the final clue to her identity. Can you help her?"

She withdrew a small bottle from her pocket, crossed to the bed, and bent over the prostrate figure. "I need you to drink this. Relevart will help you to sit."

Sunken eyes blinked open. The woman frowned. Relevart leveraged her halfway to sitting. Henri held the bottle to her lips. One small sip at a time, she drank until a round of coughing left her gasping for air.

Henri motioned Relevart to lower her onto the pillow. "This cannot undo the damage you have done to your body, but it will give you a reprieve."

The twins and Esán made a hesitant entry and waited beside Shyllee. Relevart waved them forward.

Ari inclined her head. "Wow. The MasTer's a woman. She doesn't look too good."

Relevart put an arm around her shoulder. "We're hoping you, Brie, and Esán can help. Henri will tell you what's needed."

"Ari, we need Efillaeh on her heart. Brielle, please stand at her head with the Remembering Stone. Esán, at her feet. Please call on the healing power of the Seeds of Carsilem. Hurry. She's fading."

Relevart held his breath. Ari placed the sacred knife. Brie held the Remembering Stone above her head. Esán rested his hands on her feet. The woman's body trembled. The years melted away. Wrinkles smoothed to finely etched lines. Hair turned a dark, rich brown with only a touch of gray. Age spots and swollen veins vanished from her hands. Eyes filled with life opened, searched those gathered around her until they found him, and flooded with relief.

Ari retrieved the knife. Brie returned the stone to its pouch, and Esán stepped away from the bed. Henri beckoned them to follow, and they slipped from the room, taking Shyllee with them.

The MasTer smiled and whispered, "Rethdun."

He took her hand. "You are so beautiful, my Rayn."

As cascading water dispersed the image, the group gathered around the fountain let out a collective sigh.

Sparrow smiled. "We should eat while we can. I've had food set out in the Reading Room." She put an arm around Elae's shoulders. "Take a break and eat something. Alli and I will watch the fountain until you return."

"Thank you, Sparrow." She and Merrilea crossed to where Voer, Wilith, Renn, and Yaro spoke together by the door. A brief conversation later, they all filed from the sanctuary.

Gerolyn and Lorsedi made no move to leave.

Sparrow clasped Alli's hand and studied her parents. "What made you come to Myrrh?"

Gerolyn glanced at Lorsedi. "We had two reasons. I felt was important to get Renn away from DerTah as soon as possible and—"

"I wanted to meet you." Lorsedi finished. "I've met my granddaughters. I wanted to meet their mother, my daughter."

Sparrow bit her lip. A spark of denial flickered. "Are you sure it wasn't Elcaro's Eye you wanted to see?"

Shrewd brown eyes regarded her. "The fountain was a motivator. However, many things have changed since I first thought of stealing it." He smiled at her mother. "I found the love of my life. Our daughter is much more important to me than the fountain." His direct gaze brought a flush to her cheeks.

Gerolyn squeezed his arm. "Let's go eat, Lorsedi. I imagine the fountain is rarely quiet these turnings."

Sparrow watched them leave. "I can't get used to the fact that *he* is my father. Standin raised me, loved me, held me when I cried. Lorsedi is..." She shrugged.

Allynae hugged her. "Standin will always be the father of your heart. Perhaps one turning, you will accept Lorsedi as the man your mother loves and the grandfather of our girls. He is a smart man. I doubt he expects more than that. One thing to remember, dearest, he did not desert you."

Sparrow moved from his embrace and kissed him lightly. "Thank you, Alli, for understanding."

Renn stuck her head in the sanctuary. "May we come in?"

Wilith and Yaro appeared behind her.

"Of course." Sparrow waved them forward. "What do you need?"

Renn smoothed her hair. "Yaro and I left our friends amid a battle, one they were in because of me. Do you think the fountain will show us if they are safe?"

"We can ask." Sparrow walked to the fountain and waited for them to join her.

Even before they had all gathered around it, the water stopped flowing. The surface grew glassy. The image of a small group gathered around a campfire gradually took shape. Nearby, a portal's faint spin glistened in the warm light of the moon, Fasfro.

Renn felt her heartbeat quicken. These were the people who had saved her, the first friends she ever had that the PPP had not hand-picked. Quickly, she counted heads. She could see Tamosh. Cayled sat across from him with his arm in a sling. Moonlight glimmered on silver-white hair, as Gregos' shadowy form emerged from the trees.

"Checked our boys and they're sound asleep. I'd call it a good turning's work."

Bibeed stepped into the ring of light and handed wooden mugs all around.

Renn swallowed. "Where's Marji? The last time I saw her, she was running for cover. What if she didn't make it?" She clutched Wilith's arm. "I could never forgive myself."

He patted her hand. "Look, Renn."

The portal began to spin. A silhouetted figure leapt into the night and walked toward the group.

Gregos called, "Well?"

Marji stepped into the fire's flickering light and shook her head. "You're always so impatient, Greg." She held up a cask. "The best ale in Trinuge!"

Gregos grinned and licked his lips.

Tamosh laughed. "You're sure one handy sister, Marji. Let's celebrate."

The picture faded.

52
Myrrh & TreBlaya

Alli and Sparrow had taken a break while Renn and Wilith watched the fountain. By the time they returned to Veersuni, everyone had gathered in small groups, chatting. Allynae joined Wilith and Lorsedi in a discussion regarding Idronatti's future. Merrilea and Gerolyn sat on a bench in quiet conversation. Voer and Yaro stood soaked in stained glass light, talking in the guttural language of ReTaw au Qa. To one side, Elae sat holding Zugo's uninjured hand. She looked up and smiled.

Sparrow examined Zugo's upturned face. "You're sure you're strong enough to be here?"

A grin lit his eyes. "Mother and Owae were driving me crazy, so I suggested they take a break. Elae promised to take care of me. Please don't send me back, Sparrow. Gerolyn and Allynae think the fountain is going to show something interesting. I don't want to miss it."

"You can stay, but please don't get too tired." She glanced up to find

Allynae watching her. Excusing herself, she joined him. "What's this I hear about something happening?"

"At almost the same instant, your mother and I got this vague feeling that—"

The statue's palms emptied of water and the fountain grew silent. Chatter in the room ceased. Allynae brought a chair for Zugo. Everyone gathered, attention riveted to Elcaro's surface, where tiny lights skittered from one side to the other, formed a rainbow of color in the air, and dove to the bottom of the bowl. When the wavelets stilled, a picture emerged.

Almiralyn observed those assembled in The MasTer's chambers. Rayn sat on the black throne, a fragile figure wrapped in deep purple. Relevart sat at her feet with Shyllee's head in his lap. Some of the most talented and powerful people in the Inner Universe formed a semicircle facing her.

Clustered at the front of the group were the young people whose gifts and talents had sparked The Unfolding. All of them had grown— transitioned from childhood into their young adult cycle. Somay had pulled up a chair within reach of Esán. Nomed stood behind his brother. Corvus sat with his arm draped over Almiralyn's shoulders. Next to her on the other side, Wolloh and Henri sat together. Teva and Lenadi were opposite, sitting cross-legged on the floor. Abarax stood to the side of the throne, cherub eyes fixed on its master.

Rayn cleared her throat. "It has taken a long time to bring all of you together on TreBlaya. If it were not for The Unfolding, I doubt it could have happened." She reached for Relevart's hand. "With the help of the VarTerels..." She smiled. "Please explain, Wolloh Espyro."

Everyone turned curious eyes in his direction.

"We have tapped into the crystal web and connected the crystals in this room to Elcaro's Eye and to crystals at Shu Chenaro where TheLise, WoNa, her brother Roandee, Stebben, and Desirol's mother, Chyneria, have gathered. Stee, Yuin, Jeet, and Mondago have joined CheeTrann and Paisley at Nemttachenn where Evolsefil resides. The Guardians have repaired Dom's crystal, so Jordett and the KcernFensians have joined him at *Antiques by Q*. Those gathered in these locations will hear and see everything that happens in Veersuni."

Rayn nodded. "Thank you." Her expression became both serious and sad. "I am about to share what the depths of despair can do to a man or a woman. I have done much that I regret." Her fingers plucked at the neck of her cape and withdrew an oval locket on a long, silver chain. For a moment, she pressed it to her heart, then let it rest against her chest, where the moonstone set in the front shimmered in the folds of her purple cloak. Her gaze traveled over the group and stopped on the Universal VarTerel.

Relevart withdrew a matching locket from beneath his shirt.

Almiralyn glanced around. Wolloh and Henri both wore knowing smiles. Nomed's eyebrow arched. Corvus' dimple deepened.

Rayn continued.

"Rethdun, whom you know as Relevart, is my birth-mate. Our host mother, Jaradee, was a young Eleo Predian rebel. Jaradee volunteered to have our fertilized eggs implanted in her womb. She carried us full term. During that time, our birther kept a journal which is in the Galactic Library in Myrrh. You can read her full account when you return. Briefly... Rethdun and I are of the Eleo Preda people from the planet of El Stroma. At the time of our birth, the Pheet Adole, the largest cultural group on the planet, had determined that our people threatened their cultural existence and were doing their utmost to wipe us out. A team of Eleo Predian Protariflee technicians secretly created Rethdun and I from the sperm and eggs of four of our most intelligent and talented leaders to insure the survival of our race. At three, to protect us from capture by the RomPeer of the Pheet Adole, they separated us. When I was a young girl, my keepers told me Rethdun had been murdered. I had seen Jaradee killed at the hands of a Pheet Adole soldier. Barbarianism was all I had ever known." She looked down at her tightly folded hands. "The event that changed me forever happened when I was eighteen. A group of soldiers raped me and left me for dead. When I recovered, I assumed the persona of a man. With the help of the Eleo Predian rebels, I gathered our people together and smuggled them off the planet. I developed a plan to destroy the continent of El SyrTundi on El Stroma and led the group that carried it out. The next period of my life I spent destroying everything I touched, including this planet. I developed the Mocendi League to help me create chaos and to search for all of you."

Relevart handed her an obsidian goblet. She took a small sip, cupped the goblet between her hands, and sipped again. Returning it to Relevart, she looked from one person to the next.

"You are here for several important reasons." She inhaled a careful breath. "One of the most important is so I can apologize to someone I love very much." Dark, tear-damp eyes found Elf. "Troms el Shiv, you are my son, created by the process of Protariflee. A trusted servant carried my egg, fertilized by the sperm of Thorlu Tangorra, in her womb. I raised you here in Soasi until you were old enough to train as a Mocendi." She sipped from her goblet. "No one knew you were my son. Thorlu does not know he is your father."

Elf flinched as though hit and rose slowly. His hand clutched his throat. Horrified eyes bored into his mother.

She struggled to her feet. "When you refused to join the League, they stripped you of your memories and your voice as required by the laws of the Mocendi. You vanished by the time I was told. I hope the twins can restore both."

He dropped to his hand to his side, sank to the floor, and buried his head in Ari's lap.

The MasTer swayed and smothered a cough. Relevart helped her to sit and handed her the goblet. A shudder ran through her as she set it aside. "I have more to share." She nodded at Abarax.

The Astican pulled a curtain aside and ushered Mairin and Lanli Nadrugia into the room.

Almiralyn started to rise. Wolloh's hand on her knee stopped her.

In Veersuni, the image froze. Allynae let out a hoarse cry. "Maman. Papa." He gripped the fountain. Eyes cemented to the image, he murmured, "Please, Elcaro…"

Rayn gripped the arms of the throne. Relevart stood beside her. "I'd like you to meet Mairin, my sister's daughter, and her husband, Lanli. Some of you are related to them and thus to me. All of you carry the blood of the Eleo Preda."

Torgin's hand flew to his heart.

Rayn smiled. "Yes, Torgin Wilith Whalend, even you." A cough shook her shoulders. She gulped a breath. "Mairin, please explain."

Mairin's gaze fastened first on Almiralyn, scanned the group, and hesitated on the twins. "Because of our Eleo Predian ancestry, the

Galactic Guardians asked Lanli and me to discover the true identity of The MasTer and to bring him to justice. The story is long and involved, one we will share another time." She allowed them a moment to absorb what she had shared, then continued. "All of us are Eleo Predian, whether full-blooded or less. Rayn has gathered us here for two reasons. One is to warn us that the Pheet Adole have not given up their desire to rid the Universe of the Eleo Preda. All of us are in danger. The second is to ask for your help. Rayn's dying wish is to regenerate El Stroma. Toward that end, she has spent time and resources developing the ship El Aperdisa. As my granddaughters and their friends can attest, it is a living organism. Once it touches down on El Stroma, it is programmed to send down roots and to begin the regeneration of life on the planet. Rayn hopes some of you will volunteer to make the journey and remain to oversee the project."

Brie gasped. A sharp pain at the base of her neck made her stiffen. Her eyes flashed to Shyllee. The dog had half risen. Brie jumped to her feet. "Something's wrong!"

Shyllee growled. The air in the room crackled. Abarax unfurled its wings and herded Brie with her friends to an alcove at the opposite side of the chamber. Chairs vanished. The adults formed lines on either side of the throne. Wards shot up around them.

A roll of thunder announced a large group of men wearing the purple-lined capes of the Mocendi League. One stepped forward. "We have come for The MasTer."

Rayn came slowly to her feet. "What do you want from him?"

The man gave a harsh guffaw. "So. It is true. The MasTer's a feeble old woman."

Others laughed. The leader raised a hand. "Silence." A triumphant gaze traveled the room. "Not only do we find a pathetic MasTer, but a room full of Eleo Preda. Look upon us, vermin of El Stroma. We are Pheet Adole." He glowered at Rayn. "We have infiltrated your Mocendi. Some MasTer you are." The wards crackled at his touch. "Do you believe these wards can withstand *our* power?"

Brie nudged Desirol and Torgin. She, Ari, Elf, and Esán surrounded them. At her signal, wards close in around them.

Blue light flashed around the fragile figure on the throne. A male voice thundered through the space. "I, The MasTer, welcome you to El Soasi, Leader of the Pheet Adole."

Flanked by the VarTerels, a tall, powerful man stood with the curved black sword gleaming in his hand. In his hand, the black curved sword gleamed. The ruby in its hilt glowed the deep red of blood. The leader of the Pheet Adole showed momentary surprise, recovered, and strode forward. An invisible wall sent him stumbling back.

Arrogant fury fired his words. "You cannot stop us. You trained us. We know your every trick."

The MasTer raised the sword. His powerful voice boomed. "But I do not stand alone."

The VarTerels gripped their staffs tighter. As though rehearsed, Corvus, Nomed, Somay, Lenadi, and Lanli stepped forward. The woman moved in behind them.

Henri withdrew a small, glowing bottle and stepped to Somay's side. On his palm, the Tabagie's eyes rested, cold and dark. Whispering a quiet word, she removed the bottle's lid. Tiny flames licked the rim and grew bigger. Somay rolled the eyes across the gap between the throne and the Mocendi. A miniature Fire ConDra shot from the bottle and ignited the long dormant embers. Circling high above the Pheet Adole, it grew to its full size and hovered.

Wolloh called out,

> *"Tabagie bring close together*
> *Pheet Adole that we may tether*
> *Them to worlds far away*
> *Do it now without delay."*

Wolloh's words ringing through the chamber ignited Torgin's memory of his conversation with Relevart in Mittkeer. Pulling the flute from its case, he brought it to his lips. With its first vibrant note, a billowing cloud of gray smoke formed around the smoldering ember eyes. A second note, deeper and longer, lifted the Tabagie to its towering height. Note by note, Torgin's music infused it with life. Long, wafting arms strengthened and encircled the enemy. A Grand Stave flowed from the flute, its ten black lines enclosing the Mocendi like a fence. Treble and bass clefs at both ends locked together.

Black notes flew toward the smoke-formed enclosure. One after another, they attached to lines or filled spaces of the stave until they trapped the Pheet Adole. The shriek and the heat of the Fire ConDra pressed them to their knees. A trill of shivering high notes joined with another piercing shriek and the deep boom of the Tabagie's roar.

The MasTer held his sword higher. The smoke roiled thicker and thicker. Relevart and Wolloh pointed the crystal tips of their staffs. Two rays of light streaked through the room, intersected in front of the enclosure, and exploded, dispatching the Pheet Adole into another dimension.

The musical fence evaporated. The Tabagie's eyes fell to the floor and rolled to a stop at Somay's feet. With a piercing shriek, the Fire Condra shrunk and shot into the bottle on Somay's hand.

Torgin's final note floated above the emptied space as the MasTer crumpled to the throne, her male form gone forever, her aged face filled with agony.

Abarax lifted her and carried her to the bed. Relevart knelt and clasped her hand in his.

Brie heard a muffled moan and turned as Somay flashed to Esán's side and scoop him up in his arms.

Eyes glazed over with pain searched his father's face. "I can't do any more. I..." Esán's eyes rolled back in his head and struggled to refocus.

Somay held him closer. "It's time to take you home to Tao Spirian and your mother's love."

Wolloh hurried to their side and placed a hand on Esán's forehead. He glanced at Somay. "I will take you via Mittkeer. We have little time to waste." He waved Torgin forward. "You have done extraordinary work this turning, Torgin. I need you to do one more thing."

"What, sir?"

"My training as VarTerel has only just begun. You and the compass must guide us through Mittkeer to Tao Spirian."

"To Tao Spirian?" Torgin looked from Esán's pale face to Somay's, slipped the flute into its case, and settled it over his shoulder. "I'm ready, sir."

Esán's eyes fluttered open. "Thank you, Torgin," he whispered.

Elf and Ari said their goodbyes and followed the silent procession of adults from the room.

Brie kissed Esán's cool cheek. "I love you, Esán Efre. Come back to me soon." She gave Torgin a quick hug and stepped away.

Wolloh tapped his staff against the floor. A door-sized portion of the wall melted in the midnight sky. Somay carried Esán through. Wolloh and Torgin followed. The portal vanished.

The memory of Torgin's first meeting with Esán and his childish behavior toward the sick boy made Brie smile through her tears. *I wonder if you realize how much you have changed, Torgin Wilith Whalend?* Wiping a tear from her cheek, she tiptoed across the black-ice floor, Rayn's labored breathing accompanying her quiet retreat.

Water spilled into the fountain, leaving it empty of images.

Sparrow led a thoughtful group into the Reading Room. Allynae brushed a tear from her cheek and slipped an arm around her. She nestled her head against his shoulder. "I hope they reach Tao Spirian in time."

He kissed the top of her head. "They will. No time passes in Mittkeer, remember. Did I hear Brie say she loved Esán?"

Sparrow moved from the comfort of his arms and smiled. "I'd say both our girls are in the blush of first love."

Allynae's jaw dropped. "Ari, too? Who?"

Sparrow brushed his lips with a kiss. "Yes, Alli, Ari, too." She looked toward the fireplace where friends and family stood in deep conversation. "I have things to attend to."

She paused beside Zugo. "I think you need to rest."

Elae put an arm around him. "I'll take him back to the healing room."

Merrilea moved to his other side. "I'll go with you."

Momentarily light-headed, Sparrow inhaled a deep breath. Energy rolled through her like a tidal current. A rush of blood to her cheeks left her feeling overheated and flushed. Allynae's eyes widened. He took a step toward her. Her mother flashed her a knowing look and smiled. Sparrow's hand flew to her heart. *I am the new Guardian of Myrrh.* Even had their expressions not confirmed it, the changes flowing through her mind and body would have.

Squaring her shoulders, she walked to the group gathered by the fireplace. They had questions. Together, they would find the answers.

In the sanctuary, the stained-glass window glowed. Elcaro's Eye stilled, and a picture formed.

Relevart looked down at the woman who would, had destiny taken a different course, have been his life-mate. He kissed her forehead.

"Rayn."

Her eyes fluttered open, and she whispered. "Are they gone?"

"They are. Your plan worked. This Unfolding cycle is complete."

A weak smile lit fatigue-dulled eyes. A shaking hand pulled him closer. "I want to fly." A cough shook her. When it subsided, she licked blood from her lips and whispered, "I want to fly one last time. I want to fly with you." Another cough rattled in her chest.

He uncorked Henrietta's bottle of healing elixir and held it to her lips. She drank the last of its contents, sighed, and relaxed back on her pillow. Energy revitalized her hair and eyes, smoothed her skin, and erased the age spots from her hands.

"Bring me the sword." Her words were breathy and eager.

He retrieved it from where it had fallen and placed it in her hands. For a moment she seemed to draw power from it, and then she handed it back. "This is yours." She touched the ruby in the hilt. "This gem carries the life blood of El Stroma—the blood of our forbearers—the blood of the Eleo Preda. Only you have the power to wield it, Rethdun. Promise you will take it to El Quil'Tran."

He stood and held it up. "I promise to return this to its homeland." Laying it beside his staff at the foot of the bed, he helped her upright. "Come, before you grow too tired to fly."

With trembling hands, she straightened her shapeless robe. "I have one more request."

Relevart sat beside her. "I'm listening."

"The Pheet Adole will not give up the hunt. As soon as they know I am dead, they will redouble their efforts to find all of you. Promise you will protect Elf. Promise you will have the twins restore his memories and his voice."

"I promise, Rayn."

She let out a long, raspy exhale. "It's time to fly. Call Abarax. I don't want to waste my energy walking."

The Astican appeared from the shadows. "I am here, my master."

Relevart moved aside.

Abarax lifted Rayn, carried her to the balcony, lowered her with great gentleness to sit on the balustrade, and bowed. "I will be close by."

Relevart took her hands in his. "I'll help with your shift. What is your favorite form?"

She smiled up at him. "I love the El Stroman Galee."

He squeezed her hands. They made the shift together. Lifting into flight, dark green feathers gleaming, golden eyes peering from red masks, they soared over the land. She shot ahead and swooped above the blackened fields. Relevart's sharp raptor eyes picked out tiny green shoots poking their fragile stalks up into the light of the TreBlayan turning. She looped higher and streaked toward a stand of charred trees. Here again, new growth pressed the decay away.

At last, Rayn banked back toward Soasi. Wing strokes faltering, she fought to keep her shifted form intact.

Swooping to her side, he began to weave a protective ward around her.

"No, Rethdun. Let me go."

His heart breaking, he withdrew his power.

The wards shimmered into nothing. A spasm shook her body. She floundered between bird and Human, regained her galee form, soared higher, and hovered. Golden eyes sought Relevart. *"I always loved you."*

Green feathers exploded around her. Heavy as stone, her Human body plummeted into the gaping mouth of the blazing pits of death. Feathers floating after burst into flame. Cinders showered like rain, glowing red, and then gone.

Heavy with grief, Relevart flew back to the balcony and shifted. For a time, he could not bring himself to move, but gazed through tears of devastating loss at the blackened landscape. *She wanted me to see the beginnings of life returning to TreBlaya. She wanted me to know she was not all bad.*

The silhouette of an Astican swooped over the fiery pit, its howl of anguish reverberating off the TreBlayan mountains.

The image in the fountain vanished in a blaze of fire, sending shadows dancing over the velvet curtains. Quiet returned to the sanctuary. Veersuni seemed to hold its breath as the alabaster statue began to change. In the flickering light, a likeness of SparrowLyn AsTar took shape, kneeling on the fountain's rim. As water spilled from the new Guardian's carved hands into Elcaro's Eye, the song of the ancients whispered through the room.

The children of many, together at last,
Learn of their ancestry, connections, and past
Their destinies blossom; their futures unfold,
Revealing adventures and stories untold.

EPILOGUE

Epilogue-Chapter 1
Treblaya

Beneath the cloud-shrouded TreBlayan sky, Relevart rested weathered hands on the balcony balustrade at Soasi. Memories of Rayn plunging to her death haunted him—feathers sizzling, cinders falling, her silent cry— He squeezed the bridge of his nose and sighed. *I honor your wish to die, Rayn.*

In the distance, an Astican soared skyward from the pit and swept over the blackened landscape. Massive wings wafting, it hovered, then landed on the balcony. Soot smeared on its forehead and cheeks, signs of mourning, surprised Relevart.

"You grieve The MasTer, Abarax?"

Rayn's personal servant recoiled. "Not The MasTer." It gazed at the pit. "I mourn my mistress, the woman who trusted me to guard her secrets." The soft sound of leather on leather whispered around it. Scaled wings quivered and settled. "Have you looked at the journals and paperwork she left for you?"

"I've done nothing else since you delivered them." Relevart studied the Astican's child-like features. "They are most interesting, as *you* already know."

Abarax narrowed celestial-blue eyes and peered down from its towering height. "How did you—" It sighed. "Never mind. You are *her* birth-mate. She, too, would have read it in me." Unblinking eyes surveyed its homeland and came to rest on his face. "I have a request, VarTerel."

Relevart raised thick, white brows.

Silvery gray scaled wings quivered again. "I wish to go with you to El Stroma. I gave my word to my mistress that I would protect you and all Eleo Preda."

"And what of your fellow Astican? Are you willing to leave them behind?"

"They will oversee the care of Soasi and the husbandry and regeneration of TreBlaya."

Relevart searched the creature's face for any sign of treachery. He found none. "I have much to consider before I make final decisions about El Stroma, Abarax. We will discuss your request again at a later time."

The Astican bowed. "I have a final document for you, one *she* asked me to deliver last."

"Please bring it to her quarters." Relevart's gaze swept over the scarred landscape and back to the Astican. "I will meet you there."

Relevart drew a steadying breath and stepped into Rayn's darkened chamber. Not for the first time, a pulsing sadness pierced his heart. He inhaled the waning scents of sulfur and musk, walked to the black throne at the room's center, and sank onto the seat. *Rayn spent her final turnings in this room.* The image of her masculine form sitting where he now sat, a hood shadowing the ravaged face, stirred more memories. *She shifted to her male form one last time to fight the Pheet Adole Mocendi.* White-knuckled hands gripped the arms of the throne. *Traitors from within her own ranks, a group determined to rid the Universe of her people—my people—the Eleo Preda.*

A flash of ruby light caught his eye. Crossing to the bed, he tugged the half-opened curtains aside, picked up a curved black sword, and hefted its weight. *The Sword of Shyteno.* A wave of emotion washed over him. He studied the ruby topping the hilt. *Rayn asked me to return it to our home planet in the Outer Universe.* He sighed. *El Stroma... We were conceived there in test tubes and implanted in the womb of the same woman.* Regret left him shaken. *We are birth-mates. That's why I feel such empathy and such loss.*

A soft knock reminded him of his many responsibilities. With a sad sigh, he replaced the sword on the bed and stationed himself beside a paper-cluttered table. "Enter."

Clawed talons clicked a rhythmic cadence on the polished black floor, then ceased. Abarax studied him, its cherubic features inscrutable. Apparently satisfied with what it saw, it passed him a document with The MasTer's seal imprinted on the folded edge.

Relevart flipped the document over and read the words scripted there. *For Rethdun's Eyes Only.* He glanced at the Astican. "You know what this contains?"

A soft chorus of leather on leather susurrated around it. "Only what my mistress shared."

"I see. Please ask my companions to join me in the meeting chamber in a full chron circle. Thank you, Abarax."

It bowed and left.

He reread the words in Rayn's careful hand and murmured, "For *Rethdun*'s Eyes Only." Rethdun, his given name, the Eleo Predan word for thunder, brought another wave of sadness. He sat down, pressed his thumb to the seal, and whispered, "*Dubinn Stersec.*"

The document fell open, showing a clutter of unrelated text. A tap and the command *"Enferi"* initiated a scurry of letters that reordered themselves into a handwritten missive. A careful study of the contents left Relevart's brow furrowed and his thoughts in a whirlwind. Laying the document on the table, he steepled his fingers and tapped his chin. "My, my, dear Rayn, what a conundrum you have created."

In a small study next to the meeting chamber, Henrietta Avetlire embraced the stone silence of Soasi. Rayn's death had left its indelible mark in the furtive glances of servants, the unspoken concern of the staff on *El Aperdisa*, and the shocked disquiet of those Relevart's birth-mate had gathered together on this planet at the Outer Rim. Sorrow and uncertainty smothered her home like a shroud.

Henri tapped her large-rimmed spectacles against her palm and sighed. "All of us are Eleo Predan." Tap, tap, tap. "The Pheet Adole pursue us." Tap, tap. "They will not stop until they have eliminated us from the Universe." Tap. She returned her spectacles to a hidden pocket and tottered into the hall. "We have important plans to make."

After knocking lightly on the door to The MasTer's chamber, she listened for the deep voice of the Universal VarTerel.

"Please come in, Henri."

She entered the darkened chamber where sadness lay as heavy as a thundercloud. The glow of a single oil lamp illuminated a pile of books, stacks of papers, and the man she sought. Wading through both the emotions and the gloom, she arrived at the table and frowned.

"Oh, my." She eyed an open journal. "May I?"

Relevart nodded.

Henri scanned the first several pages and sank into a chair. "Are they all this detailed?"

Another nod. He handed her a document with The MasTer's seal.

She skimmed it once before withdrawing her spectacles and rereading it. A startled exhale left a soft mist on her lenses. Taking them off, she tapped the document, watched the words reshuffle, then placed it on the table.

"Well now, that certainly complicates things. Does Elf know?"

"No one knows except you and me, and perhaps Abarax." He pursed his lips. "Although it may have been telling me the truth when it told me it didn't know the contents."

After returning the spectacles to their pocket, Henri massaged her aching knees. "When will you inform the boy?"

He stood, offered his hand, and assisted her to her feet. "First, I will require your help to restore his voice and his memory. Then I must share other important news with our companions. We have many decisions to make before *we* leave for El Stroma."

Henri cocked her head. *"We?"*

"Of course, we." He raised his brows. "You would never let me leave you behind."

She peered up at him, her violet eyes alight with laughter. "I will consider that the unbreakable promise of an old friend."

Brie stood beside a gothic-style window in the assembly chamber of Soasi, staring up through the glass dome protecting The MasTer's home. She scanned the heavens. *I wonder where you are, El Aperdisa. I miss you.* She tugged a red curl. *Imagine a living, breathing ship! A ship that pulses with life.* In stark contrast, the decimated landscape of TreBlaya presented her with a view of blacks and grays, of death and decay. *I wonder if El Stroma looks as bad as this?*

She touched an index finger to the window, sighed, and turned to observe those gathered to hear Rayn's last will and testament. *We all hope to learn more about what lies ahead.* Without thinking, she searched for Esán and frowned. *Wolloh, Somay, and Torgin took him to Tao Spirian right after the battle in Rayn's chamber.* She brushed a tear from her cheek. His illness had reached a critical stage, one that could end his life, and only healers on his home planet had the means to cure him. *I miss you, Esán Efre. I hope you're feeling better.*

With a lingering wave of sadness, she refocused her attention. At the end of the table, Ari sat with Elf, fingers intertwined in his and a softness in her expression Brie had rarely seen. *I believe you are in love, Arienh AsTar Nadrugia.*

Her twin caught her eye and smiled, then spoke to the young man at her side. He laughed a silent laugh, shot a twinkling look in Brie's direction, and grinned.

Henri appeared at the door. All heads turned. She raised a hand, clutching her spectacles. Conversation ceased.

"Relevart asked me to inform you he will be a bit longer." Perching her spectacles on her nose, she let magnified eyes roam the room. "Please Ari, Brie, and Elf, come with me."

Once in the hall, Henri laid a hand on Elf's arm. "Are you ready to regain your speech and memory?"

Hope, fear, then hope again played tag on his expressive face. *"I'm ready to get my voice back, but I fear what the memories might reveal."*

Ari squeezed his hand. "I'll be with you, Elf. We'll remember together."

Relevart met them at the door to Rayn's chambers and guided Elf to the bed. "I believe you will discover much good in your memories, young Elf." He looked from one twin to the other. "For the safety of all concerned, please keep what we learn to yourselves. Understood?"

Ari moved to Brie's side. Both nodded.

Relevart's gaze shifted. "Elf?"

"I understand, and I promise to keep secret what occurs here." He touched his heart. The bed sighed under his weight as lay down. He smiled at Ari and closed his eyes.

Henri took charge. "This is a two-step process. We will first attempt to return Elf's voice and then his memories. Ari, you will, at Relevart's command, put Efillaeh on Elf's throat and step away."

Ari withdrew the sacred knife from its scabbard. Relevart gave the command. She placed it and retreated.

Henri drew a symbol in the air and began to chant:

> *"Efillaeh, return to Elf*
> *That which lets him speak of self.*
> *Heal what's been torn by choice;*
> *Give Elf back his words, his voice."*

As the words faded and the silence intensified, Elf's eyes flew open. He gripped Efillaeh's jeweled handle, sat up slowly, and stared in surprised astonishment from it to Ari.

She removed the knife from his trembling fingers and sat down beside him. "What happened?"

Awe-widened eyes sought her face. *"I—"*

Ari shook her head. "Not telepathy. Speak the words." She secured the knife in its scabbard and clasped his hands in hers. "Tell *me* what happened."

Elf glanced at Relevart.

The Universal VarTerel nodded.

Elf's expression changed from fear to determination. He squeezed his eyes shut, swallowed, and then looked straight into Ari's eyes. "I haven't—" Surprise registered. He exhaled a long, emotional breath. "I...haven't... spoken...aloud..." A tear slid down his cheek and onto the tip of his finger. "For five of my seventeen sun cycles, I have known only the words in my head. When you placed the knife, my throat began to tingle." He touched a spot on his neck. "Something stirred here. In my mind, I saw my vocal cords hanging limp and atrophied; and then they, too, began to tingle and quiver! The next thing I knew, they had returned to their natural form." He released Ari's hand and pulled her into his arms. "Thank you, Arienh. Thank you!"

Relevart cleared his throat. "We have another goal to accomplish, Troms el Shiv. Please lie down."

When Ari tried to leave his embrace, an inner shiver shook him from head to foot. "I'm afraid to know what they have taken from me." He lowered his arms and ran a shaking hand through his hair. "What if..."

Ari faced him square on. "Elf, even *I* know what-ifs are pointless. All of us care about you. We're here to help. Let's get this done."

After flashing the VarTerel and Henri a sheepish smile, Elf lay down and closed his eyes. Ari rested her hand on his arm.

Relevart moved to the end of the bed. "Brielle, at Henri's command, place the Remembering Stone on his brow. Both of you will stay by his head. Do not touch him. Ari, once the stone is in place, join me. We do not want to color his memories with our thoughts. Please, Henri."

At a nod from her great aunt, Brie placed the stone and stepped back. Blue light flowing from the stone's center formed a halo-like haze around Elf's body.

Henri donned her spectacles.

"Remembering Stone, do your work
Pull back memories from where they lurk
Bring them from those hidden places
Clarifying all names and faces.

> *Let each returning fill a gap;*
> *Sharpen memory with a snap;*
> *Heal all loss and hurt and trauma*
> *End Elf's long and tortured drama."*

Elf's body twitched and grew still.

Brie held her breath, her gaze fixed on the boy lying on the bed.

The return of his memories reminded Elf of an ancient water pump building pressure as the handle moved up and down. Images dripped into his mind one at a time, then two, then a gush of color and sound. Faces and voices, laughter and tears followed in rapid succession. The pulsing of the Remembering Stone grew more insistent. A rush of images left him gasping for breath. A hand gripped his. Someone removed the stone. He lay motionless, bathed in what seemed like a life's worth of memories.

A finger tapped his brow. Relevart's voice filled his head. "Open your eyes, Troms el Shiv. Your memories will not disappear."

His eyes fluttered open. Ari filled his line of vision. He drank in her familiar features and clasped her hand tighter. Henri, Relevart, and Brie stood behind her, observing him with patient interest. He squeezed Ari's hand before he released it and pushed himself to sitting. Bent legs to his chest, he rested his forehead on his knees. Memories once again held him motionless. A quick shake of his head cleared them. Scooting to the edge of the bed, he planted his feet firmly on the smooth, black floor. "So, so much..." He released a long breath. "I need time to digest and to understand everything that happened in those early years."

Relevart sat beside him. "Tell us the most important thing you have discovered."

Elf studied his hand, rubbed the palm against his pant leg, and sighed. "A woman named YanaLoma cared for me. I called her Yanni. She lavished her love and attention on me and—" Puzzlement creased his brow. He tipped his head. "I remember a little girl about my age." Again, his brow furrowed in thought. "Ahhh. Her name was Penee. She spent all her time with us. Yanni loved her as much as she loved me. One turning, The MasTer hid me in a secret place and warned me not to make a sound. Much later, when he came for me, I could sense the anger and sadness battling in his heart. I never saw Penee or Yanni again."

Relevart leaned closer. "And?"

Elf straightened. "I now understand Yanni and Rayn were the same person. Rayn loved me. And so did Penee. I loved them both. Who was Penee, Relevart? When I think of her, my heart aches."

The Universal VarTerel and Henri exchanged glances. The elderly woman turned to the twins. "I believe Elf and Relevart need some time alone. Come, my dears. Let's join the others."

Ari moved closer to Elf. "I'm not leaving. Elf needs me."

Elf rose and hugged her. "I'll be fine. Go with Henri. We'll join you soon."

When Ari hesitated, Brie linked arms with her. "Come on. The sooner we go, the sooner Elf can tell us what he learns."

Elf walked them to the door, closed it after them, and leaned his back against the hard wood. *I want to know what Relevart knows. Why am I so uneasy?* He peered through the gloominess to where Relevart waited by a paper-cluttered table, a folded document in his hand. *Come on, Elf. It can't be all that bad.* Straightening, he marched to the table and sat down.

Relevart took the seat opposite. "You've been through much today, Troms el Shiv." He offered the document. "This will answer most of your questions."

Elf hesitated, accepted it with shaking hands, and turned it over. His brows drew together. "It says 'For Rethdun's Eyes Only'. Is it from my mother?"

"Until you open it, Elf, you won't know what it says or who it is from."

His lips pressed together, Elf unfolded the paper and stared at a mix of letters that made no sense.

The VarTerel tapped it and whispered, *"Enferi."*

Excitement replaced Elf's trepidation as the words on the page rearranged themselves into a coherent message. Chills raised goosebumps on his arms and neck as he read the missive written in his mother's hand.

Rethdun,

What I am about to reveal must remain a secret, one you may only share with those whom you trust with your life.

When I decided I wanted a child and realized that, as The MasTer, I could not do so and maintain the masquerade, I selected to use the process of Protariflee. The more I thought about it, the more I realized a solution to the battle between the Eleo Preda and the Pheet Adole lay within my reach. As I have shared, Elf is my child. Thorlu is his father. We are all full-blooded Eleo Preda. Elf has a birth-mate, Penesert el Stroma, who is a full-blooded Pheet Adole. She was kidnapped at five. Even with my many resources, I've never discovered who took her or where they hid her. I leave that in your capable hands.

Rethdun, I am entrusting you with the lives of my children and the future of El Stroma.

I am your birth-mate. You are my heart, now and forever,

Rayn el QuilTran

PS: You will find the details you require in a journal hidden in a place only Elf knows.

Elf pressed a hand to his hammering heart, drew in a deep breath, and placed the letter on the table. Tumultuous thoughts and emotions left him bereft of speech. Fear that he had become mute brought a gurgling sound to his throat. He swallowed. "N-n-now w-what?"

Relevart tapped the letter with a forefinger. "Do you know this hiding place?"

Elf crossed to the throne, knelt behind it, and pressed his thumb into a small indent in the floor. The throne glided forward. Descending a flight of steep stairs, he felt his way along the rough stone wall, pressed another indent, and listened for the quiet rattle of a panel opening. At the back of a deep recess, he found what he sought. After closing the panel, he returned to The MasTer's chamber. The pressure of his toe on the back of the throne returned it to its place. He handed a leather-bound journal to Relevart, who took it with a questioning glance at the throne.

"A secret get-away. The place The MasTer hid me the turning Penee disappeared—the last turning I saw my mother." He sat down and dropped his head in his hands.

The soft sound of pages flipping, the inhale and exhale of Relevart's breath, and his own heart beating held him motionless.

Relevart put the journal on the table. "What an interesting read."

Elf raised his eyes to the VarTerel's face. "Is Thorlu truly my father?"

"Only in the sense that his sperm fertilized your mother's egg. You may dislike him, but he is a highly intelligent and talented man. His ancestors were leaders on El QuilTran."

Elf allowed himself a moment to gain control of his emotional response to Thorlu. "And what of Penee? Who are her parents?"

Relevart pressed a palm against the leather cover. "Prior to leaving El Stroma before the persona of The MasTer took over completely, Rayn asked friends in The Protariflee Center to steal samples of several distinct family lines, hide them in cryogenics flasks, and smuggle them from the laboratory. Your mother brought them to TreBlaya and set up a lab here. Penee's blood parents are the RomPeer's favorite daughter and his most trusted advisor."

"So my mother expected me to marry Pheet Adolean royalty, hoping we could bring the two opposing cultures together."

"She did." Relevart's serious expression intensified his words. "I believe you understand the magnitude of what we have learned. Whoever gains control of you not only has a hostage, but gains control of The MasTer's wealth and property. You top the list of those the Pheet Adole want to destroy or control." He picked up the paper, whispered, *"Debrin Stersec,"* and tucked it inside the journal. "I believe you and all of us will *be* safer if the others assume you are still voiceless, with no memory of your past."

A shiver of excitement and dread traveled the length of Elf's spine. "What of the twins and Henri? I trust them, but Brie carries the Star of Truth."

A frown deepened the lines around Relevart's mouth. "As we speak, Henri is instructing the twins to keep the results of their time with you to themselves. They will play their parts well. If it becomes necessary, I will remove the recollection of Penesert from Brie's memory."

"What happens if we discover Penee and I aren't compatible? I love Ari, and I believe she cares for me. How do I..." He shrugged.

"We don't know yet if Penesert is alive." Relevart's brows raised. "Or do we?"

Elf stared at his hands. "She's alive, Relevart. I can sense her as I know you sensed my mother."

The Universal VarTerel observed him from under bridged brows. "This complicates things, doesn't it? And it makes it imperative that we share her existence with our companions. The knowledge will help them keep themselves and you safe. As far as your feelings for Ari and hers for you, time is the revealer of all things. If The Unfolding taught us anything, Troms el Shiv, it is to live one turning at a time." He stood.

Elf rose and met Relevart's understanding gaze. "Thank you for everything you're doing. You hardly know me, yet you have trusted me with your life and the lives of our companions. I will not fail you or them."

"I trust you to do your best, Elf. You and I will speak more of this later. From this moment, we will communicate only telepathically."

Side by side, they left The MasTer's chamber.

Epilogue-Chapter 2
Myrrh

In the Dojanack Caverns on Myrrh, SparrowLyn AsTar Nadrugia stood alone in the sanctuary of Veersuni. Staring into the depths of Elcaro's Eye, she watched rippling wavelets disperse Almiralyn's image. Myrrh's former Guardian's brief appearance to teach her how to shrink the fountain and bring it back to size and how to restore the cottage had left Sparrow wishing she didn't feel so alone.

Behind her, the sanctuary door opened and closed. Allynae strode to her side, draped an arm around her shoulders, and touched the open palms of the kneeling statue on the fountain's rim. "She looks just like you. How are you coping now that you're the *official* Guardian of Myrrh?"

She drew him with her to stand in front of the wall-sized stained-glass window. A snap of her fingers sent colored shapes flying to hover in front of the new drapes, which covered the sanctuary's walls. The clear glass panes formed a mosaic of night sky, stars, and spiraling galaxies. She grinned and glanced up at her companion and life partner. "I never expected that to happen."

He kissed the top of her head. "Better get used to it. Almiralyn may not be coming back to Myrrh. Have you spoken with her?"

"Yes, she provided instructions about the fountain and the cottage. She said Relevart has called a meeting to discuss what will happen next. Almiralyn has already made her choice, Alli."

Allynae turned her to face him. "And that is?"

"She and Corvus will go to El Stroma on the ship *El Aperdisa*."

"What about the girls? Do we know what they've decided?"

Sparrow stared at the vastness of space. A wave of sadness washed over her. "It's been a little over two Myrrhinian sun cycles since The Unfolding sent them on this journey. They're only sixteen, Ally. They need to finish their education and decide what they would like to do when they are adults and..." Allynae's expression made her stop. Her heavy sigh fogged a pane of glass. She touched it and gasped as the glass sparkled with the light of a shooting star.

She looked at her finger. "Did I do that?"

Allynae grinned. "I doubt the star was your doing, but..." He shrugged.

A snap of her fingers brought the color back to the panes. She watched them reassemble into a new design and drew Allynae back to the fountain. "The girls have their own destinies, Alli." Her gaze met his. "I want them to come home, don't you?"

"I do." He pulled her close. "The new cycle of balance and integration will have its own challenges. I'd like to visit with *everyone* before they head off in different directions."

Sparrow rested her head on his chest. "New challenges like the Pheet Adole Mocendi will not rest until they obliterated every Eleo Preda, including all of us." A shiver prickled over her scalp.

Allynae released her. "Look."

The water spilling into the Elcaro's Eye stopped. Sparrow gripped the rim. A large bubble floated to the surface. Within its shimmering shape, dark flecked with flames, peered through the eyeholes of a bronze mask.

Sparrow whispered a clipped command. The bubble burst. The eyes exploded into nothing.

Allynae put a protective arm around her. "And so it begins. I was hoping for a few peaceful turnings. I wish Somay were here to help rebuild the wards."

The water whirlpooled downward. A spout shot an immense bird, composed of stars and sky, into the air. It soared in a wide circle and landed in front of the stained-glass window. The cock of its head sent the window's colors flying. Starry eyes blinked. The figure melted into the universal mosaic as a door-shaped opening formed.

Sparrow gulped an astonished breath and stared. A man she had seen only in Elcaro's Eye limped forward, followed by Somay. Esán preceded Torgin into the room. The door faded and color filled the window.

Wolloh motioned the group into the Reading Room, closed the door, and drew an invisible sign on its surface. His good side to Sparrow, he bowed and offered a hand. "I am most delighted to meet Myrrh's new Guardian. Wolloh Espyro at your service."

Sparrow placed her hand in his. "And I am glad to meet you, VarTerel of the Inner Universe."

With the courtliness of another age, he kissed her hand, released it, and with a second bow, turned his attention to Allynae and Somay.

Her gaze moved to Esán and Torgin, where they stood together, recovering from their journey through Mittkeer. Torgin had grown taller and filled out. Anxiety, once his constant companion, no longer enshrouded him. Esán, whom she had first seen in her painting riding on the back of an owl, and then only in the fountain, had also matured. Although still too thin, his cheeks held a hint of color and the ever-present crescents under his eyes had faded, no longer exemplifying his illness. *He doesn't look fully recovered, but he appears to be making progress.*

He raised eyes the color of the sunlit sea, spoke to Torgin, and followed him to her side.

Torgin smiled down at her with a formality that made her suppress a desire to hug him. "SparrowLyn AsTar, it is so good to see you. Congratulations on your new position. I believe you know of Esán but have not met him in person."

Sparrow extended a hand. "I've wanted to meet you for a long time, Esán Efre. Thank you," she smiled at both boys, "for taking care of my daughters."

Esán touched his palm to hers. "Congratulations on your appointment as Guardian of Myrrh."

A twinkle lit her eye. "I have a favor to ask. All the formalities are wearing me out. Please relax. Tell me about..." She grinned. "I want to know everything about the girls and TreBlaya, and... *El Aperdisa*." She gave them each a quick hug. "How did you like sailing on *SeaBella* with the Senndi brothers?"

Pulling chairs into a circle, they sat down. With animated faces and bright smiles, the boys shared their adventures. Sparrow hadn't heard nearly enough when Allynae interrupted.

"Wolloh would like you to join us in Veersuni."

Sparrow pushed her disappointment aside. "Tell him we'll be right there."

He nodded, grinned at the boys, and hurried into the sanctuary.

With a rueful smile, Sparrow stood up. "I expect we are about to be very busy. But first...What is the one thing you would love to experience again?"

The boys exchanged glances and grinned. "Sailing!" they chorused.

Sparrow smiled. "I would love to sail on the sea." She edged between chairs. "We'd better not keep the VarTerel waiting."

Wolloh stabilized the wards around Elcaro's Eye, gripped his staff, and, motioning everyone to follow, stepped away from the fountain.

He stared unseeing, then blinked. "Relevart is about to meet with your families and friends in TreBlaya. He feels you should be present."

Esán spoke up. "What about my Aunt Merrilea and Torgin's parents? They were here, right?"

Sparrow answered. "They have returned to Idronatti to help plan for the city's future."

"And Yaro?" Torgin asked.

"Lorsedi released Yaro from his service. Your heart-brother is now on ReTaw au Qa, beginning preparations for his initiation as the Nep Rin Tese Venerat. I have arranged—"

Veersuni's door flew open. Zugo, his burned arm in a sling, launched into the sanctuary. Pale eyes gleaming, he strode up to Esán and Torgin. "I am so glad you're here." He glanced around. "Where are the twins? "

Wolloh cleared his throat and narrowed his good eye. "You are Zugo, if I'm not mistaken."

Zugo wrapped the dignity of his lineage around him. "I am Zugo, the son of Yookotay, the Redael of the DeoNytes. Welcome to the Dojanack Caverns, VarTerel of the Inner Universe."

Wolloh stifled a spontaneous laugh. "Thank you for your most gracious welcome, Zugo." He raised his staff. "The meeting is about to begin."

Everyone congregated around Elcaro's Eye. The sound of dripping water stilled. Reflected on the gleaming surface were those whose destinies would be determined by the reading of Rayn's will.

S parrow gazed at Relevart's countenance, filling Elcaro's bowl.

White hair moved with the water's final ripples. Stillness brought his dark russet eyes into focus. His gaze came to rest on the young DeoNyte.

"I am glad to see you are doing so well, Zugo. Soon, I will bring Ari and Efillaeh to heal that arm and hand." The astute gaze moved to Esán. "Ahhh. You are looking much better, Esán Efre. After you return Evolsefil to Canedari, your father will take you back to Tao Spirian to complete your recovery." He waved a hand.

The fountain zoomed out. On the surface, Almiralyn, Corvus, Mairin, and Lanli sat on one side of The MasTer's assembly table. Henri, Nomed, Teva, and Lenadi sat on the other. Ari, Brie, and Elf had arranged chairs in a small semicircle at the end opposite Relevart. At the table's center, a large, shallow bowl of water with a round crystal at its center mimicked Elcaro's Eye. Like a split screen, it showed those in Myrrh on one side and those at Shu Chenaro on the other. A charged silence permeated the room, and those linked by the Crystal Web.

From Veersuni, Sparrow searched the faces of her daughters. They had grown so much since the turning they and Torgin had gone to DerTah to rescue Esán. Ari's hair, cut short to help her maintain her boy's shifted form, brushed her shoulders. Elf draped an arm around the back of her chair, his expression bemused. Brie sat next to her twin, her attention riveted to the bowl at the table's center. Esán smiled as they connected briefly across the dimensions.

Torgin cleared his throat. "Desirol isn't with the others. Is he alright?"

Wolloh smiled. "Desirol has recovered well from his encounter with the Mindeco." He indicated the bowl at the table's center. "He has joined his parents at Shu Chenaro."

Elcaro framed the bowl within its alabaster rim. On one side, Desirol sat between his mother, Chyneria, and Gerolyn. Lorsedi stood behind them. Stebben and TheLise sat opposite. The Eye reverted its focus to Relevart and the pile of papers in front of him. The Universal VarTerel selected an official-looking document and cleared his throat.

"Let us begin. Rayn, The MasTer and my birth-mate, left us considerable information to contemplate and much to accomplish before the Cycle of Dovi brings portal travel between planets to a halt until ten turnings from now." A long finger tapped a stack of papers. "I have family trees for everyone here, in Veersuni, and on DerTah, and will deliver them to you as soon as I am able." He scanned the document. "The MasTer's estate is massive and complex. Rayn had holdings on most planets in this solar system. She owned the mineral rights here on TreBlaya and on the El Stroman continent of El QuilTran. I have been in contact with her financial and resource reckoner and her legal advisors. Most of her wealth and holdings she left to me with the stipulation that it pass to Troms el Shiv when I feel he is ready to take the reins. She has bequeathed each of you a small gift, which I will distribute individually. Questions?"

When no one spoke up, he continued. "Rayn's biggest concern, and the reason she used her resources to gather us together on TreBlaya, is that we represent the power structure of the Eleo Preda. Although many Eleo Predans escaped to this side of the Décussate, the majority reside in other solar systems and other galaxies. We are the closest to the Outer Rim. We are also the descendants of El QuilTran's brightest minds and most revered leaders. The Pheet Adole fear we might seek revenge and use our combined power to wipe *them* out. If the persona of The MasTer still lived, he would do exactly that. Rayn's true personality, however, had other plans." He placed the document he held on top of the stack and glanced in Elf's direction, his expression questioning.

The boy removed his arm from Ari's chair, clasped her hand, and nodded.

"Rayn's goal was to end the war and unite the opposing cultures on El Stroma. Toward that end, she used the process of Protariflee to not only provide a child for herself, but to create a birth-mate for Elf, a birth-mate from the egg and sperm of the RomPeer's daughter and his most trusted counselor. Someone discovered Penesert el Stroma's whereabouts and kidnapped her when she was five sun cycles."

Everyone's attention focused on Elf. Ari tried to pull her hand free. Elf held fast. His dark eyes sought hers. Her spine stiffened and her chin went up. "You have a birth-mate. You have no need of me."

He gripped her hand in his. "If you run, you'll never know if what we share is strong and true." His gaze embraced everyone at the table. His voice rang out. "With all present as my witness, I state that I, Troms el Strom, love Arienh Lynae AsTar Nadrugia." He held her gaze and continued. "*We* cannot know what the future brings, but I swear to stand by you until my last breath."

Ari paled. Then a flush crept up her neck. "*You* have a birth-mate." She glanced at Brie. "I know the loyalty that comes with gestating in the same womb, of being born on the same turning, of sharing a bond that is deeper than the breadth of the Universe." She pulled her hand free. "Do not make promises, Troms el Shiv, you cannot keep." Head held high, she walked from the room.

Elf's dismayed gaze flew to Relevart. "I'm so sorry. I forgot..."

Murmured sound pervaded the chamber.

Relevart raised a hand. The murmur of voices quieted. "I believe a break is in order. Let us reconvene in one quarter chron circle."

The image in the fountain faded, leaving those in Veersuni and Shu Chenaro wishing for more.

While those in Veersuni dispersed to think and clear their minds, Sparrow and Allynae remained in the sanctuary. Seated on a bench, her gaze fixed on stained-glass color, Sparrow waited for her companion to join her. Instead, he stared into the fountain and cracked his knuckles one at a time. When at last he faced her, puzzlement clouded his eyes.

"The twins are only sixteen sun cycles. How can Ari think she's in love? Elf isn't much older, is he? And Brie and Esán?" He sank onto the bench.

Sparrow clasped his hand. "Our girls are not much younger than I was when we first met, Alli. Do you remember how much in love we were? Time will tell if their first love is their last. Don't fret. I'm more interested in learning our ancestry and how it affects them and us. I'd also like to know if they'll be coming back to Myrrh soon." She sighed. "I know they have their own destinies, but I'm not ready to let them go."

The sound of dripping water ceased. Allynae pulled her to her feet. "Here we go, Guardian of Myrrh."

They moved to the fountain.

Almiralyn smiled up at them. "Good to see you, Alli."

"And you, Sis. How are Maman and Papa?"

"They're fine. I'd be surprised if you don't see them soon." Her attention shifted to Sparrow. "How are you holding up?"

Sparrow smiled at her Sister-by-Joining. "Wolloh will work with me before he leaves. The Galactic Guardians have been in contact. They tell me my gifts are maturing." She cocked her head to one side. "Are you coming to Myrrh prior to leaving for El Stroma? Are the twins?"

"I'm not sure, Sparrow. Relevart has made no decisions yet."

Corvus appeared at her shoulder. The dimple in his cheek deepened as his smile widened. "Good to see you both. Congratulations, SparrowLyn." He turned to Almiralyn. "Relevart would like to confer with us before we reconvene."

Almiralyn waved. "We will know more soon. Take good care of each other."

The tranquility of Veersuni settled over its occupants as the fountain's drop, drip, drop drifted through the room.

Epilogue-Chapter 3
TreBlaya

Ari straddled a stone balustrade, gripped the edges, and swung her legs like an angry child. This balcony, the only place at Soasi where the crystalline dome was not apparent, had become her getaway. Although she had encountered Abarax and knew Relevart retired to it, few others came here. The memory of the sadness on the Astican's face ended the agitated swing of her legs. *I believe it cared for The MasTer, for Rayn...* She bit her lip. *For Relevart's birth-mate.*

A silhouetted figure blocked the doorway. Elf stepped into the light. "May I join you?"

An intentionally disinterested shrug preceded her reply. "If you like."

He traversed the balcony and climbed astride the balustrade, facing her.

His presence, so close, too close for comfort, sent her scooting back. She folded her arms across her chest and said in a flat voice, "How may I help you?"

A flinch raised his shoulders. "Ari, we know nothing about Penee. I feel her enough to sense she's alive, but I don't have the same closeness you have with Brie. Penee and I are *not* twins. I have memories of us as children, and yes, I loved her—but as a sister or playmate."

His imploring tone and the tenderness in his expression eased the pain in her heart. She traced an infinity symbol on the black stone. "I don't want to lose you. But if it is inevitable, then..." She raised her eyes to look into his. "Let's end it now."

Earnestness filled Elf's voice. "Ari, we don't know what the future will bring. Can't we face it together and see where events take us?"

Pressing her palms against the smooth stone railing, Ari scanned the landscape where Relevart had seen tiny green shoots pushing up through the blackened soil. The image of life's return to TreBlaya gave her hope. She swung her back leg over the balustrade, jumped down to the balcony, and held out a hand. "I can try."

His relieved expression when he landed in front of her and clasped her hand brought tears to her eyes. He wrapped his arms around her and rested his chin on her head. Warm breath rustled her hair. The steady beat of his heart vibrated against her chest.

Brie hurried onto the balcony, stopped short, and shot her a knowing smile. "Relevart sent me to find you. He's ready to proceed."

Elf held Ari at arm's length. "I need to talk to Relevart. I'll meet you there." He brushed a kiss across her lips and strode through the door.

The heat of a blush made Ari bluster, "I...we..."

Brie grinned. "Looks like you made up. I'm glad." She grabbed her hand. "Come on. I want to hear what else Relevart discovered in Rayn's papers."

Ari let her twin lead her down the hall, preparing as she went to enter a room where all eyes would be on her.

Relevart glanced up as Elf entered, looking elated then contrite. Setting aside the journal he had been reviewing, the VarTerel presented a stern face and waited for the apology he knew was on the way.

"Relevart, I am so sorry." Elf's contrition mimicked the look of a young pup that knew it had erred. "I didn't mean to speak aloud. My emotions... Well, sir, I just couldn't help it."

Had Elf been younger and the situation less worrisome, Relevart might have ruffled his hair and sent him on his way. "Your behavior has placed you and us in danger. What do you think should be done?"

Rayn's son squared his shoulders. "I believe I should explain and apologize, sir. It won't undo the damage, but perhaps it will remind everyone to be vigilant."

The twins appeared in the doorway.

His expression stern, he allowed a twinkle to spark in his eye. "I'm glad you and Ari sorted things out." He once again picked up the journal. "Take a seat. I'll call on you soon."

Through half-closed eyes, Relevart regarded his companions as they entered and gathered in small groups. *The power assembled in this room, on Myrrh, and on DerTah, is formidable. How do we make the best use of it, protect ourselves, and accomplish everything that must be done?* His eyes came to rest on Nomed. *I have a surprise or two for you, my friend.* He reread the passage that had caught his attention, returned the journal to the stack, and waved a hand above the oval bowl of water at the table's center. When the image had focused, showing those in Myrrh and DerTah, he gripped his staff and tapped it against the floor. "Please, everyone, your Eleo Predan family history is at your place at the table. Take a moment before we will begin."

Excited interest and the sound of turning pages filled the room. Anxious observers on the water's surface watched with a touch of envy. Relevart smiled. "Those in Myrrh and Shu Chenaro, patience. You will receive your histories soon."

As he spoke, Wolloh limped into the study at Shu Chenaro and handed a file to Stebben. "From the Universal VarTerel..." He lifted his staff, stepped into the astral beauty of night, and reappeared in Veersuni with a second file under his arm. But for an occasional gasp and the crinkle of paper, tense quiet reigned.

Nomed shook his head, gave a soft laugh, and peered into the bowl. In Veersuni, Torgin walked to the fountain. Surprised interest flashed between them.

Torgin broke the silence. "We are cousins. Your father is my mother's uncle."

Nomed grinned. "We are indeed cousins."

Esán joined Torgin. "I think that means we're cousins as well. How unexpected, and how wonderful."

Relevart stood and motioned Nomed and the boys to sit. The room grew quiet. "You may explore your histories further at a later time. Right now, we must proceed with our agenda. Please give Elf your attention."

The boy squeezed Ari's hand and came to his feet. "I owe you an apology and an explanation. For our safety, yours and mine, Relevart asked me to continue to use telepathy to communicate. He hoped our enemies would focus less on finding me if they continue to believe I remain mute and unaware of my past." His gaze rested on Ari. "In a moment of high emotion, I gave myself away. I am asking you to keep my secret. Please forget I regained my voice. *From this moment onward, I will use telepathy until Relevart tells me it is safe to do otherwise.*"

"Thank you, Elf." Relevart scrutinized those at the table. "I trust all of you to protect Elf's secret. If it leaks out, the Pheet Adole will descend on us and many others." He picked up a document and perused the contents. "I have a list of those who wish to accompany Henrietta and me to El Stroma on our initial voyage. Let me know if I've missed anyone... Almiralyn, Corvus, Mairin, Lanli, Teva, Lenadi and his life mate, Akeri, Arienh, and Troms el Shiv. Brielle will make the trip to El Stroma at a later date. It is vital that she spend time at the Temple on KcernFensia and also continue training with Wolloh. Somay will take Esán back to Tao Spirian. When Esán fully recovers from his illness, he will go into seclusion until the Quickening of his dual Seeds of Carsilem is complete. For those of you who may not know, in order for the Seeds to achieve maturity and for Esán's formidable talents to achieve their full potential, he must spend time away from humanity."

He consulted his list. "Ah, yes. Nomed will return to DerTah." Focusing on the bowl, he said, "TheLise, by now you will have discovered your mother was Eleo Predan. Do you wish to travel to El Stroma?"

"I am responsible for Trinuge, Wolloh. I must remain on DerTah."

"Thank you, my dear." Relevart placed the list on the stack of papers in front of him. "Next: who wishes to return to Myrrh before heading to your next destination?"

Relevart recited the names of those who raised their hands. "Ari, Elf,

Nomed, Brie, Mairin, Lanli, and Lenadi." He nodded at Henri, who scribbled a list. "Add yourself, Henri. Good. We will leave after our morning meal. Almiralyn and Corvus, please stay. The rest of you take some time to ponder all you've learned. I will be available for questions following supper."

Chairs and feet shuffled; the room emptied.

Brie slipped away. The news Esán would return to Tao Spirian and then go into seclusion left her reeling. *Will I ever see you again? Will you join us in Myrrh? Oh, Esán...*

She discovered a small, dark room down the hall from The MasTer's chamber, and stepped inside.

A soft voice stopped her. "Can I help you?"

"I am so sorry. I didn't mean to intrude." Brie prepared to withdraw.

"Please don't go."

She tiptoed forward until she could make out the shape of a single bed.

"It's alright, my dear. I won't hurt you." The breathy voice paused. A quiet inhale gave its owner the strength to continue. "Open the curtains, and you will see I am quite harmless."

Brie pulled the heavy drapes aside, squinted in the sudden brightness, and turned. Tucked in the bed, a frail, old woman peered at her from fading honey-brown eyes. Brie stepped closer. "Who are you?"

The aged, dark-skinned face crinkled into a toothless smile. "I might ask you the same question, my dear. Please come closer so I can see you better."

Brie moved to the bedside. "I'm Brielle AsTar from the planet of Thera."

"Ahh." The woman looked Brie up and down, licked her parched lips, and blew out a tired breath. "You are here with the VarTerels?"

"I am. And you?"

She licked her lips again and smacked her gums together. "I am Rasiana from..." A furrowed brow redefined the deeply etched lines in her skin. "El Stroma. I am from El Stroma." Satisfaction brightened her eyes. "Abarax tells me The MasTer is dead?"

Brie nodded.

Arthritic fingers plucked at the bedding. "It is good." She shook her small fist. "*He* was an evil man." Tears made her eyes bright. "But I miss

Rayn. She came to visit me every turning." Her face hardened. "She cared. He wanted me dead." Venom filled each word. "He tried to kill me." White-knuckled hands gripped the comforter. Her frightened gaze darted from side to side. Tears traveled deep wrinkles to soak her pillow. The withered hands relaxed as her expression morphed from hatred to love. "Rayn saved me. Took care of me." A conniving look wiped the love away. She beckoned Brie closer and patted the bed beside her. "If you promise to tell only *her* birth-mate, I will tell you a secret."

Brie touched the Star of Truth. A warm tingle and nothing. No pain. No warning sting. She sat on the bed. "Are you sure you want to share it?"

Rasiana wrung her hands, then grabbed the comforter and clutched it to her chest. "I've told no one else." She worked her lips and gums in a rolling motion. "What did you say your name was?"

Brie started to speak. A raised finger stopped her.

"Brielle," she whispered. "I've been waiting, Brielle. *She* told me you were coming. *She* told me to tell you." Gums smacked. Eyes rounded. A hand as dry and brown as an autumn leaf gripped Brie's. "I carried babies." She patted her concave belly. "Carried babies for Rayn. First there were two. She named one Elf and one Penee." Her expression grew sad. "Then another." She shook her head. "Dead before it birthed." She brightened. "The last one—so special—so perfect..." The hand tightened on Brie's. "*The MasTer* found out. *He* sent it away."

Brie leaned closer. "What was the baby's name?"

"Rethson." She coughed and sagged onto her pillow. "The MasTer... " She spit the words into the air. "A wicked man took the baby away. Wicked man's name—" Her head dropped forward. The hand on Brie's arm relaxed, then gripped harder. Unexpected strength made Brie gasp. The head came up. Frightened eyes flew open. "Not yet, Rasiana. Tell all." With fierce determination, she pulled Brie closer. "Baby—her son and Rethdun." Her hand groped beneath the comforter. Distress puckered her wrinkled mouth. "Where are you? I put you right here. I... Yes-s-s-s." She withdrew a small, black lacquer box and clutched it to her heart. "For him..." Pale lids drooped and fluttered open. "For Rethdun."

Confusion left her licking her lips and muttering. A hiss accompanied her struggled to focus on Brie. "Rethdun and Rayn..." Her eyes rolled back in her head. Shaking hands clutched the comforter. "Jaradee's Legacy. Story in journ—"

Collapsing onto the pillow, she drew in a shallow breath. Blank, staring eyes lost their luster. A whispered exhale left the fragile body deflated and lifeless.

"Rasiana?" Brie clasped the delicate wrist, found no pulse, and rested it on the bed. *I have never seen death claim a soul. It was so quick.* She stared at the inert body. The emptiness stunned her. Tears ran down her cheeks as she removed the box from flaccid fingers. *I have to find Ari.* At the door, she turned and whispered, "May your journey be filled with grace." Taking a moment to compose herself, she stepped into the corridor.

Almiralyn and Corvus joined Relevart at the end of the table and waited for him to begin. He sat deep in thought, then straightened the papers in front of him and placed the journal on top. When he looked up, Almiralyn's heart jumped.

Corvus rested his arms on the table, attention unwavering. "What do you need, VarTerel? You know Almiralyn and I will do our best to help."

Relevart adjusted the angle of the journal and glanced at the door. "Please, Corvus, bring another chair. We are about to have company."

Corvus placed the chair next to the VarTerel and returned to his seat.

"Thank you. I—" A soft knock interrupted. "Come in, Brielle."

Almiralyn watched her niece enter. Overly bright eyes drifted from her to Corvus and came to rest on Relevart. She brushed a tear from her cheek, stared at the wetness on her palm, and crossed to the table.

"Rasiana is dead. I've never seen a person...I..." A tear rolled down the side of her nose and dispersed over her lips. "I went to find Ari, but..." Another tear and a hiccuped inhale.

Relevart patted the seat next to him. "You have sustained a shock, Brielle. Take a moment to collect your thoughts."

Like a sleepwalker, she sank onto the chair, clutching a small, black box in her hand.

"Take your time, Brie." The VarTerel's gentleness eased her agitation. "Almiralyn, please pour her a glass of water. Corvus, would you summon

Abarax? Ask him to check on Rasiana. You will find him on the balcony overlooking the fire pits."

Corvus hurried from the room. Relevart pushed his chair back. "Why don't I step outside and let you have a few minutes?" He motioned Almiralyn to take his seat and left her to support her niece.

Brie heaved a sigh, heavy with sadness. "I'm alright, Aunt Mira, just stunned by how swiftly life exits the body. I've never seen a person die." A tear slid down her cheek. "Buster died, but I wasn't there." She rotated her water glass one way and then the other. "I haven't thought about death or where we go when we die or..." She picked up the glass, sipped the cool fluid, and replaced it on the table.

Almiralyn listened to her niece and remembered her first experience, the sense of loss, the time of grieving. "Death makes us look at life from a different perspective. We must cherish each moment, Brielle. Why don't you and I talk more later? I believe you have something to share with the VarTerel." She moved back to her seat.

"I do."

On cue, Relevart entered and lowered his rangy body onto his chair. "Are you ready to continue, Brie?"

"I am. Thanks for understanding." She studied the small box she continued to hold. "You know Rasiana?"

Relevart stroked his chin. "Abarax mentioned her to me."

Almiralyn nodded. "I checked on her this morning."

Brie continued to stare at the box. "Rasiana told me a secret, one I am to share only with you, Relevart."

"It's alright, my dear. You can tell us both."

Brie blew out a breath and described her visit with the elderly woman. When she reached the part about the babies, she paused. At a nod from the VarTerel, she continued her tale. "Relevart, you and Rayn have a son."

The VarTerel's hand flew to his heart. He closed his eyes. A hushed silence wrapped around him like a robe. As though he had thrown a stone into a pool, his emotions began to roll to the surface. He opened eyes misty with tears. "Rayn left a hint in her last journal, but I thought she was delusional." He rubbed the center of his forehead. "Tell me what else she shared, Brielle."

She explained that the first attempt had failed. "The baby was stillborn.

The second attempt succeeded. Rayn snuggled your beautiful son in her arms; she named him Rethson. When The MasTer discovered the boy and realized Rayn intended to abandon her male persona, he sent the baby away."

Relevart's piercing, dark eyes hardened. "Who took the child away?"

"I don't know. Rasiana died before she could tell me." She set the small black box in front of him. "She asked me to give you this."

Relevart studied the box, removed the lid, and withdrew one dark sable curl. His hand trembled. "So, it is true. And you say she called him Rethson?"

"Yes. And just before she passed, she said two things: Rethdun and Rayn, then Jaradee's Legacy. Story in journ—" Brie brushed a tear from her cheek. "She died before she finished what she wanted to say."

He returned the curl to the box, replaced the lid, and held the box to his heart. "Another mystery to solve; another complication to untangle." Tucking it in his jacket pocket, he turned his astute gaze in Brie's direction. "You look puzzled, my dear. How may I help?"

Brie bit her bottom lip. "When Rasiana spoke of Rayn and The MasTer, it sounded like they were two separate people. They weren't, right? I mean, Ira was Ari's shifted form, but he was still Ari." Her brow wrinkled as she looked from Relevart to her aunt.

Relevart sat back. "Almiralyn, I believe you might explain Ari and Ira better than me."

Almiralyn rested her forearms on the table. "You know that when we shape shift, Brie, as you do to the Water ConDria or I do to Mira, it is vital that we not stay in our shifted forms too long. If we do, we can lose touch with the essence of who we are."

Brie's brow smoothed. "You mean like when the Sebborr trapped Corvus in his Karrew form?"

"Exactly. We would have lost him to the raven if you hadn't reached him." Almiralyn shuddered and then continued. "Before I sent you, Torgin, and Ira to rescue Esán, I gave Ari a trigger...the pain in her finger...to warn her subconscious she needed to change."

"So Rayn didn't have a trigger?"

Relevart answered. "Correct. Her journals are clear. Her anger and hatred at those who had hurt her and supposedly murdered me brought

The MasTer forth. The longer she remained in his form, the more of herself she lost. It speaks to her strength and determination that she could reassert her female personality at all. Her desire to have children was so great that she overpowered her shifted form. When Elf was in danger, her mother's love again brought her to the surface. What Rasiana described sounds like a split personality, in this case a duel between her mistress' feminine and masculine aspects. Her journals suggest there was more to it. Rayn thought so, too. She asked me to have the genetic technicians test her DNA to make certain." He paused. "Does that help?"

"A little. So, was Ira Ari's masculine aspect?"

Almiralyn smiled. "We all have feminine and masculine sides. When our emotions are healthy, these aspects remain in balance. If polarized to either side, our dual nature can cause instability."

"Poor Rayn."

"Don't feel sorry for her, Brielle." Relevart fixed his steady gaze on her. "Learn from her instead. Choose with care in each moment. Rayn's life was what she made of it. Choose wisely, Brielle AsTar." He swiveled to observe Corvus and the Astican entering the room.

Abarax bowed. "The Lady Rasiana has indeed passed, VarTerel. My mistress left instructions for the care of her body. It is being done as we speak."

"Thank you, Abarax. Please take a seat and share her story."

It moved to the table, waited for Corvus to sit, arranged its wings to accommodate a chair, and lowered onto the seat.

Almiralyn watched memories gather around the creature like a mist. She settled back, prepared to listen. Rasiana's story not only intrigued her; on some level, she knew it would affect all their futures.

Epilogue-Chapter 4
Myrrh

Sparrow lounged in the Reading Room, enjoying the warmth of the fire. Allynae perched on the arm of her chair, listening to Wolloh and Somay discuss plans for Esán's return to Tao Spirian. Her thoughts strayed to the twins. *How soon will you be home?*

Wolloh's good eye found her. His odd mouth formed a crooked smile.

"Your girls will be here sooner than you think. In fact, you have a decision to make."

She smothered a yawn. "Decision?"

The frontal view of his face penetrated her weariness. A hint of amusement lit his eye. "Would you rather everyone descended on you here or at the cottage?"

"Oh my, I hadn't thought of that." Another yawn caught her by surprise.

The VarTerel raised a bristly brow and teased, "Sleepy, my dear?"

An easy laugh preceded her thoughtful pause. "I suspect the cottage would be best, but what of Elcaro's Eye? Will it be safe there?"

"It might be even safer." Wolloh's eyes narrowed. "Those searching won't be looking in that direction, at least not for a time. Thoughts, Somay?"

Esán's father smiled. "I believe you are correct, VarTerel. And with your help, we can build formidable wards around the fountain and the cottage."

Wolloh leveraged his body to standing. "Then I suggest we let Relevart know our plans. After that..." He bowed to Sparrow. "You know how to shrink the fountain and bring it back to size, correct?"

Sparrow smiled. "I do. Almiralyn taught me that and how to make the cottage visible, as well."

He reached for his staff and offered his good hand. "Shall we, Madame Guardian?"

With a saucy smile, she took it and rose. "Thank you, VarTerel. Alli, will you join us?"

Allynae stretched and came to standing. "I'll inform Yookotay of our plans. Anything else?"

"Yes. Zugo will need to accompany us so that Ari can heal his burns. Make sure Lisseta and his father are comfortable with that. We'll meet you..." She deferred to Wolloh. "Do we travel through Mittkeer, teleport, or use the Intersect?"

"Those who may watch will expect us to use Mittkeer. Teleporting a large group will alert our enemies to our position. I suggest we use the Intersect. I have not experienced that particular pleasure and have wanted to." He looked pleased.

Sparrow gave Allynae a quick hug. "We'll meet by the fountain in the Meosian Central Square. Somay, please help find everyone and have them gather their belongings." She watched them go with a touch of trepidation.

"You will be fine, SparrowLyn." The gleam in Wolloh's good eye encouraged her to relax. "Shall we take care of business?"

Walking beside him, she gathered her courage. *I am the Guardian of Myrrh. I will indeed be fine.*

The lips on his uninjured side curved into a knowing smile.

After apprising Relevart of their plans and making certain Sparrow had tucked a small Elcaro's Eye in her pocket, Wolloh hobbled after her from Veersuni and down the Hall of Priestesses. In the Cave of Canedari, his limped gait carried him around the space.

"So this is Evolsefil's home. I'm certain it will be glad to return to this quiet safety." He tapped his staff against the floor.

A square opening appeared. Water sloshed and whirled. A baritone voice boomed. "I, the Lake of Rorret, welcome you to the Cave of Canedari and the Dojanack Caverns, Wolloh Espyro."

The crystal Froetise sent radiant shafts of light shooting through gaps in its leafy cocoon at the tip of Wolloh's staff. He took an awkward step. "I am honored to meet you at last, Rorret. Soon you will continue your guardianship of Evolsefil. We thank you for your service and for your diligence."

"The honor, VarTerel, is mine." Tendrils of water licked at Sparrow's shoes. "Congratulations, SparrowLyn AsTar Nadrugia. You will do well in your new role as Guardian of Myrrh." The tendrils withdrew. "I will protect the crystal heart of Myrrh and the Caverns of the Dojanacks." The opening disappeared, and tranquility settled over Canedari.

Wolloh moved to Sparrow's side and placed his staff between them. "Since we are but two, I suggest we teleport to Meos."

As her fingers curled around the rowan wood, the cave blurred and Yookotay's council chamber came into focus.

To one side, the ReDael stood with his back to the room, hands clasped at the small of his back. Zugo fingered a gemstone marker on the round table, his spine arrow straight. Tension screamed through the gap between them.

Wolloh cleared his throat.

Both DeoNytes turned. Stubbornness obscured Zugo's usual exuberance. Yookotay, the picture of fatherly frustration, hurried toward them.

"Welcome to Meos, VarTerel." He touched his heart. "Congratulations, SparrowLyn, on your appointment as Guardian of Myrrh."

"Thank you, ReDael. I am—"

"I want to go to El Stroma." Zugo blurted out and shot a defiant glare at his father.

Stern determination lit the ReDael's pale eyes. "You are my heir and the future leader of Meos. Please curb your need to explore. You belong at my side."

Wolloh looked from one to the other. "Yookotay, I know you and SparrowLyn have things to discuss. Why don't you adjourn to your office while Zugo and I confer?"

The ReDael hesitated for only an instant, motioned Sparrow ahead of him, and followed her through the open door.

Wolloh pulled out a chair and lowered his crippled body onto it. "Please sit down, Zugo."

Obstinacy thrust Zugo's chin forward. "I don't want—"

Angling his smooth cheek to the young DeoNyte, Wolloh tapped rowan wood against the floor. "I may understand your dilemma better than you realize, young Zugo." He used the end of his staff to push a chair from under the table.

Zugo sank onto it and repositioned his injured arm.

Wolloh nodded his approval. "You want to go to El Stroma? Why?"

The DeoNyte's mulish expression dissolved into eagerness. "When I joined the twins and Torgin to fight the DiMensioner, I'd never been Outside. Unlike my father, I love doing new things and seeing other places." Again, the chin went up. "He desires only the safety of the Dojanack Caverns. Why doesn't *he* understand I'll be a better leader if I experience more?" His brow wrinkled. "I want to travel like my friends. At least when Elcaro's Eye was in Veersuni, I could observe their adventures. Now that it is gone..." A shrug propelled him to his feet.

Wolloh remained silent, his expression neutral.

Zugo gripped the edge of the table. "The DeoNytes cannot stay hidden forever, Wolloh. You said yourself that Mocendi search for Myrrh. They *will* find us. Please help me learn what I need to know to protect my people. Take me with you to El Stroma."

"Sit and we will talk."

With a hopeless sigh, Zugo slumped back into the chair.

The VarTerel noted the scars forming on his chin, cheek, and chest and the badly burned arm that refused to heal. "Look at me, Zugo. What do you see?"

The DeoNyte's eyes widened. "The VarTerel of the Inner Universe…a man who has experienced much in his lifetime."

Wolloh presented only his disfigured cheek. "You see, a man whose curiosity and stubbornness almost destroyed his life. Like you, Zugo, I disobeyed and paid the price. *You* are fortunate that Efillaeh has the power to heal your wounds. It will not, however, erase the scars. You, like me, will wear them as a warning to others. Choices made because of stubborn rebellion rarely profit anyone."

"But, Wolloh, you have been *everywhere*. *You* are the VarTerel. I know I have to return to the Dojanacks to lead my people. I accept and honor that. All I want is…" He lifted his uninjured hand and let it fall back to his lap.

Wolloh studied the youthful face. *We are more alike than you know, Zugo.* Seriousness cloaking his words, he said, "If I take you with me, how do I know you will not disobey and bring danger to yourself and others?"

Zugo stood and walked to his father's sapphire marker, placed a hand on it, and lifted a steady gaze to Wolloh. "I swear on the ReDael's Sapphire of Ascendancy to do as I am told by you and those representing you."

Wolloh leveraged himself to standing. "I can promise nothing, young Zugo, but I will speak with your father."

As though in answer to a summons, Yookotay ushered Sparrow into the chamber. "You need me, VarTerel?"

"I do, ReDael. Sparrow, please wait here with Zugo. We won't be long."

Zugo paced around the table, touching each marker, adjusting each chair, and glancing repeatedly at his father's door.

Sparrow's understanding gaze tracked his progress. "Pacing won't help, Zugo. Your father will decide based on what he believes is best for you and the DeoNytes."

"How did you know?" He laughed. "Of course, Wolloh told you, right? I mean, you are the Guardian and…"

Sparrow's warm smile stopped him. "They're almost ready. Are you?"

He hurried to her side as the door opened. Wolloh entered the council chamber. The ReDael beckoned his son into the office and closed the door.

· · ·

Zugo still couldn't believe his good fortune. A difficult conversation with his father left him breathless with excitement. He grinned. *I'm going to the Guardian's cottage with my friends.* Dark fingers touched his burned arm and hand. *Ari will be there! She'll use Efillaeh to heal my burns.* A tingle of anticipation skittered up his spine. *Then Wolloh will meet me in Meos and take me with him to DerTah.*

The idea that his dream of traveling was about to come true made him want to dance like his friend Skipt, the Enots. Instead, he waited with a pretense of calm at the chamber entrance, while his father conferred with the VarTerel and Sparrow.

A glance in Zugo's direction brought a glimmer of understanding to the ReDael's eye. With a quiet comment that made his companions smile, Yookotay waved him from the room.

Through the throng of bodies milling around the square—DeoNytes going about their daily business, his companions gathering to return to the cottage—Zugo spotted Esán and Torgin sitting on the lip of the fountain. Running up to them, he grinned. "Wolloh is taking me to DerTah. I wanted to go to El Stroma but... It doesn't matter. Wolloh will introduce me to the DerTahan leaders, and we might visit RewFaar and..." He gulped in a mouthful of air and grinned even wider.

The boys jumped up. Torgin thumped him on the back. "Good for you!"

Esán smiled. "I'm excited for you, Zugo. I know how much this means to you." He glanced beyond him. "Looks like we'll be leaving soon."

Zugo turned.

SparrowLyn and the VarTerel exited the Council Hall with his father and walked toward the square. His gaze followed Wolloh's halting progress. *When I watched him in the fountain, I never expected to meet him in person. Now, he is my mentor.* Anticipation, trepidation, and humility washed over him. He studied the divided face. *The man with two faces...*

Wolloh glanced his direction and nodded.

Zugo grinned. "Wolloh is sure interesting, isn't he?"

Esán laughed. "Interesting is not even close. Right, Torgin?"

Torgin slung his flute case over his shoulder. "I'd say extraordinary... remarkable...astonishing...incredible...a little scary..."

Zugo punched him in the arm and dodged a playful return punch. "I have missed you two!" His father caught his eye. "Father needs me. I'll be back."

Sparrow counted heads. Everyone but Allynae awaited instructions. He had gone ahead to make sure Katerrace and Feela, Almiralyn's handyman and her housekeeper, had returned. She pursed lips. *Alli will also make sure Mondago and his men have moved their camp beyond the pond.* She frowned. *It will be strange to have RewFaaran soldiers around. But since Relevart, Wolloh, and my father feel it's important...* She shrugged. Her frown deepened. *I still can't believe Lorsedi Telisnoe is my father, and that Mother is going with him to RewFaar.*

A hand on her arm made her jump. "Somay! You startled me."

His smile, so like Esán's, evaporated her negative thoughts.

"Changes are rarely easy, SparrowLyn." He looked around the square. "All of us have experienced a few."

Wolloh joined them. "Everyone is here. Shall we go?"

Sparrow thanked Yookotay one last time for his hospitality. "I will take good care of Zugo and bring him back to you safely."

The Redael of the DeoNytes motioned his son forward. "I look forward to your return, healed and healthy. Take care, my son. Please lead our friends to the Intersect entrance."

When at last they stood on the Intersect platform and Sparrow had divided her companions into two groups for the trip, she linked elbows with Wolloh. "Are you ready? We arrive on three different platforms before we reach Nemttachenn Tower. Allynae will meet us there—a precaution, just in case there's trouble."

Wolloh, his good side to her, grinned like a boy. "Nemttachenn. I've always wanted to see it."

She smiled at the VarTerel. "I bet you'd like to meet CheeTrann, too."

"And Paisley. I am looking forward to meeting CheeTrann's chess opponent." Wolloh gripped his staff and smiled at Zugo. "Our young friend is as eager to be off as I am."

Sparrow glanced over her shoulder. Somay, Esán, and Torgin stood ready to follow. She took a breath, repeated the Key for the next platform, and stared in wonder as the geode-like space flashed above her.

Wolloh absorbed the glimmering beauty of malachite and sapphire, emerald and topaz. Flickering stars rekindled memories of traveling through Mittkeer. From the next platform, he fought the urge to reach out and touch the slender tubers beneath the grasslands. Moments later, the long, tangled roots of the Terces Wood surrounded them, and they prepared to climb a steep stairway.

Somay and the boys flashed into view as Zugo jogged up the steps. Esán and Torgin dashed after him. The door swung open, and they darted through.

Wolloh held back. "Somay and Sparrow, please go ahead. I'll join you in a few minutes." Breathing in the scents of dark earth and burrowing vegetation, he contemplated the vastness stretching around him. "It is rare these days to experience the innocent freshness of the Intersect," he said to no one but the stars sprinkling the night sky. "A small corner of Mittkeer, I believe." One halting step at a time, he climbed the stairs and ducked through the opening into the Terces Wood. The chirp of birds and wind in the trees greeted him. He savored the smells of late autumn, the blue of the Myrrhinian sky, and the feel of mulch and soil beneath his feet. A subtle wave of enchanted energy urged him around a leafless maplenut tree. He stared up at a tall, granite tower. "Nemttachenn."

Crossing to where Sparrow, Somay, and the boys waited by the tower's arched entryway, he stepped into the dim interior. A curtain of invisibility brought him up short. Its subtle shimmer into nothing exposed a majestic quartz spire on a light solid gold base. Wolloh presses a hand to his heart. "Evolsefil." A throbbing wave of energy coursed through his crippled left side. Gasping, he felt the pain, his constant companion since his first attempt to shape the osprey, drained away. He stepped closer, pressed his twisted hand against the coolness of the spire, and closed his eyes. "Thank you, Prima Crystal. Now, I truly understand why you and your power are coveted by so many."

Pivoting, his limped gait carried him to the tower's center. "CheeTrann, Sentinel of Myrrh, come forth!"

Hazy blue light swirled up from the ground, formed a frothing cone of light, and coalesced into the shape of a giant man. A deep voice rumbled, "I, CheeTrann, welcome you to Nemttachenn, VarTerel of the Inner Universe. I see Evolsefil has made itself known."

"It has." Wolloh scrutinized the impressive stature of Myrrh's Sentinel. Froetise's crystal glow highlighted the rugged features and brought a gleam to the dark eyes. Wolloh lifted the staff in a salute. "Alvin Enus sends this message to you." His voice took on the tenor and cadence of the Universal VarTerel. "The Pheet Adole search for Myrrh. Be prepared for trouble. Protect and defend SparrowLyn and Allynae Nadrugia and Myrrh's connection to Thera." The crystal's light faded.

Serious eyes fastened on Wolloh's face. "I give you my word that I will heed the message, VarTerel. Myrrh's new Guardian waits outside. I must congratulate her."

Wolloh bowed and positioned himself nearer to Evolsefil.

Chee Trann called out, "Guardian of Myrrh, make yourself known."

Sparrow motioned Somay and the boys to follow and walked into the dim interior of the tower. Evolsefil gleamed to her left. CheeTrann knelt on one knee and bowed his head.

Shrewd wisdom washed over her as he lifted his gaze. "I offer you my loyalty, Guardian of Myrrh. I am your servant and your protector."

Sparrow experienced a wave of astonishment. "Thank you, CheeTrann. I accept your loyalty and your protection."

He rose to his full height and boomed, "Spirit Boy, you have been to Tao Spirian. Health and vitality stir within you. Do not linger long on Myrrh, Esán Efre, or you will undo that which has been done." He nodded to Somay and fastened his intimidating gaze on Torgin. "You have gained much power since you were last in my tower. Your adventures have honed your skills. One turning, I would hear you play that flute." His gaze shifted.

Zugo quaked beneath his sudden attention. "Yookotay's son, you once again journey into the Outside." His eyes narrowed. "Beware the desire for adventure. It may well bring more than you can handle."

Allynae strode into the tower and stopped at Sparrow's side. "Hello, CheeTrann. Paisley sends his regards. He looks forward to a rematch soon."

The imposing figure pursed his lips in annoyance. "You are, as always, impetuous, Allynae Nadrugia. Tell our friend I await his return and look forward to our game."

The throbbing hum of Evolsefil shook the tower.

CheeTrann's piercing eyes swept to the crystal and back. "VarTerel, it senses Spirit Boy and calls to return to Canedari."

Wolloh beckoned Esán forward. "The ancient writings state that the one who removes the crystal from the cave must be the one to return it. We will all help, but you must be the one to accompany it to the caverns. I do not want you to deplete your energy reserve, so your father will go with you. Torgin, please prepare to play the flute. Sparrow and Allynae, stand on either side of me. Zugo, join our circle and lend your support. CheeTrann, remain alert. Warn us of any strangeness in the forest."

Evolsefil began to vibrate. Gold filaments within the spire quivered and gleamed brighter. The gold pedestal glowed. Torgin lifted the flute and began to play.

Esán placed his hands against the silky crystal surface. The tower faded as Evolsefil's energy flooded his consciousness. Memories flashed from one to the next...his escape from Seyes Nomed, the journey to Nevah Efas, and Elae's battered body... He blew out a shaky breath. Music building in volume and intensity chased the memories into abeyance. Each note etched a clearer picture of the Cave of Canedari in his mind. Zugo's presence brought clarity to the image. His confidence steadied.

Opposite him, his father's energy merged with his. The support of Wolloh and Sparrow, of Allynae and CheeTrann bolstered his inner resources. Molecule by molecule, he learned the crystal's structural make-up. Coherence of thought coupled with visual precision straightened his spine. Inhaling a cleansing breath, he thought the Prima Crystal Evolsefil through time and space.

Total silence held him motionless. A soft whispery sound followed by water's rhythmic lapping left him weak-kneed with relief. He opened his eyes and exhaled. The walls of Canedari enclosed them.

"At last you return to my care." The Lake of Rorret's bombastic voice echoed through the cave. "It has been too long since its magic filled these caverns." The lake withdrew. The floor pane closed.

Dazed from relief and exertion, Esán stumbled backward.

His father caught him, steadied him, and drew him away from the power of the crystal. Tears came unbidden. "We met here for the first time, Father."

Somay smiled through his own tears. "The Unfolding has changed so many lives, Esán. The most important thing of all—it brought me you."

Esán threw his arms wide. "I have met my mother, and I have seen my home planet." He dried his tears. "I have learned about friendship and love and..." Laughter bubbled up and spilled into Canedari.

Understanding and pride shone in his father's eyes. "You saved Evolsefil, Esán Efre, by removing it from harm's way. Now you have returned it to its home, as the ancient texts dictated." He rested a hand on his shoulder. "We must go back. Are you ready?"

"I am."

The next instant, they stood on the edge of a field of sunflowers.

Esán and Somay materialized at the Guardian of Myrrh's acreage as Sparrow raised her arms and began to recite,

> *"Time is illusion—Something but not.*
> *It holds things together. I retie the knot.*
> *Returning the cottage, no trick of the sight;*
> *The spell that's unbroken, I now make it right."*

Diffused light glistened. Where the cottage had once stood, vague shapes and muted colors wavered, grew more distinct, wavered again. The illusion shimmered; the cottage appeared and solidified. From its perimeter, the gardens spread outward like ripples in Elcaro's Eye. When they reached the borders of the sunflower field and the Terces Wood, grass and flower beds flowed into focus.

Sparrow led her companions around the side of the cottage as the swing and tree house took shape in the ancient maple tree. The red barn and the paddock, the pond and the caretaker's cottage, glistened into being. The chicken coop sprang up by the barn. A rooster crowed. The pounding of horses' hooves sounded, and Gemlucky trotted into the garden with Tam and four horses in his wake.

Wolloh rapped his staff against the ground.

Sparrow called out, "Seal and Secure."

The VarTerel raised the staff. "And it is so." Lowering it, he acknowledged Myrrh's Guardian with a slight bow of the head. "Well done, SparrowLyn."

When at last she walked their direction, Esán caught his breath. Her resemblance to the twins brought a sharp pang of loneliness. *I miss you, Brielle.*

Sparrow greeted them with a tired smile. "How did things go?"

"Evolsefil is safe in the cavern." Somay brushed a strand of chestnut hair from her cheek, erasing her fatigue with the touch of a finger.

She grinned. "Somay, you are magic. Thank you." Her attention switched to Esán. "Are you content the Prima Crystal is where it belongs?"

"I am. The Cave of Canedari feels alive again. And Rorret is thrilled."

"Then you have accomplished your task. Enjoy your friends while you can."

Zugo waved as he jogged across the back garden. A grinning Torgin greeted him with a slap on the back. "It is good to be here." He ran a hand down Tam's back. "Isn't she beautiful?" Not waiting for an answer, he rubbed her nose. "I have missed you, Tamboreen."

The tan and cream pony tossed her head and flicked her tail. Ears twitching, she swung her head toward the barn and gave a soft whinny of recognition.

A man, well past middle age and bristling with energy, strode from shadow to sun. A shy woman stepped from the safety of the barn and clutched his hand. They made their way along the garden path to the horses. He patted Gemlucky's gleaming hide and murmured a quiet word. The big stallion tossed his head, snorted, and led his charges through the barn and into the large back paddock. The man returned to the woman.

"Hello, Esán. You are looking well. You remember Feela, my wife."

"Hi, Katerrace,Feela. I don't believe you've met my friends, Zugo and Torgin."

Zugo smiled and nodded. Torgin offered a hand.

Katerrace shook it. "Friends call me Race."

Feela peered timidly at Torgin. "Tam told me about you. She has missed you." Her shyness dissolved as she told him how Tam had shared her name when Almiralyn first came to Myrrh.

Race observed her with an indulgent smile. Tidy as a pin in his overalls and blue plaid shirt, he exuded the aura of a man comfortable with himself.

Esán met him once before The Unfolding sent the couple back to their village. He had liked him then; he liked him now.

Allynae strode up to them, shook hands with the caretaker, and smiled at his wife. "Feela, Sparrow is in the kitchen. She would love to have you join her. Race, I'll take you to the RewFaaran camp and introduce you."

Torgin offered his arm. "May I walk you to the kitchen, Feela?"

Her shy smile flickered. "I would like that."

Esán sensed Zugo's energy flagging. "Come on. We need a quiet place to rest."

Zugo touched his scarred chest. "I could use some time to recoup."

Leading the way to the barn, Esán climbed the ladder to the loft, pitchforked hay into a nest, and plopped down next to his friend. Zugo's soft snores, like dust particles in sunlight, soon drifted through the barn. Esán stretched out and let his mind draw an image of Brie. *Will I ever see you again?*

Epilogue-Chapter 5
TreBlaya

A curious quiet settled over the meeting chamber at Soasi. Relevart leaned back in his chair, his attention fixed on Rayn's personal servant. Almiralyn rested a hand on Corvus' knee. He covered it with his. Brie tugged at a red curl, her brown eyes searching the Astican's face.

Abarax sat as though preoccupied, clawed fingers massaging his chin. With a sigh, he lowered his hand to the table and began.

"Rasiana traveled with Rayn from El Stroma in the last wave of rebels that escaped. The more venomous The MasTer's personality became, the fewer appearances Rayn made. Rasiana learned to stay hidden. One turning, Rayn's form and personality materialized and held firmly to reality. She asked Rasiana to carry her son and his birth-mate. He paused.

Brie leaned forward. "She had a protariflee lab built on the ship, didn't she?"

"She did." Abarax looked pleased. "Genetic professionals from El Stroma were recruited, and they set up a secret lab."

Relevart gazed at the Astican over steepled hands. "Where did she get specimens for implanting?"

"Rasiana discovered The MasTer's plan to destroy the lab and its contents. With my help, she rescued and hid several cryogenics canisters. As soon as the new lab was ready, she informed our mistress. Together, we transferred the canisters to *El Aperdisa*. The genetic team obtained additional specimens from hand-selected Mocendi. When everything was ready, the team impregnated Rasiana with Elf and Penee. For some time after their birth, the MasTer's personality and form remained in a state of dormancy unless circumstance demanded he emerge."

Corvus put an arm around Almiralyn. "What made her decide she wanted another child?"

Abarax's cherub-blue eyes narrowed in thought. "Even though Rayn loved her son and daughter, the longing to have her birth-mate's son haunted her. Eggs and sperm collected from her and from Rethdun when they were children were among those Rasiana had saved. Rayn had already directed a team to experiment with specimens taken from kidnapped children to see if they would mature in the lab. After many failures, they succeeded and perfected a process. Again, they impregnated Rasiana, the only other human woman still living in Soasi. When the first baby died, The MasTer raged to the surface, squelched Rayn's personality, and went on a rampage across the Inner Universe. Upon his return, he grew more and more suspicious of everyone around him."

Abarax scowled and sat in silence, lost in memories of that unpleasant time.

Relevart cleared his throat. "Do you need a break?"

"Just water."

Corvus filled a tumbler from the large pitcher on the table. The Astican quenched its thirst and set the glass down. "Vygel Vintrusie became The MasTer's most trusted Mocendi." The cherubic features dissolved into an acrimonious mask. The gray scales covering its body quivered. It shook itself and continued.

"When Rayn finally reasserted herself, she ordered a second try. Her delight when she held the newborn Rethson threatened The MasTer's personality."

Corvus refilled the Astican's glass. "Why did Rethson's birth threaten him when Elf and Penee didn't?"

Abarax dipped a finger in the water and let a drop fall back into fluid anonymity. "Rayn's love for her children, her birth-mate's son in particular, consumed her. Her decision to abandon her male form forever caused a battle between the two personalities. The MasTer emerged triumphant, found the baby, and ordered Vygel to take it someplace Rayn would never find it. He didn't want it destroyed in case it might be useful at a later time."

Almiralyn frowned. "Where did Vygel take the child?"

"Not even The MasTer himself knew." The creature flexed long, clawed fingers, curled them into a fist, and continued the story. "Over the course of the next two sun cycles, The MasTer made certain Rayn's appearances to visit Elf and Penee were rare and of short duration. *He* lavished affection on the boy and ignored the girl. The turning of Penee's kidnapping, he hid Elf and soon thereafter sent him to *El Aperdisa* to train as a Mocendi."

Sadness broke over Relevart like a storm. "It must have been horrible for Rayn. All her children gone." *My son, too.* Losing parenthood he had never considered flooded his heart in a torrent of anguish. He blinked tears away and motioned the Astican to carry on.

Abarax pursed rosebud lips. "Rayn never recovered from losing them. Her desire to hold on to her own personality faltered. The MasTer dominated for several sun cycles. It was during this period that he burned the flesh from his body—Rayn's body—and developed The Reach."

Brie bit her lip and asked a quiet question. "Where was Rasiana during this time?"

"She hid and waited for the chance to help our mistress assume her true identity. Opportunity arrived the turning Vygel Vintrusie brought the news that Thorlu Tangorra had made an example of Elf. Tangorra had ordered the boy's vocal cords cut and his memories eradicated. But before he could execute the ultimate step—throwing Elf in the fire pits of TreBlaya—the boy escaped.

"Rasiana realized the news would trigger Rayn's persona to fight. She created a sleeping draught that I put in The MasTer's wine at dinner."

Its angelic countenance appeared child-like, but only for a moment, before it twisted into an ugly sneer.

"That night Rasiana snuck into The MasTer's chamber and used her Eleo Predan training as a hypno-healer to tap into Rayn's personality. The news of Tangorra's plan and Elf's escape brought Rayn up from the depths of her subconscious. From then on, she ruled. Rasiana and I became her only companions."

Its wings ruffled. The scales clicked into place. "That is all I know. Unless you have questions, I should oversee the preparations for Rasiana to join our mistress."

Relevart tapped his lips. "I have one question. Did Rasiana ever mention Jaradee's Legacy to you?"

The Astican's cherub blue eyes squinted as he peered into the distance. "She told me a bit of Jaradee's story." His gaze widened. "Ahh. Jaradee was yours and Rayn's host mother. Her life history is the story of El Storma's demise." He pursed his rosebud mouth, then shook his head. "That's all I remember."

Relevart stood. "Thank you, Abarax. You have been most helpful. I want to be present when you take her to the fire pit."

"I will keep you informed." Bowing, it swept from the room, wingtips brushing the floor behind it.

Relevart laid a hand on Brie's shoulder. "You are looking worn, Brielle. Go. Rest until supper. I will see you there. And, Brielle, you may not share what we have learned here with anyone, not even Ari. Am I clear?"

"Very clear." She left, shutting the door behind her.

Almiralyn reached for Corvus' hand, her eyes on the VarTerel.

Brie smoothed red curls back from her face and sagged against the corridor wall. Exhaustion threatened to leave her asleep on her feet. Voices headed her direction jerked lassitude to action. *Ari. Elf. I can't see them yet. They'll both know I'm hiding something.*

She dodged into Rasiana's room, where someone had stripped the sheets and comforter from the bed and remove all of her belongings. Nothing remained to suggest anyone had lived in the austere space.

Hesitant to lie down where a woman had died, Brie wandered the room, peered between the drawn drapes, and tried to ignore her weariness. A yawn left her eyes stinging and fatigue weighting her body. She glanced at the bed and yawned again. *Rasiana wouldn't mind if I rested for a few minutes.*

Curling up on her side, she gave in to her exhaustion. Sleep lulled her, cradled her, plunged her deeper and deeper until dreams shifting like colors in a kaleidoscope dumped her into a barren place smelling of acid and decay. A curious quiet settled over the meeting chamber at Soasi. Relevart leaned back in his chair, his attention fixed on Rayn's personal servant. Almiralyn rested a hand on Corvus' knee. He covered it with his. Brie tugged at a red curl, her brown eyes searching the Astican's face.

Abarax sat as though preoccupied, clawed fingers massaging his chin. With a sigh, he lowered his hand to the table and began.

"Rasiana traveled with Rayn from El Stroma in the last wave of rebels that escaped. The more venomous The MasTer's personality became, the fewer appearances Rayn made. Rasiana learned to stay hidden. One turning, Rayn's form and personality materialized and held firmly to reality. She asked Rasiana to carry her son and his birth-mate. He paused.

Brie leaned forward. "She had a protariflee lab built on the ship, didn't she?"

"She did." Abarax looked pleased. "And she had genetic professionals from El Stroma recruited, and they set up a secret lab."

Relevart gazed at the Astican over steepled hands. "Where did she get the eggs and sperm for implanting?"

"Rasiana discovered The MasTer's plan to destroy the lab and its contents. With my help, she rescued and hid several cryogenics canisters. As soon as the new lab was ready, she informed our mistress. Together, we transferred the canisters to *El Aperdisa*. The genetic team obtained additional genetic specimens from trusted Mocendi. When everything was ready, the team impregnated Rasiana with Elf and Penee. For some time after their birth, the MasTer's personality and form remained in a state of dormancy unless circumstance demanded he emerge."

Corvus put an arm around Almiralyn. "What made her decide she wanted another child?"

Abarax's cherub-blue eyes narrowed in thought. "Even though Rayn loved her son and daughter, the longing to have her birth-mate's son haunted her. Eggs and sperm collected from her and from Rethdun when they were children were among those Rasiana had saved. Rayn had already directed a team to experiment with specimens taken from kidnapped children to see if they would mature in the lab. After many failures, they succeeded and perfected a process. Again, they impregnated Rasiana, the only other human woman still living in Soasi. When the first baby died, The MasTer raged to the surface, squelched Rayn's personality, and went on a rampage across the Inner Universe. Upon his return, he grew more and more suspicious of everyone around him."

Abarax scowled and sat in silence, lost in memories of that unpleasant time.

Relevart cleared his throat. "Do you need a break?"

"Just water."

Corvus filled a tumbler from the large pitcher on the table. The Astican quenched its thirst and set the glass down. "Vygel Vintrusie became The MasTer's most trusted Mocendi." The cherubic features dissolved into an acrimonious mask. The gray scales covering its body quivered. It shook itself and continued.

"When Rayn finally reasserted herself, she ordered a second try. Her delight when she held the newborn Rethson threatened The MasTer's personality."

Corvus refilled the Astican's glass. "Why did Rethson's birth threaten him when Elf and Penee didn't?"

Abarax dipped a finger in the water and let a drop fall back into fluid anonymity. "Rayn's love for her children, her birth-mate's son in particular, consumed her. Her decision to abandon her male form forever caused a battle between the two personalities. The MasTer emerged triumphant, found the baby, and ordered Vygel to take it someplace Rayn would never find it. He didn't want it destroyed in case it might be useful at a later time."

Almiralyn frowned. "Where did Vygel take the child?"

"Not even The MasTer himself knew." The creature flexed long, clawed fingers, curled them into a fist, and continued the story. "Over the course of the next two sun cycles, The MasTer made certain Rayn's appearances to visit Elf and Penee were rare and of short duration. *He* lavished affection on the boy and ignored the girl. The turning of Penee's kidnapping, he concealed Elf's presence and soon thereafter sent him to *El Aperdisa* to train as a Mocendi."

Sadness broke over Relevart like a storm. "It must have been horrible for Rayn. All her children gone." *My son, too.* Losing parenthood he had never considered flooded his heart in a torrent of anguish. He blinked tears away and motioned the Astican to carry on.

Abarax pursed rosebud lips. "Rayn never recovered from losing them. Her desire to hold on to her own personality faltered. The MasTer dominated for several sun cycles. It was during this period that he burned the flesh from his body—Rayn's body—and developed The Reach."

Brie bit her lip and asked a quiet question. "Where was Rasiana during this time?"

"She hid and waited for the chance to help our mistress assume her true identity. Opportunity arrived the turning Vygel Vintrusie brought the news that Thorlu Tangorra had made an example of Elf. Tangorra had ordered the boy's vocal cords cut and his memories eradicated. But before he could execute the ultimate step—throwing Elf in the fire pits of TreBlaya—the boy escaped.

"Rasiana realized the news would trigger Rayn's persona to fight. She created a sleeping draught that I put in The MasTer's wine at dinner."

Its angelic countenance appeared child-like, but only for a moment, before it twisted into an ugly sneer.

"That night Rasiana snuck into The MasTer's chamber and used her Eleo Predan training as a hypno-healer to tap into Rayn's personality. The news of Tangorra's plan and Elf's escape brought Rayn up from the depths of her subconscious. From then on, she ruled. Rasiana and I became her only companions."

Its wings ruffled. The scales clicked into place. "That is all I know. Unless you have questions, I should oversee the preparations for Rasiana to join our mistress."

Relevart tapped his lips. "I have one question. Did Rasiana ever mention Jaradee's Legacy to you?"

The Astican's cherub blue eyes squinted as he peered into the distance. "She told me a bit of Jaradee's story." His gaze widened. "Ahh. Jaradee was yours and Rayn's host mother. Her life history is the story of El Stroma's demise." He pursed his rosebud mouth, then shook his head. "That's all I remember."

Relevart stood. "Thank you, Abarax. You have been most helpful. I want to be present when you take Rasiana to the fire pit."

"I will keep you informed." Bowing, it swept from the room, wingtips brushing the floor behind it.

Relevart laid a hand on Brie's shoulder. "You are looking worn, Brielle. Go. Rest until supper. I will see you there. And, Brielle, you may not share what we have learned here with anyone, not even Ari. Am I clear?"

"Very clear." She left, shutting the door behind her.

Almiralyn reached for Corvus' hand, her eyes on the VarTerel.

Brie smoothed red curls back from her face and sagged against the corridor wall. Exhaustion threatened to leave her asleep on her feet. Voices headed her direction jerked lassitude to action. *Ari. Elf. I can't see them yet. They'll both know I'm hiding something.*

She dodged into Rasiana's room and stared. Someone had stripped the sheets and comforter from the bed. All of her belongings had been removed. Nothing remained to suggest anyone had lived in the austere space.

Hesitant to lie down where a woman had died, Brie wandered the room, peered between the drawn drapes, and tried to ignore her weariness. A yawn left her eyes stinging and fatigue weighting her body. She glanced at the bed and yawned again. *Rasiana wouldn't mind if I rested for a few minutes.*

Curling up on her side, she gave in to her exhaustion. Sleep lulled her, cradled her, plunged her deeper and deeper until dreams shifting like colors in a kaleidoscope dumped her into a barren place smelling of acid and decay.

A strange creature leapt from the top of a rockslide. Its growl shook the landscape. Its teeth glinted razor sharp in the eerie light. Terror propelled her over charred terrain, up endless hills, and along dry riverbeds to the top of a ridge. Hot breath burning her back sent her slipping and sliding down a steep embankment. Fighting to regain her footing, she hit the bottom and dodged down a crooked path bordered on both sides by flame-blackened stumps. She came to a standstill, where the mouth of a cave yawned wide. A withered, misshapen figure blocked the way. Dark eyes peered through holes in a featureless bronze mask. A high-hitched note emitted from a rounded orifice stood Brie's hair on end. Her stalker whined. Cowering, it crept away.

Menace as thick and tangible as molasses choked her. Danger and hatred lurched toward her. Her body's refusal to obey her command to run left her gaping in horror.

An impaired voice burbled, "You, destroyer, will suffer like so many suffered."

A twisted appendage reached toward her. Pain piercing her mind left her trembling. Forcing herself to think, she focused on the Star of Truth. No pain. No warning. An exhaled breath hissed between chattering teeth. The figure wavered. She shook her head. "You're not real. You're a dream!"

The landscape quaked and dissolved. The figure scrabbled forward. Her wards shot up. The stump of a hand struck the invisible wall, jerked away, and decomposed. One after another, malformed limbs disintegrated until only the bronze mask remained. Hatred blazed in the eyeholes as cracks splinter the mask into pieces, and they, too, crumbled into fine, gray dust.

Brie jerked to sitting and stared. A strange man towered over her.
"You did well, Brielle."
She shot to her feet, wards shimmering and her mind masked. "Who are you?"
"I am CharElgan Chealim. I have a secret for you to guard until the time is right."
"How do I know you aren't lying?"
"You are the bearer of the Star of Truth, Brielle AsTar. You know I speak the truth, as you knew you were dreaming only moments ago."
Instinct carried her hand to her neck. The Star, cool to the touch, tingled. "And what is this secret?"
A quick mind touch left her dazed and the room empty.
Brie rubbed her forehead and straightened her tunic. "I can't wait to go home tomorrow. I hope you're still in Myrrh, Esán Efre."

Relevart pinched the bridge of his nose and sighed. When he looked up, Almiralyn's sympathetic gaze searched his face.

"I think you need some time alone. We'll take a walk and come back in a quarter chron circle." She pushed her chair back and followed Corvus into the hall.

Relevart withdrew the black lacquer box and with shaking hands tipped the contents onto his palm. Quieting his racing thoughts, he contemplated the silky fineness of the sable brown curl, raised it to his nose, and breathed in the subtle scent of his son. *Rethson.* A soft sigh gave the curl the illusion of life. *You, too, are part of Jaradee's legacy.* Relevart cradled it between his palms and tried to envision a child carrying his genes and Rayn's. *What do you look like? Are you tall or short? You are almost sixteen sun cycles.* He opened his hand and narrowed his eyes. *The real question is: how do I find you?*

As solitude soothed his frazzled nerves, an answer emerged. He tucked the curl in the box and murmured, "How to make it happen is the question."

A knock, followed by a respectful pause, alerted him that Almiralyn and Corvus had returned.

"Come in."

Almiralyn stuck her head around the door. "Are you ready for us?"

"Yes. Please join me."

Corvus followed her into the room and sat down. "I hope we gave you enough time."

Relevart set the box on the table. "Solitude helped. Thank you. I never imagined having a son. Life has kept me too busy for a family. This news has left me shaken."

Corvus scooted his chair closer to Almiralyn. "What do you need us to do?"

"My first thought was to ask you to discover the whereabouts of Penesert El Stroma. Now I am in a quandary." He tapped the box. "I have a son. Which is more pressing...finding Elf's birth-mate or finding Rethson?"

Almiralyn traced the weave of her long braid. "I believe they are of equal importance, Relevart."

Corvus nodded. "I agree. Our enemies can use both young people against you—us—to gain control of The MasTer's wealth and of El Stroma.

If the Pheet Adole have Penee, as I suspect, that leaves you with one hand tied behind your back, and if they find Elf—"

Almiralyn straightened. "They trap you between the young people and the Galactic Guardians' wish to restore El Stroma and bring about a peaceful settlement between the planet's two warring factions." Her tone became more urgent. "I believe, Relevart, that my parents would bring an informed perspective to this conversation. They have spent much of their adult lives in secret pursuit of The MasTer."

Corvus's dimple deepened. "They might have stumbled on important information that would help us."

Relevart brushed thick, white hair off his forehead and turned toward the door. "It just so happens that they are—"

A knock, and Mairin stepped into the room ahead of her mate. "Did you call us, Relevart?"

"I did." He indicated chairs across from Almiralyn and Corvus. "Mira, will bring you up to date."

Corvus observed the exchange between Almiralyn and her parents with interest. He remembered meeting them for the first time at their estate in KcernFensia soon after Almiralyn's birth. Their disappearance when she was fifteen sun cycles and Allynae was ten had been devastating for both. Rayn brought them back together.

Almiralyn's narrative reached its conclusion. Mairin's eyes, the same sapphire blue as her daughter's, narrowed when Almiralyn explained Vygel had taken Rethson and secreted him somewhere out of reach. Lanli's expression, unchanging throughout her account, grew thoughtful.

Relevart sat back. "I imagine you have already guessed why I asked you here. Did you on your travels to uncover The MasTer's identity hear any rumors that might pertain to either Penee or Rethson?"

Lanli glanced at his life-companion and received an affirming nod. "Over the course of our travels, we met a group of younger Pheet Adole rebels. Unlike their parents and older relatives, they hoped to reestablish contact with the Eleo Preda and try to mend the rift. Rumors that an unknown party stole a girl child from right under the nose of The MasTer had come to their attention."

Mairin continued the story. "Those responsible had hoped to kidnap twins, a girl and a boy. Although there was a discussion about another attempt, they only managed one. Our source believed the person on the inside who helped them must have disappeared."

Relevart frowned. "Did you hear anything that might help us locate Penee?"

Lanli shook his head. "Not that I recall. Mairin?"

"A boy who worked in the stables in Soputto, and I became friends. He hinted at something, but I didn't pursue it. If we could find him, he might help."

"I know you want to go to El Stroma—"

"Relevart, we understand that finding Penee is important." Lanli put an arm around Mairin. "The resettling of El Stroma depends on all factions working together. We *will* find her."

Almiralyn stiffened. "But Maman—"

Mairin stopped her with a reassuring smile. "This is our way of life, Mira. We're good at what we do; we'll be fine." She turned to the VarTerel. "Relevart, we'd like to see Allynae and meet Sparrow. How do you feel about us leaving from Myrrh?"

"I believe it's a splendid idea. No one will suspect you are off on an errand for me. We can meet after this evening's meal to discuss details and avenues of contact."

Lanli pushed back his chair. "Good. We can use the time to develop a plan." With an air of purpose, he followed Mairin from the room.

Corvus observed the satisfaction in Relevart's shrewd gaze. "So, one problem down and one to go, VarTerel. What are your plans for us?"

"I need you to find Rethson, which means you must track down Vygel and Thorlu."

Almiralyn grimaced. "My two favorite people. Do you know where they ended up when you dispatched them from Mittkeer?"

"In another dimension, one that parallels Thera prior to its connection to Myrrh."

Corvus frowned. "That means you sent them through Time and

Dimension. We would need to travel through Mittkeer, and we are neither one VarTerels."

A blaze of white-blue light flared by the windows. CharElgan Chealim, a flash flood of power and ethereal beauty, smiled down at the room's occupants. "I am here to remedy that, Corvus Karrew Castilym. The Galactic Council has declared it is time to replace the VarTerels destroyed by the Pheet Adole." He beckoned Almiralyn forward. "We also feel it is time we had a female VarTerel. Avlin Enus, your staff please."

Relevart passed it to Chealim.

The Guardian peered down at Almiralyn. "You are hesitant, Almiralyn Nadrugia?"

"I vowed not to become a member of the Order of Esprow. Although most of its members are dedicated and honest, I do not wish to join the ranks."

Chealim's blue eyes twinkled. "Knowing you as I do, I have secured permission to provide you and Corvus with the required initiation independent of the Order. The Outer Universe will be your focus, and thus you will be answerable to Avlin Enus, the Universal VarTerel. Will that suit your desire for personal autonomy?"

Sapphire eyes widened with surprise and pleasure. "Yes, Chealim, it will."

"And you, Corvus? Will this arrangement work for you?"

Corvus moved to Almiralyn's side. "I am honored to accept the initiation under your stated conditions."

Froetise began to glow. "VarTerel, stand between them. We do this work together."

The crystal's dazzling light moved toward them. Corvus closed his eyes. Energy immersing him in color and light left him breathless. His body ceased to be solid. Molecules danced, spun, streaked through All Time.

Almiralyn gasped. Vibrant colors infused her mind as pulsing energy enveloped her. Marrow to bone to muscle to skin surging power saturated her body. Every molecule vibrated. Tears streamed down her cheeks. The thrumming in her brain sang a chorus with the rush of blood through her veins. Her heart's pounding rhythm vibrating her ribcage left her breathless. The flood of effervescent beauty gradually withdrew until only the soft hum of Froetise tingled over her skin.

Relevart squeezed her hand. "Open your eyes, girl."

Chealim smiled down at her. "We knew you had more talent to develop; but as always, Almiralyn Nadrugia, you surprise us. As do you, Corvus Castylim." He returned the rowan wood staff to Relevart. "They will serve us well, Avlin."

A corona of light surrounded him. "Be safe and be successful. The peace and prosperity of the Outer Universe depends on what you accomplish." The light imploded, leaving the spot where he had stood empty.

Almiralyn sank into a chair and accepted a glass of water from Corvus. "My legs feel as wobbly as a colt's."

Relevart laughed. "It's no wonder, my dear. You have assimilated more energy in the past few cron-clicks than most DiMensioners experience in their entire careers." Relevart fingered his staff. "On this trip, a staff could be more trouble than it's worth. When you return, yours will be waiting."

Almiralyn finished her water. "I imagine there are things we need to learn prior to using Mittkeer on our own."

The VarTerel whispered a word and waved a hand. Shimmering starlight ushered them into the Land of All Time and No Time, where their lessons began.

Epilogue-Chapter 6
Myrrh

Sparrow gazed out the kitchen window at the garden and pond. Wolloh had excused himself to rest; Allynae conferred with Race and Feela about preparations for guests; and the boys sprawled in the loft, reminiscing about their adventures. Alone for the first time since their return, she wandered the cottage, marveling at how it had already begun to take on her personality. She picked up a small, framed picture from the mantelpiece in the front room. Standin and her mother smiled back at her. Next to it, the portrait of the twins made her heart ache. "You have grown up much too fast. Sometimes I wish we were a normal family." She laughed out loud and returned it to the mantel. "There is definitely nothing normal about any of us."

In her studio, she placed a clean canvas on the easel, arranged her paints, and picked up a brush. Allowing her artist's trance to enclose her, she began to paint. Shape and color, highlight and texture created a collage of memories. The step drag of Wolloh's limped gait heralded his appearance in the doorway. Brush in hand, she turned.

Full face in view, with none of the posturing for affect she had observed so often in the fountain, his straightforward gaze met hers. "I believe it is time to bring Elcaro back to size. Company will arrive sooner than we expected. Do you need my help?"

"I don't believe so. Almiralyn taught me what to do." With deft movements, she cleaned her brush and secured her paints.

Wolloh accompanied her to the foot of the stairs. "I think I will take a quiet stroll through the garden while I can. Call if you have need of me." He left her to ponder the fact that the VarTerel of the Inner Universe trusted *her*.

Mounting the stairs, she noted the creak of the fourth step, made a mental note to keep it, and continued to the sanctuary. Once inside, she stopped to revel in a few monumental truths. "I am the Guardian of Myrrh. This is *my* cottage and *my* sanctuary. A full Myrrhinian sun cycle has passed since Almiralyn took Merrilea and me to hide in the Dojanack Caverns. Several moon cycles have passed since she left for TreBlaya with Relevart, and I assumed the role of acting Guardian."

She crossed to the map of Myrrh painted on the wall. "I'm the steward of *this* land. I didn't see that coming when I returned here to help my daughters."

She turned and withdrew the miniature fountain from her pocket. Awed by its beauty, she held it up and watched tiny rainbows glint in the purest white alabaster in the Inner Universe. "It's time to bring you home, Elcaro's Eye." Placing it on the floor at the room's center, she positioned it with the statue on the rim facing the windows. After a quick review of Almiralyn's instructions, she recited:

> *"Elcaro, the All-Seeing-Eye,*
> *Grow to size that I may spy,*
> *Within your depths, the heart of things,*
> *And all that coalescence brings.*

> *Expand your width and height to be*
> *My eyes that I may know and see.*
> *I clap my hands to call you forth.*
> *Spring to size from your true north."*

Three brisk claps snapped through the sanctuary. The miniature fountain trembled. Quick as the flick of a cat's tail, it achieved its normal size and sat glistening in the late turning sun.

Caught between astonishment and delight, Sparrow paced its circumference, stopped with her hands on her hips. "I did it! You are beautiful, Elcaro's Eye." She touched the tip of the Vesen crystal embedded in the pedestal. *"Rappae."*

Water surged up from the bottom of the alabaster bowl, swirled, and calmed, reflecting her face on the mirror-like surface. Another clap brought water to the upturned palms of the statue. The song of its fluid drip, drop, drip filled the room.

Entering Mittkeer always left Brie's senses reeling. A glance at her companions told her she wasn't alone. Only Relevart seemed unfazed. A wave of nausea gripped her. With a long exhale, she cast her thoughts back through time. Surprise at the swiftness of her nausea's departure left her smiling.

"Ah, Brielle, you have learned the way of Mittkeer." The Var Terel's dark eyes sparkled. "I believe Arienh would like to know it."

Brie hurried to where her sister stood with Elf. Neither looked happy. "Concentrate and send the pain and nausea into the past. It will be gone in an instant."

Ari groaned. "I'm not you, Brielle."

Brie winked at Elf, who already looked better. "But you are my twin, and you have every bit as much talent."

Her sister groaned, shut her eyes, and clasped Elf's hand. A soft guffaw and she placed a kiss on Brie's cheek. "Thanks, sis. That's a trick I will remember."

Elf's quick hug expressed his thanks. He took stock of his surroundings and his fellow travelers. *"I believe we have all discovered the secret."*

Relevart raised his staff. "Please form a tighter group."

Henrietta, Nomed, Mairin, and Lanli formed a snug circle with Ari and Elf. Brie clasped her Aunt Henri's hand on one side and Ari's on the other. Froetise's glowing light encircled them. A soft word from the VarTerel and a gateway opened. Relevart led the way into the alley between stalls in a barn.

"Look who's here!" Torgin scrambled down the ladder from the loft, helped Zugo down the last rungs, and met them midway to the open double doors into the garden.

Brie's welcome caught in her throat. She stepped to one side, her eyes fixed on Esán, the one person she had feared would already be gone. She knew Evolsefil was back in Canedari. Esán had no reason to stay.

As though suspended in time, he gripped the rung of the ladder and grinned.

Ari gave him a hug, threw a glance over her shoulder, and grinned. Elf herded her ahead of him. Still, Esán did not move.

Nomed looked him up and down. "You seem much better, nephew." He winked and strode into the garden.

To Brie, a world of space stretched between them—held them apart, their eyes fastened on each other. Esán took a step. The next instant, his arms wrapped around her. He lifted her up, put her down, and buried his face in her hair. "I have missed you so much, Brielle AsTar!"

Her delight bubbled up and burst into laughter. She touched his cheek. "You look great! Your hair has grown. You don't appear to be sick anymore. You are better, aren't you?"

He released her and cupped her face in his hands. "Things are moving slowly, but I'm improving."

His gentle kiss left her grinning like a fool. *"He loves me!"*

He kissed her again. "Yes, Brielle, I love you." He clasped her hand. "We should say hi to your parents before they start to wonder—"

Her quick kiss cut him short. Fighting to regain her equilibrium, she blurted out, "Did you know Father has not seen his parents since he was ten?"

Grinning, he grabbed her hand. "I've never seen you flustered before, Brielle AsTar."

The laughter filling Esán's eyes as they walked from the barn made her heart sing.

Excited voices drew Sparrow to the window. A glint of red hair sent her jogging down the stairs, through the kitchen, and out the back door. Ari waved, grabbed the hand of the boy next to her, and together they sprinted across the garden. Tears streamed down Sparrow's face as she hugged her daughter. "Where's Brie?"

Ari gave a deep guffaw. "She and Esán are discovering how much they missed each other." She nudged the boy forward. "Mother, this is Troms el Shiv. Elf, this is my mother, the Guardian of Myrrh."

Sparrow observed him with a touch of relief. She liked what she saw. *"Welcome to Myrrh, Elf. I was hoping to meet you."*

"I wanted to meet you and Ari's father."

Allynae strode around the end of the pond and gathered Ari into a bear hug. "I'm so glad to see you, Arienh."

Her joyous laugher made him hug her again before extending a hand to her companion. *"It is good to meet you in person, Elf. Thank you for taking care of our daughter."*

"It has been my pleasure, sir."

Ari cocked her head to the side. *"I didn't know you used telepathy, Father."*

He put an arm around Sparrow's shoulders. "All in a turning's work. Right, Guardian of Myrrh?"

Brie and Esán exited the barn and hurried toward them. Nomed and Somay finished their conversation by the maple tree and followed. Sounds of greetings and laughter filled the back garden.

Torgin eyed the joyful reunion with a touch of envy. A hand on his shoulder changed it to a gasp of surprise. "Mother. Father. I didn't expect you to be here." He hugged Renn and offered a hand to Wilith, who took it and drew him into an embrace. Torgin, eyes wet with tears, returned the first hug he could ever remember receiving from his father.

Sparrow's heart overflowed. All those she loved most, except her mother and Standin, milled around the garden. She bent to tickle Majeska under her chin. Amethyst eyes gleamed; her long tail twitched. With a clipped meow, the smokey gray cat trotted to her favorite place by the front door. Sparrow's gaze roamed the garden. Greetings, tears, smiles, and laughs created a party feel in *her* garden. *It is a party...a reunion. Speaking of reunion...*

Henrietta caught her eye and whispered something to Mairin and Lanli, who waited with Relevart in the lengthening shadow of the old maple. She dropped her spectacles in a pocket and placed a hand on Relevart's arm. With a nod to Allynae's parents, they ambled toward the cottage, where Wolloh waited by the back door.

Sparrow stood on tiptoe and whispered in Allynae's ear. With the efficiency of a sheepdog, she herded her family and guests around the cottage to the front garden, where a banquet awaited. A glance back assured her that Allynae and his parents had found each other. Embracing her role as hostess, she prepared to take good care of her guests.

Allynae placed one foot in front of the other. His dry mouth tasted pasty. Sweat or tears—he couldn't tell which trickled down his face. The moment his mother's arms encircled him, he knew they were tears. His knees turned to jelly. The warmth of his father's hand on his shoulder cancelled their sudden weakness. The young boy he had been when they left wanted to sob.

Mairin smiled through her tears. "It's alright to cry, Alli."

He let down. Tears bottled up for sun cycles rolled down his cheeks and soaked through his shirt to his heart. Lanli guided them to a bench by the pond, where his mother sat on one side of him and his father on the other.

Mairin clasped his hand and inspected his features one at a time, as if she could read the past in every line and wrinkle. "When the Guardians requested we find The MasTer, we realized it would be difficult. You were young, but strong enough to handle our absence. You had Lenadi and Teva and Mira to help. The job took longer and was more dangerous than we expected. We couldn't contact you, Alli, without putting you and everyone around you in peril."

Lanli stretched his arm along the back of the bench. "And returning prior to finishing the job would have brought the Pheet Adole down on all our heads. We hope you can forgive us. We didn't intend to be gone so long."

Allynae stared over at the pond. "Sometimes I hated you for leaving me. I'm lucky; Mira was always there. Lenadi became my best friend. When I went to live at the Temple of Mahyinaeh, it got easier." He sighed. "If I have learned anything from Mira and now Sparrow, it's that life takes you where you are needed. There is nothing to forgive. You did what had to be done. The Guardians realized you were the best ones to do the job. I'm just glad the girls will get to know you." He stood up and faced them. "I look forward to—"

Mairin clasped his hand. "We won't be here long, Alli. Relevart needs our help."

Allynae linked his arm through hers. "In that case, I suggest we make the most of our time together. Come and meet SparrowLyn."

They strolled together as the sun underscored its descent to the horizon with wide swathes of salmon, pink, and orange. In the front garden, Katerrace had already placed lanterns on the tables and hung glow-globes in the trees. Sparrow walked their direction, stopped to confer with Feela, and then hurried to Alli's side.

Allynae followed her movements with a touch of pride, then looked to where the twins and their friends gathered at a table, enjoying the calm of Myrrh's dusk. *At this moment, my life is perfect.*

Sparrow caught his eye. *"Life is always perfect."* With a gracious smile, she turned to his parents. "Welcome to Myrrh. I'm SparrowLyn AsTar Nadrugia. We are so glad you're here."

Epilogue-Chapter 7
Myrrh

Sparrow pumped the swing higher, soaking in the beauty of moonlight that painted the garden with silver and shadow. *My life is so full.* The reuniting of family and friends earlier made her smile. Hugging her daughters; seeing the health shining in Esán's eyes; watching Torgin, now so grown up, talking to his parents.

The swing reaching the top of its arc made her grin. *As a child, I loved seeing the world from on high. When it plunged to the bottom, my stomach jumped into my throat. The sense of freedom and flight when it shot higher made me giggle with sheer joy. I hated leaving it behind when Standin moved us to the Central Mountains.*

While it slowed of its own accord, she thought about her parents, about Allynae's reunion with his. The joy in his eyes when he introduced them to her made her heart sing. He was with them now, catching up on many sun cycles of living apart. She had listened while Alli described his shape shift to

Starfire. Ari and Brie plopped down next to him on the sofa and chimed in, eager to let him and their grandparents know their father was special. Sparrow had slipped from the room. Mairin and Lanli would leave in the morning. Family time would be much too short.

She pushed off and pumped the swing until the wind kissed her face and tangled her hair. *I miss the mother who raised me.* She leaned back and gazed up at the sky. *I miss you, Standin.* She jumped from the slowing swing, enjoying the surge of childish laughter bubbling in her throat.

Biting her bottom lip, she considered returning to the cottage. *I'm not ready for people.* She wandered to the edge of the pond and watched the moonlight dancing on the water. A small, flat stone glistening at her feet caught her eye. She picked it up, savored the smooth curve of its edges, threw her arm out, and, with a flick of her wrist, let the stone fly. One, two, three skips rippled the calm surface. She grinned. *Haven't lost my touch.*

Autumn's cool breeze ruffling her hair made her tug her sweater tighter. She sank onto the bench and let her thoughts return to the events of the turning. Midway through the wonderful meal Feela had prepared, Merrilea and Major Jordett had arrived from Idronatti, bringing with them Akeri, Lenadi's life-mate, and a PPP officer named Sagus.

Sagus spoke with Relevart about being part of the team going to El Stroma. She sensed Teva was the reason for his interest.

A chill prickled the back of her neck, a chill engendered by her sixth sense. Eyes narrowed, she sent a subtle mind probe sweeping over her acreage in search of a reason for her unease.

The RewFaaran camp was quiet. Demrach Gateway, guarded by Mondago's men, spun undisturbed. Nemttachenn gleamed silent and majestic in the moonlight. *What am I feeling?*

A shadowed figure descended the back porch steps. Henrietta flashed to her side.

"Relevart needs us." She touched Sparrow's arm. The sanctuary replaced the garden.

Wolloh placed a finger on his lips. The fourth stair creaked. Somay, Allynae, and Nomed arrived. Relevart materialized and waved a hand above the fountain.

"Our adversaries search. It is time to construct wards around Elcaro and the cottage. We must also obscure Myrrh's portals. He counted on his fingers. "Tropal, Demrach, Nervac, and NiaDisbo. Did I miss any?"

Allynae shook his head. "You got them all. There used to be five, but the Pentharian destroyed Kao." He turned to smile at Mairin as she and Lanli preceded Akeri into the sanctuary.

Brie appeared in the doorway and noted adults gathered in the room. "Do you need *me*, Relevart?"

"I do, my dear. Your presence brings our count to the power number eleven." He gripped his staff and moved to the fountain. Everyone, please form a circle and repeat after me,

> *"Wards and shields form—protect!*
> *Evil's quest you will deflect.*
> *Obscure all portals near the Eye;*
> *Foil attempts to good defy.*
>
> *Eleven is our number strong;*
> *We weave these shields to fight all wrong.*
> *Around the cottage and the grounds,*
> *Henceforth, our power now abounds."*

The room vibrated with the sound of eleven voices. Elcaro's Eye grew quiet. On its surface the soft shimmer of wards taking shape floated up from the bottom of the bowl, spilled over the alabaster rim, and like dawn's mist, drifted out the windows and around the land, the cottage, and the four portals. When water once again flowed from the statue's palms, Relevart and Wolloh raised their staffs. Eleven voices called out, "Seal and Secure." An alert hush stole over those gathered.

Finally, Henri removed her spectacles; Nomed rubbed the scar on his cheek; and Relevart and Wolloh lowered their staffs.

Relevart gave a small bow. "A job well done. Thank you. I suggest a good night's sleep. Tomorrow, the CoaleScent Cycle enters its beginning stages, and new journeys begin for many of us."

Allynae spoke to his parents, then put an arm around Sparrow. "I can tell you're not ready to settle down. How long will you be?"

She kissed his cheek. "Go. You need to share every moment you can with your parents. I'll let you know when I'm done." A brief hug and he was gone.

Nomed and Somay followed him into the hall. Wolloh's careful stride carried him to her side.

"I leave tomorrow with Nomed, Somay, Esán, and Torgin. Zugo will go with us as well. We cannot afford to be trapped by the Cycle of Dovi. We have much to accomplish at Shu Chenaro before the next phase of this adventure." His good eye found Somay. "Esán and his father will leave from DerTah. The boy requires more time on Tao Spirian to complete his healing."

Beside the map of Myrrh, Brie and Relevart conferred. The VarTerel finished talking and tapped her forehead. Somewhat dazed, she left the sanctuary.

Wolloh's good eye followed her exit. When his attention returned to Sparrow, his sympathetic expression was unyielding. "You know the girls must leave soon. Do not let Dovi catch them in Myrrh." When he reached the door, he turned his full face to her. "You are the perfect choice to follow in Almiralyn's footsteps, SparrowLyn. Never doubt that."

Henri, who had been staring into the fountain's bowl, looked up. "He's right, Sparrow. You are the right person to oversee the last piece of Old Earth." She gazed at the gentle ripples on the water's surface and stroked her wrinkled cheek.

"Are you alright, Henrietta?"

She rested a hand on the rim. "I was just wishing I had not lost quite so many years in Idronatti."

Sparrow experienced a stab of guilt. "I'm sorry you had to..."

Henrietta shook her head. "Oh, my dear, I would not have missed a moment with you and your girls, even though I had to remain incognito." She sighed. "So many adventures await us, but—" A deeper sigh whispered over the water. "I am feeling my advanced years."

Relevart guided Akeri to the fountain. "I have explained to Akeri that Teva and Lenadi remained on TreBlaya at my request." He patted the hand resting on his forearm. "In a couple of turnings, my dear, I will take you to rejoin your mate."

Akeri responded with a professional nod. "I am excited to be part of the team. Thank you, Relevart." Somay stuck his head in the room. "Akeri, let me show you Sparrow's studio and her prophetic paintings. They will help you to understand why The Unfolding accelerated."

When they had gone, Relevart stroked the rim of the fountain. "Sparrow, would you mind giving Henri and me some time alone with Elcaro's Eye?"

"Of course, I don't mind. I'm happy to take a break. Let me know when you're finished." She regarded Henri. "I will never forget your sacrifice, Henrietta. I'm grateful that you were there for the twins and me."

Relevart walked her into the hall. "Thank you." He paused and seemed to listen. "The cottage has accepted your presence and your new role. Almiralyn will be pleased."

Sparrow jogged down the stairs, smiled at the creaking fourth step, and murmured, "I like your gentle warning." Walking into her empty studio, she stopped to inspect the paintings Somay had lined up for Akeri. *My brush captured so many memories. When I arrived in Myrrh, I didn't know that my art would play a major role in the Unfolding.*

Ari and Elf stood with Zugo on the Intersect platform beneath the red barn. With Wolloh's help, she had used Efillaeh to repair the DeoNyte's burns. His arm, though better, needed more time to heal. The VarTerel had explained that The MasTer's fire did more damage than an ordinary blaze. Zugo would bear the scars on his face, chest, and arm for the rest of his life.

The DeoNyte's expressive face looked momentarily sad. "I said goodbye to everyone but Brie. Please tell her goodbye for me." The sadness vanished into excitement. "I may see her in DerTah, depending on how long I am there."

Ari smiled. "I am so glad your father is allowing you to travel. DerTah is an interesting place. You'll like TheLise od Trinuge. Between you and me, I think Nomed is in love with her; so keep your eyes open."

Zugo draped his uninjured arm around her shoulders. "Thank you for using Efillaeh on me, Ari."

"I'm sorry I couldn't erase the scars."

"I don't mind the scarring—*Wolloh* has scars." He flexed his damaged fingers. "I'm just glad I have the use of my hand."

Ari glanced at Elf and smiled at Zugo. "Elf says you're lucky to have Wolloh as a mentor."

"We're all lucky. You and Elf have Relevart. Esán has his father. Brie…" Zugo squinted into the distance. "I believe Brie will have many mentors." His pale eyes searched her face. "We've all changed since the turning that the DiMensioner and Wodash invaded the Dojanack Caverns."

"Haven't we just!" She looked at Elf. "You wouldn't have liked me then. I was…" She laughed. "Torgin would say I was a Drotti."

Elf's teasing smile made Ari blush.

Zugo looked from one to another. "I wish…" White fur floated around him as he shook himself. "I need to go home. I want to spend time with my parents before I leave for DerTah."

Ari hugged him. "Don't know when I'll see you again. Stay away from fire."

He gave her a mock salute, whispered the key to the intersect, and flashed from sight.

Ari slipped a hand into Elf's and gazed at the scattered stars. *Never thought I'd travel through time.*

A kiss brushed her cheek. She looked at Elf. *I never thought I'd fall in love either.*

Henri waited by the fountain. The cottage, though quiet, reverberated with the vitality of its occupants. *Rayn brought all this power and talent together.* Again, she stared into the fountain. *I want to travel to El Stroma. I want to—* Relevart's silent appearance startled her. "My goodness, you are quiet for a big man."

His shoulders shook with silent laughter. "You never cease to astonish me, Henri." He sobered. "I have something to propose, Henrietta Avetlire."

She traced the roundness of Elcaro's rim. "A proposition?"

Humor sparked in the VarTerel's dark eyes. "Before I present it… I'll understand if you say no," his tone teased, "and so will the Galactic Guardians."

Henri choked down a churlish quip, dipped a finger in the water, and flicked a drop into the air. "Relevart, you are a clever man. How can I refuse the Guardians? You'd best present your plan so I know what lies in store for me."

A smile softened the angles of his rugged features. "I promised the Guardians I will find a companion to share the role of Universal VarTerel—a partner to help bring balance to the Universe." He hesitated and seemed to gather courage around him. When he spoke next, his voice was steady and confident. "I would like you to be my companion and life-mate."

Henri's eyebrows shot up. Emotions hitting her stomach like a storm of butterflies sent her toddling to the window. Diamonds of light on the garden pond sharpened. The heightened scents of autumn tickled her nostrils. Night sounds amplified until she could hear the spider weaving its web in the old maple tree. She donned her spectacles and turned to regard him. Startling clarity replaced any uncertainty that might have been lurking around her heart.

"My, my, Avlin Enus, you truly know how to take a woman by surprise." She hobbled to the fountain and peered once again at her reflection. "As a young woman, I imagined my prince charming; what he would look like; where he would come from; all the things we feminine creatures fret over. While you talked to Sparrow in the hall, it hit me even harder than usual how my stay in Idronatti has cut short my longevity." She glanced at him from under half-closed lids. "I yearn for more adventures and to explore the Universe." A heavy sigh steamed her lenses.

Amusement shaped Relevart's mouth into a teasing smile. "Hmmm. Feeling a bit of self-pity, are you?" He paused and smiled. "As I recall, the Old Earth saying is 'I am no spring chicken,' Henri. I've lived my life without ties of any kind, and I am set in my ways. You are the only woman who continues to delight me. We will make a great team."

Henri heard no pleading, only conviction and caring. She removed her spectacles and tapped her palm. *The Unfolding has changed me, given me the opportunity to use my training and talents for the good of others. I liked it. I like adventure. Relevart has always held a special place in my heart.* She tucked her lenses in a pocket. "Please answer one question. What about your feelings for Rayn?"

The weathered features grew thoughtful. "Rayn is gone. Who knows how we would have felt if they hadn't separated us for so long? She was part of me. But, Henrietta, I did not—do not—love her. You have the potential to enrich my life in ways I can only imagine. I need your talents and skills to help me do my job well. I *want* your companionship to fill my sun cycles, however many, with the energy, intelligence, and humor you bring to everything." His eyes flooded with hope. "I know I've surprised you but..."

She chuckled. The clarity she had experienced earlier sharpened. Her heart gave a leap of delight. "Avlin Enus, VarTerel of the entire Universe, I would adore the adventure of being your companion."

An elated laugh rumbled up from his chest. He drew her close. "I am more happy than I can express."

She swallowed a girlish giggle. "So, what's next?"

He turned her to face the fountain, retrieved his staff, and placed it between them. "Please hold on to the staff."

As he spoke, water ceased to drip from the statue's hands. The surface grew silky smooth. Chealim's angelic countenance took shape and steadied. "You have made a wise choice, Avlin Enus and Henrietta Avetlire. The Galactic Council is well pleased. With your permission, we will recite the Psalm of Joining."

Henri drew in a breath and nodded. Relevart bowed his head.

Chealim's voice began softly and grew louder.

"This man and woman once apart
Now make a promise of the heart:
To honor each and share their lives,
To stand as one through all divides.

We join them now that they may fight
To help the Universe reunite
Their strengths and talents thus define
A partnership that is divine."

Heat whirling through Henri's body created the sensation of skin pulled taut, of muscles strained to the point of tearing, of blood boiling through her veins. Blazing color robbed her of sight. A deep, continuous hum canceled all sound. Clutching the rowan staff, she fought to absorb the information surging through her mind like a spring melt-off over a waterfall. Giving herself up to the process, she focused her attention inward and waited. When at last coolness stole over her skin and goose flesh tingled up her spine, she opened her eyes. Relevart filled her line of vision. Youth gleamed in his eyes. Hers sought the fountain.

Mirrored on the surface, an image of herself in her prime smiled up at her. Her gaze darted to Relevart's face. Fine lines around his eyes had replaced the deep wrinkles of moments before. Dark hair streaked with silver fell in waves to below his ears. She looked again at her reflection: smooth skin, bright blue eyes, pale golden curls, a charming smile she knew could quickly become an impish grin. Laughing out loud, she released the staff and spun around. No aches, no pains, no weakness in her right knee left her shaking her head in astonishment.

"How long?" she asked.

"Our bodies and minds will keep this level of health and vitality. The illusion of aging will return to our skin and hair. The important thing to remember is that our soul essence is eternally youthful." He held out a staff. "The Guardians are happy to have another female VarTerel. With you and Almiralyn, they believe the Universe has the potential of attaining balance much faster."

She accepted her staff, a replica of Relevart's, but for the crystal contained by leaves and tiny branches on the top. Hers glowed the pink of rose quartz. He clasped her hand. Together they watched age etch fine wrinkles in their skin and silver-white replace the youthful color of their hair.

Henri glanced up at Relevart from beneath her lashes. "Nothing like growing old together to cement a relationship. Do you think anyone will notice we're different?"

Relevart guffawed. "I believe everyone will, my dear. You look more radiant than I've ever seen you. Shall we join our companions?"

Brie reclined on a bale of hay in the loft. Close by, Ari, Elf, Esán, and Torgin teased and laughed and exchanged stories. Unable to make herself join in the fun, she chewed a piece of straw and pondered the past two sun cycles. *I'm different.* Ari's deep chortle rang out. Brie couldn't help but smile. Twirling the straw between her fingers, she reminded herself that all of them had grown more powerful. *Esán moved Evolsefil from Nemttachenn to the Cave of Canedari. Elf carries more untapped power than anyone I know. Torgin creates magic with his flute, not only musical magic, but power strong enough to imprison the Pheet Adole.* She studied her twin. *And you, Arienh, have more talent than you have even begun to realize.*

Brie flipped the straw in the air, picked up another piece, and worked it through her fingers. Her thoughts carried her back to the discovery of the amethyst cavern in the Dojanacks, where she sat upon a tourmaline throne. *The Throne of ReNin RepPosu showed me the Ari of the future. I wish I could remember even part of it.* She sighed. *I only remember subtle imprints of people and events.*

Another chortle amplified Brie's perplexed thoughts. *All my peers have talents equal to my own. Why do I feel estranged and alone?*

Ari shot her a smile, punched Elf in the arm, and pushed him down in the hay.

Torgin grinned and stood, brushing bits of straw from his pants. "I need to spend time with my parents. Tomorrow, I leave with Nomed and Wolloh to return to DerTah."

Ari sat up and regarded him with surprise. "I understood Zugo was going with them. I thought you were returning to Idronatti, not DerTah."

"You don't know everything, Arienh Lynae. You only think you do."

She launched herself at his legs, knocked him down, and straddled his chest. "Tell me where you are going, or I'll tickle you until you squeal."

"Get off, and I'll tell you."

She tumbled off and pulled him to sitting. "Well?"

Brie noted the confidence he exuded. *He looks so alive.*

"My parents have given Nomed permission to take me to ReTaw au Qa to be part of Yaro's Venerat initiation. Nomed and I are cousins, you know."

Elf touched Ari's arm. She nodded. "Elf says that is pretty great. He says the ceremony is supposed to be beautiful."

Torgin scrambled to his feet. "We leave early, so I might not see you in the morning. I'll miss you." He looked around. "All of you, please take care of yourselves."

Elf helped Ari to her feet. Hands on her hips, she regarded Torgin with a teasing smile. "You sure have changed, Torg. You're definitely not a Drotti anymore. Take care."

He laughed and hugged her. "And you never were a Drotti, Ari." He winked. "Except maybe once in a while." He offered his hand to Elf. "She's a handful. I wish you the best."

Elf grinned. Ari laughed. "He says he knows just what to do."

Esán looked up at him and smiled. "Take good care of yourself, cousin. Don't forget me."

Torgin sobered. "Never. Get well. I mean *really* well. By the time you come out of seclusion, I'll be conducting the symphony. I hope you'll attend a concert or several." He gave Esán a quick embrace and whispered, "Take care of Brie."

"I will. Tell Yaro I said hello."

Brie hugged him goodbye. He kissed her lightly on the cheek. "I can't wait to see where life takes you." Not waiting for a reply, he descended the ladder.

Ari nudged Elf toward it. "Later, you two."

In the sudden quiet after their friends left, Esán pulled Brie down on the hay bale beside him.

"I leave tomorrow, Brielle. Although I'm not sure when, I promise we will be together again."

She plucked at the hem of her tunic. "How long will the Seeds of Carsilem take to mature?"

He put an arm around her. "I don't know. Father says the Unfolding has given them a kick start and the CoaleScent Cycle will escalate the process.

His took fifteen sun cycles. I'm hoping for less than half of that, but they will mature in their time, Brielle."

She brightened. "My training will be done by then." Doubt assailed her. "How will we find each other, Esán? It's a vast Universe. I may be in El Stroma. You need to return to Tao Spirian. I—"

He put a finger on her lips. "Shhh. How can you believe for a moment I won't find you? Leave the worrying to others, Brie. Tonight is beautiful. Look at that moon!"

Brie snuggled closer, gazing in wonder at Myrrh's creamy white moon framed in the loft doors. She envisioned Fasfro, Calegri, and Lunule, DerTah's three moons, and the two that orbited TreBlaya. *Will I ever stand beneath them again? Will I truly see El Stroma and its moons?*

An autumn breeze tangled her hair. Esán blew a curl off her forehead and pulled her down to the hay-strewn floor to recline against the bale beside him. She leaned her head on his shoulder and watched the huge white orb rise higher and higher until only the night sky, with its sprinkling of stars, remained framed in the arched opening.

Realization washed over her. *Someday, I will travel back through time.* The silence of middle-night wrapped the cottage in a protective cloak. In the upstairs room, the alabaster statue gleamed on Elcaro's rim. The fountain's surface glistened like a moonlit mirror. At the bottom of the bowl, an image took shape and, in slow motion, began its journey upward.

The finished Unfolding leaves questions behind
For those who fulfilled it to sort and unwind,
But forces of evil will not let them rest.
They now must prepare to persist in their quest.

GLOSSARY LINK

A searchable glossary for the
VarTerels' Universe™ is available online at:

www.skrandolph.com/glossary

ACKNOWLEDGMENTS

To the following, I express my heartfelt thanks and gratitude:

To my editor Linda Lane, for every moment spent editing VarTerels' Universe and for mentoring my developmental as a writer

To Leslie Randolph, my critique partner, for discussing, reading, and rereading, every sentence and paragraph in *MasTer's Reach*

To Debbie Stilson, my tireless copy editor, for her time, energy, and great sense of humor

To those who have contributed their artistic gifts to *MasTer's Reach*:

Emma Randolph, Watercolor Artist
Linda White, Clay Artist
HellBentPuppet, Aerial Photographer
(see his work at www.youtube.com/user/HellBentPuppet)

To Charles Lawrence, who inspired the character Wolloh, for granting permission to use his image

To Courtney Krantz and Brenden Crane, for allowing me to use their pictures

To Captain Dennis Rogers whose strength of personality and knowledge of boats and the sea inspired the character Gregos Senndi

To Deb Alexander and Dragon Fly Ranch, for a fabulous weekend filled with horses and many opportunities to capture their magnificence in photos.

To the National Aeronautics and Space Administration, www.nasa.gov, for inspiring and nurturing my fascination with the wonders of the universe and for allowing the use of photos of our galaxy and beyond

ABOUT THE AUTHOR

FROM DANCE STAGE TO WRITTEN PAGE

STORYTELLER

Dance, humanity's most ancient narrative art, captivated S.K. Randolph as a child living and dancing in the British Crown Colony of Bermuda. After graduating from the University of Utah with a BFA in Ballet, her dance career spanned four decades of performing, mentoring, teaching, choreographing, and directing. Over sixty of her original choreographic works were brought to life for theatre audiences around the globe, establishing her deep foundation in pacing, movement, and narrative structure. She was the Ballet Mistress of the Colorado Ballet and the Alberta Ballet as well as cofounder of the Bermuda Dance Theatre. For the last two decades of her dance career, she educated the next generation of creatives, as Director of Dance at Interlochen Center for the Arts, named the "#1 Best High School for the Arts in America", and at St. Paul's School.

S.K. at the helm of her forty-foot boat leaving Seattle, Washington on a transformative seventy-five day voyage up the Inside Passage to Sitka, Alaska. Then a decade writing while living afloat swinging on the anchor rode in one remote Alaskan cove or another.
2010

DIGITAL ARTIST

S.K., a pioneer in the digital art sphere, has been creating original digital art since 1997. Utilizing a unique, self-taught technique, she transforms photographs into vibrant, otherworldly masterpieces using Adobe Photoshop. Today, her VarTerels' Universe™ series features nearly 500 of these hand-crafted digital illustrations.

VOYAGE TO WRITING

In 2010, S.K. retired from the dance world to live with her partner on their boat in the world's largest temperate rainforest along the remote and rugged coast of Alaska. Isolated in nature, she spent a "gap decade" afloat honing her writing, refining her digital art style, and mastering shipboard skills (including catching dinner). It was during this creative voyage that she transitioned her storytelling from the dance stage to the written and illustrated page, self-publishing her first novel, *DiMensioner's Revenge*, in 2011.

TODAY

Now, in 2026, S.K. is currently writing the twenty-first installment of her saga. She and her partner reside in the lower-48 states, living on the side of the largest flat-top mountain in the world. From her mountain studio, she continues to cultivate her "Illustrated by the Author" Science Fantasy series, VarTerels' Universe™, dedicating her life to the timeless journey of a true storyteller.

S.K.'s website
www.skrandolph.com

Facebook
facebook.com/skrandolph11

Substack
skrandolph.substack.com

Wanted

VarTerels' Universe™ Book 9
Part I - UnFolding
Novella
33 pages

A fugitive with a dark past escapes prison only to discover he's being hunted by a powerful mystical league that wants to control his untapped ability to bend reality itself.

Available in the paperback *Agothany 1* and as an individual eBook.

An epic science fantasy saga told through art and words
in companion shorts and illustrated novels,
available as paperbacks and eBooks.

Illustrated by the author, color in eBooks
and black and white in paperbacks.

Presented in suggested reading order.

DiMensioner's Revenge

Illustrated by the Author
VarTerels' Universe™ Book 1
Part I - UnFolding
Novel
642 pages, 73 illustrations

Four young people from a regimented city discover their destiny when they journey to Myrrh—the hidden remnant of Old Earth—only to find themselves hunted by a vengeful DiMensioner, his death shadow, and alien mercenaries determined to destroy everything they've come to cherish.

Available as a paperback with black & white illustrations and eBook with color illustrations.

Gifts

VarTerels' Universe™ Book 2
Part I - UnFolding
Novella
34 pages

A pregnant art student must deceive a ruthless surveillance state about her twin daughters' true father, the brother of a powerful Guardian, or become the perfect hostage in a deadly political game.

Available in the paperback *Agothany 1* and as an individual eBook.

Discovery

VarTerels' Universe™ Book 3
Part I - UnFolding
Novelette
32 pages

Fourteen-year-old Torgin must choose between protecting his passion for music and spying on the only friends who understand him in a dystopian city where the government controls every aspect of life.

Available in the paperback *Agothany 1* and as an individual eBook.

Rescue

VarTerels' Universe™ Book 4
Part I - UnFolding
Novella
31 pages

In a dystopian city where surveillance is constant and conformity is mandatory, twin sisters Ari and Brie must navigate secret portals and evade ruthless patrollers to rescue a lost boy and return him home before their forbidden act lands them all in the dreaded Five Towers.

Available in the paperback *Agothany 1* and as an individual eBook.

ConDra's Fire

Illustrated by the Author
VarTerels' Universe™ Book 5
Part I - UnFolding
Novel
504 pages, 59 illustrations

Kidnapped to a hostile desert planet, Esán must survive while his friends race to rescue him, unaware that their rescue mission will unleash ancient powers and reveal family secrets that could destroy three worlds.

Available as a paperback with black & white illustrations and eBook with color illustrations.

Encounters

VarTerels' Universe™ Book 6
Part I - UnFolding
Novella
29 pages

When a vengeful DiMensioner forms an unholy alliance with a death shadow to steal a legendary crystal and destroy the Guardian who banished him, he discovers that the children he saves along the way may hold the key to his own redemption—or his ultimate damnation.

Available in the paperback *Agothany 1* and as an individual eBook.

Metamorphosis

VarTerels' Universe™ Book 7
Part I - UnFolding
Novella
31 pages

Wrongfully banished from his home planet and left disfigured by a catastrophic magical accident, Laurent must shed his arrogance and accept his broken reflection before he can master the ancient art of dimensional magic and discover his true purpose.

Available in the paperback *Agothany 1* and as an individual eBook.

MasTer's Reach

Illustrated by the Author
VarTerels' Universe™ Book 8
Part I - UnFolding
Novel
686 pages, 60 illustrations

As the UnFolding reaches its climax, teenagers wielding legendary artifacts must evade deadly hunters across multiple worlds while uncovering shocking truths about The MasTer's identity and a centuries-old conflict that threatens to destroy the Eleo Preda people forever.

Available as a paperback with black & white illustrations and eBook with color illustrations.

Wanted

VarTerels' Universe™ Book 9
Part I - UnFolding
Novella
33 pages

A fugitive with a dark past escapes prison only to discover he's being hunted by a powerful mystical league that wants to control his untapped ability to bend reality itself.

Available in the paperback *Agothany 1* and as an individual eBook.

Jaradee's Legacy

Illustrated by the Author
VarTerels' Universe™ Book 10
Part I - UnFolding
Novel
336 pages, 51 illustrations

Separated as children during a brutal genocide, birth-mate twins Rayn and Rethdun must survive across galaxies while carrying the genetic legacy that could save their dying civilization or destroy them both.

Available as a paperback with black & white illustrations and eBook with color illustrations.

Agothany 1

An anthology of
the Companion Shorts
Gifts, Discovery, Rescue Encounters,
Metamorphosis, and *Collision*
in VarTerels' Universe™
Part I - UnFolding
256 pages

Available as a paperback.
Each Companion Short also
available as an individual eBook.

Incirrata Secret

Illustrated by the Author
VarTerels' Universe™ Book 11
Part II- CoaleScence
Novel
428 pages, 45 illustrations

Racing against ruthless enemies across mystical dimensions, the Universe's youngest VarTerel and a prophesied leader with legendary eyes must rescue kidnapped mentors from a cloud-shrouded island where a phantom octopus guards secrets that could reshape their world—or destroy it.

Available as a paperback with black & white illustrations and eBook with color illustrations.

Lessons

VarTerels' Universe™ Book 12
Part II- CoaleScence
Novella
26 pages

On the desert planet of DerTah, blind oracle WoNadahem Mardree must overcome devastating loss and her deepest fears when a mysterious shape-shifting DiMensioner arrives seeking knowledge, challenging everything she believes about fate, power, and love.

Available in the paperback *Agothany 2* and as an individual eBook.

Corps Stones

Illustrated by the Author
VarTerels' Universe™ Book 13
Part II- CoaleScence
Novel
438 pages, 52 illustrations

A young VarTerel and her friends journey to 1969 New York City to recover three stolen Corps Stones before their entire solar system collapses into chaos.

Available as a paperback with black & white illustrations and eBook with color illustrations.

Fishing

VarTerels' Universe™ Book 14
Part II- CoaleScence
Novella
30 pages

A twelve-year-old boy with extraordinary powers must survive slavery, betrayal, and the relentless pursuit of a deadly league that murdered his parents and will stop at nothing to control him.

Available in the paperback *Agothany 2* and as an individual eBook.

Duplicity

VarTerels' Universe™ Book 15
Part II- CoaleScence
Novella
30 pages

A sworn protector with shapeshifting abilities and a future Guardian destined to unite worlds must outwit a ruthless League of sorcerers determined to claim her before she can fulfill her destiny.

Available in the paperback *Agothany 2* and as an individual eBook.

Mocendi's Gambit

Illustrated by the Author
VarTerels' Universe™ Book 16
Part II- CoaleScence
Novel
328 page, 35 illustrations

Stripped of her protective Star of Truth and held captive aboard an enemy ship young VarTerel Brielle AsTar must trust an unlikely ally—a former enemy seeking redemption—and escape through folded time before The MasTer's followers destroy everything she loves.

Available as a paperback with black & white illustrations and eBook with color illustrations.

Destiny

VarTerels' Universe™ Book 17
Part II- CoaleScence
Novella
32 pages

Brielle AsTar, the youngest VarTerel in the Inner Universe, must hide her genetically engineered babies and their surrogate mother from ruthless spies while battling a dangerous gene threatening to resurrect an ancient evil.

Available in the paperback *Agothany 2* and as an individual eBook.

Cimondeli

VarTerels' Universe™ Book 18
Part II- CoaleScence
Short Story
12 pages

Sixteen-year-old Desty has never seen the sky, but when she ventures beyond her underground refuge for the first time, she discovers her telepathic gifts, befriends a majestic flying lizard, and learns that healing a poisoned world may begin with bridging the divide between enemy tribes.

Available in the paperback *Agothany 2* and as an individual eBook.

Queen's Quest

Illustrated by the Author
VarTerels' Universe™ Book 19
Part II- CoaleScence
Novel
420 pages, 44 illustrations

A young VarTerel, a bearer of cosmic seeds, a musical genius, and a street-smart boy with magical spectacles must unite their extraordinary powers to shatter an impenetrable dome, defeat a rogue demi-god, and complete a universal cycle before time runs out.

Available as a paperback with black & white illustrations and eBook with color illustrations.

Collision

Prequel to VarTerels' Universe™
VarTerels' Universe™ Book 20
Part II- CoaleScence
Novella
64 pages, 14 illustrations

A genius physicist barely out of university must lead a team of Galactic Guardians wielding ancient instruments of power to rescue Earth from total annihilation, even as enemies from his past conspire to ensure the planet's destruction.

Available in the paperback *Agothany 2* with black & white illustrations and as an individual eBook with color illustrations.

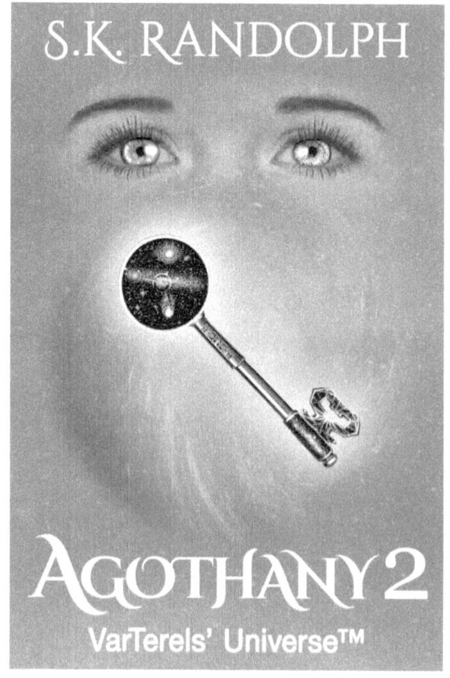

Agothany 2

An anthology of
the Companion Shorts
Lessons, Fishing, Duplicity
Destiny, Cimondeli, and *Collision*
in VarTerels' Universe™
Part II - CoaleScence
284 pages

Available as a paperback.
Each Companion Short also
available as an individual eBook.

Divided Destinies

Illustrated by the Author
VarTerels' Universe™ Book 21
Part III- QuicKening
Novel
a Work In Progress

Divided Destinies is a work in progress with a targeted release date of late 2026. An illustrated novel, it starts QuicKening, Part III of the VarTerels' Universe™.

See www.SKRandolph.com for current status and subscribe to S.K.'s newsletter to receive progress updates.

www.ingramcontent.com/pod-product-compliance
Lightning Source LLC
Chambersburg PA
CBHW061102310726

48974CB00002B/360